3M   14.00 9.00

More praise for *Boys & Girls Together*

"An extraordinary achievement . . . [that] will break your heart . . . will make you laugh . . . will make you weep . . . It is impossible to praise this book too highly. If you care at all about people who have blood in their veins, it is imperative that you read it. If you are nostalgic for novels of plot and structure and commitment, then you can't afford to do without it."
—*Cleveland Plain Dealer*

And acclaim for William Goldman's classic thriller, *Marathon Man*

"Superb . . . One hell of a read . . . There are two literary virtues that one wishes hadn't become cliches: 'It's a good read' and 'It exists on several levels.' One wishes these hadn't become clichés because they are two obvious virtues of William Goldman's *Marathon Man*."
—*Washington Post*

"An exciting—often funny, often sad—chase . . . Goldman does a masterly job."
—Associated Press

"Well-plotted, expertly characterized, and fast-paced."
—*Los Angeles Times*

"A slick, professional job . . . Goldman has [his] craft well under control."
—*The Boston Globe*

"A cliff-hanger . . . International skullduggery, clandestine mayhem and sweet revenge."
—*Fort Worth Star Telegram*

D0958534

ALSO BY WILLIAM GOLDMAN

William Goldman's

Boys & Girls Together

BALLANTINE BOOKS · NEW YORK

A Ballantine Book
Published by The Ballantine Publishing Group

Copyright © 1964 by William Goldman
Copyright renewed 1992 by William Goldman
Foreword copyright © 2001 by William Goldman

All rights reserved under International and Pan-American
Copyright Conventions. Published in the United States by The Ballantine
Publishing Group, a division of Random House, Inc., New York, and
simultaneously in Canada by Random House of Canada Limited, Toronto.
Originally published by Atheneum Publishers, New York, in 1964.

Ballantine is a registered trademark and the
Ballantine colophon is a trademark of Random House, Inc.

www.randomhouse.com/BB/

Library of Congress Catalog Card Number: 00-111113

ISBN 0-345-43973-2

Cover design by Carl Galian
Cover art by Tom Nikosey

Text design by Holly Johnson

Manufactured in the United States of America

First Ballantine Books Edition: August 2001

10 9 8 7 6 5 4 3 2 1

FOR

My
Father

East Side, West Side, all around the town,
The tots sang "Ring-a-rosie," "London Bridge is falling
*   down";*
Boys and girls together, me and Mamie Rorke,
Tripped the light fantastic on the sidewalks of New York.
JAMES W. BLAKE (1894)

Contents

Foreword to
Boys & Girls Together

In 1938 I was seven, and my family had recently moved to the then very small town of Highland Park, outside of Chicago, and why I cannot tell you, but for either one week or several, we got the Sunday *New York Times.*

I was already a movie nut, had been to the theater more than a little and right now, as I write this, sitting in 2000 at a machine undreamed of then, I can still see the seven-year-old child, turning page after page of *Times* movie ads and theater ads and thinking, "I must try and live there someday."

I remember where I was in the room, the pattern of the yellow rug, the light coming in from the bay window at the far end. And as anyone who knows me will tell you, I don't remember what I had for lunch yesterday, much less rug patterns.

But the kid of that moment and that wish have been inside ever since.

I think the original working title was *Magic Town.* I think I had this much: a bunch of young people come to New York. I know I knew it went badly for them.

That's it, folks.

Oops, sorry, one more thing: I knew more than anything that the novel *had to be long.* If it ran over a thousand typed pages, fine. Ask me now where that lunatic notion came from, I know not. But long novels, I have survived to tell you, are the worst to write.

I've always been good at guilt, but I think when I began *Boys & Girls Together,* I must have had Olympic records in mind. You see, I *had* come to the city. When I was twenty-two. And I *had* miraculously become a writer. And the first three novels, though short, had also been successful. I was going great, no question.

But all around me, my friends were falling to earth.

And so, around thirty, I set out to write my book of atonement.

Because I was programmed all my life to fail, to finish, if I got to the line at all, at the back of the pack. When I was maybe six or seven, I went to playgroup and at the end, they had parents' day and there was a running race, I was in it, and it started and I took off—

—entering a nightmare—

—I looked around—no one was near me—*I had gone in the wrong direction*—

—can you imagine the humiliation? I could. I did.

—and then blessedly came Minnie's voice, Minnie, who had worked for my family close to half a century was shouting now, "run Billy run"—

—so I ran, and I won—because I had *not* been going in the wrong direction at all, I was simply out in front, far out in front, winning if you will—and I simply could not conceive it.

Hiram Haydn, my beloved editor for fifteen years, was a novelist himself and quick to understand the problems of fellow fumblers. Usually I presented him with a completed novel and we would then go to work.

Since I had no idea what *Boys & Girls Together* would be, he pretty much directed the way the book might go. Take the five characters and write a chapter about each of their childhoods, he'd say. So I would. Then we'd go on to the next period of their lives. The process of writing the book took three years—I stopped in the middle to do a play and a musical on Broadway, both of which stiffed, you will be thrilled to learn—and he was essential all the way. He might say "What's happening to Walt, how's Walt doing, that's what I'd like to know," and off I'd go, trying to figure for myself how Walt was, in point of fact, doing, and I'd come up with a Walt chapter, write it down.

My first three novels—*The Temple of Gold, Your Turn to Curtsy, My Turn to Bow* and *Soldier in the Rain* had not been well received critically. Except by Dorothy Parker who, bless her, could not have been kinder.

Hiram thought *Boys & Girls Together* would establish me as one of the serious American novelists of my generation.

Wrong. It was . . . how shall I put it . . .

Slaughtered.

The most crucifying reviews up and down the line. I was truly on the verge of tears for weeks. But out of that came a wonderful decision—

—fuck 'em!

I have not read reviews for over thirty-five years now, good or bad. I remember being sent an entire package of raves for the film of *All the President's Men*.

—fuck 'em!

Never opened it. I don't want to read what those assholes have to say. And if any of you want to write, I cannot give you better advice. Don't read anybody.

Just fuck 'em!

And go write some more.

Two final *Boys & Girls Together* stories, both involving Princeton.

The first involves finishing the book. It was 1963 and I was not in great shape. I'd rented a house in Princeton for the summer to complete the writing and I was, of course, exhausted from finally almost getting it done but more this: I had a bad back then and it had chosen to go out. So I lived on red wine and pain pills to force sleep, caffeine to get me going.

Plus this: I had to wear a girdle to get through the day.

Didn't do a lot for my good old masculine sense of self-esteem.

Anyway, the day I was done I was alone in the house and stared at "the end" when I wrote those blessed words, got up, went outside to the backyard, where we had a child's swing set up for daughter Jenny, then all of a year. I sat in it, smoking, and suddenly I had this realization:

I had told all my stories.

Every one.

I sat there thinking it couldn't be true, because that would mean the end for me as a writer, then luckily I remembered the story of the mother who dressed her son in her clothes . . .

No, I'd put that in the novel, given it to Branch.

I went through them *all* and I'd given them *all* away. That's my chief memory of that afternoon. Knowing what I'd done, wondering what I was going to do with the rest of my life. (I did not realize at the time that two years down the line, in that same university town, over Christmas vacation, these two outlaws named Butch and Sundance would ride up from South America to save me.)

We moved permanently to Princeton in early 1965, when Susanna, Daughter Number Two, was born.

Shortly after, the regular writing teacher came to me and said he had gotten a sudden shot at sabbatical and needed a quick replacement. Would I do it?

I had always wanted to teach. Easy yes answer.

I had a bunch of kids for creative writing, wanted them to remember me kindly, so I stopped writing for the year and just taught. I must have done well because the visiting writing professor (there were two at Princeton in those days) came to me on a Spring afternoon and asked if I would like to be the permanent professor of writing there.

My decision was that if I did not have any heavier a workload than I'd already had, yes. Any more, and I would never be able to get back to my own work.

He said he would get back to me.

Now you must know this—that summer, *Boys & Girls Together* was *the* beach book in paperback. Huge success. A very sexy cover for those days. And was the book salacious? Sure, the gay characters I guess were more shocking then. But no more than that.

Days kept going, as they do, by.

No answer about becoming a writing professor.

Finally (we are well into May) I ran into the visiting teacher and asked what was going on. "I've been avoiding you," he said. "I'm just dreading this."

What he was dreading was that one of the top professors in the English department, old and gray and gay, had heard about *Boys & Girls Together*, and rejected me with these words:

> I WILL NOT HAVE OUR CHILDREN
> WORSHIPING AT THE SHRINE OF
> A PORNOGRAPHER.

I took my family and left Princeton that week. Back to Magic Town where I belonged. Been to Princeton one time since.

As someone must have said: fuck 'em!

Boys &
Girls
Together

Part I

I

Aaron would not come out.

Nestled inside his mother, blind and wrinkled and warm, he defied the doctors. Charlotte's screams skimmed along the hospital corridors, but Aaron, lodged at his peculiar angle, was mindless of them. Charlotte vomited and shrieked and wanted to die. As that possibility became less and less remote, the doctors hurriedly decided to operate and, deftly cutting through the wall of Charlotte's abdomen, they slit the uterus and reached inside.

Pink and white like a candy stick, Aaron entered the world.

It seemed to be a great place to visit. His father could not have been gladder to see him. Henry Firestone, universally known as Hank, was a big man, confident, with a quick smile and a loud, rough voice. Aaron never forgot that voice; years later he would still spin suddenly around—on the street, in a restaurant, a theater lobby—whenever he heard a voice remotely similar.

Hank was a lawyer, for Simmons and Sloane, the Wall Street firm, and when he was thirty-one Mr. Sloane himself made Hank a full partner, Mr. Simmons being bed-ridden that day with gout, a disease to which he noisily succumbed some months later. The week he became a partner, Hank was sent to Roanoke, Virginia, for a three-day business trip.

He stayed two weeks and came back married.

Her name was Charlotte Crowell, of the Roanoke Crowells, or what once had been the Roanoke Crowells, the family having been comfortably poor since shortly before the turn of the century. Charlotte was tiny, barely five feet tall, with a sweet face and a voice as soft as her husband's was harsh. Her hair was black and she wore it long and straight, down her back; even when it began turning cruelly white (she was not yet thirty) she wore it that way.

Hank and Charlotte lived in New York for a few months but then, the summer after they were married, they moved to a large white colonial on

Library Place, a gently curving tree-lined street in the best section of Princeton, New Jersey. Mr. Sloane himself lived in Princeton, on Battle Road, of course, and when he saw that the house on Library Place was up for sale he mentioned it casually to Hank, who immediately took Charlotte for a look-see. Charlotte loved it—it reminded her so of Roanoke—so Hank bought it for her. He couldn't afford it but he bought it anyway, partially because Charlotte loved it and partially because she was pregnant and everybody told them New York was no place to bring up children. They moved into the house the week after Deborah was born, all waxy and red, the only time she was ever unattractive. The wax soon washed away, the red softened into pink, and she became a beautiful baby, fat, spoiled and sassy. Charlotte adored her and Hank liked her well enough—he cooed at her and carried her around on his big shoulders and gently poked her soft flesh till she giggled—Hank liked her fine, but he was waiting for his son.

The wait took over two years. Hank worked hard at the office, making more money than he ever had before in spite of the depression, and Charlotte hired a full-time maid and then a gardener to tend the lawn on summer mornings. They entertained a good deal and they entertained well; Charlotte had the gift. Hank gave up tennis for golf, which bored him, but it was better for business. A lot of things bored Hank until the evening Aaron emerged.

Before the boy was a month old his room was crammed with toys and dolls and music boxes, and a menagerie of stuffed animals pyramided against the foot of his canopied bed. Almost every afternoon Hank journeyed north to F. A. O. Schwarz's for more and more presents, and when Charlotte warned he was in danger of buying out the store he only nodded happily and told her she had guessed exactly his last remaining ambition. Nights Hank spent in the boy's room, rocking him to sleep, singing soft lullabies in his big rough voice. Whenever the boy was sick—and he was sick a good deal—Hank would go to work late and return early, calling in constantly from New York, always asking the same question: "Aaron? How is Aaron? How is my son?"

Hank loved Aaron; Charlotte loved Deborah. There were no troubles on Library Place.

For Aaron's third birthday Hank bought him a jungle gym. They set it up together, the two of them, in the back yard. It was a marvelous structure, more than six feet high, and Hank used to take Aaron and lift him, setting him on the very top rung. "Hold tight now," Hank would say. "Hold tight and stay up there all by yourself." So Aaron would hold tight, sitting on the top rung, his tiny fists gripping the bars for balance. Hank would back away from him then, calling out "Scared?" and Aaron would yell "No, no," even though he was.

One Saturday afternoon the maid was out and Charlotte was watching Deborah perform at ballet class, so Hank and Aaron played cops and robbers for a while, shooting each other, falling, suddenly up again, running pell-mell across the lawn. After that it was time to play on the jungle gym. Hank lifted Aaron, carried him on his big shoulders, carefully placed him on the very top rung. Hank started backing away. "Hold tight now," he said. Aaron held tight. "Are you scared?" he said. "No," Aaron cried; "no." Hank stood a distance from the jungle gym and smiled his quick smile. Then, thoughtlessly, he paled, falling to his knees. He gasped for a moment, then slipped to the grass. Gasping louder, he crawled forward, crawled toward the jungle gym, saying, "Aaron. Aaron." He raised one big arm, then dropped it. Reaching for his son, he died, sprawled full length, white on the green lawn.

Aaron giggled. "That was good, Daddy," he said. He did not know the name of the game, but whatever it was it was obviously still on—his father, after all, had not answered—so he giggled again and stared down at the dead man. It was a fine summer day, windy and warm, and Aaron stared up at the clouds a moment, watching them skid across the sky. Grabbing on to the bars with all his strength, he looked down again—it frightened him to look down, it was so far—but his father still had not moved. "That's good, Daddy," Aaron said. He giggled once more, lifting his head, staring at the clouds. His fists were beginning to get sore from holding the bars, but he did not dare loosen his grip. "Down, Daddy," Aaron said, looking up. "I wanna come down." The game was still on; his father did not move. Aaron gazed at the clouds and started to sing. "How sweet to be a cloud floating in the blue. It makes you very proud to be a little cloud." It was a song from *Winnie the Pooh*—Aaron knew all the songs from *Winnie the Pooh*—and Pooh sang it when he was floating up after the honey on the tail of the balloon. But he never got the honey because the bees found him out and Pooh fell all the way down. Pooh fell. Aaron's hands ached terribly. "Daddy," he said louder. "Take me down, Daddy. Please take me down."

His father made no move to do so.

"Daddy," Aaron said, frightened now. "I'll drink my milk I will I will I promise but take me down." He hated to cry—his father never cried—but suddenly he was crying, the tears stinging his eyes. "Take me down, Daddy." He began to shake and his hands were numb and the tears would not stop. "TAKE ME DOWN DAH-DEE." His chest burned and the clouds were monsters diving at him so he closed his eyes but he thought he might fall so he opened them, alternating his stare, up to the diving monsters, down to the still figure, up and down, up and down. Aaron began to scream. "DAH-DEE DAH-DEE DAH-DEE TAKE ME DOWN DAH-DEE TAKE ME DOWN TAKE ME DOWN DAH-DEE DAH-DEE DAH-DEE DAH-DEE TAKE ME DOWN."

He was still screaming when Charlotte found him an hour later. She ran across the lawn, took him down. Then she dropped to her knees beside the still white figure on the grass.

Soon she was screaming too.

For a short period after the funeral there were no changes in the life at Library Place. Then one morning the gardener didn't come; a high-school boy was hired to mow the lawn. Two months later Charlotte let the maid go. There was no money coming in now, no money coming in. They had always lived beyond Hank's income and probably Charlotte should have given up the big house sooner, but she determined to keep it, working desperately, cutting corners, cleaning and patching and cooking until finally, eight months after the death, Charlotte, exhausted, found a new place to live, the first floor of a yellow frame house on Nassau Street, close to the center of town.

Deborah wept as her mother packed her clothes. "Now, Deborah Crowell Firestone, you stop that, hear?" Charlotte said in her soft Southern voice. Aaron stood silently in the doorway of Deborah's room, watching. "Oh, baby," Charlotte sighed, opening her arms. "You come to me." Deborah ran into her mother's arms. Charlotte rocked her gently, back and forth. "It's all right, baby, hear? Mother's going to make it all all right. Everything's going to be wonderful, baby. Mother promises. Mother loves you and she swears it's going to be all right. Mother loves—"

Aaron crept into the room.

"Get out," Deborah said.

Charlotte said, "Now, Deborah, you stop talking that way."

"Get out," Deborah repeated.

"Aaron is your brother. Aaron is my son. Aaron is a part of this family. Have you packed your games, Aaron?"

"No."

"Well, maybe you better pack your games, do you think?"

Aaron turned and said, "All right."

"And stay out," Deborah called after him.

The yellow frame house on Nassau Street was owned by Miss Alexandra Hamilton, an elderly lady who had been teaching high school in Princeton since before the First World War. Miss Hamilton had been married twice, both times to the same man, an irresistibly handsome plumber from Newark. He was still alive and plumbing, but after the second divorce Miss Hamilton resumed her maiden name. She met Charlotte and the children as they moved in, set down the law of the land— "There is to be *no noise*"—and promptly departed to the second floor via the outside stairway, which she always used. They heard her occasionally, going in and coming out, but they saw her only once a month, when she stopped by for the rent.

Shortly after Aaron was five, Charlotte went out and got a job. The money from the sale of the white colonial was going much too quickly, so one morning she combed her long black hair, put on her best white hat— from behind she looked like a school girl—and left the house "to seek her fortune," as she told her children, giggling nervously while she said it. When she returned to the house several hours later she reported that she had "acquired the enormously responsible position" of saleslady at the Browse-Around, an expensive shop on Nassau Street catering to girls and young women. From that day on she seemed forever to be talking about the Browse-Around, about style and color and cost and the women who brought their little girls in for clothing and how much they spent and "not one of 'em's as pretty as you, Deborah; not one holds a candle to you." A month after she had been at the store she brought home a playsuit for Deborah. It was marked down, she said, and, besides, she had her employee's discount, and a week after the playsuit came a dress, and then there followed other dresses, and pajamas and shoes and gloves and socks and blouses and coats and hats.

Aaron began to read.

All the time, lying on his bed, his thin arms holding the books upright on his stomach, his thin fingers turning the pages. He was tall and bony and long, and he ate only when forced. He had no interest in food. Charlotte forbade his reading at the table and at night she forced him to turn out his bed light and sleep. He would obey partially, lying still, waiting for her to go to bed. Then he would read into the night until his eyes burned.

One hot summer day when he was seven Aaron Firestone sat on his bicycle, staring hypnotically at the traffic on Nassau Street. The street was crowded; the cars seemed hardly to be moving at all. A truck lumbered noisily toward his house. The truck stopped, then started again, but slowly, slowly. Aaron pushed hard on the foot pedal and the bike left the sidewalk and skidded over the curb, down into the hot street. Aaron fell backward, balance gone. The truck braked, stopping, but not before its great wheels rolled up and over Aaron's legs.

He awoke in the hospital to find his mother leaning over him, weeping. Looking away from her tears, he muttered, "I'm sorry, Mama." Charlotte sobbed aloud, reaching for her son, cradling him. Hidden beneath the folds of Charlotte's dress, Aaron found himself smiling.

He was in the hospital over a month. Charlotte came to visit every day and sometimes Deborah came too, but mostly it was just his mother. Aaron got to like it in the hospital until Charlotte told him that his hips had been damaged, crushed somehow by the truck, and he would be able to walk again, not well, probably not without some pain, but he would be able to walk.

Aaron started practicing with crutches. Then canes. Finally he was able to move unaided. It hurt, a lot at first, and the pain never completely left him, especially when he was tired, but by the time they brought him home from the hospital he walked by himself.

It was a steaming afternoon, and Charlotte, first seeing that Aaron's needs were accounted for, excused herself and hurried to the Browse-Around. Deborah appeared briefly, wearing a new dress, and she modeled it for Aaron before going down the street to play. Aaron lay on his bed and tried to read. The room was very hot. His throat felt dry and there was a different dryness deep behind his eyes, and perspiration poured off his thin face.

Aaron shut his book and his eyes. He lay perfectly still until a fly buzzed near him. He lunged for it, missing, but managing by the sharpness of his movement to cause his hips to hurt. Aaron bit his lip until the pain was gone. Then, taking a deep breath, he moved slowly off the bed to the telephone. When he got the Browse-Around he asked for his mother, and when he got her he said, "Did you ask me to call you? I forgot."

"Aaron, whatever—"

"I couldn't remember if you asked me to call you at the store to tell you how I was or not, I'm fine."

"Good. Of course you are."

"I'm reading this book. It's a very thrilling adventure story."

"It's my son," Charlotte said.

"What?" Aaron said.

"I was just explaining who you were to Mrs. Cavanaugh, Aaron. Mrs. Cavanaugh is buying the cutest—"

"I loved Deborah's new dress."

"Oh, good. Aaron? Thank you for calling; I'm very glad you called—"

"Bye-bye, Mama," Aaron said, hanging up. He moved back to his bed and lay down. Then he got up and walked very slowly out of the room, out of the house. On the sidewalk, he paused for a moment to stare at the spot where the truck had hit him. Aaron turned and, forcing his legs to obey, began to limp along Nassau Street. He was sweating terribly and his legs hurt more and more with each slow step, but he dragged himself along.

Almost an hour later he reached the white house on Library Place. Aaron stopped. In the yard he saw three children playing, and their high laughter reached him on the thick summer air. He hated to cry—his father never cried—but suddenly he was crying, bitterly, painfully, out of control. Aaron dropped to the cement sidewalk and wept. When he was done, he vowed not to let it happen again.

His word was good for close to twenty years.

The days that followed proved easily endurable. He read books. Quickly at first, but by training himself he increased his natural speed until, by the time he was twelve, he could finish almost any book in a single day. He began to draw, his thin fingers fluttering hurriedly across white notebook paper, leaving behind an accurate image of a tree or a gun or an elegant car. He taught himself to play the piano even though he never had a lesson. Deborah got the lessons, one each week from a university student who didn't really need the money but who liked to look at Deborah for an hour each Tuesday; even at fourteen, Deborah was something to see. During the lessons Aaron would stand outside the living-room door, never making a sound—he was good at that; he would regularly frighten his mother by appearing suddenly in doorways or dark halls, making her spin around, making her gasp. And while the lesson went on inside, Aaron would listen, and when the university student said "Cup your hands, no, relax them, relax them," Aaron would cup and relax his hands. Then, when the student was gone, he would rush to the piano and practice. He had a good ear. Deborah had none, but the lessons continued for more than a year because Charlotte felt the playing of Chopin to be a minimum basic requirement for any young lady worthy of the name. By the end of the year, Aaron could play. So he played, and he read, and he drew.

But his greatest love was writing.

He had begun to write quite by accident. He had been to the movies alone one night and, as was his ritual, he crept silently into the house. When he heard his mother's voice he stopped.

"I'm worried about Aaron," Charlotte said.

Deborah grunted.

"What are we going to do about Aar—stop fiddling with your nails and help me, Deborah—he's your flesh-and-blood brother after all."

"That," Deborah said, "is not my fault."

"He should go out with other people more," Charlotte said.

Deborah laughed. "What other people? Aaron's a joke, Mother. I just dread having him in high school with me next year."

"People shouldn't laugh at Aaron," Charlotte said. "Why do they?"

"Look at him. He's ninety feet tall and his clothes never look like they fit and he thinks he's so smart and he's all the time *appearing* behind your back like a spook. He's a nut, Mother. I'm ashamed to be seen with him and that's the truth."

"If only your father had lived," Charlotte said. "If only he hadn't—"

Aaron slammed the front door.

"Is that you, Aaron?" Charlotte called.

"Yes, Mother," he answered.

"Howza flick?" Deborah asked him.

Aaron smiled. "Yummy."

That night he drew a vicious picture of his sister. He looked at it. It wasn't enough. He began to draw another picture, then, suddenly shifting from one form to another, he started writing. He wrote for hours. About Deborah. And Charlotte. Page after page, crushing them beneath the weight of his erudition, slashing the remains with his wit. It was nearly dawn when he finished. Aaron walked outside and waited for the sun. He felt wild.

He began writing character sketches of his fellow students, the shift into high school serving only to widen his choice of subject matter. He was protected from everyone now; as long as he had paper, he was safe. In school he was brilliant, and if his teachers were frightened of his habit of asking difficult questions, then smiling at them while they stumbled through an answer, they also admired his brilliance. His fellow students simply feared him. Sometimes, as he limped through the halls, he could hear them whispering about him. "That's Debby Firestone's brother. Him. Yeah. Can you believe it?" Whenever he met his sister on his way to class the pattern was always the same. She would do her best not to see him until he moved almost directly in front of her. Then she would smile. Aaron always smiled back.

He was a freshman in high school when he discovered his name. He was reading in study hall, doing his homework for the day, when he chanced across the names of the four elements: earth, air, fire and water. He studied the words. Earth, air, fire and water. Earth and air. Air and fire. He said them to himself. Air and fire. Aaron Fire. AARON FIRE. He shrieked. Heads turned to face him. AARON FIRE. That was his name. Aaron Fire the writer. He was Aaron Fire, the writer.

At last he knew his immortality was assured.

Charlotte decided the time had come for Deborah to get married. Deborah was eighteen, halfway through her senior year in high school, and there seemed little point in her going to college. Her grades in high school had been barely average, and, more than that, what was the point of going to college when there were all the eligible young men right here in town, in Princeton. "And you must have an eligible man, my baby," Charlotte said. "It has got to be an eligible man."

"You mean rich," Deborah answered.

Charlotte grabbed her daughter's shoulders and turned her. They faced each other, standing close. "Now you hear me," she whispered. "You listen to your mother. I want you to marry for love, you understand that? For love." Charlotte smiled. "But you might as well fall in love with a rich man."

And so the search for a suitor began. Not that there was any shortage of candidates; Deborah was pretty, with pale red hair and a lithe body, and boys flocked to the yellow house on Nassau Street. High-school boys and Princeton sophomores and even a few graduate students all the way from Columbia University. But the rich ones were too young and those old enough didn't quite seem eligible enough.

Aaron watched it all, watched as his mother entertained the men in the living room while Deborah applied a final touch of lipstick, a last dab of perfume. Charlotte was at her most charming—she seemed to speak more Southern than in the past—as she gently probed the young men, inquiring as to their homes, their interests, their parents' occupations. "Mr. Firestone was a fine lawyer," she would begin. "Is your father by any chance in law?" Occasionally she would bring Aaron into use, calling to him as he stood by the wall outside the living room. "Oh, come in, Aaron. Do you know my son Aaron? Aaron's the smart one in the family." But always, after Deborah and her escort had gone, Charlotte would frown slightly, shaking her head. "Not for my baby," she would mutter. "Not good enough for my baby."

Generally her disapproval went only that far—a quick shake of the head. The one time it exceeded the limit was when Deborah went out with Dominic Melchiorre. He was a big man, broad and swarthy, and he came to the door wearing a striped double-breasted suit. Ill at ease, he stumbled through a few minutes' conversation with Charlotte. Then he smiled at Charlotte—he had a dazzling smile, white teeth flashing against dark skin—and moved outside. "Tell Debby I'm in the car," Dominic Melchiorre said. Charlotte watched him through the screen door as he got into an old sedan and began smoking. Deborah dashed after him a few minutes later. "Bye, Mama," she said. "Don't wait up."

But Charlotte waited.

Aaron listened to the scene from his room. Deborah got home after three and Charlotte was ready. "An Italian?" she began. "I brought my daughter up so she could be escorted by an Italian? I bought my daughter clothes so she could look nice for a . . . a . . ."

"Say it," Deborah urged.

"Catholic," Charlotte said.

"I like him."

"You like him. Oh, baby, you don't know what you're saying. What does he do?"

"He's in the construction business."

"Day laborer, you mean. A common sweating day laborer."

"But I *like* him."

"There's nothing to *like*! He does not exist. This did not happen. Not in our world. He is gone, hear? He is dead and forgotten and long, long gone. You tell me that. Deborah Crowell Firestone, you just tell me!"

There was a long quiet.

"Gone," Deborah whispered then. "He's gone."

They wept that night. Both of them. When they retired to their bedrooms, Aaron could hear them weeping.

Aaron smiled.

Jamie Wakefield appeared the following week, as if divinely ordered. Charlotte met him first, at the Browse-Around. "This wonderful young man came in today," she began, the minute she got home. "Listen to me, Deborah, while I tell you about him."

"Who?" Deborah took her gum out of her mouth and began rolling it in her fingers.

"Jamie Wakefield, that's what I'm trying to tell you. Jamie Wakefield, he bought a coat—Deborah, stop playing with your gum this minute, hear?—a cashmere coat. For his mother. It's her birthday and he bought her a one-hundred-percent cashmere coat just like that. We got to talking, and he is a real charmer and nice-looking and—"

"I'll bet," Deborah said.

"And it turns out he's from Dallas. Well, I had his address, of course—he was sending the coat to his home—and you remember my cousin Millie—well, she lives in Dallas, has all her life, and she told me today—"

"You called her?" Deborah said. "To check up on this boy?"

"I did no such thing as check up on anybody. I owed Cousin Millie a letter—have for the longest time—so I called her to chat and if I happened to mention the Wakefield boy, well, I certainly don't see anything unusual in that. Deborah, you're going to love this Jamie Wakefield—I know it. I told him all about you—he's very interested—he's a premedical student and I mentioned how you loved biology and all. He's coming on Friday to see you. I knew you'd be free, so I took it on myself—"

"I'm busy Friday," Deborah began.

"Not anymore you're not," Charlotte said. "Not after what Cousin Millie told me today you're not."

"What did she say?"

"He's eligible, baby. That's what she said."

Jamie Wakefield arrived promptly at seven o'clock on Friday, wearing a dark tweed coat, a dark tweed jacket and dark gray pants. Shy, obviously nervous, he waited with Charlotte and Aaron in the living room.

"I think the role of a physician is a noble one, Mr. Wakefield," Charlotte said. "My husband, Mr. Firestone, was a lawyer. That's noble too."

"Yes, ma'm," Jamie Wakefield said. He was of medium height, with brown hair and a bland, even face.

"My son Aaron here hasn't decided yet what he wants to be, have you, Aaron?"

"Not yet," Aaron lied. He had never told her about Aaron Fire. There was no point in telling; she would never have understood.

"Aaron's the brains of our little family," Charlotte went on. "Deborah's got the beauty and Aaron's got the brains." She laughed softly. "I don't know where I fit in."

"I'm sure they both take after you, Mrs. Firestone," Jamie Wakefield said.

"Gallantry," Charlotte said. "Undeniable gallantry. See, Aaron? It's true what I say about Southern men. They have—what would you call it, Mr. Wakefield?"

"I don't know, ma'm."

"Flair," Charlotte said. "That's as good a word as any. Style. Southern men have style."

"If you say so, ma'm." Jamie Wakefield nodded.

"Why, I remember some of my beaus when I was growing up in Roanoke. I remember . . ."

Fortunately, Deborah appeared.

Jamie Wakefield stood silently, looking at her. She was wearing a dark green dress and it contrasted perfectly with her pale red hair. "Mr. Wakefield, my daughter Deborah," Charlotte began. "Deborah, this is Jamie Wakefield from Dallas."

"How do you do, Mr. Wakefield," Deborah said.

"Yes, ma'm." Jamie nodded, looking at her.

Charlotte saw them to the door, and when they were gone she whirled around, eyes bright, arms stretched wide. "Aaron," she said, "we have great expectations."

For the next month Deborah and Jamie dated several times a week and every weekend. Jamie was inexperienced, backward at times, ill at ease. He took her to the movies and for coffee after, where she did most of the talking, chattering on about whatever came into her mind, while he simply nodded, sipping his coffee and nodding, looking at her. Then they began going to New York. They ate sometimes at Le Pavillon—Jamie's father liked Le Pavillon—and they went to the theater on Saturday nights, and everything seemed to be living up to Charlotte's hopes until Deborah found out she was pregnant.

Charlotte's reaction to the news was quite remarkable. They were having dinner, Deborah and Charlotte and Aaron, sitting at the small table in the corner of the kitchen, and Charlotte was commenting about how happy she was and how happy Deborah was and how even Aaron seemed happier than usual and wasn't it wonderful what one person like Jamie Wakefield could do for the spirits of one family and the high cost of weddings and was there ever a better time of day than suppertime with a family all together when Deborah burst uncontrollably into one quick wave of tears and then gave forth the news. In the ensuing silence, Deborah half closed her eyes, tilting her face up toward her mother, ready for the blow.

Charlotte simply put her fork down. "You're sure?"

Deborah nodded.

"Jamie?"

Deborah shook her head.

"Who, then?"

Deborah sat frozen.

"Tell me—" Abruptly Charlotte stopped and said "No."

Deborah nodded yes.

"The Catholic, I might have known," Charlotte said, and she put the tips of her fingers against her closed eyes, talking very quietly. "It is not going to happen and that is all there is to it. I simply will not allow . . ." She opened her eyes. "Are you sure it isn't Jamie?"

Deborah nodded.

"How do you know?" Charlotte asked, no longer talking quietly.

"Jamie's never touched me," Deborah whispered.

Charlotte reached across the table and took her daughter's hand, stared at her daughter's eyes. "We can remedy that, can't we, baby?" Deborah said nothing. "Can't we, baby? Can't we, baby?" Staring and touching, Charlotte went on. "Can't we, baby? Can't we, baby? Can't we, baby?"

Deborah was never one to argue with her mother.

When Jamie arrived that night Deborah was waiting for him, sitting in the living room. "Where's your mother?" Jamie asked. "It doesn't seem as if I deserve to see you without talking with your mother a while first. Sort of a price of admission."

"Mother had to go to New York for the evening. Some cousin of hers is in town."

"Well, I'll miss her," Jamie said. "I'll truly miss her." He took off his tweed coat and folded it over a chair. "You look very pretty, Deborah."

She smiled at him. "You always say that."

"It's the truth is why."

Deborah wore a black sweater open at the throat with a thin strand of pearls around her neck. "Hey," she said, giggling. "Guess what I discovered today. Guess. Mother keeps a bottle. Isn't that amazing? Do you want a drink?"

"No," Jamie said.

"True blue Jamie Wakefield," Deborah answered. "Lips that touch liquor will never touch his. I'm going to have a drink. A big strong one."

She disappeared into the kitchen and Jamie could hear the sound of an ice tray splitting open. He rubbed his palms against his trousers. Deborah came back carrying two glasses. "I brought you one anyway. In case you change your mind." She handed it to him and they both sipped in silence for a while.

"Aaron's at the movies," Deborah said. "Like always, Aaron's at the movies."

Jamie nodded.

They sipped a while longer.

"The lights bother my eyes," Deborah said. "Jamie, turn off the lights."

"What's got into you anyway? 'Jamie, turn off the lights.' "

Deborah giggled. "I'm just trying to get you alone in the dark, silly. That's all."

Jamie looked at her. "You are?"

"I are."

"Oh." Slowly he walked to the wall switch and flicked it off. The room was dark momentarily, but then they began getting accustomed to the moonlight. Jamie sat across the room from her, holding tightly to his glass.

"Jamie Wakefield, you win the blue ribbon for stupidity. The world's championship."

"What did I do?"

"Why are you sitting over there? What's the point of being all alone in the house with no lights anywhere to be seen if you're going to sit a million miles away?"

"You want me to come sit beside you?"

"No. Move farther away if possible."

He moved through the darkness and sat beside her. "Here I am," he said, taking a long drink of bourbon.

Deborah began to laugh. "It's just like kindeegarden. I swear it is." She laughed louder. "You might as well turn the lights back on. Never mind. I'll do it."

She made as if to move, but he took her hand. "No."

"Well, why not?"

Her pearls glistened in the moonlight.

"Why not?"

Jamie put his drink down. His hands were trembling terribly.

"Why not?"

Jamie grabbed her. He dug his fingers into her shoulders and her face turned, moving up to meet his.

"Jamie," Deborah said. "Jamie."

He kissed her again and she pressed her body against his body, her arms locking around his neck. Her tongue flicked at his mouth while his hands pressed against her flat stomach. Slowly, hesitantly, his hands began moving higher until they were cupped around her breasts. "Yes," Deborah said. Jamie began unbuttoning her sweater.

Aaron saw it all.

Standing in the darkness of the foyer, he saw it from the first rough kiss. There were times when it was hard to keep from laughing at what they said, at Deborah's pseudo passion, Jamie's overpowering sincerity. But he did not laugh. He watched instead as they disrobed, throwing their clothes to the floor, lying on the couch in the moonlight. Deborah still wore her pearls and Jamie had his socks on, but Aaron did not laugh. He moved closer as their bodies locked, Jamie astride her, Deborah moaning wonderfully beneath him.

When they were done Aaron left, slipping out of the house. Alone on the sidewalk, he began to howl.

They waited three weeks before Deborah made the phone call. Three weeks seemed suddenly an incredible length of time. Charlotte would stare at Deborah's stomach in the mornings, then quickly look away. But finally the time came and Deborah made the call.

"Jamie?" she said. She was crying softly; the tears were real.

"Yes?"

"Jamie—"

"What? What is it? Tell me."

Deborah told him.

"Are you positive? It can't be. It's too soon."

"I'm positive" was all Deborah said.

Jamie said nothing for a while.

"Come see me," Deborah managed, crying harder now. "Come see me tonight, Jamie Wakefield. I'll be waiting."

"I'll be there."

He found the note as he came back to his room after class. A folded piece of paper, it had been slipped under his door. Jamie stooped, picked it up. Then he read it.

SHE LIES

SHE LIES

IT ISN'T YOUR BABY

IT ISN'T YOUR BABY

They waited for him on the front porch of the yellow frame house, Charlotte and Deborah and Aaron. It was a warm night. Deborah sat very still. Aaron paced. Charlotte could not stop talking. "Now don't you worry, baby. Just as soon as he gets here we'll go inside—won't we, Aaron?—the minute he arrives you know we'll just disappear—you understand, Aaron?"

"Yes, Mother," Aaron said.

Charlotte turned to Deborah. "What time did he say he'd come?"

"Seven. He always comes then."

"Lots of time, baby."

Aaron paced faster.

"Aaron, you're making me nervous," Charlotte said.

"Terribly sorry, Mother." Aaron sat.

"Lots of time," Charlotte said.

"Maybe he won't come," Aaron said.

"Hush," Charlotte told him.

"Well, maybe he won't. Maybe he knows."

Charlotte snapped, "Impossible."

"I guess you're right, Mother." Aaron's fingers squeezed the arms of the rocking chair.

"Lots of time," Charlotte said at seven o'clock. She said it again at a quarter after and again at half past. "Lots of time. Lots of time."

Aaron waited with them. He could not remember having been so wildly happy. He had never known until then how splendid was his hatred, and the strength of it surprised him, almost frightened him a little. Taste it, he thought. Go on. His sister stared straight into the quiet night. His mother turned constantly, gazing down Nassau Street for the boy, the expression on her face growing more and more desperate as the hours went by. Aaron's body flamed. Giddy, he waited, exultant; he watched, enraptured, triumphant, revenged. Taste it. Go on. Go on. Taste it, bitch. Taste it, whore. Taste the wrath of Aaron Fire!

II

Walt was trailing Big Nose Tim Connery while his mother died.

The June sun felt cold on Walt's freckled skin and he knew his teeth were just aching to chatter. He was scared; no use denying it. But he was not ashamed of his fear. Who wouldn't be afraid of Big Nose Tim Connery, wanted for grand and petit larceny, arson, fraudulent use of the U.S. mails, and who was—according to the poster in the post office where

Walt got all his information—KNOWN TO BE ARMED. Big Nose Tim Connery stopped. Walt dashed behind a tree. Big Nose turned. Walt held his breath. A dozen or so lush streets away, in St. Louis' wealthiest suburb, Walt's mother lay dozing in her white bedroom, a nurse in an easy chair sitting close beside. The doctor, on his morning visit, had pronounced Emily Kirkaby to be "resting comfortably"—can you rest comfortably with terminal cancer?—but no one was kidding anyone anymore. It was simply a mathematical matter—seconds, minutes, perhaps days—until Emily died.

Big Nose Tim Connery started walking again, faster now. Walt, on the far side of the street, pushed his glasses up snug against the bridge of his nose with his left thumb, then dashed forward into the shadow of the next protective tree trunk. He continued on, from tree to tree, and as he passed some kids playing marbles on a lawn the thought crossed his mind that he must have looked like a nut. But what did kids know anyway? It was lonely work, gangbusting, and you just couldn't care about appearances; you had your job to do and you did it and that was that.

Big Nose stopped again. Walt froze behind a tree. Big Nose took out a handkerchief and wiped his forehead. Walt noted the action down in his notebook with his pencil stub. He had a list of Big Nose's activities for the past twenty minutes and it probably would come in handy at the trial. Walt peeked out from behind the tree and, seeing his quarry back on the move, darted out of the shadows toward the next tree, but Big Nose Tim Connery turned and Walt, caught between shelters, was momentarily visible, so he casually dropped to his knees and began searching for four-leaf clovers. Big Nose Tim Connery never suspected a thing. Walt had to smile. Walt the Whizzer. That was his favorite name for himself: Whizzer. His full name was Egbert Walters Kirkaby, and he hated it. Most everyone called him Walt, which was O.K., except his lousy brother Arnold, who called him Egbert or Berty. But Whizzer was the name he cherished above all. Walt the Whizzer. The Whizzer strikes again. Walt the great whizzer Kirkaby. *Whizzer!* That was a *name.* Up ahead of him, Big Nose was moving, so Walt got up from the clovers, confident now that the end was in sight, because Big Nose Tim Connery swung up the walk leading to a large bastard-Tudor house, knocked once and, when the door opened, disappeared inside. Walt made a note of the house number, then dashed to the house directly across the street. He rang the bell and when the door opened he said, "Pardon me, ma'am, but my name is Walt Kirkaby and could I use your phone please?"

The woman knew the name Kirkaby—everyone in the town knew

that name—so she said "Certainly" and led him to the living room. Walt peered out the living-room window; it was perfect, the Tudor house across the street was completely within his sight so if Big Nose tried a getaway, the Whizzer would be on him in a flash. Walt picked up the phone, and when he got the police station he whispered, "Gimme Sergeant Quinlan. It's life and death. Gimme Quinlan. Right away."

Across town, in the white room, Emily Kirkaby sighed. It was a soft sound, trivial; for just a moment her numb lips almost parted. The nurse, roused, stood up, looking down on the still, gray woman. The nurse nodded and shook her head, a silly gesture, but what else could she do because the woman was dying and that was a shame. Tiptoeing to the door, she opened it and gestured to the large Negro lady keeping watch outside the door. The Negro lady nodded and shook her head too, then went downstairs to spread the untidy news. The nurse crept back, still on tiptoe, and assumed her position of command by the bedpost. In a moment the door opened and P. T. Kirkaby entered, *the* P. T. Kirkaby, followed by his older son, Arnold.

"How much time she got left?" from P.T.

The nurse moved her hands. Not very much.

"She say anything?" P.T. again.

"No."

P.T. grunted. "Go outside if you want," he said to Arnold.

"I'm O.K.," Arnold answered, readying his tears.

Emily sighed a second time. This sound was so frail as to make the first seem like thunder. But they all heard it, and though they had no reason to be sure, they knew it was the last sound she was ever going to make.

"Emily," P. T. Kirkaby said.

"I don't think she can hear you." The nurse.

"Nobody asked you, did they?"

"I'm sorry, Mr. Kirkaby."

"So are we all." He turned his big body. "Arnold, where's Walt?"

Arnold let go with a few tears.

"Stop that and answer me. Where's Walt? Wherever he is, get him! Get him! That crazy Walt, where the hell is he?"

"Sergeant Quinlan speaking."

"Sergeant Quinlan?"

"Yes."

"I've got Big Nose Tim Connery for you." Walt tried very hard not to hear Sergeant Quinlan's tired sigh.

"Is that you, Kirkaby?"

"Yessir, it's me."

"You again, Kirkaby?"

"Yessir, me again."

"And you've got who this time?"

"Tim Connery. Big Nose Tim Connery. Wanted for grand and petit larceny, arson, fraudulent use—"

"Are you sure you've got Big Nose Tim Connery? Because I don't believe you, Kirkaby. I'm not calling you a liar, understand; I just somehow do not—"

"But, Sergeant—"

"You remember last week, Kirkaby? Last week you had Willie 'the Shiv' Fusari. You called me and you swore up and down—"

"Please, Sergeant Quinlan. Before he gets away."

"You swore up and down you had Willie 'the Shiv' Fusari, but when we checked it turned out you'd been trailing Rabbi Silverman of the St. Louis Synagogue. And two weeks before that you trapped Harry 'the Weasel' Trockman in the card room of the St. Louis Country Club. And—"

"It's going to look awful bad on your record, Sergeant Quinlan."

Another weary sigh. "What's going to look bad on my record, Kirkaby?"

Walt pushed his glasses up snug against the bridge of his nose with his left thumb. "Oh, just that you had a red-hot tip on Big Nose Tim Connery and you let him get away."

"Kirkaby, you are one smart boy."

"Thank you, Sergeant Quinlan."

The weariest sigh of all. "All right, Kirkaby, where's Big Nose?"

"He's lurking in the house at 274 South Elm. I'm calling from right across the street, so if he tries a getaway, I'll stay on his trail. Don't worry about that."

"Hold on, Kirkaby." The line went quiet. Walt stared out at the house across the street. "WHIZZER DOES IT AGAIN." That would be how the *Post Dispatch* would put it. In big black type the size of the whole page. "OH THAT WHIZZER!" That would be the *Globe-Democrat*'s headline. "Topping off his already unbelievably fantastically incredible career, Walt the Whizzer Kirkaby today brought to justice the worst criminal we've ever had around here . . . the modest Whizzer . . . the handsome Whizzer . . . the absolutely superb but shy Whizzer . . . the ever-popular Whizzer . . . the . . . the . . . ooohh*hhhhh that* WHIZZZZZZZZZERRRRRRRR!"

The nurse, embarrassed by the frail face of the dead woman, began to pull the sheet up and over, but she stopped, frightened, when P.T. said, "Don't."

"I'm sorry, Mr. Kirkaby."

P.T. stood over his wife a while. He felt moved and he didn't like that, not P.T., so he turned then and went to the bedroom door. "It's over, Maudie," he said to the large Negro woman.

"Well ..." Maudie began. But she had no place to go with her thought. "Well."

"Tell Arnold to forget about looking for Walt."

"Um-hmm."

"That's all, Maudie."

She nodded and turned, then, after a step, turned back. "I'm sorry, P.T."

"Yeah-yeah-yeah," he said and he gestured for the nurse to get out. When she was gone he pulled a chair over beside the bed and studied the dead face. He had been unfaithful to her so often, so many times, always, almost, that it came as a shock to him that this once she had beaten him. He had never lost well; it wasn't in his nature. But she had beaten him, the tiny bird lying dead before him. God, but she had been a sweet thing once, then, before, whenever it was, ago, long, long ago, and probably he had loved her. No. Not probably. He had loved her. That was a fact. A dead fact. A sad one. He had loved her back aways. When he was young and she was younger and that was sad too. Everything seemed suddenly sad to him. He looked again on the quiet face of his wife. "Aw, nuts," P.T. said aloud. He did not cry; but the thought crossed his mind.

"Kirkaby?"

"Yes, Sergeant Quinlan."

"I've just spoken to the people who live at 274 South Elm. That man you've been following? He sells the Encyclopædia Britannica, Kirkaby. He goes from door to door selling the Encyclopædia Britannica. Are you wearing blue pants and a tee shirt, Kirkaby? ... Kirkaby?"

"Aw, nuts."

"He saw you following him. You scared him, Kirkaby. He says you were hiding behind trees. Is that what you were doing?"

"No." Nobody spots the Whizzer. Walt looked down at his blue pants. "I'm wearing a green suit, Sergeant Quinlan. A green suit with a green tie and maybe he just claims he's selling that thing. Maybe—"

"The case is closed, Kirkaby."

"He looks an awful lot like that picture of Big Nose Tim Connery they got hanging in the post office. It's a really fantastic resemblance."

"I'm sure it is. But will you let us try to keep crime out of the area, Kirkaby? After all, it's our job."

"I'm just trying to help, that's all."

"I know you are. Goodbye, Kirkaby."

Walt hung up the phone, thanked the lady of the house and trudged on out the door, his hands shoved deep in his pants pockets. He paused a moment in front of 274 South Elm. He shoved his glasses up snug against the bridge of his nose with his left thumb. Then he began retracing his steps to the corner of Oak and Archer, where he'd left his bicycle. You couldn't follow crooks on a bicycle. It was a pretty day, so he started singing. "A wand'ring minstrel I, a thing of shreds and paaaa-tches, of baaaaa-lads, songs and snaaaaaatches, and dreeeeee-meeee luh-ulll-a-bies." He loved Gilbert and Sullivan and knew all of *Trial by Jury* by heart, plus most of *The Mikado* and *The Gondoliers*. "My ca-ta-log is long . . ." Some kids were playing marbles up ahead of him. He was a terrific marble player, the best in the world when he wanted to be, so he reached into his hip pocket for his favorite shooter, a cat's-eye, worth eight agates any day. Fatso Moran had offered him eight agates for it, but no soap. Nobody got the Whizzer's cat's-eye. "How about me playing?" he said to the kids. "You're too good, Kirkaby," one of them said—which was victory enough, Walt decided, so he muttered "Chickens" and moved on. How about that? Everybody knew you didn't mess with the Whizzer at big pot. He broke into a run then, because if he was ever going to break the four-minute mile he had to stay in shape. Ladies and gentlemen, they're entering the last lap and Gundar Hagg has the lead and it looks like it's another victory for Gundar the Wonder—*But wait!* Somebody's moving up. Just a moment, ladies and gentlemen, while I consult my program. It's—it's the Whizzer, ladies and gentlemen, Whizzer Kirkaby and look at him fly. It's fantastic! Broken leg and all and he's gaining on Hagg. Hagg looks like he's standing still. Here he comes. Here comes the Whizzer. Will you look at him flyyyyy . . .

Walt reached his bicycle and paused until he got his breath. Then he took a running start, vaulting onto the seat, pedaling hard. He took off his right hand, steadied himself, then slowly removed his left, sitting back on the seat, curving off Archer Street, heading for home. "I am the monarch of the sea; the ruler of the queen's nay-vee. Whose praise Great Britain loudly chants and so do his sisters and his cousins and his aunts . . ." He stopped singing when he got to Linden Lane, pedaling in silence along the tree-shaded pavement. When he reached the end of the lane he rode slower. "You've just got to learn to slow down on that bicycle, Walt, or you'll hurt yourself." That was what his mother always said because she didn't know he was the greatest bicycle rider of all time although once he had almost told her. At the end of the lane stood the great stone posts, and Walt experienced, as he always did, a flash of acute embarrassment because of the wooden signs that read PRIVATE DRIVEWAY. NO TRESPASSERS. TRESPASSERS WILL BE PROSECUTED. They had always been there, those signs nailed to the great stone posts, and once, at Christmas, Walt had asked that they be taken away but P.T. thought he was just trying to be funny. Walt pedaled for a while along the paved driveway until the house came into view. The house would have embarrassed him except that nobody could see it from the street because of all the shrubbery and trees. He stopped the bicycle and got off, wheeling it into the garage, parking it in the corner of the garage next to the limousine. The limousine he classed with the wooden signs. Brushing his hair with his hands, he cursed his curls good, then straightened his pants. Presentable, hopefully, he walked in the back door, through the kitchen and the butler's pantry and the dining room to the front hall.

The hated Arnold was waiting for him.

"Mother died," Arnold said.

"She did not." Since he refused to believe in the possibility of death, how could she have died? Besides, Arnold had told him and Arnold was a liar. Besides, he had kissed his pale mother on the cheek that morning and she was breathing then.

"She died."

"She did not either." God, how he loathed his brother, his three-years-older and twice-as-big brother, his handsome, picky, graceful, strong, sniveling, popular, "Walt, why can't you be more like Arnold?" brother.

"Dammit, dammit."

"No, she didn't."

"You don't care!" Arnold screamed, because he didn't care, not remotely, and the thought that it would show made him wet with fear. So he screamed it again, louder, straining his throat: *"You don't care!"*

"Boys." Maudie standing black at the top of the stairs. Walt glanced up at her face and was forced backward two steps, stunned by the knowledge of death. "Boys."

Walt glanced back at his brother, who was crying now. "I care," he said. More than care. I loved her. I did. If I love her, why don't I cry? He stared at his brother's tears, and suddenly their transparency was clear to his good, quick mind. But his face always betrayed his thoughts, always, so before he could say, "You don't fool me, Arnold, you don't fool me with those tears, you got an onion in your hand, Arnold, huh?" the thought was on his face and perhaps Arnold saw it because in three great steps he was on top of Walt, slashing out with his thick hands, bruising Walt's face, drawing blood, splintering Walt's glasses on the expensive parquet floor.

Walt had retreated at the realization of death, but he took no backward steps on his brother's account. Rather he stood firm throughout the onslaught, ignoring Maudie's high yells, the blurring of his vision, the sharp, surprising taste of blood. He stood firm, and when his brother had spent his anxious fury, before his brother could turn his false tears to the papered wall, Walt slipped it in good.

"You're a shit, you know that, Arnold?"

"All right, cut it, Walt." Big P.T. standing beside Maudie on the landing. "You too, Arnold."

"Yessir," Arnold said. "He just gets to me sometimes."

"Wipe your face, Walt. Go to your room."

Walt mounted the stairs, smiling at black Maudie, nodding to big P.T., moving past them in silence. When he reached his door he paused, then crept forward again until he reached the room where his mother had breathed that morning. He got inside quick enough but it took a while before he was able to travel to her side; he had to think about it first as he leaned, eyes wide, his back against the door. Finally he moved, eyes on the floor, to the bed edge. A chair was placed close alongside, so, eyes still on the floor, he sat, surprised at the sudden numbness invading his body. He looked at his mother and she looked like his mother except she was dead. Frail and dead. He was the only frail one left now. Before there had been two frail ones; now there was one. Before there had been someone to cling to; two frail ones are never as frail as one. Before there had been quiet support, and that was needed for survival in this great rough house. Walt looked at the thing on the bed (she was that, that only now, a thing, just a thing, like any other thing, useless, dreamless, without animation) and he almost thought, I love you so, but that was wasteful since you chose to leave me, but he killed the thought ruthlessly before it developed fully, so only the first part filled his mind. I love you so . . . I love you so . . .

He left her when Maudie called that it was time for dinner, first washing the blood from his face before going downstairs not to eat.

By midnight he knew he was falling asleep and he cursed himself for his weakness because he planned to stay up all night (it seemed the least you could do the day your mother died). Ten, tired and funny-looking, Walt drowsed, aware that the day had been an important day and not just because of what she had done. His awareness was sound. He did not know that he would be sent away to school now, that the tight knots of Missouri—it's my home, Missouri's my home—would never be quite so tight ever. He did not know that his mother's will made him nine-tenths a millionaire, but if he had been told, the news would only have conjured up black signs on stone gates, so he might have nodded but he never would have smiled. Nor, most immediately painful, did he dream that the Whizzer was dying—no . . . not you, Whizzer . . . never you—but it was true.

What was important was a simple thought that entered him forever sometime that night, a thought which later was to cause him such pain, such pain. Try as he would—and he did try, and mightily—the thought would not vacate his mind; nothing, not even medical reports which proved that the gluttonous cancer had eaten her frail body to pieces, would shake it free. It would not go. He had loved his mother, and maybe, just maybe, just possibly, if only he had been there, *there,* near her, near her to help fight that final onslaught—two frail ones are never as frail as one—then perhaps she wouldn't have died.

Ten, tired and funny-looking, Walt slept.

P. T. Kirkaby was worth considerably less than a million dollars when he married Emily Stahr Harding, who was worth a million dollars and considerably more. But P.T. (he was that even when he was poor, and who wouldn't be with a name like Phineas Thaxter?) had prospects as blazing as the air on his wedding day—*the* social event of a typically inhuman pre-air-conditioning St. Louis summer—so no one thought once to whisper that Emily's money was a factor in the love match. And it was not a factor. P.T. was aware of her wealth, of course, and its existence caused him no pain, but he was correctly confident that in not too many years she would be the poorer member of the family. If he had a motive in addition to what he hopefully assumed was his undying devotion (and he did) (and who doesn't?) it was simply the cliché of social position. Her father was a Harding, her grandfather a Stahr, while his father was an organ grinder (yes, with a monkey) and his grandfather a nameless Union soldier who stopped off in St. Louis one night on his way north after the Civil War.

They met on a spring afternoon at the St. Louis Country Club, the year before P.T. became a member. He was playing golf with Joe Manchester, who was shortly to become his partner for a while, and even though he had lost, P.T. was in fine humor; he never minded losing at golf because it was such a stupid game. Who the hell cared about putting the ball onto the green into the cup? Distance off the tee was what interested him, and though his score was much higher, he had outdriven Manchester on every hole. After they finished the eighteenth, they started back to the men's locker room and on the way they passed a woman dressed in white. Manchester stopped to talk; P.T. waited, watching.

She was a small woman—no, she wasn't, when you looked at her carefully; she just seemed small. Thin, but the legs looked strong. P.T. liked that—good strong legs. He could never understand the lure of the bosom or the butt. Her face was not a pretty face, but it didn't miss by much. Probably the nose was the spoiler—it was too small—because the eyes were good and blue and he found no complaint with the wide mouth.

"Miss Harding, Mr. Kirkaby."

"Miss Harding." He smiled at her.

"How do you do, Mr. Kirkaby." She looked up at him.

P.T. knew that look, so he broadened his smile. He was handsome, and he knew that, too. They stared at each other until she had to break it, almost jerking her head toward Manchester. Manchester must have suspected something, because he coughed unnecessarily—nobody has to clear his throat that many times—and took a step away toward the locker room. P.T. continued staring at her, sadistically, though he did not know the word, fully aware that the one place in the world she could not look was back at him. He was tempted to ask her for dinner that evening but he resisted; they didn't do that kind of thing, the rich, and he was almost one of them now. Manchester said goodbye and she echoed it. P.T. nodded and moved a step ahead of Manchester, walking toward the locker room. Abruptly P.T. turned, calling out to the retreating white figure.

"Miss Harding."

She turned, shading her eyes from the sun, waiting. P.T. crossed to her, tempted to stop halfway, tempted to make her cross to him, because he knew she would, and quickly, but he decided not to. Although he usually struck at the throat there were times when he enjoyed subduing more slowly, and this seemed like one of those times. When he reached her he took an extra half step so that he was right on top of her, and it pleased him vaguely that she held her ground.

"Dinner tonight, Miss Harding?"

"I'm sorry. I'm busy this evening."

"Some other time then." He started to turn away, but her hand touched his arm.

P.T. waited.

She fidgeted.

"What?"

"I had to say that."

"Come again?"

"That I was busy. I had to say it."

"Why?"

"It wasn't proper of you. To ask me like that. I had to put you in your place."

P.T. laughed. "O.K. I'm in my place. Now what about dinner tonight?"

"You really should give me more time to—"

"Going once. Going twice."

"Yes. Please. I would love to."

"Seven o'clock," P.T. said, and this time he did turn.

"Don't you want to know where I live?"

P.T. laughed again. The Harding house was as famous as any in St. Louis—thirty-five rooms, so they said, piled in the center of six green acres along Kingshighway. "Don't you worry," P.T. told her. "I'll find you."

And, promptly at seven—he had never been late in his life—he pulled his new Packard into her driveway. She was ready for him and, after fencing with her father—not that it mattered but they liked each other; they both went for the throat—P.T. took her to dinner.

They dined at the Chase Hotel. She ordered lobster and against his judgment, he did the same. She badgered him into it. "Oh, you'll love the lobster here. It comes straight from the shores of Maine in New England. Take the lobster. Please, Mr. Kirkaby. Please." Reluctantly, he submitted, but with vague fears; he had never ordered lobster or chicken in a restaurant before. While waiting for their food they danced some. Dancing bored P.T., but she liked it and was adept, cool, elegant, in his arms. Finally the lobster came and they sat down. She picked up a red claw and deftly dug out the rich white meat, chattering on all the while about what a fine dancer he was for such a big man. He watched her gut the claw and then, emboldened, commenced his own attack. Alas. His hands were too powerful and he cracked the claw with ease, sending splinters of red shell onto the floor, the tablecloth, her plate. Hurriedly P.T. sipped some water, then forked his vegetables into his mouth. She was eating the tail of the lobster now and he watched her carefully, searing the sharp hand movements into his brain. When he was sure he knew how, he began again. Alas. Again the red splinters scattered. P.T. covered his face with his napkin, staring down at his plate. He thought he heard her laughing and when he could bring himself to look at her he saw that she *was* laughing, and hard, tears streaming from her eyes.

"What're you laughing at?" P.T. managed, though he might just as easily have hit her a good one.

"You eating lobster."

The honesty of her reply embarrassed him still further, so for a while all he could say was "Oh."

"It really is funny," she assured him.

"It is, huh?" He watched her a moment. "I never would have ordered the damn thing except you insisted."

"I know that. That's why I insisted. Of course, it was an outside chance at best, that you might not be familiar with the niceties of lobster demolition, but I had to take it."

"I don't like being laughed at," P.T. said.

"Neither do I, Mr. Kirkaby."

"P.T."

"P.T."

"I never laughed at you."

"Oh, come now. When we met, and you just looked at me. You were laughing then. And when you asked me to dinner you were practically standing behind me, you were so close. And that was cause for laughter too. Wasn't it? *Wasn't it?*"

"Maybe."

"Yes or no?"

"Yes."

"All right." They looked at each other across the table and he was surprised by the brightness in her eyes. "We're all trying to survive, aren't we, P.T.? You do it your way, I'll do it mine. Don't you mock me. I won't mock you. Fair?" Then, without waiting for a reply, she smiled and reached out to take his hand. "You poor man, you must be famished. Order yourself a steak."

P.T. held her hand and laughed and snapped his strong fingers clear and loud and three waiters scurried out, converging around him, nodding while he ordered a sirloin. When the steak came, P.T. released Emily's hand. But not before.

At ten-thirty he drove her home, walking her up the great stone steps to the great stone house. Thirty-five rooms. He believed it now.

"I enjoyed myself," P.T. said.

"I'm glad."

"You too?"

"Does it matter?"

"Goddam right."

She flushed at that, opening the front door, moving inside, turning. "Then I did."

"I'm glad."

"Yes." She hesitated in the doorway.

"Tomorrow night?"

"Was there ever any doubt?" she said, smiling her sweet smile, closing the door behind her.

P.T. cackled as he hurried down the steps to his Packard. He gunned the motor in farewell, then drove by memory to East St. Louis, parking on a side street. He didn't bother locking his car; he was known in East St. Louis and nobody was going to tamper with it—nobody had yet and nobody was about to. P.T. walked quickly up the street. As he moved along people called to him, "Hiya, P.T.," and he winked back at them or nodded, as the fancy took him. He paused outside Randy's for just a moment, feeling an unaccustomed twinge of what he did not know was guilt. Then he went inside. Randy goosed him, bellowing her laughter as he swore. His favorite girl was busy, and, impatient, he did not wait for her but took another, another nameless one with no chest but with good strong legs and a supple body, and when they were upstairs behind the locked door she moaned entirely to his satisfaction.

P.T. had been a customer at Randy's since long before he could afford it, and he had been aware of the place's existence, and what it was, since he was a child. He was born and brought up right around the corner, and one of his early games had been simply to hoot at the rich men from St. Louis as they hurried out of Randy's at two or three o'clock on a summer morning. P.T.'s home was an oblong room—fifth floor, 71 steps—with a single dark window where he lived (lived?) with his father and his father's monkey, a surly brown bundle of hair named Belinda. P.T. had never known his mother; either she had died or the oblong room had proved too much for her to bear. When he was young he had been afraid to ask his father for the truth, and when he was old enough to shame his fear his father's mind had started playing tricks so the answer was unreliable.

Since home was someplace you didn't go, P.T. spent his life on the streets. They were dangerous streets, but not to him; he was big and he was strong and he was fast and he was smart so he was safe. He roamed, scavenged, stole, alone or with a pack, by day or by night, and it seemed only inevitable that he would, according to the countless fat housewives who screamed it at his fleeing form after he had tipped their garbage cans for laughs, "rot in the jailhouse with the other scum."

P.T. had no intention of rotting. And there were signs. School, for example. He liked school. Not the work, not the studying, but the building itself. He liked being inside it, warm on cool days, cool on hot. He was never absent or tardy, and although his grades were indifferent, there were occasional flashes of a mind operating behind the darting eyes. More than one teacher took him aside, urging hopefully, whispering, "Now, Phineas, if you would just apply yourself, if you would only *try*, Phineas . . ." So the mind was capable of survival and certainly the body was strong, but what gave P.T. his confidence was that he had dreams. Great sun-drenched dreams.

He was going to be a soldier.

A general someday, but before that a captain, a decorated captain, chest bursting with ribbons and stars, a stern captain, hard, but beloved by his men. He attempted enlistment when he and the century were both twelve, but although they were kind to him he knew he had made himself a fool. Two years later, when the Great War broke, P.T. used to pray at night that it would wait for him. Thoughtfully, it did. Within the week after St. Louis and the rest of the country declared war, P.T. marched with tears in his eyes to meet his glory.

He had flat feet.

The shock of being rejected was too great to cause pain. P.T. wandered dumbly along the streets of East St. Louis, the ribbons and stars withering, falling from his chest row by row. If, during this mute journey, some intimate had seen him and asked him to join in a robbery or a mugging, P.T. would have likely gone along, and from there, who knows? But luck was with him (luck was always with him, only he did not know it yet), for at precisely four-fifteen on that April afternoon of nineteen and seventeen, P. T. Kirkaby stumbled (quite literally) into his salvation.

It was a toaster.

Someone had left a toaster on the sidewalk, and P.T., blind, had stumbled over it. For a moment he was tempted to kick it to bits with his flat feet, but he didn't. Instead he stared at it—it didn't look all that old—eventually stooping, picking it up, tucking it under a strong arm. Then he began to wander again. At half past five he paused on the sidewalk in front of Kindall's Garage.

"Hey, P.T." P.T. turned at the sound of George Kindall's voice. George had been a friend, more or less, in high school, until he quit at the age of sixteen to tend his father's garage.

"Hey, George."

"Watcha got?"

"Toaster."

"Looks broke."

"Is."

"Hey, you enlisting today?"

"Flat feet."

"Oh. Sorry, P.T."

"Can I use the toolroom?"

"Why not."

P.T. nodded and walked to the toolroom in the rear of the garage, closing the door tight behind him. Setting the toaster on a workbench, he examined it a while. He had no actual knowledge of its workings, but soon he started taking it apart, confident that he could get it back together without much trouble; he had faith in his fingers. And wires and bolts and plugs never bothered him much; he understood them somehow. This part just had to fit into that one, and the two of them together went snugly over this dingus here. Like that. He understood. Concentrating fully on the toaster left no room in his mind for the beaten captain. First making certain that the door to the toolroom was still shut, P.T. began to sing.

The sound was surprising. It seemed to have no connection with his speaking voice, which was ordinary. The singing voice was sweet and pure and most at home with Irish ballads. "The Last Rose of Summer" or poor, fat "Molly Malone." It was his father's voice—theirs were so similar as to be identical—and on occasional evenings when the monkey was still, they would sing old songs, sitting close together in the oblong room, harmonizing tenderly until the crazy lady living downstairs banged her broom into her cracked ceiling, quieting them.

At a few minutes after six, P.T. left the toolroom, toaster in hand. "George?" he called.

"All finished?" P.T. looked around, finally locating the feet extending from below the running board of a black Chevrolet. P.T. waited, and in a moment George Kindall rolled out into view. "Fix it?"

P.T. held out the toaster. "Better 'n new."

"Buy it from you?" P.T. was about to say "You can have it," but again luck was with him (luck was always with him), because before he could speak George Kindall said, "A buck," and he reached into his overall pocket, pulling out the money.

"Done," P.T. said, and they swapped.

"If it don't work, I get my money back."

"Yeah-yeah-yeah."

"O.K. See you, P.T."

"See you, George." He left the garage and started slowly toward the oblong room. Halfway there he stopped dead. Jerking the grease-stained bill from his pocket, he stared at it. A *dollar*! And for what? Just a little tinkering. Hell, at that rate he could be a millionaire in no time.

It was almost that simple.

The next morning he was up by dawn, scavenging from the streets. By noon he had found an iron and several coffeepots and by nightfall he had fixed and sold them, "Better 'n new." Profit: six dollars. By the end of the first week he had made nineteen dollars. The following week he entered into negotiations with a small junk shop on the South Side, so after that he didn't have to scavenge anymore. He worked all day every day in the toolroom of the garage, paying George Kindall five dollars per week for rent. When he had a group of appliances in working order, he would wander the streets shouting "Better 'n new! Better 'n new!" until he had customers enough to go around. Inside of three months the junk shop he had dealt with could not supply him sufficiently, so he struck a bargain with another, then another. By January the toolroom in the garage was too small, so he rented a loft and set to work there, working nights now, straining his brute's body to the limit. ". . . if you would only apply yourself, Phineas . . . if you would only *try* . . ."

Phineas tried.

The brain that lurked behind the darting eyes grew tired of sleeping; day and night it burned. P.T. slaved sixteen hours a day, and in November 1918, when the war was over, the image of the soldier was dead. He watched the returning heroes as they marched the streets of St. Louis and he felt neither envy nor pain. Because he had money now. And he was going to have more. By his twentieth birthday he could afford the highest-priced girls at Randy's on a biweekly basis, and how many who were twenty could do that? Damn few. Damn few. He had a staff now, three mechanics working under him, and they worked, not as hard as he did, of course, but he was P.T. Kirkaby and look out up there. Before he was twenty-two he opened his first store, on a side street in East St. Louis. (He wasn't ready to make the move across the Mississippi yet; not quite yet.) Painted across the entirety of the store front, in great white letters, was his name—K I R K A B Y—and underneath that, in letters slightly smaller, BETTER 'N NEW. The store did surprisingly well, but not well enough for P.T., and, several months later, when a sales representative thought to interest him in buying new appliances in large lots and selling them for less than standard price, P.T. was way ahead of him. But he feigned doubt, got a better deal, and from then on there was no stopping him. He sold decent stuff and he sold cheap, so the housewives loved him. He had three stores before another year went by, and the week of his twenty-fifth birthday P. T. Kirkaby rented a suite in the Park Plaza Hotel, where the rich people lived. It was a glorious day for him, the only difficult moments being caused by his father, who did not understand much of what was going on and who was deathly afraid of elevators. The old man tried fleeing across the lobby, and P.T. had to grab him and lift him into the elevator, where his father trembled, eyes closed, until the journey to the eleventh floor was safely over. P.T. had six stores by that time, half of them in St. Louis proper (he had crossed the Mississippi now), the largest of all being right on Maryland Avenue in the midst of the most expensive shops in town. He never failed to smile when he saw, at night, his name— K I R K A B Y—flashing red on Maryland Avenue.

On their second date P.T. took Emily Harding to watch the Cardinals play the Giants. He bought peanuts and hot dogs and when the game was about to begin he nudged her, gesturing toward the Giant manager. "There he is," P.T. said, awed. "There's McGraw."

"Yes," Emily said. "Of course."

"You never heard of John McGraw?" P.T. was stunned. McGraw was one of his special heroes, along with Fairbanks and (privately) John McCormack. Shaking his head, he handed her some peanuts.

"Thank you," she said, but it was immediately evident that she did not know what to do with them. She glanced several times at P.T.'s big hands, at the way his fingers pressed sharply on the proper seam, making the shell split. Then she tried it herself, suddenly talking very fast. "I had no idea baseball could be so much fun. I really never thought it. I'm not much of an athlete, I'm afraid. Of course I played field hockey at school, but then everyone played field hockey at school."

"Like this." P.T. demonstrated his peanut technique.

"Oh yes, I see now," but she still could not do it. Finally she dropped the peanuts to the concrete. "I know I must look silly, but my father was very strict. He would never let me come to this kind of thing. You understand that."

But the game had started and P.T. was not aware of her talking until she pulled several times at his arm. "What?"

"I was just asking about your father."

"What about my father?"

"Nothing. It's just that you never mentioned him. So I wondered . . ." She shrugged.

Dead. That was what she was asking. "Yes."

"Oh. I'm sorry."

P.T. nodded and turned back to the game. They sat in silence through the rest of the inning, and when the Cardinals took the field P.T. said, "He's alive."

"Pardon?"

"He's alive!" Why so loud? "My father. He's retired now but he's alive. He played the organ. He was a musician. A fine musician. O.K.?" She was looking at him and he didn't much like it, so he shoved the peanuts at her and said, "Have some more lobster," and, happily, she laughed.

That night, after he had pulled his Packard to a halt in her driveway but before she had a chance to push at the door-handle, he kissed her. She was surprised and at first made token resistance, but as his strong arms held her in their circle, she honestly faced her own desire and kissed him back. When that was done, P.T. walked her up the stone steps to the great front door. Awkwardly, he kissed her hand (Fairbanks did it better) and probably it was funny, but she did not laugh.

Later, P.T. stood outside Randy's, frozen. He was unable to think why he was unable to move, so he simply stood still, waiting. Eventually a gang of children began hooting at him from across the street and their derision freed him. P.T. reached into his pocket, scattered a handful of change into the street, roared as the children scrambled for the silver. Turning abruptly, he returned to his Packard and drove back to the Park Plaza Hotel, singing.

They were married in merciless heat and honeymooned for three months in Europe. P.T. spent a fortune—"You're only *nouveau riche* once"—and on their return their house in the suburbs was finished, so they all moved in, P.T. and Emily and Emily's Negro maid and P.T.'s father and an English couple named Saunders, who were to be the first in an endless stream of servants. In their second year of marriage Emily gave birth to their first son and three years later Walt came along, but between the two the crash came, hitting P.T. hard for a while. Three stores had to be closed and two more were on the verge, though he managed to avoid the shattering losses that claimed most of his competitors. Emily gave a lot of parties in between her seemingly constant social work, and the marriage looked exemplary for several years. It wasn't, of course, but the initial decay went unnoticed. It was not until their seventh-anniversary party, at which P.T. arrived late, drunk and with several female companions, that his whoring became very common knowledge. Once it surfaced, however, he no longer took pains to hide it—Emily's public humiliations were almost ritual now—and people took to shaking their heads in silent commiseration whenever Emily walked by.

Once—it was the day after a swimming party at the Kirkaby pool at which P.T. had struck Emily (it was the first time he had ever done that, in public)—Emily's best friend, Adele Hosquith, asked her point-blank why she put up with it all. Emily—who was probably the person at the party least surprised by P.T.'s action since he was always at his cruelest right after he had "been bad" (her word for it)—was embarrassed by the question and tried not to answer. But when Adele pursued, Emily simply stated what she understood to be true: that although he was undeniably at times somewhat less kind than she would wish, still, her admiration of him and for him was more than sufficient to cover any occasional imperfections. But underneath the explanation lay sadness, for the first time he had been bad (they had not been married a year) he had come to her and told her, painfully, explicitly. He told her and stood before her, waiting, a gigantic moppet, impatient, almost, for his whipping. And she should have whipped him, she knew that now. She should have doled him his expected portion of scorn. But she piled his plate high with forgiveness, and that night, when he wept in her arms, she joyously mistook his hatred for penitential tears.

When Emily first noticed the small ump on the underside of her left breast she immediately decided not to think about it. She was vaguely aware of the possibility of the lump being a harbinger of a certain disease (the clean image of a crab flashed across her mind, but she would not think the word) but she doubted it. No one in her family had ever had the disease (dirty thing) and, besides, she was still under forty and it was an old people's sickness. There was no question about it: the lump would go away. To make absolutely certain that it would, she vowed never to look at her left breast again.

P.T. discovered it, months later. They were (for some reason) in her bed and his hands moved slowly across her body. Suddenly the hands stopped.

"Hey," P.T. said.

She pulled away from him.

"Hold still."

She tried getting up.

"I said 'still.' " Forcing her back, he flicked on the bedlight. "What the hell."

"It's nothing."

"You're a doctor?"

"Please."

In answer, he took her gently in his arms. "Hey, honey?"

"What?" she said, though she knew what he wanted. A checkup. Just a little checkup, huh? Take a little trip to Chicago and let them have a look at you. Emily resisted, but he had no intention of losing, so eventually she succumbed. She took the train to Chicago, where P.T. had arranged for a suite at the Ambassador East, and she toured the Art Institute and bought some clothes on Michigan Avenue and went to the theater twice and after a week the doctors were done testing. A sweet Jew named Berger was in charge, and when he called her into his office they lied to each other for a while.

"I'm going to be absolutely honest with you," Dr. Berger said. Lie number one.

"I want you to be." Number two.

"Well, it could be a lot worse." Number three.

"I believe you." Four.

They went through seventeen lies without once mentioning *that* name (Emily stopped counting after seventeen), and when they were all done they both smiled and shook hands and as she waved goodbye and started for the elevator she knew she was a dead woman. Back at the hotel, she was tempted to call P.T. but she did not. Instead she packed, paid her bill and took a taxi to the railroad station. She arrived in St. Louis at a few minutes before seven and took another taxi to her home. P.T. was out, but the boys were glad to see her and she talked and played with them until they tired. Then she put them both to bed. After that she unpacked, carefully folding her clothes into their proper drawers. She showered, dried herself thoroughly, ran a comb through her hair. Finally, naked (no sense in hiding it anymore), she lay down in the dark to wait. She waited from ten till eleven till one till two, motionless, staring at the ceiling, feeling it build all the while inside her. She would gladly have waited a month or a year because the look on his face was going to be worth it. When P.T. came home at three she made no sound of welcome. She listened, rather, to the sounds of his undressing. When he entered their room and turned on the overhead light, she still did not move. He did, though. He saw her and his mouth dropped and he stumbled with surprise.

"I'm going to be unfaithful to you, P.T." The tone in her voice thrilled her. She had never thought herself capable of such honest open loathing, but now her body throbbed with it. He flattened against the far wall, watching her, and the look on his face *was* worth it. After all these years she had loosed her flood of venom and she loved it. Arms outstretched, naked and dying, she advanced on her husband. "The ultimate infidelity is mine!"

Through and around all this, Walt grew up.

When he was not yet four, he spent the entirety of Easter afternoon staring at a piece of pastry. It was an exquisite piece of pastry, a delicate chocolate with a pink Easter bunny etched on top in confectioners' sugar. The bunny had little pink eyes and big pink ears and Walt thought it prettier than any picture. But he was hungry. He was incredibly hungry. So he stared at the bunny, aware of its beauty, aware, also, of the rumbling of his stomach. Walt walked out of the big living room. He roamed around the house (careful to avoid Arnold) and then went back to the living room. There was the bunny, still beautiful. But his stomach would not stay quiet. Walt made a circuit of the house again. Oh, what a beautiful bunny. He licked his lips. Gently lifting the bunny, he brought it close to his face. (Not to eat it, just to look at it better.) The bunny grazed his lips. He restored it to its position on the table and left the room again, hurrying this time, making another tour of the house. Arnold was outside now playing catch with his father and he thought of joining them, except Arnold would probably kill him later if he tried, so he watched them through a window until it was time to go look at the bunny again. Oh, he was hungry. His stomach thundered. Walt ran from the room. Arnold was still playing catch but he might stop any minute and come in and eat the bunny, so Walt ran back into the living room and, more gently than before, lifted the bunny and moved on tiptoe up the stairs to his bedroom. He placed the bunny in the very center of his pillow and climbed up on the bed to stare at the little pink eyes and the sugary ears. Oh, my. It looked even more beautiful than before now, lying graceful and chocolaty in the very center of the white pillow. Walt stuck his nose close to the bunny and stared at it cross-eyed. My, my. He got up from the bed and went to his closet and put on his gun belt (low on the hip) and, creeping to the window, fired a few hundred silver bullets into Arnold. This done, he took off his gun belt and climbed on his bed again. He was weak from hunger now, so he closed his eyes, holding his breath until his lips burst apart and he lay still, gasping. Then he grabbed for the bunny and gobbled it down. The rich taste of chocolate still lingered in his mouth as he started to cry. Burying his head in the very center of the pillow, Walt wept.

It was more or less the story of his life.

His life, or at least the early years of it, should have been pleasant. Deprivations were few, mothers were warm, fathers omnipotent but *in absentia* more than not. Yet his early years were filled with an almost perennial fear.

Arnold.

"Hey, Ugly." (They were four and seven and Walt had just eaten his first meal without spilling, an event that caused parental disbelief, then joy. Walt lay in his dark bedroom, ready for sleep.) "Hey, funny-looking, I'm talking to you."

"What is it, Arnold?"

"You're gonna cry, Ugly. You know that? Every day till you're dead."

"I am not."

"Y'are too." Arnold's fingers began pinching him.

"Stop it, Arnold."

"Make me."

The fingers dug at the flesh on his ribs. He tried to struggle but Arnold was strong. "Stop it, Arnold."

"Shut up. If you ever tell them, I'll make you cry twice as bad."

"Arnold, you're hurting."

"Cry."

Walt bit his lip but it hurt. It really hurt. Disobeying his orders, the tears came. But Arnold continued to pinch. That was the thing about Arnold: he enjoyed it.

"Hey, funny-looking." (A summer noon and he had his first real suit, fresh from the store all the way in St. Louis.)

"What?"

"C'mere and help me a sec."

"Why?" Already wary.

"Just c'mere and hold the hose. I gotta spray the garden."

"You gonna get me wet?"

"How can I get you wet? The water's not turned on."

That was true. Walt took the hose from his brother. "Now what?"

"Just hold it. Whatsa matter, doncha trust me?"

"No."

"Well, just hold it." Arnold walked toward the house. "That's a nice suit, Walt. I really like that suit."

"You do?"

"Yeah. You really look good in it. No kidding."

"It comes all the way from St. Louis."

"It does?"

"Mama helped me buy it. She drove me in the car."

"No kidding?"

"You really like it?"

"I'll say I do. I wish I had a suit like that. Hey, Walt, is there something stuck in the end of the hose?"

"I don't see—" The water gushed from the nozzle, drenching his body, turning the blue suit a darker blue.

Walt fled toward the house but Arnold grabbed him. "Don't you tell them or you'll really get it."

Walt broke free and continued his run, Arnold's laughter keeping him company.

"Hey, Goofy." (It was Walt's birthday, and he was in his room, getting ready for a boat ride on the Mississippi with his mother.)

"What'd you close the door for?"

Arnold leaned against the door. "No special reason."

"What do you have behind your back?"

"Nothing."

"Then let me see your hands."

"Sure." Arnold brought one hand out, opened it, put it behind his back, then brought out the other hand. "See? Nothing."

"Both at the same time, I meant."

Arnold crossed to the bed, keeping his hands behind his back. "That boat ride sure oughta be fun."

Walt continued getting dressed, keeping an eye on his brother.

"Ice cream and cake. All you can eat. That's what I heard Mother tell P.T."

"You did?"

"That's right. All the chocolate cake you can eat. Hey, Walt. Guess what I found today?"

"I give up."

"Oh, go on, guess."

"I'm late, Arnold."

"Guess."

"What have you got behind your back, Arnold?"

"Jar."

"What's in it?"

"Guess."

"Cut it out, Arnold."

"You know what I got."

"Don't."

"Doncha know?"

"*Spider!*" Walt said and he bolted for the door but Arnold blocked him. Walt retreated.

Arnold waved the jar at him. "Baby. It can't hurt you. Not while it's in the jar. I wonder what would happen if it got out?" He twisted the cap and then the spider was crawling crazily on the rug.

"Arnold—"

"If they hear you, you're dead, you know that."

"Please, Arnold."

"Eat the spider."

"No."

"Yes. Eat the spider."

"Please."

Arnold scooped it up and ran for Walt, grabbing him, forcing him down, pushing the twisted black mass toward Walt's face. Walt screamed and got sick on the rug.

"Hey, four eyes." (It was suppertime and Maudie was feeding them at the kitchen table while she and the other servants served cocktails to company in the living room far away.)

Walt silently finished his mashed potatoes.

"You better answer me, Egbert. You know what'll happen if you don't."

Maudie came in, big and black, and took their plates, depositing them in the sink. She crossed to the icebox door and brought out two large bowls of chocolate pudding. "Surprise," she said as she set the bowls in front of them.

"Oh boy," Walt said. "Oh boy." Maudie turned and left the room. Walt picked up his spoon.

"Wait!" Arnold said.

Walt looked over at him, spoon poised.

"Don't touch that. There's something wrong with it."

"Oh, you don't fool me, Arnold. Not this time, you don't."

"I'm not trying to fool you."

"You just want my pudding, I know. Well, you can't have it."

"I don't want your pudding, Berty. I don't even want mine." He pushed his plate a few inches away.

"Why don't you?"

"Because there's something wrong with it." He sniffed his pudding. "It's spoiled or something. Smell it yourself if you don't believe me."

Walt stuck his nose close to the pudding and that was when Arnold pushed his face down, right into the bowl. The pudding splattered all over and Walt's glasses were caked with chocolate so he could hardly see.

"All right now, what's the fuss?" Maudie, big and black, stood by the table.

"Walt had an accident," Arnold hollered. "He thought the pudding smelled funny and then he had an accident."

"I do believe you're right," Maudie said, picking up Walt's bowl, sniffing it. "I must have used spoiled cream. It sure does smell funny."

"It does?" Arnold said, and he sniffed at his bowl of pudding until the great black hand slammed down, shoving his face into the chocolate. Arnold kicked but the hand held firm, forcing his nose flat against the bottom of the plate. Arnold flailed his arms but the great black hand did not move. It pushed and pushed and only when Arnold began coughing convulsively did it raise up.

Arnold ran sobbing from the room, crying, "P.T., P.T." over and over.

"He's going to tell them," Walt murmured. "He's running right to them."

Then Maudie had him, shaking him hard. "You! You are so gullible I want to cry. You know what that means? Gullible? It means sucker and you stop being one!"

Then Arnold was back in the kitchen, screaming, "You're gonna get it now, you're gonna get it now!" and then P.T. strode in, followed by Emily.

P.T. pointed to his eldest son. "You do that, Maudie?"

"Bet yo' ass!"

P.T. hesitated, staring at the folded black arms. "Oh," he said finally. "Well, you probably had a good reason."

"That's my feeling."

"Just checking," P.T. said, and he returned to his guests.

Emily approached Maudie. "Maudie," she whispered, "you must try to watch your language in front of the children."

"You're absolutely right, Emily. I gotta do that."

"Yes," Emily said, and she followed her husband. Arnold just stood there, staring around.

Walt looked at him. "Chicken!" he said. "Yellow chicken!"

Arnold began to shake. Then he (1) stamped his foot in anger; (2) burst into tears; (3) fled.

"He's yellow," Walt said. "I never told them. Never even once."

"Shut up and eat your pudding," Maudie said.

Walt ate his pudding. And didn't it taste good!

Gino Caruso was the only marble player in school as brilliant as Walt. Gino never fudged or spit during an opponent's turn. He simply knelt by the perimeter of the big pot circle, his chin resting on his knees, his dark eyes bright. Then, when his turn came, he would knuckle down fairly and begin to shoot, his deadly fingers cleaning out the pot with startling speed. He and Walt would usually battle around the big pot circle late in the afternoons, after they had beaten all other comers soundly. Then, their pockets crammed with spoils, they would engage each other in epic struggles that sometimes lasted till dark. Gino won some, others Walt won; always the caliber of play was outstanding. But Gino was more than just a marble player; he was quick, brighter than most, and easily the most graceful on the jungle gym or at tag or pom-pom-pullaway.

"Hey, Gino," Walt said. It was autumn and they were standing together on the playground during recess.

"Hey, Walt."

"Hey, Gino," Walt said again, feinting with his right, sending a straight left that grazed Gino's arm.

"Pow," Gino said, moving his lithe body this way, then that, getting Walt off balance, delicately landing a light right to the chin.

"Watcha doon?" They continued to spar.

"Watcha mean, watcha doon? When?"

"After."

"School?"

"Yeah." Walt drove in with a right and left to the body, but Gino was much too fast, so both punches missed.

"Some stuff for my old lady."

"That take long?" Walt tried a roundhouse right, but it wasn't a good idea; Gino gave him three fast ones in the ribs and was gone from range before the right arrived.

"Half hour if I hurry."

"You wanna do something after that maybe?"

"Sure. What?"

"I don't know. Something."

"Fine with me. Where? Here?"

"How 'bout my house? We got trees."

"Where's your house?"

"End of Linden Lane."

"I'll find it." The recess bell rang. They started back to school, still fighting. "Zonk." A right to the breadbasket. "See you, Walt."

"Whap." A final errant left. "See you, Gino."

As soon as school was over he hurried home. His mother was back by the pool with Mrs. Hosquith. She waved to him, gesturing toward the water, but he shook his head, shouting, "Gino's coming to play" before turning, starting for the kitchen. He let the screen door slam shut with a bang because that always got Maudie good.

"You let that door slam one more time and you are d-e-a-d."

"Hey, Maudie." He entered her domain.

"Don't you 'Hey Maudie' me, whoever you are. I don't associate with people so stupid they let the door slam."

"Hey, Maudie."

"Hey Maudie what?"

"What we got to eat?"

"Food, stupid. That's what we generally eat, ain't it?"

"We got any cookies or cake or anything?"

"Who wants to know?"

"Gino's coming to play and maybe he'll be hungry."

"The famous marble shooter you told me about?"

Walt nodded.

"Is he as stupid as you are?"

Walt shook his head.

"Then don't you worry. I'll feed him."

Walt dashed out the back, letting the screen door slam again, waiting till he heard "d-e-a-d" loud and clear. Then he ran around to the front and started inspecting trees. He decided that the old maple would be best to climb, and, the decision made, he tore into the house again and up to his room. He got out his collection of baseball cards and tossed them casually across his dresser top. Then he brought his game of Photo Electric Football from his closet and stood it in a corner of the room. Ready at last, he mussed his hair, made sure his hands were dirty and walked to the window seat on the landing. From the window he had a clear view of the long driveway along which Gino would have to travel. Walt waited. After a moment or two he began to sing. "I'm called little Buttercup, sweet little

Buttercup, though I shall never tell whyyyyyy; but still I'm called Buttercup, dear little Buttercup, sweet little Buttercup I-I-I-I-I-I." No Gino. He dashed downstairs and looked at the grandfather's clock that dominated one corner of the foyer. It had been half an hour. Gino was due. He took the stairs two at a time and slid safely onto the window seat. It was a beautiful day, warm, with the leaves still striving for green. A light wind blew across the great lawn. Walt slid down the banister and examined the grandfather's clock. Forty minutes now. He climbed back to the window seat. The maple tree was begging to be conquered; its low arms reached out toward him, bowing before the mounting wind. "You're mad, Kirkaby. No one has ever climbed Everest. Much less at night. Much less in a blizzard like this one. Great Scott, man, you won't have a chance." The Whizzer's eyes narrowed. "You've got to listen to me, Kirkaby. It's two hundred below on the slopes tonight. And that wind! Just listen." The Whizzer listened. Then he donned his ear muffs. "Kirkaby, come back. Kirkaby, don't. Kirkaby . . ." Fifty-five minutes. Walt drew back his foot to kick the clock, then thought the better of it.

"Ain't your friend here yet?"

"He'll come!"

Maudie looked at him. "Course he will, sugar. Don't you worry."

Walt walked to the window seat and stared out. Nothing. Just the wind. At that moment he could have cried, so he vaulted off the seat and ran out into the front yard. The maple tree was no fun to climb alone, but he pulled himself up over the bottom limbs just to see better. Nothing. Just the wind. Had he said Linden Lane? Maybe he had said the wrong address. Walt shook his head. He remembered. End of Linden Lane. That was what he had said and Gino had answered I'll find it. Walt jumped out of the tree and did an awkward somersault on the grass. They always made him dizzy, but the grass was soft so he didn't mind. He lay on his stomach and pushed his glasses up snug tight against the bridge of his nose with his left thumb before he began looking for a four-leaf clover. He was terrific at spotting four-leaf clovers, probably the best in the world. He never cared much for them but his mother loved them, so whenever he had nothing better to do he hunted them down and gave them to her. She always made a fuss and thanked him and that wasn't so bad. Walt looked for a little but then stopped because where was Gino! Walt rolled onto his back but the clouds were too thin to hide any animals. And wasn't that always the way? When you were in a hurry there'd be a whole menagerie over you and when you had time, nothing. Not even a cow; not even if you cheated. Walt stood and started spinning around and around. That really made him dizzy, much worse than the somersaulting, but he kept on until he almost fell back to earth. He lay in a heap, eyes closed, heart thumping. *Where was he?* Why did he say he was going to come if he wasn't going to? He should never have told his mother and Maudie. Walt stood and thrust his arms out straight, making airplane noises. He was good at it but it bored him then, so he shoved his hands into his pockets and started walking aimlessly across the perfect lawn. "*Gino!*" he yelled suddenly, all he had. From somewhere came an answer, soft and far. "Walt? Walt?"

Walt ran. He tore down the lawn to the driveway and then sped over the gravel toward the great stone posts at the end. Gino was standing framed between the posts at the edge of the driveway.

"Hey, Gino!" Walt cried.

"Hey, Walt!"

"How long you been here?"

"Hour."

"You have? You been here an hour, Gino?" They were standing side by side now and they shook hands. "Why didn't you come in? You crazy?"

"I just been waiting for you here."

"But you should have come *in*. That's what you should have done. You crazy Gino."

"I can read."

"Read what?"

Gino pointed.

Walt stared at the wooden signs. PRIVATE DRIVEWAY. NO TRESPASS-ING. TRESPASSERS WILL BE PROSECUTED.

"I ain't no trespasser," Gino said.

"Oh them. They're just there, y'know? Now c'mon."

"I ain't no trespasser."

"Will you forget about them, huh?" And he pulled at Gino's arm but Gino did not move. Walt pulled again and then he let go and ran at the signs. "I tell you they don't mean anything! See?" And he started pulling at them but they were nailed in, so he grabbed a rock and started pounding with all his might until the wood began to splinter. "See? See? They don't mean anything! Not a goddam thing! See! See, Gino! See!" He switched the rock to the other hand, crying like a fool, smashing until the wooden signs fell from the pillars to the ground, where he stamped them to death beneath his feet.

Maudie approved of Gino and Emily was very kind, so the next recess Walt asked him over for lunch.

"Got my lunch," Gino said.

"You got milk? You got dessert?"

"No."

"Then come on."

So they walked to Linden Lane, quizzing each other on batting averages. (They were both fantastic on batting averages.) When they got to the house Walt opened the back screen door, careful not to let it slam, and preceded Gino up the steps. "Hey, Maudie."

"Hey Maudie what?"

"Guess who I got with me?"

"I got my own lunch," Gino said quickly, holding up his brown paper sack.

"He's gonna have milk and dessert."

"That's right," Maudie said. "Course he is." They sat at the kitchen table and she brought Gino a plate. He unfolded the brown paper bag, took out two sandwiches, then folded the bag again on the same creases and stuck it into his back pocket. Maudie busied herself with Walt's lunch.

"Watcha got?" Walt asked.

"Same as always."

"What?"

"Peanut butter and jelly sandwiches."

"They any good?"

"You never had one?"

"No."

Maudie brought them both glasses of cold milk. Then she brought Walt's lunch. It consisted of a slab of roast beef and mashed potatoes and gravy and fresh green peas.

"Lemme taste," Walt said.

Gino handed him a sandwich.

Walt took a small bite. "So this is peanut butter and jelly."

Gino nodded.

Walt could say nothing more.

Then Gino said, "You ate my whole sandwich."

"Gimme the other."

Gino hesitated.

"Here," Walt said, and he shoved his steaming plate of roast beef across the table. "If you don't like it, you can have something else. But I gotta have that other sandwich."

Gino started eating the roast beef.

"Oh boy," Walt said. "Oh boy." He finished half the sandwich, then forced himself to slow down. "You get these every day?"

Gino nodded. "Whaddya call this?"

"Roast beef."

"Oh, sure," Gino said, and then neither of them spoke until the meal was done.

The next day, Maudie made Walt peanut butter and jelly sandwiches and he ate them, but all the while he was watching Gino eat his. Because Maudie's weren't the same. Peanut butter is peanut butter; jelly, jelly; bread, bread—but they just weren't the same. After lunch, he took her aside while Gino waited for him in the doorway.

"Those were terrific sandwiches, Maudie. I really liked those sandwiches."

"Go on."

"Well." Walt smiled at her. Finally he whispered, "I think it's that brown bag gives them the flavor, you know what I mean?"

"I know what you mean." She sighed. "And ask the marble shooter how he likes his steak. We aim to please around here."

"Yes, Maudie. I'll ask him, Maudie."

From then on it was hot lunches for Gino.

Afternoons, they played in the yard, the two of them. (Once Arnold tried to ruin it, but they were stronger than Arnold, the two of them together, so he tried it only once.) They played marbles, of course, battling grandly on the gravel driveway, or tag or two-man touch, or they lay on the grass adding numbers or counting animals in the sky. One afternoon it rained so they ran up the stairs to Walt's room and lay on the floor.

"Ducky Medwick in '35," Walt said.

".353. My turn. Pepper Martin in '34."

".296. My turn."

"Belinda . . ."

"No, it isn't your turn. He hit .289, so it's still my turn."

"Aw, nuts," Walt said.

"Dizzy Dean in '34."

"Belinda . . ."

"Dizzy Dean in '34," Walt repeated. "Thirty wins, seven losses. O.K. My turn. Daffy Dean in '34."

"*Belinda . . .*"

"What is that?"

"My grandfather. He lives in the back. Sometimes he yells a lot."

"Daffy Dean in '34." Gino closed one eye, then sat up. "Who's Linda?"

"Not Linda. Belinda. A monkey. Grandfather's a little . . ." And he twirled his index finger around his ear.

"Is he really . . ." Twirl of the index finger.

"Don't you believe me? You want to see?"

"Can we?"

"Follow me." Walt stood and crept out of the room down the long hall to the back of the house. He stopped in front of a partly open door and turned to Gino. "Don't be surprised at how the room looks. It's all his stuff. Very old."

"O.K.," Gino whispered. "I'm with you."

Walt knocked and gave the door a push. "Grandfather?"

"Belinda?"

"No, it's me, Grandfather. Walt. You remember me?" He moved into the room a step at a time.

"You. Yes. I remember." The old man sat in a corner by the window. A torn blanket comforted his shoulders. The room was furnished sparely, a bed, a tired chair, a trunk without a lid. The old man peered at Walt, his eyes very pale, very wet, hardly blue.

"Can I get you anything, Grandfather?"

"Belinda has gotten out. Have you seen her?"

"No. I'm sorry but I haven't."

"Well, she has gotten out and it is too cold for her. It is very cold to-day, yes?"

Walt ignored the perspiration on his face. "Yes," he said. "Very cold."

"Belinda is dead," the old man said then, waving a hand. He shook his head and smiled. "I just remembered that. She is dead, Belinda. Sometimes I forget. It comes and it goes. Everything." He began to mutter at the windowpane. "Everything comes, everything goes, yes?"

"Grandfather?"

No response.

"Grandfather, I'd like you to meet somebody." He gestured for Gino, who crept forward till he was even with Walt. "This is Gino Caruso."

The old man turned suddenly, wet eyes wide. "The great singer?"

"No," Gino said.

"No." The old man nodded. "He was taller than you. Not so young."

"Yes," Gino said.

"You sing? I sing. I was a great singer. Not so great as my son. But I was great."

"That's wonderful, Mr. Kirkaby," Gino said.

"Sing for me, Caruso."

"I'm not so good, Mr. Kirkaby."

"Do you know 'Blessed Assurance'?"

"No. I'm sorry, I don't."

And then the old man was singing. Sitting on a dying chair by a wet window, in a room filled with ruins, the torn blanket held tight, he sang, his voice old, unsteady, dry. " 'This is my story, this is my song; praising my Savior all the day long.' " He paused. "You remember it now?"

"No, but it's very pretty, Mr. Kirkaby."

"Yes," Walt echoed.

"All together now. A trio. 'This is my sto—' Don't be shy. Come. A trio. Now. 'This is my story . . .' "

" 'This is my song,' " Walt sang.

" 'This is my song,' " Gino sang.

" 'Praising my Savior all the day long.' " The old man nodded. "That was all right. This time we do better. Now; one, two, three," and they all sang, " 'This is my story, this is my song; praising my Savior all the day long.' "

"Do you know 'Rock of Ages'?" Gino asked.

"Of course." And they all sang " 'Rock of ages cleft for me, let me hide myself in thee.' " They sounded better on "Rock of Ages" than they had on "Blessed Assurance," but "Shall We Gather at the River" was the best yet, although "The First Noel" topped it by a mile because they were beginning to feel each other now, Gino's voice soaring high in makeshift harmony, the old man growing stronger, his voice beginning to swell. The rain stopped but they didn't, segueing into "Silent Night," then "We Three Kings," which was followed by seven of the "Twelve Days of Christmas" and "Deck the Halls with Boughs of Holly," really rolling now, demolishing "We Wish You a Merry Christmas," pulverizing "Hark! the Herald Angels Sing," bringing new life to "O Little Town of Bethlehem," etching "It Came Upon a Midnight Clear" so that you could almost see it, and when they finished with "Joy to the World" there was joy.

P.T. ended all that.

P.T. or the rain; either way it ended. He had been golfing but the rain had stopped that, so he got home early. Walt never heard him but there he was suddenly, standing in the doorway.

"What's all this?" P.T. said.

"We're just singing," Walt told him.

"Well, I think the old man's tired." (He did not mean father, not the way he said it; he meant the man who is old.)

"No," the old man said. "Come sing."

P.T. snapped his fingers.

"This is Gino Caruso," Walt said.

"Hello," Gino said.

P.T. snapped his fingers.

Walt nodded and he and Gino left the room.

That night Walt and his father had a talk. Walt had been expecting it, more or less—the old man probably was tired; maybe they had excited him, although Walt didn't think so. Still, he prepared an apology so that when P.T. called him into his study after dinner he thought he was ready.

"I'm sorry we got him all tired," Walt said. "It was my fault."

"Nice-looking boy."

"Pardon?"

"That boy you were with."

"Oh, Gino? I don't know."

"Italian, isn't he?"

"No, he's Greek."

"You said his last name was Caruso."

"It is."

"Caruso's an Italian name."

"But he's Greek."

"Don't argue with me."

"His name is Caruso but it really isn't Caruso. It's Gianopolous. That was his father, but he died and his mother married this Mr. Caruso and—"

"Greek, Italian—that's beside the point."

"Yessir." Walt nodded. Then, almost in a whisper: "But you see, he really isn't Italian."

P.T. got up from his big chair and walked to the fireplace. Above it, hung high on the wall, were the head of a deer and a fat bass. The bass had set a record—the biggest ever caught in the state of Wisconsin. "What's his father do?"

"He runs the school."

"You mean he's superintendent?"

"No, no; he runs the school."

"You mean he's the janitor."

"Yes, but he runs the school, doncha see?"

"Now listen, Mister!" P.T. left the rest unfinished. He reached up with a big hand and stroked the face of the brown deer. Walt watched the hand and waited for the voice. When the voice came it was friendly, fatherly, false. "Walt?"

"Yessir?"

"Do you trust me?"

No. "Yes."

"Have I ever lied to you?"

Yes. "No."

"Have I ever done anything to hurt you?"

Yes. "No."

"You'll believe me, then, when I tell you something."

Why should I? "Yessir."

"You don't want to bring kids like that around here. I can't tell you who to play with when you're away from home, but when you're here, you don't want to bring kids like that over."

"But he's my friend."

"You'll have lots of others."

"But he's my friend."

"Are you listening to me?"

"Yessir."

"Bring home whoever you want to, but you don't want to bring home kids like that."

"No. I don't."

"O.K.?"

"O.K." He was about to say O.K. for you, old man. That's what he should have said. O.K. for you, old man. Tough about you, old man. He's my friend, old man, so to hell with you, old man. That's what he should have said.

But he didn't.

Walt discovered his salvation on the second day of second grade.

The first day, he tried not to think about. His mother had driven him in the big black car, depositing him right in front of the school. (He had sensed even then that it was too far, that he should have made her stop a block away, but he did nothing.) The early hours in school were uneventful, but recess was not. He was standing by the jungle gym when somebody pushed him from behind. Walt stumbled forward, managing not to fall. Then he turned to find Wimpy Carlson advancing on him.

"I seen ya," Wimpy Carlson said. Wimpy Carlson was fat and probably slow, but, unfortunately, big.

"Hi," Walt said.

"I seen ya," Wimpy said again.

Walt made a smile.

"In that car. Ya goddam rich kid."

"I'm not," Walt said. "Rich."

"Yes, y'are. Think you're so good, doncha, 'cause you're rich, doncha?"

"No," Walt said.

"Yes, you do," Wimpy replied, and he pushed Walt again.

"Cut it out."

"Gonna make me?"

"Cut it out."

Wimpy pushed him again, very hard, and this time Walt did fall. As he got up he calculated his chances of making it safely to the school door. The odds seemed definitely in his favor, but by now a crowd had gathered so he had no choice but to charge. He ran at Wimpy's stomach with all he had and his aim was good. Wimpy said "Ooof," more or less, as Walt collided with him. They both went down, rolling across the gravel playground for a while before Wimpy's weight began to tell. Soon he was sitting astride Walt, punishing him as best he could, but Walt had been hurt by masters so he did not cry. In time Miss Allenby pulled them apart, with Wimpy hollering, "I'll getcha, I'll getcha good," Walt hollering back, "Just you try," but his heart wasn't in it.

At noon, when Miss Allenby dismissed them for the day, Walt hurried out of the room onto the playground. There, dead ahead, was the big black car, his mother waiting behind the wheel. Walt stuck his hands into his pockets and began to walk away from the playground, not bothering to turn as Wimpy shouted after him, "Don't worry. I'll getcha tomorrow." Walt walked down the block just as fast as he could—he didn't run; no one could accuse him of running—and by the time he reached the corner the great black car was cruising alongside. "Walt, what's the matter? Get in." He continued to walk. "Please, Walt." He shoved his hands deeper into his pockets, staring straight ahead; his glasses began sliding down his nose, but he didn't bother pushing them back. "Now, Walt. Enough of this. Get in the car." Walt walked the second block without breaking stride. At the corner he glanced back. Sure that no one saw, he dashed around the front of the car and got in.

"Now what in the world," his mother began, but that was all she said.

"Don't you ever—and I'm not kidding, no sir, I mean it—drive me to school, not me, I'm walking, or maybe my bicycle—but you're not driving me, not in this car—I mean, you're not!" He did not mind the fact that she was smiling, but when he added, "Except when it rains," he would have much preferred it if she had not laughed.

The hours before recess on the following morning were spent partially in trying to pay attention to Miss Allenby, partially in trying not to pay attention to Wimpy. Wimpy would turn in his seat and clench his fat fist, scowling, and Walt did his best not to show fear. He scowled or shrugged or yawned ostentatiously, but when Miss Allenby said "Recess" he was the first one out of the room. Hurrying around the corner from the playground, he found a dark place behind an open door and crept into it. Hiding. He could not deny it to himself. He was hiding. He was afraid of goddam fat Wimpy so he was hiding. He—Walt the Whizzer Kirkaby. Shame. The one and only Whizzer was hiding. Walt pressed deeper into the shadow behind the door and closed his eyes, swallowing air. When he guessed that recess was over, he sauntered as casually as possible back to the playground and up the steps into school. Wimpy was waiting by the door and Walt said, "Where were you? I was looking for you" as he passed by into the room to take his seat.

As Miss Allenby clapped her hands for quiet, Walt leaned forward on his desk, cupping his chin in his hands, watching her. She was quite young and pretty and had a nice soft voice. "Printing can be fun," Miss Allenby said, and Walt nodded in absolute agreement. She turned to the blackboard and Walt watched as her hand made marks with a piece of yellow chalk. "That is an 'A,' class. Say 'A.' " "A," everybody said. "Good," Miss Allenby said, and she turned to the blackboard again, commencing to write more letters. Walt was watching her closely when his belch began.

Miss Allenby had received her degree in Education from Washington University the summer preceding, so this was, in actuality, her first class. Of course she had had many sessions in practice teaching, but this was her first *real* class. She was even-tempered and she liked children, so she felt she would be a fine teacher, given time. She was, however, worried about enforcing discipline. She never much cared for punishing pupils, and if they ever found that out, they would obviously take advantage of her weakness, and who could blame them? Consequently, her initial reaction to the start of the belch was confusion. Should she punish the offending belcher? Or should she ignore the whole thing, make believe it never happened? She decided on the latter course of action (or inaction), which seemed sensible because, after all, belches were brief, and in a few moments the whole incident would be forgotten. Miss Allenby printed a

"C" and a "D." But the "D" was a sloppy "D"—by now her hands were shaking, she hoped not too noticeably.

Because the belch was growing louder.

Miss Allenby started on an "E," but she was just not up to it. She dropped her writing hand to her side. Really, it was the most incredible belch she had ever heard. The duration, the resonance, the sheer blasting power! Reluctantly, Miss Allenby turned to face her class. She was about to ask, "All right now, who's belching?" (a difficult thing to say under the best of conditions) but there was really no need. And so, summoning her fiercest face, Miss Allenby stared at the nice little boy with the glasses.

Walt had always been able to belch. There was really nothing to it: open your mouth, swallow some air, belch. These were average belches, indistinguishable from any other. The superhuman belch (later to be known far and wide as the "Kirkaby Special") he had not discovered until one afternoon when Arnold was chasing him with a garter snake. Walt had taken refuge in the toolshed behind the greenhouse, where, in order to quiet his heart, he had begun swallowing air. How many swallows he took he never knew, but ten minutes later the first Kirkaby Special gave his position away. Arnold traced the sound and frightened him plenty, but Walt didn't mind so much because the belch was such an impressive sound he felt an undeniable pride of ownership. To his knowledge, no one else in the world could belch as well. Being dimly aware of social amenities, however, he hid his light under a bushel; P.T. would doubtless have been unimpressed, and even though his mother or Maudie might have shared his pride, there seemed to Walt no point in putting them to the test. So his belches he kept private and secret, used only when he had to quiet his heart (as from Arnold) or when he wanted to remind himself of his limitless capabilities. Hiding from Wimpy, that second recess, he had needed to quiet his heart, so, without really knowing it, he had swallowed air for perhaps ten minutes.

The resulting belch was, even by his standards, fantastic.

Walt looked up at Miss Allenby. She was obviously not happy. He turned his head from side to side, watching all the eyes. There was no other sound in the room, which only served to make his seem all the louder.

Without warning, the belch ended.

The classroom stayed silent. Walt was less aware of it than of the look on Miss Allenby's face. Slowly he stretched out his hands toward her, as if saying, "Whatever you decide to do to me, I'll understand."

Miss Allenby began to laugh. At first she resisted it, but not long, and as she leaned against her desk and dropped her head, the girl in front of Walt started laughing and then the boy across the aisle and then the boy behind him, and as the pandemonium built even Wimpy laughed and after that Walt himself went, putting his face on his desktop and howling like a fool. More laughter came, louder; there was simply no stopping it now, and when Miss Allenby realized this she managed to announce that class was dismissed for the day. But no one moved. Eventually Walt stood, and then so did everyone else. He moved toward the door, and as he did they surrounded him, the circle thickening as he left the school and walked down the steps to the playground. "Hey, Kirkaby, howja do it, Kirkaby? Do it again, Kirkaby. Once more, huh, Kirkaby—just one more time, please, Kirkaby—please." They peppered him mercilessly and he stood there safe inside them, waiting for them to pause.

"You really want me to do it again?" he said then, trying not to beam at the shouted cries of *"Yes!"* "Well, I hope I'm up to it, but it takes time." Walt started swallowing air. "It's not as easy as it looks. I learned how when I was a child in India, living at the Taj Mahal." They laughed. He moved to the teeter-totters, sitting in the very center of one, balancing cross-legged while they grouped around him, breathless. (It was the first of such gatherings; they were to come often, with word spreading for hours beforehand—"Hey, didja hear? Kirkaby's gonna do it after school.") When he had swallowed sufficient air, Walt had nothing to do but wait for the belch, so he filled the time with stories (they laughed) and imitations (he was terrific on Humphrey Bogart, so they laughed) and occasional snatches of song. Walt sat above them, chattering on, pausing for his laughs, timing them instinctively, hurrying on as they reached a climax—the Whizzer triumphant, hiding no more.

So what if he was funny-looking? Who cared about being small? And what did it matter if he was never able to punt a spiral? (he) Or hit a flat backhand? Or make the pivot on the double play? Or move with grace? (he) Or dance the rumba or get A's without studying (he was) or win contests or elections or friends or wars or climb a rope hand over strong hand or fight without losing or lie without suffering or be President or King or Champion or strum banjo or play drum or mournful trumpet (he was . . .) or do great things or even good things or run fastest or throw farthest or jump highest or skipper a ship or fly naked up through cool night air to sleep on clouds or love his father or not love his father or write or paint or sketch or slash beauty from stone?

HE WAS FUNNY.

(yeah!)

III

From the first, Sid and Esther were at war.

Sid was the declarer. He entered Turk's Delicatessen, planted himself at the counter, looked around, and there, standing on a ladder reaching up for a can of sauerkraut, was Esther Turk. Of course, Sid did not know her name then. Nor was he aware of the color of her hair (black) or her age (nineteen), height (she claimed five three but the three was a lie) or disposition (unstable). His total concentration was reserved for what he immediately termed "the sweetest little ass in Chicagoland." Sid stared at it, expertly, his bright eyes dancing. Esther turned, sauerkraut in hand, saw the bright eyes, read their message and immediately sent forth a message of her own: You should live so long.

Not remotely daunted, Sid let fly a smile.

Esther caught it nimbly, swatted it to death with a yawn.

"Hello, Tootsie." He did a Valentino with his eyes.

"Hello, Sport." Obviously she was not a fan of Valentino.

Sid surveyed the selection of cold meats. "What's good?"

"Everything. What do you want?"

Sid ogled her ripe bosom. "What do I want?"

She withered him and walked away down the counter.

"Back or front, either is perfection."

She stopped, hesitated, turned sideways.

"No complaint with the profile," Sid said.

She faced him, hands on round hips. "You're a smart guy, aren't you?"

"That's right. Also good-looking." The eyes danced again.

"Tall, too," she replied. "A real skyscraper."

Sid reddened, sensitive about his height, or lack of it, and her open laughter only colored him darker. "Five foot two, eyes of blue, that's me."

"Little fella's blushing," she said, laughing on. "Fancy that."

"Pastrami!" Sid told her. "Heavy on the mustard."

"Pastrami for the skyscraper."

Vulnerable, Sid was; but not permanently. "So after dinner, do we go to a movie or a walk along the lake?"

"Pest," she gave him.

"That's right."

"Neither. We do neither."

"A little wager?"

"Listen to Mr. Irresistible."

"That's right. I'm Sid Miller, the world's greatest door-to-door salesman.

I can sell anything. Ice to Eskimos, you to me. On account of I got the secret ingredient."

She was obviously not going to ask him, so he told her anyway.

"Charm," Sid said. "I am loaded with charm." And he smiled at her, knowing it was a good smile, knowing he was handsome. Small? Sure, but, dammit, he was handsome.

"Catch me, somebody, before I swoon."

"Esther, quit fighting with the customers." The man standing at the far end of the counter was obviously the morsel's father. The resemblance was unmistakable, in spite of the fact that the old man had the largest nose Sid had even seen.

"Not a customer, Father. A gnat."

"Well, quit fighting with him and let him go."

"If he'd go I'd quit fighting."

The old man took two steps toward them and started to speak, his voice kind, explaining. When he spoke, his nostrils dilated. Sid watched them. "My daughter is the local lure. Granted she is ripe, she is also, believe me please, sour."

"I am helpless before her charms," Sid said.

"I assure you, you have no chance. Is your suit cashmere? If not, strike three goodbye."

"Persistency is my middle name," Sid said.

"Then I weep for you and also wish you joy." Old Turk gestured softly and retired.

"Nice man," Sid said.

"He's word-happy. A frustrated philosopher." She handed him the sandwich. "Two bits you owe me."

"You can have my heart."

"A quarter is preferable."

Sid held the change in his hand. She reached out and took it. Even her fingers, soft and pink and round, aroused his passion. "We touched," Sid said. "Your hand and mine. Now I can die."

"Outside, not here." She moved down the counter, disappearing behind a barrel of pickles.

Sid pursued her to the pickles and beyond until their eyes met over a chunk of Swiss cheese. "When shall we two meet again?"

"Whenever you're hungry, feel free."

"Looking at you, I starve." Now she was starting to color, so he pressed on. "My name is Sid. Say the word. Let me hear you say it."

"If you're not outta here before I count two, I'm calling the cops."

"I want a corned-beef sandwich," Sid said. "Heavy on the mustard."
He smiled. "Now the law's on my side, so call who you want."

She backtracked to the corned beef and he followed along on the outside of the counter. "You really think you're something, don't you?"

"What's my opinion against thousands of others?"

She hacked at the corned beef with surprising vigor. "I wish you eternal indigestion," she said.

"She cares for me," Sid said.

Esther snorted.

"Movies tonight or a walk along the lake?"

"I'm busy tonight."

"Tomorrow night, then."

"I'm busy."

"This week sometime."

"All week I'm busy."

"I never ask a girl out more than a week in advance. That's a rule. Break one of your dates or you lose me."

"Here's your corned beef." And she slammed it on the counter. "Two bits and get out."

Sid paid her and started for the door. "The week after," he yelled, whirling.

"I'm busy the week after."

"Goodbye. You'll never forget me." He was halfway out the door.

"Two weeks from Thursday."

Sid jumped back inside. "What?"

"I happen to be free two weeks from Thursday."

"Why not say next year?"

"That's the best I can do. Take it or leave it."

"Sold!" Sid said and he stormed out pursued by her laughter. He did not like her laughter. But when she laughed her body shook. And he did like that. He did indeed. He liked that fine.

He had, however, no intention of keeping the rendezvous. Pride was pride and he had plenty, so even though he called her on the phone later that week to reconfirm and set seven as the time, it was all show. Set her up high, let her down hard. He was much too successful with women to let a garlic maiden ruffle him. He called her again to inquire innocently about the color of the dress she might wear. Naturally, she would envision flowers. Sid chuckled as they hung up. (Set her up high, let her down hard.) His normally busy social life—he had a string of succulent South Siders—became abnormally busy: Tilly one night, Adele the next, Adele again, then mysteriously Claudette, and Esther Turk disappeared from his life during the day.

But at night, on his bed, he had visions.

Oh, that ass, Sid would moan, seeing it twinkle. And he would rise and grope through the darkness to the kitchen sink and there attempt to drown his passion with glasses full of Chicago water.

So, in the end, he kept the date. He had to make her suffer for her lip and he plotted this tiny revenge, then that. His final decision was simply to keep her waiting. She had, after all, asked him for the date, was undoubtedly looking forward to it, and the idea that she had been stood up (or worse—that he had simply forgotten all about her existence) would be punishment enough. So Sid, a prompt soul, arrived at the deli at a few minutes before seven, smirked up at the lighted window over the store and took a walk. The night was steaming, but he did his best to ignore it, strolling around and around the block. At a quarter of eight (no point in making her hysterical) he presented a slightly perspiring version of himself at the Turk door. Sid knocked. There was a pause. Then the nose peeked out.

"Young Lochinvar," Old Turk said.

"I desire your daughter," Sid said, entering the apartment.

"A worthy ambition," the old man allowed. "Hardly unique, but worthy." He gestured around the living room, at the sofa, at the two overstuffed chairs. "Pick. Each is uncomfortable."

Sid settled on the sofa, the old man on a red chair. Sid glanced around. The room was very neat. "Your daughter is a fine housekeeper," Sid began.

"Nothing could be further from the truth. Cleaning vexes her. I clean." And he bowed.

Sid glanced at his watch.

"She is anointing her body," the old man said. "Sometimes that takes a while."

Sid nodded. He loathed being kept waiting; one of his notions of Hell was a waiting room with him at the end of an infinite line.

"I believe I warned you she was sour."

Sid nodded again, folding his hands in his lap, his left wrist turned so he might stare at the plodding second hand.

"What would you like to talk about? Please, choose your subject. I pride myself on versatility. History, politics, astronomy. Pick. You'll find me equally dull on everything." When Sid made no reply the old man smiled. "Some prefer silent suffering," he said and he opened the Chicago *Daily News.*

Sid transferred his stare from the second hand to the front-door knob. His legs wanted to leave, and if his mind could have stopped envisioning Esther Turk's backside, his legs would have carried him away. But his mind could not stop, so he waited.

And waited.

And waited.

And waited.

And precisely at thirty-one minutes after eight, she appeared.

"Shall we go?" Esther said.

Sid took her in a while before rising. A pale-blue dress, tight across the bosom and the butt; a single strand of phony (but who could really tell?) pearls; black hair loose and long, tumbling down between the young shoulders; black eyes shadowed and bright; lips red.

Sid stood. Across, Old Turk dreamt, the world his bed, the *Daily News* his blanket. Sid led her quietly from the room. They descended the stairs, exchanging the apartment's heat for the night's, walking down the street toward the bus stop. As he paused, she said it.

"*Bus?*"

There was a world to be read in that word. Sid browsed through some of it. You mean we're going to take a bus? You mean you are such a short little two-bit piker you're going to let me ride on public transportation? Big talk, little do. Phony. Faker. Mouth. Hot, hot air.

"Who said anything about a bus? I got a stone in my shoe." He ripped off his shoe and deposited the imagined blister maker onto the baking cement. Then, battling for aplomb, he hailed a cab.

As they rode silently north (who needed talk when there was that Mozartian meter to listen to) Sid pondered killing her. She had kept him waiting and she had as much as called him a piker, and to top it all off she looked so sexy he was weak. She sat—lush, plump, ripe, rich, ready— staring out at the city. Nineteen and already she had designs on the whole world. Sid watched her, passion mounting. He was not used to women giving him trouble and it upset him. And when he got upset, he got upset right smack in the pit of his stomach. So when they reached the Red Star Inn (to Sid's mind the best German restaurant in captivity, no question) his stomach was as knotted as a basket of snakes. He ordered the duck but picked at it only, and the apple pancake for dessert went so untouched as to be salable all over again with maybe a little reheating. Esther, however, ate like a wrestler. Oblivious to his torment, with delicate fingers she spooned down the sauerbraten and potato pancakes and red cabbage and applesauce and strudel. When she was done, Sid paid (bitterly) the bill and they walked out of the Red Star, crossed Clark Street (here Sid took her soft arm, the shock of contact almost electrifying—can a mere arm be voluptuous? Ye gods!) and headed east toward the Gold Coast. The uniformed doormen filled Sid with even more than customary envy (he saw her eyes, saw them covet the shined doorknobs, the carpeted entrance-ways, the spotless elevators beyond), so he walked faster, quickly leaving Esther paces behind. She noted the separation but made no attempt to catch up. Finally, Sid dropped back until they were parallel again.

"We gotta crawl?" Sid said.

"After a big meal I don't speed."

"Yeah."

"You should learn to enjoy your food."

"What?" Sid stopped dead.

"If you're not going to eat, don't order."

"You kept me waiting!"

"What?"

"For an hour and a half. A lousy hour and a half she keeps me waiting and then she tells me to enjoy my food!"

"You lie!"

Somehow her venom equaled his; her eyes burned just as bright. Sid quailed. "Huh?"

"I know you big shots!" She moved up right next to him, almost touching (but not quite), and let fire. "I knew you were gonna keep me waiting. You wait two weeks to see me, you wanna make me suffer. I read you, Mr. Big Shot. You kept me waiting forty-five minutes. Well, I kept you waiting forty-six. One minute more. Just one minute. But one minute *more.*"

"Just you hold your water, Tootsie."

"You hold yours. Nobody made you see me. Nobody but you. I'm the belle of the ball, Sport. Everybody wants me. Everybody wants little Esther. Well, goody for little Esther is what I say. She's king of the mountain and she's happy up there." She stopped talking but her eyes still burned.

Sid looked away. "I'm sorry, Esther," he mumbled, hoping like a bastard it sounded sincere. "I'm really sorry. I should be shot, talking to you like that. Forgive me, Esther. Please."

"Forgiven," she said, and they started walking again, neither speaking. She was busy dreaming again of the life inside the doormanned buildings. Sid was busy making plans.

Obviously she craved him as he craved her. (Why else the outburst?) And obviously he was going to satisfy her cravings (the little bitch) because he was a gentleman and liked leaving the ladies happy and because nobody yelled at him like that and got away with it. Nobody mocked him. Not her; not nobody.

"I hate myself sometimes," Sid said, the words catching in his throat the way they always did when he wanted them to. The last syllable, "times," had an almost authentic sobbing quality. She looked at him but he turned away perfectly, his face to the wind. The wind made him blink and luck was with him—one tiny tear formed in the corner of his eye. Sid turned back to her, made certain she saw it, then shook his head. "You pegged me, Esther. From the very start."

"I did?"

Sid nodded. "Dead through the heart."

He pointed toward the lake and she nodded, so he took her arm gently, guiding her toward the water. The night was cool here, the great dark waves muffled against the shore. Sid smiled shyly at her and the sight of Esther in the moonlight spurred him on. "I'm a phony," Sid said. "I talk too much like a big shot. But I'm no big shot." He blinked furtively, waited a moment for the tears to glisten, and then faced her, whispering, "I'm nothing, Esther. Nothing. Just like you said."

"Oh, I never said that."

Sid shook his head, dropped his chin to his chest, and moved a few paces away from her. She was interested now, but he had to be careful. Slow and easy. One step at a time. Women had always been a snap for him. Always. Always.

"Maybe it's because I'm short."

She moved to him. "What, Sid?"

He moved away. "The whole thing. All the talking, all the front. Maybe if I was taller—"

"What's tall got to do with it?"

He shrugged. "Nothing. I don't know. I'm always afraid people are going to laugh at me. Because I'm strange-looking."

"Strange-looking? Oh, Sid, you're not. Believe me, you're not."

Bet your ass I'm not, Tootsie. "You really think that, Esther? Don't kid around now."

"I promise you. I wouldn't ever kid about that."

"You're sweet, Esther, you know that? You're afraid to show it—you try like hell to hide it—but I see, Esther. I see." That particular ruse had never failed to score him points, so he let it sink in and moved away from her again, along the lake. She hesitated, then followed.

"Sit here a while?" Sid pointed to a rock. Esther nodded and sat.

When she was down he joined her, but a considerable distance away. Come to me a while, Tootsie. You will. You will.

"It's pretty," Esther said quietly.

Sid nodded. "I love this lake. It's like part of my family. The day my mother died, I came here. To hide, I suppose."

"When did she die?"

Sid took a deep breath. It was just about time for the stories of his life. But which stories? Which life. "You don't want to hear about me, Esther."

"I do, though."

"After my father died, I guess my mother didn't want to live either."

"Oh," Esther said, moving closer to him across the rock.

Sid's voice was very low. "See, my father never came back from the Great War." That was absolutely true. Of course, his father had never departed for the Great War either, having been shot over a crooked crap game in Pittsburgh. "The Germans killed him." That was also true. His father's slayers, the brothers Neumann, Fritz and Erich, were one-hundred-percent German. (They were tried for manslaughter but acquitted. Or, at least, so his mother informed him.)

"Damn the Germans," Esther said, moving next to him, her tender leg brushing Sid's. "I hate them."

Sid nodded. "You sure you want me to go on with this, Esther?"

"Please."

"Well, like I said, once he died, my mother gave up."

"Gave up?"

"A broken heart." Medically, that was true. Her heart had been broken. Along with the rest of her body. By a North Side streetcar as she rushed heedlessly across a busy intersection because she was late for her nightly tryst with the grocer.

"First one, then the other?"

"Yes," Sid whispered. "First one, then the other." Whenever he chose this story he carefully omitted that there were seven years between the two fatalities.

"Oh," Esther said. "Oh."

Proud that he had correctly guessed she would be a sucker for *schmaltz*, Sid hurried on. He spoke of his boyhood struggles, of making his lonely way, of nights spent shivering on benches and in doorways, of days spent searching through garbage cans for food, of the beatings he absorbed, the whippings and the scorn, of the times he had been cheated and lied to and left for dead by the Wayside of Life. But never once in the recounting of his tragic journey did he allow a note of self-pity to enter in. (That was his secret. Let them supply the pity. Every so often women wanted to feel like women. Happens in the best of families.) He was closing in now, the end in sight, so he stood up abruptly and, as if deep in thought, moved close to the shore of the lake. On cue, Esther followed. Sid faced her. The setting couldn't have been better: moon, water, clean cool air. She stood before him, gazing, her head tilted ever so slightly to one side. Sid was about to make his move.

"Don't even try!"

He couldn't have heard her. She could not have said that.

"Keep your hands to yourself, Sport, O.K.?"

"My hands?" Sid's fingers flew into an innocent knot behind his back. He tried to appear confused, which was easy.

And then she started laughing.

"I tell you the story of my life and you laugh?"

"I laugh at what's funny."

Whipped, Sid brought her home. It took forty minutes on the bus (enough was enough) and not one word was spoken. When he got her to her door he told her he would never see her again but somehow it came out, "When can I see you again?" Her reply was "A week from Tuesday" and his answer to that was "Never." Except someone said, "O.K., a week from Tuesday," and then she disappeared into the apartment, wagging her tail behind her.

Sid muttered his way back to his place, undressed and went to bed. Six glasses of water later, he slept.

Their second escapade was no improvement on the first. Not to Sid's mind. If anything, it was worse. Esther's dark skin was stained shades darker from the summer sun and she served herself up totally in white—skirt, blouse and shoes—and the blouse was of such flimsy material, sheer almost, that as they walked through the Loop (Sid surreptitiously eyeing her profile) he had to restrain himself actively from roughly unveiling her then and there, on State and Madison, for all to see. But the sweetness of her body had not sugared her tongue. Lip she gave him, in full measure. Whatever pose he tried, she mocked. (Nobody mocked him.) Gallant, worldly, humble, witty, sad, fey—she mocked them all with obvious relish. But he endured her tongue with false smiles (visions of her body in rhythmic action supported him and his strength was as the strength of ten) and spent his money (too much, too much) on her like a fool (filet, she had to order) and when he followed her, at evening's end, up the stairs to her apartment (that ass, ooooooooohhhhhh) he asked her meekly when he might again have the pleasure, and her reply of three weeks from yesterday brought from him a nod, a grin (false), a thank-you, a goodbye.

The third time around was no cause for hosannahs. Esther went Mexican—sandals, black swirling skirt, red peasant blouse scooped low. Standing up straight, she was enough to wet his palms; but when she bent over . . . when she bent over . . . (Did she bend over more tonight than she had in the past? Sid wasn't sure. Yes or no, the flash of white at the top of her bosom blinded him.) They dined on the steak for two at Barney's and took in a movie at Balaban and Katz's Chicago (Garbo's face was better, but Esther won the body) and walked along the lake again. As they walked she did her customary skillful job of scorning him, but Sid did not seem to mind so much. Because a very sad dawning had commenced to flicker way back in his head and it told him intermittently to prepare for second place; he, the mighty Sid, conqueror of countless breasty maidens, had maybe come a cropper at last. Sid looked longingly at the fiery body clad in swirling black and flashing red. Nobody got the best of him, but without exceptions, where would rules be? So when he took her home he honestly hesitated before inquiring after her future freedom, and her surprising answer of this coming Saturday filled him with less than joy.

But he arrived for the joust punctually (and subdued—three strikes are out, four are ridiculous) to face Esther in yellow. Esther in yellow was better than Esther in anything except maybe Esther in nothing. Her shape jutted and curved sublimely; she was a masterpiece (and Sid would have chuckled at his pun had she not been so ruthlessly unobtainable).

"You look wonderful, Esther. Absolutely wonderful."

Sincere sincerity is not usually difficult to spot, and in Sid's case, because of the rareness of its appearance (he, like most, was long on the other kind), the occasional truth gleamed like a wistful star.

But he scored no points with Esther. She simply accepted the gratuity with a nod (though Old Turk must have detected something, because he grunted to life in his soft chair, the *Daily News* tumbling down around him in disarray). They left the apartment, Sid and Esther did, Sid then hailing the hated inevitable cab, instructing the driver to take them to Chicago's feeble answer to Coney Island. They wandered through the summer heat, licking ice cream, and the screams of the myriad children saddened Sid. It was a bad idea coming here, and his wish that Esther might cling to him during a roller-coaster ride (hope springs eternal) was dashed brutally as she sat bravely throughout the entire journey with her arms crossed, her eyes wide open. The Ferris wheel was no better, and Sid missed the target with a rifle, so Esther won no doll. Four teenagers followed them for a while, whistling at his yellow dreamboat, but Sid did not bother discouraging them; experience had taught him that Esther was fully capable of defending herself, capable and then some. The evening spun painfully along. Sid, without half trying, was able to list at least thirty-two *zoftig* succulents with whom he had been unquestionably successful, so why with this one, this yellow vision, did he have to fail? He would gladly have traded at least twenty-five from his list for one turn with Esther. Twenty-five, hell; all thirty-two. Sid sighed.

"What's the matter? I'm boring you?"

"No. I'm just tired. Hard day."

"I'll bet."

"The exit's over this way," Sid said.

"It's Saturday night. Not even eleven o'clock."

"Hard day," Sid repeated, and he started toward the exit. He was not remotely fatigued, but he wanted to remember one affirmative action on his part. In his future daydreaming he could expand on it, amplify it, color it to his advantage, removing at least part of the sting from the shellacking she had so skillfully inflicted. He chatted with her as amiably as he could, and when the taxi stopped before the deli Sid held the door open for her, paid the driver and followed her up the stairs, waiting politely by the door of her apartment as she fumbled for the key, waiting only to say goodbye. When she had the key held firmly, the yellow dress tilted abruptly, carrying the encased juts and curves into his arms as her red lips ambushed his mouth. Her strong tongue fired barrage after barrage while her shape locked itself against him. Sid reeled before the ferocity of the *blitzkrieg*, the apartment door finally halting his backward voyage, and, braced, he launched an attack of his own. His arms had barely touched her warm flesh (at last, oh, at last) when she broke from him, inserted the key, opened the door, told him she was free next Friday and, eyes fiery (yes, with passion; it had to be that), disappeared.

Sid could not move. He sent a tentative order to his legs but, when they were slow to respond, rescinded it. His body still felt her pressures, and he closed his eyes briefly, pushed back through time for thirty seconds and relived the moment, framing it forever in his mind: shock, surprise, pleasure, heat—all. Finally he turned, descending the stairs to the warm street, and started to walk. For a block or two he basked, a smile curling his strong mouth.

The night heat was not oppressive; actually, it was relaxing, and Sid swung along at a loose gait, close to humming, for he had kissed Esther

Turk, he had, he had. And this coming Friday he would kiss her again. Definitely. Sid stopped. Would she let him? Sid nodded and resumed his walk. Of course she would let him. Who ever heard of one kiss? Impossible. But he had to be careful—he could not assume it was his God-given right; then she would squelch him like a bug. Back to the Red Star Inn. (Women loved going back. Memories . . . memories . . .) Sid hummed the tune aloud. And after the Red Star they might just happen to walk along the lake again. And again they would sit on the rock. And they would laugh (a little off-color joke was always good for openers) and stroll and stop and then into his arms with her. What a kiss it was going to be! Here an hour before he had been happy to accept defeat and now he was back in the running. What a kiss. Whaaaat a kiss. A kiss to end all kisses. Suddenly Sid stopped dead. What? What? A kiss? "Christ," Sid said aloud. "A *kiss!*" The humiliation! He, the one and only Sid Miller, the killer of the South Side, was plotting a kiss; he, who unquestionably could make a living as a full-time gigolo, was working up a sweat over a nineteen-year-old delicatessen keeper's daughter. "Christ," he said again. With one flick of her body she had sent him spinning. One seemingly unplanned embrace (she knew what she was doing, that tootsie did; she knew all right) and God's gift to women was grappling for another peck on the lips. It was like Rockefeller scheming over a gallon of oil. But there it was.

She had hooked him.

The little bitch had hooked him.

But good.

Schmuck! That was the word for him. Sid seethed. Ohhh, she was clever. A shrewd slut, that little Esther. She saw he was getting away, leaving her in the lurch, beating her at her own game, so she threw out a little smooch to string him along. "Hah!" Sid said, and he spun into a candy store, ordered an egg cream and downed it in a swallow. Quenched, Sid pierced the hot night, fingers snapping fast. Well, he would take her anyway. Take her, then leave her; have her to the hilt, then drop her by the wayside. He had tried being charming, he had tried being sweet; kindnesses he had showered. Could anyone have been nicer? He had wooed as a gentleman woos, and where were the results? In return for his investments she had paid him with ashes. But no matter; he would still win the day.

By being evil.

Because he had to have her. He just had to.

That, or go mad.

•

Wellington never mapped a campaign with more care. Sid stayed up late every night, pondering, fretting, pacing the floor. By Wednesday he had his plan and Thursday evening he went over details till he was bleary. No plan is perfect and neither was Sid's; he needed one break from the Almighty.

Heat.

Chicago was in the midst of an August bonfire and Sid prayed for it to hold. He listened to the weather forecasts on the radio every hour on the hour. At one in the morning he first heard reports of a cold front moving down from Minnesota and that news sent him quickly toward despair. The two-o'clock news repeated chill words of the arrival, but Sid, exhausted, could not wait for further bulletins. He fell asleep, the radio still going full blast. When he awoke, groggy, he staggered to the window and said hello to Friday.

It was a steamer.

For the rest of the day Sid moved. Down to the Loop for a furtive transaction with Whittaker, the Negro train porter, then back north for peanuts, quickly to another store for dry potato chips, then a long bus ride west for the best tomato juice in town. When he arrived back at his apartment he forced all the windows shut and tried to nap, first going over everything one final time. The alarm woke him on schedule and, not taking time to stretch, he burrowed through his closet for his oldest suit and, with surgical care, ripped the left trouser leg along the seam. That done, he rumpled the coat, dirtied his face good, dressed, eyed himself one final time in his full-length mirror and went forth to do battle.

"What happened to you?" Esther said, opening her apartment door, staring out.

"I tripped." Sid hesitated in the doorway, looking at her. She was dressed all in black; black was his favorite color.

"What do you mean, tripped?"

"Fell down. I fell down. See, I was a little late getting over here so I ran across the street a block back and my foot didn't make the curb, I guess. Anyway, I skidded and ripped the pants and—"

He stopped at her laughter.

"I don't think it's so funny, Esther."

"You don't, huh? You should see yourself."

"Esther, I might have got hurt, Esther. All right, all right, go ahead and laugh."

She did.

Sid waited. "Listen, I can't take you to dinner like this. Tell you what. I'll go home and shower and change and get back here as fast as I can. Shouldn't be more than an hour."

"An hour!"

"Maybe a little less."

"I don't much feel like waiting around, if you don't mind."

"I'm open to suggestions."

"Why don't I come along with you?" And she went for her purse. Now why didn't I think of that? Sid thought, and while her back was turned he allowed himself to beam.

They taxied through the heat, Esther grousing about food and the heat and being kept waiting. When they stopped in front of his apartment house she pursed her lips with evident disdain. Sid paid, led her up the steps and into the building. "Second floor," he said, and he mounted the stairs ahead of her, unable to ignore the strong smell of onions clouding the hall. "Italian people live next door," Sid explained and Esther nodded. Sid took out his key, smiled at her, unlocked his apartment and ushered her in.

"My God, it's a steam bath." And she retreated quickly to the hall.

"It'll cool off quick," Sid said, and he plunged through the still air, throwing both windows open. "In this neighborhood, leaving your windows open isn't so smart."

"That I believe."

"Kitchen, bathroom, living room, bedroom," Sid said, pointing as he spoke.

"Palatial," she gave him.

"Now, Esther, I never once said it was a palace."

"Maybe not, maybe not."

"And it's clean. You got to admit that."

Finding no dust, she had to shrug agreement. "Still, I've seen better."

"I ain't gonna die here, Tootsie; you better believe it." He slipped off his suit coat and hung it in the closet.

She wandered around the room. "Sid?"

"Huh?"

"You got anything to *nosh* on?"

"We're going to a good restaurant; leave your appetite alone."

"I asked did you have anything to *nosh* on."

"Esther—"

"I'm *hungry*."

"All right, all right, check the cupboard."

"Umm," she said a moment later. "Peanuts."

"Well, go easy."

"And potato chips."

"I said go easy."

"Peanuts I love." She returned with a handful. "Want one?"

"I'm not spoiling my appetite." He took off his shirt and tie, then covered himself with his robe.

"Modest fella." And she returned to the cupboard for another handful of peanuts.

Sid tied the robe and moved to the bathroom. Closing the door, he leaned against the wall opposite the mirror and looked at himself, waiting.

"Sid?" He let her try again. "Hey, Sid."

He opened the door a crack. "What is it? I'm trying to take a shower."

"I'm thirsty."

"I don't wonder with all those peanuts."

"What have you got that's cool?"

"Water."

"What else?"

Sid opened the door. She was sitting on his couch, eating peanuts. "I got some cold tomato juice."

"Great. Nothing I like better." Didn't I know that, Sid thought. Didn't she order it (the large glass, twice as expensive) with almost every meal he'd ever bought her?

"I'll get it for you."

"That's all right. Take your shower." She started to rise.

"You're in my house, Esther. I'm the host, O.K.?"

"O.K." She sat back down.

Sid sauntered to the kitchen, but, once out of sight, he started to fly. Out came the tomato juice and the ice cubes and the biggest glass he owned (bought today special), and once they were assembled he took a deep breath before reaching far behind the stove for the secret ingredient.

Vodka.

It almost amused Sid, years later, when the North Shore bridge ladies discovered the stuff. "Try it," they would urge him. "It has no taste at all." "No taste?" he would reply, unable not to smile. "I can't believe it." How could they sense that he'd known about it all his life, that he had first used it (successfully) on Midgie Greenblatt when they were both seventeen, that his father had taught him of its loosening qualities, that it was Sid's only worthwhile legacy from his old man?

Sid poured a lot of vodka into the big glass. After came a handful of ice cubes; finally the tomato juice, sweet and cold. He gave it a quick stir with his finger, felt the glass's exterior starting to chill, hesitated one moment more, then walked back to Esther.

"Here," he said. "Don't drink it too fast."

She gulped it down. (She had to. He said drink it slow, so she had to.) Sid watched her, a dark creature of infinite curves, a sour, tantalizing bitch about to go into an unsuspected heat. God, but he wanted her, and the proximity of fulfillment did not make life any easier.

"I'm a new woman," Esther said, putting the glass down. "Was that good!"

"You can't taste anything when you drown yourself in it like that."

"Let me have a little more."

"Why don't we just forget all about dinner," Sid said, approximating annoyance.

"I'll eat, don't worry; just a little more."

Sid grunted, took her glass and made her another drink, except with half again as much vodka. She took it from him, and as he headed for the shower he could hear her humming softly behind him.

What a shower! Sid (no singer) sang "Great Day," "When the Organ Played at Twilight" and "Singin' in the Rain." All the time the water cascaded down, dancing across his shoulders, sliding along his shapely legs to the final safety of the porcelain. When he had taken as much time as he could without arousing suspicion, he turned off the knobs, threw the robe around his shoulders, a towel around his neck and gave a quick check to his pigeon.

She was sitting heavily against the back of the sofa, arms at her sides, eyes staring blankly out the window. Sid stood before her, waiting while she slowly turned her heavy head up to face him. He smiled at her and, wonder of wonders, she returned it. (That vodka, it's fabulous.)

"I won't be much longer," Sid said.

She waved a hand. "Take your time, take your time."

Without asking, Sid picked up her glass and made her the crusher in the kitchen. Half and half (at this stage, who could taste?) and easy on the ice (dilutes). Setting the drink carefully into her hand, he nodded approvingly as she sipped steadily away.

"Bes' damn tomato juice," Esther said.

"For you, Tootsie, only the very finest." Sid zipped back to the bathroom and dried himself good before carefully applying exotic oils to his face, imported cream to his armpits. He hummed "Five foot two, eyes of blue" as he combed his hair, getting it to lie just right. Then he brushed his teeth with Colgate's and stepped back, eying himself, trying to be critical. He had never looked better and he knew it as he scurried to his bedroom for his only pair of genuine silk underwear. (For you, Tootsie, only the very finest.) Then, donning his blue sharkskin slacks, he hid his belt in a bureau drawer and closed in for the kill.

"Esther?"

"What?"

"I leave my belt out there?"

"I don't see it."

He walked into the living room, bare-chested. He was well muscled and she noted him with what he knew was pleasure as he approached. "Where the hell's my belt?" He searched the room, circling closer to the couch.

"Where did you leave it?"

"That's a bright question, Tootsie."

She thought about it a moment before commencing to laugh, her entire body going into the action, quick tears shining in her eyes, and while she was amused (no time like the present) Sid slid down beside her, grabbed her tight, pulling her against his bare chest, and, taking dead aim, went for her mouth.

It all made for a sloppy kiss.

Not that she resisted; rather, it was a matter of her being unable to control her lower lip. It sort of lay limp across Sid's cheek, like a wet fish. Ye gods, he thought; have I maybe overdone? A quick glance at the table showed that the third vodka was gone. Sid stared at Esther, who could not stare back, being able only to blink in slow rhythm. Sid kissed her again and, when it ended, held her close. "Oh God," he said carefully into her ear. "Oh God."

"Sid," she came back. "Sid."

"Esther, I love you. Oh, I love you, believe me, Esther, I love you, do you believe me? Say you do."

"Sid," she said. "Sid."

"Esther, my beloved," and he started with the hands, moving tentatively along her shoulders, then down. "My darling, my darling, I love you so, oh God, Esther, I just love you."

"Sid," she said. "Sid."

"My sweetest, dearest, beloved Esther," and he repeated that a while as he fiddled with the buttons. She didn't resist him (or help him for that matter) but just kept saying "Sid, Sid," over and over, and as he was well along with depriving her of her dress he felt a momentary fear that maybe she wasn't all real; maybe cotton padding had given Mother Nature a helping hand. But the fear in no way crippled him, and when she was naked on the couch (slumped, but naked) he saw joyously that his fears were groundless. "Oh, my beautiful sweetest sweetheart," Sid said. "You creature from my dreams, I worship you and love you." And she kind of nodded with her eyes closed, and he knew she wasn't paying too close attention, but he always felt sound was important in and for itself, so he talked a blue streak as he perused her shape. "Oh, oh, you Esther, my Esther, my sweet Esther, I love you, I love you," and she nodded a little but she wasn't doing much talking anymore. The couch was no longer required, so Sid (at heart a true romantic) started to carry her (with style) to the bedroom. "Esther, my own, my own," and he shoved one arm under her back, which shouldn't have tickled her, but she did manage a small laugh. "I'm taking you to dreamland, beloved," and the other arm struggled under her dimpled knees. "We're going now, my sweet," Sid said. "To dreamland."

It took a while to get there.

Sid lifted her halfway off the couch, but his grip on her back proved untenable and down she slumped. "Yes, my sweetheart, we're flying off to heaven," and he attacked her again, trying to get her off the damn couch. Finally he managed to brace his knee under her and with one final tug he had her up in his arms. Sid staggered back under his burden. "Only a moment more, dumpling, and we'll floating on heavenly clouds." He banged her knees against a wall and her eyes half opened with distant pain, so he kissed them closed. "A little accident was all, my beloved; now rest up for dreamland." He was strong enough and she wasn't *that* heavy, but there was no denying that she was one hundred percent dead weight and bulky at that. "We're at the door to dreamland, my sweet," he said (wheezing a little now). "Heaven, here we come." But the narrow door presented an unexpected problem in logistics and, try as he would, he could not solve it. He tried her first, him first, sideways, backward, front, but nothing came of it. His arms aching, he finally bulled his way through, scraping her knees again and banging her head for good measure. Again she came to life, but by now he was a little weary from all the talking so he didn't bother to speak. Instead he fell forward, dumping them both on the bed. Immediately he assuaged her with tender kisses and then pulled off the bedspread (first maneuvering her to one side of the bed, then rolling her to the other), revealing sheets both cleaned and ironed. Sid stepped out of his pants, ripped off the clinging silk underwear and, sweating like a pig, leaped to his revenge.

Sweet it wasn't.

Sid had to maneuver for both of them, never the Platonic ideal, but he was professional enough to manage it with reasonable success. And Esther lying like a lump was not the Esther he envisioned. But lump or no, she was still Esther, delectable as any plum. So if the battle was not an overwhelming rout, still it was a victory, clean and tasty. And when Sid deposited her at her doorstep (first filling her with several bowls of chili) he could feel the laurel wreath resting on his curly head. And that night, as he fought sleep alone in his bed (one more time—he had to go over it all just one more time), he knew he could give cards and spades to Valentino and not come out behind.

The way Sid lingered in bed the next morning, Greta Garbo might have been there. He had no Swede, of course, nor, for the first time in his life, did he want her. He had his daydreams; he was rich enough. Said daydreams consisted of the scene he was about to play with Esther, which would begin with his saying. "So long, Tootsie," to which, shocked, she would reply, "So long? So long? You're leaving me?" "That I am, Tootsie." "But my . . . my *maidenhead*—you took it." "Better me than the garbage man, Tootsie." "You . . . you *deflowered* me." "You should feel proud, Tootsie." "Proud? Why proud?" "Because, Tootsie, you were planted by the greatest goddam gardener in the world."

Luther Burbank stretched in bed. Gloating was a terrible habit, and whenever he did it (often) he felt, ordinarily, pangs. But not this morning. For Esther had been an adversary worthy of his guile (worthy? My God, for a while she looked a winner) and only genius had brought her to her knees (pun), so why should a genius feel guilty? Rising, he allowed the rug to cushion his pink feet as he journeyed to the bathroom. Inside, he gave the mirror a longer than usual look at his baby blues while he selected the proper Sid to enter Turk's deli and bid humped Esther a fare-thee-well: Grinning Sid, Sober Sid, Modest or Brilliant Sid—there were so many, each more perfect than the last. He decided finally on Sid the Wandering cavalier. (The element of mystery was what appealed most to him; after all, who could explain Napoleon, Charlemagne, mighty Alexander?)

He dressed with great care, combing his curly locks to perfection, brushing his teeth till they glistened. (Let her remember him at his most beautiful; might pain her just a speck more in the long run.) Then, jaunty as d'Artagnan, he mounted a trusty taxi and set off in quest of his final fillip, that terminal burp which always signals the settling of a perfect meal. Next to the delicatessen was a shoeshine parlor and there Sid dismounted, letting the rhythmic Negro touch up his Florsheims. Flipping a quarter to the grateful black, Sid invaded Salamiland.

Old Turk was armpit deep in his pickle barrel (maybe he'd dropped a penny?), and the way his monolithic nose was screwed over to the left indicated his displeasure in his task. At Sid's approach he gratefully removed his withered arm from the brine. "Pickle man's coming tomorrow," he explained. "Therefore the census."

"A job for a lesser man than you," Sid said. "Counting cucumbers."

"Agreed." The old man nodded, sponging his dripping arm. "But—" and he shrugged—"a little humbling is good for the soul."

"Perhaps, perhaps no. Where is your beauty this morning?"

"Up." His dry thumb indicated the apartment above.

"I would speak with her."

"I would not."

"I must."

"She is bursting with alum, I promise you."

"I'll sweeten her."

"Doubtful."

"It's a chance I have to take. We must have words."

"Then go to your doom," Old Man Turk said, plunging back into the pickle barrel.

Sid left him and sauntered up the stairs. Knocking, he waited. Nothing. He knocked again. More of the same. Sid tried the door, found it open and entered. Striking a pose in the center of the living room, he called softly, "Esther." No reply. "Esther?" He moved toward her closed bedroom door. "Esther! It's me. Sid. Esther, you in there, Esther?" The sound of inner thrashing indicated that she was. "I'm out here, Esther," Sid said and when her stumbling had become consistent, he retreated toward the living-room window, posing himself so that the sun streamed in around his curly head, burnishing him an almost solid gold.

If he had never looked better, she had never looked worse. She leaned in the doorway, eyes half closed, pale, a torn gray robe flattening her curves. "Yeah?"

"Esther, you all right?"

"It looks like I'm all right?"

"What's the matter?"

"I'm sick, fool."

"I'm sure sorry about that," Sid said seriously while someone inside him laughed. "Esther . . . ?"

"Yeah, what?"

"I'm leaving, Esther."

"Leaving? What leaving?"

"Town. I won't be seeing you for a while. Maybe longer."

"You bothered me for *that*?"

"You're not hearing what I'm saying, Esther. I said I'm leaving town."

"So go."

God, but she was tough. Sid had to give her credit. Not much, though. Her puny attempt at pride only made him smile.

"What's so funny?"

"Nothing. Goodbye, Esther," and he turned for the door, knowing he would never get his hand on the knob, knowing she couldn't let him (and still survive), knowing the silence would be broken by her crying out his name.

"Sid?"

Why was he never wrong? Sid smiled again. The mark of genius, probably. Did Charlemagne make boo-boos? Sid continued toward the door, waiting for her to plead. She did. On cue.

"Sid. Sid, please. Wait."

At the door he pirouetted (who's this Nijinsky anyway?) and gave her his Sunday smile. She stood across the room, still leaning against her doorway. "Yes, Esther?"

"What happened last night?"

When Dempsey cold-cocked Willard in the summer of '19, there came a moment—halfway through the first round—when big Jess was done, gone, out; only he didn't know it yet. His body had the message, probably, but his brain, stubborn, absolutely refused to answer the phone. "What do you mean, what happened last night?"

"Just what I said—what happened last night?"

"You mean you don't remember?" Left to the head, right to the heart, right to the head.

"I'd ask if I remembered?"

"You don't remember anything?"

"It was hot, I remember that. You took a shower. I felt funny. Then later I got sick on some cheap chili."

Sid leaned against the door. Willard was falling; Charlemagne too. "Nothing in between?"

"Quit with the games!"

"You don't remember . . ." What could he ask? His hands gripped the doorknob for support. ". . . kissing me?"

"That was a week ago. Outside the front door. You aroused my pity."

"Pity."

"What else?"

"Pity!"

"Fool."

"*Pity!*"

They charged toward each other like fighters, standing in the center of the hot room, panting, circling, measuring.

Sid stared at Esther. (Nobody got the best of him.)

Esther stared at Sid. (Nobody got the best of her.)

Eventually (inevitably) they married and got the best of each other.

IV

Jenny grew up in Cherokee, Wisconsin.

When she was born, Cherokee's population was 182; when she left home, nineteen years later, the population was 206. Aside from that, nothing had changed. The town consisted of a general store, a meeting hall, a drugstore, a saloon, all clustered together on a dirt road. Gray wooden structures, square in shape, they differed from one another only in size, like children's building blocks. The climate was dry, the weather clear—cool in summer, painfully cold from November through March. The houses of the town stretched feebly along both sides of Cherokee Lake, one of the endless small bodies of water that pockmarks the flat face of northern Wisconsin. The entire area was distinguished by two things only: on one side of the lake stood an exclusive camp for boys, while directly across was Cherokee Lodge, a small, luxurious retreat catering to vacationing businessmen who hunted or fished, as the season demanded.

Jenny's home was near the lodge. Her father had built it himself. When he became engaged he set to work, and when the living room, bedroom, kitchen and bath were finished, he got married. Then, each time his wife became pregnant, he would build another room for the new baby. It was an ample house, sturdy and clean, set in the woods above the shore of Cherokee Lake.

Jenny's was a quiet family. Mary, her mother, was a plain, quiet woman, tall, big-boned. Her brothers, Simon and Mark, were quiet brothers. But her father was the quietest of all. Carl Devers rarely spoke. He was a giant, with light blond hair, great thick shoulders and long, surprisingly thin hands. The hands were remarkable—powerful, supple; there seemed to be nothing they could not do. His large face was unusually expressive; emotion ran close behind his blue eyes. With his hands and his eyes, he could answer almost anything; there was really little need for him to speak. When he did talk, one syllable kept recurring: "Auh?" He said it quietly, always with a rising questioning inflection. "Auh?" Jenny came to know the sound and its almost limitless meanings—yes, no, I'll think about it, I love you too, good night. "Auh?" It was his word.

Carl Devers was a guide. Businessmen came from all across the Middle West to fish with him or hunt in the hushed, snow-covered woods. Partially because of his skill, partially because of his size, stories grew up around him. "Carl Devers," the businessmen would say, back again safely in the comfort of their clubs. "Let me tell you about Carl Devers. Big, blond sonofabitch. And strong. Why, I've seen him grab a couple of packs and hoist a canoe and take off through the woods on a portage and there I am, running like hell to keep up with him, and all I'm carrying is a goddam fishing rod. But that's nothing. This guy is fantastic. Why, I've seen him . . ." And so the legend swelled.

Jenny grew up in the woods. Running. Barefoot across the pine-needled ground, then down the gentle slope to the beach, then along the narrow stretch of sand, then up again, back into the tree shadows, darting. She ran like a willowy boy, the movements long, controlled, filled with quick grace. Sometimes she would plead with her brothers to chase her and then she would shout with joy, scampering past trees, bolting through bushes, under limbs. By the time she was five, Mark, who was nine, could barely catch her, and even Simon, eleven, would have to set his mind to his task, biting into his lower lip, scrambling after her. Her hair was long and still light blond, her father's color, and it flew behind her, sometimes swirling across her pale skin as she turned abruptly, spinning, changing direction. She was tall, but she did not mind it then, and her legs were good, thin-ankled and long. Days she spent with her mother, Simon and Mark being off to school, Carl usually having left before any of the others were awake, at dawn, not to return until near suppertime. One night, after he came home, Jenny copied him. She stuck his pipe into her mouth and slipped into his boots and clumped through the front door, then she kissed her mother on the cheek, as her father did, and said "Auh?" as her father did, and nodded to her brothers the way he nodded. At first they just watched her. Mark was the first to laugh, staring as she sat in her father's favorite chair and knocked the ashes from his pipe into the ashtray. "Auh?" she said again, and by this time they were all laughing, Carl loudest of all. Jenny was trying hard not to giggle as she put the pipe back into her mouth, adjusting it to her father's angle. Carl came over to her then and lifted her from the chair, holding her high with his great arms. Slowly he brought her down, folding her gently against his chest, while the others applauded. For a moment Jenny wanted to cry.

It was her first performance and she never forgot it.

Jenny's best friend was Tommy Alden. Frail, dark, he was one year older than Jenny but not nearly so fast a runner. His father, Richard K. Alden, had been a successful clothing manufacturer in Chicago until a heart attack made the further creation of dresses, coats and suits a perilous venture. Recuperating, he had come upon Cherokee Lodge and decided almost immediately to buy it. So he did, enlarging it, installing his family in one wing, throwing the rest open to his former colleagues at outrageous prices. Because of Carl Devers, the lodge was an immediate and continuing success. They were close, Mr. Alden and Carl. Different as they were—Mr. Alden was short, paunchy, vocal, aggressive—they were close.

And so were their children. They were always together, Jenny and the boy. He was studious, shy, given to periods of silence followed by quick bursts of speech that only Jenny could understand. He loved to read, and late afternoons they would sit by the water and he would recount tales of knights and kings while she listened, nodding when he glanced at her, urging him to go on. Tommy was the one who wanted to be an actor, a career in which Jenny, at first, had no interest, preferring to run or swim or creep through the woods on an Indian raid. They compromised, eventually, spending the mornings running, the afternoons perfecting their talents as performers. They had a place, halfway between Jenny's home and the lodge, a semicircle thick with shrubbery, the open half facing the water. There they would act, stumbling through Robin Hood or Cinderella, listening as their words echoed back across the water.

All too quickly Jenny's childhood passed. She grew taller, towering half a head above her classmates in school. She took to slumping, rounding her shoulders, but she was still tall. Too tall. Taller even than the boys. Then, when she was eleven, her body absurdly began to develop. At an age when everyone else was flat, Jenny's breasts were slowly starting to fill. She rounded her shoulders even more and did what she could to ignore it. One afternoon when she was alone in their acting place Mr. Norman found her. It was a red day, hot, and even as the sun began falling the heat lingered. Jenny sat cross-legged on the ground, staring out. She wore a white blouse and a summer skirt and her pale skin was stained dark. She turned as she realized a man was watching her, smiling down. "Hello," the man said.

"Hi," Jenny answered. "You staying at the lodge?"

"Maybe I am," the man said, "and maybe I'm not." He smiled again. "What's your name?"

"Jenny."

The man opened his mouth wide. "Isn't that amazing? That's my name too."

"Jenny? Your name is Jenny?"

"Absolutely. What's your last name?"

"Devers."

"Curiouser and curiouser," the man said, shaking his head now. "So's mine. Jenny Devers. That's my name."

"You're kidding me. You are."

"Word of honor." He raised his right hand as a pledge. It was a short hand, white and soft, with little pudgy fingers.

"But Jenny's a girl's name."

"Sometimes. Not always. Why, some of my best friends are called Jenny and they're not girls. I'm not a girl either." He smiled. Jenny said nothing, staring up at him. "The thing that worries me," the man went on, "is that we've got the same last name too. Maybe we're the same person. Did you ever think of that?"

"You're crazy." Jenny giggled.

He laughed with her. "There's one way of finding out. How old are you?"

"Eleven and a half."

"Whew." He gave a tremendous sigh. "We're not the same person. I'm not eleven and a half, so that proves it. I'm only six. Six going on seven, really."

"Oh, you're not either six. You're way older than I am."

"I just look older than you are, Jenny. I'm really just six going on seven and I can prove it. Here." He reached into his shirt pocket and pulled out a cigarette. "See that? That's my birth certificate."

Jenny giggled again. "That's your cigarette. You really are crazy."

"It's my birth certificate and I can prove it," the man said. He pulled out a lighter. "See? I'm going to smoke it and I don't smoke cigarettes. Never smoke cigarettes. Only smoke birth certificates." He lit it and inhaled deeply, sitting down quietly on the ground beside her.

"If that's your birth certificate what does it say on it?"

The man peered closely at the cigarette, squinting, cupping his hands around it so Jenny couldn't see. "It says on it, 'Jenny Devers is six going on seven.' "

"It says 'Chesterfield,' " Jenny cried. "I saw the package."

"You're not very logical, Jenny, are you, Jenny? It did say 'Chesterfield' on the package. I admit that. But I always keep my birth certificates in a Chesterfield package."

"Why?"

"So they won't fly away, Jenny. Like you, Jenny. Are you going to fly away?"

"I can't. I don't know how. Anyway, people don't fly."

"What about pilots? Don't they fly?"

"Yes, but they're in air-o-planes, silly. They couldn't fly if they didn't have an air-o-plane around them."

"Have you ever asked a pilot if he needed an air-o-plane, Jenny-o-Devers? Have you?"

"No."

"Well, I have. Some of my best friends are pilots and I've asked them and they all say the same thing." He picked up a long pine needle and skimmed it along the ground.

"What did they say?"

He touched the tip of the needle to Jenny's skin and ran it down softly along her leg.

"Don't do that. What did they say?"

"What did who say?" He touched the tip of the needle to her skin again. Jenny moved away from him.

"The pilots, silly. The pilots."

"They said you have lovely legs, Jenny. That's what they said. Every last one of them. That Jenny Devers has lovely legs. Do you want to see my legs, Jenny? Would you like that? Say yes."

She tried to scramble clear but he was too quick for her. With one hand he flicked the cigarette away and grabbed her ankle, pulling her down. She was about to scream when his other hand clamped down hard across her mouth and for a moment she could not breathe. He held her with surprising strength, the palm of his hand imprisoning her mouth, his other arm locked around her kicking body. Then he threw one of his own legs over hers, pinioning her. He smelled of tobacco and she wanted to open her eyes but she was afraid of what she might see. Then his hand began moving up her leg. "Relax, Jenny," he whispered. She tried to kick but she couldn't and his hand was under her skirt, above her knees, moving slowly higher. He was breathing harder, the heavy sound exploding in the quiet afternoon. The sun must be beautiful now, Jenny thought, all red and beautiful, and she wanted to look at it, but she knew his face would be in the way and the thought of his face made her shiver. "You stop that," he whispered. "We're friends, Jenny, so you stop that. Nobody's going to hurt you." But you are, Jenny wanted to scream. You are. His hand hurt her and the weight of his body hurt her terribly and she could feel herself growing faint with the pain when suddenly the pain was gone. Jenny opened her eyes. The man was suspended above her in midair and Carl Devers was holding him. Carl's great shoulders shrugged and the man spun upward through the air, crashing down like a rag doll ten feet away. Carl was on him quickly, lifting him, and the back of Carl's hand caught the man flush on the mouth and he spun toward the earth again, starting to bleed. Again Carl was on him, dragging him silently to his feet. Again Carl's great hand swung and again the man spun down. Blood dripped from one side of the man's mouth as Carl took him by the shirt front and slowly, with his left arm, lifted him off the ground. Clenching his right fist, Carl drew it back slowly and carefully, taking dead aim.

Abruptly the man started to cry.

Carl hesitated. The man was sobbing, his face wrinkled up, tears streaming down his cheeks, mixing with the blood along his mouth. Carl watched him a moment. Then he put the man down.

"I almost hurt you, Mr. Norman," Carl said.

Mr. Norman turned and ran into the woods toward Cherokee Lodge. Carl dropped to one knee beside Jenny. Gently he lifted her, carrying her down to the lake. A canoe was half dragged up on shore, Carl's fishing rod and tackle box lying alongside. He put Jenny down, gestured for her to get in. She did. "Face me," he said. She faced him. Pushing off, he began effortlessly to paddle in an easy rhythm, and the canoe sped along the shore of the lake, gliding through quiet patches of shadow as the red sun settled. He watched her with concern, and every so often he smiled, nodding his great blond head, and she smiled back at him, her hands gripping the sides of the boat.

"I'm all right," Jenny said. "I am."

"Auh?"

"Yes. I'm fine."

He nodded, continuing to paddle. The rhythm was faster now and the canoe cut through the still water. Jenny turned, staring out ahead of them. Then she looked back at her father.

"That's the end of the lake," she said. "The very end."

"Auh?"

"I've never been there before. Never. Not once."

He smiled, slowing as they approached the shore. Holding the boat steady, he gestured for her to step out. He handed her his rod and tackle. Quickly he lifted the canoe, shouldering it, setting off through the woods, Jenny skipping alongside.

"Where ever are we going?"

He shrugged his great shoulders.

"Wait till I tell Tommy about this," Jenny said. "He'll just die."

They moved through the woods a minute more and then Jenny stopped, staring. They were on the shore of another lake. Very small, almost perfectly round, it seemed, as she stared at it, with the final soft rays of the sun splashing it deep red, to be a magic place if ever there was one. Carl lowered the canoe, beckoned for her to get in. He pushed off from shore and they glided quietly toward the center of the circle. The sun was gone suddenly. Shadows slipped out to meet them, covering them. The constant summer sound of insects and birds seemed distant, muted. Jenny locked her arms around her knees, rocking gently back and forth.

"Princess lives in there."

Jenny looked at her father; his hair seemed almost to shine in the dusk. He sat holding the canoe paddle in one hand, pointing with it toward an area of shore where the trees were thickly bunched, interlaced with bushes. It was a dark place. Jenny stared at him, then at the dark place, back and forth, back and forth.

"A princess?"

"Auh?"

"A real princess?"

"Auh?"

"How do you know?"

"Seen her. Met her. Took her fishing once."

"You took her *fishing?*"

"Auh?"

"What does she look like?"

He shrugged his shoulders. "Like a princess."

"What's her name?"

"Name?"

"Well, what did you call her?"

"Princess, I guess. I'd just say, 'Reel in slow, Princess. Good cast, Princess.' Like that."

"Oh, I don't believe you."

Carl leaned forward. "Have I ever lied? Ever?"

Jenny looked at him. Then she turned, squinting in at the shore. "No," she said. "Not ever."

"Well, then."

"Tell me about her hair. How long was her hair?"

"How long?"

"Yes."

Carl twisted the canoe paddle in his hands. "Well, it was long enough."

"Oh, no. No. More. It has to be more than that. Princesses have long hair."

"Well, as a matter of fact, now that you mention it, it was very long. Very long indeed. Longest hair I ever saw."

"And was it golden?"

"Yes. Very long golden hair."

"She must be a princess, then. No doubt about that." Carl began to paddle slowly, and they glided in closer to the dark shore. "Why ever is she living here? What's she doing?"

"Hiding, I guess. Waiting."

"Auh?" Jenny said.

Carl nodded. "That's what she told me anyhow." He moved the paddle slowly through the water and they edged still closer to shore. " 'Carl,' she told me—"

"She called you by your name? Fancy that."

"Very informal princess," he said. "Not the least uppity. Anyway, she said, 'Carl, everybody wants me because I'm a princess. Everybody's always grabbing for me on account of that. Well, I'm sick of it. I'm going to hide out here and wait for a gentle man. I don't care how long it takes, I'm waiting. Gentle people, they're harder to find than you think.' 'I guess so, Princess,' I said. 'I guess maybe you're right.' " He pulled the paddle sharply in the water and the canoe glided up on land. "Hungry?"

"Here? Won't she mind?"

" 'Carl,' she told me, 'The shores of my kingdom are yours. You ever want to bring your wife or daughter—' "

"She knows about me?"

" '—your wife or daughter Jenny—' "

"Fancy that."

" '—for a meal, go right ahead.' " He gestured with his long hands. "Now get us some wood for a fire." Jenny stepped out and he pushed off, stroking down along the shore. She gathered some good wood, then turned, arms full, watching her father. He was casting out, reeling in, whipping the lake white, a gigantic figure kneeling in the center of the canoe. Again and again he cast and she heard the slap of the bait striking the water, the whisper as he reeled in. The moon began rising, catching his pale hair, holding the color. All the rest of him was dark, shadow, but the pale hair glistened. Fish began hitting the bait and he brought them carefully up to the boat, effortlessly scooping them from the water, dropping them on the floor of the canoe. Then he was casting again, steadily, in perfect rhythm.

Jenny watched her father.

When he had half a dozen fish he returned, started the fire, then set to work. She stared at his hands as they scaled and cleaned the fish, moving by memory, cutting, scraping. The fire began to snap, sparks spinning away, as her father, caught in the red glow, concentrated on preparing their dinner. When it was ready, they ate.

Jenny could not remember having had a better meal.

Later, as she tired, they paddled back. He led her through the dark portage, then they were on water again. She napped. When they got home she went straight to bed. She slept well until she began to dream. She was running through the woods down to the lake. Far, far on the other side she saw her father and she ran across the lake, but not fast enough because now she could see what was behind her and it was a hand. She fled but the hand was much too fast and it was grabbing at her, pulling her down. In the water there were more hands, hundreds of them, all of them pawing, and she tried fighting but they had her feet and her arms and were covering her mouth when she screamed. She screamed again and he heard her. Carl heard her and started for her and now they were frightened. The hands were frightened and they began swimming away but she kept on screaming until she woke.

"There, there," she heard. "There, there, baby." It was Carl and he was sitting on her bed, stroking her face with his strong fingers. She relaxed. She could never remember him calling her that before—"baby."

"Baby," Jenny said, and she slept.

Two months later she made her first dress. Until then her mother had always made her clothing, working quietly at the sewing machine that stood permanently in a far corner of the living room. But when Jenny asked could she please do one by herself, Mary assented. Jenny worked very hard on the dress, carefully copying the pattern, sitting bent over by the machine, squinting hard at the fluttering needle. Finally one afternoon it was done and she tried it on. They were in her bedroom, Mary sitting on the bed, Jenny pivoting before her mirror. "What do you think?" Jenny said.

"It's very nice," her mother answered. "A very nice job, considering."

"Considering what?" Jenny pivoted sharply before the mirror. The dress was plain blue cotton and the skirt swirled softly around her long legs.

"It's your first try, Jenny."

"What's wrong with it?"

"Well, look." Mary got up and approached her daughter. "Look, Jenny." She put her hand to the back of the dress and gathered in a handful of material. "It's a little loose. A little big."

"No, it isn't."

"Jenny, be reasonable. It's much too big for you. You look lost in it."

Jenny smiled at herself. "I like it this way."

"But—"

"I like it."

"Don't shout, Jenny."

"I just want you to hear me. I like it. The way it is. And I'm going to make all my clothes. From now on. Just the way I like them. Do you hear me?"

Mary Devers looked at her daughter a moment. Then she looked away. "Yes, Jenny," she said. "I hear you."

When she was twelve she told Tommy about her ambition. They were walking to school together when she said it. They always walked to school together, down through the woods to the lake, then around the narrow shore half a mile to the school yard—Jenny carrying her books across her chest, shoulders rounded, Tommy walking straight alongside her. Sometimes he would slump his shoulders and press his books to his chest, mocking her. She didn't mind it when he mocked her; anyone else, yes, but not Tommy.

"I'm going to be an actress someday," Jenny said. It was late March but the ground was still thickly covered with snow.

"An actress?" Tommy said, scooping up a handful of snow, packing it hard, tossing it out into the lake.

"Yes."

"Where'd you get that nutty idea?"

Jenny thought a moment. "I don't know, I guess. Besides, it isn't nutty. And anyway, it's what I'm going to be."

"Have you told your folks?"

"No."

"Well, don't. They'll have a bird."

"I won't. This is our secret."

"Oh God, Jenny, we got a million secrets already."

"Now we've got a million one."

"Why does everything have to be a secret with you?"

"Because it's more fun that way, that's why."

"Who says?"

"I do. And I also say I'm going to be an actress. You just wait."

"Course I will," Tommy said. "Course I will."

Jenny hated high school. She was indifferent about studying and the other girls ignored her and the boys whistled after her or snickered as she walked by, her books clamped to her chest. She was terribly conscious of her height. When she was a freshman she was already five feet eight, her mother's height, and at night she would pray silently, kneeling at the edge of her bed, her fingertips pressing against her eyes. Please, God, let me be small. Please, God. Please. When she was fourteen her body was wildly ripe and the sound of derisive laughter seemed always to follow her. Cherokee High was small, the percentage of attractive girls astonishingly small; the boys still whispered about Laverne Elias, a delicate redhead who had graduated five years before and who now gave weather reports weekday evenings on a television station in Minneapolis. Jenny, of course, was no delicate redhead. Her hair was dark blond and it looked peroxided. Her lips were full and pouty and her eyes offered unintentional suggestion. The boys, she knew, thought her face cheap, and she could not disagree. At first, when they asked her out, she accepted, successfully fighting off their inevitable advances. In spite of her defenses, the backwash of stories about her behavior grew too much to bear. Completely untouched, she managed to gather in a few short months the worst reputation in the entire school.

If it weren't for Tommy Alden, she would have had no friends. They saw each other constantly, walking to school together, walking home together, studying together at night either by the fire in the lodge or at her house. He was terribly smart and terribly kind.

They were inseparable.

Then, one morning, everything changed.

They were walking to school together, hurrying along the lake. It was May and the sun was surprisingly warm.

"Listen to me," Tommy said.

"What about?"

"Nothing," he answered finally. They walked quietly along for a while. Tommy crossed his arms on his chest, rounding his shoulders, imitating her walk.

"Stop that," Jenny said.

"You're blushing."

"Well, stop it."

"Listen to me," Tommy said again.

"I'm not talking to you until you stop walking that way."

Tommy dropped his arms to his sides.

"What about?" Jenny said then.

"You doing anything Saturday?"

"When Saturday?"

"Night."

"No."

"Wanna go out?"

"With you?"

"What the hell kind—"

"Don't swear so much," Jenny interrupted.

"What kind of question is that? Yes, with me."

"But we spend Saturday nights together anyway. So what are you asking me out for?"

"Because this is different. We're not going to study or anything this Saturday. We'll go out someplace."

"Together? Just the two of us?"

"You want me to bring my father along? Boy, are you a nut."

"A *date*?" Jenny said. "With *you*?"

"Forget the whole thing, fatso. O.K.?" He grabbed a stone and skipped it out across the water.

She touched his arm. "I'd love to, Tommy. I mean it. It just surprised me, that's all. I'm sorry. I'd love to go out with you. I would."

"It's a deal then," he muttered. "Saturday night."

"Saturday night," Jenny echoed. They looked at each other a moment. Then, suddenly, he broke into a run, racing away along the sand.

He picked her up at eight o'clock but she wasn't nearly ready. She had started preparing at a little after five, but when she heard him knocking at the front door she was still only half dressed. She didn't know what to wear, so she tried on every dress she owned, staring at herself critically in her mirror, sharply shaking her head. She finally decided on a white dress she had made herself and that was only a little too big for her. She wore white shoes, with high heels, and earrings and when she finally entered the living room everybody stopped talking and looked at her.

"Don't bother waiting up for us," Jenny said. "There's no telling how late we'll be. Good night, all," and she swept to the front door.

Tommy opened it for her. He was wearing white buckskin shoes and a blue suit and a blue striped tie. As she stood beside him, Jenny realized suddenly that the high heels were a mistake. Without them they were the same height; with them, she seemed to tower over him.

"Where are we going?" she asked when they got outside.

He gestured with his arm and they moved through the woods away from the lake. When they got to the road Tommy stopped, pointing to a new Pontiac that was parked on the shoulder. "Mine," he said.

"Yours?" Jenny looked at him.

"The old man gave it to me. On loan. As long as I don't drink or smoke I get to keep it." He pulled a cigarette out of his coat pocket and lit it. "If the old bastard thinks he's going to buy me off he's crazy."

"You're too young to be smoking."

"I knew you'd say that." He got into the car. "I just knew it." He inhaled deeply on the cigarette, then began coughing. "Dammit," he muttered.

Jenny sat beside him and they started to drive. "What's the matter with you?" she said. "Smoking and swearing."

"That ain't all, sister." He opened the glove compartment and pulled out a pint of whisky. "Want a snort?"

"No, I don't. I most certainly do not."

"Chicken," Tommy said, raising the pint to his lips, drinking.

"Watch the road," Jenny cautioned.

"Chicken," Tommy said again.

"Sometimes I don't think I know you, Tommy. Lately—"

"Call me Tom. My name is Tom, not Tommy. Call me that."

"Tom," Jenny managed to say.

He took another swallow of whisky, then replaced the bottle in the glove compartment. After that, they drove in silence for a while.

"Where are we going?" Jenny said finally.

"Dancing."

"Auh?" She was conscious again of the white high-heeled shoes. "Wouldn't you rather go to a movie or something?"

"Nope."

"I'm not a very good dancer," Jenny said.

Tommy shrugged, continuing to drive. Every Saturday night the meeting hall in Cherokee was used for dancing. A phonograph was placed on the platform and popular records were blasted through the night, until one in the morning. It was nine o'clock when they got there but the hall was already crowded. Tommy parked the Pontiac, took another long swallow of whisky, stuck a Lifesaver in his mouth and led her toward the noise.

There were a number of high-school students grouped around the perimeter of the big room. Jenny stood very close to Tommy in the entranceway, conscious of the stares, trying not to hear the whispered laughter. A group of boys were standing in a distant corner and Tommy left her, moving to them, talking, gesturing. She waited, alone, feeling awkward, oversized. A man came up and asked her to dance but she shook her head. The man looked at her closely, his eyes traveling up her body. Jenny gave him a nervous smile and retreated back to the wall, standing rigid. When Tommy came back he grabbed her arm and they moved onto the floor. He put his arms around her, pulling her very close, pressing his body against hers. She pulled away. Patti Page was singing "The Tennessee Waltz" and they struggled on the floor.

"Not so close, Tommy," Jenny whispered. "Please. Whatever is the matter with you?"

He glanced over to the group of boys and waved one hand.

They moved awkwardly across the floor. Jenny began to perspire lightly. "I remember the night and the Tennessee Waltz," Patti Page sang. Jenny stepped on Tommy's foot. A burst of laughter exploded in a corner of the room.

"I'm sorry," she muttered.

He tried pulling her close again, her breasts grazing his shirt. She resisted a moment, then let him hold her. She buried her head in his neck and closed her eyes.

"Attago, Tom, boy," somebody shouted.

The song ended. Another record began, louder, and they danced, awkwardly as before. When it was over, Jenny dropped her arms. "I want to go outside," she said. "Right this very minute."

They walked to the car and stood listening to the music as it pierced the soft evening. Tommy got out the pint and took a long swallow. Then another. His face was beginning to redden.

"You'll never be able to drive if you keep that up."

In answer, he drank again.

"I'm not going back in there," Jenny said. "I promise you. I won't."

"Why did you have to wear heels?" Tommy said quietly. "I don't want to go back in there either. I never wanted to go there in the first place but word got out. About us. Tonight. They dared me to bring you. So why did you have to wear heels?"

She touched his hand gently.

He jerked his hand away. "Come on, let's get outta here." They got in the car and began to drive.

They drove for a long time without speaking. The night was warm and bright, the moon a tilted crescent spilling yellow light across the ground. Finally he pulled off the main highway onto a dirt road that curved continually west. At the end of the road Tommy stopped the car, parking at the edge of a narrow river. The river was filled with rocks and the water whispered as it rushed along. Jenny listened.

"There's trout in there," Tommy said. "Sometimes your father, he brings people here to fish. Pretty, huh?"

Jenny nodded.

"You're pretty, too, Jenny. Did I ever tell you that?"

"No. Not ever."

"Well, you are. Especially tonight. I love your dress. I like white. I do." Abruptly he reached over and grabbed her, forcing her face toward his, trying to kiss her. She pulled away sharply, breaking his hold, moving to the opposite side of the car.

"Boy," Tommy said. "Boy." He grabbed for his pint and began to drink, shaking his head, glaring at her. "Boy."

"I'm sorry," Jenny began.

"Just shut up," he told her.

Jenny nodded, staring out the window, away. She suddenly had no idea whom she was with and it frightened her. She could hear him drinking, the liquor bubbling in the bottle, rushing down to his lips.

"Maybe we'd better go home," Jenny said.

"Maybe we'd better go home," he mimicked.

"What's the matter with you? What?"

"You did it with Pete Johansson. He told me. I know." Before she could reply he had opened the car door and thrown the pint viciously into the river. It hit a rock and splattered, showering glass. He got back in the car, slamming the door. "And Whitey, too."

"That's not true," Jenny said. "You know very well they're lying. Boys talk."

"I'll say they talk. I'll say."

"They never touched me. On my word of honor. Not ever."

"They didn't, huh?"

"They didn't."

"Liar."

"Don't do this to me!" Jenny was surprised at her voice. "You're my friend, my best friend in the whole world, so don't do this to me."

He edged over to her, their legs touching. The whisky smell was terrible, so she stared out at the river.

"Look at me. You like me so much, look at me."

Jenny looked at him.

He lunged at her, his arms circling her neck. For a moment she stiffened but then she stopped, letting his lips press against her mouth. His hands left her neck and they kissed, his mouth punishing hers.

Jenny pulled her head back. "That's enough, Tommy."

"Tom."

"Tom. That's enough, Tom."

"No, it isn't," he whispered and he kissed her again. She tried to force herself into enjoying it, but the smell of whisky was too strong.

"I like you, I do, but—"

He kissed her a third time, his body crushing hers, and she closed her eyes as tightly as she could and then his hands were on her breasts. She jerked her head away again, staring mutely down at his hands, cupped on her breasts.

"Not you," Jenny said. "Please not you."

They stared at each other a moment and then his hands began digging into the soft flesh, ripping at the white fabric. Jenny shoved at his hands, but they only dug in deeper, so she threw open the car door and tried escaping. He was still touching her. Finally she burst free. She ran a few steps but he came after her, grabbing her from behind, his hands tearing at her breasts again. They fell to the ground, wrestling, rolling over and over.

Jenny was stronger.

In a minute she was sitting on Tommy's chest, pressing his arms into the ground, pinning him.

"Please stop now," she said.

He kicked on the ground. "Get off me."

"If you'll stop."

"Get off me, you cow."

"Will you stop?"

"Yes."

"Promise?"

"I promise, I promise. Now get off."

She let him go, rolling off him. He started to sit. "You promised, now. Remember."

They sat beside each other and in a minute they were both crying. He lay back down on his stomach, his head in his hands, his hands pressing into the soft earth. Jenny brought her legs up and wept openly, rocking back and forth. Tommy rolled over on his back and dried his eyes. Then he stumbled down to the river and knelt beside it, ducking his head into the cool water. His coat was getting wet, so he took it off, his shirt too, and ducked his head, over and over. After a while, he came back to her.

"I'll take you home."

"Yes."

He put on his shirt and coat and they drove east along the dirt road to the highway. Then slowly he drove toward Cherokee. Neither of them spoke until he had the car parked on the shoulder of the highway above her house.

"I'll walk you to the door."

"It's all right. You don't have to."

"Please."

They got out of the car and entered the woods, moving slowly.

"I'm sorry about calling you a cow," Tommy said.

"Oh, that's all right."

"I had too much to drink was the reason I did it. I'm not much of a drinker. As a matter of fact, I think I'm going to be sick any minute."

"Auh?"

The house was visible now, framed between the trees and the lake.

"Will you ever let me take you out again?"

"I don't think so."

"Why?"

"Why should I?"

"Well, at least you know you'll be safe with me. I mean, you're stronger than I am, so you've got nothing to be afraid of. That's something."

Jenny shrugged.

"I mean, I promise I won't try to rape you again. You can take my word on that."

"Auh?"

"Absolutely. Never again."

"I'll think about it."

"Do that. It's very important to me."

"Why?"

"Because you're my best friend too, Jenny. I love you. I have ever since we were eight years old. But it couldn't go on like it was. You understand that?"

"No."

"Well, it couldn't, that's all." They were nearing the front door now and he lowered his voice. "Please let me see you again. I've got to. We're something to each other, Jenny. Don't let it go."

Jenny stopped and looked at him for a long time. "You ripped my dress," she whispered finally.

"I'm sorry."

"Here," she said, taking his hand. "See where you ripped it?" There was a small tear in the fabric over her left breast. She raised his hand, placing the tips of his fingers on the tear. "Gently," Jenny said.

"Yes."

Again she took his hand, raising it, touching his palm to her lips. Then she moved quietly to the front door and opened it.

"Jenny?"

She turned in the doorway.

"I'm going to marry you, Jenny."

He waved.

She waved.

They were inseparable again.

V

"You will sit here," Miss Dickens said, indicating the receptionist's desk. She spoke like a teacher addressing a class full of children, and Rose almost felt as if she ought to repeat what had just been told her, to prove she had learned her lessons well.

I will sit here, Rose was tempted to say.

Miss Dickens, an overpowdered maiden lady in her fifties, drummed her fingers on the desk top. "Have you any questions, Miss Mathias?"

"Mathias," Rose corrected. "Accent the second syllable. Not *Math*ias. Math*ias.*"

"I'm sorry." Miss Dickens cleared her throat. "I shan't do it again; I never make the same mistake twice."

The telephone rang.

Miss Dickens was about to say "Answer it," but Rose was too fast for her, and by the time Miss Dickens got the first half of "Answer" out, Rose was already talking on the phone. Miss Dickens converted the "Ans-" into a general all-around throat-clearing. "Ans-ah-um-um."

"West Ridge Real Estate," Rose said. "Good afternoon." She listened a moment, then handed the receiver to Miss Dickens. "For you."

"What's that?" Miss Dickens said a moment later. "Your basement is filling with water again? Call the plumber. He'll fix it. . . . He what? The plumber said what?"

Bored with what the plumber said, Rose strolled around the office. It was small, two rooms, but the ceilings were high. The office was located on Central Street in West Ridge, set between a dress shop and a hardware store. West Ridge, in turn, was located in northern Ohio, thirty miles west and a little south of Cleveland, a comfortable forty-five-minute drive on Route 10. Rose had only made the trip by bus; by bus it took an hour and a half.

Although it was her first day on the job, she was not particularly nervous. She knew how to type, file—whatever was necessary. Rose looked at her short, strong fingers, then smoothed her skirt. Her skirt was a pleated green cotton (she favored green). Her blouse was also green, neatly pressed, as was the skirt, and her short hair was carefully combed. Rose was neat, proper and clean.

She was also plain.

Her nose was too big. Her eyes were too small. Her hair was brown. Just brown. Not dark brown or light brown or curly brown or straight brown. Not even mouse brown. Brown. Brown was the color of her hair. Her lips were thin, but not thin enough to be memorable. Her chin was ordinary, neither weak nor jutting. Her skin was gray. Her body was straight and square and flat, completely devoid of mystery. Only her legs were good—rounded at the calf, trim at the ankle—so good that they came as a shock after the rest of her, as though, at birth, someone had said, "Good God, give her something." She was not yet twenty-five.

She looked thirty.

Plain Rose.

Miss Dickens was finishing the phone call when the front door of the office opened and Mr. Scudder walked in. He moved up quietly behind Miss Dickens, and as she put the phone down he whispered something in her ear and whacked her on the fanny. Miss Dickens flushed, a pale hand hiding her thin face.

"The new girl," she whispered. Mr. Scudder turned. Rose stepped forward.

"Hello, new girl."

"Hello, Mr. Scudder."

"Howard."

"Howard."

He held out his hand.

"Miss Mathias," Rose said. "Rose." She held out hers.

"Glad to have you aboard, Rosie. Dickens show you around?"

"More or less."

"You'll like it here. We don't make money but we have a helluva lot of fun."

Behind him, Miss Dickens inhaled audibly.

Howard turned on her. "Helluva," he repeated. "I said it and I'm glad."

Miss Dickens flushed.

"Anything happen of late?"

"Mr. Traphagen called. It seems his basement is flooded again."

"Poor Mr. Traphagen," Howard said. "Anything else?"

"No."

He walked into his office, returning a moment later with a briefcase. "I'm off to show a house. Hold the fort." He winked at Miss Dickens and left.

"Mr. Scudder is a terrible kidder," Miss Dickens said when he was gone.

"I can see that."

"He's very nice, though."

"Yes."

"You'll like him, I'm sure."

"I wouldn't be a bit surprised," Rose said.

It was late afternoon before Howard returned. He breezed into the office, patted Miss Dickens on the head and disappeared into the back room. A moment later he stuck his head through the doorway. "We eat," he announced. "I sold it." Then he pulled his head back and closed the door.

Rose waited until it was nearly time for her to leave for the day. Across the room Miss Dickens was already adjusting a faded spring hat, decorated with what once must have been flowers. Rose walked to Howard's door and knocked.

"*Entrez, s'il vous plaît.*"

Rose closed the door behind her.

"If you're trying to hit me for a raise," Howard began, "your timing is bad."

Rose made herself smile.

"What is it, Rosie?"

"I just wanted you to know," Rose said, "that I take dictation."

"You do?"

"Yes."

"That's wonderful, Rosie." Howard smiled at her. He had a nice smile. He was better than average looking to begin with, but he was handsome when he smiled. Medium tall, he had a trim, athletic build. Even though it was still only early April, he was deeply tanned.

"So if you want, you can dictate some letters tomorrow."

"I can't do that, Rosie."

"What do you mean, you can't do that?"

"I get flustered. I have to write everything out in longhand."

"But I *take* dic*ta*tion."

"Maybe Dickens has some letters she'd like written. Why don't you ask her?"

"Miss Dickens is an employee. You're the boss. There's all the difference in the world."

Howard pulled at his chin a moment. "We seem to be at an impasse, Rosie. What do you think we should do?"

"I think you'd better learn to dictate. That's all there is to it."

Howard stared at her.

She could feel herself starting to blush, so she stopped it. "After all, Mr. Scudder, there's no point in wasting me."

"Right you are, Rosie. No point in wasting you. I'll just learn to dictate and that's all there is to it."

"Thank you," Rosie said, and she turned, starting for the door.

"You're a funny girl, aren't you, Rosie?"

Rose glanced back at him. "Funny?" she said. "Me?" she said. "No," she said.

It was a pretty day, so she decided to walk home. She walked along Central Street, then turned two corners down, crossing over to Beach, then to Elm, then to Cedar. When she reached Oak, she turned again, moving to a house in the middle of the block. A sign in front of the house read "Furnished Rooms." Rose moved under the sign. Her room was on the top floor. Small, perfectly square, it reflected nothing. The small closet was neatly filled with clothes. The bed was made and already turned down for the night. On her bed table were a book and a picture from a newspaper. The book was the Bible. Rose never read it, but she was never without it either. The picture was clipped from the West Ridge *Weekly Sentinel*. Dated mid-March, it had already begun to curl. "Returns from vacation," the picture said. And underneath, some society doggerel that began, "Howard Scudder, one of West Ridge's most eligible bachelors, returned recently . . ." Rose did not bother reading the rest. She knew it by heart anyway.

Instead, she stared at the picture.

•　•　•

The next afternoon, on her way home from work, Rose stopped at the West Ridge Public Library. Ordinarily she did not read much; books made her impatient. She stood in the doorway of the library for a moment, quietly looking around. Rose always did that; whenever she had to enter a new room she would stop and fix it carefully in her mind, so that when she moved she could move directly. Rose had little patience with indecision. Nodding to herself, she walked quickly to the library desk and made out a card. When it had been processed, she hurried to the shelves. She took out two books on selling and two more on the fundamentals of real estate. They were heavy, and she resented their weight, but she took them anyway, charging them on her card, nodding curtly to the elderly librarian behind the desk. When she got home she brewed herself a pot of strong coffee—strong coffee was a weakness of hers—and began to read.

It was nearly four in the morning before she allowed herself to stop.

Two days later Miss Dickens came down with the flu, and the day following that Rose appeared in the office carrying a large paper bag. She worked efficiently for an hour, answering the phone when it rang, typing correspondence, changing the photographs of houses for sale that served as a display in the window facing on Central Street. It was after eleven when she made her move.

Howard emerged briefly from his inner office, watching her as she typed. "Slave on," he said.

Rose finished the letter she was copying.

"New dress?" Howard asked. "It's very nice."

"Thank you." Rose brought the paper bag up and set it on her desk.

"What's in the bag, Rosie?"

"You were supposed to ask that."

"Always on cue. That's me."

"Food," Rose said. "You see, I had some friends to dinner last night and we had roast beef, except that I bought too much, so instead of letting it go to waste—I could never finish it all—I made sandwiches for us. And potato salad. A picnic lunch. Right here in the office." Howard was watching her and she wondered briefly if he knew that there had been no friends, that the food was purchased early that morning from the grocer on the corner.

"Sounds great, Rosie."

Rose allowed herself a smile.

"But I can't make it."

Rose said nothing.

Howard hurried on. "I eat lunch at home, Rosie. Every day. Rain or shine."

"At home? Alone?"

"With Mother, of course," Howard answered.

"Oh," Rose said, looking at him. That was all. Just "Oh."

Late in the afternoon Dolly Salinger appeared.

Rose was alone in the office when the front door opened. Rose glanced up. The woman in the doorway looked to be twenty-one or -two, tall, slender, dark. Her skin was pale and clear, her lips red, her hair raven black. She entered the room and Rose examined her. She was almost unfairly pretty, and she moved with athletic grace. My legs are better, Rose thought. My legs are better.

"Yes?" Rose said.

"Howard here?"

"Mr. Scudder is out just now."

The other woman shrugged. "Just tell him Dolly stopped by."

"I certainly will," Rose said, jotting it down on a note pad. "Dolly who?"

"Salinger."

Jew, Rose thought. "I'll tell him, Miss Salinger."

They stared at each other a moment. "You do that," Dolly said. She continued to stare.

Rose busied herself with some papers. When she heard the front door close she looked up. "Stay away," Rose said out loud. "You hear me? Stay away."

•

The next morning Miss Dickens returned, more powdered than usual. "The doctor urged me to spend another day in bed," she began, hanging up her coat. "But I told him 'Absolutely not.' I can be very stubborn when I want to."

Rose waited for her to sit down.

"Influenza is a dreadful disease. I seem to get it at least once each year. Usually I get it in the wintertime and—"

"Who's Dolly Salinger?"

"Dolly Salinger?"

"That's right."

"Why, she and Mr. Scudder are keeping company."

"For how long?"

"Several years now."

"She rich?"

"I don't believe so. Not anymore. Her family was hit badly by the crash."

"Oh, that's a shame," Rose said.

"Yes. Yes, it was. Her father took his own life soon afterwards. Or so the story goes. At any rate, he died."

"We all have to go sometime."

"She's a lovely girl, don't you think? So pretty."

"Beauty fades," Rose said.

One morning late in May Rose walked into Howard's office. "If you promise not to ask me how old I'm going to be, I'll let you take me to dinner on my birthday. What do you say?"

Howard smiled. "Who could refuse an offer like that?"

"You promise?"

"Cross my heart, Rosie. When's your birthday?"

"Today."

"Stabbed," Howard said.

"You promised."

"You're a hard woman, Rosie."

"I never said I wasn't."

"I've been working since I was sixteen," Rose was saying. "Full-time. Before that I worked part-time. I don't remember anything of my childhood except working. I never had much." She took another sip of her

Pink Lady. They were sitting in a dark corner of a cocktail lounge off Euclid Avenue in downtown Cleveland. In the middle of the room a fat Negro man played softly on the piano. "Tea for Two" and "Dardanella" and "Blue Skies." "No," Rose said, "I never had much."

"What did your father do?" Howard asked.

"As little as possible right up until he died. My mother, she was dead too by that time." Rose realized that she was talking too much and she paused, staring down at her Pink Lady. Ordinarily she did not drink and this was her third cocktail. "Am I acting drunk?" Rose said.

"You're a perfect lady. Besides, it's your birthday."

"I hate birthdays. Not this one. But the others I hated."

"How many others have there been?"

"And you promised you wouldn't ask."

"See?" Howard said. "You've got a mind like a trap. You can't be drunk."

Rose sipped her cocktail.

"You were talking about your family."

"Oh, them. To hell with them. I got a bunch of aunts. They used to shift me around every so often. House to house. I bet I've lived in most every town in Ohio. You ever move much? I hate moving."

"West Ridge is my home, Rosie. I've never lived anywhere else. Never want to."

"Your father dead too?"

"He's dead too."

"What did he do?"

"You're kidding."

Rose looked at him blankly.

"You can't have lived long in West Ridge without knowing about my father. He delivered nine-tenths of the population."

"That's a good thing to be. A doctor."

"Yes."

The piano player started into "Make Believe." Rose hummed along softly. "You would have been a good doctor, Howard. You got good hands. I look at people's hands a lot. You can tell about them from their hands. Did you know that?"

"Bumps on the head are a lot more scientific, Rosie. Phrenology."

"You're kidding, but I'm serious. You should have been a doctor with your hands."

"I tried. I went to medical school for a year after college. I flunked out. So you see, you're wrong."

"You're very good at selling houses, Howard."

"Damn right I am. I know every house in West Ridge. I used to bicycle around when I was a kid. All over town. Ask me any corner in town and I'll tell you about the houses there. Go on. Ask me a corner. Ask me any two streets that come together."

"All right. Cedar and Lincoln."

"Cedar and Lincoln." Howard closed his eyes. "There's four corner lots and two houses. One of them's owned by the Fergusons. Brown house. Three floors. They bought it from the Slocums in 1926. The other house is empty now, but Old Man Mahnken built it back in 1915 and—"

Rose laughed. "I believe you."

"I can do that for hours," Howard said.

"I believe that, too."

"Damn right," Howard said. "Damn right."

They finished their drinks. "Do you think we should have another, Howard?"

He raised his hand for the waiter. "What the hell, Rosie. It's your birthday."

"It really isn't."

Howard lowered his hand.

"My birthday is in December. I was a Christmas child. I lied to you, Howard. Are you mad?"

"What did you do that for?"

"Better work relationships. I'm a firm believer in better work relationships. Are you mad?"

Howard raised his hand again. Then he smiled. "What the hell," he said. "It's May. That's almost your birthday."

"You drink a lot, don't you?" Rose said. It was two hours later and she was on her sixth Pink Lady.

"Yes. I drink a lot."

"Does your mother like for you to do that?"

"I don't believe we've ever discussed it."

"But you live with her."

"That's right. But she goes her way pretty much and I go mine. She doesn't pry."

"You're very lucky."

"Yes."

Rose swallowed half her drink. "I love these. They get better and better the more you drink them."

Howard sipped his Scotch.

"How old are you, Howard? I never promised *I* wouldn't ask."

"Thirty-one."

"You ever want to get married?"

"What the hell kind of question is that?"

"I just wondered."

"Damn right I want to get married."

Rose took another swallow of her drink. Then she said it. "You can do better than Dolly Salinger."

Howard looked at her.

"A lot better."

"What are you talking about? What do you know about Dolly?"

"I've seen her. That's enough."

"Did her hands give her away?"

"Are you serious with her?"

"Dolly's my fiancée. We're more or less engaged."

"What does that mean?"

"It means we're going to get married."

"When?"

"Soon, I hope."

"Do you want to marry her?"

"It's really not much of your business, Rosie. But since you stuck your nose in, yes, I want to marry her."

"But she won't have you?"

"She'll have me."

"When?"

"Dolly's got this thing about money."

"You're not rich enough for her. Is that it?"

"Now, look, Rosie—"

"Don't talk about it anymore. If you don't want to, don't. Change the subject."

Howard took a long swallow of Scotch.

"I'm going to be getting married myself one of these days."

"Who to?"

"I got me some ideas," Rose said.

When they drove up to the house on Oak Street it was early in the morning. Rose opened the door for herself and stepped out. Howard moved around the car, holding on to it with one hand as he went. They started up the walk, moving past the "Furnished Rooms" sign. The night was bright, the moon full. Rose stepped up the steps but lost her balance, falling against him. He steadied her as best he could. They were standing very close together.

"I never had a better time," Rose said.

"My pleasure." Howard started a bow, then thought better of it. "I'd never make it back up again," he explained.

"I'd help you," Rose said. She stood a step above him, staring into his eyes. "I meant that, Howard. I never had a better time. Not ever."

Howard smiled.

"Thank you, Howard." She closed her eyes, waiting.

"Welcome," he answered, but she knew from the sound of his voice that he was moving away from her.

Rose opened her eyes. He was backing down the sidewalk, waving. She returned it. " 'Night, Rosie," he called.

Rose turned, entering the house, climbing the steps to the top floor. Flicking on the lights in her room, she went to the mirror and stared at herself. She looked worse than usual. I wouldn't kiss me either, she thought. Taking a step closer to the mirror, she began examining her face. Plain. God, it was plain. With a wild burst of anger, she grabbed a handful of her brown hair and pulled it until the pain began to numb. "Easy, Rose," she said aloud. "Easy." Her temper frightened her when it came like that. She breathed deeply, trying to bend it under control. In the mirror she could see her room. Square and dull. She hated it. She hated everything about . . . No. No, that wasn't true. (Her temper was going.) She didn't hate it. (She was breathing easily again.) After all, she had had worse. A lot worse.

And by Christ she was going to have a lot better.

The morning of the seventh of July, Rose talked to Howard's mother for the first time. She and Miss Dickens were in the office when the telephone rang. Rose answered it.

"This is Mrs. Scudder," the voice on the other end said.

"Oh, Mrs. Scudder, how do you do?" Rose said.

The question was ignored. "My son will not be in today."

"Is he sick?"

"He is not sick. He is fine."

"Will he be in tomorrow?"

"I'm not in the least sure." There was a click on the other end.

Rose hung up the phone. "She's a sweetheart. Howard won't be in today."

"I don't wonder."

"Why don't you?"

"Haven't you heard? Dolly Salinger ran off and got married. He's quite a bit older than she is, but very rich, or so the story goes. I imagine he's all upset, poor Howard. It's really very sad."

"Tragic," Rose said.

Howard did not come to work the next day. Or the day after that. But when he finally did return, a week later, it was obvious what he had been doing with his time.

Drinking.

The smell of alcohol in the early morning made Rose want to retch.

"Good morning, harem," Howard said. "Miss me?"

"You must never desert us again," Miss Dickens began.

Howard held up his right hand. "Scout's honor."

"You O.K. now?" Rose asked.

"Fine," Howard said, making a smile. "Fine, fine, fine." And with that he went into his office and closed the door.

Later that morning, when Rose went into Howard's office, she caught him hurriedly shoving a bottle of whisky into a desk drawer.

"You better knock next time, Rosie."

"You think so?"

"What is it, Rosie?"

"You got any letters you want to send?"

"Not just yet. I'll call you if I do."

Rose hesitated in the doorway.

"Anything else, Rosie?"

"It can wait," Rose said, and she closed the door.

At eleven-thirty Rose looked over from her desk. "Time for your lunch," she said.

Miss Dickens looked at the time. "But I never go to lunch this early."

"Yes, you do. Today you do."

"But—"

"Out you go. Don't argue."

Miss Dickens looked at Rose's face for just a moment more. Then she hurriedly put on her summer hat, her summer gloves. Picking up her purse, she was gone.

Rose waited for a moment, her eyes closed. Finally she stood and walked to Howard's office, throwing the door open.

"Didn't I tell you to knock?"

"Did you? I forgot."

"What's got into you, Rosie?"

"That's not the question. What's got into you?"

"That's my business."

Rose said nothing. Howard sat back in his swivel chair, his hands folded on his stomach. Rose stared at his puffy eyes. Howard looked away.

"I'm busy right now, Rosie. So if it's not important, let's postpone it."

Rose moved closer to him.

"Don't make me order you to get out, Rosie."

"Order me. See what happens."

"Dammit—"

"You're scaring me."

"Please."

"Beg some more," Rose said. She could feel her temper breaking loose inside her, a thing unto itself, anger building. She let it come.

"For the last time, Rosie—"

"I hate weakness! Howard. It makes me sick." And suddenly her voice was out of control. "You lousy *lush!*"

Howard closed his puffy eyes. "I never said I was strong, Rosie. Did I, now?" He forced a smile. "Under stress I tend to drink. It's my pattern."

"It is, huh? It is, huh?" And she whirled around the desk, jerking at the drawers, opening them, slamming them shut, moving to the next drawer, jerking and slamming until she found the bottle. "Here," Rose cried and she shoved the bottle at him.

Howard's eyes were still closed. "Don't do anymore. Please."

Rose grabbed him. "You're through with that stuff! Never no more, not while I'm around. You ever touch that stuff again you'll have to answer to me and you don't wanna do that, Howard." She let him go.

Howard began to shake.

"Aw, Howard," Rose whispered then. "Aw, come on."

"She left me, Rose."

"Good, I say."

"She left me."

"Rest easy, Howard." She reached out, gently touched his cheek. "I'm here."

After that, they were together. Most of the time they spent in the office, working until ten o'clock at night, six nights a week. Sundays he took her driving in the country or swimming in Lake Erie. But even then they talked about work. How to sell houses. How to sell houses. During the week they would tour West Ridge at lunchtime, driving slowly down street after street, Rose watching and listening, Howard explaining about who lived where and when it was built and what kind of a price it would bring on the market. Howard talked. Rose absorbed it all.

In October she sold her first house. It was small, on the north side of town, but still she sold it. That night he took her into Cleveland again, where they had dinner and then went to the symphony. Afterward he drove her home, his right arm draped over her shoulder most of the way. When they reached the front steps of her place on Oak Street, he hugged her briefly, then kissed her quickly on the cheek.

As she walked up to her room, Rose could not help smiling.

Toward the end of that month Rose got a second phone call from Mrs. Scudder.

"Miss Mathias?"

"Speaking."

"This is Mrs. William Scudder."

"I recognized your voice."

"I would like to see you."

"Anytime."

"Tomorrow, then? Four o'clock. Can you get away?"

"If you'd like me at four, then I'll be there at four."

"Until tomorrow, then. And, Miss Mathias . . ."

"Yes?"

"I don't see any reason to tell Howard about this, do you?"

"Is that an order, Mrs. Scudder?"

"That's an order, Miss Mathias."

At four o'clock promptly, Rose arrived at the Scudder house on Waverly Lane, one of the two most exclusive streets in town. The Scudder house was large and white, with four white columns in the front. Rose walked up the path along the lawn and rang the bell. A middle-aged servant lady opened the door.

"To see Mrs. Scudder. Miss Mathias. I'm expected."

"This way, please," the servant lady said, turning, walking through the foyer. Rose followed her.

Mrs. Scudder was waiting, seated in the library. She was a small, heavyset woman with white hair. "Miss Mathias," she said.

Rose sat in an easy chair across from her, carefully folding her hands in her lap.

"Coffee?"

"Please. Black."

Mrs. Scudder poured a cup of coffee from the silver pot on the table beside her. Rose took the cup and balanced it carefully, making sure not to spill.

"Lovely fall," Mrs. Scudder said after she had poured herself some coffee.

Rose allowed as to how it was indeed a lovely fall.

"I felt the summer was a trifle hot."

Rose allowed that too.

Mrs. Scudder talked on, holding her coffee cup gracefully, sipping from it gracefully. Rose followed along as best she could. The room seemed uncomfortably warm and she wanted to wipe her brow, but she decided against it. The walls of the room were lined with books, the great majority of them bound in leathers of red and green.

Rose commented on the books.

"Dr. Scudder was a great reader," the older woman said.

"I wish I could say the same," Rose said.

"You don't read, then?"

"I know how, if that's what you mean."

Mrs. Scudder smiled. "Books can be a comfort, Miss Mathias. In times of stress."

"Some people read, some people drink." Mrs. Scudder flicked her eyes across and for a moment they stared quietly at each other. "And you can call me Rose."

"Rose," Mrs. Scudder said.

Rose finished her coffee.

"Would you care for another cup?"

Rose shook her head.

"I myself happen to have a passion for coffee. I drink coffee most of the day. In the morning when I awake, then again at lunch, then—"

"Get to it."

"I beg your pardon?"

"The point."

"I prefer reaching the subject gradually."

"I don't."

"That's more than obvious."

"What's the subject?" Rose said.

"Come now. We both know the answer."

"O.K.," Rose said. "What about Howard?"

Mrs. Scudder poured herself another cup of coffee before she spoke. "I owe you a debt of gratitude for what you've done with him. I could never have done it. I know that."

"Go on." Rose got up from her chair and started to pace.

"I prefer you to sit."

"I prefer not. Go on."

"You're too common for my son," Mrs. Scudder said.

Rose nodded. "What was the matter with Dolly Salinger?"

"What has that to do with anything?"

"Plenty. Answer my question."

"She was half Jewish, for one thing. I disapprove of mixed marriages."

"What kind do you approve of?"

"I wish you'd sit down, Miss Mathias."

"And who was the girl before Dolly and what was the matter with her?"

"I'm not going to continue this until you sit down."

"Then just listen, lady, because you're right. I am too common. And I'm too plain. And I've got a rotten sense of humor and I've got a temper that could send you right up the wall, so don't make me lose it. O.K.?" Rose was moving faster now, back and forth, ranging across the room. "But if I was perfect you'd still find something wrong. Because there's nobody no place good enough for your son. Howard is a weak man. We both know that. We sense it. Because we're just the opposite. At least, I am. I'm strong, lady. I'm so strong you wouldn't believe it and that's why I'm going to marry your baby boy whether you like it or not."

"Somehow I doubt that."

"Who the hell cares what you doubt? I'm going to marry him."

"You can leave whenever you're ready."

"When I'm ready I will. I got more to say. I got some instructions for you. You know what you're gonna do? You're gonna tell Howard that little Rosie is the girl of his dreams. You're gonna push little Rosie every chance you get. Rosie, Rosie, Rosie, that's all you're gonna talk about. You want him to marry me more than you ever wanted anything."

Mrs. Scudder stood. "If you'll excuse me." She took a step toward the door.

Rose grabbed her. "Don't you want to know why? I'll tell you why. I'm going to get Howard one way or another, with you or without you. And if it's with you, I'll move in here. He'll still be under your roof, lady. Just like he always has been. But if it's without you, I'll take him away. I don't care if he kicks and screams, I'll drag him all the hell across the country and you'll never see him again. I'll make sure of that. No visits home to see mommy. Not for little Howard. You understand me? One way you got half; the other you got nothin'. Your move, lady."

Between the two of them, Howard never had a chance.

They were married early in January and they honeymooned in New York. Rose didn't want to go to New York at all but Howard insisted, so she decided it would be best to give in to him. They arrived at Grand Central Station and took a taxi to the Waldorf-Astoria Hotel. Their suite at the Waldorf was on the thirty-fifth floor, and from the window you could see all the way uptown to Harlem, Howard said, if you looked close enough. Their first night in the city they went to dinner at Luchow's. The next morning, after several hours of walking, Rose formed her impression of the city.

She hated it.

The women were strange-looking and they wore too much makeup and the men walked too fast and looked down their noses at her and everyone knew she was from out of town and took advantage of her whenever she walked into a shop to ask the price of anything. And worst of all, the city was cold. The thermometer read close to the zero mark and sharp winds cut up the wide streets, stinging her eyes.

That night Howard wanted to go to the theater but Rose said that she didn't feel up to it. Instead they had supper sent up to their hotel room and went to bed early. Howard seemed nervous and Rose was too unhappy to sleep. They lay side by side in bed, staring up, neither of them moving for fear they would disturb the other.

The next morning Howard had a business appointment for lunch.

"Take your time," Rose said. "I'll be here when you get back."

"You ought to go out. Buy things. That's what women do on their honeymoon."

"Not this woman," Rose said.

"What will you do here?"

"I don't know. Maybe I'll write a letter to your mother."

"You said goodbye to Mother day before yesterday. What have you got to tell her?"

"How much I love New York. I could fill pages about that."

Howard kissed her lightly on the forehead, "Suit yourself, baby."

Rose nodded. "Haven't you noticed? I usually do."

•

A few hours later she found herself on Fifth Avenue. What drove her finally from the suite was the fact that there was no one to write to. There was Howard's mother, of course, and there was Dickens back at the office, but they didn't really care. Not that much, anyway. Not enough. The thought that there was no one, not one person anywhere on the entire face of the earth, that gave a sufficient damn about her sent her onto the street.

Rose wandered through the cold on Fifth Avenue, gazing in shop windows. Nothing intrigued her. She ought to buy something, she realized, but what? Maybe Howard wanted a wallet. But then, he already had a wallet, not to mention half a drawer full of others at home. Or shirts. He had shirts, though. Stacks of them. What, then? What? She was trying to make her mind up one way or another when she saw him.

With Dolly Salinger.

They were hurrying across the sidewalk toward an empty cab, laughing very hard. Rose watched them a moment. They made a handsome couple; there was no use in trying to deny it. He held the door open for her while she got in; then he followed her, closing the door. The cab drove up Fifth Avenue. How typical it was of Howard, Rose realized, to worry about whether she would be happy while he was out with another woman.

Embarrassingly close to tears, Rose returned to the hotel.

Howard returned after four, smiling. They embraced and she held him very tightly for the longest time. She asked how his appointment had gone and he answered that it went as well as could be expected and all the while they chatted Rose wondered whether to tell him or not. The question stayed in her mind through dinner and the theater and after when they returned to the hotel. Finally, when they were getting ready for bed, she asked him a question.

"Do you remember Dolly Salinger?"

"Certainly. Why?"

"No reason. I just saw someone today who looked a lot like her and I wondered whatever became of her. After she got married, I mean."

"She came east, I think. Boston, maybe."

"Well, then, it could have been her that I saw. Boston isn't that far away."

"I doubt it," Howard said.

"Oh, I doubt it, too," Rose agreed. And for the while she let it rest.

But the next afternoon, when Howard remembered another business appointment, she had to go on with it. They were in the suite, Rose sitting in a chair by the window, Howard standing by the closet door, selecting a necktie.

"You certainly have a lot of appointments."

"Not so many, really."

"I didn't know you knew that many people here."

"This is just my second time. I know two people."

"Both named Dolly?"

Howard found a tie to his liking and inserted it beneath his collar.

"Yesterday—"

"I know. We were getting into a taxi. I saw you too. So you see, New York really isn't much bigger than West Ridge."

"How can you do it? How can you be so calm about it?"

Howard finished knotting his tie. "At the risk of seeming trite, I'd just like to say that it isn't what you think."

"It isn't, huh?"

"Scout's honor, Rosie."

"You're just good friends, is that it?"

"That's it."

"Is she the reason we came here?"

"Good God, of course not."

"Just because I know, that doesn't change your plans or anything?"

"This is the last time. She's got to be back in Boston by tonight."

"One final roll in the hay, is that it?"

"Don't talk like that. I told you, it isn't what you think."

"Does her husband know, since it's all so pure and upright?"

"No. He wouldn't understand."

"You expect me to?"

"No, Rosie."

"This is all just too damn sophisticated for me, Howard. If you think I'm gonna straighten your tie, you're wrong."

"I'll be back for dinner. We're just going for a drink and then I'll put her on the train. I'd let you come along but you'd probably be bored."

Rose stood by the window, staring down at Park Avenue. "Howard, don't go. You're making me do this but I forbid you, Howard."

"Look at me!"

Rose turned.

"In the taxi," Howard said, his voice growing louder, "when I told her you'd seen us, Dolly, she predicted that. She said you'd forbid me. And she said I'd never disobey." Howard slapped his gloves into his open palm. "She said I *liked* being ordered around. I got very irritated. I almost lost my temper right there in the taxi. Because it's so untrue. I'm really sick of people—women, I'm talking about now—telling me what to do. I'm the man in the family, Rosie. And if I want to go out that door, I'll go out that door. Mother thinks she can order me around and so do you and so did Dolly. Well, if I want to see Dolly off on the Boston train I will and if I want to stay here and order Room Service to bring me a double portion of Jell-O I will and if I want to do anything else then by God this once I'm gonna do it."

Rose hurried to him, took his hand. "Howard, will ya listen to me a minute? You remember? That first night in Cleveland? What I said? That I never had much? I was lying. I never had anything, Howard. Not really one thing ever in my life. I've got you now. But if you go out that door, I won't want you quite so much. Nothing will ever be the same again, Howard."

"You don't think that's a little melodramatic?"

"I warned you, Howard. Always remember that."

Rose watched as he moved to the door and out. She stood very still, and when it did not reopen Rose ran to the mirror and hated her face for a while. Then she stepped back, raised her skirt above her knees and whispered, "My legs are better, my legs are better," until, in spite of all she could do, the tears came.

After two hours of walking alone through the streets of Manhattan, Howard came back. He stood in the doorway of the darkened suite and said, "I didn't see her off, Rosie. Honest, I just walked." Then his hand flicked on the light.

"Turn it off," Rose commanded.

Howard obeyed. "What is all this?"

Naked, Rose advanced on him. With terrible efficiency, she got him out of his clothes. When he was naked, she put her arms around his waist. Together they fell back onto the bed. Through it all, Rose never said a word.

Nine months later to the day, her son was born.

When Howard came to the hospital later that day, he kissed her on the cheek and sat on the foot of the bed. "What do you think of William?" Howard asked.

"For what?"

"His name."

"Not for my boy. Anyway, he's already got a name. Last night it came to me. Branch. His name is Branch."

"Are you kidding, Rosie?"

"Do I look like it?"

"But what kind of a name is that?"

"Strong, Howard. You know what that means, don't you? A branch from a tree. Strong."

"But William was my father's name."

"Your mother's named Flora. You wanna call him Flora?"

"Listen, Rosie—"

"It's settled."

"Branch William maybe? Would that be all right?"

Rose relented. "Branch William would be fine."

When the boy was ten months old he contracted pneumonia. For sixty hours Rose sat by his bed, never sleeping. The doctor came several times and Howard hired a full-time nurse, but Rose never left his side.

"For God's sake, Rosie, get some sleep. You'll kill yourself if you don't watch it." This was the second day.

Rose stared at the boy.

Howard took her hand.

She jerked free.

"The nurse is right here."

Rose reached out and touched the boy's fevered skin.

"Get some sleep. Please. Come to bed."

"I can't."

"Why can't you?"

"If I leave him, he might die. But he won't. Not so long as I stay right here."

Rose stayed right there. Then, halfway through the sixty-first hour, the fever broke.

"See?" Rose said, staring triumphantly up at her husband. "See? I told you."

He was her baby; there was never any doubt about that. As he began to grow she let his hair remain uncut, long and curly. She dressed him in elegant clothes, making sure that he was always immaculately clean. "Little Lord Fauntleroy," Howard said time and again. Not that it did much good.

Branch was a verbal child. He spoke sentences by the time he was two, and he knew all the letters of the alphabet by sight. Whenever company came over Rose would get out his blocks and he would say the letters in order while Rose beamed. Branch was thin and his appetite was poor and he cried a lot. But other than that he was fine.

Flora spoiled him terribly, worse than Rose almost, and Miss Dickens would stop by from the office after work with presents several times a week. Howard endured it until one spring Saturday when Branch was almost four.

Howard awoke that morning with a particularly bad hangover and at breakfast he yelled at the maid, a nervous young Negro girl who burst into tears on the spot. Shortly afterward Branch ran in. He was dressed in perfectly pressed short pants and a clean white shirt and his hair seemed to Howard to be longer and curlier than usual. "Hi, fella," Howard said.

Branch paused for just a moment, then ran out of the room and upstairs.

Howard got up from the table and went into the foyer. "Hey, Rose," he shouted. "Come on down here."

While he waited for her to appear, Howard paced.

"What is it?" She stood halfway up the stairs, dressed, as usual, in green.

"Let's talk."

"What about?"

"Our son. Oh, pardon me." Howard bowed low. "I mean your son."

"If you can't hold your liquor, don't take it out on the rest of us."

"I've had it with the kid," Howard said then.

"What are you talking about?"

"He's spoiled, he's bad-mannered and he's just about to blossom into the biggest sissy in the whole state of Ohio."

"Shut up," Rose said.

"Why doesn't he play ball or something?"

"So he can grow up to be Babe Ruth? Thanks."

"Other kids play ball."

"What is this ball business? Since when are you such a fan?"

"I just don't like the way he's acting."

"Branch," Rose called. "Come here, baby." A moment later he was standing alongside her on the stairs. "Do you want to play catch with your father?"

"No," Branch said.

"But you'd like it," Howard said. "Come on. Give it a try. Just for a little, Branch. Out in the back yard. We'll quit whenever you want to."

Branch looked up at Rose.

"Humor your father," she told him. "He's having a hard day."

"I'll play for a little," Branch said.

But there wasn't a ball in the house. Howard looked in all the closets and in the basement and up in the attic and the best he could do was an aged tennis net, gray and moldering.

"Some athlete," Rose said when he told her.

"I'll drive uptown and buy one," Howard said. "You want to come along, Branch? We'll have fun."

"No," Branch said.

"It'll only take a second," Howard said, and he hurried to the garage.

It took close to half an hour. Branch was painting a picture when Howard found him. "O.K., fella," he said. "All set."

"I'm doing a pitcher now, Daddy."

"That can wait."

"So can you," Rose said suddenly, coming up behind him.

Howard waited.

Finally they moved out onto the back lawn. Rose stayed on the porch, watching them. Howard moved a few steps away from his son. "Now I'm going to toss it to you, fella. And you catch it. Here she goes."

He lofted the ball gently into the air. Branch watched it. It bounced off his stomach onto the grass.

"That's pretty good, fella. Shows you're not afraid of it. But you're supposed to catch it with your hands. Like this." Howard cupped his palms together in demonstration.

Branch shook his head. "That would hurt."

"No, it wouldn't. I promise you. Just toss it to me and I'll show you." Branch picked up the ball and threw it at Howard. Howard caught it. "See, fella? It doesn't hurt a bit. That was some toss. You've got a good arm. Now you catch it this time." He lofted the ball toward his son. Branch turned his head as the ball dropped to the ground a few feet to his left. "Bad toss on my part," Howard said. "Give it here. I'll do it again." He was starting to sweat and his head ached slightly.

Branch threw the ball toward his father. Howard picked the ball up and tossed it gently back toward his son. The ball struck the boy in the chest.

"Now, you could have caught that one, fella. You're just not trying."

"I must be careful of my hands. So I can paint. Mamma tells me to."

"Well, I'm telling you to do something now. So you do it."

"Have you had enough?" Rose called from the porch.

"We just started," Howard yelled back. "We're having a wonderful time." Howard retrieved the ball and tossed it to Branch. Branch half turned, and the ball missed him. "Now come on, fella. Try."

"I don't want to play anymore," Branch said.

"You hear that, Howard? He wants to quit."

"We just started!" There was a crazy tone in his voice and Rose must have heard it too, because after a pause she called out to her son.

"Play with him a little more, Branch. Just a little more."

Howard walked over to Branch and put an arm around his shoulder. "You're going to learn this now," he said. "You're not leaving till you learn to cup your hands. A baby can do it. You can do it." His headache was worse now, the pain moving down, camping close behind his eyes. "Cup your hands." Branch did as he was told. Howard dropped the ball into the hands from a foot above. "Now, did that hurt? Tell me the truth."

"No."

"All right, then. Catch it this time." He threw the ball harder than he meant to and it struck Branch on the knuckles.

"That hurt, Daddy."

"No, it didn't. Now throw the ball back here."

"But it hurt."

"Dammit, it didn't. Quit being such a baby and throw me the ball."

"Howard . . ." It was Rose calling from the porch.

Branch threw the ball back to his father. Howard dropped it. Perhaps the sun had suddenly blinded him or perhaps he had been staring at the shadow of his wife on the porch. At any rate he dropped it.

And then the lawn was loud with Rose's laughter. "You're some teacher, yes, you are."

"Shut up."

The laughter grew louder and suddenly Branch joined in and then blindly, with all his might, Howard threw the ball toward the sound.

The ball crashed against Branch's temple.

Branch screamed and fell.

Howard rushed toward him, tears in his eyes, kneeling beside the writhing body of the boy. He reached out to touch him, but the body rolled away and Howard was about to reach out again when Rose was on him.

"Lush," she said. "Lush!" Cradling Branch in her arms, she carried him away.

Howard stayed where he was, embracing the grass where his son had fallen.

Branch began dreaming of a black prince.

For weeks on end he would wake in the middle of the night, the dreams vivid in his mind. They were all more or less the same. He was always bound up, either with belts or chains or cords of fire. Nothing could save him. Not this time. But then, always at the last second, a figure would appear.

The black prince.

The beautiful black prince.

With a slash of his silver sword, Branch's bonds fell dead. Then the prince would step forward and they would stare at each other. Then the prince was gone.

Awake, Branch shivered in the night.

Waiting . . .

"Sal-*lee*."

"What?"

"Come out and play." Her name was Sally Baker and she was five when he was six and she lived across the street.

"No."

"Why?"

"I hate you, that's why."

"I promise I won't pull your pigtails."

"That's what you always promise. Bully. Branch is a bul-ly. Nyah-nyah-uh-nyah-nyah."

Later, Branch in pursuit.

"Sal-*lee*."

"What?"

"I'll let you play with my train if you'll come out and play."

"Your fingers are crossed."

Branch held his hands up high. She stood in the window of her room on the second floor watching him.

"Your legs are crossed."

Branch uncrossed his legs.

"I won't play with you. Bully."

Later.

"Sal-*lee*."

"No."

"I'll let you play with my train and I'll give you a lollipop if you'll play with me." He held up the lollipop.

"What flavor is it?"

"Grape."

"No."

Still later.

"Sal-*lee*."

"No. You'll just pull my pigtails."

"But I'll give you three lollipops and nineteen red rubber bands if you'll play with me."

"Nineteen?"

Branch opened his hand. "I've got 'em right here. All red. Every last one."

"You promise you won't pull my pigtails?"

"Scout's honor."

"And you've got nineteen rubber bands and they're all red?"

"Yes. Yes."

She stuck her finger in her mouth.

"You coming?"

"Just for a little while." She disappeared from the window.

As soon as she was outside he gave her the lollipops and the red rubber bands. While she was counting them out loud—"ten, 'leven, twelve"—he stepped behind her and grabbed her pigtails. Then he started to pull. He yanked and pulled until she cried. Then he stopped. She whirled around and began to hit him. She slapped him in the face and kicked him in the shins, and the more she did it the more he wanted to smile.

When Branch was seven Howard took to drinking much too much and gambling on Saturday nights. Once, as Branch lay in bed quivering from the closeness of his escape—he had been bound with snakes and as the black prince struck them they doubled in size and number until they almost overwhelmed him and he had to kill them all with his bare hands—he heard his mother and father talking in her bedroom. It was a hot summer night and the windows were open, so he heard every word, starting with his mother's voice saying, "I couldn't care less about what you did Saturday."

"You're lying."

"Like hell. Just so long as you don't enjoy yourself, I don't care what you do. And you don't enjoy yourself, do you, baby? You haven't enjoyed anything much since Dolly."

Then his father's voice, suddenly soft. "I didn't put her on the train. I just walked around all by myself. That was eight years ago. Can't you forget that?"

"Can Hell freeze?" his mother wanted to know.

Howard took to washing his car.

Every day after work and every Saturday afternoon he spent in the driveway, hosing down his red LaSalle, then sponging it off, cleaning the whitewall tires, shining the chrome. It got to be a joke on Waverly Lane and he knew it, but he went right on, day in, day out, washing his car. "Get it good and clean, Howard," the neighbors would call out when they drove past. "Shine it up good." And he would smile, nodding to them, waving. If the Japanese hadn't bombed Pearl Harbor, he probably would have gone on washing it forever.

"I was thinking of enlisting." Howard stood in the doorway of Rose's bedroom. It was night on that cold December Sunday. The room was dark.

Her voice from her bed. "Think all you want to. Just don't do it."

"I'm serious, Rosie."

"You're a laugh."

"Tomorrow morning. I think I'm going to do it."

"They don't takes lushes in the Army."

"I can stop drinking."

"Funnier and funnier," Rose said.

The next day he enlisted.

"Fool!" Rose commented when he told her.

"Probably."

"You'll regret it. Leaving us here like this."

"You can take care of yourself, Rosie. We both know that from long experience."

"You left me once before when I told you not to. That was just for two hours. This could be for years."

"Or a lot longer," Howard said.

Early one snowy morning he left. Rose kissed him goodbye at the front door. Branch sat on the stairs, watching. Howard looked at his son. "Say goodbye to your Daddy, Branch? Will you do that?"

For a moment Branch sat still.

Then he was flying, down the steps, whirling around the banister, running, running to his father, arms out wide. Branch leaped into his father's arms and clung to him.

Howard blinked at the quick tears that suddenly covered his eyes.

Monday of the following week, Rose went back to work. The real-estate office was larger now. Several years before Howard had taken over the hardware store and broken the wall between them so that now there were five women working at desks and a young Italian girl sitting as receptionist. Rose took Howard's old office and soon was busy from early morning until night. Lunchtime she always drove back to Waverly Lane, eating with Branch in the quiet dining room, smiling at him, touching him, asking him about his day. "How was your day, Branch?"

Branch's days were going badly. He never told her that, of course, but he began to dread school. He was dreaming a good deal, and time after time he would stare embarrassed as his teacher caught him unprepared. "I'm sorry. I wasn't listening." He was chubby now and bad at sports and other boys were always picking on him. There was something that made them pick on him regardless of how he acted. "Fat ass." That was what they called him. "Fat ass."

"Fine, Mamma. My days are fine."

Once Rose returned to the office, business improved. Several factories opened on the outskirts of town, and even though the new members of the community were not of the highest type, still, they needed houses. And Rose sold them. Between early in 1942 and Christmas of that year, three thousand people came to live in West Ridge. Rose drove herself viciously, working until late at night now, and the office on Central Street hummed. Rose made more money that year than Howard had ever been able to do and 1943 was even better. She wrote him notes, keeping him abreast of business affairs, but he never answered them. From time to time he wrote to Branch, but never to Rose.

In the summer of 1943 she was informed, via wire, that he had been killed. She opened the wire slowly, sensing the contents, and she read it through once before tearing it to pieces and throwing it into the fireplace. Bending down, she lighted a match and watched it burn. "I'm not sorry, Howard," Rose said, staring at the little yellow flame. "I can't say that I'm sorry."

She told Branch that night. He was lying in bed and she came in and sat beside him, taking his hand. "Your father won't be coming back, Branch."

He looked at her. "You mean he's dead."

"Yes."

Branch said nothing for a while. Then he closed his eyes. "How did he die, Mama?"

"I don't know, Branch."

"Tell me, Mama. How did he die?"

Rose kissed him. "Go to sleep, baby."

Later, when he was sure no one could hear, Branch pushed his face into his pillow and wept the night away.

Howard died superbly.

On a steaming island, the name of which Rose could never quite pronounce, he made a wild lonely trip across a steep ravine. Alone, he stormed screaming down one side and up the other, running, grenade in hand, toward a machine-gun nest that lay camouflaged on the far ridge. An opening burst of fire tore his chest open, but he crawled forward, still screaming with what was left of his voice. When he reached the nest he pulled the pin on the grenade and threw himself onto the gun.

He was awarded the Distinguished Service Cross.

And the citizens of West Ridge honored his family with a parade. Rose tried to squelch the idea but there was nothing she could do. But endure.

The reviewing stand was set up on Central Street, in front of the office. Rose, resplendent in green, stood, Branch beside her, while the parade marched by. It was hot and sunny and there were five brass bands providing music. The American Legion marched by and the Boy Scouts and the Girl Scouts and the mayor gave a speech and the Lieutenant Governor of the state of Ohio gave a speech. The parade dragged on and on, flags and tubas, words and drums. The Lieutenant Governor pinned the Distinguished Service Cross on Rose's green suit and in the crowd Branch could see the boys from school smiling up at him and waving. No Fat Ass today. Then Rose was standing in front of the microphone, clearing her throat.

"No one knows what I'm feeling at this moment," she began. Across the street two women began to weep. "But my husband—" and here she paused—"my late husband would want me to tell you that he loved this town. And I'm sure you have made him permanently proud. Thank you." There was a burst of applause and cheering and then the band started again, blaring away. Rose waved. The crowd waved back. Then, suddenly, two little boys with bugles were standing in front of the reviewing stand. Everything grew quiet as they began, badly, to play taps. Day is done . . . gone the sun . . .

Goddammit, it's touching, Rose thought.

The parade ended.

As soon as they got home, Rose went to her room and changed into something more comfortable. When she came downstairs, Branch was standing in the back yard, tossing a ball up into the air and catching it.

"What are you doing?" Rose called from the porch.

"Nothing."

"Well, stop it."

Branch tossed the ball up into the air again.

"Where did you get that?"

"It was Daddy's."

"You just find it?"

"No."

"Speak up, Branch."

"I've had it. In my room. In my desk."

"And you never told me?"

"I guess I didn't."

"Well, come in, baby. You've been in the sun enough for one day."

Tossing the ball, Branch came in.

"Would you like some lemonade, Branch?"

"No."

"You hungry?"

"No."

"What do you want to do?"

"Play catch."

"I already told you you can't do that. Give me the ball."

"No."

"Branch, give me the ball."

"No."

Rose held out her hand.

Branch shook his head.

"You know what we do with naughty boys?"

"I won't give it to you. It's mine."

"Then go to your room, Branch."

"I won't give it to you. You'll throw it away and I won't—"

"Go to your room!"

Clutching the ball in both hands, Branch went to his room. Lying down on his bed, he stared at the ball, rolling it around on the blanket. Then he sat up. It was hot in the room, so he took off his shirt and pants and lay on the bed clad only in his shorts. He tossed the ball and caught it a few times, then stood and went to the door, opening it, walking down the hall to his mother's room. Branch walked in and looked around a while and was about to leave when he saw her clothes and undergarments on her bed, so he got a hanger and took her green suit and hung it neatly in her closet. He went back to her bed and picked up her brassiere and was glancing around for a place to put it when he saw himself in the mirror. Walking close to the glass, he held up the garment. Then, out of curiosity, he tried to put it on. The brassiere was too big for him and he reached around to his back, trying to get it to fasten. He couldn't do it. He reversed the brassiere then so that the hooks met on his chest. He gazed at himself for a long time. He looked stupid, standing there in his shorts with the brassiere on. But he continued to stare. He was breathing faster than he should have been and his body was wet with perspiration.

"You've got it on backwards," Rose said.

Branch screamed.

Whirling, seeing her standing there, he ducked his head and ran out of the room. He ran down the corridor to his room and slammed the door and ran into the bathroom and slammed that door and stood trembling in the corner with his eyes shut tight. The Black Prince. Where was the Black Prince?

Rose opened the door and stood smiling at him.

"Come here, baby," she said. "Come to Mama."

Branch could not move.

She walked to him and took his cold hand. "Follow me," she whispered, and she led him out of the bathroom. Branch dragged his feet and tried pulling against her, but in a moment they were back in her bedroom again. Rose sat on the bed and held him close. "You must promise never to be afraid of Mama again. I don't care what you do, I'll understand. Now answer me."

"Yes."

"Yes what?"

Branch could think of nothing to say.

"Everybody else is afraid, baby. Everybody else in this whole world. But not you and me. Now tell me, why did you run away from me like that?"

"I was embarrassed."

"Why were you embarrassed?"

"Because you caught me."

"Caught you doing what, baby?"

"You know."

"Say it to me."

Branch shook his head.

"Trying on Mommy's clothes? Is that it?"

"I never did it before. Never. I swear."

"You don't have to swear, baby. Mama believes you. And there's nothing to be embarrassed about. Lots of little boys do it. Because they're curious. Isn't that how you were?"

"Yes."

"There's nothing wrong with curiosity, baby. So there's nothing wrong with what you did. The only thing wrong in this whole world is running away. You ran away from me, Branch, and you must never do it again. If we just face things, nothing can ever go wrong. If we don't face things, they fester. You were curious. Fine. Curiosity must be satisfied, baby. That's the best thing for it. Face it. Come." She stood. "Let me help you."

"Help me?"

"Stand still now."

Branch stood still while she took the brassiere off. He looked out the window. The sun was very bright.

"This is how it works," Rose said, and she slipped the brassiere over his arms, fastening it in back. "Go look at yourself in the mirror." Branch obeyed. The garment hung limply down his chest. "Remember, Branch; I'm just showing you there's nothing wrong with what you did. Here. This is a slip. Step into it." She held it for him. He did not raise his legs. Finally she took one leg and set it into the slip, then the other leg. Then she pulled the slip up until it held around his waist. She took a green skirt from the closet. "You get into this the same way, baby. You do it. Show Mommy you know how." Branch put on the skirt. "And here's a beautiful green blouse, baby. Made of pure silk. See how smooth it feels?" She put his arms through the blouse and buttoned it up the back. "And now for a hat." She rummaged through her closet before choosing a wide-brimmed white sunhat. She was about to set it on his head when she stopped. "Just one more thing, baby, and we'll be all set." He stood frozen while she dabbed rouge on his cheeks and carefully lined his mouth with crimson lipstick. The hat went on. Rose took his hand and they walked up close to the mirror. "We could pass for sisters now, couldn't we, baby? All right, let's see you smile. Come on. Let's see. Look—Mama's smiling. You do the same. Come on. Come on now. We've had a hard day but it's all over. We're together, baby, just the two of us, always together. With nothing to be afraid of ever again. So smile. For Mommy. Smile."

Branch wanted to die but he smiled.

"Oh God," Rose said happily, hugging him tight. "Ain't we got fun."

Part II

VI

Esther didn't much want the baby.

She was, in the first place, too young, a scant twenty-one, not ready yet—not nearly. And, besides that, there was her figure to consider. Her waist had never been smaller (a scant twenty-one, like her age), her pink-tipped prizes never so full and firm. The thought of her flat stomach swelling from Sid's sting deprived her of sleep, while the image of her sublime bosom sagging, webbed with blue veins, provided her with night-mares. (Her mother's breasts had sagged, nipples and navel a level line; Esther remembered little of her mother, but she remembered that, and it chilled her, it chilled her.) And who the hell liked babies anyway? Not her. Not little Esther. How could you like them? Ugly wrinkled brats, cry-ing all the day, all the night, tying you down, jailing you, and for what crime? Carelessness. Simple stupid carelessness. So where was Justice any-way? Out *noshing* bagels with cream cheese and no one watching the store.

And how could she support a kid after her divorce?

There was no doubt in her mind she would soon be divorced. Her marriage *(Ha!)* had been one titanic nothing, but after it was over, what then? Back pushing pickles in the deli? Better to die. Sid (the piker) would never come across with anything resembling alimony. Talk? Sure. Hot air? Sure. Money? Don't hold your breath. She could always marry again (no sweat, not with her looks) but marriage meant another husband around the house and Sid had soured her sufficiently on that score. More than once she fiddled around in her mind with the idea of letting some *holvah* baron keep her, but that (if you pursued the notion to the end) always seemed unappetizing. Nice Jewish Girls didn't do it and she was a Nice Jewish Girl. Besides, everybody would whisper. Besides that, where would she be at forty when her looks started going? And (finally) besides that, she had never met a *holvah* baron.

As she idly brushed her long hair each afternoon from three to four,

126

Esther stared in her mirror and dreamed. The brush caressed the rich black curls, and Esther, wistful, prayed not for a young knight in shining armor but for an (a) old rich man who would (b) change his will, making her the beneficiary, (c) marry her and then, thoughtfully, (d) die. (Quickly, without suffering; Esther was part romantic.) The chances of all this befalling her were, she knew, remote. (She was also part realist.) Still, she wished it with all of her sad heart, every afternoon, from three to four.

The rest of the time she busied herself loathing her husband.

Sid. Good old Sid. Sid old kid. How could she have said "Yes" to his pleas? Compared to her, General Custer was Alfred Einstein. Sid with the bad jokes and his bad breath and his bad taste. Sid the Yid. A child of six could hold a job; could he? If it weren't for his luck playing poker, his good fortune at snooker, they would have starved long ago. All day long she spent alone in the apartment, the same crummy apartment he seduced her in with that poisoned tomato juice. How could she go out when there was no money? Could you get mink from Marshall Field's on credit? And no new clothes to wear. Nothing to wear but promises. "Tootsie, I'm working on a deal and if it comes through . . . Tootsie, I'm onto something hot, big money, so much if you went into training you couldn't lift it all. . . . Tootsie, tomorrow, if everything goes right, I'm buying you the biggest . . . the best . . . the finest . . . the most . . ."

Baloney. That was all he was. Esther had married a sausage and it was killing her. As bad as he was when they were together, when they went out to one of his crummy friends' crummy parties he was unbelievable. Telling her how to dress—"No girdle, Tootsie. Let it shake. And wear the black dress without the front. Let the boys drool a little." And then, always in public, he pawed her, pinched her round bottom or, for variety, slapped it loud with the flat of his hand. Of course, he pawed her in private too. Nightly there was sexual solace, but the thought that she was supplying him pleasure deprived her of hers.

So there she was, married to the all-time loser, King Schlemiel, and with the possibility of a "little one" an interval of unhappiness might easily become a lifetime of grief. (After all, what were the odds on a rich old bachelor with a heart condition knocking on the door to her apartment?) Life, once the color of wheat, was now rich milk chocolate. With no marshmallow topping in view.

The first month, when she missed her "time" (her word), she ignored it. It had happened before when she was nervous and she was nervous now. She buried the thought beneath a heaping mound of bile and slept, all things considered, soundly. The second month, though, she began to panic. She felt well enough; there was no morning nausea; her stomach was still beautifully flat. But her carefully tended red fingernails took to clawing the base of her thumb, and sudden sounds gave her a start. All this was endurable, but when her complexion began spotting and the skin beneath her eyes started to darken unattractively, Esther hied herself to Dr. Fishbein. The good doctor borrowed some urine, played around for five days, and then reported the good bad news.

In the privacy of her apartment, Esther wept. She might have gnashed for hours except that on passing her beloved mirror she noted the dark skin beneath her dark eyes was both wrinkled and puffed and that was too much. Calling down vanity, she showered, perfumed her soft body, donned her best bra, her sheerest slip, ironed a black dress, draped it subtly over her curves, and slaved over her face, disguising it, banishing the dark skin, so that when Sid returned flush from a triumphant afternoon of eight-ball, had he bothered to give her a glance, he would have seen a dark vision, scented and soft and round. But the *Racing Form* held more allure for his blind eyes and he buried himself in half-mile résumés and abilities to leg it in the mud. But when Esther said "Hey, Sid, guess what—I'm pregnant" it was goodbye to all that.

• • •

Sid didn't much want the baby.

He was, in the first place, too young, a virile twenty-five, not ready yet—not nearly. Inside him, he knew, were those same seeds that formed all the titans, the Rockefellers, the Fords, the Julius Rosenwalds. He was a Man on the Move; direction: Up. And he doubted whether Greta the great Garbo could have provided him with permanent joy, much less the dark shrew he had bedded himself with, a voluptuous monster who could play Lady Macbeth without makeup. Witch Esther was certainly part of his present, but his golden future? Thanks but no thanks. Of course, Esther was good in the sack (but not that good. Winifred Katz, a remarkably athletic secretary he had met one night peddling cutlery door to door, was at least her equal). And there would be others, just as pretty, not as tart, just waiting to be plucked (joke) once he had the loot. But baby spelled complication, baby spelled not-only-alimony-but-support-yet (oh, and she'd kill him with that; just for spite she'd kill him), baby spelled Esther.

So no baby.

On warm nights, when Esther was asleep, Sid would sometimes pull the sheet away from her body, open the curtain wide so the moon touched her skin, and stare. Partly he did this for pleasure, but partly it was to reassure himself that anybody might have slipped the way he had, anybody might have married this rounded slut, anybody. She looked so sweet that, if you tapped her veins, maple syrup would run out. No flaws showing; all inside. *How could she look like that and still be like that?* How could she fail to see why the selling jobs he quit were nowhere? Couldn't she tell just from looking at him he was going someplace? And all the *kvetching* about money. Did she have to buy out Field's every day? Didn't he make enough at pool and cards to keep any ordinary hunk happy? And the way she dressed when they went out. It was humiliating. No girdle and dresses cut to the navel. "Jesus, Esther. Why don't we just go naked, Esther?" And at parties, slapping her body up against every available man, inhaling and bending over all night long. Did she have to give away what he had married her to get? Well, forget it and smile. Divorce was just around the corner. And fame was right there too. And love and money and trips around the world and cashmere suits and half a million broads and . . .

"What'd you say, Esther?"

"I said guess what—I'm pregnant."

Down went the *Racing Form.* "For sure?"

"For sure."

"Oh God, Tootsie, that's wonderful," and he took her in his arms.

"Isn't it? Isn't it?"

Sid ran his hand across her stomach. "I can feel it. I swear."

Esther giggled. "Oh, Sid, you're crazy."

Sid held her very close. "It's just like a dream. You've wanted a baby so bad."

"So have you."

"I know. After all the talking we've done about it and now it's here. Oh, Esther, it's a dream come true."

"A dream come true."

"Do you love me, Esther?"

"Yes, yes. And do you love me?"

"Oh yes." He raised his hand from her stomach to her breasts. Then slowly he began to undo her buttons.

"Sid. Careful."

"I'll be careful. You're a mother now. I've gotta be careful."

Esther unbuttoned his shirt, pulled it out from his trousers, running her hands across his chest. "You're a papa now. I'll be careful too."

"You know what I'm gonna do now, Tootsie? To celebrate? Something I've never done before."

"What, Sid?"

"I've never done it before but I'm gonna treat you like a queen, Esther—I'm gonna carry you in my arms into the bedroo—What's the matter, Esther? What're you looking like that for?"

"Nothing. I just was afraid you might drop me."

"Never." Sid picked her up. "Esther the queen."

"You happy, Sid?"

"I'm happy."

"I'm happy."

"We'll be that way forever."

"Forever."

"Say it again."

"Forever. Now you."

"Forever."

"Forever."

"Queen Esther."

"King Sid."

The next morning, His Highness was awakened by the Queen's groans.

"Ohhhhhh," Esther said. "Ohhhhhhh."

"Hey, Tootsie." Up on one elbow. "What is it, Tootsie?"

Pale smile. "Nothing. Nothing, darling. I'm fine."

Two mornings later, the King awoke alone. "Esther?" he called.

No answer.

Again: "Esther?"

No Esther.

Out of bed he hopped and into the next room. The Queen lay doubled up across the sofa, her arms gripping her stomach. "Esther, what?"

She bit her lower lip hard. "It's nothing."

"But, my God, you're in pain."

"What's a little pain?"

"But—"

"Women get this way. It's natural. Don't worry."

"I'm human. I worry."

"My sweetheart."

"Can't I do something?"

Pale smile. "I'm fine."

. . .

The next morning he again awoke alone. But this time the sofa was vacant. Likewise the kitchen. Sid pounded on the bathroom door, then opened it.

Esther knelt by the toilet.

"Esther?"

"Get out."

"No."

"I said get out!"

Sid stood in the doorway. "But—"

"You think I like having you see me like this? Get out. *Out! Out!*"

Sid closed the door, heard it lock. Then the sink was going full, both faucets hard. Sid pressed his ear against the wood. He did not hear her retch, but later the toilet flushed, so she must have. When the door opened she came (weakly) out, looked at his face and then dazzled him with her smile.

At two o'clock on Saturday morning Esther began to scream. Sid jumped from the bed in panic, staring at the creature clawing at the sheets.

"What?" Sid said. "What?"

"I hurt," Esther muttered. "Oh God, I hurt. I want to die."

"I'll call the doctor."

"No."

"But, Esther—"

"Some women have difficult pregnancies. I'm like that. There's nothing wrong. I just hurt, that's all."

"Where?"

"Here," and she clutched her left side.

"A second ago you were grabbing your stomach."

"I hurt all over."

"God," Sid said.

"Oh, Sid. Make it stop."

"Tomorrow you go to the doctor."

"It's nothing."

"Tomorrow you go!"

"I hate doctors."

"Tomorrow!"

"All right. All right."

"Promise?"

Esther nodded. "You take such care of me."

"We don't want anything to happen to the baby now, do we?"

"Sweet Papa," Esther whispered.

"Good Mama," Sweet Papa said.

"Well?" Sid put down the *Racing Form* and waited.

Esther said nothing, took off her gloves and her hat.

"You saw the doctor?"

Esther unzipped her dress and stepped out of it, hanging it in the closet.

"You saw the doctor?"

"I saw him."

"And?"

Esther shrugged.

"And? And?"

"I want the baby. Do you want the baby?"

"As God is my witness."

"Good."

"What did the doctor say?"

Esther tried to smile. "It's going to be a difficult pregnancy."

"What does that mean? I don't understand."

"It means . . ." And she shrugged again, disappearing into the bathroom.

"It means?" Sid shouted through the door.

"The baby is fine" came Esther's voice. "Couldn't be better."

"Go on."

Nothing from the bathroom except perhaps a stifled sob.

"Esther, for God's sake go on! The baby is fine and—"

"Chances are I'll be fine too."

"Chances are! Chances are!"

The door swung open and naked Esther raced into his arms. "Hold me. Sid, don't talk—just hold me."

"You mean you're liable to . . ."

"Don't say it. Just hold me."

"You mean it's possible that you might—"

"Anything's possible," Esther said.

•

"Esther?" Later that night, lying side by side.

"Yes, darling."

"There's something I've got to say."

"Of course, darling."

"This is very important, Esther. Now you've got to listen to me. Every word, it's that important. Will you promise to hear me out?"

"What is it, Sid?"

"You've got to promise to hear me out. No matter what, I've got to finish telling you what I've got to tell you."

"I promise."

Sid sat up in bed, locking his hands around his knees. "My father's closest friend all his life—I can't tell you how close, like brothers they were—well, this man, he had a daughter and she got, you know, like girls do sometimes, and, well, she was ashamed to tell him about it, so she went to a butcher and he did this thing to her and she died."

"Oh, that's terrible." Esther shook her head. "The crazy things kids do. A story like that, it just makes me want to cry."

"Yes, well when that happened to this close friend of my father, he swore that it would never happen to anybody he knew and cared for, what had happened to him."

"Don't go on, Sid."

"This man is a doctor, Esther—"

"Don't say any more. Not one word—"

"He's a surgeon."

"No!"

"He's a great surgeon. A great surgeon, you hear?"

"Nothing! I hear nothing. I want my baby. I want my baby."

Sid pulled her close. "You think I don't," he said.

"Esther?" The next night.

"Uh-huh."

"Last night what I said?"

"Yes?"

"I didn't say it."

Esther (into his arms): "You're so good."

Sid (rubbing her fanny): "Solid gold."

"Oh God." Esther writhing on the floor. "God . . . God . . . God."

"Tootsie, can't I help?"

"Make me stop hurting. Oh God."

"The doctor. Can't he give you something?"

"Oh God."

"Tomorrow. You go see him."

"Sid . . . make it stop hurting, Sid . . ."

"You make him give you something for the pain. Understand? I don't care what it costs. Something for the pain."

"Yes . . . tomorrow . . . something for the pain . . ."

"Well? Where are the pills?"

"He wouldn't give me any."

"Wouldn't give you any?"

"Pills won't help, he said. Nothing will help, he said. Just for me to be brave."

"I'll call up that doctor right—"

"No!"

"But, Tootsie—"

"Just hold me, Sid. And tell me you love me. That's the best medicine."

"I love you."

"Do you really mean it?"

"Have we ever lied to each other?"

Some Thursdays Old Turk would come to dinner. Or, more accurately, bring dinner, since Esther, never Fanny Farmer, doubled up now in agony whenever she caught sight of the kitchen. So Old Turk came, and with him he brought corned beef and cole slaw and rolls and more than a dozen crisp garlic pickles (his weakness), plus three celery tonics to wash it down.

"What have you done to my daughter?" Old Turk inquired. "She just sits and stares." Chomp-chomp-chomp—the old jaws on the new pickles.

"Worries she has," Sid explained. "A dear friend of hers makes Job look chipper."

"So?" Chomp-chomp-chomp.

"Yes, this dear friend of hers is with child, and the child is fine, but this dear friend is in terrible danger and the husband of this dear friend has a dear friend of his own who is a great surgeon sympathetic to such dilemmas but as yet no one has done nothing. What do you think?"

"I think they're both *meshugah*," Old Turk pronounced. Chomp-chomp-chomp.

•

As they were walking through the Loop a few nights later, on their way to a Ronald Colman, Esther began to slow. Sid, now a few paces ahead, turned to watch, stopping as she stopped, following her stare.

She was looking at an elevated train.

Sid returned to her. "What?"

Esther's voice was soft, far away. "I wonder . . ."

"Yes?"

"About trains. I've heard stories that it isn't good to sit on trains."

"I have heard the same."

"The bumps, they're not good for you."

Sid took her arm then, starting toward a flight of steps that led up to the station. Esther let him lead, slowly, to the steps, then up one, two, another.

Halfway to the top she came alive, her fingers gripping his coat. "God will strike me dead!" She screamed and fled down the stairs, across the street, running, running. Sid pursued, chasing through the crowd, trying to smile at the people he passed (because it *was* embarrassing), muttering explanations as he went. "It's all right, everything is all right, just a little misunderstanding, everything is really fine . . ." He caught up with her on the corner of Randolph, grabbing her, pulling her around to face him. Her eyes were dry.

But wide.

"Sid?" A shake at four in the morning. "Sid?"

"Huh-huh?"

"I woke you; I'm sorry."

"What is it? You all right?"

"I just wanted to talk to somebody, that's all."

"Time?"

"A little after four."

"How come you're up?"

"Oh, I've been awake for hours. Thinking. I had a dream, Sid."

"A dream?"

"Yes. I dreamt I was going to die."

"Now, Tootsie—"

"I dreamt I was going to die but the baby was as healthy as can be."

"Esther, a dream's nothing. You can't go getting upset because of some silly dream."

"I'm not upset. Really. I'm not. But if that happens you're going to have to take care of the baby."

Palms across the eyes. "Will ya stop with this crazy talk."

"You don't even know how to change a diaper and I'm worried about the baby. Who's gonna change the diapers? Who's gonna feed it? Who's gonna walk it when it cries?"

"You are! Now go to sleep."

"I'm gonna die, Sid. You'll see."

"Goddammit, Esther—"

"Who's gonna walk the baby? I gotta know that. I don't want it catching cold and getting sick and all like that. You've gotta promise to take care of it."

"Like hell!"

"Sid—"

"I'm not gonna take care of it 'cause there ain't gonna be any baby!"

"I told you. The baby is as healthy as can be."

"You wanna die?" He took her shoulders, squeezing hard, trying to meet her eyes, but she dropped her head. *"Answer me, you wanna die? Yes?"* The shoulders commenced to tremble beneath his fingers. Slowly the head raised, the mouth loose and torn, the eyes wide, dry no more.

A whisper. "... no ... nnnn ..." Again the head dropped.

"Then I'm going to see this doctor. This great surgeon friend of my father's. Tomorrow."

The head shook. "That's wrong."

"You wanna die?"

"No ..."

"Then it ain't wrong."

"You're ... sure?"

"Yes! Yes!"

"You swear it's all right?"

"I swear."

"You're making me do this."

"That's right."

"Tomorrow?"

"Tomorrow."

"This doctor. He's really good?"

"Best in the west." Sid smiled.

A package tucked tight under an arm, Sid entered the tiny pharmacy. "So, Manfred," he called out.

"So, Sidney" came the answer from the sweet-faced cadaver behind the counter.

"How's with the pill pushing?"

"Slow on the Trojans since you took your business elsewhere."

Sid examined the aging face. "Good to see you."

"I suppose likewise."

"So," Sid said.

"So."

"Listen, Mannie . . ."

"Here comes the touch," the druggist said. " 'Listen, Mannie, how's about a ten-spot?' "

"Nothing like that."

"I wouldn't have given it to you anyway."

"Mannie . . . you interested in a little work?"

"Of which nature?"

Sid took five twenties from his pocket, laid them on the counter. "Guess."

"Hot afternoon at the snooker table?"

Sid nodded.

Mannie shook his head. "No," he said.

Sid smiled, picked up the twenties, waved them under the other's nose, asking, "Smell good?"

"My answer stands, Sidney. No."

"Why no?"

A shrug. "The heat, shall we say, is on. My place is, I do believe, under surveillance."

"Use mine?"

"Can't be done."

Again Sid waved the green. "They have brothers, Mannie. Nestling in my pocket. Each has a twin."

"Two hundred?"

"That is correct."

"Not that I don't trust you, but can I see?"

Sid produced them.

Mannie grabbed the bundle. "I'm weak and greedy."

"Nonsense. You're rich with character."

"Will tomorrow evening be satisfactory?"

"Not nearly so as tonight."

"It so happens I'm free." Mannie shrugged. "So who's the lucky girl, Sidney? Be sure your wife is gone for several hours at least. In case of complications."

"If I did that, we would have to talk to each other, and much as I love you, at these prices it ain't worth it."

"Ah" from the druggist. "The dutiful and loving husband."

"That's right, pill-pusher. I'm rich with character too."

Mannie produced some capsules. "Give her these at nine. I'll arrive at ten."

"They are?" said Sid, pocketing them.

"For sleep. To dull pain."

"A humanist in the bargain."

"Tell me, loving father, how far gone is she?"

"Just barely."

"Good. I'll see you at ten."

"Just one thing."

"So?"

"Before you ring our bell, don this," and he tossed over the package.

"What is it?"

"The white robe of the physician."

"There's a reason, I'm sure."

"I told her you were a doctor."

"A doc—"

"A great surgeon."

Mannie began to laugh. "A great surgeon. Oh, that's funny. That's very funny." The laughter grew and grew. "Me a great surgeon. Oh Jesus, Sidney, you're a killer."

Sid saw the joke.

But he did not laugh.

• • •

"Dr. Lautmann, good evening," Sid said, shaking hands with the man in the white coat.

"Good evening to you, Mr. Miller."

"Come, Dr. Lautmann, in here," and Sid led him toward the bedroom. "See, Esther, who is here? The great surgeon Dr. Lautmann that was the dearest friend of my father I told you about."

Esther lay on the clean white sheets, doped, limp, pale. "Doctor," she made with her lips, but soft. "Doctor," and she tried to nod, tried to smile.

"Everything will be fine, I promise you," the surgeon assured. "But first a few words with your husband." The two men hurried to the living room, closed the door. "We'll need noise," Mannie said.

"Noise?"

"Fool! You think she won't scream?"

"Easy," Sid said. "Easy." He scampered to the tiny Victrola in the corner, slapped on a record. "Russ Columbo," he explained. "A favorite of Esther's. Very soothing."

"I have been happier," Mannie said.

"Ya think I'm ecstatic?"

Mannie drummed his fingertips together in no rhythm. Sid rubbed his palms against his pants legs. "It's this coat," Mannie said. "This goddam doctor's coat."

Sid's palms wouldn't get dry.

"I never wore a doctor's coat before, don't you see? That makes it . . ." He paused for a shrug. "Different is the word. Don't you see, I'm not a liar. I don't . . ." He pulled at his earlobe. "I'm an honest man. I pride myself on being an honest man."

"The friendly neighborhood abortionist," Sid said.

Mannie smiled, the corners of his sweet mouth rising, then freezing there, suspended, the smile fixed, like a photo. No sound. Then he released the smile and it fled. "Yeah," he said after a while. "Who'm I kidding anyhow? Yeah." He tugged at the white coat. "My size. Perfect fit."

"Like a glove, Mannie."

"Shit," Mannie said, and he disappeared into the next room.

Sid flicked on the Victrola, slid a record down, turned the volume up full. Music. Sid sat beside the machine. Now Columbo, with that great rough voice. He could really sing, that Dago. "I can't forget the night I met you," Russ sang. "That's all I'm dreaming of. And now you call it madness. But I call it love." Esther was showing her fanny when they met, standing on a stool reaching up. For what? Sardines maybe. Sauerkraut. Something. And he'd done a Valentino with his eyes. She wasn't buying and that was when he should have quit, canceled the account before it opened. When the cock gets hard, the brain gets soft. His father had told him that. "Sidney, listen and don't you forget. When the cock gets hard, the brain gets soft." He had been six or eight at the time, so what the hell was the old man bleating about? He remembered the moment, understood it at last, when he was about to score with his first piece, some pig a year ahead of him in high school. It was good advice. The old man was no fool. No. The old man *was* a fool but still it was good advice. That and vodka. Some inheritance.

A noise from the next room. Esther? Yes, Esther, and he didn't know what she was doing but it wasn't laughing. Sid started the record over and this time he joined in, making it a songfest. "You made a promise to be faithful, by all the stars above. And now you call it madness. But I call it love." Madness. The whole *megillah* was that. Crazy. He, Super Sid, tossing his life after a round butt and a pair of cans. *Meshugah.*

Another scream from Esther.

Sid, no drinker, bolted for the kitchen and poured himself half a glass of vodka. He swilled down a goodly portion, but aside from steaming his throat a little it did nothing to relieve. Sloshing the stuff around in the glass, he returned to the Victrola and switched to a couple of Paul Whiteman instrumentals. When they had run their course he repeated them, tapping his foot to the beat, downing the remainder of the vodka. In a way, it was a shame; if the kid had been a girl with Esther's looks and his brains she might have been President, Jew or no. He would have steered for her, separating the bums from the worthwhile suitors, ending her up with maybe a Rosenwald, maybe a Lehman (or a Rockefeller if they'd decided to mix the blood strains a little), and that would have been something, Sid hobnobbing with old John D. himself, riding the hounds, then a little whist, finally a little three-cushion billiards with Napoleon brandy. He'd take John D.'s ass at three-cushion, no doubt about that, and that (definitely) would have been something to tell the boys in the neighborhood, so it was, in a way, a little shame.

"Annnhhh!" Sid cried out loud.

Esther answered with a scream.

Back came the Columbo, full voice, with now a little record scratch adding to the fun, Sid singing so his throat burned worse than from the vodka and then sweating Mannie stood in the doorway, pale like Esther. He moved to the sofa, standing over Sid.

"So soon?" Sid said, rising.

"I can't," Mannie said, and he sank.

"Whaddya mean, ya can't? What kind of talk is that, you can't? Get back in there. Finish it off. What have you been doing? Having, for crissakes, tea?"

"I can't." Columbo was still singing, "You made a promise to be faithful . . ."

"Why? The coat? Take off the coat."

"Nix."

". . . by all the stars above . . ."

"What've you been doing in there?"

"Probing. I have been examining the patient."

"Yer not gonna get more money, you kike son of a bitch!"

"I can't! Don't you understand? Nix. Nix!"

". . . but I call it love . . ."

Sid kicked the goddam Vic and it fell. "Why?" He kicked it again and this time the cord came loose from the wall. The record broke and Sid gave the machine another good one because he liked the record more than almost any. "Why?" Panting. "Why?"

A whisper. "You lied to me."

"What-what?"

From Esther in pain: "Doctor . . . Doctor . . ."

"You lied to me. You said she was just a couple weeks' pregnant."

"She is."

"Doctor . . ."

"Three months," Mannie said, shaking his head. "Three months if she's a day."

"The little bitch. The little bitch lied to me, I swear, Mannie. She knew two months, she kept it secret."

"That may be, but it's too dangerous now."

"Doctor . . . please . . ."

"No."

"The longer you wait, the more dangerous to all concerned."

Sid stood still.

"She's liable to die."

Sid sat.

"If I do it, she's liable to die."

"What are the odds?"

"In her favor, but still . . ." Mannie shrugged. "You haven't got enough grief on your conscience?"

A wail from Esther. "Dr. Lautmann . . . Dr. Lautmann . . ."

"Have the baby, Sid. Worse things have happened."

"Dr. Lautmann . . ."

"I don't want the kid."

"I'll give her a sedative and maybe—"

"No. You can't leave now."

"Doctor . . . Please, Doctor . . ."

"It's best, Sid."

"I can call the police. A good citizen. 'I know where there's this dirty abortionist.' You'll go to jail. I can do that."

"I know you can."

"Mannie, I don't want the kid. I don't want nothing to do with any goddam kid."

"Don't make me go back in there, Sidney. It could turn out very bad. Bad for me, bad for you, worse for them in there."

"Oi, God, Doctor. Come . . . please . . ."

"What am I gonna do, Mannie? You tell me." He threw the empty vodka glass against the wall, where it shattered. Sid threw it, Sid was watching it, but when the noise came he jumped with fear. "Tell me, Mannie."

"I'll give her a sedative. You get drunk, she'll sleep. Tomorrow . . ." And he shrugged. "Can things be any worse?"

"*Shimah Yisroel . . .*"

Again Sid jumped. "All of a sudden she's religious."

"When people hurt, they get religious. No pain, no God."

"*Baruch adonoi eluhenu . . .*"

"So what do I do, Sidney?"

No quick answer.

"It's best. I promise. Please take my word. Who needs grief? God gave us enough."

Sid sat. Then, finally, he said, "Yeah. Enough."

"You're doing the right thing, Sidney."

"Yeah." It was hard for him to breathe.

"Please, God, Dr. Lautmann . . ."

"Coming," Mannie said. "Coming." He stood and started moving for the door. "Coming," he kept saying. "Coming. Coming," over and over, which was probably why he did not hear Sid leap up, why he was so surprised when Sid's hands spun him so viciously around. "What?" he managed before Sid took over.

"Kill it! Now, now, now, kill it, kill it, kill it, kill it, kill it now!"

Mannie quietly closed the door to the bedroom, took off the white coat, folded it carefully and dropped it on the sofa beside Sid, who sat too stiffly, nodding his head, nodding his head. "The bloody deed is done," Mannie muttered.

Sid continued to nod.

"Some instructions, Sidney. Listen. Keep her flat on her back. Don't let her move around much. Tomorrow I'll come back and finish it off. I couldn't scrape, she was too far along, but this works as well; it just takes a little longer. Bamboo expands, you see, and so in time . . ." Mannie shrugged. "I think all went well. I'll see you tomorrow, Sidney."

Sid heard the door close.

He sat, still stiff, not knowing quite what to do, where to go. Esther lay behind the bedroom door and there was his place, he knew, beside her in this time of . . . Time of what? Grief? No, something . . . something . . .

Sid crossed to the corner of the room and picked up the shattered vodka glass. His hands moved quickly, carelessly almost, asking for a cut. Pain. A little pain would have felt good, but his fingers were too deft and no blood spilled. Dumping the slivers into the trash, he went to the bathroom and combed his hair, then suddenly threw the comb down hard and dashed into the bedroom.

Esther didn't look so hot.

"Oh, Tootsie, God," Sid said, the words out before he knew it. He dropped onto the bed beside her and gently touched her hair. "You O.K.? Huh?"

Esther wasn't saying much.

She tried with a smile but missed and after that she just lay there while Sid touched her hair, her skin, while he kissed her eyes. He offered her some food but the idea didn't thrill her; neither did liquid of whatever nature.

Sid, though, felt the need of a little pick-me-up, and with a little kiss, a quick muttered " 'Scuse me," he dashed for the kitchen, returning with the bottle of vodka, which he swilled liberally. He held her very close, muttering love, rocking her mutilated body. The motion was pleasing and soon her eyes half closed, her fatigue battling the pain, winning little by little, so that by one in the morning she fell into a dizzy sleep. Sid continued to drink, holding the bottle in one hand, her soft shape with the other, until the bottle deserted him and he dropped it empty to the floor. Then, undressing, he slipped into bed beside her, resting his handsome head on her handsome bosom, hearing only her soft breathing growing louder, louder as his own eyes closed. Sid slept then, along with Esther, their bodies close, their breathing a unison. The sight of the two was close to idyllic and the evening, considering what it might have turned into, wasn't half bad.

Until Esther started hemorrhaging.

Sid woke to find her writhing, biting down like a crazy woman on her lower lip, drawing blood almost, her small hands kneading her stomach. "What-what?" Sid cried but she would not answer, continuing to writhe, moaning in spite of herself, unwanted tears trailing down across her cheeks, dipping for a moment into the tight crease of her lips, then on again, falling down her chin, where they mixed with the sweat that glistened on her taut neck. "Esther, Esther, what can I do?" But still she twisted, her head shaking now as the vowelless groans grew louder, higher in pitch, approaching the kingdom of the scream. Panicky, Sid bolted from the bed, running around to her side, but she turned away from him, digging in with her fingers, grabbing her stomach, trying to rip it away. Sid ran like a fool around the bed again, jumping onto the mattress, grabbing her as she tried to turn, but she was deep in pain now and too strong, so his hands slipped from her wet shoulders as she began to cry out, "God-God-no-no" and Sid hollered along with her, "Esther, my little Esther," until she managed to clamp her teeth back down on her lower lip, leaving Sid to shout alone, "Esther, sweet Esther," and no telling how long that would have gone on if her sexy legs, kicking on their own to some secret rhythm, hadn't swiped him good and sent him sprawling off the bed to the hard floor. Sid rose and stared at the kicking thing on the mattress. Whatever resemblance she had once had to Esther was rapidly disappearing as the thrashing and the biting picked up tempo. The entire body was coated with pale sweat and the tendons in her neck awed him. He watched her until he realized that very likely she was going to die and once that thought took hold he threw himself into his clothes, shouting, "Hospital! Hospital!" hoping he could get through to her.

"No," Esther screamed.

Sid jammed his shoes on, buttoned his shirt, buttoned his fly, hands never once stopping until Esther said "No hospital."

Sid tried to take her hand and lift her from the bed but she fought him.

"Esther, for God's sake."

"No hospital!"

"Es—"

"Father might find out. Somebody else. No. No. Please don't."

Sid grabbed her with all his might and pulled her into a sitting position. "Quit now."

"I don't want people to know. Leave me here. Leave me here."

"Come."

"No. Please. Leave me be."

"Come." Sid lifted her as well as he could, looping her arm around his shoulder, forcing them toward the door.

"I want to die. I want to die."

Sid grabbed the front door, flung it open, started out along the corridor and down the stairs. The Dago woman next door appeared beside him but he shouted for her to get the hell away and she did as he took the stairs one at a time with Esther screaming every step, "No hospital, let me die, no hospital," until suddenly she sagged semiconscious, just weight now, all fight gone. Sid staggered with her out onto the street praying for a cab and it worked, the driver helping to lift Esther inside, then breaking all records on the way to Michael Reese. When they reached the emergency ward Sid said, "My wife, miscarriage, miscarriage," to whoever would listen and insisted on a private room for his beloved. As they started to wheel her away, Esther, who had staged a mild comeback, held his hand as long as possible. "Miscarriage," Sid said to the wheeler, a young man in a white coat. "A private room. The best." The white coat nodded. Sid indicated a desire for privacy and the white coat retreated. Sid bent to taste his wife's pale lips. "Sleep, dumpling," he whispered.

"We killed it," soft into his ear.

"Sleep, dumpling," Sid repeated, and he smiled. His was a helpful smile, a smile of reassurance.

So why was she smiling back?

As she awaited the arrival of the doctor, little Esther half dozed. The knotting pains of the bedroom were loosening now, and she was able to breathe again—a luxury. She remembered the piker yelling "Private room, private room" and that was something to look forward to. Also she had gone through, in her mind, those young interns and potential physicians she had known before E. Scrooge had worn her down, and none of them worked at Michael Reese, so she could relax on that score, confident that neither Maxwell Baum nor Tommy Sternman nor any of the other surgeons-to-be who pursued her on their nights off would come popping in and thereby provide her with an unnecessary humiliation. (Maybe the private room would have a view of the lake. In any case, she hoped it was wildly expensive; a little apoplexy would do Sid good.) Maxwell Baum and Tommy Sternman. Esther drifted. Doctors always appealed to her— more than lawyers, dentists, architects. The only trouble with doctors was it took so long before you started cashing in. The young *goy* pushing the wheelchair had looked at her with lust in his blue eyes, and that was flattering; if you could lure them at your worst, you were really something. That was what she was: a real something. Married to a real nothing, true, but everybody fumbles on occasion. The thought of divorce made her smile. In a month, probably, she would be looking herself again, and that was the time to make the move. Let Sid pay for the convalescence (do him good), then off to the races. Toot, toot, tootsie, goodbye. Let him crawl a little first, beg awhile (do him good), lead him on, let him think he's still got a chance of keeping her, then out the door. Stick him for what she could on alimony (her smile broadened)—every penny. God knows she was deserving, living with the little letch the way she had. Esther began laughing softly but it hurt, so she stopped. Those pains. Never would she forget those pains. No matter what they told you about childbirth, it couldn't be as bad. That Dr. Lautmann: some *schlemiel* of a surgeon he was. But that was typical; you marry a third-rater, you travel third class.

An intern walked by.

Esther returned his smile, watched him until he was gone. Tall, good head of hair, nice springy walk. Next time around, a doctor. Definitely. A surgeon; if possible, a specialist on the brain. If you made one thousand for an operation, and you did five operations a day, and you worked five days a week, that was . . . mink for little Esther, that's what it was. A mink coat and a mink stole and a mink blanket. A mink blanket? Did people have such things? She shrugged. Why not? Give one good reason. It would supply warmth; it would last and last, so it really wasn't such an extravagance. No. In many ways, it was sensible. Her stomach began to hurt and she pressed down with her hands. Not so bad this time. The worst was over. The good days were coming up hard on the horizon. She had her looks, her good brain; that was plenty. From now on, nothing but doctors, early thirties at the youngest, maybe a little gray at the temples. The good days. From now on, nothing but good days. The future glistened before her, colored bright mink. She felt good. For the first time since the Shrimp had cast a blight on her life, she felt good. No Sid, no kid, no nothing to remind her of the past. Take an apartment on the near North Side and let the suitors come. She was a divorcée, now, a woman of mystery as well as beauty. What a combination. Mystery and beauty. She felt wonderful. Really wonderful. Really incredibly fantastically unbelievably wonderful.

So why, all of a sudden, was she crying?

The ex-papa danced a jig on the sidewalk in front of the hospital. It was late, five, six in the morning (who cared), and he was brimming to the top with piss and vinegar. "Toot, toot, tootsie, goodbye," he sang, breaking into a little soft-shoe. (He was one helluva dancer when he wanted to be.) A cab cruised by and Sid whistled it dead, hopped inside and slammed the door behind him. To the cabbie's "Where to?" Sid said "Drive," and he settled himself in the back, content to watch the dying moon over Lake Michigan. Home was probably the place to go (wouldn't be so bad with the Bitch gone) but who could sleep? They drove along the lake, Sid whistling a little Gershwin, a little Kern, punctuating the concert with occasional bursts of laughter. The thought crossed his mind to go beat the shit out of Mannie for doing a lousy job that was going to cost him a hospital bill, but was tonight a time for vengeance? Mannie could pay the bill when it came (if he balked, a little phone call to the cops), so why sweat? Sid's fingers danced across his knees, and Sid, heeding their call for action, directed the driver to the Loop, where he got out at Painter's, the best pool hall in the city, open all night. Ordinarily Painter's was a little stiff for Sid, the sharks a little too tough, but tonight, his fingers told him, was no night to be chicken. So he mounted the inevitable steps, confident that he could kill any shark alive. Painter's was empty, or nearly so, and Sid grabbed a cue (first testing the weight, making sure the balance was perfect), then proceeded to a table, where he hacked away like an amateur, whistling all the while. His act was good enough to lure a shark, an old man with watery eyes and not much hair, and after the usual pleasantries (Care for a game? Well, I'm not much good. Neither am I. Et cetera) they got down to business. The old guy could shoot and in the dim, low-ceilinged room he seemed quite at home as he moved his tired bones around the green, but Sid panicked not. No reason to with his fingers dancing the way they were, and when the watery eyes emerged the victor in the first clash at straight pool (they were both trying to give it away) there followed round two of the chatter (Christ, I stink. No, I was lucky. Shall we try it again? If you want to. I wouldn't mind. You break. Here goes nothing) and Sid won the second game (still for free) but by the fourth they had ten bucks riding (a pittance) and the old man won, so they doubled up to twenty and he won that too but when it got to fifty bucks a game, Sid released his fingers and they went to work. They banked, they drew, they applied follow English, the touch elegant, precise, caressing the cue with genuine devotion. True love always finds a way, and by the eighth game Sid was up two hundred and roaring. The old man called for coffee, Sid for Scotch, and the night gimp (they gotta be gimps—union regulation) returned with their orders, getting a fiver from Sid for his pains. The old man, hyped by the caffeine, staged a little comeback, but Sid hung in there, erasing the Elder's earnings with a hot streak of his own, increasing the bankroll to two-fifty. "Last game double or nothing," Sid (ever the sportsman) said and the Elder nodded, chalking his cue, lifting his watery eyes (maybe praying to Hoppe), sipping a fresh pot of tea (always change a losing game). The preliminaries done, they began.

Under pressure, the old guy acted like a colt, his hands like rocks. He broke, left Sid nothing, and Sid's return safety enabled the geezer to run a quick seventeen balls before he played safe again. Again Sid was blanked and this time the old man pounced on Sid's shot and ran fourteen more, making it thirty-one to goose-egg. When Sid's turn came, he had no shot except a wild bank the long way that a genius couldn't make five times out of ten, which, besides, if missed, opened the rack for slaughter. Sid talked to his fingers, inquired after their health, and when they seemed sound he heard his voice saying "Eleven ball the long way," after which he took a practice cruise with the pool stick, felt the need maybe of a touch more chalk, applied it, bent down low over the table, sighted for just the proper angle, found it, stood up, smiled at the old guy, inhaled, held it and shot.

The ball banked like it had eyes. The rack split open and there he was, the one and only Super Sid, chuckling, smiling, making good swift chatter as his fingers fired ball after ball, the run growing from ten to eighteen, then thirty, forty-five, and with five balls to go the old guy was reaching into a pocket and counting the bills, licking his thumb in obvious pain with the departure of each C note. Sid polished off the last five, making an unnecessary bank on the last ball, taking a big risk but what was life without them?

So there he was, on the streets again, five hundred nestled neatly in his right front pocket with the sun pouring down from all over, the time ten o'clock on a beauty of a morn. Probably some sleep would have been helpful but you can't order its arrival, and if he was high when he left the hospital, now he was looking down at the stratosphere. With a wave of his finger he materialized a taxi and sat back humming while they journeyed to the Blackstone, a good enough hotel which housed, along with businessmen and rich old ladies, a legendary blonde, supposedly French and definitely expensive, ordinarily far out of his reach but today his arms were infinite. He buzzed her from the lobby, tasting her wrath (he roused her from slumber), but she sweetened when the subject reached *dinero* and falling victim to his appeal, invited him to visit. Supposedly she had (according to Pinky Katz, who had a rich cousin who had once tasted of her charms) great tits, and Sid, ever the connoisseur, licked his chops during the upward ride, anticipating what only money can buy, and when he knocked and she answered he saw (she met him in a negligee) that she was sufficiently top-heavy (slim in the waist though—that was good) to slake any appetite. The blonde was big, much taller than he and probably as heavy, but he was used to that, so unafraid. They got comfortable with a minimum of chatter, which suited Sid, and after a little financial exchange they set up housekeeping. She was practiced but lacking in inspiration, devoid of vision, and Sid rode her deftly into submission without the expected kick. Her body, great from any distance, was lacking on contact; softened by too much wear, no tone to the muscle, just flesh piled decently enough, but flabby, not remotely as satisfying as Esther on her bad days, let alone the good. Still, as Sid dressed he knew it was money well spent—the story should be good for months if he doled it out decently to the droolers across the poker table, so he noted carefully the décor, the perfume, the color of the rug. As he headed for the door, the stack accompanied him, urging him a speedy return (she knew a master when she saw one), and he had not the heart to tell her she was over the hill, so he smiled and whacked her a good one on the fanny and they both laughed loud as he departed, her probably for the sack to rest her weary flesh, he for the Palmer House, where he blew twenty-eight bucks for lunch (which wasn't easy), such was his hunger. Belching, Sid sauntered across the Loop for a while, stopping into Field's briefly for a silk summer jacket, then on again to Florsheim's, where a pair of black leather wing-tips soothed his feet. He had not slept, not really, in forty hours or more, but he was, if anything, even more chipper than earlier and he danced along the street in his wing-tips until he remembered Esther in the hospital.

That soured him.

It was an unhappy prospect, but a visit did seem required; so, grumbling, he taxied to Michael Reese, stopping outside to buy a bunch of posies for his beloved.

She was sitting up in bed when he got there. He handed her the flowers and received the barest of thanks (gratitude for you!), but, undaunted, he went on with the charade, kissing her dutifully on the cheek, then sitting in a chair beside the bed, holding her hand, throwing her little kisses (what the hell, why not?).

"Well," Sid said, "how are you?"

"Well," Esther answered, "we're fine."

The room, as hospital rooms go, was better than nice, being light and almost (but not quite) cheerful and possessing two windows overlooking the Illinois Central tracks and, beyond them, Lake Michigan. From where he sat Sid could see the lake, immense and solid blue save for the slits of white foam tumbling from time to time toward shore.

"Pretty fancy, dumpling," Sid said, smiling at the spouse. She looked good, almost all right again, though her face was stern. "Just like the Blackstone," and he allowed himself a solid laugh. A train bumped by outside on the I.C. tracks and Sid followed its progress awhile before returning to the calm blue of the lake. "You get my phone message? I called you to tell you I might be a little late. Business appointment at the Palmer House. Otherwise I would have been here a lot—"

"We're fine."

"I'm sure glad of that, Tootsie. I didn't go to sleep last night for worrying." He flashed her a smile but it died when he realized her meaning and he sat gaping, suddenly a fool, the last to get the joke, the wearer of the dunce cap, the ass. "We are?"

"We are."

"How come?"

"You got me here in time. Those things Dr. Lautmann did to me, they didn't have a chance to work."

Why was he so tired? Where had it come from?

"A day or two rest here and I can go."

"Ah," Sid said. "Ah." He got up and moved to the window, staring at the blue, his head resting against the cool pane. He closed his eyes, intending a blink, but it felt so good he kept them shut a while. How long had he been without sleep? Too long. Too long. From somewhere far behind his eyes, a red ache started, complete with its own little throb. Sid pressed harder against the pane.

"The baby is fine."

"The baby is fine," Sid repeated.

"You O.K.?"

"The baby is fine," Sid said again.

"Come away from the window."

"Sure thing." He groped back to the chair, fighting the pain in his head. All for nothing. Everything for nothing.

Another train went by.

Sid stared.

"Sid, I got to talk to you—"

"Maybe we'll take a trip—"

"I didn't sleep either—"

"A nice trip on a train—"

"Sid, I've been doing some thinking—"

"A long trip while you recover. We'll sit back and relax—"

"Are you *listening*?"

"My head. It hurts so."

"Sid, this is important."

"I can't hear so good, my head hurts so, go on, go on."

"All those things I had in the beginning that went wrong with me? You remember how I screamed and threw up and everything?"

"Sit over the wheels. Sure, we'll sit over the wheels. Take a long trip and sit over the wheels. Have a lot of fun, nice scenery, sit over the wheels, watch the nice scenery . . ." Something in her face, some look, made him trail off, waiting, trying to concentrate on the red pain creeping up behind his eyes and then the hush of the hospital was ended and Esther was shouting:

"Are we animals?"

"No," Sid said, "no-no," and then the dunce was crying, weeping unaccustomed tears as he fell across her body, clutching at her hands.

"I faked, Sid! All those pains, the throwing up, I faked so you'd get a doctor!"

"Butcher!" Sid cried. "He was no doctor. I led you to the slaughterhouse and you'll never forgive me!"

"I forgive!"

"I forgive!"

"Do you love me, Sid?"

"I dunno, I dunno."

"Me either. But we can't do anymore. We can't."

"No, we can't."

"Sid, we're not animals," and she was crying too.

"Not us," he managed as he crawled blindly up on her bed beside her and they wrapped their arms tight around, joining their private griefs, rocking, keening, seeking forgiveness from their ancient gods, twin sinners, Sid and Esther, for a moment together, all bullshit gone.

So they had this kid.

From the first he was different.

Not that he didn't soak his diapers twice an hour; not that he didn't cry; not that he didn't smile when bounced or laugh when poked or shriek when tossed or wail when startled or hungry or wet or sleepy or afraid or alone; not that he preferred Pablum to his mother's milk; not that he liked beets or turnips or spinach or lima beans; not that he didn't like sounds, rattles or music boxes or voices that went "Row, Row, Row Your Boat" during the day or "Rockabye, Baby" at dark; not that he didn't lift his head to stare fascinated at the blank sides of his cradle or, when he could roll over, at the sunny particles of dust floating softly in the air; not that he didn't give endless inspection to the soft pink skin on his hands or, later, suck his sweet thumb; not that he didn't cry out in the night with the pain of teething or, when he was able to crawl, gnaw passionately on table legs; not that he was able neatly to master the spoon or guide the cup on its two-handed journey from table to lip to table without occasional mishap; not that he didn't like to bounce and catch a red rubber ball or run or kick or jump up high or open a door or close a door or snip newspapers with tiny scissors or skip or hop or balance on one foot with one eye closed or climb unaided up long flights of stairs. What made him different was simply this:

The child was impossibly beautiful.

The boy's appearance certainly pleased Sid, but it by no means surprised him. One of those things was all it was, one of those remarkable father-son resemblances that crop up from time to time, knotting two generations. Oh, maybe the kid's hair was a little darker, maybe his eyes a little bigger and brighter, maybe the limb formation a spec improved here and there. But these were trivia, nothing more—minor impediments in a major thesis, that thesis being that the kid was a carbon of his old man, a mint replica, detail for perfect detail. And when he took the kid out for walks, something he did continually—and *without* Esther tagging along if you don't mind, gumming things up—when he took the kid out, Sid beamed. Not just because of the compliments the kid received (compliments which, he knew, were as much for him as for the offspring); no, it was the kind of compliment, that was what did it. With most kids, all you got from the gassing grandmas in the park was "Oh, isn't he cute?" or "My, how adorable," or "That's a handsome young man"—junk like that. But when Sid strolled by with Rudy, the old ladies always started to speak, but then they stopped, looking closer at the kid, up to the papa, back to the kid again, staring hard now, and after that they either nodded or shook their gray heads. Whichever they did, Sid beamed.

Esther, for her part, was also pleased by the boy's appearance. But by no means surprised. Astonished, yes; she was that, for in all her short life she had never seen a boy who so resembled his mother.

When you push encyclopedias door to door, either you have good days or bad, no so-so's. On the eleventh of July, Sid met and charmed an overfed, education-starved Polish lady from Cottage Grove Avenue, leaving her house at two in the afternoon with the preliminary papers signed and sealed in his briefcase, thereby making the eleventh of July one of the good ones. On the street, Sid wiped his brow and pondered further charm-spreading, but it was hot and if there was one thing he wasn't, it was a greedy pig, and one encyclopedia set per day was enough for any man. So he decided to quit early and go home and take his almost five-year-old for a jaunt through the neighborhood.

On his way to the apartment he passed Solomon's Delicatessen. Now he passed Solomon's more than occasionally and usually it wasn't so painful, especially in wintertime when the door was closed. But this was July, the door was open and as Sid ambled by he was ambushed by the aroma of Solomon's corned beef. Sid paused, took a step, stopped and approached the store window. Inside it was busy as usual, stuffed with stuffed *hausfraus* buying goodies. Sid peered through the army of salamis hanging at rigid attention, guarding the shop window, his bright eyes wandering from pastrami to tongue to good garlic pickle. Sid sighed. He had long ago sworn that when he finally struck *gelt* he was going to plug a movie star all night and eat at Solomon's all day—a double orgy.

The aroma of corned beef was stronger now and Sid was terribly tempted to fight the mob inside. But it was so expensive. A rapist, old man Solomon was, a pastrami peddler who drove a Cadillac, who lived like a merchant prince on Lake Shore Drive. The prices he charged! Sid scowled. Ridiculous. Unfair. Illegal. The one and only reason he got away with it was that somehow, through some miracle of curing, he produced the absolutely finest corned beef the world had ever tasted. Someday, Sid told himself, someday I'll be bored with it. "What?" I'll say. "Solomon's corned beef again? Pitch it. Get rid of it and bring me some *food.*" But that, alas, was for the future, and Sid, very much, alas, in the present, stood riveted before the salami sentries, his stomach rumbling. What he wanted was corned beef for supper. What he needed was a reason to buy. He noted that the flow of fatsos was primarily out of the store, leaving it momentarily less than crammed, which meant he stood a good chance of dashing to and away from the counter without getting ground to death between the expansive corsets of the regular customers. But that was no reason. He did have in his hot pocket, however, sufficient money for a moderate purchase. But simple possession was no reason either. Hold it, Sid thought. Hadn't it been a good day? Hadn't the sweet Pole from Cottage Grove fallen victim to his charms? So wasn't that reason enough for a little celebration? Who could object to that? Sid took a step forward. Esther could object to that. Sid took a step backward, hearing her unbell-like voice belting away—"Celebration? For what a celebration?

Just because you did your job for once in your lazy life which every other man in the world does every day, that's why we should go crazy in Solomon's, just because *you did your job*? Fool. Fool!" Sid shook his head. There was no reason for supper to come from Solomon's, so he started to walk away, head down, feet scuffing the sidewalk for six steps before he whirled and entered Valhalla, buying not only too much corned beef but also cole slaw and a whole loaf of thick dark rye and a boatload of Russian dressing and half a dozen scented dills and three slabs of pineapple cheesecake. He spent every penny, Sid did, his conscience so clear you could see your face in it. Because he had his reason.

The kid. That was his reason. The kid loved corned beef. They had both discovered it some weeks ago when, out for lunch one day, Sid had given the boy a nibble of his corned-beef sandwich and the boy had lit up like a top. He loved it. He loved it and it wasn't even Solomon's, just some inferior junk from around the corner. Well, Sid thought as he hurried home, a brown paper bag under an arm, tonight, my son, tonight you dine in heaven.

Esther was out when he reached the apartment, so, after tenderly placing the brown bag of treasures in the icebox, Sid crossed to the living-room window and opened it, peering up to the top of the fire escape, looking for his son. The kid spent all of his time there, every free second, alone at the top of the fire escape, but now he was not there. Sid cursed mildly. Esther had probably taken him for a long walk. She was always doing that, taking him for marathons, showing him off to shopkeepers or the old ladies in the park. It wasn't good for the boy, all that walking, not that Esther cared. One thing you had to say for Esther: she was a lousy mother. It was just like her, taking the kid out the one day *he* got home early. She probably planned it that way. She had a sixth sense, Esther did; she was a great depriver. Hell, Sid thought, I wouldn't have taken him to any lousy park; I would have taken him to the *zoo*. But down was down and what was the point of aggravating yourself? The afternoon was his; he had to do something with it.

It was well after six before he got back from the poolroom. He hadn't meant to stay that late but a couple of young wiseacres thought they could shoot pool and it had taken him that long to show them the error of their ways. He closed the apartment door and hurried to the kitchen, but when he got there he stopped dead: Esther was frying chicken.

"You're frying chicken?" Sid said.

"I'm frying chicken."

"You're frying chicken?"

"Smart, my husband," Esther said, tapping her temple. "He walks in and sees his wife frying chicken and before you can say Jack Robinson he's figured out she's frying chicken."

"For dinner?"

"No, breakfast; I thought we needed a change. Of course for dinner, fool." She flipped a thigh from one side to the other and the grease spat.

Sid edged to a safe distance from the stove, shaking his head as he saw the gravy, the peas, the mashed potatoes. "I already bought dinner," he said.

"You what?"

"I already bought dinner. A special treat. It's in the icebox. Didn't you even look in the icebox to see if I might have bought dinner?"

"If I opened the icebox door every time I thought you might have bought dinner, the hinges would rust and fall off." She jammed a long fork into a breast and turned it. "Ouch," she said, rubbing the grease from her forearm. "Get out of my kitchen. I can't concentrate with you in my kitchen."

"A special treat," Sid repeated. "You should have looked. Corned beef and cole slaw and pickles and cheesecake. All from Solomon's."

"Solomon's?" Esther shot him a look.

"On sale," Sid answered quickly. "Everything was on sale."

"If you've bought it, you've bought it," Esther said. "We'll have it to-morrow for lunch."

"We'll have the chicken tomorrow for lunch."

"Corned beef keeps. Chicken's no good cold."

"Chicken's no good cold? *Chicken's no good cold?* Are you crazy?"

"Don't shout. The boy will hear you." She gestured toward the fire escape.

"Chicken is delicious cold!"

"I said don't shout."

"Chicken is delicious cold," Sid said. "And we'll have it tomorrow for lunch. Just because you were too stupid to look in the icebox—"

"Don't argue with me," Esther said.

"Who's arguing? I'm telling."

"That stuff from Solomon's isn't healthy. No good for a growing boy."

"Chicken fried in grease is so healthy? Potatoes are so good for you? I notice the Irish are conquering the world, they're so healthy."

"The boy likes chicken."

"*You* like chicken."

"And you hate corned beef, I suppose."

"I bought it for the boy."

"Who am I cooking this for?"

"The boy loves corned beef."

"He's never even *had* corned beef."

"That's a lie and he loves it and he's eating it for supper."

"He's having chicken for supper because he loves chicken."

"Corned beef more. I know my son."

"You know nothing about your son. He prefers chicken."

"Corned beef."

"Chicken."

"Corned beef!"

"Chicken!"

"Corned—"

"Chicken—chicken!"

"—*beef!*"

"Rudy," Sid called out the window.

"Yes, Father."

"Supper," and he watched as the child nodded, rose from his seated perch at the top of the fire escape and raced down the steps to the apartment. Ducking his dark head, the tiny creature slipped through the window, landing silently on the fraying rug, clean palms exposed to his mother's inspection even before she said "Hands?" Ordinarily when he beat her she smiled. Tonight she did not.

"Sit," Esther said.

The child approached the dining table and stopped, staring at the serving plates filled with chicken and corned beef and mashed potatoes and cole slaw and gravy and Russian dressing and peas and dill pickles and pineapple cheesecake and chocolate fudge cake that his mother had made early in the afternoon. The boy stared at the table, which was small, so that none of the serving plates was lying fully flat but instead tilted and balanced against each other, barely leaving room for the three clean plates from which they would eat. All the plates were crammed on top of his mother's best tablecloth, beautiful and white, with delicate lace edges. The boy stared at all this for a time, then quickly looked up for his parents' eyes.

"A feast, isn't it, Rudy?" Sid said.

The boy nodded.

"All for you," Esther said.

The boy smiled.

"Sit down, sit down," Sid said. "Everybody sit down."

Everybody sat down.

"Now listen, Rudy." The boy looked at his father. "There's two different kinds of meals here; maybe they won't go together so good. So you pick whichever you want. But first—"

"Let him alone," Esther said.

"First just a word about the corned beef. It's from Solomon's, Rudy. You remember me talking to you about Solomon's, how they make the finest corned beef in the world, let alone Chicago? Well, I bought it today for *you*, because you'll remember your first taste of Solomon's corned beef all your life, I promise you, but if you'd rather have your mother's chicken, I won't mind a bit. Of course, you've *had* your mother's chicken many times before and you've *never* had any of Solomon's corned beef— you've only heard me speak about it—but like I said, eat what you want, I don't care one way or the other."

"Eat the chicken, Rudy," Esther said.

"The boy can make up his own mind."

"You call what you just said letting him make up his own mind?"

"Rudy, I didn't try and influence you just now, did I?"

The boy shook his head.

"Rudy and me, we understand each other," Sid said, and he forked some corned beef onto his plate. "I don't know about anybody else, but I'm hungry."

Esther reached for a piece of chicken and put it on her plate. "I love fried chicken," she said. "And this looks awfully good, if I do say so my—"

"Oh," Sid interrupted. "Oh, oh, oh, this corned beef. Oh. Oh, my God, that old man Solomon is a genius, oh, oh, it melts in your mouth like ambrosia, it's so tender and—"

"My best chicken skin," Esther cut in. "Just so crisp."

"I'm in heaven," Sid said. "Eat, Rudy."

"Yes, Rudy, eat."

The boy hesitated, his hand hovering first over the corned-beef platter, then over the chicken, back and forth, back and forth, and then it hawked down, plucking a chicken leg. Esther started to smile but stopped as she saw her son's other hand gathering up corned beef, the two hands depositing their loads simultaneously onto his plate. Isolating a piece of meat, a piece of fowl, he stuck them both onto his fork and gobbled them down, smiling at his parents briefly before reaching out for the cole slaw and the mashed potatoes and the pickles and the gravy, and when his plate was heaped high he began to eat.

"Not so fast, not so fast," Esther said as he downed a spoonful of potatoes, an equal helping of cole slaw.

"That corned beef's so good it brings tears to your eyes, huh, Rudy?"

The boy ate a piece of corned beef and there were tears in his eyes.

"You like my chicken?" Esther said.

"It's . . . all . . . so . . ."

"Don't talk with your mouth full," Esther said.

"Wonderful," the boy mumbled. "Wonderful." And he continued to eat, gulping everything down as fast as he could, all the food, hot and cold, bland and sharp, staring at his plate, and when it was empty he looked up at his parents, saw their eyes, hesitated a moment before reaching out, filling his plate again, filling it with everything, everything.

"It's my best chicken, isn't it, Rudy?"

The boy nodded, continuing to eat.

"You ever taste corned beef like that before, Rudy?"

The boy shook his head, eating relentlessly.

"It looks like any other corned beef," Esther said.

"Yeah, well, it ain't."

Esther reached for a piece of the meat and nibbled. "It is good," she said. "I've got to admit it."

"Chicken's perfect," Sid said, munching on a wing.

The child closed his eyes briefly, continuing to eat. He opened his eyes. His plate was still half full, so he took a deep breath and dug in, forking the stuff into his mouth until finally, finally, his plate was empty and then he closed his eyes again.

"Some meal," Sid said.

"Rudy, clear the table," Esther said, and the child stood and carried the plates to the kitchen. It took him many trips, but when he was done the table was empty except for the chocolate fudge cake and the pineapple cheese. Esther cut a piece of fudge cake and put it on his plate.

"Try the cheesecake, Rudy," Sid said.

"Later, if he's still hungry," Esther said.

"The cheesecake is a specialty of Solomon's. Cut him a piece of cheesecake."

"Go on, Rudy," Esther said. "Eat."

"*I'll* cut him a piece of cheesecake," Sid said, and he grabbed for the knife.

"Rudy loves my fudge cake." Esther pulled the knife out of Sid's reach.

"Some people love junk."

"Are you saying my fudge cake tastes like junk?"

"I don't know. What does junk taste like?"

"Junk tastes like junk."

"Sounds like your fudge cake."

"What do you know? What do you know? You don't know anything except how to ruin a meal. I fixed this marvelous meal and you ruined it."

"Who said it was marvelous?"

"You did! You said the chicken was perfect. And so is my fudge cake. I make the best fudge cake! Nobody makes fudge cake like I make fudge cake! I'll stack my fudge cake up against any fudge cake in the—*Rudy, not on the tablecloth!*"

Too late, the child clapped both hands to his mouth, jumped up, ran to the bathroom and dropped to his knees over the toilet, shutting the door. The toilet flushed, but the door did not immediately open. Several minutes passed. Then there came a sound from the bathroom, the toilet flushed again, and then slowly, slowly, the door opened.

"My mother's best tablecloth," Esther keened, sponging at it feebly, shaking her head. "My mother's best tablecloth. An heirloom ruined."

The child took a step toward them.

"It's all over the fudge cake," Sid said. "The cheesecake too. Both of them."

Another step forward.

"What's the matter with you, what's the matter with you?" Esther glared. "Are you an animal? A pig? You can't eat without getting sick all over my mother's best tablecloth? What's the matter with you?"

"I'm . . . sorry," the boy said. For a minute he shook. Then he was gone, whirling and gone, out the window and up the fire escape, gone.

"What's the matter with you?" Esther shouted after him, staring at the window a moment before throwing the sponge onto the tablecloth, slumping back in her chair, her arms clasped behind her, breasts jutting. "What's the matter with him? What is it with that boy?"

"Easy, Esther."

"I'll talk how I want to. He can't hear me."

Yes, I can. Yes, I can. Every word.

"Done is done, Tootsie."

"Look at this tablecloth. Made by hand. Priceless. Look at it."

"It don't exactly whet the appetite."

"I just don't know what it is with that boy. Don't I try?"

"Don't we both?"

"Yes. Both. And look at the thanks we get. Just . . . don't do that."

"Don't do what?"

"Sid, I mean it, Sid—"

"That's my name."

"The blinds are open."

"Not in the bedroom."

"I'm just too upset—don't *doooo* that." Laughter.

"Dessert. I'm still hungry. I want a piece of Esther. Beats cheesecake all hollow."

Laughter.

"Come on, Tootsie."

"First let me clean this up."

"The kid made the mess. Let him clean it."

"The kid. Chicken and corned beef and look what he does with it. Spoiled, that's all he is. How many kids get chicken and corned beef? Hash he'll get from now on. Hash he understands. That's all he deserves, hash."

Outside and above them, the tiny face nodded, mouth open, eyes closed, yes, yes.

"I'm terribly hungry," Sid said. "Faint from hunger. Dangerously weak."

"Not *that* weak, I hope."

"Never *that* weak, Tootsie."

Laughter. Fabric. Then a door.

Silence.

The dark child clung to the fire escape. His tiny hands gripped the rusted red bars; his feet dangled in space. Pushing his head through the bars, he stared at his feet and, below them, the narrow back alley. Slowly at first he began to kick his feet, and when they were running he raised his eyes, challenging the setting sun. Eventually, of course, his legs tired and the sun forced him to look away. The boy fell back then, lying flat, facing the gentler sky. He did not know the word "unworthy," but the feeling was familiar.

After six years of being his grandfather, Old Turk one day became his friend.

The transformation was brought about primarily, if indirectly, by the depression, which did not exactly balloon the door-to-door-encyclopedia-selling business. Nor was it much help to the door-to-door-imported-china-marked-down-to-one-tenth-its-actual-value profession, which Sid tried next. He was still a great salesman, incomparable as always, but the goddam Republicans had loused up the goddam economy (probably not with his specific ruin in mind, but he wasn't 100 percent sure even of that, Republicans being what they were) and *people just weren't buying.* No money; was it his fault? Didn't he try everything? Refrigerators after china, magazines after refrigerators, newspaper subscriptions after magazines? (Get a job, Esther berated, but what job? Behind a desk, behind a counter? Strangulation. Even if he could have found one, he would have said nix. He was a salesman, a door-to-door executive, best in the west, and there was money in it too if the goddam Republicans hadn't etc.) After unsuccessfully pushing newspapers, Sid retired, because he had his pride, and besides that, if he worked full-time, pool playing could more than pay the bills. So he took the little cash remaining and he started playing pool, nice and easy, no big plunging, a few bucks at a time.

But his touch was gone! Sid found it difficult to believe. Always before, when it had been for laughs, he had had it, right there, right in the sensitive tips of his fingers, but now, when it was for a lousy loaf of bread, he couldn't sink a six ball in a bushel basket. Until he was totally broke, he always managed to answer Esther's shouts with shouts of his own, coupled with assurances that he was on the trail of something hot and tomorrow would, indeed, be another day, but once his last pennies had fled, he had no antidote for her venom, sitting head bowed, dumb, taking it like what was left of a man, and when Old Turk's offer of *gratis* room and board was voiced, Sid could do nothing but submit silently, all the time trying to incorporate the somewhat sullied image of a failure forced to living off the dole into the larger truer picture of the Super Sid he knew himself to be.

The boy, when informed of the coming shift, was troubled only until he remembered that Old Turk's apartment also possessed a fire escape. After that he didn't really care.

They made the move one bitter spring morning, Old Turk delaying the opening of his deli to come over and help. He came in a small truck, on short-term loan from Rosenheim, an old and sometime friend who ran a Chinese laundry down the block from the delicatessen. They moved with a minimum of chitchat, Esther pointing here, pointing there, Sid and the old man gathering up whatever it was she indicated, lugging the stuff downstairs to the truck. The boy did what he could to help, then, just before the final journey, he slipped out the window, up to his rusted place, standing in the cold, looking down and around and all over until Old Turk stuck his head out the window and said, "Come. Mine's got a better view." The boy joined the old man, the two joined the others, the four squeezed wordlessly into the truck and Rosenheim's motor took care of the rest.

When they reached the deli, they unloaded onto the sidewalk, Old Turk returning the truck to behind the laundry, while the others began to trek the belongings up to the second floor. The old man rejoined them, helped them finish the chore, then said, "Welcome, make yourself at home, excuse me" and hurried downstairs to open the store. Sid carried a suitcase into the bedroom and began to unpack, grabbing two hangers of pants, opening a door to hang them up. "That's a closet?" Sid said, pointing. "*That?*"

"Shut up," Esther said.

"Six handkerchiefs would fill it. That's not a closet, it's a crack in the wall."

"It will hold our clothes," Esther said. "And shut up."

"My wardrobe it might. Your wardrobe would strain the *Normandie*. If I had half the money I've spent on your clothes—"

"You'd lose it at pool. My father gave *us* his room. *His* room. He's sharing the living room with the boy so we can have—"

"The living room's bigger," Sid said. "He's no fool, that *cocker*."

"What's lower than contempt, I wonder? Whatever it is, that's what I feel for you."

Sid turned away from her, mumbling, "Why d'ya gotta say things like that for?"

"I speak what's on my mind."

"If that were the case," Sid said, whirling back in triumph, "you would have nothing to say and wouldn't that be a blessing?"

"How does it feel to be a failure?"

Sid turned away again, slumping onto the bed, the hangers of clothes wrinkled across his lap. "I can't live in a place like this, Esther."

"You're talking about my home, Failure. I was brought up here."

"Don't say that word anymore."

"There's work to be done, Failure. Do it."

"I'm used to better things."

"The world's only Jewish maharajah, that's you."

"Esther, it may come as a surprise to you but you're getting to me."

"Not only a failure, but sensitive yet. My cup runneth over."

"Bitch!"

"Bast—Rudy? Rudy, darling?"

"Yes" from the living room.

"Go down and see if you can help your grandfather in the store, will you do that?"

"Yes." The apartment door closed.

"Bastard!"

The boy heard the word through the door, and the words that followed too, but they faded as he raced down the stairs to the store. Old Turk was sitting in his chair by the pickle barrel, reading a thick book. He held the book in his lap, and his chin was dropped onto his chest, so that as he read he looked as if he were using his gigantic nose as a pointer.

"Can I help?" the boy said.

Old Turk lifted his nose, aiming it first at the boy, then slowly around the empty store. "Thank you," he said. "But I think I can handle things."

"Mother sent me down to see if I could help."

Old Turk said nothing.

"They're very busy unpacking."

Old Turk nodded, and for a moment they listened to the muffled shouts from the room directly above. "Yes. I can hear."

The boy said nothing.

Old Turk dropped his nose and began to read.

"Mother sent me down to see if I could help."

The old man pulled a toothpick from behind his ear and dropped it into the book, marking his place. Then he closed the book, resting both elbows on it. "We could talk if you like. That might be considered helping; it would pass the time."

The boy said nothing.

"I somehow feel that that idea doesn't thrill you."

"No—"

"Please." And Old Turk raised a finger. "I understand. When we talk, I do all the talking. But that is as it should be. I'm old. It's my right. When you are old, then you can do all the talking." He picked up the thick book, holding it out a moment before setting it on the counter. "Philosophy," he said. "Are you knowledgeable on the subject?"

"I don't understand."

"Neither do I, and I am very knowledgeable on the subject. Philosophy is what you study when you desire to increase your ignorance. Why aren't you out on the fire escape?"

"It's very cold."

"Yes. So it is. Sad for you, joy for the coal man."

The boy stared at the wooden floor, standing on tiptoe, moving his feet a little this way, a little that, avoiding the cracks.

"Since there is little in the way of help at the present, I release you."

The boy continued to avoid the cracks.

"You may go," Old Turk said.

"Yes." But he did not move.

"I see," the old man said. "Where will you go? Upstairs is 'unpacking,' outside is cold, here an old man jabbers." He sighed. "At best, an unappetizing selection. But perhaps if the old man quieted, that, at least, would be something. You could go read labels and pretend you were alone. I recommend the tinned fish. They swim here from all over the world, a lesson in geography." He pointed to a far corner. "Read in peace. The old man is shut."

The boy moved to the indicated corner and sat cross-legged on the floor, staring at the shelves.

"One thing more," the old man said.

The boy turned.

"A pledge, a promise, as God is my witness what I have to say is so."

The boy waited.

"I want nothing from you."

The boy stayed by the shelves until it was time for lunch. Then the old man made sandwiches and the boy carried them upstairs, leaving Old Turk to munch alone by the pickle barrel. The boy entered the quiet apartment and put the sandwiches on the small dining table. His father was sitting on the sofa, looking out the window; his mother was lying down in the bedroom, looking at the walls. "Food," he said to his father, and again "Food" to his mother, and then he sat down at the table to wait. He was very hungry but they did not come. "Food," he repeated to his father, who still sat across the room, still staring out the window. The boy reached for a sandwich, salami on dark rye. He waited a moment longer, then nibbled at the sandwich. It was delicious and he tried to wait some more but he couldn't, so he took a big bite, then another, and by the time his parents got to the table he was done eating.

Sid picked up a salami sandwich and looked at it. "You call this food?" he said.

"I'm all done, may I go?" the boy said.

"Go," Sid said.

"Stay," from his mother.

"If I'd said stay, you woulda said go, right?"

"I'm not talking to you," Esther said.

"How I only wish that were true," Sid said.

"May I please?" the boy said.

"Sure, kid, sure, Rudy. I'm your father and I say you can go."

"Yes, Rudy, go before you catch whatever he's got."

"Are you saying I'm diseased?"

"I'm not talking to you."

The boy darted for the fire escape but as he opened the window he started to shiver at the cold air and when his father shouted, "You want to freeze us all? Close the window!" it was already shut. The boy crossed the room to the front door and skipped down the stairs into the store. "Good salami," he said to his grandfather, who sat, as before, reading by the pickle barrel. The old man nodded with grace and the boy sat down again on the floor in front of the tinned fish. A few minutes later he heard a sound, so he turned to see Old Turk devouring a dill. The old man caught the turn and pointed to the barrel and the boy nodded, so Turk reached down for a pickle, discarding several before making a selection, then threw his choice end over end across the store. It was not a perfect toss, too high, but the boy reached up with one hand and made the catch.

"In my youth I was more accurate."

"It wasn't a bad throw."

"Thank you." He returned to his book.

The boy began to eat the crisp pickle, taking little bites.

"They're *that* interesting, the labels?" Old Turk said later when the pickle was gone.

"What?"

"Can you read?"

"Yes. Of course I can read." He picked up a tin. "This is salmon."

"Almost."

"It isn't salmon?"

"Tuna fish. But they're very close."

"Oh, of course. Look." He pointed to the label. "Tuna . . . fish. I wonder why I said salmon."

"Slip of the tongue. Everyone is prone."

"Tuna . . . fish."

"That is correct," and he returned to his book.

"I can't exactly read," the boy said then. "But the labels are very pretty."

"Beautiful," the old man agreed. "Sardine labels—there, two stacks to the left—they're my favorite. Genuine works of art."

"They are nice. But I think I like the tuna . . . fish better."

"You may well be right. Taste is a peculiar thing. Some people prefer the salmon—the stack in between—the salmon labels to either."

"Oh, I don't think so," the boy said. "Not the salmon labels. The tuna is much prettier. The sardine too." He brought a sardine tin close to his face and stared at it. "Maybe the sardine *is* the prettiest after all."

"The tuna is certainly lovely. If I were forced to choose I think—" And he stopped as a sudden burst of screaming came from above. The old man shook his head. "They're at it again?"

"At what?"

"You've got to listen to that every day?"

"Listen to what?"

"Nothing," the old man said, and he picked up his book. "Nothing. But it can't be much fun."

"No," the boy said, "it isn't much fun."

The next day was cold, so after breakfast the boy left the apartment and went downstairs. Entering the store, he approached the pickle barrel and stopped. Old Turk looked up from his book. The boy nodded. The old man nodded. Then the boy moved to the canned-soup section and sat down. After a moment he picked up a can and held it up. "This is . . . ?"

Old Turk sat forward, squinting. "Bean," he said finally.

"Bean," the boy repeated, staring at the letters on the can. "Beeennnnn. B-e-a-n. Bean."

"Last night, how was my snoring?"

"You snore very well."

"I meant, did I keep you awake?"

"I wasn't really tired. This is . . . ?"

"Pea. You are given to rolling around."

"I am? Pea. I'm sorry. P-e-a. Pea soup."

"Forgiven. I snore, you roll, some gnash; who amongst us can lay claim to perfection?"

"What does that mean?"

"It means that if you jump up and down long enough, eventually you'll smell. Good morning, Mrs. Feldman." He smiled at the large lady entering the store.

"Good morning, Mr. Turk."

"The little Feldmans?"

"Bigger."

"As it should be."

"Three quarts milk, a loaf of rye and a pound of your good Swiss cheese."

"A tasty order," the old man said, leaving his beloved chair. He set the milk on the counter and was going for the cheese when a can of soup floated into view above a shelf of appetizers. "Beef," Turk said.

"What?" Mrs. Feldman said.

"Beef," came a voice.

Mrs. Feldman peeked over the appetizers. "Who?" she whispered.

Old Turk shrugged. "A stray," he replied. "Either a small boy or a midget. Backwards in either case."

"B-e-e-f. Beef."

"All he does is read soup labels. I checked the symptom in a medical text. There is a disease. Rare. *Cogito ergo sum* is the Latin name. In English it's called Double Stupidity."

Was that a laugh? From behind the shelf of appetizers? The old man listened. There was no more sound. The old man sighed.

"I'm not hungry," the boy said as Old Turk finished making the second sandwich. "I'll just take those up to them and come on back down."

Old Turk wrapped the sandwiches in a paper napkin, opened two bottles of celery tonic and pushed them across the counter to the boy. "What will your mother say about your not eating?"

"She won't mind," the boy said, and he cradled the food in his arms and hurried up the stairs to the apartment. His father was in the living room playing solitaire. "Lunch," the boy said, and he set the food down. His mother came out from the bedroom. "Lunch," he repeated.

She approached the table. "Only two sandwiches?"

"I already ate," the boy said. "Downstairs." His stomach started rumbling.

"Why are you coughing like that?" his mother said. "Is it too cold for you in the store?"

"Frog in my throat," and he turned for the door. "I'm helping Grandfather. I've got to go now. Goodbye."

"Don't work too hard," his mother called after him as he skipped on down the stairs. The old man was sitting in his wooden chair, eating a sandwich. The boy sat down by the canned soups.

"Chicken noodle," the old man said a moment later.

"Chicken noodle," the boy repeated.

"Campbell soups, not only are they tasty, they're educational."

"Could I ask you a question?"

"Ask me a question."

"In the meat counter? I wonder what do you call what's between the salami and the tongue."

"This, from a Jewish boy? Corned beef. In some communities you can be ostracized for such an inquiry."

"I wonder, is it any good?"

"Taste for yourself," and he stood up, slicing a piece of meat.

The boy approached, took the meat and ate it. Then he shook his head.

"What's the matter?"

"Well, you just can't tell about corned beef unless there's bread around it."

"Wisdom," the old man said, and he cut some more meat and two slices of dark rye bread.

"I have had corned beef from Solomon's. I wonder is yours as good?"

"I await your decision."

The boy bit into the sandwich. "No," he said. "Solomon's is better."

"You have just," the old man said, "hurt my feelings."

"Of course, I'm not hungry," the boy said quickly. "That has a lot to do with it. Probably if I was hungry, yours would be at least as good."

"The pain is lessening."

"I have never been hungrier than when I ate the Solomon's."

"Miraculous," the old man said. "The wound is healed. A pickle?"

"Yes, please. Sometimes a pickle makes food go down easier, especially if you're not hungry."

"Nothing like a dill to make the food go down." He reached down into the barrel, found a pickle, then handed it back over his head to the boy on the counter.

The boy sat quietly on the counter, kicking his legs, biting into the sandwich, nibbling at the pickle, keeping them even, until, with one last swallow, both were gone. "Sometimes I wonder," the boy said presently.

"About?"

"Well, why is it, I wonder, that sometimes I start to eat and I'm not hungry and then I eat and I'm still not hungry, but when I'm all done I could probably still eat some more."

"Most mystifying," Old Turk said, rising, moving around the counter to the corned beef, starting to slice.

"Is it all right, my sitting here on the counter like this?"

"Do you hear the customers complaining?"

"Why aren't there more customers?"

"Why do you never smile?"

"I smile."

"You do? I can't remember having seen it. Perhaps you just don't smile around me."

"Why aren't there more customers?"

"Anti-ss-ss-ss-Semitism."

"I don't understand." The boy took the sandwich and began to eat.

"Don't you know that joke? About the Jew who applies for a job as a radio announcer. Only he has the stutters. And when he doesn't get the job his friend asks him why, and the Jew says, 'Anti-ss-ss-ss-Semitism.'"

The boy took a bite of his sandwich.

"You didn't laugh."

The boy looked at him.

"At my joke. You didn't laugh." He slumped in his chair, nose pointing to the wooden floor. "Do you know what the worst thing in the world is? I'll tell you. The worst thing in the world is to be a fool."

"Why are you a fool?"

"Because you didn't laugh at my joke."

"But I didn't get it."

"I accept that as a possibility. But it is *no excuse* for not laughing. When someone tells a joke there are four possibilities: either you don't get it or you get it but you *don't* think it's funny or you get it and you *do* think it's funny or you've heard it before. Of those four, only one relieves the listener from the obligation of laughing." He reached into the pickle barrel, gave a pickle to the boy, took another for himself and began waving it in the air.

"Thank you," the boy said.

"If the joke is funny, then you *don't* have to laugh. Because a man telling a funny story is not a fool. Oh, you *can* laugh if you want to; no law against it. But you don't have to. The funny man, he doesn't need your laughter." Around and around went the pickle in the air, circling high, swooping down, suddenly pointing straight at the boy, who stopped in mid-bite, eyes and mouth wide. "I see a rich man with a limp and I think, my, what an expensive cane he uses. I see a poor man with a limp, and I think, oh, how that must hurt." The pickle was swooping again. The boy gobbled the remainder of the sandwich. Then the pickle was back on him, and he froze. "I see a pretty woman weeping and I say, 'How pretty!' When an ugly woman weeps, I say, 'How sad!' The winners of this world, they can adjust their own laurel wreaths. The losers go bareheaded. The winners need only a mirror; the losers need your laughter. Vegetable," he said to the boy, who was back at the canned-soup shelf.

"Vegetable," said the boy, staring at the can. "I know a joke."

"Tell me."

"It's dirty."

"I'll forget where I heard it."

"All right, here goes. Have you read *The Yellow River* by I. J. Daily?"

"No."

"That's the joke," the boy said. "*The Yellow River* by I. J. Daily."

"Oh, of course, of course," and he started to laugh. "I . . . hah . . . I see—yes—ho, hah—*The Yellow River*—oh yes—I. J. Daily." The old man rocked back and forth in his chair. "Oh, I love that—wonderful, wonderful— yes, hah, ho." He laughed until he stopped.

"I thought you'd like it."

"Clam chowder," the old man said.

"Clam chowder," the boy repeated. "C-l-a-m . . ."

Old Turk rose from his chair and walked to the front of the store, staring out. "*The Yellow River* by I. J. Daily?" He shrugged. "That's a joke? That's funny?" He shook his head. Back and forth. Back and forth.

"Did I say 'I. J. Daily?' " the boy called.

"Several times."

"Oh. Well, I told it wrong. I meant 'P.' *The Yellow River* by I. *P.* Daily."

"Yes, that's a decided improvement. Not only is it dirty, it also makes a little sense."

"But you're not laughing."

"Of course I'm not laughing. Why should I laugh? Now it's funny."

"What kind of crap is that?" Sid stormed.

"Shhh," Esther said. "They'll hear you." She sat up in bed watching her husband crisscross the tiny room.

"I tell a joke and nobody laughs. I mean, what kind of crap is that?"

"They might not be asleep yet. Come lie down. It's late."

"Was it a funny joke, Tootsie? I ask you. My joke about the camel. Didn't I tell it perfect? Is there a better joke-teller than me living any-where? And then my kid, my flesh and blood, he says it's funny but he don't laugh. I mean what kind—"

"Maybe he didn't understand the joke."

"Didn't I offer to explain? Didn't he say he understood the joke? I like to hear people laugh when I tell jokes." Sid glared at the door. "It's that fa-ther of yours. I'm telling you, he's no good for the boy. Why don't he spend his time on the fire escape like he used to?"

"It's too cold."

"Yeah?" Sid said, the door still holding his glare. "Well, it'll warm."

It did, but not for ten days, and during the first five the boy continued his canned education. He moved from the soups to the fruit, then the vegetables. The condiments gave him trouble, but eventually he mastered them, advancing from there through the spices and the meats, finally to the cartoned dairy products, to the cheeses and the creams. Quite by accident, one afternoon, he and the old man invented "Seek the Seltzer," a simple enough game—it evolved somehow out of "Pin the Tail on the *Kreplach*," an earlier invention that after less than a day had already started to pall—in which Old Turk shouted the name of a product and then counted slowly while the boy whirled around the store, seeking the product before the old man reached ten. "Mushroom soup," the old man would shout and then the boy would flash from the counter to the soup section, searching desperately for the can with the eight-letter word. In the beginning he lost more than he won, but by the second day he had pulled even and the day after that found him beating the game, sometimes winning before the count of seven, sometimes before six, and once he located the pickled herring before the count of three, grabbing the jar from the dusty shelf, holding it triumphantly over his head for all the world to see. They played "Seek the Seltzer" all day long, day after day, even on the morning the weather turned warm. It rained that morning, rained hard, and there were fewer customers than usual to interrupt the game, and at lunchtime the boy took food up and then came back down to dine with the old man, and after lunch they played until the sun came out. As it broke through the clouds, they both stopped and stared into the brightness, and then the old man shouted "String beans! String beans!" very loud and the boy hesitated by the counter. "String beans!" the old man yelled and then the boy moved, toward the string beans and past them, past the dairy case, out the door, gone.

"String beans," the old man said, softer now. He looked at the door a while, and then he shook his head. He groped for his chair, found it, sat down heavily. Again he shook his head. Then he nodded. Then he shrugged. Then he reached for a pickle and ate it, shaking his head until the pickle was gone. Then he reached behind him for his book, opened it to the toothpick and started to read. He read the same sentence half a dozen times before closing the book. Mrs. Feldman came in and he smiled until she said what a hurry she was in so could she please just have a quart of milk, and though he tried to entice her with conversation she would have none of it and, plunking down her pennies, she toted the milk out of the store and he was alone. Again Old Turk sat down, but he wasn't comfortable. "Too many pickles," he muttered, and he patted his stomach. Then he went to the shelves and began straightening the cans. Widow Kramer came in, evil Widow Kramer who always accused him of overcharging, of stocking only junk, of weighing with a heavy thumb. Old Turk looked at the harpie, at the skeletal destroyer of his equilibrium, and he smiled. "Widow Kramer, a pleasure."

"You got any cheese that isn't rancid?"

"So nice to see you, Widow Kramer. Have I got cheese? Here. Take a knife. Taste. Take your time."

"You sick?"

"Never better. I just thought we might pass the time chatting and tasting—"

"A pound of Swiss and be quick about it. And I'm not buying your thumb."

Turk weighed the cheese, wrapped it, nodded with each insult, bade her farewell. Alone again. He started to sit, thought the better of it. He had craved the Widow Kramer's company. Begged for it almost. Turk sighed, and the sound filled the empty store. He was not partial to the sound, but he sighed again. He could not stop sighing. Abruptly he turned and started for the door, half running, bent over in an old man's shuffle. He closed the door and locked it and hurried outside through the sunshine around the building to the back. When he reached the alley he stopped, peeking around the edge of the building. There, feet dangling in space, was the boy, head through the bars of the fire escape, staring. At what? What was there to see? Turk shook his head. Where did it come from, such beauty? Not from Sid or Esther; God knows they didn't resemble him. And God knows *he* didn't. So where did it come from? "God knows," Turk muttered. And then, with a shake of the head: "Beautiful." Tiny and dark on the fire escape. Turk turned, trudging back to his store. "The boy should have some air," he said. "Yes." He unlocked the store and stepped inside. Enormous it was—suddenly enormous. Bleak and plain and too big. Much too big. "The boy should have some air," Turk said. He wandered into the tiny store. "Fool," he said then. "Fool." He sat down in his beloved chair and tried to close his eyes, but they preferred to scan the labels on the shelves across. "The boy should have some air!" the old man shouted, immediately feeling better for the exercise, stronger, for now his eyes did close and he slumped, hands in his lap, nose aimed at the floor. Good times he thought of. Not good times gone, but good times as they happened, for the conjuring of past pleasures was the secret of long life. He heard his father's laugh, his mother's song; he tasted duck for the first time, and chopped liver lightly salted, and beer; he rolled in snow, he kissed a breast, he raced the dog to water, rode the horse, won from his sister at checkers, lost to his brother at chess; he talked on a telephone, listened to a radio, saw Toscanini, walked beside Casals—and held his breath as his grandchild said "I was wondering" from the delicatessen door.

"What—you were wondering what?"

"What I was wondering was, you couldn't come out to the fire escape, could you?"

"I could. But who would watch the store?"

"Mother?" The boy stood on tiptoe, avoiding the cracks.

"In her present mood your mother would frighten away the few customers we have."

"Father?"

"That strikes me as vaguely impossible. In his present mood your father would frighten away your mother."

"We could hire somebody."

"We could do that."

"Why don't we?"

"Because we would starve, because it would cost us more money than we have just to pay his salary."

"Well, maybe we could both go out on the fire escape except that we would tie a string around the front door and take the string with us so that every time the string moved we would know it was a customer and you could run down the fire escape to the store and fill the order."

"Now that's a marvelous notion, except that I am not as young as some people and chances are all that running up and down would kill me."

"Well, we could do the same thing with the string except I would do the running up and down and fill the order."

"That, I think, is a perfect solution except that, even though you are a first-class label reader, you are not quite so brilliant at adding up numbers and therefore you would probably either overcharge the customers, in which case they would yell at you, or undercharge them, in which case they would cheat you, and after a while they would either be so angry at us they would go to the A&P or they would have cheated us out of everything and we would starve."

"You know what? This is more fun than 'Seek the Seltzer.' "

"More intellectual," the old man agreed.

"Could I have a pickle? I mean, you do want to sit on the fire escape?"

"Nothing would give me more pleasure."

"Well, we'll just have to figure it out."

"All problems are solvable."

"And I'm going to stay right here until we do. I mean, I could stay outside, but I'm going to stay right here. Stores are better for thinking."

"Infinitely."

"Yes. We'll get it. But it may take days."

"Weeks, even."

"Months."

"Years."

"What comes after years?"

"Perhaps we'll find out, you and I."

So they pondered the problem of the fire escape, and they slept in the same bed, and they did what they could to cheer Sid and sweeten Esther, and they played "Seek the Seltzer" until the boy was perfect and after that they waited on customers together, the old man saying "Spinach for the Widow Kramer," the boy running down the vegetable, swooping it up, dashing back to set it on the counter, then waiting for the next labor, "Granulated sugar, monkey, five pounds for the Widow," and he would retrieve the sugar and whatever followed the sugar and whatever followed that until the list was done. Then he would say "Add," and the old man would obey, and then the old man would take the money and give it to him and he would gently open the money drawer and tuck it safe inside, and then they would sit until the next customer. And while they sat, they talked. They talked about why there were cracks in the sidewalks and what happened to letters once you dropped them in the mailbox, and prehistoric dinosaurs and railroad trains and sharks and squid and slinky barracuda. They talked about how they were going to spend the reward money they were going to get after they captured the gangsters who might try to rob the store and how they would subdue any frothing mad dog who happened to wander in and what did the Lone Ranger really look like and just *what was* in Fibber McGee's closet. And men from Mars. And Stanley Hack. And the Italian the evil Yankees had found to run in center field. And the great Bronko Nagurski. And J. Donald Budge. And rain. And they talked about the old country. And Old Turk's childhood. And the awful boat ride across when he was eight. And how he happened to come to Chicago. And they talked about his father. And they talked about his mother, who died on the trip. And his sister, who died in Cincinnati. And they talked about his brother and they talked about his wife.

But mostly they talked about his nose.

"My nose? You want to know how I got my nose?"

"Yes."

"You really want to know how I got—"

"Tell me—tell me!"

"You're absolutely positive you're interested in hearing how—"

"Yes-yes-yes."

"God gave it to me personally."

"No, he didn't either."

"Since you obviously already know the story," Old Turk said, leaning back in his soft wooden chair, "there doesn't seem to be much point in going on with it."

"But you've got to go on," the boy said. He was sitting on the floor by the chair and he reached forward and pulled the old man's trousers like a bell rope.

"You called me a liar. I said God gave it to me personally and you said no he didn't either. A man likes to be believed."

"But you always lie when you tell about your nose."

"I do?"

"Yes."

"Well, this time I'll tell the truth."

"Promise?"

"Of course not. I'm a man of my word. I don't have to promise. So anyway, one day when I was nine years old, I was plowing the fields and—"

"When you were *nine*? You said you came over on the boat when you were *eight*, so how could you be plowing the fields when you were nine?"

"In the old country we counted differently."

"Oh," the boy said. He moved in closer to the chair.

"So, this particular day when I was plowing the fields God came up to me and said—Good morning, Widow Kramer."

The boy jumped to his feet and ran toward the woman. "What do you need? Tell me and I'll get it." And she gave him the order and almost before she was done telling it was filled.

"Add," the boy said.

"The service is certainly improved," the Widow allowed. "I'm sorry I can't say the same about the food."

"Always a pleasure, Widow Kramer," Turk said, and he gave the money to the boy, who threw it into the money drawer, then pulled the old man back to the chair.

"God came—I hate those interruptions—God—"

"You never interrupt?"

"Never. God came—"

"Yes, he came up to me one day when I was plow—"

"How did you know it was God?"

"What you just did, that wasn't an interruption?"

"A question. I asked a question. Go on."

"How did I know? Well—"

"I mean, he could have just been somebody *pretending* he was God. A practical joker. Or a movie actor maybe."

"I doubt that He was a movie actor, since when this happened no one had yet invented movies. And although what you say is possible, I think He was legitimate."

"Why?"

"There was this *blinding light* around Him," Old Turk said. "And it was a *cloudy day.*"

"Oh." The boy nodded. "Well, why didn't you say that in the first place?"

"I should have. I'm a poor storyteller. My apologies."

"That's all right. Go on."

"So I'm in the fields plowing and all of a sudden God came up to me and He said, 'Hello there, Joel Turk,' and I said, 'Hello there, God,' and He said, 'How are things?' and I said, 'You mean, *You* don't know?' and He said, 'Of course I know. I know everything. I was just making conversation, that's all. Let me tell you something, Joel Turk. This business of knowing everything, it doesn't leave much room for surprises. If I didn't make a little conversation every now and then, I think I'd go *meshugah.*'"

"Means?"

"Meshugah?"

The boy nodded.

Old Turk whirled his index finger around his temple.

The boy nodded again. "And what did you say?"

" 'Well,' I told him, 'God,' I said, 'we could all of us do with a little more strudel, even You.' And He said, 'Joel, you are so right. Being God, it's like being the family doctor, except the whole universe is your family.' And I said, 'Have You ever thought of delegating the authority?' and He said, 'I tried that once, only it didn't work out so good. No; if you want to get something done, you've got to do it yourself, and I've got a lot to do. So, much as I'd like to stand and *schmoose* with you—' "

"*Schmoose?*"

"Chat. Talk. Pass the time."

"Thank you."

" 'Much as I am enjoying our conversation,' God said, 'it's time we got down to business. I'm worried about your village, Joel. I am genuinely concerned.' 'Our village?' I said, and He said, 'Yes. Have you noticed that in your village no one smiles, no one laughs?' 'Since I've lived here all my life,' I said, 'it has come to my attention.' And God said, 'Do you know why?' and I answered, 'Well, God, no one has any clothes, and no one has any money to buy any clothes, and the weather is stern, and in the winter everyone freezes, and the fields are solid rock, and nothing grows, and everyone is dying of starvation; I think that might have something to do with it.' And God said, 'Well, I'm going to change all that,' and I said, 'You mean You're going to make things grow, so we can have food, and money for clothes; You're going to change the solid rock into topsoil, yes?' and He said, 'I could. I could do all that and more. But I don't want to spoil you.' 'You know best, God,' I said, 'but it sure sounded nice while I was saying it.' 'If I did it for them,' God said, 'then they would become lazy; they would become fat. But if only their hearts would buoy, then their spirits would swell, and their strength would be as the strength of ten, and the rock would crumble, and there would be nothing but rich black topsoil for as far as the eye could see and instead of being fat they would be youthful and instead of being lazy they would be proud.' 'Oh, that's beautiful, God,' I said, and there were tears in my eyes, 'but why would that happen? Why do their hearts buoy?' 'Joel Turk,' God said, 'what do you think of yourself?' Well, I thought a minute, and you must realize, monkey, that when I was young I was pretty special, not ugly like you, but I didn't want to sound cocky to God, so I just said, 'I guess I'm not so bad.' 'You're nothing!' God said. 'A shadow. A lump. A cipher, Joel Turk, is what you are, and as you age you'll disappear and when you die no one will care because no one will know you were around.' 'I'm that bad?' I said. 'I wish you hadn't told me. Getting the word from you, God—that banishes hope. I can't even dream anymore; not now. What have I got to look forward to?' 'Misery,' God said. 'Misery, loneliness and grief, coupled with gradual decay.' 'Please, God, stop!' I said and I couldn't help crying. 'No more. I beg you.' And then God came right up next to me, blinding He was, and He said, 'Would you like a different fate, Joel Turk?' 'Yes,' I said. 'Anything.' And God said, 'Would you like to be much admired?

Would you like to be much adored?' 'Yes. Yes. Much admired, much adored, yes.' 'And would you like to help your village, Joel Turk? Would you like to make them strong and proud?' 'Yes, but what can I give them? What do they need?' 'They need only one thing. One thing alone.' 'What, God? What?' 'They need something to smile at, Joel Turk; they need something to make them laugh.' "

"Your nose!" the boy cried. "Your nose!"

"Yes." The old man nodded. "God's words exactly. But I didn't understand. 'I've got a nice nose,' I said. 'It's small and cute.' 'Agreed,' God said, 'but if you like, I could change that. I could give you such a nose. Such a nose! And when the people of the village see it they will smile and then laugh and then their hearts will buoy and the rock will turn into topsoil and you will be much admired, much adored.' 'You mean You're going to make me funny-looking, a buffoon?' 'Something like that,' God said. 'Along those lines, anyway.' 'But, God,' I said, 'why the nose? I mean, the nose, it's so . . . visible. Couldn't you maybe do something clever with my ears instead?' 'Has to be the nose,' God said. 'Don't you know that famous Shakespeare poem, perhaps the greatest poem he ever wrote?

> *The ears are for hearing,*
> *The lips are to smile,*
> *The nose is for laughing,*
> *The tongue is for guile.*

" 'Now do you see, Joel Turk? The nose is for laughing. Has to be the nose.' 'I see, God,' I said. 'And that certainly is a *great, great* poem but—' And God said, 'Make your choice, Joel. A free choice. A life of unbelievable, incredible agony against a life of being much admired, much adored. Choose!' 'God,' I said, 'You are indeed a true God, a fine God, fair and in all ways sublime . . .' " Old Turk quieted.

"Go on."

"No more. My choice, I believe, is obvious to this day."

"You mean all of a sudden you had a nose? Just like that?"

"As I remember, there was an accompanying flash of light."

"The people in the village, did they laugh at you?"

"They laughed at me."

"And did the rock turn into topsoil?"

"Well, the next morning there was a little dust."

"Have you been much admired, much adored?"

"Sometimes God is given to exaggeration," the old man said.

·

The flag stood in the corner of the first-grade classroom. Mrs. Witty gestured toward it. Rudy stared down at his desk, listening as Mrs. Witty said, "Now, this morning is our first assembly, so we'll need someone to carry the flag. *I* could pick that someone if I wanted to, but I don't do that in my classes. *You* will pick that someone. Right after recess, we'll have our own election; we will make nominations and then we will vote. And whoever we select will carry the flag into assembly at the head of the class. Yes, Naomi?"

"Can a girl do it?"

"I won't say absolutely *no*," Mrs. Witty replied, "but I will say that *generally* boys carry the flag. I have never, in all my years here, had a girl carry the flag, but that doesn't mean a girl *can't* carry the flag. Whoever you select, he or she, will have my wholehearted approval. Does that answer your question, Naomi?"

Naomi indicated that it did.

"Well then," Mrs. Witty went on. "Once we get into the auditorium our flag-bearer will carry the flag up the steps onto the auditorium stage, and he—or she"—a smile toward Naomi—"will remain there along with the other flag-bearers while the principal addresses the school. So, although this is our first election, it is a very important one. And I know we've only known each other for less than a week, and that isn't much time, but it will have to do. Now go to recess and think about your vote. Dismissed." Mrs. Witty sat down at her desk as the class fled toward the door. "Gently, gently," Mrs. Witty cautioned, not looking up. "Nobody likes a pusher." And she continued filling out the daily attendance report. She had been filling out daily attendance reports for twenty-seven years, and she loathed the chore, especially in the early fall, before names had attached themselves to faces and faces had attached themselves to desks. So although she wrote with undue speed, it still took time, and her finishing sigh would have been louder than usual had it not suddenly changed into a start of surprise. "Oh," Mrs. Witty said. "Oh." Then: "Rudolph, you didn't go to recess."

The boy shook his head.

"You've been here all this time?"

The boy nodded.

"Well, Rudolph, what is it?"

"I don't think I should carry the flag."

"I'm sorry, Rudolph, I didn't quite hear you."

"I don't think I should carry the flag."

"Well, I guess I did hear you. I don't understand, Rudolph."

"The flag." The boy pointed to the corner. "I don't think I should carry it."

"I understand *that*, Rudolph. But don't you see, you haven't been elected yet."

"I will be," the boy said.

"Well, confidence is a wonderful thing, Rudolph, and I'm not trying to destroy yours, but there are, after all, thirty students in this class, and that makes your chances one in thirty, so I don't think we need get excited." Mrs. Witty opened her purse, making sure her cigarettes were inside.

"Please."

Mrs. Witty stood. "I'd like to help, Rudolph, but there's really nothing I can do." She started for the door.

"Please."

Turning, Mrs. Witty looked at the boy. "Are you all right, Rudolph? I mean, do you feel well?"

"Yes. Yes. But I don't think I should carry the flag."

"I'm sorry," Mrs. Witty said. "This is just too premature," and she hurried from the room toward the Teachers' Lounge.

After a moment the boy moved to the window and stared out at the playground. Hidden, he watched the others as they talked, their lips moving, heads nodding, arms waving in the air. He stared until he heard Mrs. Witty ringing the recess bell and then he hurried to his desk and sat down, his hands in his lap, his eyes on his hands.

"All right now," he heard Mrs. Witty say when it was quiet. "I hope you've all thought carefully. Nominations are open. Yes?"

"Petey Steinem."

"Peter Steinem. Yes, Naomi?"

"Rudy Miller," and she reached forward from the desk behind Rudy, pulling at his shirt.

"Rudolph Miller. Yes?"

"Naomi Finkel."

"But I'm a *girl*," Naomi said.

"As I explained to you earlier, Naomi, this is a free country. Anyone else?"

"Dopey Sternemann."

"*Daniel* Sternemann," Mrs. Witty said over the giggling. "All right now, anyone else? No? Then nominations are hereby closed. All right, everybody, shut your eyes. No peeking. As I say each candidate's name, raise your hand when I come to your choice. Ready? Peter Steinem. . . . Rudolph Miller. . . . Naomi Finkel. . . . Daniel Sternemann. . . . All right, you may open your eyes. Now we none of us like being kept in suspense—"

"Rudy, Rudy," Naomi whispered. "I peeked. You won. It was practically *umanimous*."

"—that Rudolph Miller has been elected. Now if you will all stand and form two rows we—"

"I don't think I should carry the flag."

"I'm sorry," Mrs. Witty said, "but we don't answer people who don't raise their hands. Now we haven't much time so . . . Yes, Naomi, what is it?"

"Rudy's got his hand up now," Naomi said.

"*Thank* you, Naomi. All right, Rudolph."

"I might do it wrong."

"There is nothing to *do* except carry the flag."

"But I might drop it."

"The *flag* is *not that* heavy."

"But I might trip. On the steps. The steps up to the stage. I might trip and drop the flag. Let it touch the ground."

"Stand up!"

The boy stood.

"Are you *ashamed* to carry the flag of your own country? Is that what I'm to understand? That you're *ashamed*? Is that it? All right, class, there's no reason for any whispering—I'm really out of patience with you, Rudolph. You're making us late for our very first assembly and in all my twenty-seven years of teaching I have *never never* had a student who was *ashamed* to carry the flag of his own country. Class! For the last time stop that whispering! Class! Oh, now I'm upset—you've got me upset. And we're late. If I didn't believe in doing everything democratically— Rudolph, get the flag! Everybody up—two lines—all right. Right. Let's go." And they straggled out of the classroom and down the hall, the boy leading them, Mrs. Witty ranging down the line, "No talking, no talking," and when they reached the auditorium most of the seats were filled but she guided them to an empty area and then pointed to the stage. "Down the aisle, Rudolph. Get up there now. Hurry. Hurry." The boy carried the flag down the long aisle. Ahead lay the steps. Five of them. He glanced around. His was the last flag. Everyone was watching. Five steps. The boy took a deep breath and started up, but the steps were very slippery and before he was halfway there his sense of balance started to go, the flag and his body tilting . . .

"So," Old Turk said. "After you dropped the flag, what happened?"

"I didn't drop it," the boy said. "I started to, but I didn't."

"Were you trying to drop it?"

"I don't know."

"So they wouldn't ask you anymore?"

"I don't know."

"In other words, all that happened that needn't have happened is that you upset your teacher and acted a fool in front of your fellows."

"Yes."

"Why was the role of the fool so alluring?"

"Who am I to carry the flag?"

"Who is anybody to . . . You're not listening to me."

The boy moved across the floor, avoiding the cracks. "No."

"If I were a man of action, you would listen, because when a man of action speaks, that in itself is unusual. But since I am a man of speech, you pay no attention. Consequently, in order that you will remember what I say, I am going to hit you. Do you understand?"

"No."

"Do you trust me?"

"Yes."

"Then come here." The old man waited until the boy stood close in front of him. "It will be a soft hit. A mere touch. But I think you will remember what I say. Now, I could answer your questions any number of ways—philosophically, historically, et cetera. But I will be brief instead and you will never again ask such a question. Who are you to carry the flag? You are you to carry the flag. Now for the slap. Are you ready?"

"Yes."

Old Turk raised his arm, hesitated, then sent it on its way. For a moment his fingers rested against the boy's cheek. As his old hand fell away, a tiny hand rose, covering the spot. The boy spun toward the wall, the hand still to his cheek. The slap could not have been gentler.

But the boy's hand did not move.

One warm October evening they lay side by side in bed, Old Turk and the boy, eyes shut tight, while in the next room Esther shouted "Failure!" for at least the fifth time.

"Sticks and stones can break your bones, so watch it, Tootsie," Sid said.

"It's a good thing we're sleeping," Old Turk said. "Else we would be overhearing their conversation."

"Yes." The boy nodded.

"Does it bother you that your looks are going?" Sid wondered.

"Guess how sick you make me," Esther answered.

"I'm sorry," the boy whispered, and he slipped from the bed to the window, then out, disappearing up the fire escape.

The old man slowly rose, clutching at his nightgown, and crossed the living room to the open window, looking up. Then he turned and made his way to the bedroom. Knocking, he opened the door and said, "You could never dream what things I wish for you." Then he closed the door, ignoring what they called after him, and crossed the living room again. Sticking his head out the window, he said, "Assuming you wanted company and assuming there was room, is it your opinion I would be warm enough?"

"Oh yes. Come. Come."

The old man began working his body through the window.

"I'll help you," the boy said.

"Next, women will be giving me their seats on the bus, thank you no," and he waved the boy away. When he was outside, he paused a moment, then walked up to the top where the boy sat, his feet dangling in space. The old man looked around.

"Do you like it?" the boy asked.

"Beautiful view of the alley," the old man said. "No wonder you're partial."

"Sit. Sit."

"And dangle my feet like you?"

"It's the best way."

"I always accept the word of the connoisseur," Old Turk said. He sat down and dangled his feet. "To my knowledge, no one is so fine as you at fire-escape sitting. And not yet eight years old. My God, think what you'll be at fifteen. And by the time you reach twenty—"

"Why do they do that?"

"Why does who do what?"

"Please."

Old Turk sighed. "Since I did not rear your father, it would be unscientific of me to speak of him."

"Mother?"

"Why is my daughter the way she is? Why is any child? Today, the fashion is to blame the parents. I myself remain unconvinced. Personally I think—you are my greatest audience, do you know that?"

"Go on."

"Heaven to me is enough dill pickles, no indigestion, and you beside me listening."

"Go on, go on. You said 'Personally I think . . .' "

"I think we are all given infinite choices. My father is cruel, so I am cruel. Or sweet. Or any stop along the way. My mother is rich, so I hate money. Or love it. I don't think we can blame our parents. That's too easy. We are the way we are. It's God's world; He gets the credit, let's give Him a little of the blame too, do Him good. God's human, just like the rest of us."

"And Mother?"

"Well . . ." Old Turk kicked his feet. The boy did the same. "There are those who would say my daughter is the way she is because of heredity, or environment—you don't know what I'm talking about, do you?"

"No; go on."

"You are such a fine listener that if I ever become King of England, I'll knight you. Heredity. Heredity is the answer. Except for one thing: for generations, we Turks were known as the cocker spaniels of our village—gentle, loyal, bland. So environment is the answer. Except for one thing: my wife—and you have only my word for this—but my wife . . . Let me put it this way: I was the savage in the family. And we raised our daughter with love. So out of this, how does your mother appear?"

"Yes. How?"

"Your mother is a bad miracle," Old Turk said.

Late on a winter afternoon, Old Turk suddenly jackknifed up from his chair, made a sound and pitched forward into the pickle barrel. The boy, watching, also made a sound, a louder sound, and ran to the body, pulling the old head from the brine, grappling with the limp flesh, trying to get it first into the chair and, failing that, lowering it finally to the cold wooden floor.

"A doctor," Turk whispered, and the boy raced toward the stairs and was halfway to the apartment before he remembered it was empty, his parents having decided earlier to douse their differences in ninety minutes of Gary Cooper. The boy whirled on the stairway, took two steps and leaped into space, landing gracefully, bolting for the street without breaking stride. On the street he paused, saw the familiar back of the Widow Kramer and was on her in an instant. Her mouth dropped open at his vehement shaking, but she nodded in understanding after he had said "Doctor—get a doctor" a sufficient number of times. The errand done, the boy whirled again and raced into the store, dropping to his knees beside the old body, lifting the old head, stroking the gray strands which were still wet from their dousing in the pickle barrel.

"To die smelling of garlic," Old Turk whispered. "For a delicatessen man, what could be more fitting?"

"You won't die," the boy said. "The Widow Kramer is getting you a doctor."

"The Widow Kramer? How fitting. Everything suddenly is fitting."

"Stop talking."

"Stop talking? Me stop talking? Are you trying to kill me?"

"Please."

"I believe," the old man whispered. "I believe I just said something funny."

"Yes. Very funny. So I don't have to laugh." He raised his head, trying to stare at the ceiling.

"Of course. Not when it's funny. You remem—Don't you dare. Don't you dare cry."

"I'm sorry," the boy whispered.

"Have we cared for each other?"

"Yes."

"Have we loved?"

"Yes. Yes."

"Then don't you dare cry. I will not have my death sullied. Not by you."

"The Widow Kramer is coming. With a fine doctor. This I know."

"Hearts wear. Mine is worn. A fault with the human mechanism. I'm seventy-two years old. Already I have bested the insurance companies. Not many can boast of besting the ins—" For a moment Turk could only gasp, his body suddenly tense, stiff, his eyes opening and closing in rhythm with the painful sounds. When he could speak again, his voice was half of what it was. "I'm dying, Rudy, I'm . . . dying and I want to . . . say something . . . wise but . . . nothing comes to mind. Smile on me . . . Rudy . . . beautiful Rudy, let me . . . see you smile . . ." The old eyes closed, and this time they did not open.

The boy waited for something, some sign. He held the body tightly in his arms. Then, when nothing happened, he riveted his eyes on the pickle barrel and began to rock silently, clutching the body and rocking, back and forth, back and forth, back—

"That is most uncomfortable," Old Turk said.

The boy looked down. "You didn't die."

"To my chagrin."

"You didn't die!"

"I swear I thought I was. I knew. In the movies they always know. Ronald Colman, he can always tell when he is dying. Spencer Tracy too. Leslie Howard. I wonder how they know in the movies? Edward G. Robinson, I like Edward G. Robinson, I have seen him die so many times, more than anybody. 'Mother of God, is this the end of Rico?' He said that and he died. How did he know? What a marvelous thing to say. I would also like to think of something marvelous. Say it and then die. Something memorable. Help me think of something memorable. Perhaps with a Biblical ring; that always lends authority. Perhaps . . ." And suddenly the gasping was back again, louder than before. "Rudy . . . Rudy . . . I've got to say . . . something . . ."

The gasping stopped. Nothing remained. The boy cradled the tired head. "Joel? Joel?" Nothing. "Please. For me. Joel? Don't die. I promise you the Widow Kramer comes. With the finest doctor in all the world. So please, Joel. Don't die. Please. Speak. A word. For me."

"I have never . . . been . . . so embarrassed in all my life."

The boy began to laugh.

"Go on. I deserve it."

"I'm sorry," the boy said.

"Where . . . the hell . . . is the Widow Kramer?"

"Perhaps you won't even need a doctor."

"That thought has crossed my mind, believe me. 'Your heart is fine,' he'll say. 'What you've got is indigestion. Too many pickles. Five dollars, please.'" Turk tried to shake his head. "I'm a fool. When a Jew is dumb, he's really dumb. There is a saying to that effect. Oh, I'm a fool. A fool."

"Tell me about your nose."

"I won it—"

"In a raffle. You've told me that one already. Tell me another."

"All right . . . I'll tell you the truth this time. The final truth. One day, when I was swimming in the desert—"

"*Swimming* in the *desert*?"

"It was the rainy season."

"Go on."

"And . . . Oh, oh, oh, my God . . . I'm wetting in my pants . . . just like a baby . . ."

The funeral arrangements fell to Sid, and they were one big irk. First of all, the old man was not at the top of Sid's hit parade. Oh, he was all right, a harmless gas bag, but bosom buddies they had never been.

And besides that, death had never much appealed to Sid. Not that anybody begged to lap it up with a spoon, but there were some, even many, who seemed not to mind the rituals—the keening, the floral decorations, the rabbinical razz-ma-tazz. Sid minded. He minded every stinking (his word, but admittedly an unfortunate choice) detail. More than anything, though, Sid minded Esther's attitude, for, after a lifetime of ignoring her father, suddenly, with the old man gone, their relationship overnight became the closest thing since God and Gideon. And what was so killing about her attitude was that it cost. Nothing was too good. The best, only, for the dearly departed. The thought of using the funeral parlor around the corner made Esther gag. No; Shapiro's had to do the stuffing. Shapiro's, the spiffiest ghoul spa on the entire South Side of Chicago. Young Shapiro himself handled the festivities and every rub of his manicured hands probably meant a fiver, every nod of his handsome greaseball head a ten-spot. The fact that it wasn't Sid's money mattered to him not at all. The old *cocker* was footing the bill for his own funeral, but when Sid tried preaching caution Esther only shouted, "It's his, shut up," because she was too dense to understand that what they were spending now would not, miracle-like, reappear untouched at the reading of the will. The estate was paltry to begin with, and with Esther digit-happy they were going to be lucky if a sou remained. So, when discussing caskets with his wife and young Shapiro, if Sid risked universal scorn by venturing to ask, Did the lining *have* to be of *quilted satin*, who could blame him?

After nearly three days of preliminaries they finally got around to the main event, which was held in a large room on Shapiro's second floor. Sid would have preferred something a little smaller, a cubicle maybe, since Shapiro's seemed to charge by the square foot, but Esther insisted on a big room, to accommodate all the mourners. Sid tried telling her not to expect the *entire* city of Chicago, lest the experience provide embarrassment as well as grief; Esther's only answer was a fervent "They'll come, they'll come," followed by a semistifled sob.

And they came. As Sid led his family into the second-floor room, he nodded in surprise, for the room was close to full. Customers all, and Sid recognized several of them from the agonizing hours he had spent the past few days minding the goddam store. Mrs. Kramer, Mrs. Feldman, Mrs. Katz, Rosenheim the laundryman. Not a multitude, but certainly a respectable turnout. I hope I do as well, Sid thought as he herded his tribe to the coffin. It was, on Esther's insistence, open, and neither Sid nor the boy had seen the old man since the demise. Esther, of course, had communed for hours the day before, weeping over the corpse while Sid had tended store. The old *cocker* looked unbelievably well, better than when alive almost, and Sid experienced a moment of something as he gazed down, because he realized then that Turk was indeed, as advertised, dead, really dead, finally and irrevocably dead: dead. Sid glanced at Esther, who stood by the coffin, Bravely Biting Her Lip, and then young Shapiro was gesturing to him. Sid approached the gravedigger, his hand moving protectingly to his wallet.

"Yes?" Sid whispered.

"Perhaps we could do something for the boy."

"What's wrong with the boy?"

The manicured fingers gestured toward the coffin. "Well, look at him."

"It's his first funeral. He'll get over it. Besides, he's not crying."

"Perhaps we could have him sit down. Generally, one is less affected when not actually viewing the deceased."

Sid walked back to the boy. "Come on, Rudy. Let's sit down." He tried to take his son's arm but the tiny fingers were tight around the coffin edge and would not move. "Rudy," Sid whispered. "Come now." The boy stayed where he was. Sid glanced toward young Shapiro and shrugged. Abruptly, the boy turned, and Sid said, "Come sit by me, Rudy," but the boy must not have heard, for he moved off by himself to the far end of the front row. Sid escorted Esther to the best seats in the house, front row center on the aisle, and they sat down. Sid looked around. It was all very impressive, but he wasn't impressed; his roving eye saw only bills. The hushed room cost money, the hard wooden chairs; the flowers cost, the organ music, the casket (mahogany yet), everything. Sid sighed. Then Rabbi Kornbluth was making with the Hebrew and everybody bowed, a few already practicing their sobs. Sid scowled at Rabbi Kornbluth; no wonder he drove a Packard. For what he charged he could have it gold-plated. Maybe I should have been a rabbi, Sid thought. A funeral specialist. Work just the spring and fall, then summer in the Catskills, winter in Miami Beach.

"We are here to honor Joel Turk," Rabbi Kornbluth said, switching tongues. "In all our lives we will have no more noble purpose."

Of course it would be tough to play around if you were a rabbi. If a broad shot off her mouth, it could ruin you; who wants a playboy rabbi? But if you wanted to play around, how could you do it? Without risk. A mistress? No; no good. One-shot jobs would be better. But the bitches might blackmail you. Kill the funeral racket. Maybe you could give them a phony name. Tell them you were a cloak-and-suiter. That might work. Or maybe—Sid stiffened in his chair. Because right then he saw it.

Turk's nose.

Curving up above the casket edge. Sid looked away, then back. It was still there. The nose. In full view of the audience. The nose. Just the nose. Sid almost laughed but managed to bite down on his lip in time. He lowered his head, fighting for control.

"I never had the pleasure of meeting Joel Turk," Rabbi Kornbluth said in his fine cantorial tone. "So in a sense I am saying hello to him today. But that is what we are all doing, saying hello. This is no time for goodbye. Joel Turk will stay in your hearts, just as he will stay in mine."

Sid raised his head quickly and peeked at the nose. Then more quickly he dropped his head again, biting down harder on his lip, causing himself mild pain. Couldn't they all see it? Couldn't everybody see it? Why weren't they laughing?

Somebody was.

Sid heard the sound at the same time Rabbi Kornbluth did. The rabbi had just said "In your faces I can see Joel Turk. Your eyes tell me everything. They tell me . . ." when he stopped, hearing the laughter. "They tell me that . . ." The laughter lingered. "That he was a fine boy," Rabbi Kornbluth said. "I mean man. A fine man."

Sid stared at his laughing son.

"The finest of men . . ."

The boy's laughter rang.

"A man who loved his fellows and his God. A man who laughed all . . . loved all living things . . ."

Sid looked at Esther, who was staring at the boy.

Sid looked away.

"A man who treated all men as equals, a man who felt superior to no one, inferior to nothing. A man . . ."

The boy could not stop laughing.

Rabbi Kornbluth took out a large white handkerchief and mopped his forehead.

Esther inhaled sharply, her eyes shut tight, her fingers suddenly digging at her temples.

"A man worthy of the name man. And now he is dead . . ."

Louder laughter.

"That is why we are here, because he is dead," Rabbi Kornbluth said, his voice rising.

Esther was gasping now, her face very pale.

"But he is not dead!" Rabbi Kornbluth raised his right hand high. "In your eyes I can see he lives on and so I say this to you: Joel Turk is alive!

The Rim Greaper will not have him!" Rabbi Kornbluth wiped his forehead vigorously. "Grim Reaper. The Grim Reaper will not have him . . ." He glared at the boy, who, helpless, could only laugh and shake his head.

Sid put his arm around Esther, listening as the rabbi droned on. She pressed her knuckles against her eyes, her head throbbing relentlessly. Rabbi Kornbluth switched back into Hebrew and Sid sighed with relief, feeling the end approaching. Then the rabbi was done. He walked over to Esther, said something and left the room. The organ music grew louder. Quietly the people filed out. When most of them were gone, Sid leaped up and ran to the boy, grabbing him by the arms, dragging him to his feet. "How could you laugh?" Sid said. "How?"

"The nose," the boy managed. "The nose."

"How could you laugh? I should beat you."

"The nose . . ."

"What nose? Oh, I should beat you. Look what you've done."

"It's for laughing. I couldn't stop, I just—"

Esther cried out then, lunging to her feet. Young Shapiro reached for her, but she shook loose and started toward the boy. One of her eyes was closed and the other could not stop blinking and the veins in her forehead throbbed. The boy retreated toward the casket but she followed him, closing the gap.

The boy reached out for the old man.

Then Esther was on him, forcing him to his knees, screaming "You killed me! You killed me!" until her voice was gone.

VII

Aaron despised Princeton University.

He had not wanted to go there at all, but none of the other colleges he applied to offered nearly so generous a scholarship, so Princeton it was. Aaron immediately opened hostilities. The other students had their hair cut short; he let his hair grow long and he kept it that way, dark and unruly, brushing it back only with his hands. They all dressed in dark gray or navy blue; Aaron bought a yellow corduroy jacket and wore it incessantly, until it became his trademark. In classes he was completely competitive, never caring what grade he received just so it was the highest in the course. Sometimes straight "A" was required, sometimes "A—" sufficed. The first semester of his sophomore year, Klein, a stubby scholar from Denver, was doing straight "A" work in Modern European History.

Aaron braced for the challenge, driving himself into the night, grinding, grinding. After the final examination the professor called him into his office.

"I could find nothing wrong with your paper," the professor said.

Aaron nodded. "I know."

"I don't believe in giving the grade of A plus . . ."

"But you're making an exception in my case."

"Yes."

"I deserved it," Aaron said and, abruptly, left the room.

For the first two years, he suffered no friends. Several made overtures, Klein among them, but he rebuffed them all, without thinking. "No, I'm busy. No, I'm busy then too. That's right. I'm busy." Aaron alone.

But that was before the coming of White.

He needed money. Always. For books. Books were his passion and he bought them a dozen at a time. His room at home was flooded with them. They spilled across the top of his desk, overflowed his shelves. He had stacks of books balanced on his windowsill, piles of books lining the floor by the edge of his bed. "Where are you ever going to get the time to read them all?" Charlotte would ask as he lugged home another armload. "Honestly, Aaron. Haven't you got enough books by now?"

"I'm paying for them," he would answer when he cared to answer at all. "It's my money."

Alone in his room, he would touch the clean jackets with the tips of his fingers, gently run the palm of his hand along the spine. Then he would read. He read them all, as fast as he could, carefully turning the pages, keeping them fresh and clean. He never felt as if he really owned a book until after he had read it through. Then it was his.

To get money, he typed. Themes, term papers, anything. He tacked little postcards up all around the campus with the words FIRESTONE TYPING SERVICE on the back. Beneath he put his phone number. He was a marvelous typist, and he would sit for hours hunched over his desk, head tilted to one side, a cigarette glued to a corner of his mouth. For a time he got enough money that way, but then, as his taste in books grew more expensive, he began seeking other work.

At the start of his senior year he took a job at the Nassau Food Shoppe. The fancy spelling was the idea of the owner, Mr. Akron, who had taken over when the old Nassau Food Shop had gone bankrupt seven years before. Mr. Akron added the two extra letters the day he took over, on the theory that it added, as he put it, "a toucha class." He was a dark, harried man and his real name was Akronopolos. The only distinguishing feature of the Nassau Food Shoppe, aside from the fact that its hamburgers were cooked in olive oil—Mr. Akron was a great believer in olive oil—was that it stayed open until two in the morning, much later than any of its competitors. Aaron worked from eleven till closing, which gave him time to catch the late movie at the Playhouse before reporting for duty. Aaron's domain was the soda fountain, at the front of the store, Mr. Akron himself handling the hot-foods department along the rear wall. "Not so much ice cream," he would shout at Aaron nightly, his voice booming across the booths and square tables that separated them. "Easy with that dipper." The customers during Aaron's working hours were almost all university students up late cramming for tests or finishing papers. Occasionally he would know one of them but mostly they were just faces. Sometimes the faces would whisper to him, "How about a little extra on the sundae?" and he would always reply, "A little extra for you, a little extra for me." They would either nod or shrug. If they nodded, he would pocket the nickel or dime they gave him; if they shrugged, he short-changed them on syrup. Either way, Aaron emerged victorious.

White found him one night in late November.

It had been snowing most of the day but that had stopped by nine o'clock. Now, well past midnight, it was clear out, clear and unseasonably cold. Whenever the front door of the store opened, Aaron glanced up, shivering. He hated winter. His body was too spare for winter. Aaron saw White when he came in, shrugged and went back to his reading. He always took a book with him on the job, propping it open on the counter, returning to it whenever he had a chance. He was aware that White was sitting across the counter from him, but he kept on reading, carefully finishing the paragraph, taking his time. Then he looked up.

"Something?"

"What's good?" White was wearing a dark tweed coat, buttoned to the throat. His hair was perfectly combed.

"Everything. You name it."

White drummed his fingers on the counter. "Make it a sundae."

"What kind?"

White smiled. "Surprise me."

O.K., Aaron thought. You want a surprise. You'll get a surprise. Grabbing a sundae dish, he moved to the ice-cream freezer. Deftly he dug out a large scoop of orange sherbet. Humming to himself, he covered the sherbet with a thick layer of butterscotch sauce. A mound of whipped cream and a cherry completed the job. Aaron set it down in front of White. *"Bon appetit,"* he said.

White nodded and fiddled with his spoon a moment. Then he began to eat. Aaron watched him. They had never spoken before—they were sharing Professor Haskell's class in essay writing that semester but they had never spoken. Aaron knew about him, though.

Hugh White was one of the two or three best-known students at Princeton. It was hardly surprising. To begin with, he had all the secondary virtues: he was a WASP in good standing. White Anglo-Saxon Protestant. His breeding was impeccable—his mother was a Boston Clarke. He dressed extremely well but casually. He was handsome, but his features were uneven, which only added to his attractiveness. He was athletic enough—a shoulder separation freshman year had ended a promising football career—and smart enough, friendly enough but not too friendly, modest but sincerely so. And of course he was rich. That was the primary virtue. Money. Uncountable money. His grandfather had founded White & Co. Steel before the turn of the century, and when the old man died, to the accompaniment of headlines all across the country, he was worth, conservatively, upward of seventy-five million dollars. Since that time, the steel business had improved. Hugh White was heir to it all.

Aaron loathed him on principle.

"What the hell is this?" Hugh White said, gagging on his sundae.

"Specialty of the house," Aaron replied. "Like it?"

"Not all that much."

"We call it 'Butterscotch Dream.' It's very popular."

"Do you charge money for it?"

"Two bits."

"Here."

Aaron took the dollar bill and rang it up on the cash register. He started back with the change.

"Keep it."

Aaron bowed. "Many thanks." He picked up his book and began to read. Once he looked up. White was watching him. Aaron concentrated on his reading. A little later three other boys came in and Aaron served them. Hugh White sat quietly, the sundae melting in front of him. Aaron stretched, then resumed his reading.

"Aaron?"

White was calling him. Aaron could feel himself starting to flush, so he kept his head down, staring at the glazed print until it was safe to look up. He was surprised that White knew his name. Surprised and undeniably pleased.

"Hey, Aaron?"

"What?"

"Like to talk to you."

"Talk to me."

"Not here."

"Why?"

Hugh gestured toward the three boys down the counter. "It's a little crowded."

"Oh, I get it," Aaron said. "We're playing Spy." He lowered his voice, speaking in a hurried whisper. "The secret formula is E equals MC squared. Pass it on."

"You finished?"

"Momentarily."

"Then let's take a walk."

"I'm working."

"It'll only take a minute."

Aaron lighted a cigarette. "You're ... uh ... I forget your name. You're ..."

"Hugh White."

Aaron shrugged. Eat that, you bastard.

"Ready?"

"Mr. Akronopolos," Aaron called out.

"Akron. Akron, not Akronopolos."

"I'm going out for a minute, Mr. Akronopolos." Grabbing his coat, he rounded the counter to the front door. Hugh held it open for him and they stepped into the cold, walking slowly along Nassau Street. "All right," Aaron said. "What?"

"You know that essay we've got due tomorrow?"

Aaron nodded.

"What did you write on?"

"Something or other," Aaron answered. "I forget."

"I couldn't find much time to do one," Hugh White said.

"My heart," Aaron said, "is bleeding."

Hugh stopped. Aaron was shivering with the cold. "Here," Hugh said. "Throw this on." Unbuttoning his coat, he handed it to Aaron. Aaron felt the soft, rich tweed a moment, then slung the coat around his shoulders. "I like this kind of weather," Hugh explained.

Aaron said nothing.

"About that essay."

"What about it?"

"How about letting me have it?"

"You mean to copy? Are you crazy? No."

"I wasn't exactly thinking of copying it."

Aaron waited.

"I thought you might give it to me."

"Give it to you? Why the hell should I?"

"Ten bucks," Hugh White said, holding two fives in his open hand.

"Thanks for the use of the coat." Aaron handed it back to him.

"I need that essay, Aaron."

"Write one, like the rest of the commoners."

"There's not enough time for me to. But you could, Aaron. You're a smart guy. You could knock one off tonight after you quit work. It doesn't matter what you hand in. You know that. You've got the prof buffaloed. You'll get your A."

"Go to hell."

"Would twenty dollars change your mind?" He started reaching for his wallet.

"No."

"Twenty-five, then." He pulled the money out. "Twenty-five dollars, Aaron. You can use twenty-five dollars, can't you?"

Aaron stared at the money.

"Twenty-five dollars. I really need that essay, Aaron. I haven't been doing so well in that course lately. So how about it?"

Aaron grabbed at the money, folding it up, shoving it into his pants pocket. "You son of a bitch," he said. "You know I'm broke."

"I'll stay in the food shop while you get it."

"I'll give it to you before class."

"I don't think so. Somebody might just see us. It's better if you get it for me now. I'll wait."

Aaron turned, hurrying down Nassau Street toward his house. "Thanks a lot, Aaron," Hugh called after him. "And take your time. No hurry."

Oh, you bastard, Aaron thought. You rich bastard. He kicked at the snow as he moved along, furious at what he had done. Yanking the money from his pocket, he counted it. Twenty-five dollars. You could buy a lot of books for twenty-five dollars. Aaron spit. Lighting a cigarette, he inhaled viciously. He was blind mad. Goddam White. Goddam all the rich ones. Aaron flung his cigarette into the snow. He was almost to his house before he realized that what riled him was not that he had sold out but that he had sold out so cheaply.

Whoever bought him next time was going to pay.

•

He worked most of that night completing a new paper. It was after two when he started and he was tired so the work went slowly. Then, around three, he remembered what White had said. "You've got the prof buffaloed. You'll get an A." It was true, of course. Aaron knew that, but he had never taken advantage of it. Now he decided to. Carefully placing a cigarette in the corner of his mouth, he half closed his eyes and typed a quick six-page essay on the joys of bird watching in Princeton. Finished, he read it aloud, laughing, retyped it carefully and went to bed.

White was waiting for him when he got to class, pacing beside the entrance to the classroom. "Morning," White said.

Aaron hurried into class without answering.

When the class was over he left the building and was halfway down the steps when White caught up to him.

"Aaron. Hey, Aaron."

Aaron slowed. "What?"

"That was a good paper you gave me. Really good."

"How would you know?"

"I read it. Twice."

"Then your lips must be tired," Aaron said. "Now if you'll excuse me," and he turned right, heading for the library. He took notes in the library for close to an hour, and when he came out White was waiting.

"Now, look," Aaron began.

"Will you let me talk?"

"Talk."

"Well—" Hugh shrugged—"I thought maybe we might get to know each other a little."

"Not in the Biblical sense, I trust. My mother's told me about boys like you."

"Will you cut it out?"

"I didn't start this conversation, you remember?"

Three seniors sauntered by, going to the library. "Hugh, boy," one of them said. Hugh nodded to them.

"Listen," he said when they were gone.

"Why? You don't say anything. And I'm getting cold standing here."

"Let's go for some coffee, then."

"I don't want coffee," Aaron said. "I've lived twenty years without you. I can probably continue for a while longer."

"I have a tremendous desire," Hugh said, "to clobber you right on the nose."

"If you do I'll never wash it again. I promise."

"Look—"

"What do I need you for? The only answer I can come up with is material. I might want to write about the other half someday. I'm always on the lookout for material. But there are limits."

"What have you got against me?"

"The way you dress, just for openers. You're so casual it makes me sick. The way you walk. You swagger."

"Go on."

"The way you always look people in the eye when you're talking to them. I'll bet you've got a firm handshake. If you do, I hate that too. I hate the way you look." Aaron warmed to the task. "I hate the way you talk. I hate the way people try sitting beside you in class. I hate the way they whisper to you, hoping you'll laugh. I hate the girls you bring down here; they're too pretty and they smile at you. Everybody's always smiling at you and I could do with less of that. I hate your money and your social background and I hate the humble act you're always putting on. I even hate your name. Hugh." Aaron said it nasally, tauntingly. "Hugh. Hugh."

"It stands for Hubert! I used to get picked on in grammar school because of my name. Hubert! What's so goddam good about Hubert?"

Aaron laughed. Hugh smiled.

Then they went for coffee.

"C," Hugh said. "You get an A on a piece of junk about bird watching and the son of a bitch gives me a C." It was a week later and they had just got their essays back.

"Can I help it if the teacher happens to be a bird watcher?"

They walked out of the building and down the steps. The day was sunny and cool but not cold. They paused a moment at the bottom of the steps, then started aimlessly across campus.

"God," Hugh said.

Aaron looked at him, then away. Briefly he wondered if Hugh was going to hit something, or burst into tears, or both. "Go buy yourself something in cashmere, Hubert. It'll cheer you."

"Don't," Hugh said. "Just don't."

Aaron shrugged. "I've got to go to the library."

"I'm mad, Aaron. Can't you see that?"

"Yes."

"I'm really mad."

"My mother always says if you do a good deed you'll feel better."

"You don't have to go to the library."

"No."

"Let's walk then."

They moved in silence for a while, circling down past the gym, along the tennis courts, then up toward Nassau Street.

"It was a good paper," Hugh said finally.

"But you didn't write it. I did. I'm the one that ought to be angry."

"Everything's set!" Hugh cried suddenly, whirling on Aaron. "Don't you see that? My whole life is set. It's like a maze. There's only one opening and I've got to follow along. I've bought papers before. Just to prove it to myself. It always turns out the same. It doesn't matter what I do. It's set. Don't you see?"

"I find it difficult to sympathize," Aaron answered, "with either the rich or the beautiful."

"I don't want sympathy. Just understand, that's all. We all of us could use a little understanding."

"Yes." Aaron nodded. "That we could." They began to walk again, slowly, changing direction, heading south, then east, wandering. The sun was warm for November. Hugh took off his coat and threw it casually over his shoulder.

"You don't like the maze, get out of the maze."

"Sure."

"What's stopping you?"

"I'm weak, Aaron. I am not strong."

"Take vitamin pills."

Hugh smiled. "It's very hard, Aaron. Try to believe that. It's very hard. Look. When I was sixteen, I got our chauffeur's daughter in trouble."

"That was precocious of you."

Hugh ignored him. "It was a terrible thing to do. For all kinds of reasons but mainly because I liked her. A lot. We'd sort of grown up together and we were close. But anyway, I did it to her and when she told me I wanted to die. I was sixteen, remember, a kid and I had sinned and when you do that you get punished. It doesn't matter if you're rich or not, God punishes you. That's what I thought. I stayed up all that night, on my bed, trembling, trying to figure out what to do. Because Deedee was pregnant and it was my fault and I had to set it right." Hugh stopped talking.

"What happened?" Aaron said.

"I'm just trying to get it straight." He closed his eyes a moment. "Yes. The second night. It was the second night after I'd found out and I was up in my room when my father came in. He was wearing an ascot—that was during his ascot phase. His tailor had told him they were coming back, so he wanted to beat the fad. We look a lot alike, my father and me. We're both of us brown, brown eyes, brown hair. Well, he came in. I nodded to him, waiting for him to say something. He fiddled with his ascot a while—it was on straight but he fiddled with it anyway—and then he cleared his throat. I just waited.

" 'I know about your difficulty,' my father said.

" 'Oh?' That was all I could answer because I was so happy. Because I knew I was going to get punished. For what I had done.

"He cleared his throat. 'You should be more careful, Hugh.'

" 'Yes,' I said. 'Yes, sir.'

"Then, as I was watching, he turned and went to the door. He got it half open before he said anything more. Then, just before he left me, he said it. His back was to me and he said, 'It's all been taken care of.'

"That was it. 'It's all been taken care of.' And the next morning when I came downstairs it was. The chauffeur was gone. Deedee was gone. A new chauffeur came that afternoon. Life went on. I found out later that what happened was father had given Deedee's old man a chunk of money and some reference letters and had paid for anything medical. As simple as that. Everybody parted happy. Nobody ever talked to me about it again. In a couple of months I began to wonder myself whether it had really happened or not."

"End of story?" Aaron asked.

Hugh nodded. "But don't you see? Why it's hard? Everything's been taken care of for me. I don't have to want anything. I'll get it anyway. That's why I need a creep like you around."

"You go too far."

"Oh, let's face it, Aaron: if they had a National Creep Championship you'd win in a walk. My God, walking around the way you do with your hair long enough to mow and that unbelievable yellow jacket. You might as well have 'I am a creep' sewed on the back."

"That jacket, knucklenose, happens to be a beacon of independence in a dark sea of Harris tweed."

"Only a creep would say a thing like that."

"Your mind is not at its best with subtleties."

"I need guys like you. It's nutty but I keep hoping you'll maybe help me. Osmosis, I don't know. You want things, Aaron. I don't. But I'd like to."

"That sound you just heard was my heart breaking."

Hugh White smiled.

From the moment they began being seen together—and they were together constantly—Aaron's position on campus abruptly changed. Boys who were never aware of his existence suddenly knew his name and called out to him as he passed; as he stood outside of classrooms, smoking, other boys came up to him and started conversations, asking questions about assignments. People were talking about him, nodding their heads in his direction. Of course he pretended not to notice and was as curt with everyone as he had been before, not returning their hellos, shrugging to their questions. He really didn't care about the simpering bastards. What he did care about was Hugh. But that was not surprising.

Twenty years had been a long time to go without a friend.

One December afternoon, as they were walking toward the library, Hugh said, "You do like girls."

Aaron burst out laughing. "Do I like girls? You're goddam right I do." He lighted a cigarette, jamming it into the corner of his mouth. "What makes you ask a thing like that?"

"No reason."

"Because I haven't been dating much lately? Is that it? Well, hell, that's just because I've been a little low on funds. Hell, I like girls as well as the next guy."

"Let's double sometime then. O.K.?"

"Great by me," Aaron answered. "Let's do that."

One night early in February they were studying in Hugh's room, Aaron sprawled on the bed, Hugh at the desk, reading. Aaron stretched. "I ought to be getting down to the Food Shoppe."

Hugh looked up from his book. "Already?"

Aaron nodded, sitting up. "It's about that time."

"Hey," Hugh said. "Your mother. What's she doing Saturday night?"

"Why? You want to date her? Don't you think she's a little old for you?"

"Just tell me what she's doing?"

"Same thing she always does Saturday nights. Baby sitting with Debby and Dominic's kid, over in New Brunswick."

"Then your house is available?"

"Available?"

"Empty."

"Yes."

Hugh nodded. "Excellent."

"Why?" Aaron began gathering his books.

"Because we've got dates Saturday night, Aaron. You and me. It's all fixed up."

Aaron smiled. "When did this all happen?"

"I've been researching the subject for quite some time. Trying to find just the perfect maiden for a creep like you. At long last I believe I have succeeded."

"I wish you'd told me about it, Hubert. Dammit. I can't go Saturday."

"Will it change your mind if I tell you this girl is absolutely guaranteed to do the trick, and no guilt feelings whatsoever?" Hugh laughed. "I ever tell you about this buddy of mine who was working in a bookstore— this is true, I swear—anyway, he answered the phone one day and there was this lady on the other end and she said, 'Pardon me, but do you have *Sex without Guilt?*' and my buddy said, 'Sometimes.' "

Aaron laughed and laughed. "No kidding? He really said that?"

Hugh raised his right hand. "Word of honor."

"What a great thing to say," Aaron went on. "That's really funny. No kidding." He burst out laughing again. " 'She asked if he had *Sex without Guilt* and he—' "

"Quit stalling and tell me you'll come."

Aaron put on his coat. "I'd really love to; I can't."

"Aaron," Hugh said, "this girl is right for you. I just know it. I've done a major screening process, Aaron. I wouldn't get you with anybody you might get embarrassed about. I mean that. This girl is bright enough and terribly friendly. A little sick maybe, I'll admit that, but that's not the end of the world—so are you."

"It sounds like a lot of fun. I'm sorry."

"Aaron, I know you're shy, it's all right. I took everything into consideration, believe that."

"I said I'm sorry. I can't go."

"Why?"

"Busy."

"Doing what?"

"That's my business."

"You're scared, aren't you? Don't be. It'll work out fine."

"No!" Aaron lowered his voice. "What the hell's to be afraid of? I just don't like blind dates. They bore me."

"Then you're not busy."

"I am."

"Aaron . . ."

"Goddammit, goddammit, quit pestering me. I said I was busy and I mean it. Busy. Now let it drop."

"Sure," Hugh said. He looked at the book he was reading. "It was a silly-assed idea, me springing it on you. Forget it."

Aaron opened the door. "Some other time we'll double. O.K.?"

"Sure. Great. Whatever you say."

"Coming down later for a Butterscotch Dream?"

"I imagine." Hugh waved.

Aaron closed the door. He started to walk, then paused a moment, leaning against the wall. He looked at his hands. They were shaking.

Why?

What was he afraid of?

Aaron lit a cigarette and decided to play Name That Fear. He walked slowly down the corridor, the cigarette jammed into the far corner of his mouth, his eyes half closed. Your friend fixes you up on a blind date, so why, Aaron old creep, do you become unstrung? Honest now. Let the studio audience hear your answer. Aaron left the building and stood outside in the chill air. He took a step, then stopped.

It was his goddam passion for perfection that was screwing him up.

Aaron nodded. That was why he was afraid. What if he tried hard to impress the girl and she didn't like him? What if he broke his butt and then he didn't like her? There were a hundred chances for disaster, few if any for success, so what was the point of getting involved in something if you knew ahead of time you were going to bomb? He had an image of himself, so what was the percentage in allowing some dumb broad to shatter it?

What if she didn't like him?

What if she didn't like him?

It was as simple as that, so he re-entered the building, hurried down the corridor to Hugh's door, threw it unceremoniously open and said, "The thing is I hate blind dates. If I said yes, it would just be a fiasco—she'd probably hate me and I'd hate her and you'd feel lousy even though it wasn't your fault. I want to really thank you, though. For thinking of me. That was nice and if I didn't hate blind dates the way I do—"

Hugh stood. "Aaron? You O.K.?"

"For chrissakes of course I'm O.K., goddammit. I'm only trying to explain how I hate blind dates. She would probably abominate the hell out of me and vice versa. I can be very caustic, especially around blind dates and—"

"Aaron, it doesn't matter. You don't have to explain. It's my fault. I should have asked you instead of sneaking around making surprises."

"How do you know she'll like me? When you get right down to it, how can you absolutely prove she's going to like me?"

"I can't *prove* it."

"Well then, see?" Aaron put his hand to the doorknob, started to close the door, stopped. "You'd be along, wouldn't you?"

"I usually am when I double date with somebody."

Aaron stood very still. Then he shook his head. "Nope," he said, "It just wouldn't work. I don't know why I should feel sorry except I sort of feel sorry putting you out after you've gone all through this legendary screening process. If I said, 'Hey, let's go pee on Nassau Hall' and you didn't much feel like it you'd be kind of a creep to feel sorry about not going along, isn't that right?"

Hugh mimed a telephone in his hands. "Let me speak to Karl Menninger," he said.

Aaron roared appreciative laughter, quickly closed the door. In the hall he examined his hands. They were very wet and they would not stay still. Aaron closed his eyes. "Hubert!" He realized he was yelling but he just couldn't care.

"Yes, Aaron?" Hugh's voice was muffled from inside the room.

"About Saturday?"

"What about Saturday?"

Aaron paused. Then the words burst from him. "I'll go, Hubert. With you, Hubert. I'll go . . ."

There were twenty-five boys waiting at the railroad station on Saturday afternoon when Hugh and Aaron arrived. Some of the boys were walking; others stood alone or in groups. From time to time they all, casually, glanced at their watches.

"We made it in time," Aaron said.

"Minutes to spare," Hugh told him. They began to pace.

Aaron stopped abruptly. "How do I look?" he said.

Hugh smiled at him. "Not nearly as creeplike as usual."

Aaron was wearing a new pair of gray flannel trousers, neatly pressed and a new tweed jacket. "I should have worn my yellow cord. I would have felt better if I'd worn my yellow cord." He ran his fingers through his hair. His hair was shorter—he had had it cut that morning, much against his better judgment. "I should never have let you talk me into a haircut. It makes my head look pointed."

"This girl loves pointed heads. She's told me as much."

"You sure she wants to meet me?"

Hugh put his arm around Aaron's shoulder. "Yes, yes, yes, for the ninety-ninth time, yes. She's crazy for writers."

"I forgot her name already."

"Shelly. Her name is Shelly."

"How do I look?" Aaron said.

Hugh sighed.

Aaron looked around. All the other boys were pacing now, back and forth along the platform, smoking cigarettes, staring out along the track. Aaron lighted a cigarette and stuck it in the corner of his mouth. It was a cool day, clear, but with a hint of approaching snow.

Casually, Hugh stuck his right hand into his pants pocket.

Aaron paused, then did the same. He looked around again. All the other boys had their right hands in their pants pockets. Hugh paced faster and Aaron hurried alongside.

"Shelly what?"

"Bingham."

"Shelly Bingham." Aaron nodded. "And she's pretty?"

"I think so."

"Good." Hugh had his left hand in his left pants pocket now, so Aaron did the same. He glanced at the other boys. There was not a hand to be seen on the platform.

Everybody stopped.

"Train's coming," Hugh said.

And suddenly the hands reappeared, flying through the air, tugging at trousers, straightening ties, smoothing down hair. Then, like dive bombers, the hands swooped low, disappearing again into pockets.

The train was pulling into the station.

Aaron grabbed Hugh, turning him. "It's going to be all right," he shouted over the noise. "Tell me that."

"What? Yes. Yes. Relax."

"Promise me."

Hugh looked at him. "I promise you." There was a pause.

Then chattering, shrieking, the girls swarmed from the train.

She was really quite a pretty girl. Tall with long brown hair, she had a delicate face, an ample body. Aaron walked beside her, following a few steps behind Hugh and his date as they crossed from the station to the Princeton Inn. Hugh's date, a dark, taut girl named Tony, clung to him as they moved, looking up at him, smiling. Aaron turned his attention to Shelly Bingham.

Shelly was from the South, New Orleans, to be exact. She pronounced it "N'awlins." And her "Daddy" was in the cotton business. She loved her daddy, her mommy, too. As he listened to her, Aaron realized that the girl seemed to love everything. She loved the East and she loved Sarah Lawrence, which was the most wonderful school in the entire world, didn't he think so? Aaron nodded. Shelly and Tony were friends at Sarah Lawrence, but then everybody at Sarah Lawrence was friends with everybody else. That was what made it so wonderful. Aaron smiled as she rattled on. She was wild about Princeton and simply ecstatic about being back again and so glad to meet him, Hugh had spoken about him so much. Hugh was a dear, didn't he think so? Aaron said he thought so. And she was so happy to meet a fellow writer. She herself was a poetess of sorts. She laughed. Poetess. Such a funny-sounding word. Aaron smiled. She loved Aaron's name. It sounded like a writer's name and that was probably why she loved it. "*Ay*-ron," she said. "*Ay*-ron Fahstone." Without warning, she smiled and took his hand.

She liked him.

She liked him.

So why was he still afraid?

They had cocktails at the Princeton Inn, two drinks apiece, and then slowly made their way into the main dining room. Shelly had another drink; Aaron joined her. He drank and he smiled and he talked, but all the while he was playing the game again, Name That Fear, and he was just finishing his shrimp cocktail when the answer came to him. She was a warm girl, a girl who was absolutely guaranteed to do the trick. Later, in his house, they would be alone; Hugh would go off to another room with Tony and then they would be alone, he and Shelly, and she would look at him and she would smile at him and she would expect things of him.

And what if he couldn't perform?

He had heard stories about that. One concerned a Princeton boy who had pursued a Barnard girl for three years, always hoping, and then, then, the night she relented, that moment as she lay naked beside him, *he couldn't perform*. Aaron sipped his water, put it down, picked up his drink, finished it off and ordered another. If he couldn't perform, then Shelly might tell Tony and Tony might tell Hugh and Hugh wouldn't tell but Tony might date other boys, Shelly too, and they would tell the other boys and then everyone would know and then everyone would laugh and I'm scared, Aaron thought. I'm just so scared.

What if I can't?

What if I can't?

Please, God.

As dinner went on, Aaron began telling tales about his mother, Charlotte Stories, most of them imaginary, and everyone laughed and Shelly was smiling at him almost all the time and he returned it, talking and laughing, and when dinner was done he excused himself and fled to the men's room, where he carefully washed his face, taking his time, pressing cool water against his fevered skin.

"You really are shy around girls," Hugh said, standing behind him, smiling. "One thing about you, Aaron, is you have absolutely no way with women."

"You know how it is," Aaron said casually.

"Just keep your hands off my date," Hugh said. "I want to tell you that rarely have I met a creep so reeking with charm."

"She does like me, doesn't she?" Aaron said.

"No, she hates you." Hugh slugged Aaron on the arm. "Creep." Together they walked back to the girls, then made their way to Hugh's eating club on Prospect. There was a dance that night, and Aaron watched as Hugh took Tony in his arms and danced away. Aaron paused, then took Shelly in his arms. He had learned to dance from his sister, who used him to practice with when no one else was available, and he danced well enough. Shelly's body was heavy against his. Pressing. After one dance Aaron asked if they might sit, explaining about his legs, how they sometimes hurt. Shelly was immediately sympathetic, so they sat in a corner of the room, watching the others. Shelly was quite drunk and Aaron forced himself to listen as she explained that she really didn't love her father because what he was was a no-good bastard and her mother wasn't much more than that and she talked on and on and then Hugh was beside them, suggesting to Aaron that they take a little trip to Aaron's house. Aaron stood. Slowly they climbed the hill from Prospect to Nassau Street, Hugh and Tony in front, Aaron and Shelly a few steps behind. Maybe his mother had come back early. Sometimes she did that. Once. Once she had done it. Perhaps tonight would be the second time. The lights would be on and she would be sitting in the living room, knitting something for Deborah's child. A sweater or a pair of socks or—

The house was dark.

They walked inside. "Nobody's home, I guess," Aaron said. "How's that for luck?"

They sat in the living room a while, talking. Aaron asked if anyone wanted a drink and Shelly said she wouldn't mind a wee one, so he went to the kitchen and slowly made two highballs. When he returned they talked some more. Tony was all over Hugh now, running her hands along his body, kissing his neck. Then Hugh stood. "Excuse us a while," he said. He and Tony disappeared into Deborah's old room. The door closed.

"We're all alone," Shelly said.

Aaron made a smile. What if I can't? What if I can't? *Please, God.* "Drink O.K.?"

"Fine."

Aaron took a long swallow. "I could use a little freshener," he said, and he stood.

She drained the glass. "As long as you're headed in that general direction . . ."

Aaron went to the kitchen. Slowly he got out an ice tray. He reached for the bottle of whisky and poured the drinks.

Then Shelly was in the doorway. "I got lonesome," she said.

"With you in a sec," Aaron said, fiddling with a long spoon, trying to stir the highballs. He could feel her standing close behind him now, moving in. Her arms went around his chest. Aaron waited.

"You must swear never to let me get lonesome again," Shelly said. "On your sacred word of honor. I'll never release you until you do."

"I swear," Aaron whispered.

She relaxed her hold and he spun around, eyes closed, blindly reaching out for her, pulling her body in toward him. He kissed her brutally, holding the kiss for as long as he could before breaking it, burying his face in her neck, kissing her hair. He kissed her ear and then her cheek before attacking her mouth again. Her arms were tight around him and they battled with their tongues. This time she was the one who broke, throwing her head back, smiling up at him.

"Hey, lover," Shelly said.

He smiled back at her and he rubbed his hands across her full body and he bit her neck but he felt nothing. No excitement, nothing at all, and he knew unless he could feel he would never be able to perform and he told himself that everything would be fine if he would just give himself time, time, but even in that moment he knew he had never been so frightened in his life, nor would he ever be again. But he was wrong. His fear was just beginning.

Because slowly, arms tight around him, she began to lead him to the bedroom.

She undressed in the dark and as she did he periodically attacked her body, caressing her breasts, her thighs, her gently rounded stomach. When she was naked he took off his clothes and then they embraced, standing by the bed. Aaron bit her lip and she winced, pulling back a moment before dragging him down on the sheets. Horizontal, the combat continued. Viciously, Aaron kissed her. Again and again he touched her breasts and fingered her soft thighs. Then, when he knew he was going to scream, he jammed his mouth down on hers and held it there until the scream died inside him.

"You're pretty," Aaron whispered then. Please, God. "You are. You're so pretty. You're pretty." Please, God.

He felt nothing. Nothing. Aaron kissed her breasts. They felt like clay. In the darkness he could see her looking at him. In the darkness he could sense her starting to pull away. Ferociously Aaron attacked her, rolling across the bed, kicking and biting, groaning for her benefit, saying her name, "Shelly, Shelly," over and over. Mechanically his hands journeyed along her body, and he continued whispering her name, louder, and he groaned and panted and sucked in air. But he felt nothing. Nothing. Nothing at—

Quite without warning he began to feel.

His eyes shut so tightly they hurt, Aaron shrieked as the excitement grew inside him, swelling like a blister, filling his body. He kissed lips—but in his mind, not her lips. He touched flesh—but in his mind, flesh other than hers.

Hugh!

It was Hugh he was touching. Hugh was beside him. Hugh was the one who was breathing his name. Aaron knelt over the other figure.

In rhythm, their bodies rocked.

VIII

"Osric!" Walt said. "Me play Osric? I auditioned to play Hamlet." He turned to the girl at his side. "Say something."

"Something," Blake said.

"You're a scream, you are. Maybe it's a mistake, do you think it's a mistake?" and he turned back to the bulletin board, turned faster than was necessary because although he thought he was probably too funny-looking to play the title role in the Oberlin College production of *Hamlet*, he had still worked very hard on the part and had given the best audition of his life, so he hoped he had a chance but now, the way things turned out, he was embarrassed and humiliated and afraid Blake might see. And if she did, he knew she would never be able to resist embarrassing him still further. Pushing his glasses up snug against the bridge of his nose with his left thumb, he squinted at the notice:

SPRING PLAY—FINAL CASTING

HAMLET...*Dennis McBride*
CLAUDIUS...*Edward Neisser*

The final listing, at the very bottom of the page, said:

OSRIC ....*Walt Kirgaby*

An additional half page, tacked to the bottom, was filled entirely by Hilton's curlicued signature: *B. Henry Hilton,* PROFESSOR OF ENGLISH.

"That lousy Hilton," Walt murmured. "He even spelled my name wrong."

"Come along, Osric," Blake said, tugging at his arm. "Buy me a hamburger and a milk shake."

Walt stayed where he was, staring at the bulletin board, shaking his head.

"Hey, you're upset," Blake said.

"Nope."

"Yes, you are, you are too."

"I'm *not* upset. It's just that I'm a senior and this is my last play and Osric—well, let's face it, Osric's just about the smallest part in the play—I mean, Osric! He's got about six stinkin' lines. *Six lines.* Well, I just won't play it, that's all, I mean, who does Hilton think he's dealing with, some freshman? I'm not remotely upset, but if you want to know the truth, when you audition to play Hamlet and get stuck with the smallest part in the play it's a little bit upsetting, especially when you've played more leads than anybody else has over the last four years, isn't that right? Who starred in *Charley's Aunt* this fall?"

"That was a comedy, Egbert. You do comedy. Hamlet ain't supposed to be funny. And now I want *two* hamburgers and a milk shake."

"I mean, if you were casting *Hamlet,* would you have me play Osric?"

"Of course not."

"Well, neither would I, so how come that crummy Hilton—"

"Personally, I think you'd make a great Ophelia."

"Will you shut up, please?"

"Let's be honest, you're too young to play the Queen."

"Y'know, whoever told you you were funny did us all a vast disservice."

"I want two hamburgers and a milk shake and a plate of French fries."

"I did one of those soliloquies for you. I wasn't bad. I wasn't. Say that."

"That."

"Why have I dated you all year?"

"I think you keep hoping I'll put out."

"C'mon," Walt muttered and he started abruptly for the door.

Blake caught him. "Now don't get mad."

"I'm sorry, but I just don't like that kind of talk. I must have told you at least fifty thousand times that I don't happen to find it hilarious, so why do you keep doing it?"

"When you get angry it proves you care. It proves you love me."

"Who said I loved you?"

"You did, buddy."

"Will you quit with the 'buddy' business? I mean, we've all read Salinger. Most of us have managed to outgrow him."

"Oh, 'fess up, secretly you think you're Holden Caulfield. Ask me where the ducks go in the winter."

"When did I say I loved you?"

"Last night. In front of the dorm. At precisely eleven fifty-two P.M."

"I don't remember."

"You said, 'I love you, Blake.' "

"Oh, *now* I remember. Sure. I was talking about William Blake, the poet. I just love William Blake's poetry. And you thought I was talking about *you*? Pardon me while I chuckle."

She nipped his ear.

"Hey—"

"I told you I was hungry."

Walt opened the door and held it while they adjusted their raincoats. Outside, the campus was intermittently visible through the gray afternoon drizzle. "What I'll miss most about Oberlin is the climate," Walt said, letting the door slam behind him. They hurried across campus toward the town. "I *should have played Hamlet!*" Walt shouted. "*I'm an actor.*"

Blake snickered. "My own little Dame May Whitty," she said.

"What's so crazy about it? I think it's a terrific idea." Walt banged his spoon against the tabletop for emphasis.

"Put on our own revue? Where'll we get the material?"

"Write it. And what we can't write, we'll steal from Sid Caesar. I know about twenty sketches he and Coca've done that'd be great." He leaned back in the booth, smiling. "And you know what else we'll do? We'll run it the same week as *Hamlet*. We'll steal their audiences. Bankrupt the Dramat. Nobody casts me as Osric and gets away with it."

"Revues have songs, buddy."

"Well, you make up poems, don't you? You play the piano, right? Aren't you always blabbing about how creative you are? Write some songs."

"I have never, in my entire life, blabbed."

"Will you just write some songs, please? Better make them funny."

"Aye, aye, sir, right away, sir, funny songs coming right up. Can we get Kazan to direct, do you think?"

"*I'll* direct the show, if you don't mind."

"Ho-ho-ho."

"Why do you always have to knock me? It so happens I am one helluva director."

"You've never directed anything in your whole life."

"I have too."

"What?"

"Plenty of things."

"Name one."

"That's not the point, don't you see? The point is, I've always wanted to be a director. I've thought about it, I've read about it, I know I can do it."

"I thought you were an actor."

"Acting," Walt said. "Who needs acting? As a matter of fact, if you want to know the truth, acting is a drag. It's not creative. You can't express yourself. All you do is spiel off something somebody else put down. But directing. That's something. In the immortal words of Peter Lorre—"

"If you start with your imitations, I'll throw up all over you."

"You don't like my imitations?"

"I loathe your imitations."

"It so happens I do terrific imitations."

"It so happens you think you do terrific imitations."

"It so happens you are asking for a belt right in the snoot, sister."

"It so happens I'm out of cigarettes." She reached across the table for Walt's pack.

Walt grabbed his cigarettes and put them in his pocket.

"Could I have one of your cigarettes?"

"Say please."

"Could I please have one of your cigarettes?"

"No."

"Will you get me a pack?"

"Will you give me the money?"

"Here," and she slapped a quarter on the table.

"Do you love me?"

"I refuse to answer on the grounds—"

"Do you love me?"

"Yes—madly."

"Get your own cigarettes."

"I have got to be part masochist. That's the only explanation." She pushed herself out of the booth.

"Hey." Walt took her hand tenderly.

"What hey?"

"Last night," Walt whispered, looking in her eyes. "Last night, when I said 'I love you, Blake,' I wasn't talking about William Blake."

She smiled at him.

"I was talking about Francis Blake."

She stopped smiling. "Who the hell is Francis Blake?"

"The Spanish Armada, fool. Fifteen eighty-eight. He saved England."

"That was Drake. Francis Drake."

"That's what I said. Francis Blake. I have a speech impediment."

"Whoever told you you were funny—"

"Yeah-yeah-yeah, a vast disservice." He ducked as she swiped at the top of his head, starting to laugh, the laugh contracting into a smile as he watched her move down the aisle toward the cigarette machine. She moved well. About that there was no question. She wasn't pretty, but she moved well. Why wasn't she pretty? Walt shrugged. She had nice black hair and bright eyes and a straight nose and the mouth was fine, but she just wasn't pretty. Not bad. Not remotely a dog. Just not pretty. Damn attractive, though. Her body was fine, slender yet full, but that wasn't what made her attractive. Probably it was the way she moved. Walt nodded. Her movements were graceful yet, at the same time, almost awkward; her movements were sudden yet, at the same time, almost languid; her movements were . . . Face it, Walt thought, she's sexy. That's all. She is a sexy girl. Of course, her name was terrible. Blake Simmons. How phony can you get? But she was smart as hell and sexy every inch of the way. Walt remembered Christmas vacation when she had visited him in St. Louis and how his brother Arnold had watched her when she walked. Walt had seen it, Arnold's lust, and once, when P.T. was watching her,

Walt thought momentarily that even his father had a couple of ideas of his own.

As she reached the cigarette machine she glanced back at him and stuck out her tongue. Walt smiled. A moment later she was intently studying the selections in the machine, one eye closed. She always did that, closed one eye, her left, whenever she was faced with a decision. In the beginning he had teased her about it, but only when they were alone. That was one of the big differences between them: she had no feelings whatever about embarrassing him in public, and when she attacked she was merciless. If it developed into a fight, then fine; she loved public combat. Private brawls, too. Fighting in general was all right with her. Walt wished she were calmer, wished she could relax, but whenever he broached the subject she shut him up quick. She was good at that. Quick and flip and always alert for openings. But never, never dull.

Blake started back down the aisle toward him. In her own way she was a good girl, as good as he was ever going to find. Bitchy, sure, and smug, at least on occasion, and spoiled, she was that, too. But just the same he was going to marry her. He had decided that morning that he was going to propose to her that evening, and it was evening now. Walt dried his hands on his gray flannels. She was a great girl, Blake Simmons, phony name or no phony name, and if he got her he was lucky, so there was no reason for his hands to start perspiring on him. No; that wasn't totally true. There was one reason. Small, but still a reason. He was not remotely sure that he loved her. He thought he did. He hoped he did. But he was not remotely sure. And that uncertainty gave him more than pause from time to time.

"Your name," Walt said as she sat down, "stinks."

"Egbert Kirkaby don't ring bells, buddy."

"You are smug, bitchy and spoiled."

"You're absolutely right. I'm a typical American girl. I also hate cooking, dread having children, intend cheating on my husband and own my own diaphragm. What else do you want to know?"

"Why do you talk like that? You don't own one of those things."

"It would rock your foundations if I did, wouldn't it, buddy? Here, gimme," and she grabbed his open hand. "Very interesting," she said, studying his palm. "Your name is Walt Kirkaby and you wear glasses. You're a senior in college and getting duller every day. By the time you're thirty you'll think golf is the nuts, followed only slightly by gin rummy. By the time you're forty you'll be potbellied and you'll talk like Casanova in the men's locker room but you'll still be scared green every time you drop in the hay with a female."

Walt tried to pull his hand away.

Blake held tight. "And she won't always be your wife, this female. Your second wife, I should say, because you'll be on your second wife and your third kid by then, and your second wife won't be any better than the first one was, because you never wanted a woman in the first place, you wanted a servant, someone to darn—"

"Cut it."

"So you'll get divorced and marry someone absolutely totally one hundred percent different except she'll be exactly the same only you won't know it until it's too late and by that time you'll have figured out that all you really wanted all your life was to bed down with your mommy—"

"I said cut it," Walt began, and he was about to say more, a lot more, but when she suddenly lowered her head, eyes closed, and kissed his palm again and again he could only stare, then blink, then quickly, quickly, look away.

At 11:31 that evening, Walt proposed. The rain had stopped and they were hurrying through the cold to Blake's dorm, after spending several hours whispering in the library, discussing the revue. After the library came a cup of coffee in the snack bar, and following that, on the way to Harkness, Walt looked at his watch, nodded and said it.

"Will you marry me?"

"What's the punch line?"

"Huh?"

"Well, obviously that's a joke. I just wondered what the punch line was."

Walt stopped. "It so happens, bright eyes, that I meant what I said."

Blake kept on walking. "Why in the world should I marry you?"

"Because," Walt began, running after her, "because you are without question a dog and nobody else is ever going to ask you."

"That may well be, buddy, but *you*? I mean, *you*? I mean, have you taken a peek in the mirror lately?"

"It so happens," Walt shouted, hurrying alongside, "it so happens—slow down, dammit—happens that I am one helluva neat guy."

"Your glasses are fogging up," Blake said.

"Right in the kisser if you're not careful, buddy old buddy." He shook a fist in front of her.

"I am literally freezing," Blake said. "Let's run."

Walt grabbed her. "What about it?"

"What about what?"

"Getting married."

"Oh, that."

"I'll kill you so help me. I'll kill you."

Blake started running.

Walt overtook her and grabbed her from behind and they stumbled off the path against a tree. "Marry me!"

"I can't. I'm really a boy. See, I went to Sweden last summer and I had this operation and—" She broke loose and started running again. "Besides," she shouted over her shoulder, "I'm already married."

"You're really gonna get it now," Walt yelled, chasing her down, grabbing her again, spinning her into his arms.

"I'm already married. I am, I am. And I will not commit bigamy. Dutch and I—"

"Dutch! Who's Dutch?"

"Dutch Cleanser. He's a nice Jewish boy." She stepped down hard on Walt's loafer and took off again.

"That hurt."

"Tough."

"See you tomorrow," Walt called.

Blake stopped. "Aren't you going to chase me?"

"No."

Blake came back to him. "It's no fun if you're not going to chase me." They started walking again. "Now what was it we were talking about?"

"I think it had to do with marriage." Walt shrugged.

"Yes. That's right. You were proposing."

"I was?"

"I think so. I don't know. Maybe I was proposing. Anyway, somebody was proposing, I'm quite sure of that."

"Was I down on one knee?"

"No."

"Then it couldn't have been me. I always get down on one knee when I propose."

"Well then I must have been the one, except I don't understand why I should have been proposing to you. You're such a meatball."

.   "True."

"Scrawny and pint-sized."

"Five-eight. The national average."

"I can't think of anything salvageable about you. Except you do terrific imitations."

Walt stopped.

"And I've always wanted to marry a man who did terrific imitations."

Walt took her hand and started to run.

"Where are we going?"

"Someplace dark." They raced across the street, Walt leading, and when they reached Peters Hall they dashed up the steps into the archway and Walt was about to embrace her when he heard another couple behind them, so he whirled and in his most menacing Sidney Greenstreet voice snarled, "You infants better get out of here unless you want trouble," and, in the darkness, a girl gasped and suddenly the other couple was gone, running down the steps and away. "Freshmen," Walt said, and then he groped for Blake in the darkness, found her, kissed her mouth. "Hey," he whispered. "We're engaged."

"Yeah."

"Don't say 'yeah' at a time like this. You're verbal. Be verbal."

"Well, you'll do for a first husband. How's that?"

Walt kissed her again, his hands fumbling with her raincoat, finally getting it unbuttoned. His fingers touched her cashmere sweater and he pressed down harder with his lips as his fingers crept under the sweater, starting the slow move up her firm body, something he had done only once before, in St. Louis, at Christmastime, and they were lying together on his bed, naked, touching each other, and if P.T. hadn't suddenly called for him, sending them scampering wildly into their clothes, God knows what would have happened.

"Remove your hands from my bosom," Blake said.

"Huh?"

"Your hands. Remove them." She stood very still, her arms at her sides.

"We're engaged. I'm entitled."

"I don't want you discovering I wear falsies until after everything has been officially announced."

"I *know* you don't wear falsies. I found out in St. Louis. Remember?"

"I borrowed those breasts for the occasion."

"Blake—"

"If you do not remove your hands from my bosom by the count of three, I shall scream 'rape.' "

"Willya please—"

"One—"

"Quit this now."

"Two—"

"Blake, I'm your fian—"

"RAPE!"

Walt scurried down the steps, his hands in his pockets. After a moment he heard her following. Then she fell in step beside him.

"Hi," Blake said.

"Nobody likes a smart-ass," Walt told her. "Bear that in mind."

"Sometimes I'm so cute and unbelievably adorably attractive I just can't stand myself."

"Yeah-yeah-yeah."

"Mrs. Egbert Kirkaby. Ye gods."

Walt kissed her. "Poetry." He kissed her again. "Hey, you know what?"

"What?"

"Nobody mentioned love."

"Clichés," Blake said. "To hell with 'em."

• • •

"Walt? You in there? It's me."

Walt lay in bed reading. "Door's open," he called, looking up as Branch Scudder, balding and pudgy, hurried in.

"Are you going to do it?" Branch asked. "Put on a revue?"

"I hope so; I'm gonna try."

"Well . . . uh . . . what I wondered is could I help?"

"Gee, Branch, we're doing it the same week as *Hamlet*. You stage-manage the Dramat. How can you do two shows at once?"

"Under certain conditions I would . . . uh . . . resign from the . . . uh . . . Dramat."

"What conditions?"

"If you would let me . . . uh . . . puh . . . produce your show."

"It's just gonna be a little revue, Branch, It's nice of you, but I don't think there's that much to be done. I thought I'd produce it."

"There are lots of little . . . uh . . . details and things."

"I really think I can handle it, Branch."

"Fine. Fine. Uh . . . don't tell anybody, please, I mentioned resigning from the Dramat, O.K.?"

"My heart is crossed."

Branch took a step toward Walt and lowered his voice. "You should have played Hamlet," he said. "That's what I think anyway." Then he was gone.

ANNOUNCING
DROP THE SOAP

A NEW REVUE
Written, Directed, Produced and Starring
MODEST WALT KIRKABY

Since it is obvious that if you had talent you would not be at Oberlin, we are looking for YOU. We need NO TALENTS. *We crave* NO TALENTS. *The success of our show depends 100% on*

NO TALENTS

THEREFORE: If you are tone deaf, sing in the show.
If you are clumsy, dance.

COME ONE

COME ALL

AUDITION'S MONDAY   4 P.M.

Walt stared off into space. "I don't get it," he mumbled. "I put those signs up myself. Noon today. Ten signs. All over campus. I just don't get it." Sadly he shook his head.

"A Communist plot, do you think?" Blake said.

Walt ignored her. "I really worked on those signs. I thought they were great. If you'd seen those signs, wouldn't *you* have auditioned?" He moved to the doorway and stared out through the drizzle at Tappan Square. The building was an old one-story affair, once the property of the Geology Department but unused for many years. The Dean himself had given Walt the key, on Walt's promising that no duplicates would be made and that no "skulduggery"—the Dean's word—would take place when the lights were out. "Nuts," Walt said.

"It probably would have been a crummy revue," Blake told him. "You can console yourself with that."

"Sometimes you thrill me less than other times."

Blake curtsied.

"Nuts," Walt muttered again as he stared out at the rain.

"You could always put on a one-man show," Blake said. "Sing, dance, do a few imitations—really stink up the joint."

"Willya shut up, please. Boy, give you an occasion and you'll sink to it."

"Crybaby cry," Blake sang.

"What is it with you? You think I like making an ass of myself? Boy, you are one helluva first-class castrator, you know that?"

"I didn't do it to you, buddy. The job was done long before I arrived on the scene."

"What's that supposed to mean?"

"It means quit moaning 'cause your great big show fell on its face."

"Big? What big? It was just gonna be a crummy little revue, that's all. I like horsing around the theater and in three months I graduate and then it's the old man's business and I just wanted something to remember, so what's the crime? And if you want to take the afternoon off, I won't be heartbroken." He turned, concentrating again on the rain.

Blake chucked him under the chin. "Wuzzy, wuzzy, wuzzy," she said.

Walt brushed her hand away.

"Hey," and she shook his shoulder. "Don't faint, but here comes Jiggles."

"Branch?"

"Who else carries an umbrella?"

Walt pushed his glasses up snug over the bridge of his nose with his left thumb and squinted. "Hey, Branch," he shouted. "Over here."

Branch scurried in through the doorway.

"What's up?" Walt said.

"Uh . . . I just wondered if you might change your mind about letting me produce the show."

"Ain't gonna be no show."

"Why?"

"Nobody wants it. Nobody came to audition."

"Uh . . . I spoke to any number of people who were interested."

"Yeah? Then why didn't they audition?"

"I . . . uh . . . I think the . . . uh . . . sign had something to do with it."

"Now hold the phone," Walt said. "I wrote that sign. I spent all last night figuring out just what to say. I think it's a terrific sign."

"Lovely work. Yes, yes. Except it didn't quite mention *where* the auditions were. That would be my only criticism. Otherwise it was perfect."

"Nuts," Walt said.

Blake started laughing.

"You see . . . uh . . . a producer tends to little things like that. Trivia. Well, do I get the job?"

"I'll think about it," Walt said.

BRANCH SCUDDER

announces audition for
WALT KIRKABY's *original revue*

```
        D              P
      R              A
    O              O
      P THE S
```

WEDNESDAY   THE OLD GEOLOGY LAB   4 P.M.

Walt and Branch stood whispering in a back corner of the geology lab while, up at the front, the eight leotard-clad girls did their best to move in unison. "Ladies, please," Walt said, and Blake, seated at the old upright piano in the middle of the room, stopped playing. "We've got to try and keep together, ladies. Everybody start *on* the beat with the *left* foot. All of you, show me your left foot." The girls showed him. "Good work. All right, again, and give it all you've got." He turned back to Branch as Blake began playing. Walt shook his head. "In the movies, chorus girls always look like Virginia Mayo. Why don't ours?"

"We'll light them dimly," Branch said. "That's bound to help."

"Nothing will help. Look at those calf muscles bulge. Where were they this fall when the football team needed them? How—ladies, ladies— hold it, Blake," and he hurried up to the front of the room, smiling at them, speaking with what he hoped was quiet enthusiasm. "Now I know this is only our second day of rehearsal and nobody expects miracles, but please, ladies, first the left foot, *then* the right. Stop hopping. O.K., Blake," and he stood in front of the girls, smiling and clapping in rhythm as they began to move. "You're getting it. Much better. Much. You're doing great, so keep it up," and he turned and started back to Branch, except Branch was talking with Imogene Felker.

Walt stopped walking.

Branch gestured to him. Walt glanced at Blake. Branch gestured again. Walt approached and Branch said, "Surprise for you. You know Imogene, don't you? She's going to be in the show."

"I've never acted," Imogene said. "I don't really know what I'm doing here, except Branch made it seem like my patriotic duty."

"I thought she'd be a perfect . . . uh . . . straight man for you. In . . . some of your skits."

"If you don't want me, I'll understand. I mean that. I probably wouldn't be any good. I'll try, though, just as hard as I can, but that's all I can promise."

"Of course he wants you," Branch said. "Good heavens, it's settled. Well, shall we begin?"

Through it all Walt never said a word.

An informal survey Walt had conducted during exam week of his junior year at Oberlin found that Imogene Felker possessed not only one of the two best bodies among female undergraduates, but one of the two prettiest faces as well. Taking both items together, she left all competition behind, since Fran McEvoy, the other head, was flat-chested and hippy, while Janine Frankel, the opposing shape, had a face like a foot. Imogene's appeal, however, was not based solely on appearances; what set her most clearly apart from her fellows was the possession of an attribute all but unique to northern Ohio.

Imogene Felker had glamour.

Just why this was so, Walt could never ascertain. There was one period, early freshman year, immediately following their first and only eight-word conversation, when he thrashed at night, trying to isolate the reason. Toward the end of that period he read *Saint Joan*, noting with some insight that the best Shaw could come up with on the Maid was that "There was something about her." Well, there was something about Imogene Felker too, and if Shaw could be vague, why not E. Walters Kirkaby, then all of eighteen? Imogene Felker arrived unknown at Oberlin, a quiet child, timid and sweet, a non-giggler who hurried alone from Talcott Dorm to the library, eyes always down, books always pressed across her priceless bosom.

In less than a month she was legend.

There was no question in Walt's mind that she would have achieved that stature eventually, but there was also no question that Donny Reilly helped speed the elevation along. Donny Reilly was something of a legend himself, a dazzling Irish giant who, because he was the only football player in school blessed with better than average coordination, found himself a gridiron celebrity in spite of the fact that he was not particularly accurate as a passer or fast as a runner and was given to fumbling on those rare instances when Oberlin found itself in the shadow of its opponent's goal. He was also something of a sexual whiz, having successfully seduced, by his own account, forty-three coeds, at least that many townies and, crown in his cap, Miss Dunhill, the only attractive associate professor in the history of the school. That Donny and Imogene should cross was hardly chance, since he made it a practice to begin each academic year by eying and then destroying the half dozen or so most alluring freshmen before moving, unscathed, to their more mature sisters. Late in September they went out for the first time, big Donny, quiet Imogene. They came to the Pool Hall, Oberlin's most sinful 3.2 beer dispensary, sitting together in the very front booth, sitting close, and while Donny joked with whatever table-hopping inferiors happened by, Imogene stayed silent, from time to time managing a sip from her glass of beer. Discreetly, Walt watched them, not only that night but in the nights that followed, and there was no doubt in his mind that he saw things in her face (Walt was always a great one for seeing things in faces). The child was lonely, the child was sad. You can't want him, Walt thought. You can do better than him, I promise you. Somewhere there's somebody better. But as they left each evening, Donny's big arm thrown possessively across her shoulders, Walt could only drown his doubts in unnatural amounts of watery brew. And each evening, after taking Imogene home, Donny would return, louder than ever, and he would gather other seniors around him at the bar and there hold forth on various subjects: the formation of Imogene's body, the smoothness of her skin, the texture of her pale red hair.

Somewhere along toward the middle of October, Imogene broke his heart.

Just how this happened, no one ever knew, for Imogene would never have told and Donny, for once in his life, shut up. But it happened, and Walt was in the Pool Hall drinking his fifth glass of 3.2 beer at the moment Donny's statue tumbled down. He entered the bar quietly, Donny did, and that was already strange, and he ordered a pitcher of beer, grabbed a stein, and had them both in his big hands, the pitcher and the stein, when someone shouted, "Hey, where's Imogene?" Walt was staring at the Celt and as the question echoed there came across Donny's face an expression so naked—he was eventually to lose it from his skin, never from behind his eyes—so full of totally deflated ego, that Walt almost felt guilty at his sudden smile. (But the lying bastard, he'd never laid a glove on her, so who could help smiling?) And that night as Donny drank himself into a silent stupor, alone in the farthest corner of the bar, Walt watched him and, while others around him evinced astonishment, Walt was not one whit surprised. For though Walt had spoken to Imogene but once (eight words), been close to her that one time only, it was enough. He knew. There was something about her. Something. An air, an aura, a way. She was a mystery. Open and sweet, yet a mystery. Not mysterious, therefore mysterious, therefore glamorous, for mystery without glamour is like love without like: false; much trumpeted, but false; much avowed, yet false; pledged, sworn, promised, still and always false; false, nothing more.

Following the breakup, Imogene went out with basketball dribblers and scholars, and in her sophomore year several slender members of the swimming team tried for the brass ring. Then, in her junior year, there began to be rumors of a non-Oberlinian, a Philadelphia lawyer, more precisely, who, according to talk, was quiet and kind and a one-time editor of the *Yale Law Review*. The rumors received substantiation as her senior year began, for Imogene returned to school officially engaged, and at Thanksgiving time her conqueror appeared, neither particularly tall nor strong nor beautiful, but, if Imogene's eyes were to be believed, kind. As they walked hand in hand across campus they were watched, studied, appraised, and by none closer than E. Walters Kirkaby. But that wasn't unusual; he had always managed to keep tabs on Imogene.

The first thing he ever noted about her was her hair. It was pale red, and it tumbled down around her shoulders as she walked ahead of him through Tappan Square, on the way to town. This was their freshman year, second day of school, and Walt was excited because he had heard of a pinball machine called Blue Skies and he wanted to test its mettle. At the sight of the red-haired girl, he doubled his speed, closing the gap between them, anxious to see her face. Suddenly he stopped, because it was really a dumb thing to do, following girls; whenever you followed a girl she always turned out to be a dog. Those were Walt's findings, anyway, so what was the point of navigating after this one, particularly since she was a redhead? Redheads were invariably at their best when viewed from behind. The thing about redheads was that when you looked at them from the front, what you saw was freckles, and what you didn't see was eyebrows. So what was the point? Walt shrugged and slowed. This hair was pale red, though, so maybe that was something. He moved a little faster. But what the hell, she had a raincoat on, so how could you tell anything about the body? He moved a little slower. I'll bet she's a dog, Walt thought. But her legs were nice. The ankles appeared thin and thank God the calf muscles didn't bulge, so probably she wasn't a field-hockey star and he began moving faster again, until he was only twenty steps behind. At that distance he noted that her pale red hair glistened in the gray afternoon, so he halved the gap, studying her with professional care. It really was a problem, because from his vantage point she looked great, and a decision would have to be made soon because they were three-quarters through the square and the chances were that she was not on her way to play pinball. To hell with her, Walt thought, and he started to slow when the girl took off her raincoat. Walt picked up the step. She was wearing a fuzzy white sweater and a straight black skirt. "Hmmm," Walt said, and he squinted at her over the upper rim of his glasses. The odds were still on an eyebrowless dog, but the fuzzy sweater looked nice, the skirt too, and she certainly wasn't fat and he could not fault her walking motion. They were nearing the end of the square, town just ahead, so it was now or never. Now! Walt thought and, pausing just a moment to attain the proper swagger, he thrust his hands into his pockets at a brilliantly casual angle and hurried alongside.

She was no dog.

Walt stared at her, walking right beside her, eyes wide, and when she glanced up at him he was unable to look away. She did, though, so he continued to stare. They walked together, stride for stride, and Walt thought that he really ought to stop this and go on about his business, but his head was practically resting on her shoulder and it was simply physically impossible for him to pull it away. The girl turned toward him again, and he was debating whether he preferred her full face or profile when she stopped and spoke.

"Yes?"

"Sorry. Thought you were someone I knew."

The eight words spoken, Walt ran. By the time he went to bed that night, he had, by casual cross-examination of other freshmen, discovered her name, age (18), place of birth (India), parents' occupation (missionaries) and shoe size (7½AA)—this last piece of data come to him because this kid who lived down the hall worked afternoons in the shoe store where she had gone earlier that day to purchase a pair of cordovan loafers. Armed with his information, Walt slept.

Or tried to.

About three that morning the thought crossed his mind that he was totally and completely madly in love, but by half past three a little of reality returned. She was one of the pretty people, sure, and it was too bad he couldn't talk to her again, but how could he, after that beginning? Still, he consoled himself with the thought that talking to her would only lead to ashes. You didn't talk to people like that; they disappointed you if you talked to them. They were for looking, only for looking, and ideally everybody should have one, one just like Imogene, and everybody should keep them around, someplace close by, so you could just turn your head and stare at them a while, to make you feel better, on those days after the bottom fell, or the roof, or the sky.

The night Imogene first came to rehearsal, Walt walked Blake home. Blake's eyes were very bright, too bright for Walt, so he looked away from them, and when he groped for her hand she pulled it from his grasp. But I haven't done anything, Walt thought. So don't fight. Please.

"You'll never make it, buddy. It's a long-lost cause. Take my word."

"What do you mean?"

"Oh, come off it, what do you think I mean?"

You mean Imogene, Walt thought. But I haven't looked at her. Not once all night. Not one time, I swear. "I don't know. You tell me."

"Right now I find you particularly unappetizing," Blake said.

"Look. I don't want to fight with you. We've got nothing to fight about. You're smarter than I am. See? I admit it. You can outwit me, so now you don't have to prove it. Just go easy."

"I hate that bitch. Her and her goddam sweetness act."

What should I say? Walt wondered. If I ask who she's talking about, she'll land on me with both feet. If I assume she's talking about Imogene, she'll land on me with both feet. "Swear some more," Walt said. "It's terrifically becoming. So feminine."

"You don't get out of it that easy, buddy. No sir, you don't. Go on. Answer my question."

"What question? What are you talking about?"

"I'm warning you. I'm just about to get angry."

"I love you. Now shut up."

"Oh, that's cute."

"God," Walt said.

"God," Blake mimicked.

"What do you want from me?"

"What do you want from her?"

"Let's change the subject, huh?"

"Let's not."

"Blake—"

"What do you want from her?"

"There's no point—"

"Making an ass of yourself. Making an ass of yourself and I've got to watch you doing it."

"Now dammit—"

"Ass!"

Walt hurried on ahead of her.

"She'll laugh in your face, buddy."

Walt whirled. "I never even looked at her!" he said, and as he said it he knew it was a mistake, but she was too angry now to catch it. That was something.

"What do you think I'm talking about? Oh God, just watching you goo-gooing around that bitch with your eyes on the floor like old Uncle Tom himself. You think she's so fantastic you'll turn to salt if you look at her?"

"If I'd looked at her you'd have yelled at me for that."

"Like hell I would."

"Admit it!"

"I would not."

"Admit it." I'm winning, Walt thought. How about that?

"Let's change the subject."

"No. Not till you admit it. You just want to blow off, right? No matter what I'd done, you'd have blown off, right? Right?"

Blake came at him then, reached for his hands. An instant later she'd placed them on her breasts and then she was kissing him, raking his mouth with her tongue, pushing her body close against him while his hands kneaded her bosom. Walt started getting aroused, biting at her tongue. She broke from him, backing away, smiling, smoothing her hair. Walt was embarrassed at the sound of his breathing, but he grabbed for her anyway. She was too quick. He started to chase her. Blake started to laugh. Walt stopped. Ordinarily the sound of her laughter ruffled him. But not now. Not tonight.

After all, he'd won, hadn't he?

Branch sat in front of the geology lab with the ticket box beside him. Walt came up. "Anybody buying?" Walt asked.

"I just purchased a pair for my mother," Branch said. "That brings our grand total to three."

"Three?"

"Yes. The third was bought by some gullible freshman."

"Three?"

"Fear not."

"Three?"

"I anticipate an upsurge this afternoon."

"How can you smile?"

"Check you local bulletin board," Branch said. That was all.

AN IMPORTANT ANNOUNCEMENT
from the cast of
D   P
R   A
O   O
P THE S

We wish to lay finally and forever to rest the following rumor:

IMOGENE FELKER WILL APPEAR
ABSOLUTELY AND TOTALLY
WITHOUT BENEFIT OF
CLOTHING

This is false
The final decision on MISS FELKER'S CLOTHES *hasn't been reached.*

Branch sat in front of the geology lab with the ticket box beside him. In front of him, seventeen people waited in line. Walt came up, counted the line and bowed low.

Branch shrugged. "Culture," he said. "It's wonderful."

"O.K., now," Walt said to Imogene. "Here's this new sketch." He beckoned her to the makeshift stage at one end of the geology lab. At the other end, out of the corner of his eye, he saw Blake and Branch in whispered conversation.

"What do I have to do?" Imogene asked.

"Well, it's like this. I'll be dressed as a magician, see? And I'll give a little introductory thing, and then I'll clap my hands and say, 'Now if my sister will be kind enough to hand me my wand,' and then you come on. And I'll talk a sentence or two more and then I'll do a double-take and I'll say, 'You're not my sister.' And then *you* say, 'I'm a friend of hers. She's not feeling well, so she asked me would I help.' Got it?"

"I think so."

"Great. Then I'll start into this trick where I make the handkerchief turn color and I'll build up to it and just before I do it I want you to stand there and shift your weight from one foot to the other—shoot your hip out, you know what I mean?"

"Like this?" Imogene said.

"Right. And I'll ogle you, and when I do the trick, not only will the handkerchief not change color, it'll rip in half. That's sort of the way the whole sketch'll go. When I make the glass bowl float, you shoot your hip and the bowl will crash and break on the floor. Every time I'm about to do something, you distract me, and the trick'll go wrong. Understand?"

Imogene nodded.

"If I can make a big enough mess, it ought to work. Art it ain't, but it might be funny. Shall we give it a try?"

"Go," Imogene said.

"O.K.," Walt began, and he moved to the center of the stage, starting to address the imaginary audience. "Ladies and gentlemen—"

"She ought to be your wife," Blake called from the rear.

"Ladies and gentlemen, it's a great pleasure to be—"

"It's not funny if she's your sister," Blake said, starting to move down the room. "She's got to be your wife."

"—to be here. What you're about to see—"

"Walt," Blake said. "Shut up a minute."

"—to see will undoubtedly amaze—"

"Walt!"

"—amaze and delight you."

"Imogene," Blake called. "Will you please get the boy genius' attention."

"Walt," Imogene said. "Blake's trying—"

"I heard!" Walt said. "I heard and I chose to ignore. Now—"

"I'm talking to you, buddy, so hold on."

"Yes," Branch said, and he moved down beside Blake.

"The whole thing is not funny this way, buddy. I mean, I know, it's your sketch, you stole it, and God forbid I should criticize, since I don't think it's going to get yucks no matter what you do with it, but I *know* it's not going to work this way."

"Will you just please let us try and rehearse?"

"The whole thing works off of you lusting after Imogene, right? The lecher, right? Well, it's only funny if you're married, don't you see? If you're married and you're hot for your wife's friend, then it's at least got a chance. This way it's nothing."

"You through?" Walt said. " 'Cause if you are, I'd like to rehearse."

"It stinks this way, buddy. Believe me."

"I'm sorry," Walt said, and he climbed down off the stage. "Forget it, Imogene. We'll try later. Tomorrow maybe."

"You won't even talk about it," Blake said.

"Please. Just forget it, will you?"

"All right. Go sulk. You're great at taking criticism, aren't you, buddy?"

"You're getting to me. That what you want? Well, hooray for you."

"Everybody thinks I'm right."

"Yeah-yeah-yeah."

"Tell him, Branch."

"Uh . . . Blake's got a point, Walt. She does."

Walt turned to Imogene. "What do you think?"

"I don't know. I really don't. It might be funnier."

"The three experts," Walt said, his voice starting to rise. "What do you know?" he said to Imogene. "I mean, you're such an expert. What do you know? I'll tell you. You don't know a thing. Not one cotton-picking thing. So you know what your job is? Your job is to shut up. You too, Branch. Got it?" He turned to Blake, about to speak, but all of a sudden he could feel tears behind his eyes. Blake must have seen them, because she started to smile. Walt ran at her until he saw she was afraid of him, for the first time afraid of him, and her fear was frightening, because he hadn't realized he was that upset, so he veered away from her, continuing to run until he was out the door and through the square and they were far behind him.

The next morning Walt found her studying in the main room of the library. She was at a back table, taking notes, and as he approached, Walt tried to remember if he had ever seen her in blue before. Probably not, and that was a shame; she looked good in blue. "Hey," Walt whispered.

Imogene looked up.

"Can I talk to you a sec?"

She nodded.

Walt sat in the chair beside her. "About yesterday," he whispered.

She smiled. "It's all right."

"No. I've gotta apologize. I shouldn't have yelled at you."

"It probably did me good. Really. You shouldn't worry about it."

"Shh," a girl down the table said.

Walt ignored her. "I didn't want to yell at you."

"I know."

"You weren't upset or anything?"

"I'm not anymore."

"I don't really know why I did it."

"Shh!" came from down the table.

"Yes, I do too. See, I was really P.O.d at Blake and—"

"I'm telling you *shhhh!*"

"Smoke?" Imogene said, rising.

"You smoke?"

"Sometimes."

"Oh, you shouldn't. Ever. Spoils the image, you know what I mean?"

"I won't inhale; how's that?"

They started out of the big room. Hey, Walt thought, I'm walking with Imogene, what do you know? He shoved his hands into his pockets and scuffed his way out of the library. It was a fine morning, blue and warm, and they moved across the street to Tappan Square and sat down together on the grass in the sunshine.

"Nice," Walt said.

She nodded.

"Here's the thing about yesterday," Walt began. "See, Blake and I, we'd had it all out beforehand. The sister-wife business. Just the two of us. In private. And I told her I was going to do it my way. I don't think it's funny, infidelity, on account of I guess I'm a prude. Anyway, I don't, so Blake, just to get to me, she brought the whole thing up again. In public. She does that. I mean, she's a great girl and all, but she does that. I was really mad. That's why I yelled at you." He dragged on his cigarette. "But I didn't mean anything." Suddenly he stood up. "I've got to be going," he said. "It's really great, though, having you in the show," Walt said as he sat down again. "I mean, you're really good. I enjoy working with you."

"Same here."

"I mean, you could have been just awful."

"You're right."

"I hate it when you see somebody on the stage and they're just awful."

"Me too."

"It's so embarrassing."

"Yes."

"Sometimes I want to hide under my seat, I can't stand it so much."

"Absolutely." She began to laugh.

"You don't laugh much."

"No. I guess I don't."

"I do. It's supposed to be good for you. Something about wrinkles."

"I'll remember that."

"Why were you laughing?"

"We sounded so stupid."

"Yes. I guess we did."

Imogene stretched her hands high into the air. "No clouds," she said. "Not one."

"Not one," Walt echoed.

Suddenly she stood up. "I've got this paper I just have to finish."

"Yes."

"This paper," Imogene said as she sat down again, "it's for Abnormal Psych and it's killing me."

"You'll get it."

"I don't know. Ever since we started rehearsing I don't seem to have any time. I don't know what my grades are going to be. That never bothers you, though, does it? Weren't you Phi Bete?"

"Pull. Pure pull."

"You never look at people. Did you know that?"

"I have a very sneaky character."

"How's your handshake?"

"Fishlike."

"Sneakier and sneakier. Why did you run away?"

"What? When? Yesterday?"

"No, no, no. Freshman year, I mean. Right at the start of school. I was walking through here on my way downtown and all of a sudden you were right next to me and I knew who you were, of course, because the night before there'd been a sort of get-together at the dorm and you were sort of the master of ceremonies and you imitated some people and you were really very funny, so when I saw you right next to me I was surprised but glad because I wanted to meet you and then all of a sudden you said that you'd mistaken me for somebody else and then you ran away before I could say anything."

"It wasn't me," Walt said.

"It wasn't?"

"No. You must have got me mixed up with some other guy."

"Oh."

"I mean, I was the master of ceremonies. I mean, *that* happened, but not the thing in the square."

Imogene nodded.

"I mean, if something like that had happened, I would have remembered."

"Yes. Well, I've never been any good at faces. Names I'm all right on, but faces, no."

"I'm the same way. Except I don't remember names all that well either."

"I read that somebody's written a book about how to get better at things like that. Remembering. Some system, I think. You connect the name with something else. I don't know."

"Cigarette?"

"I really should get back to work."

"So should I."

"One more won't hurt, though."

"No." Walt handed her a cigarette and cupped his hands around the match until she'd managed to get it lit. Then he lit one for himself.

They smoked a while.

"I almost did it," Imogene said finally.

"Did what?"

"Asked you what you were thinking. I hate it when people ask you what you're thinking. That and 'what's the matter?' People ask that too."

"Constantly."

"It's really nobody's business what you're thinking. Don't you think so?"

"I was embarrassed," Walt said. "That's why I ran away."

"Yes."

"You knew, didn't you? That it was me."

"Yes. Are you nervous?"

"Absolutely. All the time. Very."

"No. I mean now."

"You mean more than ordinarily?"

"Yes."

"No. Why?"

"I don't know. I am. I just wondered if you were."

"Well, as a matter of fact, if you want to know the truth, I am, too."

"Why are you?"

"I don't know. Why are you?"

"I don't know. But we're sounding stupid again."

Imogene smiled, nodding. She ran her fingertips over the grass, back and forth, back and forth.

Walt stared at her face.

When she turned to him again, he was still staring, and he tried very hard not to move.

"See?" he said. "Sometimes I look at people."

Then he looked away.

"I never do this," Imogene said. "Not often, anyway."

"Do what?"

"Just sit. Just talk."

"Why don't you?"

"I don't know."

"In the dorm at night? I thought girls did that. Sort of their national pastime. Hen parties, aren't they called?"

"Yes."

"Girls don't much like you, do they?"

"Not much."

"That's too bad, isn't it?"

"Yes."

"Have you always been pretty?"

"Yes."

"One of my big problems is that I never ask personal questions."

Imogene said nothing.

"Listen. You can't help the way you look. It's your cross, that's all. I understand. It's the same with me. I've always been fantastically handsome."

"You're not fantastically handsome."

"Oh, I am too."

"You're not handsome at all. You're funny-looking. And you're always pushing your silly glasses up over the bridge of your nose. And if you're not going to comb your hair, why don't you get a crew cut? And shine your shoes once in a while. And tuck in your shirt—it's always hanging out in the back. And look at me."

Walt looked at her.

"And smile."

He did that, too.

"No, it doesn't help. You're just awful."

"I know."

"You can stop smiling."

"I will if you will."

"Nut," Imogene muttered, and she threw her head back. "It's just such a beautiful day."

"If you like beautiful days."

"Except I've got so much to do."

"Likewise."

"I mean, I've just got to get back to work."

"You're not the only one."

"I mean, if I don't get that paper done I won't pass the course, and if I don't pass the course I won't graduate. Just think of that."

"All right. I'm thinking."

"So what."

"Huh?"

"So what if I didn't graduate from Oberlin? Lots of people didn't graduate from Oberlin. Winston Churchill didn't graduate from Oberlin."

"Neither did Johnny Weismuller."

"Or Shoeless Joe Jackson."

"How do you know about Shoeless Joe Jackson?"

"My father wanted a boy. I'm going to swear. To hell with Abnormal Psychology."

"Sing it out."

"I mean, after all, the sun *is* shining."

"That it is."

"And Vitamin C is good for health."

"Nothing better."

Imogene clapped her hands. "And besides, it's nice here."

Walt stretched full on the grass. "It'll do," he said.

When Walt got to the geology lab that evening, Blake was waiting for him. He kissed her lightly, unlocked the door and followed her inside. Walt began setting up the stage for rehearsal while Blake, after watching him work a while, began to play "The Volga Boatman" on the piano. "So what'd you do today?" Blake said.

"Nothing much."

"Oh?"

"Just goofed around."

"I saw you," Blake said then, playing high trills on the piano.

"Oh."

"That's right. In the square. From eleven till two. The poor girl must have been starving. Why didn't you buy her lunch?"

Walt said nothing.

"Oh, I bet I know why. You're probably still putting on your poverty act." She began to play "Brother, Can You Spare a Dime?" "Why don't you tell her that your old man's loaded? Might score a few points."

Walt continued setting up the stage.

Blake banged out "The Wedding March." "Tonight you make the pass, right? That the plan? Tonight, when you walk the bitch home."

"What are you talking about? I walk you home at night. You know that."

"Not tonight, buddy. Tonight I'm leaving early. Does that make your little heart go pitty-pat?"

"I really—and I know you couldn't possibly believe what I'm about to say, but I honestly, cross my heart, et cetera—do not want to fight with you."

"Who's fighting? I'm flying the dove of peace myself."

"Yeah-yeah-yeah."

"Tonight's your chance, buddy. There'll be just the two of you under the moon. No me around, cramping your irresistible style. Think you'll make it? What do you figure your chances are?"

"In the first place, I'm not gonna walk her home—"

"Bet me—"

"Shut up. And in the second place, I am engaged to this slightly erratic nut and since even an attempted seduction might be considered an act of infidelity, I would doubt—"

Blake began to play "The Star-Spangled Banner."

Walt started out of the building.

"Who said I was finished?" Blake began.

"You're so nasty sometimes it still surprises me."

Blake smiled. "A bitch like her, you know what she'll do if you make a pass, buddy? She will laugh, right in your—you should pardon the expression—face."

"You mean like you do?"

"That's right."

"Why do you like to see me squirm?"

"You do it so good," Blake said.

Walt worked that night. He directed the rehearsal with what he hoped was gentle but firm efficiency, going over skits again and again, staging and restaging song after song, driving himself without letup. He worked harder than he had ever worked before, because Blake might be right, of course, about him making a pass at Imogene, and he didn't want to think about it. He had thought about it every moment as they lay chatting on the grass, and if it had not been daylight, if they had been alone, well, he just didn't know.

For the first half of the evening, as Blake sat at the piano, he began to think that she had changed her mind, that she wasn't going to leave, but then quietly she was gone, and somebody else was playing the piano, and Walt immediately sought out Branch and made an appointment for after rehearsal and Branch was free so that was that. He continued rehearsing, moving from skit to song and back, chain smoking, giving a suggestion here, throwing out a notion there, never raising his voice, never looking at anybody, and he was surprised at quarter of twelve when Branch told him it was time to stop, that the girls had to be back in their dorms, so with reluctance he let them go and they went, and when he turned to start talking with Branch, Branch wasn't much interested in prolonging the discussion, partially because Walt really had nothing new to say and partially because Branch felt a cold coming on and in spite of Walt's pleadings Branch nodded and stammered and left, leaving him alone in the room, alone except for Imogene, who quietly was cleaning up, disposing of coffee cups, cigarette butts, the usual debris.

"You're gonna be late," Walt said. "You better get home."

"It's all right. I got a special Per."

"I'll clean up. You better get home."

"I don't mind, really. It's woman's work, tidying."

"Get on home!"

Imogene looked at him then, nodded and started out the door.

"Hey."

She stopped.

"I'll clean it up tomorrow. It's too late now. I'm bushed." He walked outside and locked the door. " 'Night."

" 'Night."

She started moving to the right while he cut quickly across the street into Tappan Square. See? Walt thought. I didn't do it. I didn't walk her home.

"Good night, Imogene," he called.

She waved.

He shoved his hands into his pockets and hurried along a few steps before he stopped again. "See you tomorrow."

"Tomorrow."

He started walking again, hands out of pockets now, fingers snapping in a soft rhythm as he started singing like Fred Astaire. "I'll go my way by myself. Here's where the comedy ends." He did a glide, then a few taps, then another glide, then he ran out of the square across the street shouting "Hey!"

Imogene stopped.

"Walk you home," Walt muttered, and he shoved his hands into his pockets.

"Thank you."

"You might get accosted, you know. Something."

"Something."

"An' I got enough guilt feelings as it is. Think how I'd feel if I found out tomorrow you got accosted or something. I mean, who needs that?"

Imogene smiled.

I can't just kiss her, Walt thought. Just lunge and grab her and kiss her. I couldn't do that. She'd never let me. Hell, I wouldn't let somebody kiss me if they just lunged and made a grab. There's such a thing as manners. "What?"

"I just asked if you thought we'd be ready. To open. It's only five days."

"Everything will be fine. We won't be ready, but everything will be fine." Gradually. That was the only way. Make contact first. Maybe take her hand. Walt shoved his hands deeper into his pockets. What if I try to take her hand and she pulls away? She might pull away. Besides, he was never any good at hand-holding. His palms perspired. Hand-holding was jerky, anyway. To hell with it. "It's really gonna be a good show. Have faith."

"I'll try."

The thing to do was put an arm on her shoulder. On or around, either one. Probably on her shoulder was better. Just rest an arm on her shoulder. Nobody could get mad if you just rested an arm on their shoulder. Just a casual resting of an arm on a shoulder, that was the thing to do. Then, if you snaked your arm right, you could get it *around*. Then, if you played that loose enough, you could begin applying a little pressure to your arm, so that she'd be a little closer to you. Then closer still. Then you started to slow the pace until you were hardly walking at all. *Then,* then you did it. Kissed her. Smack on the old lips. Right smack—did she just say something? She was looking at him as if she'd just said something. Quick, Walt thought. Quick, answer her. "Maybe," he said. "Maybe not."

"What?"

"Didn't you just say something?"

"No."

"I thought you just said something."

"I didn't."

"Oh." He smiled quickly. "I do that a lot. All the time, as a matter of fact. I'm all the time thinking people are saying something when they're not, you know what I mean?"

Imogene smiled.

God, you're pretty. You really are pretty. You're really a pretty—the arm! Get to work on the arm. The arm on the shoulder. But casually.

Casually. Walt took his hands out of his pockets. His palms were wet, so he rubbed them on his trousers. Now it was just a matter of raising the arm, and almost by accident, plunking it down on her shoulder. Just as natural as can be. Just raise the arm and let it settle on the shoulder. Easy apple pie.

Except why the hell should my arm be on her shoulder? What's it supposed to be doing there? I'll never make it. Never. What if she doesn't want it on her shoulder? What if she says "Why is your arm on my shoulder?" How do you answer a question like that? What do you say? "What arm?" That's no answer.

"I didn't hear you," Imogene said.

"Huh-what?"

"Your lips were moving. Just then. But I didn't hear what you said."

"Oh, you mustn't pay any attention to that. I do that all the time too. Move my lips. My whole family does that. We're all the time moving our lips. You should see us. Just sitting around quietly, moving our lips."

"Sometimes I don't always follow you."

"I'm very mysterious," Walt said.

Imogene nodded.

Kirkaby, you're a fink, you know that, Kirkaby? Fink first class. Now cut the screwing around and do it. Do it! Move that arm! Get that arm on her shoulder! To hell with what she says! She'll probably love it. She'll probably say, "I'm so happy you put your arm on my shoulder." Something like that. So do it! Walt took a deep breath. Then another.

Then he moved his arm.

If he had been paying attention to the fact that they had reached the end of the block and were stepping down to cross the street, the chances are that he would not have elbowed her in the neck. But he was not paying attention. So he elbowed her. Hard.

"Ow."

"I'm sorry."

"It's nothing."

"I'm sorry."

"It's all right. Really." She smiled at him while she rubbed her fingers against the side of her neck.

"I was just stretching. I'm kind of clumsy. I mean, I didn't mean to elbow you. But like I say, I'm not the most graceful guy in the world, so sometimes I elbow people." As they started up the street Walt saw she was walking faster than before. And farther away from him. "Nuts!" Walt said, and he kicked at a small rock, sending it flying ahead of him.

"Don't be upset."

"I'm not upset. What made you say that? Just because I said 'nuts'? I always do that whenever I kick a rock. Sort of a password. I'm a terrific rock kicker. When I was a kid I was the greatest rock kicker in the world. Once I kept the same rock going for more than a mile without once breaking stride. I mean, anybody can kick a rock, but to not break stride, that's something."

"Jacks were my specialty."

"I played Jacks too. Not so much in public. I mean, it's a girl's game, so I stuck more to marbles in public, but I played Jacks when I was by myself. I was good at it, too. Not great. Just good."

"I was fantastic," Imogene said as she pointed. "There's the dorm."

Walt stayed even with her as they cut toward the building. Fifty yards to the front door. Sixty at the most, so you better do it. If you're going to do it you better get on the stick. Sometimes you just have to take the plunge. Kiss them right off. No working up gradually. Just do it without the preliminaries. Now. Right this minute now—

"What comes after ten-zees?" Walt said. "I remember you work your way up to ten-zees, but then what?"

"Eggs in a basket, then pigs in a pen."

"Oh, sure, that's it. Eggs in a basket, then pigs in a pen." Don't be a fink, fink. There's thirty yards to go. Twenty-five and you'll never get another chance, so make up your mind. One way or the other. Do it or don't do it. Make up your mind. Think. Think—

He was still thinking when Imogene turned her body.

It was such a graceful movement that for a moment he wasn't even aware that she had done it, but suddenly she was ahead of him, one step ahead, and then her body turned, pivoted, stopped, and she was facing him—facing him in the darkness. During the moment it took for him to realize her action, he completed one final step toward her. The gap closed. There they were.

Omigod, Walt thought. She's making a pass at me.

They stood quite still, not looking at each other. Walt waited for her to move, but she didn't, and then he realized that she was waiting for him to do it, move, act, something. *I wonder what I'm going to do,* Walt thought, because whatever quandary means, I'm in one, because I'm engaged and that's important, to me, it is, even though I don't know if I love her or not, Blake, and Blake says she's a bitch, Imogene, but if she is I've never seen it so I don't think so, what I think is that she's beautiful and sweet and kind and maybe even cares for me, not much but maybe a little, maybe, so *I wonder what I'm going to do.* I mean, of course, I won't do anything. I just couldn't. Except she's right there. Imogene. Waiting for me. The two of us. Together. In the dark. Alone.

Hey, Walt thought. Hey, I better remember this.

The pressure of her breasts against his body; he could feel the tender pressure. They were standing close together, almost but not quite touching, except where her breasts grazed the front of his shirt, and even though the pressure was light, so light, he could feel it. And the date was the eleventh of May; the time: half past twelve. Place: Oberlin, Ohio. More specifically, the lawn of Keep Cottage. More specifically still: close beside a tree, the biggest tree on the lawn, to the left of the front door, deep in shadow. The weather was warm, and a warmer wind washed them from the south. Except for the leaves overhead, there was no sound. The sky? Clear, with the usual number of stars, a wedge of moon. The moonlight was not strong, and the tree branches cut off most of what there was, but a bit of it managed to spot her shoulder, paling her pale red hair. She wore white, a man's shirt, much too big for her, the sleeves rolled up over the elbows. Her red hair cascaded down, covering the collar of her shirt. Her eyes were bright—pale blue in sunlight, bright only now. Bright was the color of her eyes.

IX

Sid at the deli was Sid at the bottom.

In all his life he hated nothing as he hated that store. Yet, every morning at eight, he descended the stairs and unlocked the door and sat in the gloom waiting for customers. The boy was no help, being off at school, and Esther spelled him only occasionally, because of her migraine headaches.

The first migraine, the day of her father's funeral, she had endured without medical aid, but a week later, after a second and more severe attack all but crippled her, she sought attention, thereby learning the name and nature of her malady. The doctor's advice, so Esther reported to Sid, seemed eminently sensible: take it easy, get lots of fresh air, try not to get excited. For a few days thereafter, she and Sid alternated in the deli, but soon it turned out that her presence in the store brought the headaches on, so Esther returned to the doctor, later coming back to Sid with both a reason and a solution. Reason: being so close to the spirit of her father caused tension and tension caused headaches. Solution: stay out of the store. So the business of clerking fell to Sid alone, and Esther began getting lots of fresh air. As spring came she took to spending mornings upstairs, resting and gathering strength, and then, on nice afternoons, she would dress up prettily and wave goodbye through the store window and never return until late afternoon. Although Sid resented her departures, he had to admit that the treatment was working. Her headaches grew rare while her disposition and appearance were unquestionably better than they had been in years.

Sid, in the meantime, declined. It was the store, the goddam store, that was doing it. He could never decide which was worse, waiting for the customers to come or waiting on them when they came. He loathed waiting on them. The indignity of it was bad enough; worse was the fact that he wasn't good at it. They didn't like him, the fat lady customers. They didn't like him, not one bit, and he could tell. They resented his presence (was it his fault he wasn't Turk), his slowness (he could never quite learn where anything was, and while he scurried frantically from shelf to shelf he could hear them muttering impatiently behind him), his jokes (they wouldn't laugh—never; no matter how funny, they just wouldn't laugh). So when they walked out the door with their brown bags full of junk, Sid wasn't sorry.

Except that when they were gone, he was alone.

Alone with his thoughts and the rotten smell of garlic. Everything smelled of garlic in the lousy store, and eventually he too smelled of garlic, no matter how hard he scrubbed his once manicured hands. Stinking, Sid sat in the old man's chair and thought. And no matter what he tried to think about, no matter where he began his daydreams, it was only a moment until his mind betrayed him and he was standing outside himself, looking down at himself, seeing only a small man who stank of garlic—a failure. A failure. A nothing. For the first time in his life his confidence was entirely gone. His dreams of gold, gone. Everything, gone. Alone in the store, Sid saw himself as what he was afraid he was: a butt, a runt, a gas bag, a clown—to be laughed at, to be pissed on.

One afternoon he closed up shop. He ran out the door, locked it good and took off for an hour. When he came back he was afraid Esther might find out, but she didn't, so two days later, when the gloom became overpowering, he took off again. He didn't go anywhere special, just walked, but he always felt better when he came back. Business, of course, fell off a little but not to the point of total disaster, so Sid kept it up, chipper with his secret, hoping only that he wouldn't run into Esther, who would flay him, he knew, if she discovered. Spring had never seemed so becoming to Sid as it did on his afternoon walks, and so the day he saw the hearse parked in an alley he stopped and shook his head, because it didn't seem right that anyone should die in such weather. The hearse, Sid noted first, belonged to Shapiro's, and as he shook his head he saw that young Shapiro himself was seated behind the wheel. And Sid saw that young Shapiro was talking, with obvious relish, to a woman. And the woman, Sid saw, was Esther.

Sid stumbled back to the store.

Esther? Esther having an affair? No, no, not possible. Not Esther. She wasn't the type and, besides, who would want her? Once it might have been conceivable, back then, when she had her body, but now her breasts sagged and her can was flabby and she was getting a gut. Sid nodded. It was absolutely impossible. What he had witnessed was an accident, a chance meeting; happens all the time. Young Shapiro was probably driving along in his hearse and he saw Esther and he gave her a lift to the alley. "Why to the alley?" Sid said out loud. He shrugged. Why not to the alley? Sure, he dropped her off at the alley and went inside and picked up some corpse. Made perfect sense. Esther unfaithful? Never.

But that afternoon, as she returned from her constitutional, Sid beckoned her into the store and they chatted amiably for a while. And as they chatted, Sid studied her—every move, every sound, every look. And it was obvious. All so obvious. Not that she slipped and called him "Eli," young Shapiro's name—nothing like that. Sid just knew. He could tell. Because she loved Eli Shapiro. Not only was she having an affair, she loved him.

Numb, Sid sank into Old Turk's chair as Esther smiled and went upstairs. She loved him. That was what almost made him cry. Hot pants he could almost understand. But love? How could she? Why? Sid hid his head. Why not? Eli Shapiro was rich and handsome. Eli Shapiro had a present and a future. You didn't piss on Eli Shapiro.

"Closed," Sid said to the woman in the doorway.

"I just want milk," the woman said.

"Closed," Sid repeated. "Go," and she left.

Sid got out of the chair and locked himself in the store. Then he turned out the overhead lights and sat back down in the darkness. Esther was leaving him. A matter of time only. She would take the child and go. How many times had he wished for just such a happening? And now the possibility was horrifying. Why? Why? He didn't love her, so why not let her go? Be glad of it? Why? Sid huddled in the dark store, his hands around his knees. He had never lost a woman. And if he lost one now,

now, with things the way they were, it could only prove that he was that lowest of all lows, a human urinal, and Sid was not remotely sure if he could bear that burden or, if so, for how long.

"Eli, over here," Sid shouted as Shapiro entered the poolroom.

Shapiro approached.

"Good to see you, Eli," Sid said, and he held out his hand. "I'm sorry to bring you all this way, but I told Esther I'd be playing tonight, and in case she calls me . . . you understand. Esther and I, we don't like to lie to each other."

"I understand nothing," Eli Shapiro said. "You telephoned me, told me to meet you on a matter of terrifying importance, you sounded upset, and here I am. Mr. Miller, I want—"

"Sid's the name and I apologize. I know I acted mysterious, but I just had to talk to you, Eli."

"I haven't much time, Mr. Miller."

"Please, Eli. Sid."

"Sid. I'm playing cards this evening with my father and we pride ourselves on our punctuality."

Sid sat in an empty chair. "We may as well get comfortable."

"I'm quite comfortable standing. All right, what is all this?"

"I want you to promise to take care of the boy," Sid said.

Shapiro looked at him.

"That's the whole thing, Eli, right in a nutshell. I just want you to promise me, man to man, that no matter what happens, you'll take care of the boy."

"What boy? What are you talking about?"

"Eli, this is Sid. Come on. Will you promise?"

"You've made a mistake, Mr. Miller."

"Eli, I *know.* I know all about it."

"All about what?"

"Eli, *please.* I'm not mad. I understand you want to be cautious, but I know. *Everything.*"

"You'll have to excuse me," Shapiro said, and he turned.

Sid grabbed his coat sleeve. "Esther's told me everything, Eli. So cut it out."

"Esther? You mean Mrs. Miller?"

"Eli, my God, Eli, will you stop with the ignorance. This is me. Esther's told me everything. Today, after you screwed her, you parked in the hearse in an alley. Do you want me to tell you what you talked about?"

Shapiro said nothing.

"Don't be upset, Eli. Esther always tells me everything. I told you earlier, we don't like to lie to each other."

Shapiro sat down.

"Oh, you are upset. Well, stop it. Esther loves you. I swear to you on my sacred word of honor, she loves you, Eli. You're not like the others."

"Others?"

"Of course others. Esther's—but you know it anyway—Esther's a nym . . . nymph . . . What's that word, the opposite of lesbian?"

Shapiro said nothing.

"Maybe she's not really that, but she needs her action. I suppose that's my fault. I don't satisfy her. Never have. Maybe that's why she does it. But anyway, the thing is, she really loves you, Eli. But I'm afraid for the boy. I mean, he's not yours, and I love him except I can't take good care of him, and I want you to promise that no matter what Esther does when the two of you are married, no matter what she tells you, that you'll love the boy and take care of him. Will you promise? Come on now, Eli, she loves you, you'll get used to this—it's not so bad. Eli, get hold of yourself. Snap out of it. Please. Aw, Eli . . ."

The next day, Esther had a migraine.

Sid did what he could to help, talked to her, soothed her, rubbed her back and neck with ice until his fingers were sore. But the headache lingered. Esther moaned, writhing and sobbing through the night and well into the next morning until finally she dropped momentarily into a dead sleep. Sid scurried downstairs and opened the store, but in a while he could hear Esther pounding on the floor above, their signal, so he closed the store and ran upstairs and rubbed her again with ice. All told, he ran up and down the stairs more than a dozen times that day.

It set a pattern. Through the next month, Sid tended the invalid *and* tended the store. The doctors were no use; migraines were mysteries. Sometimes ice was good, sometimes heat. Try this, try that, try anything. Sid tried. He stumbled exhausted from week to week, losing sleep, weight, hair. There was never a minute to relax. If it wasn't some old bag in the store screaming his name, it was Esther. Up the stairs, down; down the stairs, up. Run, run, all the day, all the night, run. He began to regret bitterly ever having spotted the hearse in the alley. For, compared to his present (non) existence, before had been splendor. At least before he had had occasional daydreams; now he had no time. Up the stairs, down the stairs. Coming, Tootsie, coming, Mrs. Feldman, coming, everybody, coming. In spite of his labors, business began falling off. He couldn't really blame the bags for heading elsewhere; nobody likes banging on the door of an empty shop, waiting five minutes for a lousy quart of milk and a half a pound of cheese. But blame or no, business was failing, and so Sid was forced to keep longer hours in the store in an effort to bring it up to his old low level. OPEN TILL EIGHT Sid printed on a cardboard sign hanging in a window, and that sign lasted for a week, when the "Open Till Nine" sign replaced it. Then it was ten. Still there was no money. Eventually the sign read OPEN TILL MIDNIGHT and there it stayed. At midnight, Sid would lock the door and trudge up to Esther, rub her weakly as long as he could, then fall back limp on his pillow, feet, more often than not, hanging over the side of the bed. Rarely did he get a full night; Esther usually shuddered between three and four, slamming her fists against her forehead. Sid, once awakened, would feel his way to the icebox and return with the cold cubes, rubbing them into her flesh until she was semi-quiet, and then he would collapse again, dreamless until eight, when the first customers began filtering into the store.

Sid was too tired for anger, but every so often, in the morning, in the shower, a vision of the past would bubble up behind his weary eyes, and for a moment he would see the Sid that was, Super Sid, in full glory. That was what made it so hard, the past. If only the broads had been less easy, not quite so soft; if only the pool cue had never been steady, the inside straights had never filled. But they had, and at the sight of what had been—without a break in the rhythm of soap and washcloth—Sid would weep. For he was dead. Sid was dead. And soon (he prayed) he would get to lie down.

Summer made things worse. The steaming days increased Esther's agony, and although the boy was home from school, Sid could never leave him alone for long in the store. He was good at reading labels, and when the orders were small, two digits, he could select the proper sum, after much pencil-point licking. But as soon as a customer wanted more than a pickle and a can of soup, the boy's mathematics failed him. So although Sid was now free to walk out of the store, he was only free to walk far enough to realize that he had to get back. And that was worse than not being able to go at all.

Sunday was the store's biggest day, since all nearby competition was closed. And the first Sunday in July was better than most, being close to the holiday. So when the nigger appeared in the entrance, Sid hid his natural prejudice with a smile, figuring on an order of at least several quarts of beer. The nigger's pistol, however, Sid did not figure on, and his smile vanished as the black rifled the money drawer and disappeared.

Stunned, Sid managed to summon the cops, who were polite but not particularly helpful, since Sid was unable to give much of a description, for in his mind niggers were like Chinamen, indistinguishable.

"Robbed?" Esther said.

Sid nodded.

"All the money?"

Sid nodded.

Esther lay back in bed, clutching at her brain.

Sid started for the door.

"Where are you going?"

"Out."

"Out where?"

"Out somewhere."

"What about the store?"

"Good question."

"Sid—"

"I can't go in there, Esther. Please. Not today. I just can't."

"I know. You've been working very hard."

"I'll be back. Later. Try and get some sleep."

"I will. And you have fun."

Sid managed a nod and closed the door, walking slowly down the stairs, holding tight to the banister. It was late afternoon and very hot and when he reached the street he paused, hands in his pockets, trying to decide where to walk. It didn't matter, and that made the decision not only difficult but painful, but finally he started to move because at a far corner he caught a glimpse of a red skirt and what might have been halfway decent legs, so he trudged to the corner. The legs and the skirt were out of sight when he got there, but he was started in a direction now, and since he could think of no reason to change, he kept on. He intended to walk forever, but in twenty minutes he was bushed. The heat. It was too much. Too hot to move, too hot to think. Sid leaned against a lamppost, searching for relief. Down on the next corner was a movie theater, and Sid sighed, squinting at the marquee. Gary Cooper. Gary Cooper and something else. A double feature. Sid nodded and crossed the street in the direction of the theater. "Air-cooled," it said, and Sid picked up the pace. Paying his pennies, he walked inside the theater and sat down. The "something else" was playing and Sid gave it little attention at first. Then he tilted his head up toward the screen. A moment later he was ramrod straight. He gaped and then the word "Yes!" escaped, much to the annoyance of those around him. "*Yes!*" he said again, and before anyone had a chance to say "Shut up" he was off, running from the theater, tears in his eyes. Tears of joy; the news was good.

Super Sid was back in town.

"A movie star?" Esther said, sitting up. "Our Rudy? A movie star?"

"Why not?" Sid cried. "Why not? Give me one good reason."

"Our Rudy?" Esther repeated.

Sid grabbed her hard. "Our Rudy! Yes! Yes!"

"But—"

"Esther—Esther, listen—I know I'm right. I can feel it. I *know*. We've been crazy not to see it sooner. Fools. Oh, Esther, I tell you, I was sitting in this movie watching this Shirley Temple and I thought, 'What's so special about her? What can she do my little Rudy can't?' And the answer is nothing. Nothing. Is Rudy gorgeous? You should see the way the people stare at him in the store. The old ladies. They stare and they stare, they can't believe it. You know how much money that little Shirley Temple makes a year? Millions. And Rudy will make more. Can't you see us, Esther, in California with a house and servants and big black limousines? Oh, we've been fools starving here when we can live like kings in California."

"How—"

"Movie people, they come here all the time. In the papers, you read about them staying at the Palmer House or the Ambassador East. Every day some big shot is in town and when he sees Rudy we can kiss this all goodbye." Sid whirled around, clapping his hands. "We're on our way. I know. I know. We're gone."

"Don't get so excited."

"I *am* excited. I can't help it. Smile, Esther, for God's sake. We'll need photographs. That will cost but nothing we can do about it. Get some good pictures of Rudy, big pictures, a foot square, in color maybe."

"Shirley Temple, she can sing and dance."

"Rudy will sing and dance. Like an angel."

"We can't afford lessons."

"Afford," Sid cried. "Afford. We're gonna teach him!"

Esther lay back on the bed.

Sid bounded into the next room, returning a moment later with a package. "I went all over getting these tonight. I traveled the Loop from end to end." He ripped at the wrapping. "Where is he? The boy?"

"The fire escape."

"Look," Sid said. "See? The sheet music to 'God Bless America.' Very patriotic. Everyone will love him when he sings it. And look still, these books. They teach you dancing. A little tap, a little ballet. Not much, just enough so he'll look cute. It's perfect. Perfect! And when he's ready, and the right man comes to town, we can start packing. God, Esther, it's so exciting."

"It is. I think you're right, Sid. It really is."

"Right! I'm right! I know. I can feel. Everything is right. Everything." He leaped onto the bed and grabbed her, twisting her across his body, kissing her open mouth.

"You're crazy." Esther giggled. "You're a crazy man."

Sid stroked her.

"Kiss me again."

"Later," and he bounced from the bed, running to the open window, shouting, "Rudy, Rudy."

"What?"

"Surprise!"

"No!" the boy cried. "No!"

"Rudy, I'm a patient man, but I'm getting tired of arguing with you. You'll like it. I promise."

"Yes," Esther said. "Really, Rudy. We'll all have fun."

The boy twisted in the chair as they walked around him. "No. Please, no."

"Rudy," Sid said, "I've explained a hundred times, there's nothing wrong with being a movie star."

"We'll teach you everything," Esther said.

"Have we ever led you wrong? Ever?"

"Please."

"You're being very stubborn, Rudy. Any other boy would be proud if his parents wanted to make him a movie star. Because it shows how much they love him."

"Yes, Rudy."

"All right now, this is the last time I'm going to ask—the last time, you understand that? The *last time*. Will you do it?"

"Please," the boy said.

"Rudy," Esther said, "for your mother—"

"I'm sorry to interrupt, Esther, but enough is enough. Rudy, do you want to go back on the fire escape?"

"Yes."

"Then go."

The boy vaulted through the window.

"But I'm locking the window, Rudy," Sid said. "Stay out there. Fine. We don't care. Just remember, you're not coming back in here until you see we're right. We're your parents and we know what's best. Stay a day, a week, stay a year. It's all the same to us. Goodbye, Rudy!" And he slammed the window down and locked it.

"Don't get mad, Sid."

Sid turned, smiling. "Mad? I love it. The stubborner the better. Shows we're right. All the big stars have it."

"Have what?"

"Artistic temperament."

The next morning there was a soft rap at the window.

"Even artists have to eat," Sid said.

So they started with the lessons, singing and dancing, an hour of one, an hour of the other, in the morning, in the afternoon, a third time at night. "God bless Americaaa," the boy sang, "laaand that I love . . ." He had a soft voice, but pleasing to the ear and always on pitch, and, at night as they listened, Sid and Esther nodded to each other. The dancing was no trouble; he picked up the Waltz Clog in one afternoon and before a week was out he could glide gracefully through the five ballet positions. "Again," Sid would shout. "Again, it must be perfect," and the tiny figure would repeat the movements as Esther hummed for rhythm. Pinkus of the Shoreland did the photography, for too much, but the results were worth it. By the middle of August Sid began reading all the papers, noting from the columns who was in town and where. Business at the store was terrible, but they managed to eat and pay the rent, so what else mattered? "God bless America" the boy sang, for the thousandth time, and he danced, moving his small body with easy grace, Esther humming, Sid nodding his head, morning and night, night and afternoon, until, at the end of September, Springer came to town.

"Mr. Springer?"

"Yes."

"My name is Miller. Sid Miller."

"Yes."

"I've got to talk with you, Mr. Springer." Sid glanced down the empty corridor, then back at the other man, who stood, barely visible, peeking out from behind the half-open hotel room door. Springer was short, shorter even than Sid. Sid smiled.

"About what?"

"It's very important," Sid said.

"It is?"

"Actually, I'm doing you a favor. You could look at it that way. You'll benefit, I promise you."

Springer closed the door.

Sid stopped it with a foot.

"Move," Springer said. "Your foot."

"Not until we've talked."

"I'll call the house detective."

"After we've talked."

"I'm a master of jiujitsu," Springer said. "I'm small, but I'm not to be trifled with."

"I'm much smaller than you are, Mr. Springer. And weak as a kitten."

"I've always hated Chicago. Always."

"I'm not dangerous, I promise. Merely desperate."

"Please go away."

"I can't."

"I'm not feeling my best today. Come back some other time."

"I said I was desperate. I spoke the truth."

"I feel like a fool holding your foot in the door."

"Then let me in."

"You've probably been sick."

"I beg your pardon?"

"I happen to be a hypochondriac. You've probably been sick."

"Not in three years, and then just the twenty-four-hour flu. I swear."

"What do you want from me?"

Sid handed the large manila envelope through the opening. "Look inside."

"Why?"

"Just look."

"Are they pictures?"

"Yes. Open it. Please."

"Pictures of you?"

"No. No. Of my son. The next Shirley Temple."

"You mean—" Springer began, and then he started to laugh. Sid saw his head shaking through the narrow opening and a moment later the door swung open as Springer leaned against the foyer wall, shaking with laughter. "Too much," he managed. "It's really too much."

Hat in hand, Sid waited.

"You went through all this just so I would look at some pictures of your son?"

"What better reason?"

"You've made a ghastly mistake, Mr. . . ."

"Miller. Sid Miller."

"I'm not a talent scout. I didn't discover Lana Turner."

"I know who you are, Mr. Springer. You're a director. A great director."

"I am a lousy director. My father helped to found the company. I am a hack. But thank you."

"Now, will you look? Will you see my son?"

"No."

"He sings like an angel. He dances like a dream. As an actor, he's a natural. And I'm not biased, I swear."

"I'm a *director*, Mr. Miller. I can't do anything for your son."

"If you liked him, you could. If you felt, as I feel, that he will be bigger than Shirley Temple, you could. You could put him in one of your movies. You could make him a star."

"It's all highly unlikely."

"Look at the pictures, Mr. Springer. And then meet my son. Hear him sing. Watch him dance. I promise you, it's an experience. What my son does with 'God Bless America' will bring tears to your eyes."

"Mr. Miller, when I repeat all this in Hollywood, you'll be famous."

"You've got to meet my son."

"I'm sorry, Mr. Miller."

"I didn't come here to fail, Mr. Springer."

"I'll write a note to the studio, how's that? You can enclose the pictures and I promise you someone will give your child every consideration."

"I didn't come here to fail, Mr. Springer."

"It's all I can *do*. Understand that."

"You can make my son a star."

"I can't make my wife a star and she also sings like an angel and dances like a dream. Southern California is crammed with dreamy dancers, Mr. Miller."

"Not like my Rudy. You notice how I haven't mentioned how he looks? That's because there are no words. You have to see for yourself. See for yourself, Mr. Springer. Do us both a favor."

"I wish I had a recording of all this."

"You wouldn't even have to change his name!"

"Don't get excited, Mr. Miller. Remember—jiujitsu."

"All his life he's been groomed for this. From birth. His middle name is Valentino, Mr. Springer."

"Valentino?"

"Rudolph Valentino Miller. Isn't that something?"

"Undeniably. However—"

"We're both Jews, Mr. Springer."

"What?"

"We've got to help each other. Jews owe that to each other. Otherwise the Gentiles will kill us all. You're a Jew, I'm a Jew, see my son!"

"Calm yourself."

"Look," Sid said, and he dropped to his knees. "I'm begging."

"Get up."

"On my knees. What more do you want?"

"Get up, get up."

"See my son."

"For God's sake, Mr. Miller—"

"I'm a poor Jew on my knees before you. No pride. Nothing. A begging Jew with his life in your hands."

"Mr. Miller, please get up. I can't take much more of this."

"Look at the pictures."

"I'm looking, I'm looking." And he ripped the envelope open. "Now get up."

Sid stood. "Well?"

Springer said nothing.

"Pinkus of the Shoreland took them. Aren't they beautiful?"

"Your son, he resembles these pictures?"

"Does a snapshot of the 'Mona Lisa' resemble the 'Mona Lisa'?"

"Photographs can be deceiving."

"These are. He is a hundred times more beautiful."

"You must be very proud."

"I love him like my life."

"Send him down."

"Poise," Sid said, tying the boy's tie. "Poise is crucial."

"Poise is crucial," the boy repeated.

"Hurry," Esther said.

Sid turned on her. "The boy cannot have poise if you all the time 'hurry' him. The appointment is for three. It is not nearly that. There is lots of time." He turned back to the boy. "Get your shoes on, Rudy. Hurry."

The boy ran to his closet and pulled out his shoes.

"They're shined?" Esther said.

The boy nodded. "This morning." He sat down in a chair, tugging at the laces.

"Don't sit so hard," Sid said. "You'll wrinkle the trousers."

The boy dropped into a kneeling position and continued putting on his shoes.

"A winning smile is as crucial as poise. Remember that."

"Yes, Father. A winning smile."

"Let me see."

The boy smiled.

"Very winning," Sid said. "Excellent. All right, after we dance, what do we do?"

"We sing 'God Bless America'?"

"And how do we sing 'God Bless America'?"

"With feeling. Not loud, but with great feeling."

"And what are our hands doing?"

"During the first half, they are clasped on my chest, like in prayer. For the last half, the left dangles while the right salutes."

"Good. The salute is very crucial."

"Everything is very crucial."

"That's right," Sid said. "Everything."

"His tie," Esther said, shaking her head.

"What's the matter with his tie?"

"It's wrong."

"I selected that tie. It's perfect. What's wrong with it?"

"Stand up, Rudy."

The boy stood. He was wearing a brand-new navy-blue suit and white shirt and dark shoes and dark socks and a red tie.

Esther studied him. "It clashes. That much is obvious."

"Clashes with what?"

"Clashes with everything."

"The tie is perfect."

"The tie is not perfect. He is a blue boy, why a red tie?"

"To give color. Contrast."

"The tie is wrong."

"The tie is right."

"The tie is wrong."

"Please," the boy said.

"See?" Sid said. "You're upsetting Rudy."

"*I'm* not upsetting Rudy. *You're* upsetting Rudy."

"Rudy, am I upsetting you?"

"Please."

"The tie should be blue," Esther said. "To match the suit."

"Blue?" Sid said. "Blue!"

"Rudy, get your blue tie."

"The boy will not dress like some goddam undertaker!"

Esther clutched her forehead.

The boy ran to his closet. "Perhaps this tie," he said, holding one up. "It has both red and blue. Do you think?"

Esther said nothing.

"Very good," Sid said. "Come. I'll put it on for you." The boy approached his father and stood quietly. Esther watched a moment, then turned away. "Where are you going?"

"To finish with my makeup."

"Your makeup? Why make up?"

"So I can be seen on the streets."

"What streets?"

"I'm going downtown with Rudy."

"No, you're not."

"Yes, I am."

"I tell you you're not."

"At a time like this, a boy needs his mother."

"His father will be more than sufficient."

"He needs me. I'll keep him calm."

"Joke."

"I'll keep him calm!"

"*I'll* keep him calm!"

"I'm going."

"You are not."

"I am too."

"Are not."

"Am too."

"Are—"

"*Stop!*" the boy said. "*Now!*"

"See?" Sid said. "See what you've done?"

"I have done nothing. Nothing!"

"Just relax, Rudy. I won't let her upset you anymore."

"He's the one upset you, Rudy. Tell him."

"Rudy, tell the truth, have I upset you?"

"Yes, Rudy, tell him. Tell him it's not me."

"You need me along, right, Rudy?"

"No, me."

"Me."

"*Neither!*" the boy cried.

"What?" Sid said.

"Rudy," Esther said.

"Neither," the boy said. "I need neither. You fight. I cannot have poise when you fight. I cannot smile. I will forget the salute."

"Rudy—" Sid said.

"No," the boy said. "I will go by myself. And I will smile. And I will have poise."

"You can't go by yourself."

"Do you want this to happen?" the boy asked.

"Yes," Sid said.

"You're very sure?"

"Yes."

"Then I will face Mr. Springer alone."

"Will you quit with the 'don't be nervous'? If you say 'don't be nervous' one more time, Esther, I don't guarantee what I'll do. Because I am nervous. So shut up."

"Well, at least stop pacing."

"I could stop breathing just as easy. You want I should do that?"

"Now, Sid. Now, honey."

"It was a goddam fool idea, letting him go alone."

"He's a big boy."

"It's still a goddam fool idea. If you hadn't stuck your fat nose in—"

"We've been through that already enough, so why go through it again?"

"Because I'm scared," Sid said. "If you wanna know the truth, I'm scared."

"The boy will do wonderfully."

"What if he forgets the words to 'God Bless America'? He could. It's possible. So what if he does? What then? Who's gonna help him remember? Answer me that."

"You'll kill yourself with a heart attack. At the very least, ulcers."

"He's a kid. Kids get nervous. Goddammit, it's way after three. Why haven't we heard?"

"No news is good news."

"If you say that one more time—"

"Hit me!" She jumped in front of him, blocking his path. "Get it over with. Hit me and shut up. Go on."

Sid pulled her close, holding her very tight. "I'm sorry, I'm sorry, but it's very important, Esther. You gotta understand that. It's gotta work. I can't take the store anymore. I need something, a change, or I'll die. I'm not kidding. I will. I'll die, Esther."

"Close your eyes, Sid."

"They are closed." He wedged his face down into her neck. "I really want this to happen, Esther."

"It will happen."

"The boy could forget."

"The boy will remember."

"He could be a movie star. The biggest. If that lousy Springer has any sense, he'll see."

"Are you crying, Sid?"

"No."

"Why are you crying?"

"I don't know. I don't know." Sid pushed her away and moved to the window.

Esther pursued him. "If you cry, I'll get a headache, I can almost feel it."

"Don't get a headache."

"Don't cry."

"I'm fine," Sid said. "Nerves."

"Don't be nervous."

"All right, Tootsie. I won't be."

"That's a good boy."

"What does he see on the fire escape? What's so wonderful out there?"

"What are you doing?"

"I don't know, going out on the fire escape." He ducked under the open window.

"Good, maybe you'll get some sun. You're very pale, Sid."

"Some sun, yes," and he waved, walking slowly up to the fire-escape landing. Sid looked around but there was nothing to see. Below, an alley ending at the street, people walking by. Beyond the alley, other houses, other fire escapes. Beyond the houses, other alleys. Sid turned his face to the sun. It was warm and he could not remember having slept the night before; maybe a catnap, but that was all. Sid yawned and stretched, leaning back against the building, closing his eyes. The sun felt good. His body began slowly to drain. Esther was probably right. The boy would do well. The boy would not forget the words to "God Bless America." No point in worrying about the boy. Worry about Springer. Maybe Springer didn't like kid actors. A lot of people didn't like Shirley Temple. What if Springer was one of them? No. You had to like the boy. You just had to. The old bags in the store, they proved that, the way they looked at him. Always looking at him, watching him as he moved. The kid had it with women; no question. In ten years, if his nose didn't grow, the kid would have his pick of the world. Any broad. Princesses, society bitches, other movie stars; he'd have them all panting. I'll pick up the pieces, Sid thought, and then he realized he had made a joke, so eyes still closed, he smiled. Any loose ends. Another joke. Sid leaned toward the sun. God, it felt good. I should do this every day, Sid thought. For as long as it's warm. Good for what ails you. What ails you? Nerves, that was all. A case of nerves could kill you quicker than a case of Scotch. That's what had ruined his pool game—nerves. From now on I'm gonna play it loose. That was the only way—

"SID!"

The moment he heard Esther shouting, he turned and started running down the rusty steps. Then he stopped. "Loose," he said, and he sauntered the rest of the way, fighting the urge to run as Esther continued to shout.

"SID! SID! SID! SID!"

Sid crouched down outside the window, about to enter the apartment, but he stopped after a look at Esther. She was standing no more than a foot from him, inside by the window, staring out. As he crouched, he dropped directly into her line of vision, only she didn't see him. Or if she did, he couldn't tell, because she continued to stare blankly out, shouting his name, "Sid! Sid!" over and over. Sid looked past her into the center of the room where the boy was. The boy was totally bald, but other than that he appeared the same as when he left hours earlier, his blue suit still neatly pressed. Sid looked back at staring Esther, then at the bald boy. Then Sid snapped. He hurled his body through the window, tripping, falling inside, rolling to his feet, lunging arms out at the boy. During the next moments he said several things, all of them indistinctly. "This to me," he said. And "Cut it all off. You had it all cut off." And "You mocked me!—Mocked me—On my knees I went to that man—I begged that man—Mocked me—You mocked me—I begged like a beggar I begged, and you mocked me—my pride I gave up and you mocked me. I fell on my knees—I crawled—Me! Me you mocked—Me!—*Me!*—*Me!*—" When he wasn't talking, he hit. He hit the boy's face and the boy stood there, and then he slammed the boy in the stomach and as the boy doubled up Sid slammed him again, this time on the neck, and the boy fell. Sid plunged down on top of him, swinging his fists at the face. Sid tried grabbing the boy's hair, but there was none, not a strand, so he had to content himself with the boy's ears, slapping them, shaking them, bouncing the boy's head against the floor. Esther fell on top of them, trying to pull Sid away, but Sid was in no mood for pulling. Esther was screaming his name still, but the meaning was different as she crawled on her husband's back, shrieking, trying to stop his hands as they pulled at the boy's ears. Sid continued to bounce the boy's head against the floor. There was much blood now, and as Esther finally toppled Sid off, they all got smeared with red. The boy lay still, breathing but still, and Sid sat beside his body, panting like an animal. Esther was whimpering, and Sid watched her a moment before he wheeled to his feet and fled. Esther glanced after him, then returned her attentions to the boy, hurrying after a cloth, wiping the blood from his battered face. Then she lifted him and carried him to the sofa and took off his clothes. The boy was aware now, eyes half open, and Esther cried, smiling down at him because he wasn't dead. She wept wordlessly as she stroked his face, kissed his eyes. The boy blinked. "Can you hear me?" The boy nodded. "Are you all right?" A nod. "Can I get you anything?" No nod. "Can you sleep?" A nod. "Try, then." The boy turned his face to the wall. "I won't be long," Esther said, and she hurried across the room, down the stairs and outside, looking for Sid.

Fifteen minutes later she found him, standing in a corner of the darkened delicatessen, his face to the wall. He did not turn when she entered. "He's all right," Esther said, "I think." Sid said nothing. "To be sure we ought to maybe call a doctor but how can I call a doctor? What can I say? 'My husband tried to kill my son'? Can I say that? Yes?"

"I didn't try to kill him."

"No?"

"I was only teaching him a lesson."

"What lesson?"

Sid said nothing.

"*What lesson?*"

"I don't know, I don't know, I don't believe me either."

"Apologize to the boy."

"Why did he have his hair cut? It was for him we did everything. Why did he cut his hair?"

"Ask him. Talk to him. Apologize."

Sid stayed standing in the corner.

Esther jerked him away.

"Don't," Sid whispered.

Esther pulled him along.

"I worship him," Sid whispered. "With all my heart. He is my son."

When they stood on the landing outside the apartment Esther said, "Go on."

Sid pushed at the door. "Loving means caring, isn't that right? If I didn't care, would I have touched him? Doesn't that prove I love him?"

Esther stayed on the landing, and, when she was alone, she pressed her fingers against her temple, trying to stop the pain.

"He's not here," Sid said, reappearing a few minutes later.

"Not on the sofa? Not in the bedroom?"

"Not here."

"Not on the fire escape?"

"Gone."

"Gone?"

"Gone."

The boy was on fire. His head would not stop burning. He moved quickly across the crowded beach toward Lake Michigan. Stripping down to his bathing suit, he slipped into the water and, when it was deep enough, fell head down into a dead man's float. The waves washed over him, cooling his body, but his head was still on fire. He held his breath and sank under water. When his breath was gone, he surfaced and floated on his back for a while, staring up at the totally blue sky. Then he ducked his body and sank under water again, his hands gently rubbing the top of his bald head. Surfacing, he stroked until he could touch bottom, and then he hurried up the beach to his clothes. Gathering them, he turned around in a circle several times before running north, north where it was cool. He ran for half an hour, cutting in and around, avoiding the others, and then he stopped, dropping his clothes, swimming out, floating, ducking, surfacing, then back, running again. The beach emptied with the falling of the sun and he walked north, throwing on his shirt, donning his pants and shoes, and when he was dressed he started to run again, running along the edge of the lake, running easily, running, running north. He swam twice more before he slept, falling instantly asleep in the warm night, his body curled between two rocks, safe from the wind. At dawn he was off, walking quickly, staring at the sun as it inched up over the horizon of the lake. The day was hot, and before the morning ended he began having hunger pangs, his stomach sounding fiercely, but he did not give in to them and by late afternoon they were gone. The second night he went to sleep shortly after sundown, again curling between warm rocks, and he slept deeply until the rain started, and then he rose and moved north through it, head down, hands in his pockets, eyes half closed. The rain stopped by midmorning and by noon the sun was strong, and he was beyond Chicago now, running up the North Shore running past Evanston, entering Wilmette, leaving it, starting into Winnetka. He swam more often than before, and for longer periods of time, trying to get cool, since his head was more on fire now than it had ever been. His forehead felt hot when he touched it, and his eyes hurt him. As he swam, he stared up over the bluff that paralleled the lake, looking at the giant houses. He stared until his eyes required closing, and then he would close them and sink under the water, rubbing them with the tips of his fingers. That afternoon he commenced to shiver, even though the sun was strong, and he was unable to run fast or far. The sun had not yet disappeared when he crept a few feet up the bluff and made a place for himself beneath some bushes and closed his eyes. But he could not sleep. He was very tired and his eyes felt as if they were swelling but the shivering was more distinct than ever, so he lay there, body foetal, awake. The moon came, accompanied by the early stars. Suddenly it was very cool and he was perspiring, the shaking almost painful, the swelling of his eyes most severe. The boy took off his shirt and pants, keeping them off until the chills began, and then he put them back on and scurried down to the beach, frantically digging a hole in the warm sand, crawling into the depression, covering his cold body. The effort exhausted him and his head dropped back at an uncomfortable angle but he was too dizzy to right it. When the perspiring returned, he managed to roll clear of the depression. He lay quietly, stretched out beside it, and as the chills began, he rolled back into the tiny hole, scraping a few handfuls of sand over him. His head was swelling now and his ears heard strange sounds, sharp whistles, muted cries. The boy put his hands over his ears and writhed. The chills increased and he could no longer stop his teeth from chattering, so he lunged away from the hole and pushed himself to his feet, starting a jagged run along the sand, running until he was on fire again, and then he ripped at his shirt, dropping to his knees, cradling his head in his elbows. At the next sign of freezing he was up, trying to run, panting, slapping his arms across his body. As his body began heating, he made for the lake, submerging in the cool water until the chill returned, worse now than before. He continued on like that, running when cold, bathing when hot, for as long as he could. But eventually he lacked the strength to reach the lake, so he slipped noiselessly onto the sand and, after a time of quiet breathing, slept.

The next day he began falling down.

The morning was perfect, warm and blue, and although the fever was stronger, he was used to it, knew its limits, was able to cope. He jogged north, stopping from time to time to gaze up at the great houses dotting the bluff rim. At noon the sun was hot, so the chilling times were easier to bear, although the periods of perspiring were probably less comfortable than ever. He swam a good deal during those periods, and it was after a particularly long swim, as he reached for his clothes, that he first fell. His face reflected surprise, but that left, and then he had his clothes in his arms and was running again until he fell. This time he paused on the sand, shaking his head weakly. His stomach rumbled and his eyes burned and the crazy sounds were back in his ears, so he lay still until he could rise. Then he walked north until he fell again. This time he stretched out full on his back, his hands shielding his hot eyes. After a while he rolled onto his stomach and pushed himself into a kneeling position. From there he made it to his feet and began walking. He tried moving straight ahead but he kept veering off, first one way, then the other. Dropping his clothes, he lunged for the lake, falling into the water, resting there. He sat in the water, the waves washing him rhythmically, the sounds in his ears growing louder. He tried to rise but slipped back into the water. Again he tried but he could not make it to his feet, so he stopped trying and lay in the water, waiting for his strength. When it came he got to his feet and broke into a wild run up the beach. There was nothing around him, nothing near, so he closed his eyes and ran. He ran faster than he had ever run before and this time when he fell he got up immediately and ran some more. He fell again and now it was harder to rise but he fought his way off his knees and ran, slower now but as fast as he could. He kept his eyes closed until he felt the lake around his legs and then he turned, because he had veered again, and he left the lake behind him, bolting for the bluff, but he never made it. He fell hard, and now there was no strength left. He tried to rise but his body hugged the sand, and all his kicking did was to move him around in a circle, around and around, his head the center of the circle, his footprints a jagged circumference. He kicked until he stopped. After that he knew nothing, not the week, the year, the time of day. Eventually he became aware of the hospital room, but how he got there he never remembered. In the hospital, however, several things became clear. He had lost eleven pounds. He had a fever of a hundred and five.

And he was deaf.

"I didn't do it!" Sid said. "You can't blame me."

"No one is blaming you, Mr. Miller," Dr. Weiss said. "Please."

Sid glanced down the hospital corridor toward Esther, who sat slumped in a wooden chair. "I love that boy. It's not my fault. I love him. I would give up my life for that boy."

"Please," Dr. Weiss repeated. "Try to get control, Mr. Miller."

"Why did it happen? What?"

"The boy showed signs of being beaten severely when he was brought in. Particularly around the head and face."

"I never touched him. Ask anybody. I have never laid a hand on Rudy."

"Undoubtedly he was beaten on the beach. Or someplace nearby. At any rate, he was beaten. And then the infection set in. He was not in good shape when they brought him in, Mr. Miller."

"Poor Rudy—God."

"The hearing loss isn't complete. Almost, but not quite. Perhaps, with the use of a hearing aid, plus lip reading—"

"God," Sid said. "Why wasn't it me? Why Rudy?"

"Would you like to see him?"

"More than anything."

"He's looking quite well now. May I ask you a question, Mr. Miller?"

"Yes, yes."

"I understand the boy's reluctance to give his name. But why didn't you notify the police about the boy's disappearance sooner? Two weeks is a long time to wait."

"I wanted to. My wife, she was against it. She kept saying he'd come back. We love the boy. He never ran away before. Every night Esther prayed for his return. It wasn't the police's affair, she said. A family business only. We have never liked washing our dirty linen in public."

"Yes," Dr. Weiss said. He gestured down the corridor. "Your son is in the last room. Don't stay long. I'll stop in after a few minutes. When I come, that will be your signal to leave."

"Bless you, Doctor," Sid said, and he turned, hurrying to Esther. "Come," he said. "Come quick. We can see Rudy now."

"Why didn't you let me call the police? Two weeks he's been alone. All by himself. We should have been with him. I should have been."

"Come," Sid said. "Every minute is precious."

Esther stood. "Rudy," she said. "Rudy."

"The last room. This way."

"What did the doctor say to you?"

"He looks fine, the doctor said."

"Then he's all right."

"Perfect. Except maybe for a little trouble with the ears."

Esther stopped. "What? What trouble?"

"Nothing. Some infection he caught."

"He can hear?"

"Of course he can hear. He'll be perfect." Sid pulled at her, but she would not move.

"Tell me."

"A hearing aid. Maybe. Now come."

"Tell me."

"He will be perfect with a hearing aid and maybe some lip reading. Come."

"You beat him deaf."

"The infection. It was the infection. Ask the doctor. Ask anybody. Don't get excited. He will be fine."

"You beat him deaf!"

"I hardly touched him. You know that."

"*Rudy!*"

"Esther—Esther, stop!" Sid chased after her down the corridor.

"*Rudy! Rudy!*" and she ran into his room.

Sid entered a moment later, standing in the doorway, watching as she cradled the boy, rocking back and forth, muttering in Yiddish. "*Weh ist mir. Weh ist mir.*"

Sid smiled. "Hello, Rudy," he said.

The boy said nothing.

"You look good, kid. I mean it. Fine."

The boy looked at him.

"*Shondeh. Weh ist mir.*"

"They treating you O.K.?"

Slowly the boy's eyes widened.

"Can you hear me, Rudy? At all?"

"*Shondeh. Shondeh.*"

"The doctor told me it isn't so bad, Rudy. Don't mind your mother. The point is it's not so bad. That infection, it could have been a lot worse. With a little help, you'll hear perfect."

Still the boy's eyes widened.

"*Oy. Oy gewalt.*"

Sid hesitated, then approached the end of the bed. "You really look wonderful. Never better, so help me God."

The wide eyes watched.

"Rudy, look, I'm so happy you're all right, I'm crying. See, Rudy? See the tears?" Sid pointed to his face. "See? That's how happy I am we found you. You had us awful worried, Rudy. Running away like that."

"*Shondeh. Shondeh. Weh ist mir.*"

"I'll make it up to you, Rudy. I swear. Look at my tears. Can you hear me? Look at my tears, Rudy. I'll make it up to you. As God is my witness, you'll never have another unhappy day. You hear that? That's a promise. I promise it to you. You're my son and I made you a solemn promise. Please, Rudy, close your eyes. Didn't you hear my promise? Close your eyes. Oh, Rudy, God, please, I'll make it all up to you. We'll be so happy. Everyone will envy us. That's how happy we're gonna be."

The eyes did not stop staring.

"*Weh ist mir. Weh ist mir. Weh ist mir.*"

"So happy. Oh, yes, so happy, Rudy. Yes. Please don't look. No more. The infection. It wasn't me. It was the infection. Ask the doctor. He'll tell you. He never mentioned the spanking I gave. That's all it was. A little spanking. It was the infection did it. On my word of honor, Rudy, my sacred word of honor, it wasn't the spanking, it wasn't me." He looked down at the floor, then up quickly, then away.

The eyes stared.

Sid made a smile. "All right, all the water is over the dam. We're just like we used to be. Can I get you something, Rudy? Anything. You just name it." Sid glanced around the room. "I'll write it down. That way we can talk. I could shout but they don't like that in hospitals. I'll write it down. Can I do something for you? Here." And he grabbed a crumpled piece of paper from Esther's purse. He rummaged through some more until he found a pencil. "See, Rudy?" and he waved the pencil. "Now we can talk. Here. Can I do something for you? I'm writing it down." Slowly, Sid printed the words then gave the paper to the boy. As the boy read the words, Sid said them again. "Can I do something for you?"

"Die."

X

Sleeping with Shelly Bingham was, for Aaron, a watershed event, since it forced him at last to face without flinching the one unendurable question: was there "something the matter with him"? That possibility had existed for quite some time, first, primarily in his subconscious, a weightless fear lying suspended inside him, a tiny spider floating darkly across his mind. Occasionally it would catch the light, but not often, and when it did he would quickly brush it back into the shadows again, praying for the darkness to kill it, kill it, make it die.

It festered.

One spring night when Aaron was sixteen the fear had exploded, shredding his subconscious. He had left the movies early that spring night, by the side entrance, and he hurried to his home via back streets, moving through tree shadows, avoiding light. Arriving at his house, he crept in through the rear door, turning the knob noiselessly, stepping inside, shutting the door without a sound. Aaron paused. From the living room he could hear talking, and he took advantage of that sound, moving a step at a time toward it. When he had moved as close as he dared he stopped, waiting, waiting.

The lights in the living room went off. Then Aaron heard his sister's voice. Deborah was saying, "Jamie Wakefield, you win the blue ribbon for stupidity. The world's championship."

"What did I do?" Jamie Wakefield said.

Aaron crept forward again, closer. Now he could see them, framed in moonlight, sitting on the couch. Aaron waited. Suddenly he saw them kiss.

"Jamie. Jamie."

Aaron held his breath. Jamie was touching Deborah's body now. They began to disrobe. Aaron moved closer, standing framed in the doorway. Their eyes were closed as they pawed at each other, breathing louder. Soon they were naked save for Deborah's pearls, Jamie's socks. Panting, they clawed each other, fingers digging into flesh. Aaron took another step forward. He was inside the room now, and had he wanted to he could have almost reached out and touched them. Jamie straddled Deborah. Deborah groaned. Aaron stared. Their bodies glistened in the moonlight. Grappling, they rolled together on the couch. Deborah's fingers tore at Jamie's back. Jamie bit her neck and then he yelled and Deborah moaned his name, Jamie, Jamie. Aaron closed his eyes. It was over, all over, and he felt . . . he felt . . .

Nothing. It had been like watching a wall.

Aaron backed out of the room, slipped through the house, mindless of noise. He opened the rear door and stepped into the spring night. He felt sick and dizzy and he staggered along the sidewalk, howling like a cretin in pain. Shades lifted as he staggered on, moving in and out of shadow, turning corners, traveling lanes. His legs ached terribly but he forced them on, glorying in the pain that gave him something else to concentrate on, something other than the one unendurable question. Eventually he lost track of time. His howling weakened. Finally he pitched forward.

Aaron on the grass.

Racked.

The night with Shelly Bingham racked him again. Try as he would to forget it, he could not. And so, three days later, desperate and weak and pale, Aaron forced himself once and for all to face the one, the only unendurable.

Was he homosexual?

Praying, Aaron walked into the university library and was about to ask the librarian for some books on the subject, except when she asked, "Yes?" he found himself too frightened to speak. He tried for a smile, finally settled for a feeble shrug and fled her sight. Later, hating himself, Aaron for the first time in his life stole the books on homosexuality from the library and crept away from the building, convinced of his perversion.

When he got the books safely inside his house he locked his bedroom door and began to read. He read the books several times through, always with the door locked, and when he had to leave his room for trips to the kitchen or into town for cigarettes he carefully hid the books in the farthest corner of the topmost shelf in his clothes closet.

After he had committed the material almost to memory, Aaron took to journeying into Manhattan, standing in the cold on 42nd Street, a cigarette dangling from the corner of his taut mouth as he watched the homosexuals prance by. Night after night he stood there, watching as they swaggered and swished, some wearing lipstick, some mascara; limp wrists and muscle men, brunettes and peroxide blondes, Aaron eyed them all.

They made him sick.

Thank God, Aaron thought, standing in the cold, and when a few approached him he sent them sharply on their way with withering scorn. For the first time since Shelly, Aaron felt alive.

I'm all right, he realized. I'm fine.

Then what had happened in his mind that night?

Aaron read his books again, and the more he read them the clearer it all came. Hugh had come after him, pursuing him down to the Food Shoppe. Hugh had pestered him after classes. Hugh incessantly talked of women and his need of them and his infinite conquests, obviously, Aaron realized now, protesting too much. Hugh's insistence on the double date, on sharing an evening of sex, that was another sign. And Hugh was always touching him, punching him or throwing an arm in a seemingly casual way around Aaron's shoulder—desperate, Aaron realized now, for contact.

He's after me, Aaron realized. And considering what had happened in his mind that night, Hugh was coming perilously close to succeeding. At last, Aaron saw it whole: he had gotten involved with (to give Hugh the benefit of any doubt) at best a latent homosexual. And who could tell how long Hugh's latency would hold? Isn't that just the way, Aaron thought: the one time you get a friend in this world he turns out to be a dirty, no-good, scheming, son-of-a-bitching fag?

Returning the books to the library, Aaron cut himself off from the world.

Until his graduation, he simply went to classes, came straight home. He quit his job. He did only what schoolwork was necessary. He lay on his bed and he stared at the walls and he thought. For the books he had stolen had told him that there was a little bit of the homosexual in every man. Through weakness, Aaron had allowed his little bit to come close to conquering. I must take stock of myself honestly, Aaron decided. No more weakness. I must set my house in perfect order.

So he cut himself off from the world. For the next months he saw, as far as was possible, no one. He was terribly lonely, of course.

But he had been there before.

Two weeks after his graduation from Princeton, Aaron received a notice of induction into the Army. The notice irked him. In the first place he was going to be 4F because of his legs, so the whole thing was a waste of time. And, most important, it would deprive him of a full day's writing. He had started a book of short stories the day after his graduation, and the way he was going there was no reason not to have it all done by early fall. Except the crucial thing was not to break the rhythm, and this absurd call to country forced him for a day to do just that, so he did not feel, as he reread the notice and crumpled it up, the least patriotic.

He was in a foul humor the morning of departure. Charlotte cooked

him breakfast and, in spite of his protests, insisted on packing an overnight bag while he stood stiffly in the kitchen, sipping coffee and practicing limping. He had been working on a particular walk ever since the
notice came, and by now he had it down to perfection. A vague pained
expression on his face, a decided stiffness in his body, Aaron stalked
around the kitchen. It was important, he thought, to appear to be hiding
the limp. He was no malingerer; the limp was real. So he drank more coffee and practiced his limp until Charlotte returned with his bag. Aaron
took it and walked halfway out the door when she called his name.

"Aaron."

"What?" Aaron said. She wore a flowered summer robe and her long
hair, totally white now, hung straight down her back. She looked at him,
saying nothing, and he was about to say "What?" again when he noticed
her tiny hands; they were in constant flight, from her cheek to her hair to
her heart. "Oh," Aaron said then as he realized she wanted to be kissed
goodbye, so he bent abruptly and touched his lips to her forehead.

Charlotte nodded. "Do you want anything special for supper? A celebration meal?" She clapped her hands. "A 4F fiesta we could call it."

Aaron grunted.

"Don't be nasty to them, Aaron. Please. Remember your manners and
don't get them mad at you and—"

Aaron waved and closed the door, starting on his not so merry way.
By the time he reached the induction center, an old gray building, pon-
derous, covered with heavy soot, he was perspiring and angrier than ever
at the Army for wasting his very good time. Limping down a linoleum
corridor, Aaron sat uncomfortably in a stiff-backed wooden chair, waiting impatiently along with more than a hundred other potential soldiers.

They were so young, so panicked, that it was difficult for him to keep
from laughing. Gawky bodies, acne-ridden faces, dead eyes. Aaron tried
not to listen to the bursts of nervous laughter which exploded intermittently, making the ensuing silences especially welcome. Finally a buzzer
sounded and a corporal with a clipboard began calling off names at the
front of the large room.

"Abbott, Henry C."

There was silence.

"Abbott, Henry C." More emphatic this time.

A high voice said "What?"

"What the hell do you think? Are you here, Abbott? If you are, say so."

"Here, sir."

"All right; down the corridor, first door to your left. Think you can handle those instructions, Abbott?"

Oh, you smug bastard corporal, Aaron thought.

"Adams, William F."

"Here, sir."

"Adderly, Morris I."

"Here, sir."

Aaron waited.

"Fazio, Eugene D."

"Here, sir."

"Firestone, Aaron."

Aaron paused a moment before standing. Then, deliberately, formally, he answered, "In attendance." There was a burst of laughter, and Aaron was conscious of dead eyes watching him. When the laughter died, he added, with infinite disdain, "Sir."

The corporal looked at him. "You'll love it in the Army, Firestone."

"Dubious," Aaron answered. "Highly." Another burst of laughter. Then Aaron nodded courteously to the corporal, picked up his overnight bag and disappeared down the corridor.

The examination was a farce. They were allowed forty minutes to complete the written test, a moronic group of multiple-choice questions. Aaron finished them in five, the first one done. He glanced around at the others; they sat, hunched over, perspiring. Illiterates, Aaron thought as he handed in his answer sheet. Limping noticeably, he left the room, heading for the physical exam. It proved to be even more ludicrous. A series of aging doctors, obviously no longer able to sustain themselves in private practice, prodded and poked him. They checked his eyes and his ears and his teeth. Aaron endured them. Finally a doctor noticed his limp. Aaron explained. The doctor touched his hips, muttered to himself, then asked Aaron to walk. Aaron walked. The doctor shook his head, then called in another doctor. The other doctor asked Aaron to walk. Aaron walked, limping magnificently. The doctors conferred, both of them muttering, shaking their heads in unison. Aaron stood very straight and tried to look patriotic. In a few minutes it was all over.

They took him.

"They took me, Mother. They took me." He sat sweating in a telephone booth, trying to keep his voice under control.

"What's that, Aaron?"

"Oh, the stupid bastards, the stupid idiotic bastards." His hands were shaking but he managed to light a cigarette. Inhaling deeply, he scowled at his hands, commanding them to be still.

"Didn't they see you walk?"

"They saw. They saw. Stop!"

"Stop what, Aaron?"

"I was talking to my hands, Mother."

"Are you all right, Aaron?"

"I am angry, Mother."

There was silence on the wire.

"When I get settled I'll want you to send me my writing." Then another silence. He sensed her tears, said, "Don't. Goodbye." Hung up. One. Two. Three.

The train ride proved dreary. For two nights and a day they traveled south, then west, then south again. The weather grew progressively hotter, but the cars were so uncomfortable to begin with that the increase in temperature didn't really matter. There was a sudden vicious thunderstorm the second afternoon, but other than that the sun remained steady. Aaron sat alone in the rear seat of his car. Originally a fat, swarthy boy shared the seat with him, but Aaron's legs were too long for both of them to be comfortable, so midway through the first night, grumbling, the other boy left.

Aaron's companions bored him. He quickly had them all pegged. Across the aisle sat a short, ugly Irish boy who boasted continually of his sexual prowess. "I had her pantin' like a bitch in heat, see, an' she's beggin' me for more. 'Go-wann, Danny,' she's sayin'. 'Yer killin' me, Danny, but go-wann.' " In front of him sat four curly-haired Jews, gamblers, devourers of salami. "Willya deal the cards, Herman, for crissakes." "Shaddup, Byron, cantcha see I'm eatin'?" "Well, I don't give a crap if yer eatin' or not, deal the goddam cards." And in front of them, two laughing Negroes who hummed and snapped their fingers and said "Man . . . man" over and over. And three sullen Puerto Ricans reading "Batman" and a quiet blond letter writer—"Dear Sis. Well, I am on the train and so far so good . . ."

You are clichés, Aaron thought. Every bloodless one of you.

Dear Aunt Lou . . .

Hey, man (finger snap). Hey, man . . .

Ohhhhhhhhh, Danny, Jee-zusssss . . .

Yer a fink, Byron, you know that . . .

Herman, yer droolin' on the cards . . .

Man, hey, man . . .

Dear Cousin Stanley . . .

Danny, yer drivin' me cray-zeeeeeeee . . .

You do not exist, Aaron thought. Not in my world. If you breathe, then I give you permission to breathe the same air. But that is all.

They reached Camp Rand the morning of the third day. Getting off the train, they marched to a line of open trucks and began climbing on. Climbing was difficult for Aaron and he felt a sharp pain as he made his first attempt at boarding. Failing, he tried again, but it hurt, and he had no success until someone started helping him, half lifting him onto the truck. Aaron turned. It was the blond boy who wrote letters. It would be you, Aaron thought; of course, it would have to be you. Should he say "thank you"? he wondered. There was always the chance that the boy might take it as a prologue to conversation. Aaron solved the problem by saying "Thanks" sharply, turning away at the same time, moving to a corner of the truck and standing rigidly, staring out.

When he first caught sight of Camp Rand, Aaron had to laugh. It too was a cliché—hot, flat, endless, just like in the movies. Not much grass, not many trees, a plenitude of dust. The trucks ground down to a lower gear, slowing, turning into the post proper. A company of basic trainees in full field uniform, complete with rifles and heavy packs, marched along a parallel road. Aaron watched them, listening as they chanted, "Lef, ri, lef, ri, ho-lef, ri, lef."

Aaron panicked.

His legs would never hold! Never. They would fail him and he would fall to earth open, exposed to laughter. Aaron rubbed his hips. They still hurt from trying to jump onto the truck. Never hold. Never. Oh, you goddam stupid doctors. You silly-assed sinecures, doing this to me. Putting me here. "*Lef, ri, lef, ri, ho-lef, ri, lef.*" I can't do it. I'll never be able to. Suddenly he wanted to cry. He had not cried since . . . since . . .

My name is Aaron Fire and I do not cry.

I endure.

The men were all delivered to the Transient Company, a squat series of dull rectangular buildings set directly across the road from the Post Stockade. Usually recruits stayed one night in the Transient Company before being shipped out to one of the other companies on post for basic training. Several times a day whistles would blow and the men would race out to the street, standing in formation, waiting for their names to be called. Then they would be marched away. Aaron stayed a week. Most of that time he spent pulling details. Twice he had KP and the strain on his legs was great. He would lie awake at night, rubbing them, pounding them with the sides of his hands, trying desperately to alleviate the pain. At first he was delighted that his name was not called and he began thinking that perhaps the Army had made a mistake, forgotten him. But as the days wore on, the delight soured. He was always being selected for some duty or other—his height betrayed him. "You, Shorty, go grab a mop." "All right, Shorty, two steps forward." He did what he was told, silently, speaking to no one. But he longed for training to begin. Anything was better than waiting; something was better than nothing.

Then, the eighth day, his name was called. Hurrying to his barracks, he grabbed his green duffel bag and dragged it back out into the company street. Several other boys were waiting. Then a bus appeared. All the other recruits had marched off, but Aaron's group silently boarded a bus. Slowly, the bus began to move. Aaron lit a cigarette. Where in hell were they going? Inserting the cigarette at the left corner of his mouth, he waited. The bus drove for fifteen minutes. Then it stopped. The recruits got out. Aaron looked around. He was standing in the street of what appeared to be the most remote company on post. There were several barracks buildings, a classroom and an orderly room. Set into the dirt by the orderly room door was a freshly painted wooden sign that read "X Company." Across from the buildings was an enormous, dusty field. Behind the buildings was another field, equally large, equally dusty. They were isolated from the rest of Camp Rand. The firing from the rifle ranges sounded louder here than at the Transient Company. It was all very strange. Aaron turned around and around, perspiring, on the dusty road. Then the bus driver asked would they please follow him, so they did, trailing along to the supply room, where they were given sheets and blankets. The bus driver requested they go into the nearest barracks, select a bed, make it and wait for further instructions. As Aaron entered the barracks he saw another busload of recruits pull into the company street. He waited for the better part of an hour and then the bus driver reappeared, asking quietly if they would please go to the classroom now. Aaron entered the classroom and sat in the rear corner. Gradually, other recruits straggled in, looking around, unsure, uncertain. In fifteen minutes there were seventy-five men in the room, smoking, talking nervously among themselves. Suddenly the talking stopped.

A figure had appeared by the lectern at the front of the room. An ape clad in the costume of a master sergeant.

"Welcome to X Company. The X, for the curious, stands for experimental, but more of that in a moment. My name is Sergeant Terry. Please call me that: Sergeant Terry. Not 'sir,' not 'Sarge.' Sergeant Terry. That is my name. Clear?"

When the man began to speak, Aaron experienced a sudden shudder of recognition—the voice was low, rough, harsh. Aaron leaned forward, studying. Sergeant Terry was of less than average height, incredibly broad. His shirt strained at the shoulders, the fabric taut. The front of the shirt was covered with ribbons; the sleeves were covered with stripes and bars. The trousers were perfectly pressed. His face was simian, small eyes, thick nose, thick lips, narrow forehead. His hair was short and reddish brown, tightly curled. Yet the man did not appear stupid. Why? Aaron leaned back, folding his arms across his chest. Why? Suddenly he knew. It was the eyes. The small eyes. The eyes were alive.

"Would you all please stand up now?" Sergeant Terry requested. The men rose. "I want you each to tell me your name. Say it loud and clear. As soon as you've done that, you may sit down. Begin here." He pointed to the front row. In five minutes they were all seated again. "This is called getting acquainted," Sergeant Terry said. "You know my name. Now I know yours." He began pacing behind the lectern, his thick hands clasped behind his back. "You are without question the most incredible group of recruits ever assembled in the Army of the United States." There was a burst of nervous laughter. Sergeant Terry stopped pacing. "I do not jest. Take a look at yourselves. Go on. Examine each other. You have sixty seconds." Aaron looked around at the other men. They were staring at one another, laughing, talking. The boy next to Aaron was uncommonly fat. The one in front had thick glasses. Aaron's eyes moved faster. They were all of them defects. Wheezers, droolers, gaspers; thin, fat, too tall, too short. Aaron felt suddenly at home.

"Did I exaggerate?" Sergeant Terry's voice cut through the laughter, dousing it. "You see? You're rejects. Every one of you. I trust you feel more at home now. We all feel at home with our own kind, isn't that so?" There was general nodding. "And here we all are in X Company. The question is why? The answer is simple." He paused. Good, Aaron thought. The proper time to pause. Whet interest. The man was a good speaker—light, casual, direct. And of course the voice helped him. The low, rough voice.

"In this great freedom-loving land of ours," Sergeant Terry said, "everyone's a slob. We found that out. By 'we,' I mean the Army. It was true in both World Wars. It simply didn't matter how low we set the physical standards, people kept getting rejected. So we had to use able-bodied men for desk work. Now, if only there were some way to free them for combat duty, the advantages would be obvious. And you, gentlemen, are the experiment to see if that way can be found. Gentlemen, each and every one of you got the shaft. I feel for you. Ordinarily, you would have been classified 4F. But now you have the supreme privilege of serving your country as guinea pigs. Don't blame me. It isn't my fault."

"Son of a bitch," somebody said.

"I couldn't agree more." Sergeant Terry nodded. "We will now have fifteen seconds in which you may swear. Please feel free." He waited a moment. "All right. Consider my position. I, gentlemen, am going to shepherd you through the easiest basic training in history. My comrades in arms will sneer at me. 'Here comes Terry with the nuts,' they'll say. You, gentlemen, are the nuts. I don't like it any better than you do. Our commander, Captain Apple, is at the present time trying to talk his way into a different assignment. He is already the laughingstock of the Officers' Club. He will be around from time to time. You can tell him by the twin bars on his shoulders and the look of humiliation on his face. Be kind to him in his time of trouble. Are there any questions thus far?"

There were none.

"Training starts tomorrow. We travel by bus, no marching. This indignity—"

"Catch the big words," a boy in front of Aaron said. Too loud.

Sergeant Terry dropped his voice. "All right. Stand up." He snapped his fingers. "You know who I'm talking to. Stand up now."

The boy stared innocently ahead.

Suddenly Terry vaulted down among them, screaming. "Stand up, goddam you! I'm talking to you, Winkler, Martin P. *Stand up!*"

Martin P. Winkler stood up.

Sergeant Terry breathed deeply a moment, staring at him. "I don't like being derided," Sergeant Terry said, his voice under control. "All of you. Remember that. Never deride me. Never deride me. You see, I know all your names now. I told you that before. I'm good at names. Names and faces I remember." He continued staring at Winkler. "I've got to punish you. You understand that?"

"Yes, sir."

"Yes who?"

"Yes, Sergeant Terry."

Terry nodded. "All right. What's your disability, Winkler?"

"Bad feet. I got bad feet."

"Then I can't make you run, can I? That would be cruel. How are your arms, Winkler?"

"All right, I guess."

"Your shoulders?"

"Yes."

"Then dig me a hole, Winkler. Go get a shovel and dig me a hole."

"A hole?"

"Good work, Winkler."

"How big a hole?"

"Ah, now that's the problem, isn't it, Winkler? How big a hole? Firestone!"

Aaron jumped. "What? What?"

"How tall are you?"

"Six four and a half. Six five."

"There's your answer, Winkler. Dig me a hole big enough to bury Firestone. Clear?"

"Yes."

"Anyplace in that field across the road will do, Winkler. Pick your own spot. I like to give my men initiative. Firestone?"

"What?"

"Do you find my order macabre?"

"No, Sergeant Terry."

Terry looked at Aaron. "Good," he said. "However, I am, from time to time, macabre." He moved back to the lectern. "All right, gentlemen, if there are no questions, we can adjourn."

There were no questions.

"Tomorrow, as I said, we start. You have the rest of the day to get ready. Relax. Sleep well. Fear not. Think of me as your security blanket and we'll all live forever."

With that, Sergeant Terry was gone.

He reappeared several hours later. Aaron was lying on his bunk, listening as a dozen other recruits exchanged Army experiences. The front door of the barracks opened and Sergeant Terry entered. The recruits quieted.

"I need a volunteer," he said.

Nobody moved.

"Gentlemen, you must have faith," Sergeant Terry said. "Nothing hideous is going to happen. I need some typing done. Now. Who can type?"

Nine boys stepped forward.

"Wonderful," Sergeant Terry said. "I've never seen such get up and go. All right, Phillips," this to the nearest boy "How fast?"

"Thirty words a minute."

"That is not what I call typing."

"Forty-five," another said.

"Fifty."

"Fifty-five."

"Going once," Sergeant Terry said. "Going twice."

"One hundred words a minute," Aaron called out.

Sergeant Terry looked at him. "Firestone, I'm impressed. I bow to talent." He bowed. "All right. Get your shoes on and come along."

Hurriedly, Aaron did as he was told. They left the barracks together and turned left, heading for the orderly room. Up ahead, five men stood clustered, talking. Two were fat, one was very short and two were myopic.

"Ye gods," Sergeant Terry muttered. "It's a zoo."

As he passed them the five men saluted.

Sergeant Terry sighed. "That's quick thinking, gentlemen," he began. "But please don't do it again. I'm not an officer. Officers have insignia on their shoulders. That's how you tell them from enlisted men. Officers have insignia on their shoulders. Say that." Raising his thick hands like an orchestra conductor, he gave a downbeat.

"Officers have insignia on their shoulders," the five men said.

Sergeant Terry nodded. "I'll put you all in for promotion." Sighing again, he commenced to walk. "I was born for better things," he muttered as he neared the orderly room. "Tell me, Firestone; what's your trouble? Neuralgia?"

"My legs. I was run over when I was little."

"That was thoughtless of you."

"Yes," Aaron said. "It was."

Sergeant Terry opened the orderly-room door. "Sit there." He pointed.

Aaron sat at a desk.

"This is the company typewriter," Sergeant Terry said, carrying it over to Aaron. "Like all of us, it has seen better days. There's paper in the top desk drawer."

Aaron got out two sheets of paper and inserted them into the aged machine.

"I'll give you one minute, Firestone. Type me a hundred words." He moved close to Aaron, standing over him, his arms folded across his chest. "Ready, set, go."

Aaron typed.

"Stop," Sergeant Terry said a minute later. Yanking the paper from the machine, he studied it a while. "This is beautiful work, Firestone. Really first rate." He shook his head. "But I needed someone who could type in English."

"Are there that many mistakes?"

Sergeant Terry squinted at the paper. "It looks like Urdu."

"I was nervous."

"Why?"

"I don't like people standing over me."

"That the only reason?"

"Why else?"

"I don't know, Firestone. Why else?"

Aaron shrugged. "Let me try again."

"That won't be necessary."

"Suit yourself." Aaron stood.

"You want the job?"

"What job?"

"Clerk."

"What would I do?"

"Little."

"Then I want it."

"Then it's yours."

"Where would the Army be without you college boys?" Sergeant Terry mused, sitting crouched, apelike, at his desk. He glanced out the window. It was after lunch three days later, and the troops were forming uneven lines in the company street.

"What did I do wrong this time?" Aaron asked.

"Nothing. Not a thing. No sarcasm intended, Firestone." Quickly he moved to the orderly-room door and shouted. "Straight lines, gentlemen. Get even with each other. Three straight lines. Try and do it right. Surprise me." He moved back to his desk and picked up his cap.

"You ever go to college?"

"No."

"Why not?"

"Pigeon-livered, Firestone. I lacked gall. I intended to once upon a time. But I was too old when the war was over. Old and decrepit. Anyway, I like the Army."

"To each," Aaron said.

"It has its advantages."

"What?"

"The chance to associate with superior people, Firestone. People like yourself. You do consider yourself superior?"

"Damn right."

"Ah, the confidence of youth," Sergeant Terry said. "You are young, aren't you, Firestone?" He put on his cap and pushed through the screen door, letting it bang shut behind him. Aaron stood and moved to the doorway, listening.

"All right now, gentlemen," Sergeant Terry began. "Let me have your attention. This is going to be one of our more grueling afternoons, so brace yourselves. It's the trench-foot movie today, so I suggest you close your eyes during the gory sections." Two buses rounded the corner of the company street. "Any of you with foot fetishes may be excused from going at all." He paused. "No foot fetishes? Wonderful." The buses stopped. "All aboard, gentlemen. We're off to see the wizard." The troops got on the buses. Sergeant Terry turned and nodded. Aaron nodded back. Then the buses drove away.

Aaron stretched. The company was quiet now. Captain Apple was up playing his afternoon golf match, so the orderly room was deserted. Aaron lit a cigarette and inhaled deeply. Placing the cigarette in the corner of his mouth, he sat at his desk. He had a little more typing to do and he would be through for the day. Wheeling the typewriter into position, he began to work.

A few moments later there was a knock at the orderly-room door. "Yes," Aaron called, continuing to type.

"Can I come in?"

Aaron looked up. "Come on."

A pudgy, balding figure marched into the room, stopped in front of his desk and saluted. "Sir, Private Branch Scudder reporting for duty as ordered, sir."

Flustered, Aaron returned the salute.

"I'm new in the company," Branch Scudder said.

"I gathered."

"Here are my orders." He handed a file of papers to Aaron. "What do I do now?"

"Relax," Aaron said. "I'm a recruit too."

"I thought so," Branch said. "But you can't ever be sure. What's your name?"

"Aaron Firestone."

"I'm Branch Scudder."

Branch held out his hand. Aaron paused, then took it.

"Where is everybody?"

"Gone. They'll be back."

"What about me?"

"You've got the afternoon off. Get some sheets from the supply room. Around to the left." He pointed.

"That's all?"

"That's all."

"You're sure? I won't get in any trouble?"

"No. No trouble."

Branch turned, walking toward the door. Then he stopped. "Around to the left, you said?"

"Yes."

"O.K. Thanks. Thanks a lot. You've been very helpful."

"*De nada*," Aaron muttered, watching as the other boy hurried out the door. When he hurried, Aaron noted, he jiggled. All over. His ass jiggled and the flesh above his hips jiggled. Everything. Baby fat, Aaron thought and he resumed his typing.

In ten minutes he was finished. Carefully filing the papers away, he lit another cigarette and got out his notebook. The afternoon was his now. To write. He had notified his mother to send his book of stories down to him, but while he was waiting its arrival he kept busy. Sketches, odd thoughts. Opening the notebook, he paused a moment, looking at the title page. *The Journals of Aaron Fire.* When he got around to his autobiography, he would call it that. *The Journals of Aaron Fire.* It had an almost Biblical ring. He turned the page and began to write. "Scudder jiggles. He is losing his hair while keeping his baby fat, which may be the neatest trick of the week. He appears to be boneless. Barbecued, he would undoubtedly prove tender." Drivel, Aaron thought. Crap. He flipped to another page. "Terry," he wrote. "Terry the Ape." He erased it, then lit another cigarette. He had been trying for two days now to write about Terry and as yet he had nothing. Why was that? What stopped him? It had something to do with Terry's eyes. They were too bright. He could not see past them. Not yet. Scudder was easier to write about. Aaron turned back a page. "Scudder was probably a beautiful baby but now the beauty is gone. He didn't grow; he simply enlarged. He . . ."

"I made my bed."

Aaron looked up. Scudder stood in the doorway.

"I got the sheets like you said. My bed's all made."

Aaron nodded.

"There's no one in the barracks at all. I . . . uh . . . felt like talking to somebody."

Aaron tilted his head to one side. Scudder had a speech peculiarity he hadn't noticed before. Either he talked too quickly or too slowly; no middle ground. "I made my bed" sounded like one word. This last sentence was filled with unnecessary syllables. "I . . . uh . . . felt . . . like . . . uh . . . talkingtosomebody."

Aaron said nothing.

"Am I . . . uh . . . bothering you?"

"Yes, frankly."

"You're working?"

"Trying to."

Branch jiggled over to Terry's chair and sat. "What kind of work?"

Aaron shrugged.

"I watched you through the screen door. You were writing. Are you a writer?"

"Yes."

"Are you writing a book or a play?"

"Listen, Scudder—"

"If you write a play I'll produce it. I'm a producer. I will be. When I'm done with the Army."

"That's wonderful."

"You know the saying, 'Those who can, write; those who can't, teach'? Well, it's different in the theater. In the theater it's 'Those who can, write; those who can't, produce.' " He laughed lightly. It was warm in the room and Aaron was sweating, but Scudder's skin was dry. "What were you writing?"

"Nothing."

"Come on. You can tell me."

"You don't sweat, do you?"

"Not very much. Why?"

"No reason."

"That's one way to tell a writer. By how perceptive they are. You're very perceptive. I just know it. I'll bet your writing is that way too. Read me something."

"I will not."

"It's all right. What were you just writing about?"

"You, Scudder."

Branch laughed again, louder. "You're kidding."

"No," Aaron said. "I'm not."

"Well, then, you've got to read it to me."

"It's hardly flattering, Scudder."

"Read it anyway."

"Dammit—"

"I'm waiting."

"All right. All right." Aaron picked up the journal. " 'Scudder jiggles,' " he began. " 'He is losing his hair while keeping his baby fat . . .' " He read it venomously. When he finished, he put the journal down.

Branch was staring at him.

Aaron smiled. "Like it?" he asked.

"I'm . . . uh . . . very sensitive about . . . uh . . . my . . . uh . . . hair. I don't like . . . uh . . . people . . . making . . . uh . . . jokes about it."

"I'll try to remember that."

"Otherwise I thought it was fine."

"I'm delighted. Now—"

"Where did you go to college? I went to Oberlin. Where did you go?"

"Princeton. Now come on, Scudder—"

"I was going to guess Yale."

"That makes us both perceptive."

"I had some friends at Princeton. Did you, by any chance, know—"

"Probably not. For the last time, Scudder, leave me in peace." He paused. "If you don't, I'll have you put on K.P."

Branch sat up. "You wouldn't do that."

"I'll give you three to get out of here."

"We're both college men. You wouldn't—"

"One."

"Besides, you don't have the authority."

"The first sergeant does. He'll do what I say. Two."

Nervously, Branch stood. "Remember, if you write a play, I'll pro—"

"Thr . . ." Aaron began.

Jiggling, Branch bolted out the door.

Alone, Aaron laughed. He put his head down on his arms and howled, tears falling onto the desk blotter. He laughed until his throat hurt. He sat up then, wiping his eyes. Hurriedly, he opened his journal, muttering aloud. "I said, 'If you don't, I'll put you on K.P.' and he said 'You wouldn't do that' and I said . . ." It was good dialogue and sometime it might be usable. Aaron lit a cigarette, continuing to write. He felt, somehow, strange. Why? He paused in his work. His shoulders itched, so he rubbed them against the back of his chair. Taking a deep breath, he held it. There was no sound in the room. Aaron listened. Yes, there was. He could hear it now. It was coming from behind him, a soft sound. What was it? There was an open window behind him and suddenly Aaron knew.

Someone was watching him.

Aaron froze. The sound was that of quick breathing but very soft, like a tiny puppy, panting after the ordeal of birth. Aaron waited. The sound stayed. "Cut it out, Scudder!" Aaron shouted. Still the sound. "I mean it, cut it out!" The panting seemed a level louder now. With a cry, Aaron flung his body around, facing the window.

He saw nothing. Nothing. He knew that he had only to go to the window and stick his head out to see who it had been.

But he did not move.

The next afternoon, Aaron sat alone in the orderly room. It was a pleasant day, warm, but with a wind, and his writing was going well. Captain Apple had called in at lunch, saying, somewhat thickly, that he would not be down for a while. In the background Aaron could hear what he assumed to be the sounds of the Officers' Club bar—soft music, loud laughter. Starting a fresh page in his journal, Aaron titled it *Apple's Fall* and set to work. He had written almost a page when Terry appeared.

"Where are the troops?" Aaron said.

"Watching a triple feature. Hygiene, Military Courtesy and something else." He sat heavily at his desk. "Ye gods."

"What's up?"

"More nuts," Sergeant Terry said. "A fresh supply. Two dozen or more. Due this afternoon."

"Where'll we stick them?"

"The last barracks down."

"That's locked up."

Terry threw him a key. "Open it." He rubbed his eyes. "And give it a once-over."

"How?"

"See that the toilets all flush. And make sure each bed's got a mattress. And make sure the sinks work. Think you can do that, Firestone?"

"With luck." Aaron stood.

"I'll be down in a while," Sergeant Terry said. He rubbed his eyes. "More nuts," he muttered. "Jesus."

Aaron left the orderly room and turned right, walking quickly. The large vacant field across the road seemed alive as little puffs of dust exploded, detonated by the wind. Aaron whistled, snapping his fingers in rhythm. When he reached the last barracks he unlocked it and stepped inside. It was stuffy, of course, but surprisingly cool. The silence was so complete he stopped whistling and listened. No sound. Nodding, he proceeded to the latrine and, moving down the row of sinks, turned on the faucets. The pipes groaned softly and rusty water cascaded out. Aaron moved into the next room where the toilets were. They all flushed. Returning to the sinks, he noted that the water was clear now, so he turned them off and headed out of the latrine to the main room on the first floor. Carefully he moved down the center aisle, counting cots. There were twenty-four of them, and each had a mattress. "Twenty-four," Aaron said out loud, breaking the quiet. The floor needed mopping but aside from that everything seemed to be fine. Aaron left the room and mounted the wooden stairway that led to the second floor. He banged his boots down heavily as he climbed, taking pleasure in the sound. There were two cadre rooms by the top of the stairs and he glanced inside. Sun streamed in through the windows. Each room had two beds and two mattresses. Aaron left them and toured the second floor. "Twenty-four," he said, again aloud, when he was finished. Making a grand total of forty-eight, not counting the cadre rooms. "Forty-eight," Aaron said.

The front door of the barracks opened and closed.

Aaron went to the head of the stairs and looked down. "Stand and unfold yourself."

"Everything all right?" Terry said, mounting the stairs.

"Yes."

"Forty-eight cots excluding the cadre rooms?"

"If you knew, why'd you have me count?"

"Caution," Terry answered. "I am, by nature, cautious. Water fountain work?"

"I didn't check it," Aaron said.

"Why don't you, then?" Terry told him. "Seeing you have the time."

Aaron descended the stairs to the water fountain. It was located in a niche outside the latrine. The water was rusty at first but then it cleared. "It's fine," Aaron called.

"Good."

Aaron walked up the stairs again. "Where are you?"

"Here." Aaron entered one of the cadre rooms. "Break time," Terry said. "Take five." Terry was smoking, his ape's body sprawled across one of the cots. Aaron sat down on the other cot and lit a cigarette. The room was stuffy, the dark shade pulled down over the window. Above, a bare bulb lit the room starkly. Aaron glanced at Terry, then away. Terry had shaved. Aaron sniffed once.

'What's that smell?"

Terry laughed. "Aftershave. French. It's imported. A weakness of mine. You don't like it?"

"It's strong, all right."

Terry laughed again. "Distinctive would have been a kinder word."

Aaron dragged on his cigarette.

"I was first given some in Paris during the liberation. A gift from an admirer. I've used it ever since. The sentimentalist in me."

"If I were writing you in a book, I'd never let you use it."

"Why not?"

"Too obvious. It's gimmicky. French-imported aftershave. My God, is that phony."

"If you were writing me in a book, what would you say?"

"I don't know yet. I haven't got you straight. But I will."

"I've been written about before," Sergeant Terry said.

"No kidding?"

"No kidding."

"Who did it?"

"Friends."

"What did they say?"

"Unkind things."

"Why?"

"Revenge, I suppose. Writers write out of revenge. Wouldn't you say so?"

"Maybe. I thought you said they were friends of yours."

"They were."

"How do you know it was you they were writing about?"

"They sent me copies of the books. Suitably inscribed."

Aaron lit another cigarette and carefully placed it in the corner of his mouth. The room was cooler now, the black shade blocking the heat of the sun. Sergeant Terry stretched.

"Maybe I'll write about you someday," Aaron said. "And send you a book, suitably inscribed. To add to your collection."

"Oh, you will," Sergeant Terry said.

Aaron shrugged.

"And yours will be just like the others. Venomous. Untrue."

"What makes you think so?"

"Trust me."

"You're pretty confident, aren't you?"

"In certain areas only."

Aaron inhaled deeply.

"The light," Sergeant Terry said.

Aaron's heart bucked.

"Relax," Terry said. "Relax, Aaron." He pointed a thick hand. "The light."

Aaron fought the trembling.

"Turn it off, Aaron."

"What are you talking about?"

"You know."

"What the hell are you talking about?"

Terry smiled.

Aaron's throat burned from the dryness.

Terry rose up on an elbow.

"You got the wrong guy," Aaron said.

Terry shook his head.

"You got the wrong guy." Louder.

"No," Terry said. "I don't."

"I'm not what you think."

"Aren't you?"

"No." Aaron slid along the bed toward the door. "I'm not. Not. I know I'm not . . . see once . . . there was some possibility . . . it crossed my mind that I might be. But I'm not! I faced the possibility. I researched it. I did. And the conclusions I reached were that . . . I'm not. And I'm sorry for you being what you are, but I'm not what you are. I may be a lot of things . . . but I'm not what you are. It has been proven. I proved beyond the least doubt—I'm not! I'm not and you leave me alone!"

"You're protesting a bit too much," Terry said, smiling again.

"I'm getting out of here."

"Go."

Aaron stood in the doorway. "I will."

"Run!" Terry shouted. "Run, then."

Aaron ran. He ran out of the room and along the hall and halfway down the stairs. Halfway down. Then he stopped. "Sergeant Terry," he called.

No answer.

Aaron pressed his head against the wall, closing his eyes. His legs ached from running and the burning in his throat made it hard to breathe. He leaned against the cool wall, gasping. "Sergeant Terry," he called again, weaker this time.

No answer.

"Please," Aaron called. Slumping down, he sat huddled on the stairs. Above him he heard footsteps, then the snap of a wall switch, then more footsteps. A mattress creaked. Then nothing. Aaron dug his fingers into his eyes. He was aware his entire body was twitching but he was helpless to stop it.

"Please," he murmured. "Please."

There was no sound in the entire barracks save his own uneven breathing. He tried holding his breath but he could not. He could do nothing. Nothing. Then, with a last desperate effort, he stood, holding to the wall for support. At last his legs began to move.

Up the stairs.

His legs were moving slowly up the stairs. They carried him along. He was helpless to stop them as they raised themselves and brought themselves down, each time on a higher stair. Finally he reached the top. His legs continued to move, turning him, dragging the upper half of him along. When they reached the doorway, the legs stopped. Aaron put a hand on the door-frame and paused, looking in. The room was dark now, the light gone. In the far corner, something moved.

"You're back, I see."

"Yes," Aaron admitted. "But not for what you think."

"Why then?"

"I just . . . I just wanted to tell you . . ." Damn the gasping. Goddamn the gasping. "That I won't tell anybody."

"Won't tell anybody what?"

"What you tried to do."

"And what was that?"

"You know."

"Tell me anyway, Aaron. Say it."

Aaron was silent.

"The word, Aaron. Say the word." Terry's voice was without a body. It came, almost mystically, from the dark room.

"It's like an oracle," Aaron muttered.

"Say the word."

"Don't you get it? I can't see you. Just hear. That's all. Like an oracle."

"The word."

"Seduction. Seduction. I said it."

"There's no such thing, Aaron." The voice was quiet now, coiled. "Nobody seduces anybody. Seductions must be mutual. Like ours."

"That's not true."

The voice laughed. "You want your pride, don't you? All right. I'll let you keep your pride. The responsibility belongs to me, Aaron. You're free and clear. Now come in the room."

"No."

"Come in the room, Aaron."

Aaron entered the room.

"Now close the door."

Aaron closed the door.

"Now we're both oracles, Aaron. You can't see me. I can't see you."

"Yes," Aaron said.

"I'm holding my hand out to you, Aaron. You can't see it, but it's there. Take it."

Aaron did not move.

"Take it."

There was a silence.

Then Terry's voice exploded. "The hand!" Aaron listened to the sound. It was wild. Wild and rough. "The hand!" Rough and, familiar. Commanding.

Aaron obeyed.

"Thank God you could type," Sergeant Terry said. He was lying sprawled on one of the cots, shirt open, smoking. "It sure made things a hell of a lot simpler." Terry laughed, flicking a stubby finger across the burning end of his cigarette, knocking specks of ash onto the floor. Obviously in good humor, he slapped his other hand flat against his chest. "Thank God."

Aaron sat across from him, watching. "It was all planned, then?"

"You might say that."

"Why me?"

Terry laughed. "I like 'em skinny. That a good enough reason?"

Aaron shrugged.

Terry slapped his chest again, harder.

"Don't do that."

"Why not?"

"You look enough like an ape. Don't push the resemblance."

Terry laughed.

"And button your shirt."

"If it pleases you." Slowly, he began closing his shirt front. "Aaron?"

"What?"

"You were . . ." Terry paused.

"I was what?"

"I'm looking for the right word."

"Well, find it."

Terry finished with his shirt and lay back. "Inexperienced," he said then.

Aaron said nothing.

"Weren't you?"

"I've slept with a woman."

"Really?" Terry said. "That must have been fun for you."

"It was!" Aaron snapped. "Damn right it was."

Terry sat up quickly. "Easy," he said. "Easy, Aaron."

Aaron took a deep drag on his cigarette.

"You all right?"

"I'm fine."

"I mean it. You all right?"

"I said I was fine."

Terry nodded.

"I'm getting the hell out of here a while, if that's all right with you." He stood, starting for the doorway.

"Sure. Sure. Take the afternoon off if you want."

Aaron whirled on him. "Thanks, Sarge."

Terry smiled. "I'm known far and wide for my leniency."

Aaron moved to the doorway, then stopped and turned again. "Just tell me one thing."

"Ask."

"What's your first name?"

"Oh," Terry murmured, slowly shaking his head. "I'm sorry. It's Philip. Phil."

"See you around campus, Phil," Aaron said, and he left the room, walking down the stairs. When he reached the front door of the barracks he pushed it. It was locked from the inside. Caution, Aaron thought as he turned the lock, shoving the door open. He stopped for a moment on the landing, looking around. Quiet. No one in sight. Aimlessly he began to move, scuffing his shoes in the dust. The wind was stronger now and far, far in the distance storm clouds scudded toward each other. I'm a homosexual, Aaron thought. Me. I am a homosexual. He said the word aloud.

"Homosexual."

Shoving his hands deep into his pockets, he ambled on. He felt curiously empty. No, not curiously. It was what he always felt. Emptiness. Nothing. Neither rage nor joy nor shimmering pain. Nothing. He felt nothing. He was moving now toward the center of the great field across from the company, dust kicking up all around him, stinging his face. Aaron closed his eyes and walked in darkness for a while.

Look on the bright side, faggot. Goodbye to self-delusion. You can run for office with a slogan like that: goodbye to self-delusion. Hell, you can be a king with a slogan like that. Maybe not a king. A queen, then. Eyes closed, Aaron howled. All the lying he had done, all the perverting of truth and fact, all in the desperate attempt to prove without question to himself that he wasn't what he so obviously was.

"I'm a fáy-reeee," Aaron shouted at the wind.

Homosexual was an ugly word, five ugly syllables, ho-mo-sex-u-al, but the synonyms were just as ugly. Ugly. Why didn't they have a prettier word for it? Like wisp. That was a pretty word. Aaron Fire is a wisp. That wasn't nearly so bad. Aaron opened his eyes a moment. Dust broke across his vision in great sheets now as the wind grew stronger. Closing his eyes quickly, he wrapped his bony arms around his bony body and threw his head back. Aaron began to shout.

"Kuh-weeeeer. I'm kuh-weeer."

"A perrr-verrt."

"Suh-wisssh."

"Faaaaaaaaaag."

The wind picked up. In the center of the great field, Aaron began turning around and around, disappearing, dry dust spotting his eyelids, caking his tongue.

He reported to the orderly room on time the next morning. Sergeant Terry was already at work, going over some papers. Aaron hung up his cap and sat down. Terry glanced over at him.

"Good day, Firestone."

Aaron nodded. "Sergeant Terry."

"I'm afraid I've got a lot of work for you this morning." He handed some papers to Aaron. "Original and five. Think you can handle it?"

"I imagine."

"A gold star for you, Firestone," Sergeant Terry said. He stretched, yawning. Then he moved to the door. "I'm off to do battle with the nuts." Walking outside, Terry took a whistle from his pocket and blew on it sharply three times. Eventually the troops began straggling out of their barracks, slowly moving into the company street, forming three uneven rows. Terry stood on the sidewalk watching them, shaking his head sadly. "Ye gods, gentlemen," he said, "you're killing me."

Aaron watched through the orderly-room window. Terry was walking in front of the troops now, scolding them, his long arms hanging limp at his sides, his stubby legs carrying him jerkily forward. All you need is a banana, Aaron thought. Terry the ape.

That night they went to a motel. Terry was waiting for him in his car when he finished supper. Aaron got in quietly and they drove off post for a while. The motel was some fifteen miles distant, small and dirty, a series of peeling gray cubicles with a hand-painted "Vacancy" sign in front. Their cabin was filthy. Aaron found a cockroach scuttling down one side of the bathtub.

He killed it slowly.

The next day Aaron was eating lunch in the mess hall when Scudder jiggled up to him.

"I'm getting my car," Scudder said.

Aaron went on eating.

"They allow us cars in this company," Scudder explained. "And I'm getting mine. I'm having it sent down. It's a convertible."

Aaron continued to eat, staring at his tin tray. "What are you telling me for?"

"Well . . . uh . . . whenever you want to . . . uh . . . use it, you can. Feel free."

Aaron looked up at the other boy. "You ought to know better than to go lending your car to anybody who wants it."

"Oh, I don't lend it to just anybody. Only special friends."

"Scudder, you and I are not special friends."

"We could be."

"Not bloody likely." Aaron resumed eating. "You're a slob, Scudder."

Branch laughed. "If you ever want to go anyplace," he finished, "feel free."

"Thanks. Now will you let me finis.1 eating?"

"You don't want me to stay and talk to you? I can." Aaron glared at the other boy. Branch smiled. "See you, Aaron," he said. Then, for no reason at all—there was only four feet between them—he waved.

Again, that night, Aaron accompanied Terry to a motel. A different motel this time, a few miles farther from post. "Caution," Terry explained it. This motel was older than the previous one, but just as badly kept. As they walked to their cabin Aaron lit a cigarette.

Terry opened the door to the cabin. "Come on," he said.

"I'm smoking."

"You can smoke in here."

"I know that."

"I'm waiting, Aaron."

"Do you good," Aaron told him. He finished his cigarette, grinding it out in the dust. Then he went inside.

Later, when they were going back to the car, Terry touched him. It was dark and Terry reached out, putting a thick hand on Aaron's shoulder.

Aaron spun around, throwing the hand off. "Don't ever do that!"

"Do what?"

"Lay a hand on me in the open."

Terry shrugged, looking around. The motel was quiet. "You see anybody?"

"I won't warn you again," Aaron said.

Terry smiled at him. "I don't get you."

"That's right. And you never will."

The following night, Thursday, as Aaron was washing up in the latrine, getting ready for bed, Branch came in.

Aaron groaned. "What is it this time, Scudder?"

"Nothing. I just wanted to ask you a question, that's all."

"Do I have to answer?"

Branch smoothed his thinning hair. "I was just . . . uh . . . wondering if . . . uh . . . if you liked movies?"

Aaron dried his hands and face. "I love movies. I'm a movie nut. I plan to write some if I ever have the time." He slung his towel over his shoulder and left the latrine, walking toward his bunk.

Branch followed him. "The reason I asked was that there's this terrific movie playing in Capital City on Saturday night."

"There is, huh?"

"Yes. A revival of *Bicycle Thief.* It's an Italian movie. De Sica directed it."

"I know who directed it."

"Have you seen it?"

"No."

"Let's go, then. Saturday night."

"It's fifty miles to Capital City."

"I've got a car. Remember?" He was speaking quickly now. "We can just go on in and see it. The two of us. I think it'll be fun. Hey. You know what? We can have dinner in Capital City. They've got some good restaurants in there. I've been told that."

"I'm a little low on funds right now, Scudder."

"Oh, I'll pay. I'll pay for everything. Dinner and the movie. Everything. It'll be worth it to me. We can get good and acquainted. I'm looking forward to it already."

"You rich?"

Branch laughed. "Not so much rich as spoiled. I'm spoiled. Rosie gives me pretty much whatever I want."

"Rosie?"

"My mother. Rosie, I call her."

"Cute," Aaron said.

"How about it? You want to go?"

"Will you quit pestering me if I do?"

"Maybe."

Aaron did not hesitate. "Sure, Scudder. As long as you're paying for it, I'll tag along."

"Good," Branch said. "You just leave everything to me. I'll take care of everything. Good." He turned and hurried out of the barracks.

Fifteen minutes later he was back.

"Scudder, old buddy," Aaron said. "What a pleasant surprise."

"I was just thinking," Branch began.

"I find that highly doubtful."

"It's a long drive back at night after the movie."

"You're right. Let's forget the whole thing."

"No, no. That's not what I meant. What I meant was . . . uh . . . that . . . well . . . uh . . . Regency House is in Capital City and that's one of the best hotels in the whole country. It is. I know that for a fact. They've got gorgeous suites in Regency House. Big and spacious. With a view of the river. Some of them even have terraces."

"So?"

"We could spend the night in one of those suites. And then Sunday we could drive back. Or we could look around Capital City and then drive back, whichever you wanted."

"They're probably all booked up by this time, Scudder."

Branch shook his head.

"How do you know?"

Branch laughed. "Because I just made a reservation. Not two minutes ago. That's how."

Whenever Aaron turned the next day, Scudder was there. He popped in while Aaron was shaving. "Don't forget about tomorrow, Aaron. Remember now." And again at breakfast. "We're going to have fun, Aaron. You'll see." And he was there at lunch and at supper. "I can hardly wait for that movie to start. Can you?" And when Aaron came back late at night after having been with Terry, Scudder was sitting on his bunk, waiting. "Saturday can't come soon enough for me. Twelve o'clock tomorrow we take off. That's just—" and he consulted his watch—"just thirteen hours from now."

And then Saturday came.

Aaron worked in the morning, typing. At noon he left the orderly room and walked slowly through the heat to his barracks. Going inside, he sat down on his bunk, unbuttoning his shirt, slowly starting to make the change into civilian clothes. He was almost finished when Scudder came in. Scudder was wearing dark pants, a blue seersucker jacket; he seemed less flabby than usual. Aaron nodded to him.

"Let's go, let's go," Branch said. "God, you're a slowpoke. I've got my pass already. Sergeant Terry just gave it to me. Have you got yours yet?"

"No. Not yet."

"Shall I go get it for you? It'll save us some time."

"I'll get it myself."

"O.K. But hurry up."

"I'm ready."

"Well, let's go to the orderly room for your pass."

"Where's your car?"

"In the parking lot."

"Go there. Take this." Aaron handed him his overnight bag. "I'll meet you."

They left the barracks, stopping for a moment in the heat.

"I can go to the orderly room with you. It's no trouble."

"No," Aaron said. "I'll meet you at the car."

"Well . . ."

"Go on!"

Aaron watched as Scudder moved away. He took a deep breath. Then he started slowly toward the orderly room, aware of the pounding of his heart. As he drew near he saw two trainees standing inside, so he stopped. He lit a cigarette. The trainees were talking to Terry. Aaron waited. The sun was very warm and he was perspiring heavily. He wiped his forehead. Finally the other trainees left the orderly room. Aaron flicked his cigarette away. Taking a deep breath, he walked inside.

"Well, well, well," Sergeant Terry said. "All dressed up." He was seated at his desk, the box of passes in front of him.

"I'd like my pass, please, Sergeant Terry."

"Going someplace, Firestone?"

"That's right." It was hot in the room. Aaron dried the palms of his hands on his trouser legs.

"Where, may I ask? It's my business to know. After all, I'm first sergeant."

"Capital City."

"That sounds like fun."

Aaron nodded.

"A little rest and relaxation, Firestone? That what you're after?"

"I'd like my pass, please."

"Certainly," Terry said. "Right away." He rummaged through the box for a while. Then he looked up, shaking his head. "I'm sorry, Firestone. I can't seem to find your pass here."

"Give it to me."

Terry smiled. "I just told you. You haven't got one. I'm afraid you're not going anyplace just now."

"I'm waiting."

"Glad to have the company."

"Game's over," Aaron said. "Let's have it."

Terry stood. "Aaron," he began.

"You'd better give me my pass, Sergeant Terry."

"Aaron, listen—"

"I mean that."

Terry walked over close to him, his rough voice low. "I had plans for tonight."

"Change them."

"We've been together every evening."

"Not anymore."

"Why not?"

"Because I said so."

The ape face began clouding. "Who is it?"

"Who is what?"

"You're going to Capital City with somebody. Who?"

"Scudder."

"Scudder?" Terry forced a laugh. "That fat-ass?"

"Correct."

"Why? Why Scudder? What's Scudder's attraction?"

"Money," Aaron answered. "As simple as that."

Terry's voice was loud again. "You a prostitute all of a sudden?"

"That's the word."

Terry was about to speak when suddenly he smiled, turning back toward his desk. Three recruits walked into the orderly room. "Gentlemen," Terry said.

"We'd like our passes," one of them said.

"Of course you would." Aaron moved to a corner of the room, waiting. "Now you'll have to sign out," Terry went on. "First and last names both. You all know your first and last names?" One of the three laughed. Terry gave them their passes, watching as they signed their names in the register. The three recruits left the orderly room. Terry stared after them until they were gone. Then he turned, walking up to Aaron. "We were speaking of prostitutes," Sergeant Terry said.

"I'm sick of cockroaches. You may love them but I don't. I'm sick of cheap motels. I'm sick of sneaking around at night like a freak fresh from a sideshow. And, if you want to know the truth, most of all, I'm sick of you."

Terry hit him.

It was not a hard blow. Aaron managed to turn his head in time so that the thick fist only brushed his face. But it was enough to split the skin. Aaron's lip began bleeding. He jammed his tongue into the cut, tasting blood. "That was a mistake, Sergeant Terry. You just miscalculated."

"Aaron . . ."

The heat in the room was oppressive. Sweat streamed down Aaron's face as he fought to keep his voice under control. "If you ever so much as come near me again—ever!—you're through. I mean it, Ape. I swear to God I'll report you. I'll go running up to the doctors and I'll cry like a baby and I'll tell them what you are. I'll tell them everything and you know what that means? They don't like faggots in the Army, Ape. They'll discharge us both dishonorably. Well, I don't give a shit. But you do. You'd be lost without the Army to mother you. We both know that. Right, Sergeant Terry? Right, Phil?"

Terry said nothing.

Aaron's voice was rising, out of control. "I'm going to hit you back, Phil. Now. And you're going to let me. You've got no choice. Apes have no choice in this world. None. And you're an ape." Aaron swung his open hand at Terry's face, slapping his mouth. "Ape," and he swung again, backhanded, catching the mouth a second time. "Ape, ape," Aaron cried, whipping his hand back and forth, lashing the other man's mouth.

Terry stood still.

"Now we can both taste blood," Aaron said. "Like it?" He swung again, then dropped his arm. "Now give me my pass."

Terry did not move.

296 · WILLIAM GOLDMAN

Aaron crossed to the box, grabbed his pass and signed the register. He moved to the doorway. "Thanks for the pass, Sergeant Terry. Have a good weekend yourself, now." Terry stared at him, frozen. Aaron opened the door, smiling. "I have an overdeveloped sense of vengeance. I should have told you that."

Aaron slammed the door.

He took a few steps in the sunshine before he realized he was on the verge of fainting. He tried closing his eyes, but that was worse. Cursing aloud, he forced his body forward through the heat toward the parking lot.

Branch was waiting in the convertible.

Aaron opened the door and sat down heavily, leaning back, staring at the sky.

Branch looked at him. "Your lip is bleeding."

"Family trait."

"What?"

"Some people get bloody noses. We Firestones get bloody lips." Branch was about to speak again when Aaron cut him off. "Drive!"

Branch drove.

The suite was lovely. As Aaron followed the bellboy into the enormous front room, he smiled. The bellboy put their overnight bags down and nodded. Branch tipped him. The bellboy muttered thanks and closed the door. Aaron moved to the large picture windows and looked out at the river beyond. Turning, he walked through the bath to the adjoining bedroom. It, too, had a view of the river.

"Very fine," Aaron said, coming back into the front room. "Very fine."

"I told you, didn't I?"

"Yes, Scudder. You told me. Which room do you want?"

"Well . . . uh . . ."

"Take this room. It's bigger."

"No. You take it."

"You're paying, Scudder. Get a little value for your money."

"Would . . . uh . . . you like a drink? I've got some Scotch in my overnight bag."

"Isn't it a little early?"

"Not for Scotch. Never for Scotch."

"I'm going to shower first," Aaron said. "Maybe later." He picked up his bag and walked into the bathroom. Undressing, he turned on the shower and quietly locked the door. The water beat against the tiles.

Aaron waited. Finally the doorknob began to turn slowly. Aaron watched. The door was being pushed now. The lock held. Quietly the doorknob slid back to its original position.

Laughing out loud, Aaron let the water cleanse him.

When he was done, he dried himself off and went to his bedroom. Pulling a sheet from the cool bed, he wrapped it around himself carefully. Then he examined himself in the mirror. Chin high, body straight, he looked, he thought, very much the Roman emperor. Unlocking the bathroom door, he entered the front room.

"Hey," Branch said. "What are you doing?"

Aaron modeled the sheet. "The very latest thing."

Branch laughed. "How about a drink now?"

"You going to have one?"

"Yes. Of course."

"All right, then."

Branch got two glasses and filled them with Scotch. He handed one to Aaron. "Here's to lots of fun in Capital City."

Aaron sat in a chair by the window. Branch lay half sprawled on the bed across the room, his head propped on an elbow. Aaron took a mouthful of Scotch, running it over his tongue. It stung sharply at his cut lip, so he swallowed it quickly.

"Like it?" Branch asked. "It's Old Smuggler. That's my favorite kind."

"Mellow," Aaron answered. "Nice and mellow."

"Does your lip hurt?"

Aaron shrugged.

"How did you cut it? Really?"

"Sergeant Terry hit me in the face."

Branch laughed for a while, his body quivering. "All right," he said finally. "If you don't want to tell me, don't tell me. Come on. Drink up. Let's toast something."

"Let's not." Aaron took another long swallow of Scotch.

"This sure beats X Company all hollow," Branch said, gesturing around the room.

"All hollow," Aaron agreed.

"You've got something wrong with your legs, don't you?"

"That's right. Something wrong with my legs. What's your problem?"

"Will you promise not to tell?"

"No."

"I won't tell you unless you promise."

Aaron sighed. "You have my word, Scudder."

"Nothing," Branch whispered. "Nothing's wrong with me. I got in by pull."

"Rosie arrange it for you?"

"How'd you know?"

"Two and two, Scudder."

"Anyway, you won't tell. You promised."

Aaron drank his Scotch.

"This sure is a big room. I almost feel like I have to shout so you'll hear me."

"Well, restrain yourself."

"You're funny."

"Hilarious," Aaron agreed.

"You are."

Aaron glanced out the window.

"That Scotch getting to you?"

"I feel a distant buzz."

"Excuse me," Branch said, and he got off the bed, moving to the bathroom. From his position in the chair Aaron could see him. Branch half closed the bathroom door but Aaron could see him as he poured his drink down the toilet. Aaron returned his gaze to the window. A moment later the toilet flushed and Branch was back. Lying on the bed, he brought the empty glass to his lips, licking the edge with his tongue.

"What river is that out there?" Aaron asked.

"I don't know. Some river."

"It's picturesque as hell."

Branch got off the bed and came close to Aaron's chair, staring out at the water. "It is at that," he said. "Yes, indeed." Again he licked at the edge of his glass. "I'm ready for a little refill, Aaron. How about you?"

Aaron finished his drink. "Love it."

Branch filled the glasses with more Scotch. Then he handed one to Aaron and sprawled down on the bed again, his head propped on an elbow.

Aaron looked at him.

Branch began to fidget. "It's sure nice this suite is air-conditioned. Imagine how hot it would be otherwise."

Aaron said nothing.

"What are you looking at me like that for?"

Aaron did not reply.

Branch was fidgeting badly now, his fingers fluttering on the bedspread. "What is it, Aaron? What's the matter?"

"Lecher," Aaron said.

"Huh?"

Aaron laughed out loud.

"What's so funny?"

"You filthy lecher. Trying to get me drunk. You ought to be ashamed."

"What are you talking about?"

"I saw!"

"Saw what?"

"Will you quit with the innocent act? I saw you. Through the bathroom door, Scudder. You should have closed the door all the way. Fool. Didn't you think I could see? Why didn't you close the door? Why didn't—"

The answer made him shudder.

"Jesus," Aaron whispered.

"Don't say any more, Aaron. Be careful now."

"You wanted me to see," Aaron whispered. "You wanted it."

"No."

"Yes! You wanted me to catch you."

"I didn't. I didn't."

"So I'd punish you for being such a bad boy."

"That isn't true."

"You love punishment, don't you, Scudder?"

Branch sat up on the bed. "No."

"Oh, it's so obvious, Scudder. It's written all over you. Admit it. You love being punished."

Branch stood.

"Sit back down!"

Branch sat back down.

Aaron smiled. Slowly he drew the white sheet tightly around him. "Do you know the poem, Scudder, about the sadistic man? 'A sadistic man had a masochistic wife and he beat her every day and they led a happy life.' Do you think we could have a happy life, Scudder?"

Branch took a long drink of Scotch. Then another.

Aaron ran his hands across his chest. Sunlight streamed in through the window, but the room was cool. Aaron smiled again. "You desire me, don't you, Scudder? Don't you, you fat fairy, you swish, you queer? Don't you?"

Branch drained his glass.

"Don't you?"

Branch spoke. It was barely a whisper. "Yes."

"Desperately?"

"Yes."

"More than you ever wanted anything ever before?"

"Yes. Yes."

Aaron stood, his chin held high, his body straight. "All right then, Scudder. You can have me."

Branch started to get up.

"But it's going to cost you."

"I don't care what it costs. I don't."

"And not just money, Scudder."

"I don't care." He started toward Aaron.

"Stop."

"But—"

"Stop!"

Branch stopped.

"Now. On your knees."

"Aaron . . ."

"On your knees, Scudder."

Branch knelt.

"All the way down. I want your head touching the rug. Bow. To me. Bow!"

Branch bowed.

Like an emperor, Aaron walked around him, studying the huddled figure. "You like being punished, don't you, Scudder?"

"Yes."

"You will be punished. Rest assured." Aaron lifted his left foot, bringing it down, his heel on Branch's neck.

"You're hurting me."

"You love it. Shut up." He held out his right hand, fist clenched, thumb extended. "Well," he shouted. "What shall it be? Thumbs up or thumbs down?"

"Aaron . . ."

Aaron pressed down harder with his heel. "Oh God," he said, and his body shook with anticipation. "The things I'm going to do to you."

Part III

XI

As soon as she saw Manhattan, Jenny knew she had made a mistake.

She sat very still, staring out, as the bus roared toward the approaching city. Oh dear, Jenny thought, what am I going to do? I still get lost in *Duluth*. What's going to happen to me here? For a moment she imagined the headline, "Girl Dies Trying to Find Radio City Music Hall."

Jenny looked away.

You stop this now, she told herself. I'm not kidding either. Millions of people find their way around, you can find your way around, right? Right! That's better. See you don't panic again, right? Right. Promise? Promise. O.K., look at it. It's not so big. Just look.

Jenny looked.

Oh dear, she thought, it's growing.

"I just love New York."

Jenny turned to the thin lady next to her. "Auh?"

"Yes, it's a wonderful place. I love to travel but New York's my favorite. Some cities, they make it so hard for you. But here it's just so easy to get where you're going."

"It is?"

"Oh, yes. The crosstown streets, they're nothing. They just go up, one number at a time."

"Fancy that," Jenny said. "You mean fifteenth is between fourteenth and sixteenth?"

"Yes. And the up and downs are simple too. First, Second, Third, Luke, Paul, Matthew, Five. That's the East Side, and—"

"Luke, Paul, Matthew?" Jenny said.

"Lexington, Park, Madison. Luke, Paul, Matthew—that's what I call a memory help. I get most of my memory helps from the Bible. Do you read the Bible?"

"Yes, I do."

"Well, then, you'll never get lost in New York."

"Fancy that," Jenny said, and she turned back to the window, whispering Luke, Paul, Matthew, Luke, Paul, Matthew over and over while she stared out at the tiny town.

I'll never make it, Jenny thought as she saw them unloading her two enormous suitcases. Her arms were already practically full, what with her pocketbook and her magazines and camera and two street maps of the island of Manhattan plus four tourist guides (three hard-cover, one paperback), so how was she ever going to manage her suitcases? Her mother had urged her not to take everything and even her father had suggested that she might leave a *few* odds and ends around the house. But she had resisted their suggestions, not because she was stubborn but rather because she knew she was, at heart, a coward, and it seemed wise to bring it all: if there was nothing to run back to, there would be less chance of running back. But as she stood between the great bulky bags, Jenny doubted her decision: after all, eleven stuffed animals was a lot of stuffed animals.

Jenny sighed.

I'll just have to get one of those redcaps, she thought. That's just what I'll do, but I wonder how much you have to pay them? "Redcap?" she whispered. "Redcap?" And she opened her purse and when she did she was glad she had whispered because all she had was a hundred dollars in travelers' checks and a twenty-dollar bill and three pennies. "Whew," Jenny said. That was a close one. I'll have to get change. She looked around for a place, but then she gasped because out of the corner of her eye she saw a titanic Negro redcap bearing down on her and he had a big scar on his left cheek and if he took her bags and she tried to give him the twenty-dollar bill he would think she was either a cheapskate phony or a girl who hated Negroes and then he would whip out his razor and she saw the headline that said "Redcap Slays Racist Girl Visitor" and he was right up on top of her now and Jenny was about to say "But I like Negroes" when suddenly a blond man came up from behind her and said "Need a hand?" and whisked her two suitcases up and started walking for the main entrance.

"But," Jenny said, tagging along after him, "but," but by the time she had actually caught up to him they were on the sidewalk and he had put the bags down and said "You'll probably have trouble getting a taxi" and then he was gone, and she could only shout "Thank you, thank you very much" after him.

"Hop in."

Jenny looked at the man in the car. "Are you a taxi?" she said finally.

"Am I a taxi. Am I a *taxi?*" The man shook his head. "You wouldn't be, by any chance, new to New York?"

Oh, wouldn't you like to know, Jenny thought. Well, you don't fool me. I've heard about you taxi drivers. How you drive people hundreds of miles out of the way and take all their money and like that. "New?" she said. "Oh, no. I'm a veteran traveler. I happen to have been here thirty-five times." She opened her purse and took out a piece of paper. "Now, I want to go to the Dixon Hotel. That's in Manhattan. On West Forty-fifth Street. One hundred and sixty-four West Forty-fifth Street. Do you know where that is?"

"Well, now, lemme see," the driver said. "That's a toughie. It's in Manhattan, you say. One sixty-four West Forty-fifth. You don't happen to know, is it on the uptown or downtown side of the street?"

Jenny consulted her paper. "The downtown side."

"Then I think I can find it." He waited while she shoved her bags in the back and when that was done he said "Dixon Hotel, I'm really nervous," and then he started to drive.

"Oh, by the way," Jenny said from the back seat. "If you get a chance, you might go through the theater district."

"The Dixon's *in* the theater district."

"Of course it is. I was just testing you."

"Franklin Truman."

"Pardon?"

"That's my name, Franklin Truman." He jabbed a finger at his hack license. "See? Franklin Truman. Easy to remember. So when I do to ya whatever it is you think I'm gonna do to ya, you won't have no trouble telling the cops."

"What are you going to do to me?"

"Little girl, listen—"

"I am not a little girl."

"All right, big girl. Listen, big girl. I'm seventy years old, with eight grandchildren and a thyroid condition, is it likely I'm gonna rob you blind?"

"I never said—"

"You got me so nervous up here I'm quivering. Forty-eight years I'm hacking I never met anybody so suspicious as you. I rode Dutch Schultz the week before they shot him and he wasn't nearly as suspicious as you and *he* had reason to be. Now I'll get you to the Dixon, but have a heart. I got feelings, lady. I never stole anything in my life. I got pride."

"Oh dear, I didn't mean—"

"My daughter I put through Bryn Mawr college, my son through Massachusetts Tech; I'm proud of that. I never once yet cheated on my wife; I'm proud of that. I ain't a bug, lady; quit making me feel like one."

Jenny bit her tongue and stared out at the traffic. "I'm sorry, Mr. Truman," she said.

"Franklin."

"I'm sorry, Franklin."

"What's your name?"

"Jenny."

"Jenny?"

"Yes."

"That's a nice name."

"Do you think so?" She leaned forward in her seat. "Can I tell you something?"

"Of course."

"It's not that I'm suspicious—no, I guess I am suspicious—but anyways, the reason that I'm particularly suspicious today is, well . . ."

"Go on, go on."

Jenny put her head up next to his. "In all my life," she whispered, "I've never been more than thirty-two miles away from home before and I'm absolutely fantastically nervous."

"You mean this is your first trip to New York?"

"Yes. My very one."

"You could a fooled me."

"I was trying to. I think it's terribly important that people think I'm a native, don't you?"

"Definitely."

"It's no good being a stranger. Why, I've heard stories about things that happened to strangers in Duluth that would make your hair stand right up on end."

"I believe it."

"It's the truth. Oh, the stories I could tell."

"Why are we whispering?"

"That's a habit I have; it prevents eavesdropping."

"Understand me, I got nothing against the practice. It's just we're all alone in the cab."

"You're probably right," Jenny said, and she sat back against the cushions. "Do you know what, Franklin? You have a very sweet face. I don't understand how I could ever have mistrusted you with a face like that."

"Happens," he said and he turned a corner.

"Stop!"

"What-what?"

"Look. At that theater." Jenny pointed to the left. "That's Stagpole's play. See? *The Left Hand Knows.*"

"So?"

"Well, he's practically my favorite writer. He's won the Pulitzer Prize. Two times. For a novel and a play. He's the only one who ever did that except for Mr. Wilder. And *I* know him. Well, I've never met him, of course, but my boyfriend—I guess you'd call him my boyfriend; we grew up together, of *course* he's my boy friend—and his father, he runs the lodge—he's very rich, he doesn't have to run the lodge, he just does, ever since he had this heart attack—and he and Stagpole both came from Illinois, the downstate part to begin with, and whenever they see each other, why, it's just as friendly as can be, and Tommy—that's my boyfriend—well, I think it's pretty impressive winning two Pulitzer Prizes, don't you, one for a novel and one for a play?"

"Your boy friend won the Pulitzer Prize? That's marvelous."

"No," Jenny said. "I didn't tell it right. But it's very exciting all the same, don't you think so, Franklin?"

"I'm thrilled, and I don't even know what you're talking about."

"New York is certainly a wonderful place," Jenny said. "Do you know a nice hotel I could stay at?"

"A nice hotel? What's wrong with the Dixon? Haven't you got a reservation?"

"Oh, I *made* one but they probably forgot all about it. I mean, things like that happen to me all the time. I lead a very perilous life. Why, did you know that when I graduated high school they forgot to give me a diploma? They just skipped right by me in the alphabetical order. The principal, he was absolutely mortified, but I expected it to happen. I just sat there while he was calling the roll and I thought, Betcha you forget my name, Mr. Lund, what do you wanna bet?"

"That's terrible."

"You should have seen what happened when I went to secretarial school. In Duluth. I was there for three months before anybody—"

"I happen to be very well connected at the Dixon," and he jumped the car ahead. "Now just relax and leave it all to me." He cut in and out of traffic, gunning the car, making a light at the last possible moment, finally pulling up in front of the Dixon Hotel.

The Dixon doorman opened the taxi door. Mr. Truman shook his head. The doorman looked at him. Mr. Truman beckoned once with the index finger of his right hand. The doorman shut the taxi door and walked around the car until he stood outside the driver's window.

"Franklin," the doorman said out of the side of his mouth.

"Mort," Mr. Truman answered out of the side of his mouth.

"Something?" Mort said softly.

"Wantcha to take care of this girl."

"Consider it done. What's her name?"

"What's your name, Jenny?"

"Devers," Jenny said.

"Devers," Mr. Truman said out of the side of his mouth.

"Devers," Mort said, nodding.

"Check that her reservation's straight," Mr. Truman said.

"Consider it done," Mort said, and he hurried into the hotel.

"This is really very nice of you, Franklin," Jenny said. "But I never meant—"

"It's no trouble. He owes me money."

"Oh," Jenny said. "Well, I hope he pays you."

He turned around and looked at her. "You're a pretty girl, you know that?"

"No, I'm not pretty."

He looked at her again. "Well, just the same, you got qualities."

"I'm very nice," Jenny said. "At least I try to be."

"Why're you here?"

"Oh, because my boyfriend's in town visiting. Well, he's supposed to be in town visiting. He's probably gone away unexpectedly, but I thought since he was here that I ought to come then because it would give me somebody to talk to. I think that's very important, don't you, to have somebody to—oh, here comes Morton."

The doorman hurried out of the hotel and around the taxi to the driver's window. "Seems there's been a slight screw-up," he said out of the side of his mouth.

"That's certainly no surprise to me," Jenny said.

"How slight?"

"Well," the doorman said.

"Why are you both talking out of the sides of your mouth?" Jenny said.

"It seems they goofed on her reservation," the doorman went on.

"Didja fix it O.K.?" Mr. Truman asked.

"Depends on how long she's staying. How long is she staying?"

"How long are you staying, Jenny?"

"Just until I find someplace. Just a couple of days."

"A couple of days," Mr. Truman said.

"In that case," the doorman said, "she can have it."

"Have what?" Jenny asked.

The doorman walked around the car, opened the door and started struggling with her luggage. "The Herbert Hoover suite," he said.

I'm in the Herbert Hoover suite, Jenny thought as the bellboy closed the door. Just fancy that. She scurried from the living room into the bedroom, back into the living room, into the closets, out, back to the bedroom, where she picked up the phone. "This is Miss Jenny Devers and I'm in the Herbert Hoover suite and I wondered could I talk to the Algonquin Hotel, please." She lay back carefully on the bed and when the Algonquin answered she said, "Hello, my name is Jenny Devers and I'm sorry to bother you but I would like to talk, please, to a Mr. Tommy Alden except that I think he's probably not there anymore, having left town unexpectedly, so could you tell me, please, did he say where he might be going?"

"Mr. Alden's in room 802."

"Oh. Thank you. Well, could I talk to him, please, if his line isn't busy?" And then a moment later she heard Tommy's voice. "Tommy?" she said.

"Hello? Who's this?"

"Tommy? It's me."

"Moose?"

Jenny giggled.

"Moose? Where the hell are you?"

"I'm in the Herbert Hoover suite."

"The where?"

Jenny giggled again.

"Listen, Bronko, you're wasting your money. Speak up."

"It only costs a dime."

"You're in *New York*?"

"Isn't that just the most incredible thing?"

"What are you doing here?"

"You know very well what I'm doing here."

"Omigod, you're going to be an actress."

"I just got off the bus."

"Have you still got your return ticket?"

"I didn't buy one, smartie."

"Omigod."

"And stop saying that. Or I won't let you see me. Do you want to see me?"

"What do you think?"

"I'm at the Herbert Hoover suite at the Dixon Hotel in Manhattan on West Forty-fifth—"

"I can find it. I'll be right over."

"Wait fifteen minutes."

"What for?"

"What for?" Jenny said. "What for? I'm in a suite. I'm a lady. A lady needs time to prepare."

After she hung up Jenny threw off her clothes and dashed into the shower and then dried herself and unpacked a little until she came to her newest spring dress, the pale-yellow one she had made just before leaving Cherokee, Wisconsin, and she put it on and had just finished combing her hair when there was a loud knock on the door. "Yes? Who is it?"

"It's me, Moose, who do you think?"

Jenny went to the door and opened it. "Miss Devers will see you now," she said.

"Hello, Miss Devers," Tommy said, closing the door. He wore a blue cord suit and cordovan loafers and a white button-down shirt and a narrow, regimental striped tie.

Jenny nodded to him. "Hello." He was a senior at Williams College, but she had not seen him since the summer of his junior year, almost ten months before, because he had gone south for Christmas, to Bermuda or Jamaica (she could never keep them straight), and though she wept when he wrote her he was going, and though she swore to end their correspondence then and there, she (frantically) changed her mind that same night and wrote him as if nothing at all had happened, in spite of the fact that she was desperately afraid of his meeting some horrible beautiful college girl and falling in love with her because it was so romantic down there, in Bermuda or Jamaica, whichever it was.

"Hey, you look good, Jenny."

"You look beautiful."

"C'mere?"

"I thought you'd never ask," she answered, and she ran into his arms.

They kissed and then he grabbed her as tightly as he could and hoisted her into the air. "God, you're a tank."

"Oh, you hush," and she made him put her down so she could kiss him again.

"I love you, do you know that?"

"Well, you should."

"Get her." He fingered her pale-yellow dress. "New tent?"

"It is *not* a tent."

Tommy kissed her. "Well, shall we?"

Without a word, Jenny walked him to the full-length mirror and they took off their shoes and stood, ritually, back to back, eying the results in the mirror.

"I'm still taller," Tommy said. "Got you by over an inch."

"Thank heavens," Jenny said, and they put their shoes back on. "Would you like to see the Herbert Hoover suite?"

He followed her into the next room. "The hotel's a dump but this room's O.K. How'd you get it?"

"It's all in who you know," Jenny answered. "How was Jamaica?"

"What did you say?"

"Nothing," Jenny mumbled, and she flicked a speck of dust from the bureau top. "I just wondered how Jamaica was."

"It was Bermuda and it was four months ago, so why are you asking about it now?"

"Just making conversation."

Abruptly he turned away. "Dammit."

"What's the matter?"

"Just dammit," Tommy said, and he led her back to the living room. "I didn't want to get into this. Not right away. What did you have to ask for?"

"I don't understand."

"Sit down, huh? Please."

Jenny sat on the sofa. Tommy sat in a chair across from her. "It happened," he said.

"What did?"

"What you were worried about that made you ask about Bermuda. What you're afraid happened. Well, you're right."

Jenny said nothing.

"I was gonna hold off telling you until this summer. I never would have written it to you; I hope you believe that."

"I believe that."

"She's English," Tommy said. "Her name is Cecily."

"Auh?"

"And nothing's set yet. I mean, no date or anything like that. I've got to go to London this summer to meet her parents. He's some rich guy. Coal business, primarily. Very snobby."

"Is she nice?"

"I think so. I don't know. It was so damned romantic down there, you know what I mean. Beach and sun and dancing all night long. I'm really torn up about it, Jenny. Honest I am. But she's so little and cute and that way she talks, it just knocks me out."

"Little and cute?"

Tommy nodded. "Like a button. Cecily Henshaw. She comes to about here on me." He indicated his chin.

"Well," Jenny said, "I hope you know what you're doing."

"So do I," Tommy answered. "So do I. I know it's crazy, but . . ." His voice drifted off.

"Just a little ago. Why did you say you loved me?"

"I'm sorry," Tommy said. "I was just trying to be nice."

"I'll always care for you and I hope you'll be very happy."

"Thanks. Oh, Jesus, Jenny, don't think this is easy for me. But there she was on the beach in Bermuda and, well, I never met anybody like her before. She's so petite and all, but with this terrific shape and great eyes and this green hair and dimples and a smile, well, I don't know how to describe her smile."

"She sounds like a very pretty—did you say green hair?"

Tommy sighed. "Long and green."

"You're terrible!"

'Tommy sighed again. "Like seaweed."

Jenny jumped up and ran into the bedroom and shut the door.

"Moose?" Tommy said. He went to the bedroom door and tried pushing it open. "Hey, Moose?"

Jenny held it shut.

"Moose, come on now."

"How dare you lie to me?" Jenny shouted through the door. "Especially when you know I always believe everything."

"You started it with that 'how was Jamaica' junk."

"I did not. Besides, it doesn't matter anymore. You went too far to ever regain my good graces. I thought you might like to know that."

Tommy threw his weight against the door, but Jenny held it shut. "Let me in."

"Never."

"*Let me in.*"

"Give me one good reason."

"I hunger for your lips."

"Oh, in that case," and she opened the door.

"Listen," Tommy said after he kissed her. "When do you wanna get married?"

"I don't know. When do you wanna get married?"

"I don't know. When do you . . ." He started to laugh. "Do you think, that maybe this conversation means we're not quite ready?"

"Probably; I don't know." She clung to him. "We really love each other, don't we?"

"Haven't we always?"

"I guess we have. That's nice, don't you think?"

"If you like that kind of thing."

"I don't even know why I bother with you." She looked at herself in the bureau mirror a moment. Then she shook her head. "Sometimes I'm not so ravishing as some people," she said.

"They've got these new things for hair I just heard about," Tommy said. "I think they're called 'combs.' Supposed to work wonders." He watched as she opened her compact. "Try not to take all afternoon."

"What are we going to do?"

"I don't know. Have cocktails eventually. First I thought you might like to see the sights. As long as you're here a few days."

Jenny said nothing.

"Let's face it. Lloyds of London says you're not liable to stay."

"I'm putting on my makeup. It requires fantastic concentration."

"I wanna talk about it if you don't. I'm glad you're here, but I don't see much point to your staying, considering we're gonna get married sometime and, anyway, you don't probably even want to stay, do you?"

"I don't know." She put her makeup away and he helped her on with her coat. "But, Tommy, so far, today, I mean, well, the things that have happened to me. Why, you wouldn't believe it."

"Try me," Tommy said as he locked the door and they walked down the hall to wait for the elevator.

"I'd rather be mysterious."

"The day you're mysterious . . ." And then he stopped, because the elevator door opened and they rode down in silence.

"I'm an enigma," Jenny said, pulling her coat collar to just below her eyes.

They walked through the lobby. "Behave yourself," Tommy told her. They moved onto the sidewalk. "Now, I thought we might begin at Rockefeller Cen—"

"Good afternoon, Miss Devers."

"Oh, hello, Morton."

"Miss Devers, Franklin was wondering if you might be wanting the car."

"Tell him 'thank you' for me, will you, Morton? I think I'm fine."

Tommy looked at the doorman, then at Jenny, then back at the doorman, then he started to run, hurrying to catch up with Jenny as she floated toward Fifth Avenue.

As they started to enter the Algonquin Jenny said, "Is the Round Table still here?"

Tommy stopped. "How many books did you read before you came?"

"About New York? Seventeen. I thought I should prepare myself."

Tommy shook his head.

"Oh, they weren't all *all* about New York. Some of them just had chapters."

They walked into the hotel and Jenny looked at the people having cocktails in the lobby, at the dining room beyond. Tommy took her arm when she gasped.

"What is it?"

"Look," Jenny whispered.

"Where?"

"There."

"I don't get it."

"*There,*" and she gestured with her shoulder to the red-haired man drinking by himself in the corner.

"So?"

"That's him," Jenny whispered. "That's Stagpole."

"You're crazy."

"I've seen his pictures."

"Come on," Tommy said.

Jenny held back. "Can't we stay here a minute? I want to watch him."

"You're probably looking at some guy from Salt Lake City who's in the butter-and-egg business."

"He looks just like his book jackets."

"Jenny, will you cut it out?"

"I wonder if I could get his autograph. You could ask him for me. It's less embarrassing for a man."

"I've had enough of this," Tommy said, and he took her arm. "I'll prove you're crazy."

"How?"

"We'll just go ask him." He started pulling her across the lobby. At first she resisted, but then as she imagined people might be staring at her she stopped, contenting herself with frantic whispers.

"Tommy, please. Tommy, now stop this. Tommy—"

"I'm sorry to bother you," Tommy said when they reached the red-headed man. "But this girl here wants to ask you a question."

"What is it, Jenny?" the man said.

"Well," Jenny said, "the thing is . . ." And then she said, "That's my name." And then she said, "You're *him*!" Then: "Tommy, you pull any more tricks on me and . . ." Then: "Fancy that." Then she just stood there.

"Sit," Tommy said, holding a chair.

Jenny sat.

"Where's Dad?" Tommy asked, sitting beside her.

"Talking too much someplace, I expect," Stagpole replied. "You know your father." He turned to Jenny. "I understand we're both fans of mine."

"Hello," Jenny said.

"She thinks you're even greater than Edgar Rice Burroughs," Tommy said.

Stagpole laughed.

Jenny put her arm around Tommy's neck and pulled him close. "Now you be nice to me," she whispered. "And, please, don't call me 'Moose.' "

"Word of honor," Tommy said.

"There she is!" Mr. Alden's voice boomed from behind them. "There she is!" He hurried up and kissed Jenny roughly on the cheek. "You and I are through."

"But—"

"Nineteen years I know this girl." Mr. Alden gestured with his unlit cigar. "I was there when she was born. And when she comes to New York, does she tell me? Hell no." He sat down and signaled for the waiter. "Through. Who wants what?" The men ordered Scotch, Jenny ginger ale.

"The reason I had to keep it secret was if I told you you would have told Tommy and he would have made some joke and then I wouldn't have come."

"That makes me sound pretty neat," Tommy said.

"Have you always wanted to come?" Stagpole asked.

"Not always, exactly. Just since I was twelve."

"Have you acted a lot?" Stagpole said.

"Not a lot, exactly. I'm too tall for most parts."

"How tall are you?"

"Oh, a little over five-seven."

"Three inches over," Tommy said.

"*Tommy.*"

"Anyway," Mr. Alden said, "you're here. How's it been so far?"

"You wouldn't believe it," Tommy said.

"That's the truth," Jenny said. "Mr. Stagpole?"

"Call him 'Wormy.' " Mr. Alden told her. "When we were growing up, that's all anybody called him. Just 'Wormy.' "

"Go on, Jenny," Stagpole said.

"Well . . ." Jenny began. Then she stopped. "Did they really call you 'Wormy'?"

Stagpole nodded. "Alas."

"I think that's terrible," Jenny said. "I saw your play this afternoon. I went right by it in my taxicab. *The Left Hand Knows.*"

"That turkey," Mr. Alden said.

Stagpole looked at him. "Have you no heart?"

Happily, Mr. Alden lighted his cigar.

"That play," Stagpole went on, "happens to be an outstanding artistic achievement. Not only has it run more than a year but Warner Brothers bought it for four hundred thousand dollars. That proves it's an outstanding artistic achievement."

"Bushwah," Mr. Alden said. "It's just like the rest of your turkeys. The men are all studs and the women are nympho—" He stopped and smiled at Jenny. "Your father would disapprove of my language. Forgive me."

"He still thinks I'm a baby," Jenny said. "But I know lots of words." The waiter brought their drinks. Jenny took a sip of her ginger ale. "I'm in New York and I'm having cocktails and I'm just so happy." She giggled at Tommy. "I am."

"Do you always say what you think?" Stagpole asked.

"Always," Tommy said. "Believe me."

"That's a bad habit, Jenny. Nice. But bad."

"Oh, I'm a terrific liar when I want to be. You wouldn't believe some of the lies I've told. Why—" She broke off suddenly. "Why are you staring at me?"

"No reason," Stagpole said.

"I don't like it for people to do that."

"Do you know why you don't like it, Jenny? I think I do."

"Oh-oh," Mr. Alden said. "He's playing God."

"Yes." Stagpole nodded. "That's a bad habit of mine. One of my better bad habits. Why did you come here, Jenny?"

"I don't know. No reason."

"It's hard to be an actress, Jenny. Hard, and not particularly reward-ing. Are you talented?"

"Oh, I don't think so. Not really. I'm—"

"She's very talented," Tommy cut in. "She just shouldn't waste her time here. She won't be happy."

"I've got to find out," Jenny said.

"You're always gassing about what a big deal you are," Mr. Alden said to Stagpole.

"You're quite right. I happen to be an enormous deal."

"Then why not give the kid a break? Let her find out fast. Give her a part in that four-hundred-grand turkey of yours."

Stagpole nodded. "That's not impossible."

Jenny held her breath.

"Not a part, really," Stagpole went on. "Just an understudy's job. And, of course, I couldn't give you the job myself; that's the director's function. But I suspect if I strongly urged it, he wouldn't buck me. Chances are you'd never go on; the show's not going to run much longer. But we do need an understudy just now, and I would be surprised if it couldn't be maneuvered. She's not altogether wrong for the part; to tell the truth, the part's so dimly written *nobody's* wrong for it. Well, Jenny, what do you say? Would you like a job?"

"You're all just fooling me; you planned it all before."

"Answer the question, Jenny," Stagpole said.

"If you did it, then this would be the happiest day of my life."

Stagpole turned to Mr. Alden. "Where do you suggest we dine?"

"What's wrong with here?"

"Nothing. Why don't you and Tom secure us a table? Now would be a good time." He flicked his hand. "Away."

"Look out, he's gonna play God again," Mr. Alden said, rising. "Jenny, you got my sympathy. C'mon, Tom."

Stagpole watched them go. Then he took out a very long cigarette holder and inserted a very long cigarette. "One of my affectations," he ex-plained. "One of an infinite number."

Jenny smiled.

"We are talking now of happiest days," Stagpole said. "Do you know what they are?"

"Yes," Jenny said. "They're—"

"That was a rhetorical question, Jenny. Now, I have a theory about happiest days, and since you *don't* know what they are, I thought I'd en-lighten you."

Jenny giggled. "You're funny."

Stagpole almost smiled. "The happiest day is that day in the past that you always run back to when the present proves unendurable. Let me give you an example. I was thirty-two. I had been famous for perhaps six months. The day was Sunday. The season, fall. I woke late, without the slightest trace of hangover—unusual; those were my drinking years. And I shaved and bathed and oiled my body and then I dressed. I chose my cashmere blazer. It was still new, but I had worn it at least twice before. And I strolled over to Madison Avenue and I had a late brunch. The food was excellent, wonderfully expensive. I had, I believe, four drinks. Then I walked. Hours of walking. And watching. Windows, faces. Then I made a telephone call. I had been, you see, to a party the night before, and I had met a blonde, a wild, wonderful blonde, and I called, and we made an assignation, and we met, and walked, and drank a bit, and then, then, Jenny, we made love. Not perfectly, not thunderously—no. Adequately only. Adequate was the word for our love-making. Am I embarrassing you?"

"No," Jenny said. "Yes. Go on."

"Very little more. We drank, dined together, separated; by this time it was late. I went home. I undressed. I went to bed. And almost immediately I knew I was going to sleep. Insomnia is one of my curses, but not that night. And as I drifted off I thought yes. I choose. I choose today. I have chosen. And then I slept." He lit another cigarette.

"Oh," Jenny said. "Well, that's certainly very interesting."

"You don't think so at all."

"Yes, I—"

"That's the whole point. That's why it's so perfect. You see—and here you must pay attention—we all get to pick our day. But we only get one pick. One time to choose. And the worst thing in the world, Jenny, the saddest thing is to choose the wrong day. You've got to pick a day that won't go bad on you; if you do, you'll have no place to run."

"And that's sad?"

"Inexpressibly. That's why you've got to pick an ordinary day. The great ones sour. Your love holds you for the first time in his arms and you think, How perfect, how splendid, but then, when your love isn't your love anymore, you think only, I let him touch me, how horrid, how vile. This isn't your day, Jenny. I promise you. You mustn't take my offer. And if I weren't quite so cruel, I'd never make it to you."

"Oh, you're not either cruel."

"You don't know about me, Jenny. But I know about you."

"What do you know? What did Tommy tell you?"

"Nothing. But I know. You're very sweet and not particularly bright and not particularly pretty either. But you've got a body that makes men gasp and you hide it, or try to, but you can't, not really, and I'm embarrassing you again."

"Yes."

"And you're probably a good enough actress, but you don't want it all that much, and if you don't accept the job you'll probably never get another one, but if you do accept you'll probably stay. Here. In this town where nobody really belongs. And this day, this happiest day, will go bad on you, and you'll have no place to run. So I beg you, choose some other time. Choose tomorrow; choose next year. But the choice is yours. Make it."

"I choose today."

"Poor Jenny."

XII

At the migraine's mercy, Esther writhed.

She lay across her bed, her fingers jabbing at her temples, probing for entrance. Suddenly she doubled up like a tumbler, straightened just as fast, her head at the foot of the bed now, her feet kicking at the pillow. Her fingers crawled up her face, paused for a moment at the temple, then scuttled on, finally getting ready to jab again, straight for the eyes this time.

The boy grabbed her hands.

"Let go!" Esther cried.

The boy held on.

"*Rudy!*"

The maid came in with an ice pack.

Rudy took it, muttered, "Thank you, Mrs. Kenton," then applied the pack to the base of his mother's neck.

At the first touch of cold, Esther cried out again, but soon she began to subside.

Sid walked in, tying his tie. "You ready?" he said to the boy. "If you want a lift, move."

The boy took his mother's left hand, clamped it against the ice pack. "I've got to go, Mother. You try and sleep; you'll be fine." He moved quickly to the doorway.

Esther watched him. He was wearing white tennis shorts and shoes, tee shirt and socks. "Watch out for the girls," Esther said.

When he was alone with his wife, Sid said, "I'm late, Tootsie; so long."

Esther muttered, "Leave me."

"Why do you always come up with a migraine whenever I go anyplace? For the love of Christ, Esther, it's just for two days."

"Who is she this time?" Esther asked.

"Who is who?"

"*I'm dying and he gives me riddles!*"

Sid retreated a step, tentatively blew her a kiss.

Esther wiped both sides of her face clean before commencing to moan.

Sid stood still, waited, said "Esther . . ." twice to no response. Then he turned, running down the stairs to the garage. The boy was waiting in the red Cadillac. Scowling, Sid slammed the car door, pushed a button, put the top up, pushed another button, turning on the air-conditioner. For a moment he looked around for more buttons to push, started for the radio with his index finger, changed his mind, dropped his hand. Who needed music? At what it cost, the sound of the air-conditioner was music enough for anybody's ears.

· · ·

Sid hit during the war.

Black-marketing, naturally, but what was the matter with that? If he hadn't done it, then somebody else would, and why should his family starve? Which they were doing, until the day his friend Mannie the druggist ran into the deli frantic with a load of hot nylons. The fact that the cops were on to the shipment fazed Sid less than little: he simply sold the deli, bought the nylons, sold the nylons, split his profits with the boys in blue and was on his way. For six months he dabbled in nylons, enriching both himself and Chicago's Finest, and then he spread into rubber tires, which he sold at prices so high it was genuinely embarrassing to him, almost. When his tire supply dwindled, he quick-hopped back to his first love, and gladly, because not only were nylons nice and steady, but the broads didn't flop as much for whitewalls, and one night, flush, he invaded the pool hall to find his touch had returned, and with just a speck of practice he was better than ever, so then he had a parlay going, stockings *and* a cue stick, and by 1943 he was able to buy his first custom-made suit and give five hundred dollars to the March of Dimes. 'Forty-four was even better, and in July of that year he opened his own store near the Loop, a hole in the wall, true, but crammed with bitches buying stockings, and he would have made a trillion except the police cut was killing him, so he sold the whole enterprise at a spectacular profit, gave a farewell party at Barney's for all his friends in the law-enforcement game and retired to his seat at Painter's, the best pool hall in Chicago, to await the next lightning bolt that he was sure now would come. Of course he was right, for in January he won half interest in an automobile agency by pulling a typical Super Sid finish (Who's this Gentile Garrison?), sinking thirty-four straight to close out the match, the thirty-fourth being a bank shot that would have given Hoppe trouble. The agency, once the war ended, was worth plenty, half of what Sid sold it for, at which point he moved his family out to the North Shore, Highland Park no less, and went into the business that must have been invented with him alone in mind.

Insurance.

Since salesmanship and charm were the twin requirements for success, was it any wonder he proved an instant sensation? Mostly he sold to the rich-bitch suburban ladies, but he also opened up a little territory in Benton Harbor, because there was money there and because it gave him a chance for a day or two away from Esther every so often, not to mention the opportunity of plugging at his leisure some Michigan lovely or other.

His kid adjusted quickly to all the changes, taking to suburban life, doing well at school, athletics too, tennis especially, at which he was, like at everything else, a natural. Sid would maybe have liked a little more noise from the kid, a little more of the old be-zazz, but even as things were, Sid wasn't complaining; he understood—it takes all kinds and the kid was just that kind, the quiet kind, except maybe for once (it was cloudy in Sid's memory), once maybe right after the kid had got the news about the hearing loss and hadn't adjusted to it yet and he'd yelled at Sid, yelled something, Sid couldn't really remember, and besides it didn't matter, because the kid had practically as much as apologized for it later and Sid, big like always, accepted on the spot.

Esther, however, submerged during Sid's ascension. Her goddam headaches drove him loony a lot of the time, so he hired a maid who doubled as nurse, a Mrs. Kenton, whom he hated, because she was old and ugly. He had always daydreamed of having someone like Theda Bara or Jean Harlow (lately he would have settled for Rita Hayworth; no one could call him a fussy man) serve him supper, because the thought of sneaking up the back stairs and whipping off a piece appealed to his senses of pleasure and thrift, except sometimes lately, when he daydreamed the excursion, he was thwarted to find his son thrilling the maid on his arrival. The kid was tiny, true, but otherwise great-looking, and it pained Sid to watch the way women watched him. Of course he, Super Sid, had had his share of looks too, when he was young, but now not so many: he was edging into middle age, a painful journey. But aging and Esther were as nothing compared to his third pain, the pain that was assuredly killing him.

Greentree Country Club.

The snotty sons of bitches, they turned down his application for membership. He applied again the next year, working overtime, charming the hell out of any members he happened to meet socially. Sid fought like crazy but he knew his chances were less than tepid, so at nights he prayed for a miracle. And when Rudy was offered a summer job working as ball boy at the Greentree Country Club courts, Sid sensed bingo!—at last the omens were all on his side, which was just and fair and good and well deserved, only that, no more.

"I'm freezing," Sid said as he drove swiftly toward Greentree Country Club. He jammed his finger against the air-conditioner button, turning it off. "Lousy crooks. I ask for a unit to cool the car, they give me one to cool the Loop. Everybody's money hungry, kid; you remember that."

The boy nodded.

"Those headaches! God damn those headaches of hers. Let me tell you something about your mother, kid."

"Did you say something, Father?" The boy touched his hearing aid. "It went off. I'm sorry."

"It always goes off whenever I say something you don't want to hear, ever notice that?"

"No; that would be a remarkable coincidence. I'm sure it couldn't—"

"She thinks I'm playing around in Benton Harbor. I look, yes. Everybody looks. But I never touch. I swear. She's trying to kill me with her accusing and her headaches whenever I set foot out the door and—"

"I'm sorry, Father. It went off again. What were you saying?"

"Those headaches are just to torture me, Rudy."

"She suffers."

"Are you saying I don't? She tells you that while I'm gone, doesn't she? While I'm gone trying to make enough somehow to pay her goddamn quack-doctor bills she fills you up with poison against me. You think I don't suffer? I'm a Jew. I bleed."

"This instrument." The boy shook it. "I really must have it looked at someday."

Sid sighed.

"It's going to be a wonderful day for tennis," the boy said.

When he reached Greentree Country Club, Sid took a right, then the first left, following the road down toward the tennis area, stopping at the far end of the bank of courts.

Rudy said "Thank you" and started to get out.

Sid grabbed him. He was staring through the fence, pointing at the man and woman hitting on the first court. "Who're they?"

"Mr. Winters, the pro, and Mrs. Marks. She takes a lesson almost every morning."

"Dolly Marks?"

Rudy nodded.

Sid continued to stare. "How'd you like to stick that?" he said.

"It's always nice to end on a religious note," the boy said, and he skipped from the car.

Sid stared a moment longer, then turned the car. He drove out of the club, pausing just a moment to look at the "Greentree" sign, until there was a loud honk from behind him. "Screw," Sid said then, jamming down on the gas, shooting the car onto the highway, narrowly missing a Chevrolet. The Chevy was dirty and several years old, and such was the scorn with which Sid eyed it that, had it feelings, it would have piled itself into the nearest embankment, killing itself on the spot, from sheer chagrin.

"You two play," Dolly Marks said, watching as the ball boy walked onto the court. In the distance, an enormous red Cadillac roared away.

"Had enough?" Mr. Winters asked.

Dolly nodded. "I've got a game in a few minutes."

"O.K.," Mr. Winters said. "Let's hit a little, Rudy. Before the heat gets me."

Dolly said, "You beat him, Rudy."

The boy smiled. "Whatever you say, Mrs. Marks."

Dolly moved off the court, lowering herself into a lounge chair, crossing her long legs. She was in all ways a splendid-looking creature, supple and sleek, tall, permanently tanned, with legitimately black hair and a stomach as flat now as it had been when she was twenty, twenty years before.

"Sorry if I'm late, dollbaby," Fran Green said.

Dolly glanced up. "*De nada*, widow Green."

Fran Green pulled up another lounge chair and stretched out. For a while the two women lay quietly, watching the men play tennis. Then Fran flicked her sunglasses up into her gray-blond hair. "My, what an interesting-looking ball boy."

"Don't harass me today," Dolly said.

"Harass? All I did was comment on the appearance of the ball boy. I don't see how that could be considered—"

"I mean it, Fran."

Fran Green nodded and was silent. Reaching up, she took her sunglasses, twirled them a moment, then rested them on the tip of her nose. "No," she said finally, "I don't see it."

"Don't see what?"

"Oh, nothing—just that my daughter reports that all the girls in high school are very big on this ball boy."

"You just never stop, do you?"

"Rudy Miller, I think she was talking about. That one. There." She pointed and laughed.

Dolly Marks said nothing.

"They're *maaaaaad* for him, so I'm told."

Dolly Marks examined her fingernails.

"Have you?" Fran asked.

"Have I what?"

"Initiated proceedings with the subject under discussion."

Dolly sighed.

"I know, dollbaby; you're gonna start something, I know all the signs, but I'm warning you, you wait much longer I might just take the play away from you. What do you think my chances might be with the ball boy?"

"You're too fat to be a cradle robber."

"*Merci.*"

"Ask a question, get an answer. Gim me a cigarette."

"Why do you smoke? You don't inhale."

"Same reason I cheat on my husband: gives me something to do with my hands." Dolly grabbed the cigarette from Fran. "I hate hearing old women mooning over infants. How old is he? Eighteen? Seventeen? Well, you're forty and so'm I. I'm forty and my husband's fifty-five and there's no law against that, but when we're alone he acts like he's a tired seventy, and that's all right too, except whenever we're in public he goes around playing like a Yale freshman and he married me because I was pretty and I married him because he had loot and in this world you get what you pay for and forget what I'm saying, I must have gotten up out of the wrong bed this morning; let's play tennis."

They played for an hour, hitting the ball like men, and then they decided to play some cards by the pool, but almost before they'd started over Dolly said, "Wait for me here" and hurried back to the tennis shack.

"Good luck with the infant," Fran called after her.

"Yes, Mrs. Marks?" Rudy said when Dolly entered the tennis shack.

"I was just wondering if you thought my racket needed restringing."

The boy examined it. "It's fine, Mrs. Marks."

"You're sure?"

"I restrung the racket myself, Mrs. Marks. It was just a few weeks ago."

"Oh, no; it was much longer than that."

"I guess you're right, Mrs. Marks."

She headed for the door. "It must really get brutal here in the afternoons. It's much nicer playing at night, don't you think?"

"I guess it would be."

"Our court's lit, you know. We play there at night all the time. If you're ever in the neighborhood, feel free."

"Thank you, Mrs. Marks."

"I mean it. It's all very casual. Just come."

"If I'm ever in the neighborhood," Rudy said.

At supper a week later, Sid made an inquiry: "What about Dolly Marks?"

"Who?" Esther asked.

"Lou Marks' wife. Tell me. A bitch? What?"

"She's very nice," Rudy said.

"I've heard wild stories," Sid said.

"She's really very nice," the boy repeated. "She even invited me to play tennis at her house if I ever wanted to."

"When was this?"

"Last week."

"And you didn't go?" Sid said.

"Why should he?" Esther wanted to know.

"Lou Marks ain't on the board at Greentree?"

"And you didn't go?" Esther said.

The Marks estate spread for twelve acres along the shores of Lake Michigan. The house was enormous and old, four-storied. There was a formal garden and next to that a pool and next to that an *en tout cas* tennis court. From there the lawn swept in an unbroken line to the bluff.

In the midst of serving, Lou Marks stopped. A reedlike man with an incongruously deep voice, he bellowed, "Who's this? We've got an intruder."

"Rudy, hi," Dolly called from net as Rudy got out of the car and walked toward the court.

"I was in the neighborhood," Rudy said.

Dolly took his hand. There were half a dozen people present and she introduced them quickly, saying, "Let's see now, you can play next set—you and I, we'll take on the winners—all right? Fran, take my place, be a dear. I'll give you the fifty-cent tour, Rudy, come on." And she whisked him away. "I'm a marvelous hostess, don't you think? Didn't I do that well?" She laughed and, when she was done, smiled. "What would you like to see?"

The boy gestured across the lawn to the bluff.

They started to walk. "I'm really surprised you're here. I never thought you'd come."

"It's the most beautiful place."

"Thank you, I guess it is. I have to ask you some questions now, do you mind?"

The boy shook his head.

"You don't talk much, do you? Aren't you even interested in why I have to ask you some questions?"

"Oh yes. Very. Why?"

"So that later, when Lou asks me about you, I can tell him. Lou's terribly curious. And I don't know much about you, actually, except that you work at Greentree. You haven't a cigarette, have you? I'm really delighted you came. And surprised. Nothing quite so dull to the young as the old, don't you think?"

The boy said nothing. They continued walking across the lawn to the bluff.

"Where do you live?"

"Over near the high school."

"Brothers and sisters? Now, don't think I'm nosy, I told you, I have to ask this—well, I suppose I am nosy. I like gossip, don't you? Except when it's about me of course. Have you ever heard any gossip about me?"

"No brothers or sisters." He moved a step or two ahead of her to the edge of the bluff. Rudy stared into the darkness.

She moved in, standing close beside him. Below them the lake rum-bled. "How did you lose your hearing?" Dolly said.

"Down there."

"Down there?"

"Somewhere. I ran away. I was very young. I got sick and . . ." He indi-cated his earpiece. "I can remember running and looking up. To the top of the bluff. Sometimes I could see the houses."

"Why did you run away?"

"For the fun of it. Everybody should once. I never had. So I did."

"Your parents must have been in a panic."

The boy continued staring down. "Oh yes. We're very close."

"Your father sells, doesn't he? Insurance?"

"Yes. And my mother is a housewife."

"Sounds wonderfully American. A *Collier's* short story. Sometimes I think wouldn't it be wonderful if life were like a *Collier's* story? And we could all be young doctors and nurses and find happiness in fifteen hun-dred words."

The boy said nothing.

"Dah-lee!" Lou's voice boomed out across the lawn.

"Coming," Dolly answered. "Lover."

"Go on—" Sid said.

"—Tell us—" Esther said.

"—Did you play?—" Sid said.

"—Of course he played, fool—did you win, Rudy?—"

"—Who cares if he won? The important thing is did you enjoy yourself—?"

"—Of course he enjoyed himself, fool; did they ask you back, Rudy—?"

"—Why shouldn't they ask him back? When are you going—?"

"—Yes, Rudy; when, Rudy—?"

"—When, Rudy, when—?"

Later. Upstairs.

Sid
It's a real break, they're taking an interest in our Rudy.

Esther
It does him good to associate with people like that.

                            SID

That's all I care about: that Rudy associates with the right kind of
people.

                          ESTHER

You can tell a man by his friends.

                            SID

The club means nothing. Who cares about the club?

                          ESTHER

Not me.

                            SID

Not me.

                          ESTHER

I just want Rudy to be happy.

                            SID

(Nodding)
A man wants the best for his son.

The second time he went to play, Rudy and Dolly stood Lou Marks
and a blond man named McCandless, who had been there the first night
too. Rudy and Dolly won and Rudy suggested a second set but Lou said
no, he wanted to play singles instead, and McCandless said I'll take the
winner and then he and Dolly were gone, so Rudy and Lou began to play.
They split the first six games and then Lou beckoned Rudy up close to the
net and when Rudy got there Lou said, "Try."

"I am."

"I said 'Try!' "

Rudy won the next three games and then suggested that they sit a
while, but Lou said no, another, and Rudy looked around for the blond
McCandless but he was still gone and Dolly was still gone, so Rudy raced
through the next six games, but they returned in time to watch the last
few points of the set. Lou was panting and flushed and Rudy said, "Thank
you. Really very much. Thank you."

"I hurt my foot," Lou Marks said.

"Oh, Jesus, Lou," Dolly said. "You and your lousy alibis."

"I hurt my foot!"

"It's true," Rudy said. "If he hadn't it would have been a much different story."

"Sure, sure," Dolly said.

Lou limped off the court. "Listen, why would I alibi? He's not that good. When I was his age—"

"You were never his age," Dolly said.

"Yeah?" Lou said. "Yeah?"

Rudy turned to Dolly. "It doesn't matter. I was very lucky. It's just a game."

Then, from behind him, Lou Marks was screaming *"Can you do this? Can ya? Can ya?"*

He was trying to stand on his hands.

"Please," Rudy said when he saw. "Please."

Lou fell down, tried again, fell again. "I can do it! I can do it! You watch! Hurt foot and all. Let's see you do it!" He kept falling, kept trying.

"I could never do it," Rudy said, and he ran to the fallen man. "Please. That's wonderful. Please stop. Please stop."

"You think I can't do it!" Lou fell down, hard this time, his shoulder slamming the ground, and he lay still a moment before trying again, kicking his feet high into the air, trying to walk on his hands.

"Please," Rudy said. *"Stop it!"*

"Hurt foot and all!" Lou Marks cried.

Rudy knelt beside him. "Please. Please!"

Lou fell again, very hard, lay still. "Hurt foot and all," he whispered.

Rudy thanked the host, thanked the hostess, ran.

"What do you mean, you're not going back?" Sid said the next morning.

"Don't ask me," the boy said.

"Of course you're going back," Esther said. "We're all going back."

The boy watched his mother. "All?"

"Saturday night," Esther said. "We're all invited to a party. Mrs. Marks herself just called to make the invitation. She insisted on us all, Mrs. Marks did."

"Please, Tootsie," Sid said. "Dolly."

"Oh my God," Esther said as they drove up the driveway to the Markses' house. "Such riches."

Sid whistled.

The boy sat in the back, quietly watching as a uniformed attendant stepped into the driveway ahead of them.

"I look all right?" Esther whispered. She was wearing a blue silk dress, new, and so well was she girdled and coiffed that from time to time the girl of nineteen made brief appearances.

"Delicious," Sid said. He stopped the car, looked at himself in the rearview mirror, gave a final quick tug to his bow.

The attendant opened the door for Esther. "Such riches," Esther whispered to Sid before she got out. The attendant took her arm, led her to a path that wound around to the rear of the house. Then he got into the Cadillac and drove it away.

"Lead," Sid said to Rudy. He took his wife's hand.

The boy followed the path around until it widened and the expanse of lawn opened to them. The lawn was lit by great flaming torches burning in the night. The torches stood at the top of long stakes and they flickered and shifted before each tiny puff of wind, casting kaleidoscopic shadows. A large tent stood near one end of the formal garden and music emanated from it, and couples danced, and more couples danced around the swimming pool and a few danced beneath the torches on the green lawn. There were other tents, for food, for drink, each tent a different size, a different color. From the people, from the hundreds of people, there seemed no sound; they seemed content with the silent grace of their movements, and as the Millers watched, a puff of wind came, and with the wind came sudden noise, a burst of laughter, a snatch of song, and with the noise came different shadows, the suntanned faces changed, but when the wind died the noise died, the faces reverted, until the next puff, so that the entire party seemed a gigantic dance, choreographed by the mindless wind.

Sid tightened his grip on Esther's hand and said "Lead!" to his son.

The boy took them to the host and hostess, made introductions, lingered for the next awkward dialogue until his father began the joke about the peanut-butter sandwiches that always got a laugh, and as his father said, "Lou, you listen; Dolly, you might enjoy this too," he slipped away, moving between the torches to the edge of the bluff, then following it, away from the pool, the colored tents, the silent dancers. He was alone now, in starless night, and he lifted his hands to the cooling wind. He spun with quick grace, then, as the wind stopped, he stopped, and continued along the perimeter of the great lawn. At the far end he turned, watching the pretty dumb show. Then he continued on, ambling until he found what once had been a path, following it in among trees until he reached its end. He saw a tiny house, dark; a teeter-totter, a swing. He walked around, trying to see into the windows of the house. Then he pushed the swing, hopped onto the teeter-totter, began walking from one end of it to the other, balancing gracefully, arms out, knees bent. "I always meant to pitch this stuff," Dolly said from the path.

"You have a child?"

"Had. I always meant to pitch it. I will too, someday." She sat in the swing and stared up at the boy through the darkness. "Careful you don't fall."

The boy continued pacing the teeter-totter, one end to the other. "This is a skill of mine. As a child I was brilliant."

"Who are your friends? I might know some of them."

"Well, I stay to myself a lot."

"Why is that?"

"Oh, it won't make any sense to you. It'll sound funny, but people, sometimes they ask me for things. And it doesn't usually work out so well. I can tell this to you because I know you wouldn't ever do anything like that. You've got so much here."

"What kind of things?"

"What kind? Oh, whatever they want, whatever they need, they ask me for."

"And it ends badly?"

"Yes."

"Why?"

"Oh, because I try to give it to them."

"Always?"

"Yes."

"Why?"

"Oh, because just once, one time, I'd like to succeed."

"You weren't gonna come back, right?"

"Right."

"On account of Lou?"

"Yes."

"I hate that phony act of his. Can you hear the music?"

"No."

"It's a wild scene. Kid on a teeter-totter, old broad in a swing, faint music. All kind of erotic." She was wearing a sheer red dress and her black hair was piled high and her perfect tanned skin seemed to glisten. She began to swing. For a moment she threw back her head and closed her eyes.

"It's too bad I can't hear the music," the boy said.

"It makes me out the bitch, you understand that?" She opened her eyes. "That's why I hate it. Old Lou falling all over on the ground and there's that bitch wife of his watching and you know she's driven him to it. I don't like being made out that way. You got a cigarette?"

"No."

"I don't inhale anyway." She stopped swinging. "You remember McCandless?"

"Yes."

"Shut up when he gets here."

"How do you know he's coming?"

"Didn't you know I was?"

Rudy adjusted his earpiece. "I'm sorry," he said. "This instrument of mine." He shook his head.

"I don't drive Lou to it. You remember that. I'm not saying that to get out of being a bitch. I am. But I'm a bitch on my own terms and he does what he does without any help from me."

"He seems very nice."

Dolly watched him. "You're very graceful."

The boy shrugged. "I'm small."

"You may not!" Dolly said before McCandless said anything.

He ran his hands through his blond hair. "May not what?"

"Talk to me."

"Why?"

"Because you're dismissed."

"What does that mean?"

"Shoo."

McCandless took a step toward her.

"Shoo!"

The blonde retreated, disappeared.

"I told you I was a bitch," Dolly said then.

"I'm getting so sick of this instrument," Rudy said.

"You didn't hear any of that?"

"Any of what?"

"O.K.," Dolly said. "O.K." She pushed hard at the ground, then lifted her long legs, pointing her toes, swinging back and forth, back and forth. "Your father's a very funny fella."

"Oh yes."

"And your mother must have been lovely—she is now, of course, but you know what I mean."

"So my father says."

"Think they'd like to join Greentree?"

"Did they mention it?"

"In passing. Your father did."

"Who knows what people want?" Rudy said, and he jumped high into the air, landed silently on the soft ground, pointed toward the path, started that way.

Dolly got out of the swing. "I play around a lot," she said.

"I know."

"How?"

"Stories."

"What do they say?"

"That you play around a lot."

"Ah, what do they know?" Dolly said. They reached the beginning of the lawn. "Do you dance?"

"Yes."

"Dance with me."

"I can't hear the music."

"I've got this thing about getting old," Dolly said.

"You'll get over it," Rudy said. "Or you won't." He started across the lawn toward the dancers.

"Rudy—"

"What a beautiful party this is; you must be so proud," and he darted in among the torches and the suntanned people, with Dolly following, and when Lou hurried over to them Rudy said, "It's the most beautiful party, Mr. Marks," and then he said, "Look! Look!" and he pointed to Sid and Esther, crying, "They're dancing," and they were, holding each other close, turning around and around. Rudy broke into a sudden run, then stopped, contented just to watch as his parents held each other. Over and over Rudy said, "Oh, isn't that pretty. Oh, oh, isn't that just the prettiest thing." And he smiled. And he clasped his hands. And he blinked his eyes . . .

The boy lay in the dark room, his naked body covered by the white sheet. It was almost five in the morning and he had been home for less than an hour, his parents being among the last to leave the party. He lay very still, the hearing aid in his hand. The door to his bedroom opened and closed, and then someone was touching his leg. "Kid," Sid said. "Put it on."

The boy mimed reaching for his instrument.

"I hadda wait till your mother was asleep. This concerns her."

The boy nodded.

"Didja see her tonight, kid? Didja ever see her so happy in years? The truth now." He sat beside his son's body.

The boy shook his head.

"That's the kinda people your mother needs. People like that. They bring out the best in her. There was no headache tonight, no nothin'. I tell you, it was like when we were young. We were awful happy then, kid, before the headaches came."

"Mother's told me."

"Now I wanna get somethin' straight, kid. I'm not telling you what to do. Nossir. You don't get that kinda stuff from me. Your life's your own, and that's that." Sid paused. "We're having the Markses for dinner next week. How 'bout that?"

"Wonderful."

"I invited them. 'Dolly,' I said, 'how's about it?' and they're coming. Esther said I shouldn't ask, but you know how Esther is. Afraid to try anything. A week from tonight. Lou and Dolly Marks, coming here. That's something, y'know? It could mean a lot to your mother."

"Yes," the boy said.

"I don't give a shit about the country club, not for myself, y'understan'? I move around a lot anyway; I meet people. But your mother. Well, it would do her so much good I can't tell you, being with people like that. She needs being with that kinda people, kid. Didja see her tonight? That's what I mean. You could really help her. You could really make your mother happy."

The boy lay very still.

"Don't blow it," Sid said then.

"Pardon, Father?"

"Kid, I see things. I hear, I see, I pick up what I can. Dolly Marks, she looks at you a lot."

"Oh, I don't think she does."

"She plays; so, she's rich, she can afford it. The latest was this *goyem* builder from Chicago, McCandless, something. He was there tonight. Left early. The word is, it's all over."

"Well, I wouldn't know about that."

"That's why I'm telling you. Listen to your father. It's your own life, but you still gotta think about other people sometimes, like your mother. So it's my guess Dolly Marks don't hate you, O.K.? There's nothing wrong with that. Now, I'm not telling you to take advantage, understand. Follow your own heart—that's the only way to move through this world. I mean, I'm *not* telling you to throw a bag over her head and do it for Old Glory. That's the farthest thing from what I'm telling you. God forbid I should ever tell a thing like that to my son."

The boy shook his hearing aid.

"You didn't miss anything," Sid said. "I was just rambling on. The main point is, kid, *don't make waves*. Be nice, that's all I'm telling you. They like you. Keep it that way. Play tennis, smile, see your dentist twice a year. You follow me, dontcha?"

"I follow."

"That's all I wanted to say, kid. Go on back to sleep." He patted his son's shoulder. "And remember: you're helping your mother. You got a chance to really make her happy. 'Night, kid."

" 'Night," Rudy said. He stared, eyes wide, at the ceiling until his mother came in half an hour later.

She shook him. "Put on your thing."

He made the appropriate gestures.

"Your father mustn't hear."

The boy nodded.

"They're coming, Rudy. Here."

"Who?"

"Mr. and Mrs. Marks."

"Ah."

"To our house."

"How wonderful."

Esther sat down heavily on the bed. "I'm very tired," she said. "I should be. Frisking around like a fool that way. I had to do it, Rudy. I couldn't let him down. He was so full of life tonight; Sid."

"Yes."

Esther sighed. "I'm so tired. Not just from the frisking. It's been a hard life, Rudy, for your father and me. A long struggle. No one has ever had to struggle any worse, I promise you that."

"I know."

She sighed again and touched her eyes. "Sometimes, way back behind the eyes, I can feel one forming. A migraine. Like a thunderstorm they tell you is over Kansas on the weather report."

"You should rest," Rudy said.

"Some parents, they push their children. Sid and me, we ain't like that. We would never be. It was very important to us. Almost a pact. We love you so, Rudy. You make us so proud. Everybody loves you. Do you know how lucky you are? Do you know what a cruel place this world is? I know. So does your father."

"I'm very lucky," Rudy said.

"He's had to fight. For everything. It crushed him when they turned him down from that silly club. I, myself, would never go. You know that. How little I care about silly things like country clubs and canasta and sitting by the pool and having someone bring you lemonade. I've always gotten my own lemonade, Rudy. You know that. We've had a lousy marriage, Rudy, your father and me."

The boy closed his eyes.

"Because he's had to fight so hard. Rudy, he doesn't know who he has to fight and who he doesn't, so he fights me. His own wife sometimes. We love each other and we always have, but sometimes we fight too much. If only he could get into that club, though. Then there'd be no place else for him to get to. He's got everything else, Rudy. And once he had that he'd stop fighting and be so happy."

"You haven't had a lousy marriage," the boy said.

"Of course not; who said that? We love each other like anything. I didn't mean we had a lousy marriage. My God, we've been so happy sometimes you could bust. But what I mean is, every so often your father—well, it would make him so happy, being at last a member. Do that for him, Rudy. Help him."

"What would you like?"

"Tell them, the Markses, tell them what a fine man he is and what a fine addition he would make. Tell them I don't care, I don't even have to set foot in the place, that would suit me, but your father—they're coming to dinner, Rudy, and you know it's going to be jokes from him and from me nothing but nerves and they won't see what a fine addition he would be. You must tell them. They like you. You they listen to. You they understand. Do this for your father, Rudy. End the fighting. Make him happy. Help him. It's up to you. You know it is. Help him." She sighed again, kissed her son on the cheek. Then she got up. "You go to sleep now."

"I'm halfway there already."

"This has been an important talk, Rudy, don't you think?"

The boy nodded. "I'm really glad you brought it all to my attention."

Late the next afternoon, as he was closing up the tennis shack, he saw her waving to him from the parking lot. He walked over. "I have to correct an impression," Dolly said.

"Pardon?"

"Get in."

The boy walked around the Jaguar.

"We all have these images of ourself, you know?" She roared up the hill toward the club exit.

"Yes."

"I didn't like the impression I made last night."

"I thought you were very nice."

"I should not have discussed my faults."

"Faults?"

"Playing."

"Ah." The boy squinted up at the billowing clouds and what was left of blue sky. Then, as the car turned, he said, "We're going to your house?"

"I thought we might."

The boy nodded.

"I spoke to your father. He said it would be fine."

The boy smiled.

"This used to be my favorite time, when I was young. Just before the rain. Everybody's in a hurry then, you ever notice that? Everybody's scurrying around just as fast as they can; they haven't got a second to notice you or anything else. They're all in this tremendous hurry. You can do crazy things and no one ever knows it, just before the rain." The car picked up speed. "One time, back in Ohio, there was this dress I hated. It made me look all fat and dumpy and you'll *never know* how much I hated that dress. Pink. For God's sake. Pink and frilly and this tremendous rain appeared way off on the horizon. All of a sudden. You could see it coming closer and closer and it got dark out and a terrible wind started and, like I said, everyone's in a hurry then, nobody notices you, so I ran upstairs and I put on this dumpy pink dress—that's all; I was barefoot and everything—and I went outside just as the wind was reaching a peak and across the street and down the block you could see everybody all hunched over, scurrying around, and I— very slowly—I took off that dumpy dress and I held it just as gracefully as I could, just like a lady, the tip of one sleeve between two fingers, and the trees were bending, and I was standing there naked, holding this dress, waiting for just the right gust of wind, and when it came I opened my hand and it flew away like Dorothy to Oz, and I stood there waving and shouting 'Bye-bye, bye-bye' and nobody noticed me or anything. People ran past, this way, that way, but I knew they wouldn't see me, and they didn't, not with the first big drops of rain coming down." Dolly laughed then. "I am known far and wide for my abilities as a storyteller. For an encore I'll shut up a while." She drove silently until they reached her house. Then she got out of the car, said "Come on" and followed the path around to the great back lawn.

Nothing had changed.

The colored tents still stood, the stakes, the torches. But the torches were dead, the people gone. Other than that, nothing had changed.

"This is the real party," Dolly said then.

The boy said nothing.

"There's no music. We can dance now."

He took her in his arms and they began to glide across the green lawn, turning and bending, silent beneath the blackening sky.

"I thought you'd like it but you don't," Dolly said.

"Why do you think that?"

"I can tell."

"You're wrong." They continued to dance. "It's very lovely, but a bad thing happened to me today. This morning. Something upsetting. I haven't gotten over it yet."

"What was it?"

"Well, this friend of my mother, she gave me a lift to the courts this morning. She picked me up and took me there. A very lovely lady. Truly. Except on the way there she stopped the car. At her house—"

"And she made a pass at you," Dolly said.

They were in the center of the lawn now, two turning spots of color, white for the boy, yellow for Dolly, white and yellow over green, beneath black. "I suppose so."

"And you don't find her attractive."

"She's very beautiful."

"But not very young." Dolly dropped her arms. "She must be a goddam fool. Doesn't she know? The worst thing in the world is to be rebuffed. You don't mind it so much when you're young, but when you're not young anymore . . . What a goddam fool."

"At any rate," Rudy said, "this is very nice here, but I'm still sort of upset."

"There are only two possibilities of why a woman does that. Either they think they're going to succeed . . ."

"Or?"

"Desperation."

Rudy turned away, faced the tents, the cold torches. "When will this come down?"

"Tomorrow. I could have had it done today but I like leaving it up as long as possible. I like ruins. Did you see my dollhouse?"

"Yes. Last night, remember?"

"But you didn't see in it. That's the treat. Come." She started walking toward the path. "Do you have a cigarette? No, that's right, you don't smoke."

"And you don't inhale."

Dolly hurried along the path, then stopped, pointing to the swing and the teeter-totter. "Not so erotic in the daylight, I guess." She pushed open the door of the dollhouse, stooped, went inside. He followed. "Sit," Dolly said. They sat on the floor. "Pretty snazzy, huh?"

The boy glanced around the tiny room. There was a sink and a stove and an icebox and a bed and dozens of stuffed animals and hundreds of dolls. He nodded.

"The dolls are mine. From since when I was a kid. Dorothy—Dolly. Get it? The rest I had fixed up when the baby came, but then she died. Stoppage of the heart. She was very small, so it didn't bother me all that much; I never got to know her all that well. I'm going to have all this pitched some—oh, I told you all that."

"That's all right."

"No; I talk too much sometimes. I should never have told you about my playing."

"That's all right too."

"When I started—playing, that is—I made a rule: I had to care. It wasn't so bad until I began breaking it. This was a long time ago."

"And your husband?"

"My husband inherited a shoe business. He buys things with the profits. Trinkets. You are looking at a trinket. He is a physical coward and a mental gull and I am in all ways his equal. If you're asking does he know, the answer is yes." She smiled. "Can you hear?"

Rudy tilted his head to one side.

Dolly pointed up. "Rain on the roof."

Rudy nodded.

"That's supposed to be romantic, rain on the roof is. I've got this thing about getting old—no, I told you that too." She pushed the door of the dollhouse wide open and stared out at the rain. "I must have a cigarette. Why don't you smoke?"

"I'm sorry."

"I've got this terrible fear you're going to turn me down."

"Shut up."

She started coming toward him, moving into his arms. He held her close and they lay flat on the dollhouse floor. "Don't laugh at me," she said. "See? My hands are shaking. Don't laugh."

"It's not funny; I ought to."

"Help me," Dolly whispered. "Help me."

And then the boy was shouting, "I . . . am . . . so . . . sick . . . of . . . people . . . asking . . . me . . . to . . . help . . . them! I am sick unto death of people asking me to help them! All my life everybody always asks me to help them but you don't want my help!" He scrambled across the doll-house floor, bolted out into the rain, sped along the path onto the great lawn. The rain was thick and steady and he stopped, staring at the ruins of the party. "Everybody says help me but nobody means it; they only mean do what I want."

Dolly touched him. "Listen . . ."

"No!" He ripped his earpiece from his ear. "I hear nothing!" He shut his eyes. "I see nothing!"

Her arms went around him.

His hands ripped at her body; he kissed her mouth. "That's what you want but that's not helping you. That is only what you get from every-body. Helping you is saying no! But you don't want that. You want my help? I'll help you—I'll say no!"

She held him tighter.

"Act your age!" Rudy cried.

She started to slap him, changed her mind, changed it back, slapped him twice, drew blood.

That evening there was a knock on the door. "Who can it be?" Esther said.

"I know this terrific way of finding out," Sid said, and he went to the door. Lou Marks stood outside in the rain. "Lou!" Sid said. "Lou! Come in."

Lou Marks stayed where he was. He wore a monogrammed white shirt and a pair of pale-blue trousers, soaked.

"What is it, Lou? My God, what happened to your hand?"

Lou Marks raised his right hand, swathed in bandages. "I just slammed the car door on it. I bandaged it myself. It hurts like crazy."

"What's going on?" Esther asked, coming up.

"Your son tried attacking my wife," Lou Marks said.

Sid said nothing.

Esther gasped.

"Earlier this evening. She managed to beat him away."

"Jesus God," Sid said.

Esther began rubbing her temples.

"Dolly's pretty upset," Lou said.

"Oh, no, oh, no" from Esther.

"The boy came home not long ago, Lou. He went to his room. He seemed upset but—"

"He tried to rape her. My wife. On the lawn."

"Lou," Sid said. "Lou, believe me when I say—"

"The boy should be punished," Lou Marks said.

"No," Esther said.

"Of course, of course." Sid nodded. "Yes. Definitely. Lou, it takes a while to adjust to—"

"He should be punished!"

"He will be."

"Sid—" Esther cried, and her fingers pushed at her eyes. "My medicine."

"I would do it," Lou Marks said. "But . . ." and he indicated his damaged hand.

"I'll do it," Sid said. "Rest easy. I'll do it."

"How do I know that?"

"You have my word," Sid said.

"Sid, my medicine—"

"The word of the father of a boy who tried to rape my wife?"

"Like son don't mean like father, Lou. Believe me. All my life I've had nothing but my word to go on. That's all that's meant anything—"

"I would love to punish him, but my hand . . ." He held up the bandages again. "Dolly told me and I slammed the goddam car door on it, I was so upset. I can't punish him with just my left hand."

"Are you sure . . ." Sid said. "There could be no mistake?"

"You're calling my wife a liar—you know that."

"No-no," Sid said. "I would rather die. *Rudy! Rudy!* Lou, this will all work out, you'll see, you'll see, I swear to you."

The boy stood above them on the landing.

"Go back, Rudy," Esther cried. "Run!"

"Did you—tonight—did you—how could you do it how—did you attack Mrs. Marks?"

"In desperation," Dolly Marks said, moving in front of her husband.

"Did you?" Sid said. "Did you?"

The boy looked down at them. "If I said no, who would believe me?"

"He didn't deny it," Lou Marks said.

"Run, Rudy," Esther cried.

"*God!*" Sid smacked his forehead. "Rudy, how could you—attack the wife of a man like Lou Marks, a woman like that. How—my God—this is not a thing you can excuse. They were nice to you—he took you into his house—this is how you repay a man like that, a man on the board of clubs, a director of companies—you get dirty with his wife. Rudy, Rudy, what must be done to you?"

"Punish him," Lou said. "I could go to the police but I won't go to the police with a thing like this. My wife's name does not get mentioned in connection with a . . . a . . ." He stared up at the boy. "I would love to punish you. I would. But . . ." He raised his bandaged hand.

"I'll punish him, Lou. You'll see. Come down here, Rudy. This is your father talking. Come down. Now."

"No, Sid," and Esther grabbed for her husband.

Sid pushed her away. "*Come down, you!* I got a belt here. I got a strong belt and you'll see, Lou. Sid Miller is a man of his word."

The boy looked at them, glancing quickly from face to face: Lou the observer, crippled and safe; Dolly smiling, about to be avenged; keening Esther, on her knees now, beginning to writhe; Sid the inflicter, innocent blue eyes bright. Isn't it wonderful, the boy thought, shuddering, descending the stairs toward them, his own eyes filling with tears; I've made everyone happy at last.

XIII

The open convertible bulleted down the dark highway. Branch sat hunched behind the wheel, driving with his left hand, using his right to lock the sleeping girl against his body. Annie Withers had a pretty face (unusual for an Oberlin coed) but a bad figure (S.O.P.). Her hips were large and her arms were too short and, worst of all, her legs were knotted and thick, dancer's legs. Branch flicked a fingertip across her small breast and she stirred, blinking up at him. He smiled, so she closed her eyes.

The speedometer read eighty, but Branch fixed that fast, jamming his foot floorward. Eighty-three, eighty-five, now ninety. The wind screamed. Branch increased his pressure on the gas pedal and at ninety-five the customary panic built inside him, wetting his palms. God, how he longed to brake, to slow, to crawl. It was out of the question, naturally; Branch Scudder drove fast. Everybody knew that. At one hundred miles per hour, the Thunderbird began resenting; the motor roared, matching the scream of the wind.

Up ahead lay Oberlin and Branch felt, as he always did upon approach, smug. Students were forbidden cars and they glanced longingly at his black carrier, just as he had glanced at other cars when he had been a student there, four years before. When he reached the edge of town, Branch slowed. Annie Withers woke, opened her eyes, blinked slowly, then self-consciously ran her fingers through her short brown hair. "We here?"

"We are."

"How's the time?"

"Peace. You've got till one-forty. It is now—" and he looked at his watch—"one-twenty-three."

Annie curled up against him, her arm around his waist. "Wow," she said. "Too many martinis."

"You college kids. No capacity."

"Amen." She snuggled up tighter as Branch drove through the quiet town. When they were almost at her dorm, she walked her fingers up his cheek, across his forehead, then up again, where his hair should have been. "Bald men fracture me," she said.

"I am not bald. I have a receding hairline."

Annie squinted at his skull. "Very." She kissed his cheek. "Face it, Branch old man: you're bald." Branch pulled up in front of Harkness dorm. Spaced along the dorm wall, deep in shadow, couples grappled. Annie gestured toward them. "How common."

Branch nodded. "Absolutely no class." Taking her roughly in his arms, he kissed her.

Eyes closed, Annie said, "You're a killer, you know that, Baldy?"

"Brat," Branch said, and he kissed her again.

"I'm smearing you," Annie whispered.

"Smear me, I'll live." He kissed her and held her close and massaged her small breasts. She whispered his name and he smiled, holding her until it was time to go in. He got out of the car, opened the door for her, then swatted her as she exited.

"Beast."

"You love it."

"Yeah," she said. "Y'know I do." She locked her arms around him and they walked slowly toward the entrance. Several other couples stood clustered by the door. "Aren't they ugly?" Annie whispered. "All that hair."

Branch smiled, conscious of the other boys, of how young they looked, how pure. And he knew they were conscious of him too. He was Scudder from West Ridge—the Guy with the Car. Branch kissed Annie on the forehead, held the door open for her, waved through the glass. Then he turned, jogged to his Thunderbird, got in, turned on the ignition, gunned the motor several times (it was expected of him). Then he released the brake and roared out of the quiet town.

It was less than ten miles from Oberlin to West Ridge, and he could make it in eight minutes if he wanted to. But he didn't want to. (Sweet Jesus, did he not want to.) One mile out of Oberlin, the road forked. The main road was, of course, the better of the two, straighter, brighter, faster. But the back road passed the Pelican.

Branch took the back road.

It was deserted, so he took his foot off the gas and coasted down to thirty. Happily, he kept that pace, sometimes dropping down as low as twenty-five until, ahead of him through the trees, he saw the neon outline of a pelican fluttering its purple wings. Branch slowed, conscious already of the pounding of his heart. When he drew even with the Pelican, Branch put his foot on the brake.

The Thunderbird stopped on the highway.

Keeping the motor running, Branch wrapped his hands around the steering wheel, rested his chin on his white knuckles, staring at the bar and the noiseless purple bird flying overhead. For an instant, Branch shut his eyes, trying to envision the inside of the bar. He saw it then, as clear as his mother's smile, which was remarkable, considering he had only been inside the bar once in his entire life, more than a year ago, the 23rd of April, a date that, like his birthday and Pearl Harbor, he knew himself incapable of ever forgetting. (He had heard about the Pelican all his life, though—whispers here, half phrases there. It was not *that* kind of place—there simply weren't sufficient personnel to support *that* kind of place in *this* part of Ohio—but it was the kind of place where, if you were looking for *that* kind of thing, you went.)

Branch gripped the steering wheel tighter and listened to himself breathe. He was afraid, just as he always was whenever he stopped to stare in at this purple place. Why do you keep coming? Branch wondered. You'd rather die than go back inside, so why do you keep coming? And then he thought of Aaron and something Aaron had said to him once: "You like punishment, don't you, Scudder?"

"Yes, Aaron," Branch said out loud. He stared a moment longer, then jammed his foot down on the gas, gunning the Thunderbird viciously, roaring down the empty road toward West Ridge and home.

Still afraid.

But then, fear was more or less his constant companion. He was afraid of so many people, everybody but Rose, really, although sometimes he even wondered about that. He had been afraid of Aaron. He had been afraid of the Army itself, yet on his Separation Day, two years ago now, Branch had been sad. Rose had driven down to Chicago to pick him up and all the way back she fairly bubbled about some wonderful mysterious surprises awaiting him in West Ridge and Branch had smiled as expected, but he was sad. He would miss the Army, or some things about it. As soon as his training in X Company was finished, he said goodbye to Aaron and the South and took a train to 5th Army headquarters in Chicago. There, life was easy. He clerked, swam in Lake Michigan and shared an apartment with a terrible-tempered sergeant named Rattigan. When Rattigan was transferred to Japan, Branch kept the apartment alone for a while, until Peter Beaumont arrived. Peter Beaumont was a private, sweet and simple, from Los Angeles. He was married, but his wife stayed in California, so she was no bother. On top of everything else, Branch liked Peter. That was why his Separation Day was sad.

Rose's wonderful surprise, which she pointed out proudly as soon as they reached West Ridge, was this: On the glass window of the real-estate office there were now two names where before there had been but one. WEST RIDGE REAL ESTATE. And underneath: BRANCH SCUDDER. ROSE SCUDDER. "Yours above mine, baby," Rose had said that day. "Yours above mine," and she waited for his smile. He gave her one, but the cost was considerable, because he had never functioned (his word) in West Ridge. He had learned the game from a counselor at boy's camp, practiced his skills on a college tour of Europe, refined his style in the Army. But never had he functioned in West Ridge.

Never near home.

Branch went right to work learning the business. He and Rose shared the inner office that had once belonged to his father. He caught on quickly. Rose was proud of him and that was pleasing, but it was not enough. He spent evenings at Oberlin, helping the Dramat with their fall production, and it was a success and *that* was pleasing, but it was not enough. The Black Prince shared his nightly dreams and that was always pleasing, but even that was not enough, for the Black Prince was dreaming and West Ridge, Ohio, was no dream.

Branch grew desperate as winter grew near.

He decided to spend a few days in Chicago with Peter Beaumont, but Rose stopped that. "Ya get out of the Army all of a sudden you can't wait to go visit. Well go! Go! Go on, go!" He had never been able to match her when she chose to overpower him, so he stayed. There was an actor at Oberlin who might have served him, but what if he talked? Branch knew the answer: it would kill him. And Rose? What if she ever found out about him?

That answer Branch knew too, but it was so hideous he never named it.

So what was he to do? Nothing. He could do nothing. But the cost. The cost. Branch began overeating, stuffing great slabs of food down his dry throat, following it with tankards of beer. But his throat remained dry. He had always tended to flesh and now the tendency flowered: a double chin appeared; the layers of flesh below his hips blistered, camouflaging his hip bones. Some nights he would slave at the office till his bloated body ached; some nights he helped at the college, building sets, trimming budgets, anything, anything.

But every so often he would drive by the Pelican and wonder.

Cruise (noun).

To cruise (verb).

Cruising (participle).

Branch loathed the word in any form. The humiliation (he, Branch Scudder, fumbling after some stranger, praying for a pick-up in some scummy bar), the danger (the police: anyone might be the police), the ever-lasting lying ("My name . . . ? My name . . . ?") and, most hideous of all, the hovering stench of guilt.

He hated being "that way," hated having to guard the secret. There were days, as he walked along the streets of West Ridge, that he wanted to scream it out, scream it out, just to end it, just to get it at last over and done. *I'm just like anybody else. I want love. Is that so terrible? Love! I want love!*

And so, in the name of love, at precisely thirty-five minutes after nine o'clock on the night of the 23rd of April, Branch drove (was driven) into the glow of the mute purple bird.

He parked in the middle of the lot and got out of the car and thought he was remarkably calm until he took a step and realized how close he was to not being able to walk. As he crossed to the front door of the bar his panic built wildly, and he was panting as he touched the knob. He froze there for a while, left hand out. Then he turned back to the car and had actually taken a step in that direction before whirling around, yanking at the bar door, shoving it open, stepping inside.

The place was almost deserted. A fat man and woman sat at the bar, talking to the bartender. In the far left corner a jukebox glowed. In the back a crippled little man was making pizza.

And to the right, engaged in a solitary dart game, stood Mr. Saginaw.

Branch could not help smiling as he hurried to the bar. Mr. Saginaw was head of the chemistry department at West Ridge High, a popular teacher, lean and witty and dry. And a bachelor. That was the fact that always preoccupied the students. Why was old Saginaw a bachelor? How they strained their adolescent imaginations for reasons: He had once been married but his wife had been killed tragically; he had once been engaged to a beautiful girl who left him stunned and weeping at the altar; he had loved a Catholic who returned his devotion but her husband was a fiend who would not die. Branch shook his head and signaled to the bartender for a glass of cold beer. Why was old Saginaw a bachelor? Seeing him here, at this time, in this place, made it all so obvious, so painfully plain. Because he was queer. That was why.

Another couple came in, younger than the fat pair, and apparently acquainted, for in a moment the four of them were laughing together. Sad old Saginaw still played his darts and the bartender busied himself drying glassware, the cross of his trade. Branch glanced at his watch. If no one came in soon, he would go. The jukebox sounded "Stardust" in response to the crippled pizza man's nickel. (A romantic, Branch thought. Well, so am I.) He finished his beer and ordered a second, a third, a fourth. Come on, Somebody—No don't no don't—yes please—no please—Somebody—no Nobody—

The door to the Pelican opened and Somebody walked in.

Branch glanced up, then back to his beer. Somebody was walking in his direction, and then the stool two down from his was occupied. By what? A thin young man with a scar. A long, puckered scar curving from the right eye down across the bony cheek to the thin mouth. A thin young man with a scar and black hair piled high, curl on curl.

Go away, Branch thought, but he smiled at the scar.

And the scar smiled on him in return.

"Beer," the man with the scar said.

Branch finished his draft. "Make that two." He glanced over his right shoulder to where Saginaw played his solitary dart game. As he returned his glance, his eyes met the eyes over the scar. There was no flicker. Nothing.

Yet.

The bartender earned his keep. Branch picked up his glass and turned it slowly in his hand. He did not speak, nor did the scar, but the air was filled with the impending inevitable conversation.

"How do you figure the Indians?" Branch said. God! Talking about baseball. He, Branch Scudder, who couldn't even catch (though he seemed to remember his father once trying to teach him), was talking about baseball. But he went right on; baseball was safe. "Think they have a chance?"

"They gotta beat the Yankees."

"That's the truth."

"They got pitching, all right."

"Sure. But the hitting's something else again."

"That's the truth."

Branch nodded and gulped down his beer. He raised his hand and the bartender came over. "One more. Two?" and he looked at the scar. A shake. "Just one." The bartender took the glass. "How do you figure the Indians?" Branch said. "Think they have a chance?"

"Who gives a shit about the Indians," the bartender said.

Branch paid him and he walked away. "Un-American, wouldn't you say? A Communist?"

"Somebody oughta notify Eastland about him."

"Absolutely," Branch agreed and they smiled at each other. "You from around here?"

A muscular man entered the bar. He sat across from Branch, absently fingering a tattoo on his forearm. The man with the scar took in the new-comer, then turned back to Branch. "Just passing through," he said.

"Same here. Just passing through."

They sipped in silence for a while. A slight, effeminate boy came in and the man with the tattoo smiled. They moved to the jukebox and put in a coin. Mantovani began to play.

"Pretty," the man with the scar said.

Which, Branch wondered, the boy or the music? He nodded, noncommittal.

"Headed for Cleveland?" the man with the scar asked.

"Wouldn't be surprised."

"Good town, Cleveland."

"If you like good towns."

"You can have fun in Cleveland, if you know how."

"I hear."

"They got some good bars in Cleveland, not like this."

Branch nodded.

"You know the Raven?"

"The Raven?" Branch had heard of it; it was *that* kind of bar.

"It's a bar."

"Oh."

"You can really have a time for yourself at the Raven. It swings."

"I think I've heard of it," Branch allowed. He finished his beer. The fencing made him thirsty. Why don't we just come out and say it? Why don't we cut the crap and just come right out in the open and say it?

The bartender came over and Branch was about to order when the man with the scar said, *"Dos cervezas, amigo."*

The bartender muttered as he filled the glasses.

"Gracias," Branch said.

"De nada."

"Name's Aaron," Branch said, holding out his hand.

"Evelyn," the man with the scar said.

Branch looked at him.

"I know, I know, it's a girl's name. My father was a joker. Besides, there's Evelyn Waugh. A lot of Englishmen are named Evelyn. It's very big over there."

"I guess."

"That's what I'm told, anyway."

"Hello there, Evelyn."

"Hi."

"Evelyn from Clevelyn."

"Hey, that's good."

"De nada." Branch's eyes roved the bar: the laughing foursome, the baseball-hating bartender, the Mantovani-loving couple across, sad old Saginaw with only his darts for company—" 'Chemistry' comes from 'alchemy,' a science which tried to prolong life; please prolong mine by staying awake during my lectures." Branch gave a little laugh.

"Aaron? Aaron?"

Branch turned. "What?"

"What's so interesting about him?" The man with the scar indicated Saginaw.

"Nothing. I'm sorry."

"We were talking about my name, remember? About how it's a girl's name."

"Yes. That's right."

"Boy's name, girl's name, it doesn't really matter, I don't think. I mean what difference does it make? Boys and girls, they're really not so different, are they?"

"No. No." *I'm just like anybody else.*

"I mean, you weren't laughing at me just because my father gave me a name like that."

"No."

"I don't much like being laughed at."

I don't much like you. "Who does?" *I don't much like you at all.*

You're not bright and you're probably not very nice either. But you're Here. That's your great charm, Evelyn from Clevelyn; you win the gold star because you're Here.

"What's the matter, Aaron?"

"Nothing. Nothing's the matter." *Love. I want love.*

"If it weren't so late I'd drive you to the Raven, just to show you what a good bar is like. But I think it's too late for that, don't you?"

"Yes. Too late."

"I don't know any fun places nearer, do you?"

"Fun places?" Branch was about to name the West Ridge Motel (nobody stayed overnight at the West Ridge Motel) but the words were hard to form. The amenities were done; now it was only the practicalities that had to be faced (time . . . place), but the words were hard to form. Branch fingered his glass. I wish I liked you better. I wish I thought you were nicer, that you might be kind. I wish . . . I wish . . . Abruptly, Branch swung off the bar stool. "Nothing goes through me like beer," he said. His hand rested briefly on Evelyn's thin shoulder. "Be right back."

"See you don't take too long."

"I'll take it up with my bladder." They both laughed lightly as Branch looked around, saw the painted sign—GENTS—in the rear of the bar, across from the pizza man. He headed in that direction.

"Pizza, mister? Wanna pizza? Lotsa cheese, lotsa tomato."

Branch shook his head at the little cripple. I'll bet you're lying, he thought. I'll bet the only thing there's "lotsa" is crust. I'll bet you're a liar, but then so am I, so in a way we're brothers, did you know that? The pizza man stared dully at the glowing juke. No, you don't know that. We're both liars, but I'm a coward too, trying to find some strength in the men's room. "Hey, I heard about a place, Evelyn; it's called a motel, but . . ." Why couldn't he say that? He knew the words. I'll say it. I will say it. I will find my strength and say it and hope you'll be kind. Branch glanced over his shoulder at Evelyn. Evelyn smiled. Branch entered the men's room and went straight to the tin mirror over the rusted sink. He was perspiring heavily, so he turned on the Cold spigot, waiting for the lukewarm water to chill.

"He's a cop, Scudder."

Branch gripped the rust. He knew that voice. Once it had come from behind a lectern; now it came from behind the closed toilet stall. Once it had linked chemistry and alchemy; now it carried a different message, echoing . . . echoing . . .

He's a cop, Scudder.

He's a cop, Scudder.

He's a cop, Scudder.

He's a cop, Scudder.

He's a cop, Scudder.

Branch died.

. . . the door . . . go for the door . . . out the door . . . the law was out the door . . . the law, the law, dear God. Dear, dear God, forgive me, for I didn't know what I was doing . . . what was I doing? . . . not the door . . . never the door . . . Branch turned for sanctuary . . . allee allee alltz in freeeeeee . . . the window was small and he was big but there was no law outside the window . . . Branch threw it open and jumped up . . . sill splinters attacked his fingers . . . he fell back . . . that sound, that terrible inhuman sound, it was coming from his throat . . . animal . . . he was an animal so he made animal sounds . . . Fear out of Guilt sired by Panic . . . Branch jumped for the window, forcing his shoulders into the blessed April night . . . at Oberlin the boys and girls were walking hand in hand . . . his hips caught . . . his fat hips jammed the frame . . . *Love . . . I want love* . . . Branch struggled in the window . . . the tough wood pierced his trousers, bruising his flesh . . . scraping his flesh . . . was he bleeding? . . . a trail of blood for the law to follow . . . Your son, Mrs. Scudder, I'm afraid I have to tell you about your son, Mrs. Scudder, your son is . . . your son is . . . Branch fell through the window onto the gravel parking lot . . . he hurt . . . but he ran . . . he ran stumbling over the gravel to the car and when it was started he pointed it home and it carried him all the way . . . out the garage and in the door and up the stairs and onto his bed . . . Branch lay face down . . . his heart . . . his poor heart . . . his poor caged heart . . .

. . . fluttering . . .

The next day he started to diet. He kept at it faithfully and after a week he took to exercising for half an hour before he slept (not with weights, of course. He didn't want bulging muscles. Someone might suspect that). In a matter of months he had lost over thirty pounds and the flesh by his hips was gone. Branch bought some new clothes, gray suits and tweed jackets, conservatively cut (nothing flashy, nothing with style; someone might suspect that). He had his hair (those few loyal strands) cut short, flat and clean across the top. He got his mother to buy him a new car, a Chevy, but he soon traded that in for a black Thunderbird convertible, paying for the switch himself. And he started with girls. Secretaries, dental technicians, bank tellers, seniors from Oberlin, juniors and sophomores, teachers, librarians, clerks from the dime store; he dated them all. Just so they were pretty, just so they looked "right" (his word) driving through town. Some he liked; some he loathed. About most he felt nothing; they were objects only, live dolls. Some he kissed, some he touched; with more than a few he got into bed (only if they wished it), and at the close of such encounters he always felt as if he had handled himself with at least adequacy, and they solidified his feeling, never once behaving as if he had short-changed them. Doing it—hell, there was no trick to doing it.

Enjoying it was the problem.

Then, one January morning, the West Ridge *Weekly Sentinel* carried an article. "Return from Vacation" was the headline. And beneath: "Looking tanned and happy after two weeks in the Virgin Islands, Mrs. Howard Scudder and her son Branch, one of West Ridge's most eligible bachelors . . ." When he read that phrase Branch beamed—he was one of West Ridge's most eligible bachelors and one of West Ridge's most eligible bachelors could not ever under any conditions possibly be "that way." As far as West Ridge was concerned, he was safe. He was someone. He had *arrived*, no question about that.

Now, getting out was the problem.

Branch drove through West Ridge. When he reached Waverly Lane he turned in with customary regret. All the houses were dark, except for his, but that was customary too. Branch picked up speed, the motor roaring, and he wheeled sharply onto the driveway, then braked just as sharply, skidding the last few feet into the garage. Flicking off the ignition, Branch examined his face in the rearview mirror. Annie Withers' lipstick still clung; his lips were smeared red and there was another long red smudge along his right cheek. Branch got out of the car and entered the house. His mother and grandmother were in the living room, playing casino.

"Hi, hon," Rose said, glancing up from the game.

"Howdy, howdy," Branch said, and he fell into an easy chair across from the card table. "Up kind of late."

"You ever found me asleep when you got home? Anyway, Mother felt like cards."

"Branch is home," Mother Scudder said. She was eighty-three, frail and gray, and her voice was very high.

"Yes." Rose nodded. "I know."

"Hello, Branch."

Branch looked at his father's mother. "Howdy, howdy."

"Your play," Mother Scudder said.

"Building sixes," Rose said.

"I've got one, I've got one," and she took the pile.

"You're crafty, Mother."

Mother Scudder nodded her head. "I had a six. Right in my hand."

"Care for a nightcap?" Branch asked, pulling himself from the chair.

"Water for me," Rose said.

"Water on the rocks coming up." Branch moved to the bar in the corner of the room, poured some water from a pitcher into a tall glass. Then, before opening the ice bucket, he reached quickly for his handkerchief and rubbed it across his right cheek. He glanced over his shoulder, saw his mother's eyes and smiled at them while he jammed the handkerchief back into his pocket. Taking some ice from the bucket, he filled the glass and brought it to the card table.

"You're a sweetheart," Rose said, and she took a long swallow.

Branch returned to the bar, first stopping by the record player. In a moment "I Could Have Danced All Night" filled the room.

"What's that music?" Mother Scudder said.

"It's from that show," Rose told her.

"Oh yes. The one with Ezio Pinza."

At the bar, Branch made himself a Scotch and water, scrubbed his mouth with his handkerchief, then turned back into the room, walking to the easy chair, slumping down.

"Such a beautiful man."

"Who?" Rose asked.

"That Ezio Pinza. Dr. Scudder and I saw him once at the Metropolitan Opera House. Building eights."

"Get any speeding tickets tonight?" Rose asked.

"Nope," Branch said. "Nary a one."

"That Annie's a brave girl, driving with you."

"She slept most of the way back from Cleveland."

"Later that night we went to an Italian restaurant and he came in."

"What, Mother?"

"This Ezio Pinza I'm telling you about. He came into the same restaurant where we were. Sat at the very next table."

"Hey, Annie got a summer job. A music tent and it'll mostly be just chorus work, but there's a chance she'll play a couple of second leads."

"She's a sweetheart, that Annie. You better be careful, Branch. She just might nab you."

"She just might." Branch sipped his Scotch.

"Who?" Mother Scudder asked.

"Annie, Mother. You remember her. The sweet little girl Branch had for dinner last week, remember? You liked her."

"I liked her," Mother Scudder said.

"Yes."

"She's sweet," Mother Scudder said.

"Yes," Rose said again. "That Scotch looks awfully good."

"Change your mind?"

"A weak one, please." Rose watched as Branch's handkerchief fell to the rug. She waited for him to retrieve it before resuming playing. "Building sixes again, and don't you dare, Mother."

"I haven't got a six. I wish I had a six."

"Annie's bought her dress for the prom," Branch called from the bar. "It cost a lot but she says only an expensive dress can really hide her figure faults."

"She's got a lovely figure, I think," Rose said.

"Yes," Mother Scudder said. "And you can imagine how well he looked on the stage of the Metropolitan."

"What's wrong with her figure, Branch?"

"I think it's terrific—here's your Scotch—but you know how girls are." He crossed to his chair and sat back, his fingers locked behind his neck. "I think her body's sensational."

Rose put her hands on her waist and inhaled and, in a voice of mock hurt, said, "Better than mine?"

Branch laughed with her, wiping his forehead with his handkerchief. Rose downed her drink.

"Refill?"

"That one did go awfully easy."

Branch took her glass and journeyed to the bar.

"Big Casino!" Mother Scudder held it high. "You must not be paying any mind, Rose. I got the Big Casino."

"Good for you, Mother."

"I got the Big Casino, Branch. See?"

Branch nodded.

"He didn't care," Mother Scudder said.

"He's a bridge player, Mother. Casino's beneath him."

Branch brought the drink and set it on the card table. "I happen to like bridge. Is that a crime? Annie and I won five dollars playing last night. At a tenth, too. She's got terrific card sense, you know what I mean?"

"She's a sweetheart," Rose said.

"That she is."

"It's my lucky day and he didn't care. You're a bad boy, Branch."

"I'm terrible." Branch sat back in the chair, folding his handkerchief in his hand, occasionally bringing it up to his forehead, dabbing it against his dry skin. He kept this up until Rose, with a cry, threw her cards onto the tabletop and Mother Scudder cackled, "I beat, I beat," over and over. Then the three of them got up and turned off the lights and went to bed, Mother Scudder doing all of the talking.

The next day was Sunday. Branch spent it with Annie. Most of the afternoon they were at Oberlin, but at cocktail time he drove her to West Ridge. Rose and Mother Scudder were waiting on the porch and when Annie came in Rose stood and kissed her and introduced her again to the old woman—"You remember Miss Withers, Mother"—and the gray head nodded and said, "She's sweet," repeating the phrase throughout the evening. They all drank gin-and-tonic for a while and when it grew dark Branch went out the porch door to the veranda and started the barbecue. In twenty minutes the fire was ready, so he put on the thick sirloin, tending it with professional care. Rose watched as Annie moved from the porch to the veranda, standing very close to Branch, whispering to him, both of them laughing, circling the grill as the smoke pursued them. "She's sweet," Mother Scudder said and Rose smiled in assent. Branch said something then that must have been funny, for Annie almost cried with sudden laughter, throwing her arms around Branch. Branch caught her, held her tight, even when the tracking smoke caught them both, framed them in rising white. Only when they started coughing did they break, and Branch looked through the smoke to the old woman sitting alone on the porch. "Rose went to the kitchen," Mother Scudder said. "Ketchup or something."

Or something, Branch thought.

Monday morning Branch and Rose went to work on schedule, talking amiably about nothing in particular. They worked together in the office until lunch, when Rose excused herself, so Branch ate alone. Rose returned in the middle of the afternoon, humming. She was not, ordinarily, musical, and Branch waited, but no explanation came. They finished work, returned home and had a quiet drink on the porch. After dinner

Branch excused himself and went up to his room to shower. When he was almost dressed, Rose walked in and sat on the edge of his bed.

"Date?"

Branch nodded.

"Annie?"

"Annie."

"Give her my best."

"Will do." He took his change from the top of his bureau and put it in his pocket. Then he carefully combed his hair, bending close to the mirror, squinting, making sure the part was right. Rose watched him, stretched on the bed, her hands cupped behind her neck.

"You're an Adonis."

"Ain't it the truth."

"Be out late?"

"You never can tell."

"Well, listen to him."

Branch smiled, starting for the door.

"Have fun now."

"I'll try."

"Oh, Branch?"

"What?"

"I was just wondering."

"About?"

"Saturday."

"What about Saturday?"

"You busy?"

"Yes."

"Oh. Well, that's too bad."

"Why? What's too bad?"

"You remember that nice nurse, Mrs. Cortesi? She's coming for the weekend to look after Mother."

"Why is she coming?"

"You're sure you're busy Saturday?"

"I'm positive."

"That really is too bad. I was lucky getting that nice Mrs. Cortesi on such short notice. Usually she's busy for weeks in advance."

"What does Granny need a nurse for?"

"You're absolutely sure you're busy on Saturday?"

"It's the prom. I told you. Annie's bought a dress specially for it."

"Oh, well, you couldn't miss that."

"Miss it? What for?"

"What kind of dress did she buy?"

"Green, brown, I don't know."

"I bet it'll be pretty. Well, I'll just have to return the tickets."

"Tickets?"

"Yes. It was a silly notion on my part anyway."

"Tickets for what?"

"That show. That musical."

"There's no musical in Cleveland."

"I don't remember saying anything about Cleveland."

"What musical? What musical?"

"Leslie Howard played it in the movies."

"You've got tickets for *My Fair Lady*?"

"I've got tickets for *My Fair Lady*."

"Saturday night?"

"Saturday night."

"New York?"

"New York."

Poor Annie.

They stayed at the Plaza (Branch's choice), arriving on Friday night, too late for the theater but not too late for a walk, after unpacking, across Central Park South to Broadway, then down Broadway, down through the theater district to 44th Street and Sardi's, where Branch thought he saw Rex Harrison and Rose ate spaghetti with meat sauce. After Branch's third stinger, they left the restaurant and returned to the hotel, where Rose, exhausted, slept till after ten, finding, on awakening, a note from her son saying that he was off to the Frick and not to worry, but she did, and when he finally returned, at noon, babbling about some Greco cardinal, she was undecided as to whether to hug him or shout him down to size, choosing the former, after some hesitation, with only a twinge of regret. They lunched at the Waldorf-Astoria (once she had honeymooned there) and went to the Radio City Music Hall (her choice) in the afternoon. That night they saw *My Fair Lady* and it was every bit what everybody said it was. Originally they planned to return on Sunday because Annie was graduating Tuesday afternoon, but they were having such a good time that Rose decided, then insisted, they stay the week, so after Branch was convinced they extended their reservation at the Plaza and Sunday was spent in Greenwich Village watching the artists and *The Threepenny Opera* at night, which Rose thought was dirty but never told

Branch because he loved it and would only have chided her for her prudish ways. Monday it rained, so they shopped, taxiing from Brooks Brothers (Branch got a coat, dark tweed) to Saks (where Rose almost got a dress but it wasn't quite the right shade of green) to Bendel's (still not the right shade) and then around the corner to Bergdorf's, where Branch selected a pair of high heels for his mother which he promised made her legs equal to Mistinguette's. They lunched at the Plaza and then took a long hansom cab ride in the rain, finally returning to the hotel and napping until it was time for the theater. Tuesday they museumed, the Metropolitan and the Modern Art, and after lunch they toured the galleries and Rose had to keep Branch in tow lest he buy something, not that she couldn't have afforded to please him, but the thought of hanging some pointless paint splattering in her nice clean house (she would have to hang it if she bought it) or, worse, having to *look* at the thing all her life pulled her purse strings tight. Wednesday (Rose was wearying) Rose slept late, letting her son roam, but they met at a matinee and saw something (she could no longer keep them straight) and ate someplace, and then saw something else, and before she slept that night she made two plane reservations home for the following evening, Thursday. Thursday morning she mentioned to Branch that she might like to go home soon and what did he think? And he thought no! Not yet! And she allowed as to how she didn't want to push him but if they could get tickets for a plane out that night she was going to take them, and when it turned out (surprise) that she could indeed get tickets she demolished his objections with a few well-chosen words and napped while he voyaged through the city, trying to get everything done in one thin afternoon. Branch ran through the heat and urged his taxi drivers to great speeds, tipping them well, because what did money matter when the city was being taken away from him and he had so much to do. He drove north to the Cloisters, south to the Staten Island Ferry, then north again for a final run through Greenwich Village, then north and east and a quick sad look at the Biltmore Bar. There was too much, too much to see, but he tried. He saw the lobby of the Mark Hellinger (I could have danced all night) and he saw the bar at Sardi's (empty). He saw the Greek's *Toledo*. He saw the shops on Fifth, the movie houses on Broadway. He saw Central Park. He saw Picasso's *Guernica*, the UN from the roof of the Beekman Tower, a Chippendale chair up for auction at Parke-Bernet. He saw poodles in Sutton Place, cats in Washington Square, blue girls from Brearley, black ones from 125th. He saw women, fair-skinned (Park Avenue), foul-mouthed (Garment District); he saw brittle men, mean men, rich men, beggar men. And, quite by accident, for but a few, few minutes late on that last afternoon, he saw:

Aaron.

"You're sure all hot and bothered," Rose said, taking a green skirt, smoothing it carefully with both hands, finally folding it neatly into her suitcase.

"Well, it's just such a great city." Branch paced nervously behind his mother. "You've got to admit that."

"It's big," Rose replied. "And you'd die without air-conditioning."

"It's not just big, Rosie. Come on. Where else can you find so many things to do? Name me any other place that compares."

"You all packed?"

"And the people. How about them?"

"Plane's got a schedule, you know. You better be ready." She picked up her new shoes, blew on them, then inserted them into a plastic bag and wedged them into a corner of her suitcase.

"Oh, this city," Branch said. "This goddam city."

"Chicago's just as nice. So's Cleveland."

"Cleveland? Cleveland! That's the funniest thing you've said all week."

"Where did I leave my bathrobe? Oh yes," and she moved to the closet, took her robe off the hook and started folding it.

"You've had a good time here; admit it."

"I'm not sorry I'm leaving; I'll admit that."

"But you've had a good time."

"Good company, good time. You didn't forget your hairbrush, did you? Double-check everything."

"I can't tell you what this town does to me."

"I hope Mother likes her surprise. Do you think she will? I got her two beautiful decks of playing cards. You can wash them when they get dirty."

"Oh, this town. This crazy town."

"You make me dizzy with all that walking."

Branch went to the window and looked out. "This beautiful goddam town."

"What's so beautiful about an air shaft? That's all you're looking at and you're swearing too much. Now double-check your packing."

Branch stooped, ducking his head toward the air-conditioner. "Ahhh."

"If you wouldn't walk around so much, you wouldn't get sweaty."

Branch spun away from the wall and toured the room, his fingertips touching the walls. "I love this hotel. I just love it."

"Branch, are you packed?"

"Can you love concrete? I love New York."

"I've asked you a thousand times, Branch. Now answer me. Are you packed?"

"Rosie . . ."

"Answer me."

"Rosie . . ."

"I mean it, Branch."

"No."

Rose turned on her son. "You're not packed, is that right?"

"I don't want to go back," Branch said. "I want to stay here."

Rose nodded, picked up a green flowered dress, tucked the neck under her chin, and folded the flowered sleeves across her body.

"I belong here, Mother."

Rose bent over the edge of the bed and folded the dress at the waist, smoothing out the wrinkles.

"I know this probably comes as a surprise to you, but believe me, I've thought about it. It's not a whim. I've really thought. A lot. The theater. I want to get in the theater. That's my place, don't you see?"

Rose lifted the flowered dress and placed it in her suitcase.

"I've known that for a long time now. Back in college. You remember back in college?"

Rose glanced at her watch, nodded, then walked to the closet, taking out her green traveling suit. Laying it on the bed, she started to unbutton her dress.

"That crazy little show we had in college? That nutty little show we put on, you remember? *I* put it on, Mother. Me. You didn't see me on the stage, but I put it on. If it hadn't been for me, there wouldn't have been a thing. Not one lousy thing. *I* got the money, *I* got the ads for the programs, *I* took care of everything. Me, myself, alone."

Rose stepped out of her dress and folded it into the suitcase. She ran her hands down along her slip, making sure it was straight. There was no extra flesh on her squat body. Her stomach was firm and flat and there was no fat puffing the tops of her arms and her breasts didn't sag. Again she straightened her slip, running her small hands down her body.

"I was happy then. That's the thing. That's the only thing, Mother. It's what counts. I was happy. Some people, they can be happy anywhere. Put 'em on a desert island, they'll be happy. But I'm not like that. You just can't say, 'Branch you go be happy.' I'm not set up that way. I was happy back then. Well, I can be happy again. Here. Here in New York. I can be happy, Mother. Don't you understand? That's important, don't you see?"

Nothing from Rose.

"Oh God, I wish you could see how important this is to me. I wish you could come right into my brain, right here, and read every single thought I have so you'd know how important it was. Believe me. Believe me."

Nothing from Rose.

"I'd still come home. I'd come home a lot. And you could come here. What's a two-hour plane ride? You could be here whenever you wanted. And we'd do things together, go all over. You'd like that. And it wouldn't cost all that much. I'm no drunken sailor. I'd borrow the money from you. I'll write you a note, nice and proper, and when I get successful I'll pay back every penny. You know I will."

Nothing from Rose.

"Rosie! You've got to do this for me. It is important. My happiness is important. And that's what I'm asking you for. I want my happiness Rosie. You can give it. I want my happiness, you hear me?"

"You're not saying anything."

"What?"

"I don't hear anything and do you know what that means? It means you're not saying anything. Not a word. 'Cause I got good ears and if you were talking I'd hear you. I don't hear you. That means you must not be talking."

Branch moved to the window, staring.

"There hasn't been a sound in this room. I've been packing and you've been walking around but we didn't speak. No sound. Just the air-conditioner, that's all I heard. Understand me, Branch. Get me now. No one has said nothing."

Branch spun from the window.

Rose waited.

"You don't love me," Branch said.

"I don't, huh? I don't, huh?"

"I belong here."

"Where? At the Plaza Hotel? With hot-and-cold-running room service and maids to fluff your pillow? Terrific. Wonderful. In a few months if you have to pinch pennies you can go rough it at the Waldorf."

"You don't love me."

"You said that for the last time."

"It's the truth. Let's just admit it. If you loved me you wouldn't make me go back to goddam West Ridge. I hate that pit."

"Watch it, baby."

"I'm dying back there."

"Please watch it, baby."

"I'm not going back. I'm staying here."

"Stay!" Rose advanced on him. Branch's back was to the wall.

"The old woman, she knows her baby. The old woman knows what's best for her baby." Rose was on top of him now and Branch stared at her fist as it beat steadily against her chest. "You say you're dying back there? You know what the old woman thinks? She thinks if you come here, then you're really dead. She had a baby but he died. The old woman's baby died dead. And after a while she'll think she never had a baby. No son. She never had none."

"Mother . . ."

"Who are you?"

"Rosie . . ."

"Do I know you?"

"Please, Mother . . ."

"You look like somebody I think died."

"I'm sorry."

"Are you dead?"

"Please, I'm sorry."

"Are you dead? Huh?"

"Mother . . . ?"

"Huh?"

"I'm alive."

"Again."

"I'm alive."

"Louder."

"I'm alive."

"That's my baby."

Branch was quiet on the flight home, but Rose let him sulk, knowing it would pass. And it did pass, for by the time they reached the house on Waverly Lane he was laughing at the frivolity of the request he had made back in the hotel room. Mother Scudder was awaiting them, and while Rose paid the nurse, Branch began telling the old lady stories of the city and the old lady almost wept because, after all, they were her family come back to her and, besides, the nurse frowned on casino. When Branch gave her the decks of playing cards she did weep, saying, "Oh, you shouldn't have, not for me," but the tears stopped at the wonder of washable kings and queens, and she could only shake her head, repeating "Just imagine—washable; just imagine" until it was bedtime. Rose watched as her son kissed his grandmother, happily waiting her own good-night kiss, and after his lips touched her cheeks he whispered, "It really is good to be home," so Rose had no trouble besting sleep that night. In the week that followed Branch worked harder than ever at the office, and in spite of the fact that she did not much believe in compliments, she found herself praising him to his face, his efforts were that rewarding. He shrugged at her words, barely smiling, but she knew he was pleased. On Friday of that week he sold a sixty-five-thousand-dollar house not far from where they lived on Waverly Lane. It was by far his biggest sale, and she was worried that he might somehow botch it through inexperience, almost taking over the transaction herself, but she didn't, and he pulled the sale off like a veteran, so that night in celebration she took him to dinner at Etienne's and from there to the Hotel Cleveland, where they danced, finally returning home well after midnight with the taste of champagne still strong on their lips. The weather turned hot the following week, but the office was air-conditioned and since they spent most of their time there they didn't mind the heat. Branch was happy and Rose herself could never remember a sweeter time, and it was probably that unusual buoyancy of spirit that accounted for the sudden cry that escaped her when, after sleeping late Sunday morning, she found, on looking out her bedroom window, her son clad in a navy-blue bathing suit, tanning his trim body on the back lawn, lying flat on the grass, one hand outstretched.

And lying beside him, holding that hand, was Annie Withers.

Rose deserted the window, but too late, for Branch's head jerked up at the cry, and though she was gone before his eyes could make positive identification, still, she knew an appearance was called for. So she dressed hurriedly, exchanging her room for the kitchen, heating some coffee, downing two cups before Branch entered, smiling.

"We've got a visitor," Rose said, smiling back.

"That we have."

"That's wonderful."

"I knew you'd be pleased."

"Did you know she was coming?"

"I thought I'd surprise you."

"What happened to her job? I thought you told me she was working at a theater."

"She is."

"Oh?"

"The theater's near Cleveland."

"Oh."

"Isn't that marvelous, Rosie?"

"That's just wonderful."

Branch beamed.

"We'll be seeing lots of her, I hope." Rosie waited.

"Lots of her."

"Wonderful," Rose said with a smile, and still smiling, arms stretched wide, she rushed to the lawn, hugging the slender visitor, accompanying the embrace with sounds of joy.

In the weeks that followed she really did not see "lots" of Annie; it just seemed that way. Once each week she and Branch would drive to the summer tent and watch Annie prancing as a nurse in *South Pacific*, then Annie as a townswoman in *High Button Shoes*. Sundays, Branch would bring her to West Ridge for the day. That was all. Twice a week. But the musicals came to be almost as dreaded as an opera in Italian, and in order to lessen the ordeal of the Sabbath Rose took to going to church. (The minister was long-winded, good for at least an hour each Sunday, and she blessed him for his dreary harangues.) Annie twice a week. But it wasn't the amount of time that deprived Rose of sleep; it was the way Annie and Branch acted when they were together.

Always touching each other.

Hand-holding Rose could ignore, but it seemed that whenever she entered a room in her house they would be starting a kiss, or ending one or, worse, in the very act. They kissed in the living room, they kissed on the porch. They wrestled on the lawn, in plain view of neighbors, laughing and kicking, skin touching skin. Right in front of the neighbors! Their attraction was understandable enough. Branch was certainly handsome and some might consider Annie pretty. But it wasn't decent. It simply was not decent. Not decent at all.

In bed, alone, Rose tossed.

One day—it was the second week of a blazing July—Branch walked over and sat on her desk and said, "Mother?" There was nothing unusual in the action, but the tone he used made her instantly wary.

"Yes, baby?"

"Could I talk to you?"

"Could you talk to me?"

Branch nodded.

Rose sat very still.

"It's about the business."

"Go on."

"Well . . . How good is it?"

"Good? What do you mean, good?"

"I mean, well . . . from a long-range point of view, what do you think? I mean, is the town going to grow the way it has been or do you think maybe the peak is over or what do you think?"

"What are you talking about, Branch?"

"Can I make a living? A good living?"

"I don't see you starving."

"Well, yeah, of course, that's true, but . . . uh . . . I mean, I don't have many expenses . . . now . . . I mean, I'm living at home, of course, and . . . uh . . . there's just me for me to support and . . . well . . . I was just wondering." Rose watched as he got off her desk and moved quickly to his own, sitting down, staring out the window.

"Branch?"

"Yes, Mother?"

"Everything all right?"

"Yes, Mother."

"Is there something you're not telling me?"

"Have we ever kept secrets from each other?"

"Then why did you ask about the business?"

Embarrassed, her son looked away. "No reason."

That night, Rose took a Seconal.

The following Sunday morning, on her return from church, Rose strolled onto the porch to find the young couple lying embraced on the couch. The kiss she was almost used to, but the way her son's hands roamed the girl's body shocked her. They broke when her presence dawned, both of them blushing, and Rose ignored the whole thing as well as she could. But she could not ignore, during the following strained conversation, the fact that though they were talking to her, they were looking directly at each other, always at each other. Lunch was salmon salad, ordinarily one of Rose's favorites.

But not today.

Late that evening Rose was playing casino with Mother Scudder when Branch returned from having taken Annie home. There were traces of red on his mouth and she tried not to look while he removed them, turning his back as he did it so she wouldn't suspect. He watched them play a hand or two, then quietly went upstairs. Rose endured the cards and Mother's prattling for a decent amount of time, then called a halt to the game. "You're tired, Mother."

"I am?"

"You were yawning."

"I was?"

"Yes."

This time the old woman did yawn. "We'd better stop, if you don't mind."

"If you like."

"I'm very tired," Mother Scudder said. "I better go to sleep." Rose escorted her to her room, saw her to bed, then went to her own room and put on a nightgown and a robe before journeying down the hall to her son.

"Branch?" She walked in.

Branch lay in bed, reading. As she approached, he hurriedly put the book down.

"You forgot to kiss me good night."

"Did I? I'm sorry." He sat up, lightly touched his lips to her cheek. "Good night, Rosie."

"Good night." She took a step, then stopped. "What are you reading?"

"Just a book."

"What's it about?"

Branch shrugged. "Nothing."

"Is it good? Should I read it?"

"I'm not all that far into it yet. Probably not."

"What's it called?"

"I forget."

"Is it dirty?" Rose laughed. "Are you embarrassed to tell me?"

"No, no, of course not."

"Then what's it about?"

"California," Branch said.

Rose said nothing.

"San Francisco, actually. Annie's from San Francisco. Her whole family lives there."

"Yes?"

"She's crazy about the place."

"She is?"

"It's her home; she loves it. There are some pictures in the book here, a few photographs. I've got to admit, it does look beautiful. The hills and the water."

"I'm told it's very pretty."

"Not only that, but according to this book, there's a real boom out there now."

"There is?"

Branch nodded and picked up the book. "If you want, you can read it when I'm done."

"Maybe I will." Rose moved to the door.

"It's a real land of opportunity out there." He blew her a kiss. "Good night, Mother."

"Good night, Branch," and she closed the door.

At two o'clock, she took her second Seconal; at three, her third. She disliked sleeping pills—they were a sign of weakness—but she had to get some rest. Somehow. Rose tossed. The sheet beneath her body felt wrinkled, so after a while she stood up and tore her bed apart, carefully tucking clean cool sheets on the mattress. She got back in and the cloth was smooth to her aching body, but still she could not sleep. Her head throbbed steadily, and that didn't make it any easier. In vain, Rose tried clearing her mind, but inevitably the picture of that girl pawing her son haunted her. She was a fast one, that Annie. Of course young people acted differently today, but any way you looked at it, Annie was a fast one. Well, what could you expect from Californians? All those movie stars setting the kind of examples they did. Rose kicked at the sheets, driving them clear off her slender legs. God knows she wanted Branch to get married. God knows she had been sweet to his girls. Hadn't Annie practically moved in with them? Branch ought to get married someday, but with that girl? A little dancer with not one ounce of common everyday ordinary decency? Rose rubbed her eyes with the very tips of her fingers. No one could say she hadn't been cordial. No one could say she hadn't been warm, hadn't encouraged Branch to go out, find girls, bring them home. No one could say she hadn't tried. But she knew what that little girl was up to. Women understood those things better than men ever could. Women sensed things. But did Branch? He was so open, so honest, so gullible, almost, that maybe he didn't see. Maybe that girl had him fooled. "You don't fool me," Rose said out loud. No, sir, she didn't. Why didn't Branch see? Rose fluffed her pillow with the flat of her hand. She didn't want to have to tell Branch; she hated being "that" kind of mother. They were so close, they understood each other so well, that having to "talk" to him that way—well, it just wasn't going to be much fun. But it was his life. One wrong move and it was liable to be ruined. She hadn't brought him up for that. She hadn't loved him to see him throw it all away, his whole life, just-like-that. "Branch," Rose said. "Branch." She got out of bed and began to pace. In a moment she was at the window, looking out at the still back lawn. There. There was the spot where Annie had made her reappearance, lying practically naked, clutching her son's hand. Rose stared at the black grass. "You don't fool me," she said again. "Not me, you don't." She inhaled deeply. There was really no choice for her. She would have to do it, tell Branch, make him see. In spite of everything, she would have to talk to him, explain to him, right away, honest and aboveboard.

Man to man.

But at breakfast the following day he was half asleep, having read most of the night to finish his book. So Rose waited. The drive to the office was too short, but the whole morning lay ahead of them, and that, she decided, was the time. But the morning was Monday, and by ten o'clock they were still swamped with work. So Rose waited. At eleven she saw they would never catch up by noon, so she called to Branch that she wanted to have lunch with him and he nodded without speaking. So Rose waited. And waited. And—

"Ready?"

Branch looked up from his desk. "For what?"

"Lunch, silly. I asked you to have lunch and you said yes."

"I did?"

"You nodded."

"My God, what time is it?"

"Half past twelve."

Branch stood quickly, shoving papers into his top desk drawer. "I've got to go."

"We're having lunch."

"I can't. Not today. Goodbye." And he was out the door.

Rose waited a moment, hesitating. Then she dashed for the door after her son. He was half a block ahead of her when she got to the street, hurrying along Central. Rose felt the fool, in broad summer daylight, in the center of her own small town, following her son. But she followed him. At the corner of Central and Tubbs he stopped, glancing over his shoulder. Rose pressed against the side of Simmon's Grocery, her back against the hot glass, hiding until it was safe. Branch turned onto Tubbs, walking faster, but she kept pace, staying close to the store fronts lest he turn again. He continued on Tubbs past Willow before he stopped again, look-ing around. Rose busied herself with a hardware-store window, hidden by the torn green awning overhead. When he got to Percy he turned again, moving out of sight, and Rose had just started to run when Mrs. Mulligan grabbed her arm.

"Hello there, Mrs. Scudder."

"Huh? Oh, Mrs. Mulligan, hello."

"Beautiful day."

"Yes. I'm in something of a hurry, Mrs. Mulligan."

"Well, it's just that Mr. Mulligan and I are thinking of moving and I was wondering what you thought you could get for our house."

"House? Please, Mrs. Mulligan, call me at the office. Do that," and she pulled loose, running as fast as her good legs could carry her up to Percy. She reached the corner and crossed the street but Branch was gone. She looked again and then she saw him, far ahead of her. Rose ran. He was walking slower now and if he turned again he would see her, but that didn't seem to matter now. She ran, closing the gap. Branch stopped. Rose ran on, panting, the air bursting from her dry throat. One hundred yards, now seventy, fifty, twenty-five. Her dress was soaked and her legs hurt and her throat, so she stopped running, pausing a moment, leaning against the window of a haberdashery, trying to get her breath. Branch moved very slowly, one small step at a time. Rose stayed with him. Then he turned abruptly and entered a store. Rose waited. In a few moments her breath was almost back to normal and she straightened her dress and did what she could about drying the perspiration from her forehead. Then, with a brisk step, she moved forward, body stiff, head held high. When she passed the place she glanced quickly to the right and caught a glimpse of her son. He was busy, so he did not notice her.

He was in a jewelry store. Rose could see the display of wedding rings in the window.

"Branch?"

"Yes?"

"We've got to have a talk." It was late the same evening and they were sitting on the back porch, prior to bed.

"Sounds important."

"I've thought about this, Branch. More than you'll ever know. It's been in my mind for weeks. Day and night, all the time."

"You're upset."

"Yes," Rose said. "Yes, I am. Do you love me, Branch? Do you think I love you?"

"Of course."

"Well, for the first time in my life I feel like a bad mother. I do. And I don't much like it."

Branch was silent.

"I want the best for you, my baby. That's all I want. Do you believe me?"

"I don't even have to answer that. You know how I feel."

"Well . . ."

"Yes?"

"It's just that . . ."

"Yes?"

"I think you should go to New York."

Branch waited.

Rose said nothing, then the words came tumbling down. "Right away. Pack up and go to New York. Just go. Now. You're not extravagant, I know that. I'll support you."

"I'm stunned," Branch said.

"Like I say, I've thought a lot about this. Ever since we had our talk in New York and you told me you wanted to stay and I said I didn't think it was a good idea. Well, I was wrong. You owe it to yourself to try and make good there. If that's what you want, you have it coming. Forget about us here. Just go there and make your mark. Will you do that?"

"I hadn't thought—yes. I'll go. If you want me to."

"I do."

"I'll fly in this weekend and find a place to live."

"Yes."

"I'll need two bedrooms."

"Why?"

"You'll come visit me, won't you?"

"I'd like to."

"Well," Branch said, and he smiled at her, "I wouldn't dream of allowing my own mother to stay at a hotel."

What could she do but smile? "I do love you, baby. I do want what's best for you."

"I know that."

"Who can tell; maybe you won't like it there. Maybe you'll miss your home." And if you don't, the money stops. After six months. Six months was a long time. Nobody could say it wasn't generous. Six months. At the outside. Maybe less.

"You're right. I probably won't like it. Once the novelty wears off."

"Time will tell."

"Yes," Branch said. "Good night." He kissed his mother on the forehead, then moved to the doorway.

"Good night, my baby."

"You know what you are?"

"What?"

"Unselfish."

Rose smiled.

Branch left her there, alone on the porch, staring at something on the lawn. Inside the house, Branch moved very slowly up the stairs to his room. Carefully he closed the door. Then he ran full tilt across the room, dove onto his bed, clutched his pillow to his body and stuffed one corner into his mouth so she wouldn't hear him laughing.

XIV

Jenny knew she was ready for something.

Monday night she forgot to go to acting class, wandering instead through Central Park, which wasn't a smart thing to do, but she did it anyway. Tuesday noon she had an argument with her temporary boss at Kingsway Press, which also wasn't a smart thing to do, especially for a secretary, but she did that too, anyway. Wednesday she simply overslept, waking at half past one—after a solid thirteen hours' sleep—still tired. Thursday she jaywalked recklessly, all day long, and had another argument with her temporary boss, whose name was Archie Wesker and who looked for all the world like Robert Mitchum.

Then, Friday morning, her dry cleaner disappointed her.

His name was Mr. Yang and he was old and very wise and Jenny loved his dry cleaning, because he showed genuine interest in her occasional spots and always returned garments when he promised. So, on Friday morning, when she dashed through the summer heat to his shop only to find that half of her clothes had not come back and the other half were less well pressed than usual, she nearly wept. Sadly, she returned to her tiny apartment and almost without thinking put on a tight blue blouse and skirt and left for work without her customary raincoat. As she waited for the West Side subway she was propositioned twice and elbowed half to death by hordes of men who all seemed smaller and darker than she was. Ordinarily the elbowing would have upset her, but this morning she took it all serenely, leaving the subway before the train came, hailing a cab, blowing her budget, going to work in style.

She had not been at her desk more than five minutes when Mr. Wesker came up and stood in front of her, arms crossed, staring. He had, of course, stared at her before, except that before, when he had stared, she had not flushed. She looked up at him. "Yes?"

"Don't attack me, Miss Devers. You didn't have to say 'yes' quite so negatively."

I really don't like you, Jenny thought.

He smiled at her crookedly, the way Robert Mitchum smiles.

There's more to a man than looks, Jenny thought.

"Good news, Miss Devers."

"Auh?"

"Yes. You're getting a new boss. I'm transferring to the textbook department."

"Auh."

"We'll still be on the same floor, of course. And if you'd like, I could probably swing having you transferred with me."

Jenny said nothing.

"That was a joke, Miss Devers. Our short time together has been more than sufficient for both of us, I'm sure."

"I haven't anything against you, Mr. Wesker, and that's the truth."

"Then have lunch with me."

Jenny almost said "Why?" but it would have been rude, so she stopped herself in time. Rude or not, it was a good question. Why in the world had he asked her? And why in the world did she accept?

That was a good question, too.

They lunched at Adela's, a long, narrow restaurant, very expensive, with red drapes lining the walls and elegant candles, one on each table, providing light. As they entered the cool darkness Jenny felt flattered. When a Kingsway editor wanted to impress someone, more often than not they lunched at Adela's. The headwaiter led them to a table in the rear corner of the room. Mr. Wesker smiled and sat down right beside her.

"Who's going to be my new boss?" Jenny asked, moving a little bit away.

"I think Fiske." Archie smiled again.

"Mr. Fiske." Jenny paused a moment. "He's supposed to be very nice."

"Who says?"

"The girls in the office."

"Charley's honest, upright and true," Archie said. "A perfect senior editor. What do you want to drink?"

"Nothing, thank you."

"Why?"

"Oh, I just don't feel like anything."

"You do drink."

"Sometimes."

"But not now. Why?"

"I already said. I just don't feel—"

"Miss Devers, we're separating as of today, so in celebration of that fact, let's be honest. You're afraid you'll get plastered and I'll lure you someplace and quote take advantage of you close quote."

Jenny was tempted to get up, just get up right then and there and say, "Archie Wesker, you think you're so smart you make me sick." But she didn't. Instead, she sat very still with her hands folded in her lap and cursed the weakness she had always had for Robert Mitchum.

"Well, let's analyze your fear," Archie went on. "You're a big strong girl. I'll tell you the truth: I wouldn't want to arm-wrestle you, at least not for money. And answer me this: where am I going to lure you that if you don't want to go there with me you can't say 'no'? How'm I going to surprise you? I'd have to have some kind of wild place, wouldn't I? Ian Fleming out of Rube Goldberg. You know, we're walking along and I push some hidden button and the sidewalk opens and you fall helpless onto this huge bed I've got stashed away under midtown Manhattan. Now all that's possible, but the odds against it—"

"Gin and tonic," Jenny said.

"Sure you're not game for a martini?"

"Gin and tonic, thank you."

Archie signaled for a waiter, gave the order. "Why don't you like me?" he said then.

"I told you before, Mr. Wesker; I've got nothing against—"

"Come on, Jenny. *Spiel.*"

"You think you're so good you make me sick. There." She felt herself flushing again and she rummaged quickly through her pocketbook.

"What are you searching for?"

"Nothing. I'm just hiding. Look away. Give me a chance—please—to get back my composure. I don't like fighting—please."

Archie lit a cigarette. "I'm cursed," he said.

Jenny went on rummaging.

"You're absolutely right—I do think I'm good. I'm cursed. I *am* good. I would love—underline love—to feel insecure every so often. A little inferiority. But I don't. When I'm honest, I'm an egotist. I've got to be hypocritical for most people to like me. It's a curse, I tell you. Where you from?"

"Wisconsin."

"Had to be. Or Minnesota. How're you fixed on composure?"

"Fine."

"You like me any better?"

"I don't know."

"I'm really a great guy."

"You're very modest. I'll say that."

"Listen: can I help it that I look like Robert Mitchum?"

The waiter came with their drinks. Jenny sipped her gin and tonic. She was to finish three before the meal was over. More accurately, she was to finish three before the meal *began*. Each time she neared the bottom of her glass Archie would make a gesture and soon another drink would appear on the table. The gesture was a wrist flick, done with what, Jenny supposed, he supposed was breathtaking nonchalance.

Actually, he was so obvious she wanted to giggle.

That was what most surprised her—his obviousness. Did he think she didn't know? Wasn't it clear that she knew when, midway through her first drink, she downed several pieces of French bread and butter, thereby coating her stomach, thereby providing immunization? Evidently it was not clear, because during the meal he insisted on their sharing a bottle of wine, which she was more than glad to do, although he was getting a little thick-tongued by then. He was obvious in other ways too: touching her a lot—his hand on her hand, on her shoulder, once, ever so briefly, on her knee. And when he asked her questions about her background, it was obvious that he was just making conversation, that he didn't really care a fig for her background, that he wasn't the least bit interested in the fact that she had been in Manhattan over a year and had had an understudy part in a Stagpole play but hadn't ever actually acted it because the play closed too soon and, besides, the girl she was understudying had had the constitution of *two* truck horses. Why am I talking so much? Jenny wondered, pausing before launching into a discussion of how much she hoped she was a good actress because that was the one thing in all the world she really wanted to be, a good actress, just a good solid professional working actress, and she was about to tell Archie Wesker how her acting teacher had taken her aside less than a month before and whispered that he thought she had the potential, except that since it was so obvious Archie didn't care, Jenny decided to keep mum on that one. She also decided not to talk about Tommy Alden being on a Rhodes Scholarship to Oxford or Cambridge (she could never keep them straight) except she changed her mind and did talk about it, because that way Archie would know she was practically for all intents and purposes *spoken for* and so wouldn't try "anything," whatever that was.

But telling of Tommy failed, for nothing Archie did was half as obvious as his approach at the end of the meal.

"Gotta pick up this manuscript, Jenny babe." His hand rested on her shoulder.

"Wherzit?" Jenny said, speaking fuzzily so as not to embarrass him.

"Thizz place. Come along?"

"Izzit onnaway tuh the offizz?"

"Sorta."

"Sher." She smiled at him. "Thank you."

"Fer wha?"

"Meal."

"Yuh travel wi' Archie, yuh travel firzz clazz." They got up and slowly made their way out of Adela's, pausing for a moment when they reached the sidewalk. "Hot azza pistol," Archie said.

"Hot azza pistol." Jenny nodded.

Archie took her hand. "Gotcha."

"Got me."

They started to walk.

"Whazzatime?"

Archie looked at his watch a while. "Four," he said finally.

"Four *o'clock*?"

Archie nodded.

Jenny pulled loose. "I've got to get back to the office. I can't take a three-hour lunch. How did it get to be so—"

She stopped suddenly, because, among other reasons, she was speaking much too clearly, but so was he when he answered, "Forget it! Just forget it! I'm your boss. We're on company business."

Jenny began rummaging through her purse. He must be terribly embarrassed, she thought. "Fresh air," she mumbled. "It really clears the head."

"What are you looking for?"

"I forget." She closed the purse after a while.

"Now just you quit worrying about the time. It's Friday and it's summertime. Nobody works. Hand?" He held his out.

She took it. "Hand." Jenny smiled. "Gotcha."

"Got me." They walked in silence for a while. Then Archie hailed a cab.

"Where are we going?" Jenny said.

"To pick up this manuscript."

"But where?"

"Listen, do you want me to drop you at the office?"

"No, no. It's Friday and it's summertime. Nobody works."

Archie nodded, gave the driver a number.

"Much cooler in the cab anyway," Jenny said.

"Much." He took her hand again. "Are you bright as a penny, Jenny? The song says you're supposed to be."

"I'm not so bright," Jenny said. "Not as some people, anyway."

"And you're going to be a great actress someday?"

"I don't know. I'd like to be."

"We should have lunched before this. Our business transactions would have been less rocky."

"Yes."

They sat quietly until the cab stopped in front of a brownstone off Park. Archie paid and they got out. "It's the garden apartment," he said. "That's where the manuscript is."

"Oh."

"Want to see?"

"Oh, yes; I love looking at other people's apartments. Mine isn't much. I think that's why." She waited behind him while he took out a key and put it in the lock. Jenny started to rummage through her purse, then stopped. She waited. He opened the door and ushered her into the hall. Then he let the front door close and moved down the hall to the apartment door. Jenny waited again. Her fingers played with the clip on her purse. She made them stop. They smoothed her skirt, made sure her blouse was tucked in neatly. Archie opened the apartment door. Jenny walked inside. Archie closed the door behind her. She stared straight ahead. He walked up behind her, put his hands to her shoulders, turned her slowly, brought her against him. As her arms went around his neck she remembered she was still holding her purse, so she dropped her arms, released the purse as quietly as she could, then embraced him again. When they broke, they looked at each other and smiled. Then they fell into another, a longer kiss. This time, as they separated, he took her hands, raised them, kissed the tips of her fingers. It was, she thought, a sweet thing to do, sweet and gentle and, from him, surprising, so when he held her close again she could feel her body relaxing. He kissed her on the mouth several times and on the neck and eyes and he had her blue blouse half unbuttoned before she spoke.

"Are you married?"

"Huh?"

"Are you married?"

"Does it matter?"

"Yes."

"Yes."

"Oh." Jenny looked around for her purse.

Archie moved to take her in his arms again.

Jenny discouraged him.

"Come on," Archie said.

Jenny rummaged through her purse.

"All of a sudden we're turned into pumpkins, is that it?"

Jenny nodded.

"Well, for Christ's sake."

"I'm sorry," Jenny mumbled.

"Jesus H. Christ!"

"Don't talk like that."

"Just can it, will ya?"

"Please. I said I was sorry."

"If I seem the least bit ruffled, Miss Devers, it's only because, with the possible exception of cancer, there is nothing I loathe more than a good old-fashioned, one-hundred-percent American teaser."

"I'm not."

"Don't get me started."

"I'm *not*."

"Then what the hell *are* ya? You been coming on at me all week. Let's just cut the crap and admit it."

"I want . . . you to know . . ." Against her will, she started crying.

"Hooray, here comes the tears."

". . . to know that . . . you have totally and . . . completely misunderstood my . . . actions."

"Sure I have. Of course I have. That story of mine makes a lot of sense, leaving a manuscript around someplace. So tell me you believed it and tell me that you couldn't have waited for me just as easy out on the sidewalk and tell me why goddammit you had to wait until the last god-dam second before asking was I married!"

"You have . . . totally . . . and completely . . ."

"Cry all you want."

". . . misunderstood my . . . actions."

"It doesn't change anything. Now I may have misunderstood yours, Miss Devers, but I'll try to make it next to impossible for you to misunder-stand mine. I used to live in this apartment before I got married. For a small fee my ex-roommate allows me afternoon privileges. I intended sharing those privileges with you this lovely afternoon until it turned out otherwise. I cannot say that I am pleased at that turn of events—you are, to use the vernacular, shapely—but I will, however, live. I will not, how-ever, wait for you to do your face so that it looks like you haven't been crying. I will see you at the office, perhaps later, perhaps Monday. Until that time, Miss Devers, may I just say shove it."

Jenny waited until the door slammed before allowing her sobbing to get out of control. Half blindly, she made her way to the sofa and dropped down, clutching at the cushions, her head buried in her arms. She cried for a long time, until her throat hurt. Then, slowly, she managed to stop. She sat up on the sofa, hands folded in her lap, breathing deeply. When she was under complete control, she stood, looked around for the bath-room, found it, turned on the faucet, and stared at herself in the mirror. Her face was, of course, a mess, but that was all right. It was the fact that her blouse was unbuttoned that set her off crying again. This siege was shorter, and when it was over she washed her face and did what she could with her hair and then went back to the sofa and sat down.

Well now.

What do you do if you're a good girl in a bad world and you're sitting in somebody's apartment and it's Friday in Manhattan and you've just been unjustly insulted and it *does* make a difference, a big difference, if he's married or not, and it's hot, and your apartment not only isn't air-conditioned, *it can't be,* because the wiring in the building is so rotten, and I could just kill that Archie Wesker.

Well, of course, I'll just have to quit my job.

I'm not going to have Bob Mitchum staring me in the face for the rest of my life. I'll quit—snap—like that—snap—and I'll live a life of luxury while the two hundred and fifty-seven dollars in my special checking ac-count lasts, and then—then—to hell with then, Jenny thought. I can't be bothered with it now.

She was suddenly in a marvelous mood, so maybe *that* was what she had been ready for all the time—quitting. She stood and grabbed her purse, hurrying across the room, because the important thing was to get right down to that office and empty that desk and leave a little note informing Kingsway Publishers Inc. that this was not goodbye, it was goodbye *forever*! "Miss Devers is bugging out," Jenny said, and she left the apartment, dashed to the street, caught a cab and urged the driver into a maximum effort as he raced her down to Kingsway.

As Jenny got out of the elevator, the main-desk receptionist was waiting to get in. They nodded to each other and Jenny hummed aloud as she made her way along the deserted corridor to her desk. Sitting down, she started opening drawers. They were empty. Oh, there were paper clips and pencils and carbons of correspondence that needed eventual filing, but, as far as anything personal was concerned, the drawers were empty. Jenny nodded. Of course they were. It was a bad habit to keep personal things in the office. Once you started spreading your worldly goods, you lost them. So the drawers were empty, and she had known all along they were going to be, so why had she rushed like a lunatic to clean out an already empty desk? Jenny wondered about that. Then she began to wonder if there was anything of her in her tiny apartment or was that just like her desk was? Then she wondered if she was going to cry again, helplessly realized the answer was going to be yes, said "Dear God" out loud and bit her lower lip as hard as she could, trying desperately somehow to stop, because even though the office was empty, it just didn't do to broadcast grief, and, besides, if the office wasn't empty, whoever was there would come around and ask a lot of silly questions. In spite of herself, Jenny wept—quietly, but not quietly enough, because from somewhere Mr. Fiske was suddenly standing over her, saying, "Miss Devers? Miss Devers? Is something wrong?"

"No."

"Then . . ."

"*I happen to be in a marvelous mood!*" Jenny shouted at him, and he nodded, and that made her mad, and then he smiled, and that made her madder, and she couldn't have been more amazed a couple of hours later when she found herself in bed with him. She was tempted to ask him if he too was married, but somehow another affirmative answer would have been just too embarrassing, so she didn't.

Charley would have given an affirmative answer, had she inquired. He was married, had one child, and had never before, not even remotely, been the least remiss. He didn't do that kind of thing (hadn't done that kind of thing).

Reprehensible; indefensible. (His way of putting it.)

"You gotta not be ashamed." (His father's.)

To the best of Charley's memory, his father had first uttered those words on a blinding autumn morning, during recess, on the playground of Covington Academy, a reasonably exclusive Connecticut boarding school for boys. Just prior to his father's utterance, Charley had been chatting with the Keeler twins, Ronald and Donald, who ordinarily ignored him. This day, however, he had just trounced them both in a relay race, he alone running against the two of them, and since their demise had been witnessed by several other members of their class, the Keeler twins were anxious to air the reason behind their setback.

"You cheated," Ronald (or Donald) Keeler said.

"It was a running race. How could I cheat?" Charley replied.

"Course he cheated," Donald (or Ronald) seconded.

"But I didn't."

"Guys like him, they always cheat." The twins were ignoring him now. "Always."

"You gotta expect that of guys like him. Cheating."

"You gotta."

"I'm not surprised. Are you surprised?"

"I'm not surprised. Are you surprised?"

"After all, his old man's nothing but the janitor around here."

"Custodian," Charley said.

They turned to look at him. "Janitor" in chorus.

Charley shook his head. "No. Custodian."

"He's the goddam lousy janitor and that's all he's gonna be and you're nothing but the goddam lousy son of the goddam lousy janitor and that's all you're gonna be too. Goddam janitor's son."

There were two of them and they were both his size, but if there had been ten and all ten giants, he still would have attacked. Charley ran at them, pummeling one until the other grabbed him from behind and pulled him down onto the playground and for a time it seemed as if their numbers would carry the day. They were sitting on him, hitting him around the face, and his nose was bleeding badly and his lower lip was cut and suddenly it dawned on him that he might just possibly lose and so he gave a terrible shout of protest and perhaps it was the sound of his own voice or the taste of his own blood or the fact that he had always associated the Keelers with the bad guys in his own private Western but as he lay there, as they hit down at his face, he knew he could beat them if he wanted to. And he wanted to. Charley twisted his body one way, then the other, back and forth, and soon one of the Keelers lost his balance, then the other slipped, and then Charley was on his feet, light and fast and on his feet, and soon one of the Keelers had a bloody nose and then the other had a swollen right eye and then the bloody one began to cry and his brother joined him and they started to turn and run away but Charley shouted again, diving on them, pulling them down, sitting astride them both, shouting and hitting until he felt a sharp pain at his ear and his father had him and was dragging him across the playground and down a flight of steps and through a door into the boiler room beneath the main building of Covington Academy.

"Animal!" Mr. Fiske said then. "Squabbling! Fighting in the dirt!" He was from the old country. He had lived in America for fewer than twenty of his forty-five years. His name, now Fiske, was once a good deal longer.

"But—"

"Before you give me your excuse, let me tell you there is no excuse."

"They called you the janitor. I tried to tell them you were the custodian. The custodian."

"Look!" Mr. Fiske held out his hands. He was tall and wiry and his fingers were long. "At my hands. Look."

Charley shook his head. "Yes?"

"They're dirty! The work I do, they get dirty! Either way, they get dirty! But I ain't ashamed. That's the main thing. The only thing. No matter what. You gotta not be ashamed."

"I'm not ashamed," Jenny said. She lay in her bed under the top sheet; Charley Fiske lay beside her. They had finished sleeping together perhaps two minutes before, and since then neither of them had said anything.

"Of course you're not." Charley rolled up on one elbow. The bed creaked. "My God, neither am I. We shouldn't be. Why did you say a thing like that?" The bed creaked again.

"That creaking. It just drives me crazy." She tried to make her fingers stop fidgeting with the sheet, tried to get her voice to sound less fretful.

"Why did you say that about being ashamed?"

"Because it's true. I'm not ashamed—I don't care what you do."

"What do you mean, what I do?"

"I had the feeling—ordinarily I'm not like this; I probably seem nervous to you but I'm not, I'm placid ordinarily and—I had the feeling that—this is very hard—that you wanted to run—there, I said it!—I had the feeling that bed play was over and you were going to run."

"Well, you're wrong."

"Good. I'm glad."

"Now, I *do* have to go."

"Oh."

"But it's because I've got a very important appointment that I simply cannot break." He sat up in bed and reached for his clothes.

Jenny watched him. "I'm not ashamed!" she said again. "This is probably one of the three worst conversations of my life and God knows what the other two were but it is not going to make me feel ashamed—"

Charley zipped up his fly. "I am a much better person—"

"*Than what?*"

"Than you have any reason to believe. Than I may seem now."

"I'm a better person too. What do you think, that I'm a quick—what's the phrase?—roll in the hay?"

"Of course not."

"*Why shouldn't you?* Haven't I acted like one? You don't even know me. Why shouldn't you?"

"Jenny . . ." Charley said, and his voice was sweet and full of compassion and very, very sad. "Come on now."

"You say you're nice. Are you?"

"Yes. I hope so. I try to be."

"Then don't leave. Not yet. Do that much. I'll entertain you. I can be very entertaining. What would you like?"

"A suede jacket for my birthday."

"I'm sorry," Charley's father said, "I can't give you a suede jacket."

Charley looked up at his father. It was dusk and they were walking to the little house that Covington Academy let them live in, the whole Fiske family: Charley, his father, and his three beautiful sisters.

"I'm sorry," his father said again. "I feel very foolish. I ask you what would you like and when you tell me I say 'no.' I promise you this, though: someday I'll have the money to give you a suede jacket. But not next month, not this birthday. Do you understand?"

"I don't really need any jacket," Charley said. "I don't really need anything. I don't like birthday presents. I think it's dumb, giving people presents just because they have a birthday. Now someday, when I graduate the smartest in my class from Covington Academy, *then* you can give me a present."

"You're a nice boy, Charley."

"I hope so. I try to be. I don't know why I said that about wanting a jacket. As long as I have this—" he reached into his back pocket and pulled out his folding carpenter's rule—"and this—" he tapped the rule against his wrist watch with the second hand—"what do I need?" Then he dashed off to try to find something to measure.

Charley had been measuring things for almost as long as he could remember. He was never without his wristwatch with the second hand and his folding carpenter's rule. He knew how big his bed was, and his room, and how many feet it was from there to the top of the stairs, and how long it took to crawl that distance as well as walk it or hop it, and he knew the length of his front yard, the width, too, as well as the length and width of each block of cement in the blissfully irregular sidewalk that passed by his home, and how many feet it was to the corner and to the next corner, and to the corner after that.

What he couldn't measure with his wristwatch and his carpenter's rule was whatever it was his father felt that drove him to take a job, an extra additional secret nightly job, as a dishwasher in downtown Covington, in order to get the money to get the suede jacket. Charley knew that his father was going out evenings, but he didn't know why, not until his birthday morning when he woke to find the suede jacket folded carefully over the foot of his bed. The minute he saw it he jumped up, touched the jacket, touched it again, then dashed downstairs to find his father, who was having his coffee, and as he lowered his cup Charley kissed him, let him go, kissed him again, then dashed back upstairs to try the jacket on. It fit, of course, perfectly, and as he gazed at himself in his mirror, he looked—he hated to admit it; it sounded conceited, but what could he do?—magnificent. Even his three sisters—Emily, Charlotte and Anne—(his mother had been, while alive, a reader) who were engaged in their customary morning squabble over bathroom rights, had to admit, as he whirled before them, that although ordinarily he did *not* look magnificent, he certainly did now. Charley left them, invaded the kitchen once more, and this time he did not kiss his father but looked at him instead, just looked at him, until the stern old man nodded, gave a small, rare smile, and then Charley was out the door to the sidewalk (twenty-four feet), then to the corner (forty-six feet, four inches), then to the lawn of Covington Academy (fifty-one seconds if you walked, thirty if you ran), where he encountered Timmy Brubaker, a dear friend of the Keeler twins, only richer. Nevertheless, Charley spun around for Timmy, let Timmy touch, and Timmy repaid his kindness with four words:

"That isn't real suede."

Charley nodded and smiled and continued on his way, walking until he was out of Timmy's sight, then running, running deep into the woods behind the Academy, where, his hands hugging the imitation leather, he wept. He was poor and his father was the janitor and, imitation or real, it shouldn't have mattered, he shouldn't have cared. Except that he did. And without thinking, he began to dig, scraping away with his fingers, making a hole, enlarging it until it was enough. He took the jacket off, folded it neatly, plunged it into the hole and covered it up with dirt. Then he stood and started out of the woods. What he would say when he got home, he decided, was that he'd lost it somewhere, which was a perfect idea unless his father happened to ask him where was the last place he could definitely remember having had it, which his father would definitely ask, so . . . What he would say when he got home was that the jacket had been stolen, and then his father would ask who stole it, and he would answer Timmy Brubaker and the Keeler twins, and his father would suggest they pay a visit, so . . . What he would say when he got home was that he had given the jacket away, to some poor kid, and his father would congratulate him for his charity except he would probably wonder, his father would, why he had worked so hard for something that meant so little.

Charley stood at the edge of the woods and stared at the sky. It was interesting, but not as interesting as trying to measure how many feet it was from where he stood back to the hole. (Two hundred and sixteen, on the button.) Charley measured the diameter of the hole (eleven inches), but in order to get a really accurate depth measurement he had to lift the jacket out, which he did, brushing it carefully before the final measurement. (Nine inches.) Then he put it on, the imitation suede, and he wore it until it wore out or he outgrew it, he could never quite remember which came first. He was poor, and his father was the janitor, but what the hell.

Besides, that fall he discovered football.

Sports were emphasized at Covington Academy, and first Charley tried soccer. But he wasn't very fast and he wasn't agile and he couldn't kick very well. He was big, though, and strong enough so that nobody ever picked fights with him anymore, so they sent him to the football field, where he tried tackling people, but he still wasn't fast, and he wasn't agile, and things looked bad for him there, too, until the afternoon they gave him the football to run with. He sighed and tucked it under his arm and ran, not fast, not with agility, just straight ahead, and it turned out, to the surprise and delight of the Latin professor who had to double as coach, that it was very hard to knock Charley down. From then on he was fullback. Freshman year of high school, when he stood six feet one and weighed close to two hundred, he scored four plodding touchdowns in a scrimmage against the varsity. From then on he was *the* fullback. He scored more points than anyone else in the history of the Academy, and everybody liked him, especially in the fall, and although he despised football he kept at it, because it was nice to have everybody like you, even if it was only especially in the fall.

He graduated third in his class, which would have been disappointing, since he wanted to graduate first, because once, years before, he had told his father that he would, except when graduation came it didn't matter because his father had died the month before. Any number of colleges were interested in him, because he was so hard to knock down, but he couldn't make a decision, and as the summer wore on, as it began to dawn on him that his good father was dead, he enlisted. He was sent, as an infantryman, to Europe, where he did nothing to be ashamed of, earning several medals, among them a Silver Star, a Purple Heart, and he advanced from private to sergeant first class and twice turned down commissions, and once a full colonel called him in to chat about making the military his career. After the war, he came back to Covington briefly before leaving again, this time for the University of Chicago, which was a very good school without a football team. He majored in English (he was, like his mother, a reader) and enjoyed the whole academic experience, except that when he received his diploma he didn't know quite which profession to attach it to. Something about writing, maybe, Charley thought, so he came to New York because it seemed like both the place to go and the thing to do. He rented himself a cell of an apartment and wrote a book (that seemed like the thing to do, too), a novel about the war. It turned out to be a bad novel and nobody showed the least interest in publishing it, but in the course of traveling from one rejection to another Charley met some people who seemed to like him even though it was wintertime, and when he was offered a job at Kingsway he with joy accepted, editing, as his first book, *The Nose Is for Laughing,* a novel by R. V. Miller. He got married, and some time after that he and his wife had a son, and some time after that the three of them moved to Princeton. The commute wasn't bad, since it gave him time to read. He worked very hard for Kingsway, eventually becoming a senior editor, and when, in the office late one afternoon, he heard Miss Devers crying at her desk, he tried to be soothing and he couldn't have been more amazed, a couple of hours later, to find himself in bed with her.

He had waited with her as she wept at her desk, her sobs shattering the quiet of Kingsway, and through the use of great patience he finally got her to stop. Since she was upset he offered to see her home. When they stood on her doorstep she invited him in for some coffee or something, and he accepted only because she seemed so lost and alone.

Jenny made the coffee or something invitation partially out of embarrassment (Mr. Fiske had, after all, caught her crying) and partially because, as he stood fidgeting on her doorstep, he seemed so lost and alone.

She brewed the coffee and they drank it. It was stifling and he asked if he might take off his suit coat and loosen his tie. She said good heavens, please. He took off his coat and loosened his tie. Then she asked if he wanted some iced coffee, seeing as it was so hot, and she laughed, explaining that she felt like a fool since only a fool wouldn't have fixed them iced coffee the *first* time. He said he would love some iced coffee. She excused herself and went to the tiny kitchen. He followed her to the kitchen entrance and stood there, talking to her while she made some more coffee. He found her face quite pretty and he wondered why he had never noticed anything but her body before. She was surprised at the breadth and thickness of his shoulders; with his jacket on he never seemed nearly so powerful. She asked him, once the coffee was ready, if he would mind getting out the ice cubes. He said he would be glad to. He stepped into the tiny kitchen and she stepped as far back as she could, but still their bodies touched. They were both about to apologize but they both stopped themselves in time. They went back into the living room and sat down and drank their iced coffee. The sun was going down and they both commented on how much cooler everything was in the dark.

He got up and moved toward the window; she apologized that there wasn't any view.

He explained that he was only going to get his coat, which was on the sofa bed, which was next to the window; she said he probably had lots of things to do.

He said lots; she said oh.

He stared out the window; she watched him.

Then she got up and moved across the room and stood so close behind him that their bodies barely touched; he decided he ought to move away from her.

Barely touching, they stood very still, staring out the window.

He wondered if he was going to do anything; she wondered, if he did anything, would he be gentle?

He decided not to do anything; she decided that, even if he was gentle, it wasn't enough.

He thanked God that his marriage was going so well or else he might have got involved; she gave thanks that although she was no genius, she was blessed with common sense.

He turned; she meant to step back.

He realized suddenly that she thought he was going to do something; she stepped back.

He reached out for her because he had to explain that she had misunderstood his intentions; she wondered if he was married.

He brought her roughly into his arms because sometimes you had to be rough with women to make them understand; she thought oh, he's not gentle, I want to cry.

Her body stiffened.

She wasn't expecting anything, he thought, and he almost released her, but not quite, and he continued to hold her, but lightly; she realized, as his fingers lightly caressed her body, how odd and wonderful it was that sometimes the biggest, strongest men were the gentlest men of all.

She kissed his eyes. She kissed his mouth.

She pulled him down.

Charley caught the Princeton train just as it was starting to move. Panting, he entered the smoker and sat down heavily. The car was not air-conditioned. Charley thought ill thoughts about the Pennsylvania Railroad while he wiped his forehead. Setting his briefcase on the seat beside him, he forced the window open, letting in the night air, which was hot, but he basked in it anyway. Then he fanned his handkerchief across his neck, doing what he could to thwart the shaving rash he could feel forming; he knew better than to run full out in hot weather; he was a big man and in hot weather he paid for his size. But Miss Devers had—no, Jenny; it was a little absurd calling her Miss Devers anymore—but Jenny had begged him to stay with her a while, so he had stayed, for too long a while, and so he had to run to catch his train. Result: he was hot and cheerless and shaving rash was already forming on his neck, ready to bloom a resplendent red when he next touched razor to skin.

Poor Jenny, Charley thought. Poor Jenny all alone in that cell of an apartment. And then he thought, No, goddammit, that way madness lies. Don't feel sorry for her because once you start feeling sorry then you'll start feeling guilty and once you start feeling guilty you'll bore me. Whatever happened happened and it ain't about to unhappen no matter how you writhe, so forget it, forget it, take two and hit to left.

Charley opened his briefcase and lifted out the large typed manuscript. He plopped it on his lap and looked carefully around. When he was sure no one was watching he quickly flipped to the end of the book and read the page number. It was a childhood habit of his, and it embarrassed him now, but he couldn't break it any more than he could forget the texture of Jenny's skin.

Now, dammit! he told himself.

But it was extraordinary skin. All right, he told himself, louder, so it was extraordinary skin. Admit it. Lots of people have extraordinary skin. You enjoyed yourself. Admit that too. She has an altogether memorable frame. Bless her for it, because when you're old, when whatever drives that drove you to do what you did earlier are dead, you'll be able to summon up Jenny Devers' body and think about it with remembered lust, the best kind. So remember her. Just stop trying to make yourself feel guilty. She started it. It was her idea. You may not resemble the driven snow but neither does she and you've got a 418-page novel to read this weekend, so hop to it.

Charley turned to the title page: *Does Your Detergent Taste Different Lately?* by Emmet Slocum. Charley had never been a fan of Emmet Slocum's novels, but they sold well, and it was a sign of Charley's advance at Kingsway that when Slocum's old editor died, this, his new novel, was awarded to Charley rather than to Ted Boardman or any of the others. Charley read the first page and a half before he sighed audibly, because it came suddenly clear that *Does Your Detergent Taste Different Lately?* was a Madison Avenue Novel. Charley skimmed the opening chapter, in which it was shown that the hero—Pete Fletcher, ace copywriter for Anders, Swivett and Bodkin (ASB to the trade)—though a good father, loving husband, handsome, brilliant, successful, rich and Protestant, was somehow unhappy. Quit your job, Pete, Charley urged; quit in the first chapter and go back to that teaching post in Massachusetts and save me from reading 400 pages of bilge. As he began the second chapter, Charley sighed again. I know the plot already, he thought. The hero's unhappy, but he doesn't know why, but he knows that he has to find out why, and it never dawns on him that the Machiavellian fink who runs the ad agency might have something to do with his unhappiness, so the hero, in desperation, has an affair with his faithful secretary—

Jenny, you're unavoidable, Charley thought.

—his faithful secretary, who's this great sweet girl who loves him from afar but in the end he stays with his wife on account of the kids and . . . Charley began thumbing through the book. Then he said "Bingo" out loud because he found the first sex scene between Pete and Helen, his faithful et cetera. Charley started reading after the dot-dot-dot double space:

    "I wanted that," Helen said. She cradled him in her arms.

    Pete looked at her. "God," he said. "God."

    "I hate her," Helen said then, and there was no denying the passion in her voice. "That wife of yours. That Doris. I wish she were dead."

    "Why didn't I meet you before?" Pete said. He grabbed her long black hair. "Darling." His lips bruised hers . . .

Charley rubbed his mouth. Our dialogue was better, he thought, Jenny's and mine, and he closed his eyes, remembering what they had said. Well, he admitted then, when you come right down to it, our dialogue wasn't all that hot either. There's not much you can do with the moment; everybody's read it before, so it's best just to hurry on by. Charley flicked a few pages farther in the book until Pete Fletcher was walking by himself at three o'clock in the morning, staring moodily at the Hudson River and . . .

I've got no patience with you, Pete. Not with you, not with me. I've edited this scene fifty times in my life and every time I edit it I have no patience with the damn man and his breast-beating, because this is a world in which you get what you pay for, so just forget what you did, because Jenny has by now, probably, and if she has, she's smart, so you be smart too. You're not the office stud like Archie Wesker. It may kill you to admit it, but you've done some things you can be proud of.

You're not a bastard! We know that already!

What he wanted, suddenly, was somebody to hit, hard, except he didn't do that kind of thing, but he wanted to anyway, the feeling was there, so naturally he thought about the night he first met Connie. He was living all alone in a cell of an apartment between Tenth and Eleventh in the West Forties, and his one and only novel, his bad book about the war, had just begun its string of rejections. He was just six months out of the University of Chicago and when he got the invitation to the Covington Academy reunion he decided not to go several times before he went. The reunion was set for a room in the Yale Club, and as he sat in his cell and fingered his invitation Charley felt very alone and wildly poor. The loneliness he was used to; the loneliness he could cope with.

Not so the poverty.

True, he had been born poor, poor in a rich kid's world, but that was all so long ago. Nobody cared in the Army and nobody cared at Chicago, and when he came to New York to live the shock of being poor again was sudden and cold and lingering. So he decided not to go, but then he changed his mind, and as he entered the room at the Yale Club he realized how right he had been the first time. He would have left then, turned and slipped out, except someone said "Charley" and took his arm and steered him into the crowd at the bar. Everyone was very well dressed, but so, he told himself, was he. Didn't he have on his good suit? Besides, from the outside, who could tell a thing about the lining? Charley ordered a Scotch and looked around. There were a number of pretty girls, some of them wives, some just girls, and the men were sleek and handsome, so Charley moved quietly to the edge of things, standing alone, watching all the rich kids play. When the totally unfamiliar girl began walking toward him he tried frantically to remember who she was, but he couldn't. "You're Charley Fiske," she said.

"How are you, you look marvelous, great to see you," Charley said, feeling completely phony and blissfully at home in the Yale Club.

"No," she said, and she flushed. "No, we've never met. I watched you play, though. You were the fullback."

"I'm sorry," Charley muttered.

"Forget it."

"No, you don't understand, coming on the way I did. I don't do things like that."

"Except you just did."

"Except I just did."

"I'm Connie Donaldson. I'm here with Timmy Brubaker."

That surprises me, Charley thought. Because you're not pretty enough, and until you told me who you were here with, I thought you might be nice. "Good old Tim."

"Yes. Well, he sent me here to fetch you."

"Good old Tim."

"Yes. Well, he'd like to talk to you but he's all tied up with that group over there and he can't get away."

"Consider me fetched," Charley said. They moved across the room. "What's Tim doing nowadays?"

"Nothing. I mean, he's in his father's business. I don't know what he's doing. Ask him what he's doing. What are you doing?"

Charley said nothing. Then Timmy Brubaker stood before them, tall and casual, a drink in one hand, a cigarette in the other, chatting quietly with the Keeler twins, Ronald and Donald, who flanked him on either side, a mirror Army. Several others milled around Timmy, who was, to Charley's disgust, both better- and richer-looking than anyone had any legal right to be.

"Hello, Fiske," Timmy Brubaker said when it was Charley's turn.

Charley nodded, wondering if Timmy remembered the day when he said, "That isn't real suede."

"What are you up to these days?"

Charley shrugged.

"School?"

"Chicago. University of. The."

"Excellent."

"Thank you. I'll write Bob."

"Bob?"

"Hutchins."

"Ah," Timmy said. "A joke."

I may just kill you, Charley thought.

"How was your war?" Timmy asked.

"My *what*?"

"You were in, weren't you? Did you fly? I flew."

"Yes, I was in. No, I didn't fly."

"I heard you did well."

I believe it, Charley thought, and he looked around at the room in the Yale Club because it helped him envision the world where one man might say to another, "Do you remember Fiske? The football ox, the janitor's son? I hear he did well in the war."

"I really don't like you," Charley said, and as he said it he thought, I'll bet you don't hear me.

"Good to see you, Fiske," Timmy Brubaker said. "You're looking well."

"Bingo."

"Pardon?"

"I made a bet with myself and I won. So I said 'bingo.' "

"Ah." He got ready to turn. "Perhaps we'll run into each other again."

"I'm unfetched?"

"Pardon?"

"Do you remember a jacket of mine? A suede jacket?"

"Yes. It wasn't real."

Charley unloaded. He was a trifle overweight at the time, two hundred and thirty, but he was by no means fat, and his hands were hard, and

Timmy Brubaker said "Oof" as Charley's left entered his stomach, "Ahh" as Charley's right contacted his chin. Then he fell into the arms of Ronald or Donald Keeler.

"Hey!" the free Keeler cried.

"And that goes for your cat too," Charley said, and he swung from his heels and connected and as his opponent slumped Charley whirled, thinking he had best get the hell out because he had caused a disturbance at his prep-school reunion and he didn't do things like that.

He walked back to the bar and ordered another Scotch. Then he moved to a chair and sat down. He sipped his drink, staring at Timmy Brubaker, who, visibly distressed, was lying sprawled in the middle of the floor in the middle of the room in the middle of the Yale Club.

Charley beamed.

"How can you smile like that?"

Charley studied Connie Donaldson a moment. She seemed to be angry, so he stopped looking at her face, which was all right, not a great face, not bad, and concentrated on her body. But she was wearing one of those black dresses that make it hard to tell.

"What did Timmy Brubaker ever do to you?"

"He insulted . . ." My poverty, Charley was about to say. "He insulted me."

"He did not. I was right there. I heard every word he said. When did he insult you?"

"Twenty years ago."

"Twenty—"

"I'm very moral. I believe in punishing the bad guys whenever possible. Sometimes it takes a while."

"I think you ought to apologize to Timmy Brubaker."

"What was your name?"

"Connie. Connie Donaldson and I think you ought to apologize to Timmy Brubaker."

"Oh, *screw* Timmy Brubaker."

She looked at him for a long time. "He is kind of awful," she said finally.

"What are you doing out with him?"

"What do you mean, what am I doing out with him?"

"Just what I said. What are you doing out with him?"

"He asked me! I'm twenty-four years of age and I'm single and when a boy asks me to go out with him, I go!"

"Any boy?"

"Within reason."

"Am I within reason?"

"I think so."

"Then go out with me."

"When?"

"Now."

"But I'm with Timmy Brubaker." She looked at Charley for a long time. "Oh, *screw* Timmy Brubaker," she whispered finally and, immediately thereafter, blushed. Then she said, "I'm embarrassed, so please . . ." And then she said, "Except I don't want to make a thing out of it. I don't like that. Do you like that? People who make things out of things? I don't. I don't even know quite what I'm saying, but I'd most enjoy going someplace with you except that if I think about it I probably won't, because I shouldn't, so get me out of here."

Charley got her out of there.

They spent the next few hours exploring Grand Central Station, because it was right across the street and because you could explore it for nothing and because, most of all, Charley had always planned on someday spending an evening exploring Grand Central Station. They did not take sixteen trains which traveled eventually through a total of thirty-seven states and would have cost them, had they been married and gone in style, more than three thousand dollars, not counting meals.

When they finally did take a train it was the shuttle, across town to Times Square, where they transferred to the uptown Broadway express, getting off at 96th Street, walking quietly to Connie's apartment, on the top floor of a five-story brownstone on 94th Street, between Broadway and West End. Her place was bigger than his, but still small, and the furniture, though in good taste, was obviously Salvation Army Modern. Before he said good night he asked her out for the following evening, Monday, and she graciously accepted, and on Monday evening he asked her out for Tuesday, on Tuesday for Wednesday. They continued, nightly, to go out, but after Wednesday he stopped asking; there didn't seem to be any real reason to ask. They both assumed that when they had free time they would spend it together, and together they endured the winter, welcomed the spring.

What he liked about her, among other things, was that she was poor. Among the other things were: a certain attractiveness, a certain wit, a definite desire to be kind. But the main thing was her poverty. They were poor, the both of them, so he didn't have to be embarrassed if his collar was frayed, his sports coat slightly out of style. And when he was able actually to *spend* some *money*, on a steak dinner or a balcony seat at a play, she *appreciated* it.

What he didn't like about her, among other things, was that she was poor. Among the other things were: she admired him too much and excited him too little, though the former bothered him only occasionally, the latter less than that. But the main thing was her poverty. He respected her and her aims. He had known many who claimed an interest in social work, but Connie was the only one who actually did it for a living. *What kind of a living, though?* Charley plagued himself with that question. He had no money, neither did she, so whenever he thought about the kind of future they might have together he quickly changed the subject.

All in all he liked her a great deal more than not. She liked him too, or so he assumed, but the exact extent of her caring was something he more or less ignored until the day she said, obviously embarrassed, that she thought it might not be a half bad idea, if he didn't mind, for him to meet her parents. He didn't mind—why should he mind?—so it was arranged for the following Sunday.

Late Sunday morning, precisely on schedule, he picked her up, and she kissed him full on the mouth, which surprised him, since she ordinarily didn't do that kind of thing. He told her she looked very pretty, which was almost true, and she examined his clothing with quiet concentration before finally nodding, one time, and kissing him again. They walked down the five flights and when they reached the street she took his hand and kissed it, explaining that although she ordinarily found him irresistible most of the time, she found him particularly irresistible on warm Sundays in April, but that he shouldn't be at all surprised, since it was a trait that ran in the women of her family, finding men particularly irresistible on warm Sundays in April and—

"What are you so nervous about?" Charley said.

"I'm not nervous. Who's nervous? Just because I'm babbling doesn't mean I'm nervous. Some people babble when they're perfectly relaxed and I'm of that ilk. Did you know I was of that ilk? 'Ilk' is a funny word. Don't you think 'ilk' is a—"

"Your folks won't hate me. I'll charm them or die in the attempt."

"I know you will. But that's not what I'm nervous about."

"Then what is?"

"Nothing. Forget it."

"Forgotten."

"Listen, the thing is I'm rich."

"Rich?"

"That's right."

"You mean really rich?"

"I guess so."

"You mean you've got money?"

"Yes. I've got money. I'm rich."

"Then what are you living in a fifth-floor walk-up on the West Side for? You're eccentric?"

"I would have said 'independent.' "

"Independent, eccentric, you're loaded, right?"

"Right."

"How loaded?"

"Sufficiently."

"One million, two million, five, ten, what?"

"Less than five."

"But more than two?"

"I guess so."

"More than two?"

"Charley—"

"Wow."

"Charley—"

"Then what were you so nervous about?"

"When?"

"A little bit ago."

"Nothing."

"Come on. You were nervous. Why?"

"Oh, because."

"Care to amplify that?"

"Well, because I hadn't told you before and I thought you might be a little upset that I'd lied to you all this time."

"A little upset? Listen: tell me you're a leper, I might be a little upset. But tell me you got two million dollars, what the hell have I got to be upset about?"

"Nothing. But you are."

"Where do they live, your folks? Fifth, Park, or both?" He looked at Connie. "That was supposed to be a joke." He smiled.

She returned it. "Then you're not mad."

"I'll tell you the absolute truth: it doesn't bother me one way or the other." They turned the corner and started walking toward the crosstown bus. A moment later a cab drove by.

Charley hailed it.

The Donaldson apartment, it turned out, was on neither Fifth nor Park but on Beekman Place, and as soon as he heard Connie giving the driver the address Charley began to prepare himself: the living room would be large and expensively furnished, the dining room too; there would perhaps be a large terrace with an unobstructed view of the East River; there would undoubtedly be servants. He thought on and on, because it was important that nothing come as a surprise because it didn't matter that Connie (suddenly) had money because a janitor's son could be just as civilized as anybody else.

But as soon as they walked through the front door Charley panicked. The Donaldsons' foyer was bigger than his entire apartment. Charley hurried after Connie, but as they entered the living room he stopped. The room was filled with vases, great, elegant vases, and Charley knew he was so clumsy he was going to break one, and then he thought he had undergone all this before. At some other time, in some other place, he had stood, trembling in fear of breaking a great, elegant thing, and then he remembered what it was, and it was Prince Myshkin, Dostoevski's poor idiot, who had trembled in fear, and Myshkin's fear had come true, and Charley whispered "Connie!" and she stopped and came back to him and smiled as he took her hand.

The Donaldsons were waiting for them on the terrace. Charley made his way through the hellos, but in the ensuing pause he heard himself saying how nice and "unobstructed" the view was, and as he said it he knew he sounded like an ass, so he blushed and shut up, feeling like the fool of all the world until from somewhere he heard his father saying that you gotta not be ashamed, and for just a moment he felt hot tears behind his eyes, but he blinked them gone, and after that he was quite himself again.

He entered the conversation and, in a few moments, found himself leading it. He spoke quietly, easily, about nothing in particular: football, fashion, the war, the peace. He accepted a daiquiri when it was offered him, refused a second when that time came. A servant appeared and Mrs. Donaldson suggested they have brunch, so they all moved to the end of the terrace and sat down beneath a large striped umbrella. Charley stared out at the East River and thought about things. Brunch was simple—eggs and livers and bacon and toast and marmalade and champagne—and as he sipped his third glass Charley suddenly stopped and realized that it didn't matter at all, Connie's money, except that he could never, not in all his life, remember having had a nicer meal.

When brunch was done Charley was aware that the ladies seemed to be making excuses for leaving, and he wondered why, until he decided that the reason must be because it was time for the two of them to have a "talk," Mr. Donaldson and he, except they really hadn't anything to talk about. But by then Mr. Donaldson was talking.

"Connie's in love with you."

"How do you know?" Charley wished he had drunk less champagne. Or more.

"By your presence. You're the first one she's brought here. Like this. She's rather ashamed of us, you know."

"I can't imagine why."

"Oh, she *likes* us well enough. We're all really quite close. In our own way."

Charley nodded and stared at the older man. Mr. Donaldson was probably fifty-five, but he looked a good ten years younger. His face was pleasant although at one time, years before, he was probably strikingly handsome.

"Actually," Mr. Donaldson said, "I knew of Connie's feelings a good deal before she brought you. She's told us about you, of course. Everything, I imagine. In the most disgustingly praiseworthy way. I was quite prepared to loathe you on sight." He smiled. "To my horror, I find you altogether likable."

Charley nodded and he smiled back at Mr. Donaldson and then suddenly he stopped smiling, because he realized that the older man was waiting for him to say something. "You're waiting for me to say something."

"That's correct."

"Well now . . . I mean, come on, Mr. Donaldson, aren't we rushing things just a little?"

"No."

"Why aren't we?"

"Don't you know what we're really talking about?"

"I guess I don't."

"We're not talking about you, Charley. Nor about Connie. We're talking about money."

Charley said nothing.

"You haven't got much, have you? As a matter of fact, you haven't any. Connie, on the other hand—"

"Mr. Donaldson, I don't love your daughter."

"That may not be as crucifyingly important as you think. You do like her?"

"Of course I do."

"And she loves you. And I love her. Something ought to work out, don't you think? There are no villains here."

"No villains."

"I'll tell you something, Charley. Not only was I totally prepared to dislike you, which, alas, I don't, but when you came in earlier I was petrified you were going to make an ass of yourself. Connie would have held that against me, you see. The money undid you, she'd say. It was my fault you were an ass and she'd only love you all the more. And you did make an ass of yourself for a moment."

"Yes. Thank you for not letting on."

"Good God, Charley, I'm a gentleman, I hope. What made you so nervous?"

Charley gestured toward the river, then the terrace, then back toward the splendor of the living room. "This," he said.

"Now I don't understand."

"We're talking of money, isn't that right? Well, I didn't know you were rich."

Mr. Donaldson got up from the terrace table.

What is it? Charley thought. Why did he look at me like that? "You don't believe me."

"Of course I believe you."

"No, you don't."

"All right, I don't."

Charley got up from the table and crossed the terrace. They stood side by side, staring down at the river. The sun was very strong. "It's the truth," Charley said.

"Connie told you you were coming to a tenement."

"No. Of course not. But today was the first time she'd let on. I swear."

"It's really not worth this much discussion."

"Yes it is. I don't lie."

"Which of us does?"

"Lots of people do. But I don't."

"Oh, Charley."

"*I didn't know.* I wouldn't have gone out with her if I'd known."

"Where did you meet her?"

"You know where. My class reunion."

"And is she pretty, my Connie?"

"Yes."

"No. She really isn't. I love her, but my eyes do not dazzle."

"She's attractive enough," Charley said.

"Let's hope so. And who was she with?"

"Timmy Brubaker."

"That's right. Now shall we add things up? Is it possible it never crossed your mind to ask why a not overly attractive girl should be at a function like a class reunion with a beautiful, socially ambitious young man like Timmy Brubaker?"

"Money," Charley said.

"Of course, money."

"I never thought it."

"Didn't you?"

"No," Charley said. "No."

"Are you sure?"

"Yes," Charley said. Then a moment later he heard himself say, "No." And a moment after that: "I'm not sure."

"Shall we go inside?" Mr. Donaldson said.

Charley followed him into the living room and they sat down amidst the vases.

"Mrs. Donaldson is vase happy," Mr. Donaldson said. "One learns, eventually, to live with things."

"I only meant I may have asked myself the question. But I didn't know she was rich. Please believe that. I'm not after her money. If I were after her money, would I have told you I didn't love her?"

" 'Get out of my house, you scheming son of a bitch!' "

Charley jumped up.

Mr. Donaldson laughed. "That was a quote, Charley. Sit back down. Please." And he waved his hand until Charley sat. "As I said, I was quoting something someone once said to me. My wife's father, to be specific. On the moment of our first meeting. Mrs. Donaldson brought me to meet her father only after months of peaceful persuasion. The man thought me a fortune hunter. Me. Just because I was poor, he thought I was after his daughter's money. But she persuaded him I wasn't. And we met. Now this was a self-made man, Charley. He didn't believe in amenities, like brunch. Out with it he came. I stepped through his front entrance and he looked at me and he screamed. 'Get out of my house, you scheming son of a bitch!' Poor man. He thought I didn't love his daughter; he thought I wanted her money." Mr. Donaldson lit a cigarette. "And, of course, he was right."

Charley looked around.

"Relax," Mr. Donaldson said. "This isn't any secret, Charley. For God's sake, if anything it's an old family story. Mrs. Donaldson and I laugh about it from time to time. Does that surprise you?"

"Yes."

"It shouldn't. You see, we love each other very dearly. Have for over twenty-five years. We are devoted; we are inseparable. I married her for her money—I was, you must believe me, dashing in those days—and then to my absolute horror I fell, as the saying goes, in love. With my wife. Oh, it was terrible. I couldn't admit it for days. Then I did, and that was that. We love each other, Mrs. Donaldson and I. We did then; we do now. Cigarette, Charley?"

"No, thank you."

"You're starting to squirm a little in that chair, aren't you?"

"No."

"Oh, nonsense. I know what you're thinking: 'The old gasbag's getting to the point.' I like you, Charley, you know that? You have such a terrifyingly honest face."

"Thank you, I guess."

Mr. Donaldson put out his cigarette. "All right, Charley, what do you say?"

"What does that mean?"

"Come, now."

"What is this? You're offering me your daughter—what kind of a thing is that?"

"I'm not offering anybody anything. I love my daughter. My daughter has indicated a preference—you—and I approve of her selection. I'm simply doing whatever I can to make her happy. You don't have to love her, Charley; that's what I'm trying to tell you. In time you will."

"Maybe."

"Take my word, Charley."

"Look at this room. What am I doing in a room like this?"

"Just because she's rich, don't hold it against her."

"I'm not."

"I was like you at one time: trying to make a virtue out of poverty."

"Listen," Charley said, and he got out of the chair. "Listen, I liked brunch. I would like to say I didn't, but I did. It's nice having people wait on you. I like it."

"And it scares you."

"Yes." He began to pace. "Damn right. Damn right."

"Relax, Charley; you needn't decide this instant."

"I gotta not be ashamed, don't you see? That's the important thing. I gotta not marry somebody unless I love them because I always thought that when I got married I'd—you know—love my wife, and then you tell me I will and look at you, you're happy, and it bothers me. I don't know. Sometimes I do crazy things and it bothers me. I hit Timmy Brubaker. I never hit anybody but I hit him and I've got to love my wife and I don't love Connie, but you say I will, and it bothers me because I think you're right. I don't know. I like it here. I like you. I don't know. If I knew what to do I wouldn't be walking around talking like I was crazy now, but I don't. You see, I was poor, all my life, poor, and I really like Connie, and . . ." He turned sharply to face Mr. Donaldson, and as he turned his hand hit a vase and the vase toppled and fell and Charley watched it shatter on the floor, listening as Mr. Donaldson said, "Forget it. Thank you for doing it. I've always loathed it. It's insured." But Charley, staring at the pieces, felt not one bit less clumsy and began shouting "Fool!"

"Princeton Junction; change for Princeton." The conductor continued the chant, moving down the car. "Princeton Junction; change for Princeton."

"Fool!" Charley said to the hero of *Does Your Detergent Taste Different Lately?* and he slammed the manuscript shut and stuffed it into his briefcase. "Fool for feeling shame."

He got off the train and transferred, and when he got to Princeton he walked to the parking lot and got into his car. As he started to drive he felt loose and relaxed and free from whatever it was he had been feeling earlier, and he hardly thought of Jenny Devers at all until he got to his house and saw Betty Jane waiting on the sofa in the living room.

"Robby?" Charley said then, meaning their son.

"Upstairs asleep," his wife answered.

Charley crossed to the sofa and she tilted her perfect face for a kiss, but he grabbed her thin shoulders with his big hands and lifted her to him and then they both fell back onto the couch and he engulfed her and she gasped beneath him and he was about to say "I love you, I love you" except he had always had a terrifyingly honest face, so he shut his mouth tight and let his body do the talking.

"Robby?"

"Upstairs asleep."

Betty Jane looked at her husband's face as he crossed toward her, and for just a moment she was afraid he was going to cry. She raised her head, but then he had her by her shoulders, and as he lifted her she wondered what in the world he had to cry about. He kissed her roughly, then lowered her back to the couch. Her arms clung to his neck. As he engulfed her, she could not help thinking, Oh, Charley, Charley, you've done something wrong.

A lot of funny things happened to Jenny that weekend. And she realized, as they were happening, that they were funny. But she didn't smile.

No more than an hour after Mr. Fiske left, Archie Wesker called her on the phone. He sounded more than a little drunk and Jenny listened as he apologized for propositioning her that afternoon and then proceeded to proposition her again, this time for later in the evening. That's very funny, Jenny thought, but instead of smiling she simply handed out a flat "no" and hung up, grabbing a pencil and paper, commencing a letter to Tommy Alden. She wrote for over an hour, six full pages and she was in the middle of the seventh when she abruptly tore it all up. Because it was all his fault, Tommy's. Everything was. Who needed a Rhodes scholarship anyway? Why couldn't he have just turned the silly thing down? Jenny went on like that a while before she realized how funny it was, the way she was thinking. But again she didn't smile. She got through the night alive, remarkable, considering the heat, and the first thing the next morning she dressed and subwayed down to Korvette's and bought an air-conditioner. She was writing out the check when she remembered that her building wasn't wired for air-conditioning. That was funny too, only the Korvette's man didn't think so.

The rest of the weekend was like that: funny.

Monday morning, she called up Kingsway to quit her job. It was hot and she felt very tired, groggy almost, and she misdialed twice before finally making connections. "Kingsway," the operator said.

"Hello. This is Miss Devers."

"Yes, Miss Devers."

"I won't be in today."

"You're ill?"

"Yes."

"Will you be in tomorrow, do you think?"

"Maybe. I don't know. If I feel all right."

"Thank you. Goodbye, Miss Devers."

Jenny hung up and fell into bed. She lay still, breathing deeply, her right hand roaming the sheet, trying to find a cool spot. I would really like to sleep, Jenny thought. More than almost anything. She closed her eyes. I feel much better, she thought, now that I've quit my job. Except I didn't really quit. Tomorrow. I'll quit tomorrow if it rains. I would like that. Some nice cool rain. And sleep. Nice cool sleep. I'm really tired too. Sometimes when you're really tired, you can't sleep. You're so tired you're too tired. I wonder if I'm too tired to sleep? "Miss Devers. Miss Devers!" Jenny heard the voice and was at first angry because it was the super come to ask something except that when she heard the voice again, "Miss Devers! *Jenny!*" she decided it couldn't be the super because he never called her by her first name, and even though, as she said "Who is it?" she knew who it was, she said it.

"Who is it?"

"Charley."

"Charley?" Jenny sat up and shook her head. It was cool in the room. She grabbed her old bathrobe and tied it tight and went to the door. "Charley?" she said again.

"Yes."

"Oh, *Charley.*" Jenny rubbed her eyes. "I've been asleep," she muttered.

"May I come in?"

"Sure." She opened the door and looked at him. He was carrying a raincoat and a hat and a large briefcase. "What time is it?" Jenny said.

"Five."

"In the afternoon?"

"Yes."

"Five Monday afternoon?"

"Yes."

"Well, fancy that. I've slept the day away."

"May I sit down?"

"I'm not awake yet. Would you like some coffee?"

"Thank you, no."

"I'd like some coffee." She hurried to the tiny kitchen. "Oh, wonderful," she said as she lifted the coffeepot. "There's some old." Jenny turned the heat up full and when the coffee boiled over she poured herself a cup. "I always do that when I wake up," she said, coming back to the other room. "Boil it over. Terrible. Sure you won't change your mind?"

"Thank you, no."

"Did it rain?"

"Earlier, yes."

"Thank heavens; it's cooler."

"Yes."

Jenny took a small sip. "I don't think I can drink this stuff. It's like solid oil." She laughed. "Except oil's a liquid. But you know what I mean."

"Go put some water on your face," Charley said.

"Why?"

"Just go do it."

Jenny went to the sink. "Any particular part of my face?"

Charley said nothing.

Jenny came back and sat down. "All wet," she said. "So?"

"You weren't sick today, were you?"

"Yes, I was."

"You didn't come to work because you didn't want to see me."

"That's not true. I like you. You're a very nice man, Mr. Fiske."

"I've been terribly upset. All day. Just as soon as I got word you weren't coming in. I decided then I had to talk to you."

"Why didn't you call?"

"Because I felt what we said might be of an intimate nature."

Jenny broke out laughing.

Charley waited till she was done.

"I'm sorry," Jenny said then. " 'Intimate nature' struck me funny."

"I don't pretend to be good at this; I admit to a certain lack of agility."

"I'm going to laugh again if you keep talking like that."

"I become overly formal under certain conditions. I'm sorry."

Jenny shrugged.

"At any rate, I want to tell you something."

"What?"

Charley hesitated. Then: "That you may return to work secure in the knowledge that there will be no repetition of Friday's actions."

"Friday's actions? What happened Friday?"

"Jenny—"

"You're married, aren't you?"

"Yes."

"Kids?"

"One."

"Happy home life in the suburbs. Right?"

"I'm afraid so."

"How embarrassing it must be for you. Coming here. A solid citizen like you. A den of iniquity like this."

"There's no reason for us to fight. We both did something. We're neither particularly proud of it. I'm sure we're equally sorry."

"*I'm sorrier!* You had the kid to play with this weekend. You had the wife to hold your hand. Let me tell you something about Friday's actions. I regret Friday's actions so much . . . so much . . ."

"I didn't mean to upset you like this."

"What did you think, coming here?"

"You won't be at work anymore, will you?"

"That's right."

"I bungled this whole thing. I'm sorry, Jenny."

"Now you're going, I suppose."

"Would I make things any better if I stayed?"

"I don't see how."

"Neither do I. Goodbye, Jenny."

"Goodbye."

"Goodbye," he said again and she watched as he grabbed his raincoat and hat and hurried out the door and was gone. He left the door partially open and for a moment Jenny thought he was coming back, back on the run, to take her in his great arms, but then she realized that he was not returning, wasn't about to return, and she wondered why she wanted him to. For she did. That much was sure. She stood slowly, shook her head, took a deep breath. The apartment was cool and that should have made her feel better but it didn't. She was alone. Alone and lonely in a cool place, and that was better than being alone and lonely someplace hot, but it still wasn't enough to warrant a hooray. Jenny started trudging toward the door, thinking that she must absolutely do something cheerful tonight. Like go to a play and sit in the orchestra or take in a foreign film. It was Monday, so getting a good seat wouldn't be hard. Yes, she thought, I must do that. And I won't cook myself dinner, either. I'll eat out. I'll eat out and I'll go to the theater and if I have to walk more than half a block I'll take a taxi. For a moment she contemplated hiring a limousine for the evening, hiring it and just telling the chauffeur to drive, and her sitting back on the soft cushions looking out at all the people, but she killed her contemplation because it was so silly and because as she was almost to the door she saw his briefcase standing by the chair where he must have forgotten it, and when she saw it she said "He forgot his briefcase" right out loud, and then she said "Charley" right out loud and she started running to the door but as she reached it he was already there and he said "I forgot my—" but that was all, because she cut him off with "Thank God," and then she was in his arms, his great arms, and he said "Thank God," and then they were saying it more or less together, eyes closed, in blind unison, "Thank God, thank God, thank God, thank God, thank God."

"I tell you," Archie Wesker said as he paced around Charley's office, "she's putting out for somebody."

Charley looked at him. "What makes you think so?"

"Think? Goddammit, I can tell. A girl starts putting out, old Arch, he knows. Just look at her. Talk to her. She's acting different than a week ago."

"Different from."

"From, then, dammit, Charley, somebody's scoring with that broad and it's *not me*."

"So?"

"So? Have you taken a look at her? *Zoftig*."

"How's Mrs. Wesker?"

"Mrs. Wesker is built like Marjorie Main, thank you."

"She is not."

"Have you seen her naked? I've seen her naked. The female frame loses its elasticity after three kids, believe me."

"You were cheating before you had any kids."

"Come on, Charley, what do you want to say a thing like that for?"

"It's true."

"I know it's true; so what? Don't make me out immoral, Charley. I want to be one of the good guys."

"No, you don't. That's what I like about you: you're an honest lecher."

"The basis of our entire relationship, Charley, is that we look down on each other. You've got a great marriage, and I don't, so you feel sorry for me, but actually all the time I'm feeling sorry for you. Let me tell you my philosophy."

"Don't tell me. Write it down. No kidding, Archie. You write it and I'll edit it and it'll be the biggest children's book since *Horton Hatches the Egg*."

Archie laughed. "Score one for you."

The intercom sounded. "Yes, Miss Devers," Charley said.

"Ready for that dictation now."

"Fine," Charley said.

Archie started for the door. "What's all this 'Miss Devers' crap? She's your secretary."

"If you think I'm about to call her 'Jenny' with a suspicious mind like yours around, you're crazy."

Archie shook his head. "I do not consider you a suspect, I promise you." Jenny knocked and entered. Archie looked at her. "How do you do, Miss Devers."

"How do you do, Mr. Wesker."

"She hates me," Archie whispered, and he closed the door.

"He's right," Jenny whispered when it was safe.

"You shouldn't."

"I don't, not really. I just wish you didn't like him."

"I guess I wish I didn't too, but I do. What's the dictation?"

"You haven't asked me where I've been?"

"All right; where have you been?"

"The lounge. Beautifying myself. Combing my hair. But more important, taking off my lipstick."

"Jenny, this is a busy office and it's three o'clock in the afternoon—"

"Put a piece of paper on your desk. Do as I say."

Charley put a piece of paper on his desk.

"Now point to it."

Charley pointed.

"Now I can't tell what the paper says from here, don't you see, so I'll have to walk around the desk until I'm right next to you." When she was next to him she said, "Then I'll bend down to see better and—"

Charley kissed her. He rose out of the chair and his arms went around her and he shoved his body tight against her.

Jenny broke free.

Charley stood very still.

She moved around the desk away from him and sat down uncertainly.

"Now will you please keep away from me? While we're here? Please?"

"I'm sorry. But I didn't intend for quite *that*. Your lips were just supposed to graze mine—that's how they tell it in novels. 'His lips grazed hers.'"

"Just stay away from me. We could have been caught then. Archie might—"

"That's part of the fun of an affair," Jenny said. "I've been reading about them this past week and it seems a great part of the fun is in almost getting caught. At least in the beginning it is."

"Don't call it an affair. It's barely a week—"

"You're right, but I don't know what else to call it."

"We're confused about each other. How's that?"

"Wonderful. And we're having a confusion."

"A confusion." Charley nodded. "Fine with me. Now what's this dictation?"

"You have that important letter to write, remember? To that nice Devers girl. About dinner. I'll read you what I thought might be a nice opening: 'Dear Miss Devers, let me begin by saying that our conference of last evening has lingered in my mind. You have a mighty brain and touching it gives me more pleasure than you will ever know. Consequently, I thought we might pick up this evening where we left off. I thought we might even go to that same restaurant—the one that seems like a tiny apartment over on the West Side. The food and the décor aren't much but you couldn't ask for greater seclusion.' I thought you might take it from there, Mr. Fiske."

"I can't."

"Can't what?"

"Miss Devers will understand."

"Miss Devers thought you were joining her for dinner. She may not understand at all."

" 'My darling Miss Devers: I must send my regrets for this evening. A certain lady of my acquaintance—' "

"You said you thought you could get home late again."

" 'I do not feel it wise to arouse the least curiosity in this certain lady, and therefore I feel our conference had best be put off till later in the week.' "

"You said you thought you could get home late again. You said that, Charley."

"I know. I changed my mind."

Jenny stood up.

"You look very pretty, Jenny."

"Thank you." She started for the door, stopped, started talking, her back to him. "I'm sorry, I'm not ordinarily like this—possessive—I'm sorry. You've got to realize something, though."

"What?"

"I care for you, Charley." She turned and gave a little smile. "But then, I guess I have to."

"I have seen happier smiles."

"The thing is, Charley, when everything goes right, that's fine; but when everything doesn't, then I have to ask myself what I'm doing. I don't much like asking myself what I'm doing."

"I banished that question from my vocabulary recently. I suggest you do the same."

"Will there be anything else?"

"Thank you, no."

Jenny opened the office door.

Charley started to call her name, then stopped. She closed the door and he nodded. There had been altogether too much last-minute calling of names lately. It was a device he had always disliked, especially in movies, when the heroine turns and goes to the door and at the last possible second the hero calls out "Jessica" and she stops, back still turned, shoulders tense, and says "Yes?" and then you're into another whole lousy scene. Well, thank God he hadn't called out "Jenny." Because he had been late getting home last night and it just wouldn't do, making a habit of it. Charley sat back in his chair and pondered the phrase, "late getting home." He had never been fond of euphemisms, but they were, like splinters, a necessary evil, and taking that into account, "late getting home" wasn't bad. True, it was vague. But at least it wasn't a lie. I'm not going to lie to Betty Jane, Charley thought. *I will not lie.* And Jenny's just going to have to understand that. For a moment he thought of Jenny, and then he thought of grabbing her the way he had, and then he reached for the phone and called his wife. When she answered he said, "This is Maxwell Perkins."

"Hello there, old Maxwell," Betty Jane said.

"I have nothing to report," Charley told her. "Nothing is new."

"Same. Oh—Robby ate all his lunch."

"Huzzah."

"I wish he weren't so skinny," Betty Jane said.

"Perhaps a new leaf is turning."

"Yes," Betty Jane said. Then: "Why are you calling?"

"No reason. To hear thy sweet voice. Really, no reason. No reason at all."

"Oh, Charley, are you going to be late again?"

"What makes you say that?"

"I know that tone in your voice and it just makes me so mad sometimes. I swear, without you that firm would fall down and die."

"They pay me."

"That's not the point. Whose work are you doing tonight? Boardman's? Or that awful Archie Wesker's? Or is it cocktails with some writer we're wooing away from Random House?"

"Now easy—"

"I don't much feel like being easy. Everybody's always taking advantage of you because you're so big. They know you won't hit them. I mean it. You work too hard."

"No, I don't."

"Yes, you do. I mean it. Someday I'm coming down there and I'm going to give them all you know what."

"Hell?"

"Yes."

"You're very sweet."

"You bet I am."

"I'll be talking to you."

"I'll be up; get home when you can."

"Bye."

"Charley?"

"Yes?"

"I love you, Charley."

Charley put the phone back in its cradle. Well, he thought after a while, at least I didn't lie.

XV

Walt sat cross-legged on the living-room floor building a house of cards.

It was a month since Blake misbehaved at the St. Louis Country Club, half that since their divorce, half that since he had heard from her. (She had buzzed him collect from New York's Idlewild to report that she was off on an extended tour of the Continent and to wish him luck. The call hadn't bothered him. Not really. Or not really as much as he thought it was going to when he picked up the receiver and heard her voice, and although he cursed aloud after hanging up for not making her pay for the call, cursed again when a couple of beautiful "I should have saids" crossed his mind, he quickly forgot the whole thing.)

Now, wearing a tee shirt and khaki pants and dirty white tennis shoes and no socks, he concentrated on the house of cards, hard work, so he stopped every little while to grab a sip from his Budweiser can. Across the room the TV set was tuned up full on a Bugs Bunny cartoon, and alongside it the Capehart clicked *Pal Joey* back into position and once again, at the top of his lungs, Harold Lang began to sing, "I have the worst apprehension that you don't crave my attention . . ." Walt nodded his head in time to the music, took another sip of beer. Then he went back to his house of cards, carefully fitting a third tier onto a none too sturdy second. When he had the third tier finished, Walt drained the last drops of Budweiser, stood, crossed the room and said, "Flynn, somebody's got to knock out that Japanese pillbox." In his best Errol Flynn voice Walt said, "My pleasure, General," and he crawled across the living-room rug to the shelter of an easy chair. Pulling the pin from his Budweiser can, he jumped up, shouted "Geronimo!" and lobbed the beer can toward the house of cards. As the can was in midair, Walt groaned, clutched his stomach and, eyes closed, dropped to his knees. "Flynn, Flynn, you'll get the Congressional; knocking out that pillbox won the war." Eyes still closed, Errol Flynn said, "Always been lucky, General," and then toppled over and died. Walt lay still a moment before getting up and looking around.

The house of cards still stood.

"Nuts," Walt said. How can you miss from six feet? The beer can lay on the edge of the rug in a little puddle of foam. Walt retrieved the can, mashed his foot into the puddle, spreading it good, then went and stood over the house of cards. "Bombs the hell away," he said, dropping the can, except it stuck to his fingertips and, when it did fall, it veered off, missing the house again.

Walt kicked the house of cards down, hurried to the telephone, flipped the phone book open, found a number and dialed. "Hello?" a lady said.

"I'm sorry to bother you, ma'am, but I'm working for the Kirkaby stores. We're taking a survey and I wondered, is your refrigerator running?"

"Yes, it is."

"Well, I'll catch it if it comes my way," Walt said, hanging up fast, falling onto the sofa, laughing and kicking his feet. Done, he lay very still and wondered if he was hungry. Eventually he decided he was, so he got up and padded to the kitchen and opened another can of Budweiser. The kitchen clock said five on the button. Walt rubbed his eyes. Morning or evening? he wondered. He continued to rub his red eyes, thinking that he really ought to be able to figure out a question like that. Morning or evening? He could always pull the drapes or look through the blinds or open a door and peek outside, which wouldn't have told him much if it was winter, since five in the winter looks the same either time, but this was summer now, definitely summer, or at least it had been the last time he'd checked, and I don't want to peek outside, Walt thought; I want to figure it out for myself. Logically. Morning or evening? Morning or . . . "You ass," Walt said out loud. "*Dumkopf.*"

It was evening. It had to be. They didn't show Bugs Bunny at five in the morning. Hell, who'd be up to see it? Nobody but milkmen and insomniacs and you couldn't get a decent rating with just them, so that was that; the time was five o'clock in the evening, but what was he doing in the kitchen?

I probably came for the time, Walt thought, and he made his way out of the kitchen, dancing like Fred with Ginger in his arms, swirling and dipping until he came to the living room, where he stopped very short because his father was there.

"Walt," P.T. said, nodding. He was a big erect man, gray-haired, tanned and handsome.

Walt nodded back. "P.T." Then he hurried to the television and the Capehart and turned them both off.

"Everything going O.K.?"

Walt nodded again. "O.K."

"Needing anything?"

"Nothing, thanks." Walt shook his head.

"Sure, now?"

Walt repeated the shake. "Sure."

"Like you to do me a little favor," P.T. said then.

Walt waited.

"Well, will ya?"

"If I can."

"I got Dr. Baughman outside in the car and I'd like you to see him."

"Who's that?"

"A very nice guy. A friend of mine."

Walt couldn't help smiling.

"What's so funny?"

Very softly Walt said, "I do not need, now or in the future, and I honestly wish you'd get this through your head, any goddam psychiatrist."

"Hold the phone, mister; he's a medical doctor."

Walt pushed his glasses up snug against the bridge of his nose with his left thumb. "Well, I won't see him, not under any conditions. I'm fine."

Very softly P.T. said, "I'm worried about you. You're acting funny."

"Say what you mean, why don't you? You think I'm cracking up. You stand there with your thirteenth-century mind and you think I'm going bughouse. Will you just please remember that I was, until recently, married three years and in the language we have a word called 'adjusting' which is what I'm doing now."

"Hiding, you mean."

"Oh, Father, I'm not hiding." He took a long drink of Budweiser.

"Walt! You stay inside the house! You pull down the shades! You draw the damn blinds! You never go out. What the hell do you call it?"

"I told you: I'm adjusting to the past and figuring out the future."

"Will ya please hurry?" He reached a big hand toward Walt's face. Walt took a step backward. P.T. jammed the hand into his pants pocket.

"Dammit, dammit, I wasn't gonna hit you. I'm worried. Don't run away from me like that. Nuts." P.T. spun around and hurried to the foyer. "Why do we fight? I ask you to see a doctor, we end up squabbling." P.T. opened the front door. "And you shouldn't have said that about me having a thirteenth-century mind." Then he was outside and gone.

Walt ran to the door and opened it and thought about saying "I'm sorry." It was a difficult decision, but as P.T. and the other man drove away, Walt made up his mind to do it and he shouted "I'm sorry, I'm sorry" to the disappearing car.

The telephone rang.

Walt sagged.

As he started slowly toward the telephone Walt said, "Hey, Walt, how about dropping over for a little chow? Gee, I'd love to but I can't. Why the hell can't you? Listen, tell you what, you stay right there and I'll hop on over and get you. Gee, I'd love to, but I just can't tonight. I'm busy tonight. I've got these plans tonight but thanks, I mean it, thanks, thanks just one helluva lot, thanks." Walt picked up the phone, closed his eyes tight, managed "Hello?"

"Hey, Walt, it's me—Marty. Listen, Sally bought about eighty times too much pot roast, so how about dropping over to bail her out?"

"God, Marty, thanks, I just can't tonight."

"Sure you can. Course you can. C'mon."

"Aw, Marty, God, wouldn't I love to. But I've got this unbreakable engagement. No kidding. I do. But thanks. Really thanks. No kidding, thanks one helluva lot, and my love to Sally, huh?"

They made the usual goodbyes and then Walt, eyes still closed, groped with his free hand, found the cradle, dropped the receiver into it. Well, Marty was taken care of. That left probably Irv and Wils and maybe Donny and that would take care of his St. Louis cronies for the night. Tomorrow night Marty, being the most persistent, would call again, Irv too most likely, and Sandy and probably Muggsy—no, Muggsy was in Europe, had been for nearly two months. "Thank God for small favors," Walt said out loud. And then, very much louder: "Leave people the hell alone!"

No. That was wrong. You had no right to get mad at them. They were your friends, and they were worried about you and they were just trying to help, so they called you and asked you to dinner or a flick or poker or maybe a box seat at the Cardinal game. You couldn't ever get mad at a friend who was trying to help you, but still it was a shame there were so many helpers, a shame he and Blake had been such a social couple, so rotten popular. Friends were great, but sometimes they didn't understand that what you were doing was thinking. For maybe the first time in your life, really honest-to-God thinking.

Walt sat down on the sofa and thought about thinking.

"Nuts," he said, getting up. What the hell business did P.T. have coming in and accusing him of hiding? Hell, he wasn't hiding. Just because he hadn't been out of the house for a while didn't mean he was hiding. Walt ran his hands across his chin. How long since he'd shaved? He tested the stubble again. A while probably. I'll shave, Walt thought, because that's probably why P.T. thinks I'm hiding, because he probably thinks hermits grow beards, and since it looks like I'm maybe growing a beard, I'm automatically a hermit, for God's sakes.

Walt finished his Budweiser, then bent into his imitation of Laughton doing Quasimodo and, his tongue sticking practically through his cheek, said, "Why wasn't I made of stone like you?" and loped to his bathroom. Spinning on the hot-water spigot, he pulled off his tee shirt and khakis, flexed his right biceps, tested the result with the fingers of his left hand.

"Nuts," Walt said, and he reached for his Burma Shave.

He had always used Burma Shave because he loved the highway signs. Blake loved them too, and sometimes, when they were married, they used to make up jingles as they drove along.

> Boys with bristles
> On their cheeks
> Often stay
> Alone for weeks.
> Burma Shave.

> Janes cannot resist
> Their cravin'
> For a Joe who's
> Freshly shaven.
> Burma Shave.

Sometimes, when Blake was quiet for a particularly long time, he knew she was working on what she called a "spicy" one, and pretty soon out she'd burst with some poem where the first word was usually "Virgins" and he'd do what he could to shush her and after a while they'd both start laughing, and as he put the lather on his face Walt could feel himself starting to go, so he quick grabbed the sink with both hands and stared at the hot running water until he was pretty sure he had control.

He heard his brother's voice then, calling "Egbert," and Walt checked his eyes to see they were dry and they were and wasn't that a break, because that was all he needed, to lose control in front of Arnold. Arnold, who was almost as big as P.T., almost as handsome too, and dumb as a barn door but nobody seemed to mind, and those were just four of the reasons Walt despised him. Walt continued to lather his beard, looking in the mirror toward the bathroom door, where Arnold would soon appear and probably say "Berty" and then throw his arm around Walt's shoulders. And of course Arnold would be smiling. Arnold had a perfect smile, even and winning, and he only used it all the time. Walt picked up his razor, held it under the hot water.

"Berty," Arnold said from the doorway. He moved into the bathroom, put a big arm around his brother's thin shoulders. "What'd the doctor say?" Smiling.

Walt cleared the stubble from in front of his left ear, then dipped the razor back under the water. *You don't care what the doctor said. You're only asking because you know it zings me P.T. tells you things. That's what you're really saying: Father confides in me. He favors me. I am the preferable son.* "Didn't see him," Walt muttered.

"Listen, it's your life, why should you?" Arnold smiled. "Come for dinner?"

Walt shook his head. "Tell Sheila thanks, I'd really love to, but I can't. Don't push it tonight, Arnold, huh? Please?"

"Why can't you?"

"I just can't, Arnold."

"Sure you can. Come on." Arnold smiled.

"You have an altogether winning smile," Walt said.

"Don't get nasty with me, Egbert," Arnold said, smiling, punching Walt on the arm. Hard. "I'm still your big brother."

I won't rub it. On my grave. I swear. "Apologies to all concerned." Walt commenced to shave again, thinking it was about time for Arnold to get around to asking whatever question it was that had brought him.

"Forget it. Didn't mean to slug you that hard either." Arnold turned, moved to the doorway. His back turned, he said, "Say, what do you think about painting the stores?"

"Score one for our side."

"What?"

"Nothing," Walt said. He shrugged. "I don't know, Arnold; if they need painting, paint them."

"I mean different colors."

"Now you elude me."

"This guy—" Arnold made a hitchhiking gesture toward downtown St. Louis—"P.T. says I should figure it out. This guy claims that if you paint walls different colors it makes people feel better. They turn a corner in a store, they see a pink wall, they feel better. So they spend more money. I think it's a lot of crap. What do you think?"

"Are you asking is there psychological validity behind color affecting mood?"

"I'm not asking you anything."

"Well, there is."

"Then you think I should paint the stores."

"I don't know, Arnold. Why not paint one? If sales go up, paint the rest. If they don't, don't."

"That's no answer; what kind of an answer is that?" Arnold shook his head. "I don't know why I bother discussing business with you; you're never any help." He smiled, punched Walt on the arm again. "Sheila'd sure love to have you for dinner." Walt made a smile, shook his head. Arnold smiled back. Then he was gone.

Walt finished shaving and thought about Sheila. God, it was irritating. Here was Arnold, rich and dumb, and he marries a girl who likes dumb rich men. And not only that, but she's built and gorgeous. Walt envisioned Sheila's face. Gorgeous was probably the right word, although there were degrees; Sheila wasn't gorgeous like Imogene Felker had been. Of course, you didn't find hair like Imogene's every day in the week, or a face like that either. Walt remembered one night when he'd walked Imogene home once after rehearsal and right out loud he said, "I should have done something!"

Abruptly he held his breath; Arnold might still be hanging around and it wouldn't have paid to have Arnold hear him talking to himself. He'd been doing too much of that lately, gassing away all alone. "I must stop talking to myself," Walt said out loud, and he quickly saw the humor in it, so he laughed. Then he dried his face and put on Afta because it didn't sting, and then he decided to shower, so he did, letting the water tingle him good and hard as he thought about Imogene, about how she put a piece like Sheila in the shade but good, and he wondered why he hadn't done anything that night, and then he remembered he had been engaged to Blake at the time and that meant something then, but now, showering, he wondered if he had ever made a bigger mistake in his life than in turning on his heels that night with Imogene, just turning and muttering "See ya" with his hands practically roped and tied into his pockets because he knew if he freed them they'd make a grab and he was engaged and wasn't that a laugh, or didn't it turn out to be one. He should have grabbed Imogene that night. He should have grabbed her and tried to kiss her and if she'd laughed at him, then let her laugh, he should have taken the chance.

"Nuts!" Walt shouted. "Nuts, nuts, nuts, goddammit *nuts!*"

"Talking to yourself again," he said, dousing the shower, drying his spindly body. Walt looked at himself in the mirror. How could you even daydream of making a pass at a girl who looked like Imogene when you were skinny with bad eyes and pimples on your back and a face that was and always had been undeniably funny-looking? Arnold had the looks in the family and Arnold had P.T.'s confidence and P.T.'s size, not to mention everything else in the world except brains.

"And where have your brains got you?" Walt wondered. You were so smart you let Imogene get away and—*will you just once and for all please just forget about her?*

Walt dressed and went into the bedroom and flopped down on the bed, looking around for something to read. Nothing looked interesting, so he picked up his college senior yearbook and began studying the pictures. He came across a shot of himself in the show he and Branch Scudder had done and he wondered where Branch was from, so he flipped to the index and found that Branch was from Waverly Lane, West Ridge, Ohio, and 23 Williams Street, Portland, Maine, was the address listed for Imogene Felker.

"Now what'd you do that for?" Walt said. Sneak up on yourself. If you want to look up the address some girl had three years ago before she got married, look it up. Memorize it if you want to.

Walt promptly forgot the address.

His stomach rumbled, so he got up and went to the kitchen. Checking the icebox freezer, he found he was running low on Swanson dinners and he reminded himself to call the grocer tomorrow and have some more delivered. Then he opened another can of beer and walked into the living room.

Sitting on the sofa, he reached for the phone and, a moment later, when he had got the long-distance operator, he said, "Listen, here's the thing: I don't wanna bother you but I wanna call somebody but she isn't where I have her being so what do I do?"

"Your call, please."

"That's what I'm trying to explain. I want to get in touch with this girl I went to school with, college, but she's not there anymore because I think she got married after graduation to some lawyer from Philadelphia, so she's probably in Philly, but I don't know where and I don't know her husband's name, do you see my problem? I know where she isn't; I just don't know where she is."

"This is my first week on the job," the operator said. "Perhaps I'd better give you the supervisor."

"No-no, please, I don't want to cause you any trouble. I just want to get in touch with Imogene Felker, except that isn't her name anymore."

"Do you have an address for where she isn't?" the operator said. Then there was a pause. "I really think I'd better let you talk to the supervisor."

Walt closed his eyes very tight. "Twenty-three Williams Street. Portland, Maine."

"You wish to speak to an Imogene Felker at Twenty-three Williams Street in Portland, Maine?"

"Yes."

"Hold the line, please."

Walt held the line while the operator did all the things that operators do, like getting in touch with other operators and talking to each other like they were really IBM machines, and he began to kick his feet a little because pretty soon he'd have Imogene's married name and phone number in Philly and then he'd be talking to her and it was always fun just shooting the breeze with Imogene, you didn't have to worry about being funny or bright or anything when you talked with Imogene, just yourself, that was all you had to be and maybe someday she'd come to St. Louis with her husband and they could all have one hell of a time, sitting around and just shooting the breeze, and he'd show them the town and maybe the Kirkaby stores if they were interested and then he'd take them to dinner to one of the artsy places in Gaslight Square, and Walt kicked his feet higher as he sat there while the operator put the call through and then the operator said "Miss Imogene Felker, please, long distance is calling," and then someone said *"This is she,"* and Walt hung up and went to the garage and hopped into his Ford and took off.

As he started to drive he realized it looked as though he was running away from something, but that wasn't it. It looked like that, sure, but the truth was he hadn't expected to talk to Imogene personally, at least not that second, and he wasn't prepared to say much of anything, and if he had spoken to her that's just what the conversation would have been, not much of anything, and he wanted to talk well when he spoke to her so that he didn't look like a complete nut, calling her cold after three years. Besides, not only would she think he was a nut, but so would her husband, except that the operator had said "Miss Imogene Felker, please," and Imogene had said, "This is she" and *not* "You mean Mrs. So-and-So. I used to be Imogene Felker but I'm not anymore." "This is she," Walt said out loud, and it crossed his mind casually that perhaps she wasn't married and that meant she was Available and so was he, Available, so you really had to prepare like crazy for that first phone call or she'd turn you down cold when you asked to see her again. I better get everything straight in my mind, Walt decided. I better drive a while.

Walt drove.

At first he just cruised along, but then he thought it might be nice to take in a ball game, so he headed for the park, except that when he got there it was empty because it wasn't time for the game yet and because the Cards were playing in Chicago and that was too bad because it would have been nice on this his first night out to see old Stan clobber one good, just swing that crazy swing of his, uncoil and *zap!* out of the park. Walt stared at the empty stadium, then turned and drove into town, Maryland Avenue, the nicest of the Kirkaby stores, and he stared at that a while and then he thought (moving again now) about what a fool he was, holing up inside his house the way he'd done. He zoomed on over to the Mississippi and took a look before driving to Kingshighway and the great old pile of stone that had once been his grandfather's house. It was kind of a museum now (P.T. used it as a tax dodge) and as he stared at it Walt wondered how his mother could ever have been happy growing up in a place like that, a big cold pile of stone, and as he stared at it he realized something: he wasn't hiding anymore; he was through with all that.

The hiding time was done.

"Son of a bitch," Walt said happily, and all of a sudden his stomach was rumbling like crazy, so he decided to hit Gaslight Square because it was lively and because he didn't figure to run into anyone he knew, so he drove there and parked and right away almost ran into Irv and his wife, so he dropped his car keys on the floor and by the time he'd retrieved them they had walked on by. It would have been just his luck, meeting someone, and then he thought that since he'd lived most of his years in St. Louis he knew one helluva lot of people and, besides, Irv had wanted to be a poet once and Gaslight Square was the artsy section of St. Louis (a contradiction in terms?). Walt got out of the Ford and started walking to the corner, but before he got there a hand grabbed his shoulder and Walt jumped and spun around, frightened until he saw that the hand belonged to Muggsy.

"Gladt'seeya," Muggsy said, doing his best to sound like Phil Silvers. Muggsy's real name was Montgomery Spanier, Jr., so the Muggsy was not only inevitable but an improvement. Montgomery Spanier, Sr., ran the bank in which Montgomery, Jr., toiled.

"Hey-hey," Walt said, and then he said "Mrs. Muggsy" to Amy Spanier, a dark, serious girl who had once written a term paper at Indiana University on Edna St. Vincent Millay, which to Walt, in some crazy way, seemed to sum her up. "So how was Europe? Think it's here to stay? What?"

"Fulla foreigners," Muggsy said.

"I whoopsed all over Italy," Amy said. "I was never so glad to get back in my life." She looked around. "Where's Blake?" she said then.

"You eaten?" Muggsy said. "Let's the four of us *mangez.*"

"Don't you know?" Walt said. "Didn't anyone tell you?"

"Know what? We just got back, Walt. Is everything all right?"

"Yeh, sure, everything's fine. It's just that, well, Blake and me, we more or less, you know, decided to *pffffffft.*" He made the sound and smiled, or tried to, but he only got halfway there because it dawned on him suddenly that he might just go, lose control, right here, on a crowded sidewalk, on a summer night, in the middle of Gaslight Square.

"Well," Muggsy said. Then he said it again: "Well." Then he said, "I'm sure as hell sorry."

Walt nodded.

"I don't think Walt much wants to alk about it," Amy said.

"Oh listen, it doesn't bother me. What bothers me—" and he started doing Peter Lorre—"is I cannot get my hands on the Maltese Falcon. And I must. I must."

Amy smiled and applauded warmly.

"So let's the three of us *mangez,*" Muggsy said. They started to walk. "How the Cards been doing?"

Walt laughed. "Come on, Muggsy, you hate baseball. You've hated baseball all your life, so you don't have to talk about it now because you're afraid I'll get all upset or something. I already said it doesn't bother me and it doesn't. To tell you the truth, I'm a helluva lot more bothered about our foreign policy than about what happened between Blake and me. Oh, I was bothered, I'll admit that. I mean, who the hell would I be kidding if I said it didn't affect me for a little, but hell, I mean, I've had time to think now, to adjust to it, so let's not restrict the conversation to the Cards if you don't mind. I mean—I mean—I'm sorry," Walt said. "I'm sorry."

He took off.

He didn't say goodbye, didn't say anything, just bolted for his Ford and when he got in he made like Fangio until he was back in his garage and then in the house and safe, because a man's home is his castle, bet your ass, and I'm safe in my castle, safe and sound and the shades are down and it's hot but I got air-conditioning and I got a grocer who delivers TV dinners and I am *safe* as long as I stay right where I am, inside, away, alone, and then the phone began to ring and Walt knew right off who it was, who it could only be, and that was Imogene, because he'd given the operator his name and number, so it had to be Imogene calling back and Jesus, what the hell am I gonna say to her, I gotta say the right thing but I don't know what the right thing is and if I say the wrong thing I might just as well kiss it all goodbye, kiss Imogene goodbye and I'm Available and so is she, maybe, and I can't mess up with her again so I can't stay here because if I do I'll pick up the phone and it'll be her and out'll come the wrong thing so I gotta take off, gotta get outta here, outta here now, gotta get out but I can't go out, I'm only safe if I stay here but I can't stay here because I'm not safe if I stay here because the phone keeps on ringing and I gotta say the right thing but I gotta be safe first so I can figure what the right thing is but time is against me, I gotta fly, I'm in a race, a helluva race, and I don't care if I win, my problem's not winning, hell, I don't even know where the finish line is.

• • •

"What's this about New York?" P.T. said. It was midnight, and he was sitting at the dining-room table in his house on Linden Lane, sipping a cup of hot cocoa. He was wearing white pajamas and a great red silk robe.

Walt cleared his throat. "I think you heard me."

"Yeah-yeah-yeah." P.T. pointed to the flowers set in a vase in the middle of the table. "Roses," he said. "I grew 'em."

Walt nodded.

"You said you were thinking of paying a visit to New York. How long a visit?"

"Permanent."

P.T. looked at him. "You'd quit working for me and just go?"

"That's right."

P.T. blew softly on his cocoa. "You've thought about this?"

"Yes."

"I don't get it. You're making decent money, you got challenge, you got responsibilities; what's wrong with a job like that?"

"It's not fulfilling," Walt said.

"Fulfilling?"

Walt nodded.

"That's a word I don't understand," P.T. said.

Walt shrugged.

"I'm already thinking about retiring, y'know. Then you and your brother, you'll have the whole business."

"Arnold can manage alone. Happily."

P.T. stood. "You never seen my garden."

"Course I have."

"Not at night. C'mon." He walked out of the room, Walt right behind. "We're gonna paint the walls of the number-three store," P.T. said.

"Oh?"

"Crazy idea. Arnold just decided tonight. Called me and told me. He's been studying the problem. There's a connection between color and mood, Arnold says. Maybe if the walls are brightened up, people'll buy more. Worth a try, Arnold says. We'll do just the one store to start. Can't cost too much."

"Well," Walt said, "since I'm quitting, that's not my concern any more."

"That Arnold is one smart kid."

Walt opened the front door. "You ought to know."

They moved into the night and as soon as the shadows had them P.T. grabbed Walt by the shoulders and shook him. "Like hell he's smart. When Arnold starts talking about color and mood you think I don't know he's heard it someplace? Why don't you toot your own horn once in a while? Aw nuts." And he let Walt go, stood still a moment, breathing deep. Then he pointed through the darkness. "These here, they're my roses." P.T. gave a laugh. "You probably think I'm batty, huh, growing roses. All of a sudden. At my age."

Walt shook his head.

"So if I made you head of the company, over Arnold—when I quit, I mean—what then? Would you stick around?"

"What the hell kind of question is that?"

"I'm trying to buy you. Yes or no?"

"No."

P.T. shook his head. "Your trouble is you got too much money. I told your mother that. She was making out her will once and I told her not to leave you so much money. It's a terrible thing when a father can't buy his own son. These are my rhododendron." P.T. laughed. "Pretty good word for a thirteenth-century mind, yes?"

"What are we doing? Can't I be excused?"

"Sit down." He pointed to an iron bench circling an oak tree in the middle of the lawn.

"Why?"

"Please."

"*Why?*"

"I want to talk to you."

"What about?"

"You don't make it easy, I'll say that. Please."

Walt sat. "Talk."

"I never showed you my petunias, did I? I mean—"

"What do we have to talk for? We never talk. Why do we have to talk now?"

P.T. sat down. "I guess we've never been what you might call close, have we, Walt? I'm not really what you might have chosen for a father."

"Would you have picked me for a son?"

"No," P.T. muttered. "I guess maybe not."

Walt closed his eyes. "Isn't it funny? That really upsets me." He shook his head.

"Nuts," P.T. said.

"Maybe you better tell me what you want to talk about."

"Yeah-yeah-yeah, maybe I better." He took a deep breath. "I want to talk about the divorce rate in California. It's very high. I read all about it in an article."

"What's this got to do with anything, Father?"

P.T. fiddled with his red silk robe. "Well, like I said, they got this very high divorce rate. And this article, it told about why. There's a lot of reasons but the one I remember is this: You see, lots of people, they got bad marriages, and they figure what they need is a new start in a new place to make it all right again. So they go to California. Except when they get there, nothing's any different. So the marriage dies in California. It didn't get sick there, it just dies there. That's why the divorce rate's so high."

"So?"

"So if you're gonna fuck up, kid, you're gonna fuck up in New York the same as here."

"No, I won't. It'll be different."

"The only difference is that here at least the postman knows your name."

"You're such an expert on New York."

"Who said? I go there every so often, I buy some stuff, I stay in some suite, I eat some French food, and I see the hit plays. I don't care what they are just so they're the hit plays. Then, when I come back here and people ask me what I did I say I saw the hit plays. That's what I know about New York. Zilch."

"Look, it's not that I don't appreciate your interest . . ." Walt started to stand.

P.T. held him. "But it'll be different for you, right? Because it's so fulfilling."

"Maybe."

"Kid, take some time. Go to Europe. Have yourself a little fun. Then, when you're not so nervous anymore, come on back and—"

"No! I've thought about that. Going to Europe would be running away."

"But going to New York isn't."

"Dammit, Father, there's gotta be more than St. Louis, wouldn't you say? There's gotta be more than sitting on your duff letting your old man's business run itself for you. In New York I'll be a director. Maybe I'll make it and maybe I won't but at least I'll have a little satisfaction—"

"*I am P. T. Kirkaby!* You make a list of the ten most successful businessmen in the city of St. Louis and you'll have one bitch of a time leaving my name off."

"No one's arguing."

"Hell. I made millions. I married millions. How's that for fulfilling?"

"That's great. You've had yours. Now I want mine."

"You little fool! God damn dumb little stupid little fool! Don't you know what I wanted to be? I wanted—son of a bitch, I got tears in my eyes."

Walt chose not to look at them.

P.T. sat very still.

Walt realized how interesting the moon was if you just took the time to examine it.

"I wanted to be a soldier," P.T. said then softly. "I wanted ribbons. I wanted my men to love me. I wanted your mother to love me too, and she did, until I whored her out of it. I whored on your mother."

"Yes. I remember once, out by the pool, you hit her. I saw."

"I have many regrets," P.T. said.

"I'm sorry, Father."

"I'm not interested in your sympathy. I have not exposed myself to you in order to gain that."

"Look, we're neither of us enjoying this. Can't we stop?"

P.T. shook his head. "I am a success. Everyone believes that. I believe, as you now know, a little different. Who's right?"

"I don't know. I guess it depends."

"Bullshit, it depends! It doesn't matter. There's only one thing that's important and that's this: I got through it. All this fulfilling stuff. Where'd you get that? Whoever told you it was supposed to be fulfilling? It's not. All you kids think so and don't ask me how I know: I play golf with them on weekends; I drink cocktails with their wives. And they don't want to be housewives either, because that's not fulfilling. Goddammit, it's not supposed to be. You . . . just . . . get . . . through . . . it. That's it. That's all. That's all and it's what I want on my tombstone: P. T. KIRKABY. HE GOT THROUGH IT."

"I'll remember everything you've said."

"Aw, Walt, come on, don't bullshit me."

"I'll try to remember. How's that?"

"It's sad, y' know?"

"What is?"

"You and me. I favored your brother. Arnold was the first. I liked that. Arnold's big and strong. I liked that too." P.T. closed his eyes. "I regret us, Walt."

"You think I don't?"

"I regret everything that's passed between us."

"You mean that hasn't passed."

"Yeah, that's what I mean." P.T. opened his eyes and smiled. Then he stood up. "So now you're off to the big city."

Walt stood alongside his father. "Looks that way."

"Follow me a sec." The two of them paraded across the lawn. P.T. bent down, picked a flower. "Here," he said. "A home-grown peony."

"I'll have it stuffed."

P.T. laughed in the moonlight.

Walt looked up at the big man. "I'm glad you understand and everything."

"Hell, kid, don't worry about me. I'm not gonna waste my time worrying about you. You'll do great."

"You really think so?"

"Course I think so. Aren't you your father's son?"

XVI

After serving almost six months of a two-year hitch, Aaron said goodbye to the military under unusual but "honorable" (the Army's word) circumstances. It was winter and Sergeant Terry saw him off on the train. In spite of everything, Terry saw him off. Somehow that was sad. Even sadder was Terry's gift, a silver flask (engraved: *To A from P: alas*) filled to the lip with good Scotch. Aaron sat in the train, Terry watching through the window (would he never leave?), and that was saddest of all, the ape staring, smiling, close to tears. The train pulled out finally, Terry walking along outside, smiling, mouthing "goodbye" while Aaron smiled back and mouthed "screw" until Terry's short legs proved unequal to the pace and he was gone. Aaron drank from the flask, finished it in less than an hour and (buzzed) tossed it into the snow at the first opportunity.

As the train journeyed east and north the snow deepened and Aaron sat shivering (God, he hated winter), trying to doze. Eventually he hurried from the train during a ten-minute layover, bought a pint of cheap Scotch, smuggled it back on board and within a half hour was sleeping blissfully enough, except once when he awoke shouting from a nightmare in which he was running naked through some jungle while a tribe of monkeys pulled him to pieces.

New York was braced for Christmas, and Aaron toured the streets, his return to civilization almost joyous. Saks Fifth Avenue was making with the carols and on alternate corners spindly Santas endlessly rang their bells. The skaters on the rink in Rockefeller Center were back (they were the same people every year, Equity members most likely, but where, Aaron wondered, did they go in the summertime?), and after he tired of watching them circle and swirl he (because it was a corny thing to do) elevatored up to the Rainbow Room and had a drink. As he sat by the window looking north at Central Park and the rest, at rich Fifth and, beside it, struggling Madison, at the west side, ugly, old (she's dead but she won't lie down), at black Harlem and the golden spire of Riverside Church, as his eyes toured east and north and all around the town, Aaron inhaled and then nodded and then smiled and then his right hand reached out, bony fingers stretched wide for just an instant before suddenly they doubled up and he had it all, the whole shooting match, safe in the palm of his hand.

His mother met him at the Princeton station. It was the last weekend before Christmas vacation and Aaron left the train in the company of twenty nervous-sweet-maybe-I-will-this-weekend young things, seasoned representatives of Radcliffe and Vassar and Barnard, clad in tweed and camel's hair and dainty galoshes with fur around the top, and even before the train had fully stopped they streamed around him, a platoon of potential flesh, to be met by twenty eager Princetonians and Charlotte. Aaron had to laugh. Twenty girls, twenty boys, me and my mother. A symbol maybe?

"What's so funny, Aaron?" after the ritual kiss.

"Just glad to be home, Mother. Just happy to be home."

"I've missed you, Aaron."

"I've missed you too, Mother." More ritual, performed with polish, and it carried them to the car and up the hill to Nassau Street and finally to the first floor of the yellow frame. His sister, Deborah, was waiting for him, along with her dark husband, Dominic, and their child, Christina, now six. (They had been trying to have more children for a long time, but nothing. Somehow that was funny.) Christina was a pretty little girl who loved Aaron, and he, although not ever certain what he felt for her, returned her warmth. Deborah talked a great deal (she was losing her looks already; hardly twenty-four and already lines were cutting in her skin. Aaron smiled) and Christina showed him her tricks, ball-bouncing and jack-grabbing, and she shrieked aloud at Aaron's praise. Charlotte hovered over it all, filling and refilling coffee cups, emptying ashtrays, talking when Deborah stopped for breath, her accent as Southern as ever.

"How come they let you out?" This suddenly from Dominic, his big hands clapping softly.

"I won a raffle."

"I mean it, how come they let you out?"

Aaron indicated his legs.

"You had that when they took you, so all of a sudden they change their minds? Doesn't make sense."

"It doesn't huh? What does?" Aaron stared at the other man. Go on, say it. Say what you're thinking, you wop son of a bitch. With a smile Aaron let a wrist go limp. Then, still smiling, he raised one eyebrow. Say it!

"Well, you're sure lucky," Dominic muttered finally, retreating.

Aaron laughed out loud.

"Food," Charlotte called, and they all trooped in to dinner. They fussed and fluttered around him, the conqueror returned, Charlotte heaping his plate high with sweet potatoes (where did she ever get the idea he liked sweet potatoes?), cutting him slice after slice of turkey breast (he preferred dark meat), and Deborah lied about how well Dominic was doing and Dominic bolted his food in rude silence and little Christina talked with her mouth full while Charlotte gave Aaron more sweet potatoes, so all in all it was a typical evening with the family, unbearable, but Aaron bore it well enough because he knew that soon it would all be a part of his past, soon he would be sipping Drambuie in the Oak Room of the Plaza, discoursing brilliantly on everything, while these creatures (were they people?) would rapidly become little more than figments of his exquisite imagination. So Aaron bore them well enough, and, though they were not aware, he studied them each, fixed them, mentally marked their boundaries. They were saying hello; he was saying goodbye.

Besides, he had his book to think about.

Books, actually, for he had two in mind (both novels; short stories bored him; he was a big boy now) and was undecided which to conquer first. The one was a comic novel, savage, to be sure, biting and pertinent, a modern-day retelling of *Le Cid* by Corneille, in which the hero was an account executive in an advertising agency, the heroine a gym teacher at Brearley, the enemy J. Walter Thompson, who was trying to steal the Buick account. Aaron was confident that *Commentary* and the *Partisan Review* would justly hail him and that Mary McCarthy, Dwight MacDonald and Edmund Wilson (three little maids from school) would outdo each other in affixing superlatives alongside his name.

But would it sell?

A little highbrow acclaim was warming to the soul, but a little Harris tweed was warming to the body, and you couldn't invade Brooks Brothers with clippings from the *Transatlantic Review*. Aaron wanted the clippings, sure, but he had been poor for a long time.

And *Autumn Wells*, he knew, would make him rich.

Autumn Wells was a romance (women buy books) that Aaron had constructed during his last days in the Army, cribbed equally from *Rebecca*, *The Great Gatsby* and *Catcher in the Rye*. A slight but winning narrative, it concerned Autumn Wells (Aaron was genuinely proud of the name, easily the best since Thackeray's Becky), a willowy creature, eerie, vague, troubled, passionate on occasion, and possessed of an altogether breath-catching beauty.

Undecided, torn between the twin clichés of wealth and fame, Aaron wandered the streets of Princeton the next few days, making up his mind. It was remarkable how the place had changed. The Army had deprived him of but six months, and yet the difference. His sexual blossoming was the key. Suddenly he knew such things. The man who ran the interior-decorating place—he was one. And the young druggist with the bad smile who was always so friendly—he was another. And the man who ran the Browse-Around, his mother's own employer—how could Aaron not have guessed before? And the students. Those seemingly proper young men who bunched together in corners of the music room, who whispered and laughed softly while he had waited on them at the Nassau Food Shoppe, he knew about them now.

And, as he walked by them on the chill streets, Aaron realized that they knew about him too. A quick glance, a stare held too long, and suddenly everything was clear. He knew about them; they knew about him. Everybody relax, we've all got blackmail on each other. Once or twice he almost tried to strike up an acquaintance (where would you go? Someplace), for they were tempting, these young men; the standard of male beauty in Princeton is surpassingly high. But he bested the temptation and then they were gone, off for the Christmas holidays. Aaron relaxed and set to work.

On *Autumn Wells*. It was the right choice; no question. The important work would come later, when the belly was properly full. Aaron arose each morning at seven, drank coffee for an hour, showered and cleaned his nails and then, with Charlotte finally gone to the Browse-Around, set to work. He wrote directly on the typewriter (if he had genuinely cared, he would have caressed a pencil during the first draft), demanding of himself a minimum of five hundred words a day (he counted them precisely), but the work went so simply that most times he doubled the minimum. The plot he kept purposely simple. The narrator, a prep-school teacher (the first chapters took place at prep school), was a young man, Willis Mumford, ugly but kind, an extraordinarily gifted painter who, one spring, took his paints and went off by himself to a desolate section of New England. There, by a swift river, he camped and painted, alone and away (he thought) from civilization. But one morning as he followed the river he saw, set deep in the woods, a great bleak castle of a house, seemingly deserted. That day he met Autumn, or saw her rather, briefly, standing in a clearing, watching him paint. When he realized her presence he started to wave but was unable to move, so did her beauty petrify him (Aaron chuckled), and when he was finally able to shout

"Wait!" she was gone. But the next day she was back, closer to him, and finally the day after that they met. Her eyes danced and his breath came hard, but he asked could he paint her and when she assented he did, falling in love with her as the portrait grew. She lived in the castle-house with her father, a cruel man, given to flights of sadism, a hunter who chose only to wound, never to kill (Willis remembered a bird he had seen, crippled and dying, crying out pitifully in lingering pain), and she made Willis promise that never, under any circumstances, would he come to her dwelling place. But even as he promised, Willis doubted his capacity to keep the pledge, for the picture was coming to completion and so was his love. And she loved him too! He knew that. For suddenly, late one perfect day, they kissed and touched, lying together by the rushing stream, and that night, when Willis was close to sleep, she returned to him, tumbling into his arms, and Willis, as the strange wonderful creature quivered beneath him, hesitated a moment before . . . (Aaron dragged on his cigarette. Should they go all the way or not? Would *McCall's* serialize it if they went all the way? Why not? Why not? What the hell!) . . . before sating his desires . . .

When he awoke the next morning Autumn was gone, and though he waited the entire day, Willis waited in vain. So that night, promise or no promise, his heart pounding with love (Aaron had to laugh), Willis crept through the dark woods toward the great house. It was dark, bleak, somehow evil, and Willis circled it once, skirting from shadow to shadow, before finally planting himself by the wooden front door. It was open and Willis shouted "Hello . . . ? Hello . . . ?" but there was no reply. He pushed the door open full and stepped into the gigantic entrance hall. Beyond lay a dark sprawling room, lighted only by the flames from the fireplace. "Hello . . . ?" Willis said again, and though there was still no reply, he knew, as he stood in the center of the room, that he was not alone. And suddenly there—there!—framed now in the red light of the fire stood Autumn's father, a giant of a man with thick brutal arms and the face of a gorilla. From the waist up he wore nothing; from the waist down he was clad totally in leather (a little something for the perverts), black leather boots and tight black leather riding pants. From somewhere above them came a scream, and Willis turned, trying to place it, and when he turned back, the half-naked giant had not moved. Except that now there was a gun in his hand, and soon the lovers were thrown together in a room deep in the bowels of the castle where terrible things had once taken place. Willis examined the strange machines set up in various corners, and when he came across a machine with blood still dripping from it he realized the father was a madman, that they had to get out, somehow, he and his beloved Autumn, that or die.

Aaron had a ball with the rest of the book. He threw in a little torture, Autumn naked and writhing, her glorious body glistening, her face pale with pain (they'll thumb the hell out of this page at Brentano's), and following the torture came an escape-chase-capture scene, then another escape, then a revelation from Autumn's bruised red lips that the giant was her husband (It's really good, Aaron knew. It is. It is!), then a long love scene, graphic: "Willis moaned as he ran his fingers across her body, such was his pleasure, the presence of death serving only to increase his passion . . ." but sensitively done: no four-letter words, lots of metaphors, and the climax ending with three dots . . . and then, finally, the confrontation, high on the roof of the house, with Willis battling the giant, almost losing but somehow summoning the strength of the desperate lover, vanquishing the enemy, grabbing the prize while the villain groaned, and fleeing into the beauty of the woods. As they ran, Willis and Autumn, they turned one last time, and Autumn screamed to see the great bleak house on fire, flames dancing across the roof where, totally mad now, her husband stood, shaking a fist at the heavens until the fire had him and then he ran, a screaming torch, to the edge of the roof and off, falling in flames to his death. Willis held his trembling Autumn, held her with all his might, all his love, and when the sun came they walked off hand in hand into the dawn . . .

"Aaron Fire. To see Mr. Boardman."

The secretary gave him a smile. "Certainly. You have an appointment, Mr. Fire?"

"For ten-thirty," Aaron said. He showed her his watch. "I'm nothing if not prompt."

She smiled again. "Please be seated just a moment," and she started fiddling with the intercom. Aaron stayed by her desk, looking around. He had always envisioned a publishing house as being a small brownstone in an old part of town, with frayed rugs on the floors and walls stuffed with books, with frayed secretaries and pipe-smoking, tweed-clad editors padding softly around chatting softly about Sartre. Kingsway Press, where he stood, looked like a Hollywood version of an advertising agency. Located on the nineteenth and twentieth floors of a new glass-and-white-brick (what else?) building on Madison Avenue in the 40s, it was sterile enough to double as a hospital. The receptionist's desk was Danish modern, the lighting indirect, the rug one of those bloodless pale colors adored only by designers, the twin waiting sofas clean, new, arm-less, almost legless, practically backless, defiantly uncomfortable—hostile modern.

And not a book in sight.

"Mr. Fire?"

"Yes." She was smiling again. What was so funny?

"There seems to have been a mix-up. Mr. Boardman hasn't—"

"Look. I'm from *Time*. We're doing a piece and—"

"Hasn't got you listed for an appointment."

"I'm going to kill my secretary."

"I'm terribly sorry, Mr. Fire."

"She called yesterday at twelve-thirty and somebody over here veri-fied the appointment for today."

"Perhaps Mr. Boardman's secretary was on her lunch hour and some-body else took the call."

"Possibly," Aaron allowed.

"You said you're from *Time*?"

"Unless they've just fired me."

"Excuse me one moment."

Aaron watched as she disappeared down the carpeted corridor. Calmly he lit a cigarette, setting it carefully in a corner of his mouth, in-haling deeply. He had never met Dave Boardman, but he knew he was about to. Boardman liked being interviewed; Aaron had read the quotes. Whenever anything newsworthy happened in the publishing business (rarely) Bennett Cerf was the first one called. If Cerf was out of town, then it was Boardman.

"Mr. Boardman can see you," the receptionist said, coming back down the hall.

"Goody," Aaron said, and he followed her along the carpet, a turn to the right, one to the left, through a door, another door, and then there he was, alone with Boardman.

At the age of forty-two, Dave Boardman had been chief editor of Kingsway Press for more than a decade and, in a field where competency was equated to brilliance, had the reputation of being a genius, which meant he was probably somewhat better than fair. He was editor for three novelists who had won Pulitzer Prizes, one of whom had a decent shot at eventually taking a Nobel when America's turn came, plus half a dozen others, three of them ladies who wrote nothing but best-sellers. And if Kingsway resembled an ad agency, Dave Boardman continued the image. His suit was dark and conservative, his tie striped and narrow, his shirt white with a button-down collar. I'll bet you're wearing loafers, Aaron thought, studying the face until he could place it. He had seen it thousands of times. It was the face of the white-jacketed television pitch-man recommending a laxative. "Doctor's reports prove that Limpo will positively loosen your stool in twenty-four hours or . . ." The Trust-worthy Face.

"Where's your pipe?" Aaron said.

"Pardon?"

"All editors smoke pipes, didn't you know that? Union regulations."

Boardman laughed. It was a good laugh. Rich. Sincere. "I thought I knew most of the boys from *Time.* You must be new over there."

Aaron smiled.

"You are from *Time.*"

Aaron laughed.

"The receptionist said—"

"I lied."

"Oh my God, don't tell me. You're a writer."

Aaron bowed.

"For crissake, why the subterfuge?"

"If I'd called for an appointment, would you have seen me?"

"No."

"Next question," Aaron said.

Boardman smiled and sat straight, examining Aaron. "How'd you know it'd work?"

"Vanity. I researched you. You like getting your name in the papers. You're vain."

"So I am. So I am. Your name is . . . ?"

"Aaron Fire."

"Goodbye, Mr. Fire."

"Goodbye." Aaron stood, grabbed his briefcase, started for the door. "One thing, though." He stopped. "How do you know my book isn't good?"

"That's a risk I'm taking."

Aaron nodded. "You," he said, "are a stupid son of a bitch," and he was out the door.

"Fire!"

Aaron let him yell it again—"*Fire*"—before he re-entered the office. "You called?"

Boardman was up, mad, but you couldn't tell it from his face. The body was angry but the face was serene, trustworthy. "You rude little bastard, who the hell do you think you are?" Boardman paced back and forth, back and forth.

Aaron moved back to the chair and sat down.

"How old are you, Fire?"

"Twenty-two."

"Twenty-two," Boardman grunted, continuing to pace. From somewhere a golf ball appeared and he tossed it from hand to hand as he moved. "That's about how long I've been in this business. Twenty-two years of writers." *Whap!* He threw the golf ball against the wall, caught it without breaking stride. "I don't like writers, Fire. I hate writers. Not because I'm jealous. Not because of their egos. Plumbers have egos." *Whap!* "I hate them because they are so childish." *Whap!* "I understand you, Fire. You fake your way in here and then when you're about to get tossed out on your ass you try a little shock treatment. Hoping to intrigue me."

"Something like that."

"I see through it. It's so childish I see the whole thing." *Whap!* "But—" *Whap! Whap!* "and this is what really irritates me—" *Whap!* "I am intrigued. I admit it. You have intrigued me, Fire."

"You're very good with that golf ball."

"Years of practice. What's your book about?"

Aaron was ready for that one. "The possibility of romance in a mechanized world."

Whap! "Bullshit. Tell me how great it is."

Great, no. There was a time, when he'd just started, when Aaron considered the book pap. But no more. It had expanded somehow in the writing, taken on a polish, a blinding sheen. If it was shallow, then it was superbly shallow. It was a clean, honest piece of work and that honesty gave it its stature. "*War and Peace* it ain't."

"Modest of you."

"I'll tell you this, though, buddy: it's pretty goddam good."

"You got an agent, Fire?"

"Who needs an agent? I'm seeing you, aren't I?"

Whap! "Title?"

"Name of the heroine. *Autumn Wells.*"

"Nice."

"I think so."

Boardman sat down at his desk, bouncing the golf ball across the glass top. "Why did you have to pick me?"

"I checked around. You're supposed to be moderately literate."

Boardman laughed. "Were you born or did you spring full grown?

You are a thorny little bastard." He dropped the golf ball into his top desk drawer. "All right, all right, give me the masterpiece."

Aaron opened his briefcase.

"Leave your number with my secretary. I'll let you know when I've read it."

Aaron closed his briefcase. "Monday," he said.

"What Monday?"

"Today's Wednesday. You can have over the weekend. Then on Monday *I'll* call *you.*"

"You have a reasonable amount of self-confidence, haven't you, Fire?"

"It's all front. Secretly I'm trembling."

"God, I hate writers," Boardman said. He held out his hand for the manuscript. "O.K. Monday."

Aaron handed it over. "You have a treat in store."

"Goodbye, Fire."

"David." Aaron stood up to go.

Boardman watched him. "Fire?"

"Sir?"

"You as talented as you think you are?"

Aaron had to smile. "I better be," he said.

"Aaron?"

"Yes, Mother."

"What are you doing?"

"Packing."

"Packing?"

"Yes, Mother."

She moved into his room and sat down on the bed, watching him. It was late afternoon but the April sun was hot. "You're going away," Charlotte said and her hands wandered a while before finally lighting on her long white hair.

Aaron nodded.

"But why?"

"Why?" Aaron whirled. Because I don't need you anymore. Because I loathe it here. Because . . . "It's best I go." She looked so pathetic, so old, fragile. Be nice.

"I don't understand."

"Well, I saw this editor today. Boardman's his name. He's reading my book. Monday we'll start conferences on rewrites. I'll have to be in New York all the time anyway, so it's best I go live there. Easiest all around."

She watched as he carried a handful of books, gently dusting them before laying them into an enormous cardboard box. There are several boxes in the room, most of them full. "All those books," Charlotte said.

"I rented a room before I came home. Right after I left this Boardman. It's not much of a room. But then I won't be there very long."

"It's probably best you go."

"Yes."

"Oh," Charlotte said, and the sound made Aaron turn uneasily. He gave her a quick smile. "Oh" again. "I'm really sorry."

Aaron busied himself with his books.

Charlotte rocked on the bed. "Both my babies."

"Now, Mother."

"Next you'll be getting married."

"I sure hope so."

"I'll miss you, Aaron."

"I'll miss you too, Mother."

"Oh," Charlotte said again, and again Aaron's features formed the quick smile. "Oh, it's sad, it's just sad."

"Yes." Aaron nodded. "I guess it is."

He packed slowly, slower than he had to, finishing the following day, Thursday. Friday morning he dragged the big boxes of books down the front steps of the yellow house and into the family car. It was hard work for him and soon his legs were aching, but he kept at it until he was done. Aside from the books he had really little to take. A few clothes, odds and ends, that was all. Friday afternoon he drove into the city. He had taken a furnished room in the West 40s, close by the Times Square area, and although it was neither particularly big nor particularly clean, he liked it; it would give him something to remember. A group of small boys watched him drag his boxes into the rooming house and up the one flight of hard stairs to his cubicle, and although at first he refused their offers to assist, he eventually succumbed, moving empty-handed alongside them as they tugged mightily at the great boxes, straining their tiny bodies. Ants. Done, Aaron tipped them, locked the door to his room and drove back to Princeton with the car. Charlotte was waiting, and they had a farewell dinner, complete with (domestic) champagne. Charlotte attempted gaiety, which might have touched him, except that she had said her goodbyes so often in the preceding forty-eight hours that Aaron had had it with them. And her, too. After dinner (sweet potatoes again!) she drove him to the train, where he muttered goodbye, vaguely angry (why wasn't she crying?) as he kissed her cheek. He boarded the train but it wouldn't start and Charlotte stood outside waving and waving *(to A. from P.: alas)* and Aaron attempted ignoring her, but he did not feel cruel then, so he waved back at her until (Thank God, thank God) the train's movement mercifully curtained the scene.

He had intended to spend the night wandering, but when he reached Penn Station his legs ached slightly and his head too, so he took the subway up one stop to Times Square and walked to his room. It was not a pleasant place and the bed was lumpy, but he slept fourteen hours. Saturday night he slept for ten; Sunday the same.

The waking hours he spent apartment hunting.

"I'll need a terrace," Aaron said. "And of course a view of the river."

"View," the renting agent said, and he wrote the word on a three-by-five card.

Aaron lit a cigarette. "I'm getting a bit desperate, if you want to know the truth. I spent the morning looking at East End, but it's so *nouveau*."

"My feeling exactly."

"And Fifth. Well, Fifth is *passé*."

The renting agent nodded. "I'm sure you'll like Sutton Place, Mr. Fire."

"I hope so. I was terribly disappointed in Beekman. Beekman and I, I don't know, we just didn't hit it off, somehow. We were not—how shall I say?—sympathetic. One has to feel sympathy with one's surroundings."

"I understand. May I tell you that many of our prospective tenants are moving from Beekman Place *to* us. Beekman Place is just not warm."

I can outphony you, buddy, any day of the week. "Like a cat. Too independent."

"Precisely, Mr. Fire." He stood. "Now you understand this building will not be ready to receive tenants for two months yet."

"That dovetails perfectly."

"We have a beautiful apartment on the seventeenth floor. Of course, it is not beautiful now. Nothing has been done to it. But I assure you it will be a showplace."

"Excellent," Aaron said.

"Follow me, please," and they went down the hall to the elevator. "The lobby will have a special quality all its own. Beautiful free-form sculpture. Soft music playing constantly."

I may vomit. "Sounds very tasteful."

"We pride ourselves on our taste, Mr. Fire. After you," and they entered the elevator. "Twenty-four-hour doorman service. Twenty-four-hour elevator-man service. The newest in automatic elevators."

"Sounds like a marvelous job," Aaron said. "Running an automatic elevator."

"That's very funny, Mr. Fire. After you. This way. Here. See. Apartment seventeen F. F as in Fire."

"Kismet." Aaron waited while the door was opened.

"After you. Foyer. Large, spacious. Dining area, nine by nine."

"I have a seven-by-seven dining table," Aaron said.

"Kismet."

Aaron moved out to the terrace. Below, the East River; above, the sun. Aaron closed his eyes. I want it. I want it.

"You're all right, Mr. Fire?"

Aaron smiled. "Fine. I'll need a few days to think, but this seems like what I've been looking for."

"Let me show you the rest."

"In time."

"Of course, Mr. Fire."

"The rent?"

"Just six hundred dollars a month."

"Reasonable," Aaron said. "Cheap at half the price."

"You recognize value."

"I try to. It's my business to notice things."

"Your business?"

"I'm Aaron Fire, the writer."

"Ah, yes."

"You've heard of me, then?"

"I pride myself on being a literate man. Who hasn't heard of you?"

"I cannot answer that question," Aaron said. Were those tears? Behind his eyes? "Modesty forbids."

Were those tears?

Monday morning Aaron woke with a headache. He lay in bed awhile, pressing his fingertips against his eyes, then grabbed a towel and hurried down the corridor to the communal bathroom, where he shaved carefully and showered, letting the water pound against his neck, lessening the tension. There was tension, no question about it, and he mocked himself for allowing it to grab him, but that did not loosen its hold.

At half past nine he called Kingsway and asked for Boardman, who was not in. No one was in, and he cursed his eagerness, for he knew better. Returning to his room, he chain-smoked for an hour, counting the cigarettes, fourteen. The room was hot, the air thick with smoke, but

Aaron lay flat on the bed, staring at the ceiling, coughing, his headache less vague than before. At precisely ten-thirty he gave himself permission to place the call again, and this time he got Boardman.

"Well, am I a genius? Be candid."

"Fire, I cannot cope with your ego in the morning. I'm a night person myself, so please go easy."

"David, I'm filled with compassion."

"If I tell you you're talented will you get off my back?"

"Say it again. I'd like a little more feeling."

"Come on up here and we'll talk."

"I'm hungry," Aaron said.

"What's that mean?"

"Buy me lunch."

Boardman sighed. "I honestly wish I could say I was busy but I'm not."

"I accept. I'll meet you at twelve."

"Any preferences?"

"Just so it's expensive," Aaron said.

Adela's was expensive. Aaron arrived at a few minutes before twelve and waited across the street out of sight. Boardman arrived promptly and went in. Aaron lit a cigarette. When he had smoked it, he lit another, smiling all the while. After fifteen minutes he decided he had kept Boardman enough, so he crossed the street and mentioned Boardman's name to the headwaiter. Adela's was a long restaurant, very narrow, with red drapes lining the walls and elegant candles, one on each table, providing light. Boardman was seated at a corner table in the rear drinking a Bloody Mary.

"I'll have one of those too," Aaron said, sliding in alongside.

Boardman signaled for a waiter.

"Talk about the book," Aaron said when the waiter had gone.

"I couldn't possibly. It's too early."

"Too early?"

Boardman held up one finger for silence. "Fire, I want to talk seriously to you for just a moment. Pay attention. What I'm about to tell you is valuable advice. So heed." He took a sip of his drink. "I'm a very successful man, Fire. Very successful. My only equals: men who are sons of publishers or men who married the daughters of publishers. I'm the top, Fire, the *crème de la crème*. And do you know why?"

"I stand a pretty good chance of finding out."

"Yes. Now you probably think I'm where I am because of my mighty brain. But you're wrong. I am not brilliant. I'm not even particularly smart. I'm not much of an idea man. I lack the social graces. All my writers are better read than I. And yet, in spite of all this, in spite of all this, in spite of my admitted mediocrity, if I chose to leave Kingsway every publishing house in town would court me, woo me, pursue me. Now, what is my secret? Why?"

"Tell me; tell me."

Boardman smiled. "I lunch superbly; that's why."

Aaron started laughing.

Again, Boardman held up a finger for silence. "I speak the truth, Fire. You are in the presence of royalty; the king of lunchers sits beside you. Notice." He waggled a finger.

A waiter appeared.

Boardman glanced down at his empty glass.

"Right away, Mr. Boardman," and he vanished.

"Did you note the smoothness of that entire operation? At the groaning board, I am a genius."

"Sire," Aaron said.

"There are, of course, certain rules for Lunching—I speak with a capital L—rules which I discovered and refined. Choice of restaurant is crucial. For example, if I am to Lunch with a virile outdoors-steak-and-potatoes writer, I always select a dainty restaurant. Make them a trifle ill at ease, follow? With a hungry yearling like yourself, I like to come here to Adela's. It's ridiculously expensive, but, more than that, the clientele is handsome. Notice the people. They all look substantial. They belong to the world you haven't made but yearn for. Of course—and this should go no further—all the people here, and I know most of them, are broke, living beyond their incomes and surviving only through the graces of God and their company's Diners' Club card. The next rule—"

"Can I have another drink?"

"That's the next rule. Always get your companion loaded." Another waggle of the finger and Aaron's order was on its way. "Not only can you have another drink, you will have a third. And wine with the meal. Which leads to rule number three: Never discuss business until dessert. Empires have fallen for ignoring that rule, Fire. The future of our country rests on that rule. Never discuss business until dessert. I speak only the truth. Lunch is what makes the world go round. You asked me to talk about your book. If I started talking business before the appetizer, I would be a ruined man. In six months, out of a job. In a year, alcoholic; next, skid row; finally, the river. So let's forget your masterpiece, Fire, at least till pastrytime. Tell me about yourself. Have you always been a monster or did you work at it? Relax, Fire; smile. You're at Lunch. God protects Lunchers. Heaven is nothing but one long Lunch. So drink to it, man; honor it. Raise that glass. To Lunch."

"Lunch!"

It was a splendid meal. Aaron chose artichoke vinaigrette for an appetizer, dissecting it with care, leaf by tiny leaf, and when they were gone he deftly separated the heart and swallowed it quickly with the remainder of the sauce. Adela's was full now and three tables away he saw a young film actor with a squat gray woman, his agent probably, and across the narrow room sat another familiar face, a financier or an ex-general, something like that; Aaron couldn't quite place it, but the face had once beamed out at him from the cover of *Time*. Aaron smiled to himself. I belong here. Here and all the other places like it. Home is where the heart is. My heart is here.

Boardman suggested the wine and Aaron went along with the choice—a strong red burgundy. For his main course Aaron took the cold roast beef; a great rare slab of it, and a delicate green salad. The wine warmed his throat; the salad cooled his tongue. Probably it was silly taking an apartment on Sutton, tying up all that money when what he wanted really was to travel, Italy, Spain, the civilized sections of the Orient. Aaron rolled the red wine around his tongue. Yes. Perhaps even South America, the less humid parts anyhow. Or was that a waste, traveling through South America? The people were notoriously backward and what if you drank the water? What disease? Malaria? No, that came from mosquitoes. To hell with South America. Just to hell with it, he decided.

For dessert Aaron chose profiterole. He had always been partial to chocolate, gorging on it even when he ran the gauntlet of adolescence, and the sauce on the profiterole was perfect, spectacularly rich. Aaron toyed with it, dipping the edge of his spoon into it, making it last as long as he could while Boardman thumbed through the manuscript of *Autumn Wells*. Boardman was smiling, talking softly, and it was hard to listen to him over the noise of the other diners. Aaron closed one eye and sighted down the long row of tables. The candles danced for him. Boardman was turning the pages rapidly now, and Aaron glanced admiringly at the neatly typed paper. He was a wonderful typist, and this was his original copy of the book, clean and new. But it was silly of Boardman to bring it along, to bring it here. You couldn't discuss rewrites in the rear of a restaurant, not after you've had drinks and good wine and a full meal. It was silly. You couldn't think under those conditions. Never. He should have left it in his office. You could talk there. Have coffee sent in and really talk. That was the way to do it. That was the way—

Aaron felt light.

"So here we are at the torture scene. Now Jesus, Fire, it's the twentieth century. A torture scene in the basement of a castle with a naked maiden? And does the villain have to drool? You call it 'flecks of spittle' and that's pretty, I suppose, but drool's drool, Fire, come on."

"You're giving it back to me?"

"What? I'm sorry, I didn't hear?"

"You're giving it back to me? The book?"

Boardman looked at him.

"You're not going to publish it?"

"That's right. Haven't you been listening? I'm just trying to explain why. Now I don't want to pick on this poor torture scene, but it's indicative of what's wrong with the book. It lacks credulity. You're writing down all the way through it. The writing's good enough, it's fine, but did you mean this stuff? Now here—"

"You've got to. Publish the book."

Boardman shook his head.

"See, you've got to publish it. I wrote it. I wrote it and you've got to publish it, don't you see?"

"You all right, Fire?"

"Sure, sure, I'm fine, it's just that I'm trying to explain to you why you've got to publish it because I wrote it, you understand."

"Fire—"

"I'll change it. Any way you like. I'll change it all around. I'm a good writer. I'm talented like you said, so I'll just change it."

"I wouldn't be blowing you to lunch if I didn't think you had something, Fire, but—"

"You just tell me what you want me to change. I'll do ten pages a day. I'll do the whole book over. Now you tell me." He pulled at Boardman's coat sleeve. "I'm listening now, so you tell me. I'll remember everything you say." Boardman was trying to get his sleeve free and Aaron wanted to hold it but he was still too light. Boardman moved away and Aaron slid after him.

"For chrissakes, Fire, cut it out."

"Please."

"Fire—"

"Please." Aaron had his sleeve again and now there was strength in his fingers. Not full, not yet, but it was coming. "Please."

"I don't want to call a waiter, so—"

"Please. Please."

"Let go before—"

"Please."

"For the last time—"

"Please. Please! PLEASE! YOU SON OF A BITCH, I SAID PLEASE! DIDN'T YOU HEAR ME? DIDN'T YOU HEAR ME? I said PLEASE!" And then he was up, Aaron on the move, running down the long, long room, running by the candles that had danced for him, by the movie actor and the agent and the financier-general, away from all the people, all the pretty people, the pretty sweet people, running, running until at last he was free and clear and out on the street and alone.

Without his manuscript.

Aaron stopped on the sidewalk. His precious manuscript. Beautiful Autumn. In there. With Boardman. Who'd tear it up. Flush it away someplace. No. Steal it. That's what he'd do. Steal it and claim it was his own. *Autumn Wells*, a novel by David Boardman.

Aaron spun, backtracked to Adela's door, threw it open. The headwaiter hurried quickly to meet him, but Aaron brushed by, took a step, only the headwaiter moved around him, confronting him again.

"Something?" the headwaiter said.

Aaron stood at one end of the restaurant, staring down the candle rows to Boardman, who sat where he was, drinking coffee. Aaron took a long step toward him, the headwaiter still at his side, but even as he moved Aaron realized his error.

They were looking at him.

All of them, all the pretty people, they were staring, tittering behind their fine linen napkins, pointing at him with their fine silver forks. Whispers in the room. The long aisle was a cage in a zoo. He was in the cage, he, Aaron Fire, was in a cage and they were all watching the funny animal as it limped along.

Aaron could feel his face flame. He blinked, tried to smile. "Just a joke," he muttered as best he could. "Just a little joke between Dave and me." But they wouldn't stop looking at him. They wouldn't stop whispering. Pointing at the funny limping animal. No pity. None. But plenty of soft laughter. The sound drummed. Aaron took another step, the headwaiter escorting him still, joined now by another flunky, a short man, but broad, with a face that was not kind. Aaron tried to ignore them, fumbling in his shirt pocket for his cigarettes, but his wet hands could not grasp securely and as the pack slipped a wave of laughter grew, building as the pack hit the floor, spilling cigarettes across the red rug. Never had he heard such laughter, never before. *Never again will you laugh at me, never again will you be afforded the chance of laughing at me. I promise you. I promise you all.* At the end of the room Boardman waited, half smiling, half not. Boardman gestured and suddenly Aaron's escorts paused, allowing him to travel the final steps alone, closer to Boardman, ten feet, eight feet, five.

Aaron smiled at the editor and Boardman smiled back, but Aaron saw the panic in his eyes. *And you're right, friend David. Because if I never do another thing in my great life, I am going to repay you. For every slight, every indignity, you will writhe and scream and pray for my forgiveness.*

"I forgot the manuscript."

"Oh, so you did. Here."

"Thanks." *Please, Aaron, dear God, Aaron, no more, Aaron, on my broken knees I beg, no more, Aaron, great Aaron, mighty Aaron, Aaron Almighty Aar—*

Aaron tripped.

As he was turning away from the table, the manuscript tight in his hands, he tripped, falling sharply, the pages spilling away from him. Boardman hurried down to help, but Aaron pushed him away—"I'll get you for this, you wait, you see"—and he scrambled solo after the pretty pages while the laughter enveloped him again but now he had nothing left, no reservoir of revenge, so he could only grab and pluck the pages from the red rug to his pale hands and then push himself up again, the beautiful book a ball of paper now, beautiful no more. Aaron lurched to his feet and, clutching the ball tight against his stomach, staggered between the candles, trying not to hear what was going on around him.

Aaron screamed.

The laughter died.

But somebody started hiccuping. It accompanied his final plunge down the long room, the hiccuping, and he finally groped for freedom, as he shoved his shoulder against the final door, as the sunlight hit him, it was the last thing he heard, the ultimate unerasable sound.

A hiccup.

Part IV

XVII

Early one evening, a month after the start of their confusion, Jenny sat in her apartment waiting for the buzzer to sound. She was nervous and excited and she finished combing her hair, looked at herself, shook her head, mussed her hair with both hands, then started to comb it all over again. She had never, not once in all her life, really liked her hair. Jenny sighed, glancing across the bed to the alarm clock. It was five after six, which meant that Charley was five minutes later than usual, which in turn meant that he probably suspected someone was following him. Whenever they finished work at Kingsway, Jenny always came straight to her apartment, but Charley always walked, for half an hour, window shopping until he was sure no one was following him, until he felt it was reasonable to taxi to her place. "Reasonable" was Charley's word; he was terribly suspicious, except that he claimed he wasn't, so sometimes she would imitate how she imagined he must look on his postwork walk: a desperately innocent figure slinking along Madison Avenue with his hat pulled over his eyes. Charley would laugh then and kiss her for her mimicry, but he still insisted on walking for thirty minutes, rain or shine. He loved for her to imitate him, and she enjoyed acting him; it was one of their best jokes, except that Jenny didn't think it was all that funny. She begrudged him his half-hour walk. Because he usually left her by nine, always by ten, and she could never quite learn to enjoy those moments after his departure when she was alone. Suddenly. Again.

The buzzer sounded.

Jenny dashed across the room, buzzed back. She straightened her skirt, said "to hell with you" to her hair, grabbed the package and opened the front door as far as the chain lock would permit. She stood pressed against the door till she heard footsteps. Then she said, "Is that you, X-9?"

"O.K., O.K.," Charley whispered. "Open up."

"What's the password?"

"You really think you're funny, don't you?"

443

"I think I'm adorable."

"That makes two of us."

"That's the password," Jenny said, and she unlocked the door and held out the package and said, "Surprise."

Charley looked at the package. It was small and rectangular and wrapped in white paper with a red bow. He took it in his hand and closed the door and kissed her. "Thank you." He hung his coat over a chair and loosened his tie.

Jenny stepped away from him. "You don't know what it's for, do you?"

"No."

"I'm really hurt." She turned away.

"You're a rotten actress."

"I'm not a rotten actress!" Jenny whirled on him. "It so happens I'm hurt and the reason I'm hurt is that today is the first month anniversary of our confusion and I got you a present and you forgot the whole thing." She began to pace. "And I'm sick that this means nothing to you. I'm tired of being hurt by you. I'm tired of being ignored and I'm tired of being used and hurt and forgotten and I think you might just as well turn around and leave right now because this is not going to be one of our more pleasant evenings and—"

Charley started after her, saying, "Jenny. Jenny, listen. Please listen—"

Jenny stopped and laughed and kissed him on the mouth. "Call me a rotten actress, will you?"

Charley looked at her.

"Had you going, didn't I? Just remember something: I have acted on the Broadway stage." She gestured dramatically. "Of course, it was just understudy rehearsal and the theater was empty. But technically, I acted *on* the *stage*. My feet rested on the floor. So there, unbeliever."

Charley took her, lifted her, held her in the air. "If you think this is easy, you're crazy."

"I know. I'm a moose. You'll break your back."

"Happy anniversary, Moose." He kissed her, put her down.

"Do you know something? I feel brazen around you and I love it! I feel like the most brazen—ordinarily I'm so timid I make me sick. Sometimes—sometimes I wake up and I think, don't be timid today, Jenny, old kid. Let the world have it right between the eyes today, Jenny, old kid. But then, when I get outside I think, well, maybe I'll let the world have it right between the eyes tomorrow instead. Aren't you even going to open your present?"

Charley began unwrapping the package.

"Wait. Don't you want to give me your present first?"

"Huh?"

"Your anniversary present to me."

"I didn't get—"

"I know what I want. You can still give it to me. Right now. Wouldn't you like that?"

"Yes. What is it?"

"Spend the night."

Charley looked at her.

"Just this once."

"I can't. You know that."

"Please."

"Impossible."

"Sometimes you're such a churl. Isn't that a great word? I just love it. I work in a publishing house. That's how come I have this fantastic vocabulary. Aren't you going to open your present?"

"You told me to wait."

"Since when do you do what I tell you? I just told you to spend the night and you wouldn't."

"Minx." He took off the red bow and shook the package. "Should I be able to guess?"

"I hope not. Charley? Before you see, I've got to explain, because it wasn't easy, getting you something, on account of our confusion. I mean, I wanted to get you something *sweet*, of course, but I couldn't get you something *permanent*, because then people might ask you questions about—"

"I understand. I do."

"All right then. Open it."

Charley opened it. "For crissakes," he said. "A Hershey bar."

"See? Sweet but not perm—"

"I get it, I get it."

"Do you like it?"

"I like it."

"Do you like me?"

"I like you."

"Then why won't you spend the night?"

"No."

"She wouldn't mind. Not for one night."

"No."

"Call her up and tell her."

"What should I tell her?"

"Lie."

"Jenny—"

"Charley, she wouldn't suspect anything. Just fib a little this once—"

"I would like to. You know that. But don't ask me. Please. Forget it."

"Forgotten. Aren't you going to eat your anniversary present?"

Charley sat down on the bed and took a bite of the Hershey bar.

"I spent eons getting ready for tonight. You might at least tell me how pretty I am or something."

Charley looked at her. She was wearing a white blouse and a white striped skirt and white high-heeled shoes. "How pretty you are," he said quietly. "How lucky I am. How pretty you are."

She smiled and slowly walked across the room until she stood in front of where he sat. Gently she reached out, put her arms around his neck, brought him close until his head rested on her breast.

He kissed her there.

"Charley is my darling," Jenny whispered.

He kissed her again. Then he locked his arms around her waist and leaned back onto the bed, bringing her down on top of him.

"I love it when you touch me," Jenny whispered.

"Isn't that nice." He kissed her on the mouth and when they broke he could hear her breathing, and with his eyes closed he touched her body and kissed her again, harder this time, harder and longer, and this time when they broke his own breathing was what he heard and he reached out for her again but she was gone. "Come back here," Charley whispered.

Jenny walked slowly around the room.

"What's the matter?"

She made a fanning motion. "It's so hot," she muttered.

"C'mere."

Jenny shook her head. "Not now. I'm just stifling. It's too hot, Charley."

"Hot? It's a cool September evening, now—"

"You must have cold blood, then. Or warm, which is it? It's too hot for me, I know that much."

"What are you talking about? Come back here."

She walked back to him.

He took her in his arms.

"Too hot," she said. "Just like I thought." She walked away again and slowly, starting at the throat, she began to unbutton her white blouse.

Charley watched in silence as she pulled the blouse out from her skirt and slid it down her arms. Her bra was very white against her skin. For a moment she cupped her hands beneath her breasts. Charley cleared his throat. "Please come here," he said.

Jenny unzipped her skirt, guided it down across her hips, let it fall into a circle around her long legs. "That's a lot more comfortable," she said. "I love it when your legs get tanned. You don't have to bother with stockings or a girdle or anything like that." She took a few long steps toward him. "See?" She ran the tips of her fingers down along her legs. "Bare."

Charley stared at her. She was wearing the bra and a white half slip and petti-pants and the white-heeled shoes. "Just exactly what is it you think you're doing?"

"Getting comfortable, that's all. You get comfortable too, if you want. Take off your shirt. This heat is terrible."

"It's not hot."

"Maybe late tonight it won't be."

"Jenny, I can't spend the night, so quit this."

"Quit what? I don't understand you."

"You can't blackmail me. I've got to go home."

"Of course you do." Jenny walked to her dresser and splashed on some cologne. "You said you loved cologne. So do I. I always feel so much cooler when I'm wearing cologne."

"Jenny, I've got to go home."

She blew him a kiss. "Bye-bye," she said.

Charley stared at her, saying nothing.

Jenny unhooked her bra.

Charley shook his head.

Slowly, Jenny slipped the straps off her arms, managing to hold the body of the bra in place, first with one hand, then the other. Then, even more slowly, she began to raise the white half slip, an inch at a time, until it barely covered her breasts. Then she removed her bra, carefully, concentrating on the action. Done, she held it out full length, flipped it around a finger, let it fall. A moment later she was naked, except for the white high-heeled shoes and the white half slip clinging to the tops of her breasts.

Charley shook his head and said, "I'll stay."

"Call her."

"Come here."

"Call her."

"Later."

"Now."

He stood, started walking toward her. "You don't trust me."

Hands on hips, she awaited him. "That's right."

He touched her.

But only for a moment. "Call her."

Charley dropped his arms to his sides.

"That's better," Jenny said.

Charley turned, went back to the bed, sat, reached for the phone. "Don't you think you might want to wait in the kitchen?"

"No."

"If I asked you to?"

Jenny snuggled up beside him.

Charley shook his head, picked up the phone. After he'd spoken to the operator he said, "Be quiet now. I mean it."

"Not a peep," Jenny whispered. "He means it."

As soon as he heard Betty Jane's voice, Charley closed his eyes and said, "This is Alfred A. Knopf."

"Hello there, old Alfred A.," Betty Jane replied.

Jenny began to take off Charley's tie.

Charley looked at her, tried pushing her hands away. "Sorry I'm so late calling."

"That's all right," Betty Jane said.

Jenny got the tie undone.

"When are you getting home?" Betty Jane said.

"That's what I'm calling about. I've got to stay in town tonight. But I'll be home tomorrow. Early."

Jenny had his shirt half unbuttoned.

"I'd like to talk to you," Betty Jane said.

Charley pulled at Jenny's fingers.

Jenny slapped his hands, put a finger to his lips. "Shhh," she whispered.

"Honey, I'm in a pay phone."

"I didn't mean on the phone, Charley."

Jenny pulled his shirt out from his trousers, slipped it down his arms.

Charley closed his eyes again. "Great. We'll talk tomorrow."

Jenny ran the tips of her fingers across his chest.

Charley sat very still, eyes shut tight. "Tomorrow," he said again.

"I was sort of hoping—"

"I can't make it home tonight."

"I guess it doesn't really matter. We haven't talked in a while, Charley."

Jenny fought with his belt, got it open, quietly unzipped his trousers.

"Charley?"

"What?"

"Why can't you make it home?"

Jenny knelt beside the bed and tried untying his shoes.

"I'm sorry, didn't I tell you? Rudy. Miller. God, I'm sorry. But I'm going down to see Rudy tonight. You know how late those sessions go."

Jenny muttered "darn" as she pulled one of the laces into a knot. Standing, she put her hands on his trouser tops.

"Did you know you were going to see Rudy tonight?"

"I never know when I'm going to see him. He just appears sometimes; you know that. He did today."

"How is Rudy?"

"He looks to be in excellent health."

Jenny tugged at his pants and drawers, pulling them down his legs, snarling them momentarily around his shoes.

"Ask him why he hasn't run off with me. Tell him I'm waiting."

"I'll tell him."

"Why can't you come home, Charley, after you see Rudy?"

"Because there's no way to get to Princeton once it's late unless you want me to taxi. That's thirty-five dollars. Do you want me to taxi?"

"No. I'll see you tomorrow. Early, you said."

"Early."

Jenny tugged at the clothes, finally pulling them around his shoes and off.

"Bye, honey," Charley said.

"Don't you want to ask about Robby?"

"Of course I do. God. How's Robby?"

"Fine. Goodbye, Charley."

Jenny took the phone from Charley and dropped it in its cradle. She sat in his lap and kissed him. "Hey," she said. "It's me. Open your eyes." She reached out, took his hand, cupped it around her breast.

The hand dropped away.

"Clumsy," Jenny said.

"Get up. Please."

"You're mad."

"No, I'm not."

"Yes, you are. Don't be."

"What the hell were you trying to do?"

"I don't know."

"Do you want her to find out?"

"No."

"Where are you going?"

"To turn off the light."

"Leave it on."

"You're still mad."

"Yes."

"You don't want me."

"I don't know."

"I want you."

"You shouldn't have done that."

"I only wanted to excite you."

"I was excited."

"Aren't you anymore?"

"No."

"You're a liar."

"Yes."

"Charley—"

"Shut up. Take off that thing."

"The slip?"

"Take it off."

"It's off."

"Yes. I can see."

"You know what's silly?"

"What's silly?"

"We've both still got our shoes on."

"Yes. That is silly. Turn off the light."

"Done."

They ran toward each other in the darkness.

Charley woke, groped for the time, found it was three, dressed. He kissed Jenny, left Jenny, checked his wallet, got a cab. At home, in the dark house, Betty Jane was weeping. When she was able, they chatted a while.

Jenny looked up from her desk. "Morning."

"Morning," Charley said. He hesitated a moment, then continued on into his office and shut the door.

Jenny stretched and looked around. Picking up a pencil and dictation pad, she looked around again and stood, moving to the office door. She knocked once, immediately entered, crossing the room quickly, sitting in the chair alongside the desk. Jenny straightened her skirt. Then she licked her pencil point. Then she opened her dictation pad to a blank page and stared down at it. "Boy, are you in trouble."

"Yes."

"It doesn't count."

"What doesn't?"

"You promised overnight, you'll stay overnight. You left. So it doesn't count."

"I see."

"Churl."

He nodded.

"Miss Devers is, as they say, 'put out.' "

"I don't blame her."

"Was she snoring or something?"

He made a smile. "No."

"You didn't even leave a note, Charley."

"I know."

"I think the least you could have done—oh, oh dear."

"What?"

"I just realized—something's the matter."

"No."

"Don't lie."

"I'm not."

"Then tell me what it is."

"There's nothing to tell."

"You look like death warmed over. What's wrong?"

"Nothing. We'll talk about it later."

"If nothing's the matter, what's there to talk about?"

"Nothing. Just like I said. Nothing."

"Tell me."

"Later."

"When later?"

"I don't know. Just not now."

"Why not now?"

"Isn't that kind of obvious?"

"No."

"Jenny—"

"I want to know. Now."

"Will you please try and understand that I'm a little upset too—"

"How did she do it?"

"Do what?"

"Find out."

"About us?"

"Yes."

"She didn't. She hasn't. She doesn't know."

"You're lying."

"Lower your voice."

"Did she threaten to divorce you?"

"Of course not."

"Then what did she say?"

"I told you, lower—"

"I want to know what she said." Jenny stood up.

"I'll tell you, dammit, but that isn't—"

"Lying bitch."

"Jenny—"

"*Tell* me."

"*Not now.*"

"*Aspirin!*" Archie Wesker cried as he staggered through the door.

Charley whirled.

"Aspirin! Aspirin!"

"Archie, what the hell—"

"Little drink-'em-up last night. The old head's not so good today. I was out of aspirin at home—the bottle in my desk's empty too."

"Well, I haven't any."

"You got to."

"I haven't."

"*The whole goddam world's out of aspirin!*" Archie slammed the door behind him.

"Betty Jane's pregnant," Charley said.

Jenny sat down.

Charley started to say something, managed to stutter over a syllable, then quit while he was behind.

"Is she positive?"

"Apparently."

"How far along is she?"

When Charley answered he said, "About a month."

"A month?"

Charley nodded.

"*One month?*" She looked straight at him. "Aren't you the busy little bee?"

"Aye."

"Forget I said that." She started shaking her head, back and forth, back and forth.

"Are you all right?"

"What do you mean, 'Am I all right'? Do you mean am I going to fall down and die? I'll survive. It's just—it's a surprise. It could be a lot worse. I'll admit I'm surprised and all, but I'm all right, I'm . . . fine, Charley, I'm going to cry." And suddenly she was. She sat bowed in the chair, her hands clasped in the folds of her black skirt, shaking her head, trying to talk as the tears dropped, spotting her white hands. The spasm built, peaked, abruptly dried. "I wonder what that was," Jenny said when it was over. She wiped her eyes. "No, I know. When you wouldn't tell me what it was, I got so frightened. Then, when you told me, I just thought, 'Oh, is that all.' And then I realized that what you'd said was the worst thing you could say, because now we're over and everything's a waste."

"Why don't you go on home?" Charley said. "I'll get there when I can. Soon. I promise. Then we'll talk."

"I can't see you anymore; you know that. Not now. There. I said it first, dear Charley. Now you're spared telling me you won't see me." She smiled at him. "I think we should strive to end this with dignity. I would like that."

"So would I."

"If you take the long view, which I can't but I'll try, all that's happened is I've postponed quitting for a month. I was going to quit when I met you; I'll quit now instead."

"And do what?"

"Leave town. I don't know. Marry the boy back home, maybe. The boy back home's on a Rhodes scholarship, is that funny?" She shook her head. "Is this sad?"

"Yes."

"I guess it is, I guess it is." Jenny made a smile. "Are we being dignified, do you think?"

"Terribly."

"It's not the easiest thing in the world, is it? I don't think I'll try it again for a while. There's such a thing as being dignified too often."

Charley went to her, touched her, pulled her into his arms.

"This isn't very smart."

"No, I suppose it isn't. But it doesn't matter anymore."

"No, I suppose it doesn't."

They held each other for a while.

•

"It's been incredible," Betty Jane said, meaning the change in Charley. It was the middle of January, she was five months pregnant and she sat in the living room of her house in Princeton, sipping sherry with Penny Whitsell.

Sprawled on the sofa, Penny said, "He was probably working too hard."

Betty Jane shifted in her favorite chair and stared first at the fire dying in the fireplace, then out the window at the falling snow. Her face, lighted by the embers, was, if possible, prettier than usual. "Aren't you right, though; of course he was." She paused, waiting for Penny's nod before continuing. They had been close since grammar school and like good wrestlers could anticipate each other's moves and pauses. Penny nodded. Betty Jane continued. "Charley's just the most conscientious man alive. For a while back in September he was working late almost every night. Now he gets home early."

Penny finished her sherry, reached for the decanter on the coffee table. "Whenever Fred worked nights it meant he was out with some broad. The bastard." She refilled her sherry glass, took a long swallow. "B.J.?"

"Wha?"

"Seriously, do you think I'm swearing more since I got divorced?"

"Hell no," Betty Jane said, and she laughed.

Outside, a car horn sounded: bump-dya-dee-ump-bump—dyump-bump.

"That's Charley," Betty Jane explained. "He's been doing that lately. He also makes puns."

"Obviously the man is cracking."

Betty Jane smiled. It was a marvelous smile, gentle and kind and understanding. The face surrounding the smile was not remotely vivacious—no one could make that accusation—but it was perfect. The eyes were brown and bright and perfect, the nose straight and small. And perfect. The skin clear and smooth, perfect skin.

Penny started to get up. "I ought to move my car; it's blocking the driveway."

"Charley will move it; he won't mind. I tell you, he's just so chipper nowadays I can't stand it." She looked out at the snow, said "Chilly" and started to push herself out of her chair.

"Sit down," Penny said. "Lemme." She got up and put another log on the fire. "Try and remember you got a gut, huh?"

Betty Jane glanced at her stomach. "I'm ballooning so. It's awful. I'll never get my figure back."

"What's that in the Bible? Something about a chasing after wind?"

"I'm not vain. You know it. But Charley likes me thin."

The back door closed and, a moment later, Charley was standing in the living-room doorway. "Who's the fathead moron who left her stupid car blocking the driveway? Hello, Penelope."

"B.J. was just telling me how chipper you are."

"Lies." He looked at Betty Jane. "I know you," he said, and he dropped to his knees and kissed her. He put his hands on her stomach and called, "Hello-oooo in there." Then he looked around. "Doesn't somebody else live around here?"

"He's upstairs. Furious with me. He wanted to go polar-bear hunting with a stick. I said he couldn't. It's practically a blizzard out. Wasn't I right?"

"As rain," Charley replied. "Or, in this case, as snow. Mary had a little lamb, its fleece was right as snow. Excuse me a moment, ladies." He stood and went upstairs and put on some old clothes. Then he walked to the doorway of his son's room. Robby had a long stick and was firing it out the window.

"Kpow. Sploom."

"Hello there."

"Lo."

"Word reaches me—"

"Splat. Kpow."

"—that you're a trifle miffed."

"Huh?"

"New stick?"

"Maybe."

"Your mother reports—"

"Wudduz she know? She wuddin knowa polar bear if it hidder."

"Well said. Aren't you Robert McGillicudity?"

"Who? *What?* No. Fiske."

"Ah. Robert Fiske. I know your father." Charley went back downstairs. "He is decidedly not in the best of humors. He said his mother was a witch, a harpie, cruel beyond—"

"He did? No, he didn't either."

"He's going to cut you out of his will," Charley said. "He told me so."

Robby ran into the room. "You *are* my father."

"Pardon, young man?" Charley said.

"Upstairs," Robby went on. "Upstairs you said—"

"Darling," Charley said to Betty Jane. "I think this young man is selling something. I'm sorry, young man, but we don't want any magazines."

"*Magazines?*"

"Don't try your high-pressure tactics on me, young man."

"But, Daddy—"

"Great Scott!" Charley cried. "There's a polar bear in the back yard!"

"For sure?" Robby said.

"It's twenty feet high and covered with white fur; what else can it be?"

"Let's go gitit."

"We can't."

"Why not?"

"I'd really like to. But we just can't."

"Why can't we? Why can't we?"

"Because we haven't got a polar-bear stick. Oh, if only we had a—"

"I got one!"

"I'm afraid you don't understand. Polar-bear sticks are very rare; just any stick won't do."

"But I got one, I got one, I do."

"Go get it, then. Let me see."

Robby tore out of the room. They heard him going to his room and he was shouting "See?" even before he started coming down the stairs. "See? See? See? See? See?"

"By George, the lad does have a polar-bear stick!" Charley cried.

"I told ya! I told ya!"

"Get your coat on. And galoshes. Hurry!"

Robby hurried, Charley too, and they ran outside, standing hand in hand on the upper edge of the white lawn, which sloped gracefully down to the icy rim of Carnegie Lake. "Look out!" Charley yelled and he grabbed the boy, diving forward into the deep snow, rolling over and over down the hill. Robby screamed at first, but then he rested in his father's strong arms, and when they reached the bottom it was hard to tell who was more pleased with the journey. They raced back to the top, where Charley grabbed the boy again, and again they rolled down, through fresh and different snow, and this time when they raced to the top Betty Jane was waiting for them, her coat thrown over her shoulders. "I thought I'd watch," she said.

"Can she?" Charley asked.

Robby shook his head. "She's a girl!"

"And a good 'thank God' for that," Charley replied before grabbing his wife, throwing her gently down, lifting her gently up, roughly washing her perfect face with chilling snow.

"Stop," Betty Jane said, somehow making the word two syllables, but when Charley did she cried, "Don't," so he lifted her again, easing her up onto his shoulder, then snatching Robby with his right arm, lifting him too, slowly starting into a spin, faster and faster, and Penny, watching them from the living room, was suddenly reminded of her childhood and one of those round glass paperweights that you shake to make the snow fall.

"Thank God you didn't quit," Charley said.

Jenny raised her daiquiri into toasting position. "Hear, hear."

Charley smiled, looked around the crowded restaurant.

Jenny stared at her glass a moment before starting to giggle. "Daiquiris make me giggle. Especially at lunch. Why is that?"

"The rum might have a little something to do with it."

"Auh?" She giggled again. "You're so intelligent. I really like you."

"I like you too. That's why it's so great you stayed on the job. Before, when—"

"Use a euphemism," Jenny warned. "Remember I'm a lady." She picked up his swizzle stick and started making designs on the tablecloth. "There's a character in a Tennessee Williams play. Sort of whory. Except every time the moon rises it makes her a virgin. She believes that. I guess, so do I."

"During the dear dead days of our confusion," Charley said. "I don't think I liked you all that much. Not the way I do now. Now, I *like* you."

"I'll tell you one thing it made me realize. Tommy? My wandering Rhodes scholar? I don't take him for granted anymore, believe me. As soon as he sets foot on American soil . . ." She made a trapping gesture with her hands.

Charley smiled. "I think I'll keep Betty Jane pregnant all the time from now on. She loves kids and she's so excited about having another. It's just great."

"Two more months?"

"Approximately." He pointed at Jenny's empty glass.

"I'll get smashed."

"That may be."

"Do I have much to type this afternoon?"

"Little."

"Another."

Charley signaled for the waiter. "Two," he said.

"What we were being," Jenny said, "was immature."

"Pardon?"

"I read this article. *McCall's* or someplace."

"Then it must be true."

"No-no; it was by a certified psy ... psycho ... That word is too much for me at the present time."

"Try shrinker."

"Thank you. A certified shrinker. And she said—"

"Beware of lady shrinkers, certified or otherwise."

"*She said* that when her patients had confusions, what they were do-ing, most of the time, was ducking reality."

"I can't think of anything better to duck."

"Anyway, it's an immature action. And it ends up horribly most of the time. Three of her patients tried to do themselves in. That's *McCall's* for 'suicide.' "

"I was hot for your body," Charley said. "I used to ogle you around the office. Secretly. Your dresses were always too big."

"I thought you were pretty cute. Before I met you, of course."

"I *am* pretty cute," Charley said.

The waiter came with their drinks. "Would you like to order lunch now?"

"The lady is on a liquid diet," Charley said. "I'm joining her."

The waiter left them.

"What we had was bed," Jenny said then.

"Before?"

"Before."

Charley nodded. "That, and we were both probably a little lonely."

"I never thought I'd get over it. When we stopped. I cried for two days. Then I came back to work and I figured I was a cinch to fall apart when you came in, except when you got there, I thought '*Him?* He's not so beautiful. Plenty of fish in the sea.' "

"I remembered you as being prettier," Charley said.

"I'm not lonely anymore," Jenny said. "My acting classes are great and I work at it. Before, I was just potchkeying. Now I dig. And I'm writ-ing Tommy every day. And once a week at least my boss takes me to lunch."

"We've been very lucky. No one ever found out. And we salvaged something from the wreckage: we like each other."

"I'll tell you one thing. If I had to pick someone with whom to have a first confusion, I'd pick you."

"Ditto."

"Was I really your first?"

"Aye."

"Miss Devers is permanently honored."

"Once I almost bedded with an English lady authoress. I think she was willing."

"Beware of English lady authoresses, beddable or otherwise."

"I beware."

"Hey—" Jenny called, and she waved, "Archie—hi."

Archie Wesker walked over. "Very suspicious," he said.

"You've caught us, Archie," Jenny told him. "We're having an affair. May we trust you to keep our secret?"

Archie shook his head. "What is it with you two? I'm not accusing anyone, you understand, but it's all very mysterious."

Jenny raised her napkin up to just below her eyes. "Me and Marlene," she said.

IT'S A GIRL
PAULA FRANCES FISKE
PRINCETON HOSPITAL
EIGHT POUNDS SIX OUNCES
THE TWELFTH OF MAY

"I thought it was a lovely announcement," Jenny said. She finished typing a letter, handed it to Charley to sign.

He sat on the edge of her desk. "I thought so too. Betty Jane was all for making a book out of it. You know: 'At home at . . .' and 'Length . . .' and so on. Who cares how long a baby is?"

"You do."

"No, I don't."

"How long was she?"

"Twenty-one and a half inches—something around there."

"You phony." She started cleaning off her desk top. "How could it be *around*? *Exactly* is what you mean; admit it."

Charley shrugged. "I do not like boastful parents. Lift?"

"You mean like a taxi? Home?"

"Sure."

"How come?"

"We're cocktailing up in that vicinity. Betty Jane's coming in. Our first gala since the arrival."

Jenny stood. "Ready?"

"Momentarily." He went and got his coat. They walked down the corridor to the elevators. "After this cocktail thing, I'm taking her to dinner. Someplace where the atmosphere's overpowering. This is basically a therapeutic meal. You see, after the baby there comes this terrible thing called 'Post-Pregnancy Pudge.' The woman feels a bit on the flabby side. She is, of course, which is why you can't tell her she's imagining things. Therefore you have to do something to make her Think Feminine again."

The elevator came. They got in and rode down in silence. "I can't stand people who talk in elevators," Charley said as they crossed the lobby to the street.

"Neither can I."

Charley was about to raise a hand when a cab appeared. "Just like in the movies." They got in and he gave Jenny's address.

"How do you feel about people who talk in taxis?"

"That's all right. Because the driver's not really there. Only the back of his head exists. He's more or less invisible."

"Don't I wish," the driver said, and he launched into an account of his troubles with his wife, a charming woman, sweet and levelheaded, except for the fact that she was very much in love with Argentina Rocca, a leading television wrestler.

"Right here," Charley said when they reached Jenny's building.

"Want to come in?" Jenny asked. "Have you got time?"

"I have, except may I tell you something? I never much liked your apartment."

"I've had it redecorated," she told him. "Repainted, I should say. I never liked it either. It's better now. Different, anyway."

"In that case," Charley said, and he paid the driver.

As they walked up to the building, Jenny held her hand out in front of her and made it shake. "This is where they resume their illicit relationship," she told him. "Notice how her hand trembles uncontrollably?"

"His breath is coming in little gasps," Charley replied. He gasped a little.

Jenny unlocked the door to her apartment and switched on the lights.

"*Blue walls?*" Charley said.

"You're supposed to get used to them, I think. At least that's what the painter promised me."

"Why blue?"

"It was just after our tearful separation. I needed a change and I begged the landlord. He also does the painting. All he had was blue. White would have meant waiting a week and I didn't feel like waiting. Drink?"

"No, thanks." He sat down on the sofa bed. "Memories flooded over him. For a moment he felt giddy . . . torn . . . confused . . ."

"She watched him and prayed she would be strong enough to resist him."

"Could he resist her? he wondered."

"She stood rooted to the spot, her loins on fire—Charley, do women have loins or is it just men?"

"Everybody do. I'll take a little vodka if you have it."

"Coming right up." She went to the kitchen. "Rocks?"

"Please." When she brought him the drink he said, "I'm sorry about the walls."

"Why?"

"They're so goddam blue. Most walls in most apartments aren't deep blue like these. They're hard to forget. When my father died the only thing I was thankful for was that he didn't have anything special, anything *his*. No pipe, no chair. I think maybe he did it on purpose. He knew it would be easier. There wouldn't be those things that you'd look at and summon him back. Nothing to remember. Nothing specific. These walls." He shook his head. "Hard."

"Maybe I'll just have a little teentsy," Jenny said, and she hurried to the kitchen and poured herself a drink. "How's that for a sickening phrase?"

"Pretty good."

"Refill?"

"He shook his head, looking at her all the while with passion."

Jenny laughed. "I'll tell you one thing," she said, coming back from the kitchen. "I mean, we're done ducking reality and all that, but I do feel a certain physical air in the room."

"You do?"

Jenny nodded. "I don't quite know where to sit, for example. I mean, if I sit on the sofa, that's next to you, and if I sit over here, in the chair, I'm protesting too much. I don't know."

"I guess you'd better stand," Charley said.

"I guess I better." She finished her drink, put it down.

Charley rubbed his eyes with the tips of his fingers.

"What's the matter?" Jenny said.

"You know."

"I guess I do. When you started talking about the walls. That's when I knew. The walls being blue, that wouldn't bother you, not unless you planned on spending some time in them, isn't that right? That's why I had the drink."

"Yes."

"Well?"

"Well?"

"Let's get on with it."

"A little while later," Charley said a little while later.

Jenny lay quietly in his arms.

Charley adjusted the sheet so that it covered them. "That's an American symbol, 'a little while later.' It's Creative Writing One for intercourse."

"Don't you have to double space?" Jenny asked.

"Usually."

"And what about the dots?"

"Three little dots," Charley sang suddenly. "Hey, you're pretty smart. Them are called ellipsis—plural, ellipses. Also symbols. 'Dot dot dot double space a little while later, he woke and stroked her soft flesh.' May I stroke your soft flesh?"

"Feel free."

"I do."

"God, are we phonies," Jenny said.

"How dare you?"

"Well, we are. Waiting all this time. All those months ago, why did we stop? I regret my tears, Charley, you bastard, Charley; you'll pay for my suffering." She nipped his shoulder. "That's just a first installment."

"We stopped seeing each other because we're good, decent, honorable, moral people."

"And today?"

"Today just proves we're human. If you'd gain fifty pounds, we could probably clear the whole thing up in a hurry."

"He finds me irresistible," Jenny said, and she kicked the sheet off them. "I find him so too." She peered at his stomach. "Even his navel is beautiful." Charley laughed and reached for the sheet, but she kicked at it again, sending it to the floor. "Puritan," she said.

"It's just that, like most men, I lose a little confidence when I'm naked."

"Fool," she whispered, and she started stroking his body. He reached out for her breasts, touching the tips of them with the tips of his fingers. She rolled her body over and lay on top of him. Then she kissed him and his arms went tight around her, squeezing her until she gave a cry. She rolled off him and they were still, hands touching, staring up at the cracked ceiling.

"I'm brilliant at finding animals," Jenny said. "Give me a ceiling, I'll find you a zoo. I'm awfully happy right now."

"Good."

"I don't think I can remember ever having been so hap—I love you, Charley, I think, and I've never told you that before, so don't say anything until I explain something to you."

"Hush."

"No, really. I've got to explain this, because I didn't use to love you. Before. But all these months we've been together—not together, but you know what I mean."

"Yes."

"Well, I didn't know you before. I do now, I think, and I love you and so I guess I'm glad we stopped seeing each other because if we hadn't I wouldn't feel this way now say something."

Charley took her in his arms.

"I didn't say anything wrong? Make a fool of myself?"

"No."

"I can't help that I love you. You can't blame me."

"No."

"Do you know how much I love you, Charley?"

"How much?"

"I love you so much that I don't even mind that you haven't told me you love me."

Charley kissed her on the mouth.

She pointed with his hand. "See? There's a camel—that's the hump—and there's the tail of a kangaroo, and that's—I'm just so goddam happy."

"That's my line."

"Because you're nice. I'm nice and you're nice and nothing awful can happen when people are like that. We'll have troubles, sure, but everything will be fine in the long run."

"Here's to a nice long run," Charley said.

"I showed you the hump of the camel, didn't I? Well, just above it, that's a lion roaring, can you see?"

"Clearly a lion."

"Jenny Devers loves Charley Fiske. I wish there were a fence around. I'd carve initials."

"Stay where you are, please."

"He wants me. I'm wanted. God damn it," she said as the telephone rang. Jenny picked it up. "Hello?"

"Jenny?"

"Yes?"

"Hi. This is Betty Jane."

"Betty Jane. *Hi.*" Jenny lay on her back and stared at the ceiling. Charley lay beside her. Their bodies were perfectly parallel, perfectly still.

"I'm sorry to bother you like this, but I thought you might have some idea about my wandering husband. Did he happen to mention where he might be off to?"

"He's meeting you for cocktails tonight. He said something about that."

"He's supposed to. Except I'm here and he ain't."

"Well, he left the office at the regular time. I remember that. We took the same elevator down."

"Then?"

"Well, I came home. I don't know where he went."

"Oh, O.K. I guess I ought to be used to Charley by now. Prompt he ain't. Sorry again. I'll be seeing—"

"You're going to have a wonderful dinner. He told me you were celebrating. He was looking forward to it. That's practically all he could talk about the whole day."

"He'll probably show up any minute. Thanks, Jenny."

"I know where he is!" Jenny sat up straight.

Charley sat alongside her.

"It was supposed to be a surprise, though. I wasn't supposed to tell, so if I tell you've got to promise to act surprised when he tells you, do you promise?"

"I guess."

"He's buying you things. Presents. That's the truth. He said he was going to order you a lot of little things."

"Charley said that?"

"Yes."

Charley reached for the phone.

Jenny shook him off. "Oh, it's going to be wonderful. He's going to buy you a thousand things. You'll see."

"Yes," Betty Jane said.

"So you just act as if nothing has happened. And don't be too hard on him when he gets there."

"All right."

"That's where he's been. Buying you things."

"Aren't I the lucky one?" Betty Jane said. "I'm sorry if I bothered you."

"Yes you are. And you didn't bother me."

"Thank you. Goodbye, Jenny."

"Goodbye." Jenny held the receiver a while.

Charley lay back down and closed his eyes.

Jenny lay down too, so they were parallel again. "See how nice you are?" Jenny said.

What he wanted her to do was go.

What she wanted him to do was not let her.

Betty Jane sat down in her favorite chair and said, "I think I'll visit Mother."

Charley glanced up from the manuscript he was reading. "Hmm?"

"Well, Paula's such a handful," Betty Jane went on. "I just think it's a good idea."

Charley closed the manuscript. "You think what is?"

"Visiting Mother. I know it sounds silly, Paula being so tiny, but she's a real tiger. I'm exhausted all the time. And Mother has that big house and Robby loves it, playing on the beach. You could come out weekends; two hours isn't such a hideous commute if you only do it weekends. And you like Long Island too. And the weather's nice in August. Don't you think it's a good idea?"

"If you do."

"I really want to go."

"I'll miss you."

"Mother's got help and it's such a big house and with the beach right there—" From upstairs, Paula started crying. Betty Jane put her finger to her lips. "Let us pray," she whispered. Paula screamed a little while, then stopped. Betty Jane shook her head. "With Robby I would have been upstairs like a shot. I feel like the worst mother sometimes."

"Nonsense," Charley said.

"No. I do. It's just that I'm so tired all the time, with the two of them both needing me. If they'd only arrange things alternately. You'd think Paula would know better; she's practically three months old."

"Backward," Charley said. "As we feared."

"But as soon as one of them wants something, it's dollars to dough-nuts so will the other." She rubbed her eyes. "I'm just shot."

"We could always get the baby nurse back for a while."

"She's on another case by now."

"Well, you didn't even like Mrs. Dreyfoos; let's get a different baby nurse."

"You know how much that would cost?"

"Let's make believe it's a tax deduction."

"No. It's better if I go out to Mother's, don't you think?"

"If you do."

"The rest *does* sound appealing."

"And maybe I could take Fridays off. Come out Thursday night."

"Do you think you could? That would be heaven."

"I really will miss you, though. This house can get awfully lonely."

"It wouldn't be long. Just until I felt really rested. I really think I ought to go out to Mother's, Charley."

"How long do you think you'll want to be gone?"

"I don't know. Two weeks maybe. Maybe less. You make me feel like I'm ditching you."

"I don't mean to. If you want to go, and you think you need it, well, you know best."

"Then it's settled," Betty Jane said. "I'll call Mother and make the arrangements."

Charley said nothing for a while. Finally he nodded. "All right. It's set-tled. Two weeks. Not one minute more."

"Fine."

Charley picked the manuscript up and opened it. "I tell you, this book: I can never find my place. This guy admires O'Hara so much, what he's done is just rewrite *Appointment in Samarra*. The main character's even called Philip French."

Betty Jane looked at him. "I don't understand."

"I'm sorry," Charley said gently. "No reason you should. O'Hara's character was called Julian English."

"Oh, how funny," Betty Jane said. "Now I see."

"Well, here goes," he said.

"Good luck," she said.

He started to read.

She started to cry.

When he heard her he said, "Honey?"

She wept silently, her face turned against the soft cushion of the chair.

"Honey?"

"Sorry . . ."

"What is it?"

"Nothing."

"Tell me."

"Tired—that's all."

Charley crossed the room, knelt down beside her.

"*You want me to go,*" Betty Jane said.

"Whaat?"

"You're trying to get rid of me."

"Where'd you get that idea?"

"Admit it."

"No."

"Yes."

"No."

"Oh . . . *Charleeeee,*" Betty Jane sobbed and sobbed.

"Who told you I was trying to get rid of you?" Charley said when she had subsided a little.

"No one told me. I just know. I could tell when we were talking."

"Honey, I was the one who suggested getting another baby nurse, remember?"

"You said that but you didn't mean it. I could tell."

"All right. Suppose you were right. Why would I want to get rid of you?"

Betty Jane said nothing.

"Why?"

"I don't know."

"You must have *some* reason. You think I don't love you? Didn't I buy you all those presents just a few weeks ago? You think I'm tired of you? You think I'm catting around with somebody else? Tell me."

"I'm a woman," Betty Jane said. "I just needed reassuring."

"We're both grownups. You come to me, tell me you're beat and suggest you might go relax with your mother. I offer a few other possible alternatives and then finally decide to let you go. How in the hell am *I* getting rid of *you?*"

"Yelling is not the same as reassuring."

"I wasn't yelling."

"You weren't reassuring either."

"I don't understand women," Charley said. "I offered a baby nurse—"

"Let's forget the whole thing."

"No. Let's be honest with each other. And I mean honest. I'll swear to tell the truth. If you will."

"All right, but—"

"Is there somebody else? Some other guy?"

"My God, of course not. Now let me ask you something."

"Anything," Charley said. "Ask."

"Do you want me to go?"

"Do you want to go?"

"I don't care. It's completely up to you, Charley."

"I don't want you to go."

"Then I'll stay."

"Good," Charley said. "Then you were lying before."

"I was not. When?"

"I don't care if you were. It doesn't matter."

"*When?*"

"You were talking about how exhausted you were. That was lying."

"No."

"You are exhausted?"

"Well, exhausted, that's a pretty strong—"

"Are you tired? Could you use a little rest?"

"Of course. Probably. Who couldn't—"

"Would it be relaxing for you? At your mother's?"

"I guess so. But—"

"Then shouldn't you go?"

"Well . . ."

"I'm not asking you to, understand. I don't want you to; we've decided that. But what I want isn't always what's best. What's best, Betty Jane?"

She said nothing.

"You don't have to decide now, honey. Tomorrow's just as good."

"I guess I ought to go," Betty Jane said.

"If it's just 'ought,' forget the whole thing. It'll be drudgery for you. You won't relax a bit. And don't go because of the kids either. You're not a rotten mother; put that out of your mind. You're a terrific mother and you know it. Nobody works as hard on the second kid as on the first. That's the truth; you know that too. So it's what *you* want. Forget about the kids."

"Well . . ." Betty Jane said again.

"We all hate making decisions. I don't blame you a bit."

"I'll go visit Mother."

"Sure? We're telling the truth now, remember."

"I want to go."

"I'll miss you."

All in yellow, Jenny stood alone beneath the movie marquee. When Charley turned the corner, she waved and said, "Why, Mr. Fiske, *hello.*"

"Hi, Jenny. What are you doing here?"

"Oh, I never miss an Alec Guinness movie. Where's Mrs. Fiske?"

"Visiting her mother on Long Island. Has been for over a week."

"Of course; I forgot." She smiled at him.

He shifted his weight from one foot to the other.

"Relax," Jenny whispered with a bigger smile. "You're doing fine."

Charley grinned at her. "This was a mistake."

"Oh, do you think so?" Jenny clapped her hands softly. "I don't. I just wanted once not to feel scrummy. Another evening staring at those blue walls—"

"We might be seen."

"We used to be seen. All the time."

"That was lunch." Charley beamed. "And we were innocent then."

"I love your choice of words," Jenny said, laughing lightly.

"If Betty Jane finds out, you think this will have been worth it?"

"The moonrise no longer makes me a virgin, Mr. Fiske. I felt the need of a little something to make me go on. Incentive, I think, is the word."

"I'm sorry," Charley said. "I'm a little panicky, that's all. Forgive me. You look lovely."

"I tried very hard. I spent over an hour getting ready." She touched her yellow dress. "New. Do you like it?"

"Aye."

"I love you."

"Bless you for that."

"Do you know, it's really exciting? We've never done this before. Talked like we were human beings, I mean, in front of God and everybody. I keep expecting Archie Wesker to put in an appearance."

"Shall we go in?" He opened the door for her.

"I'm going to hold your hand," Jenny whispered. "Once it's dark."

"Have you your ticket, Miss Devers?"

"No, Mr. Fiske, but—"

"My pleasure." He paid for them, smiled, walked to the ticket-taker. "Really the most marvelous coincidence, running into you like this," Charley said, loud, for the ticket-taker's benefit.

"You're indicating," Jenny told him. "Actor's term. Quit it; relax."

"We'll find our own way," Charley said as an usher approached them. They started along the aisle, toward the blank screen. "Here?" he asked, halfway down.

Jenny sat.

After a moment Charley sat beside her.

"I'll bet I know what you're thinking," Jenny said then. "You're thinking, 'Why is it so *bright* in here?' "

Charley nodded.

"Your hand, please," Jenny said, reaching out, taking it. "It gets darker when the feature goes on." She rubbed his palm. "Dampish."

"One of us is."

"I'm really happy, Charley."

"Good."

"This is really fun."

"Yes."

"Aren't you glad I talked you into it?"

"Of course."

"Then quit looking around."

"I wasn't looking around."

"Your head was turning and your eyes were open. I call that looking around."

"I'm sorry. I keep trying to think of this like you told me to—an acting exercise—but—"

"You'll get better with practice. And stop being silly about this. I mean, what are the odds against your running into someone you know? Enormous. At least."

"What are we doing, Jenny? Have you any idea?"

"You mean now?"

"You know what I mean."

"Keep your voice down."

"I shouldn't have let you talk me into this."

"What are you getting angry about?"

"Nothing. Nothing." Charley took a deep breath. "I'm sorry—for the eight hundred and forty-fifth time."

"I'm big on forgiveness."

"I care for you, Jenny." He paused. Then he added, "God damn it."

"Miss Devers is touched, she thinks."

The lights got lower; the movie began.

"Dark enough for you?"

"Where's the cartoon?"

"This is an East Side art house; are you mad?"

"In Princeton we get a cartoon."

"Very academic town, Princeton."

A couple sat down across the aisle from them.

Charley froze.

"What—" Jenny began.

"I know them," Charley whispered.

"You can't."

"They're the Hagners. He teaches at the university; she's a friend of Betty Jane's. They live down the road, so—"

"Are you sure?"

"You want me to go over and introduce—"

"I just want you to be absolutely—"

"Now you lower *your* voice," Charley snapped.

"I was whispering."

"What were those odds you were talking about? How high were they?"

"I'm sorry." Jenny got up and moved back two rows. "God forbid you should be seen with someone like me."

Charley sat very still.

The couple across the aisle stood, looked at him, moved two rows closer front.

Charley watched them go.

Jenny stared at the silver screen.

Charley turned toward her. "Jenny?"

She looked at him.

"It wasn't who I thought."

She nodded.

"I thought it was but it wasn't."

She nodded.

"Shut up," a nasal voice from behind them said.

Charley faced front.

Jenny's head began to shake.

"Come back?" Charley asked, turning to face her.

Jenny's head continued to shake from side to side.

"Are you still mad?"

Jenny shook her head.

"What is it, then? How do you feel?"

"Negroid," Jenny said.

"I'm gonna call the usher," the nasal voice said.

Charley faced front.

When he looked back again, Jenny was gone.

"I'm packing now," Charley said. "I no sooner started than you called." He tucked the receiver between his chin and shoulder and continued folding a shirt.

Betty Jane said, "What did you see last night?"

"Some Alec Guinness picture." He sat down on the bed, gazed out the window at the setting sun.

"Any good?"

"I can't remember it today, so I guess it wasn't."

"Remember now: bring your swimming trunks *and* your tennis shorts. You're always forgetting one or the other."

"Nag."

"We're all so excited you're coming."

"I'll leave straight from work tomorrow. I'll catch the four-o'clock. Meet it?"

"If you'll blow me a kiss."

"Ye gods—"

"Well, it's not as if I asked you in public. You are alone, aren't you, Charley?"

"Aye." He blew her a kiss.

"You should hear my heart," Betty Jane said. "This has been very good, this separation. I feel I'll be better able to endure you now."

"Well, aren't you feeling frisky."

"I ought to. My husband's coming tomorrow. On the four-o'clock train. Goodbye, husband."

Charley hung up. He stood, folded his shirt, then tossed it into his suitcase and left the bedroom, walking downstairs to the screen porch. He sat stiffly down, staring out at the sloping lawn and, beyond it, Carnegie Lake. At the bottom of the lawn was a man-made waterfall. Charley listened to it rumble. He closed his eyes. The rumble grew. He touched his fingertips to his closed eyes and rubbed and rubbed. When the phone rang again he sighed and stood and went inside and answered, saying "Where have you been?" as soon as he heard Jenny's "Hello."

"Here and there. Around and about. Hither and yon."

"I've been trying to get hold of you since last night."

She made her voice very English. "I stayed with an acquaintance—a fellow thespian."

"You could have at least called in at work today; let me know you were all right."

"Who said I was all right? We've got to talk, Charley."

"When? You know I've got to go to Long Island tomorrow."

"How about now? I could come out to Princeton."

"Gee; that's a swell idea."

"We might be seen; is that it?"

"Well, what do you think?"

"Same old song. Goodbye, Charley."

He hung up, shook his head, smiled, stepped to a small mirror and put his fist through it. A moment later there was blood on his big hand. He stared at it, licked the cuts, then held his hand high over his head until the blood dried. He went to the kitchen, got a broom, swept up the splintered mess. His hand was swelling slightly. He made a loose fist, tightened it until he winced. Then he went upstairs to the bathroom and soaked his hand in cool water. After that, he came back downstairs to the porch and was in the act of sitting when Jenny said, "What happened to your hand?"

"Son of a bitch," Charley said.

Jenny hurried on. "Pretty here—view of the waterfall. There's a gas station a little ways back. That's where I called from. What happened to your hand?"

"I cut it." He sat very still, eyes closed.

"Oh. That accounts for the blood."

"Yes."

"Don't say it."

"Don't say what?"

" 'How could you come?' 'What are you doing here?' Any of those. The point is, I came."

"That's the point, all right."

"Rest easy: no one saw me. I took the bus to New Brunswick and taxied from there. I got off two houses down. Clever?"

The doorbell rang.

"Son of a bitch," Jenny said.

"Excuse me," Charley said. He got up and moved to the front door. "Who is it?"

"Me, Charley. Mac Clendennon."

Charley opened the door. "Hi, Mac."

Clendennon gestured across the street to his house. "Milady said you was taking off. Want me to look after anything?"

"I'm just going the weekend."

Clendennon shook his head and gestured again. "Milady got things a little screwy. She thought you was gonna be gone a while."

"No—just the weekend."

Clendennon shook his head again. "My wife has this thing about being neighborly. Sorry, Charley."

" 'S all right. Thanks, Mac."

"See ya."

Charley watched the other man walk across the street. Then he closed the door, locked it and returned to the porch.

"I think I was just explaining how clever I was," Jenny said.

He made no reply.

She went right on. "This chat. My reasons for having it. Some things have happened. For example, I'm changing roles. From Whore—"

"Dammit, Jenny—"

"Whore to Other Woman. See, we're changing pastimes. Fun in Bed is over. From now on, Divorce is the name of the game."

Charley nodded.

"What does that nod mean?"

"That I heard you."

"Well, hear this: Last night, after fleeing the cinema, I decided to stretch my giant brain. I tried figuring, since I'm an actress, how I'd play me. And what I found was I couldn't, not really well, because I'm inconsistent. Look at it this way. Here I am, in love with you and wanting to marry you, except all I do is lie there flat on my back in bed and get used. Now I know that there are a lot of things a girl can get by lying flat on her back in bed, but a husband isn't one of them. So if I want you for a husband, why am I acting in the best possible way not to get you? Answer? There isn't one. I'm inconsistent. That's when I decided to change roles."

"I liked you the way you were."

"Enough to marry me? Don't answer; let me. Because you'd answer 'No,' but you'd be wrong. The correct reply is 'Not yet.' I'm gambling you'll switch. In time. And in order to hurry that time I am going to summon up all the little bitchy wiles of the Other Woman, but subtly. My life is dedicated to making you choose me, so look out!" She started into the living room.

"Where are you going?" He hesitated a moment, then followed her.

"Do you remember once telling me about your father? About how he didn't have any favorite things. Is she like that?"

"Make sense."

"Well, this nice green chair, for instance. Does she always take it?" Jenny sat down. "How does it look with me in it?"

"Like a chair."

"Don't you know why I came here? To her home grounds? I had to check the competition, Charley; you know—take in the talent in the room." She stood and hurried upstairs, turning into the nearest bedroom. "Robby's?"

Charley nodded. "Quit this."

"It bothers you? Me in your son's room?"

"Of course not."

"Liar." She hurried out and down the hall into the master bedroom. "Packing?"

"That's right."

Jenny opened a closet door, grabbed a dress, held it against her body. "Tiny," she said. "On me, anyway. But then, I'm such a horse." She gestured to a picture of Betty Jane on Charley's bureau. "God, she's pretty. Pretty and petite. I could kill her."

Charley said nothing.

Jenny started to laugh.

"The joke?"

"The joke is that I can't remember a time when we've disliked each other more than we do now. And what's the subject under discussion? Why, divorce, naturally. That's funny, Charley. Think about it. I'm furious with you for last night; you're furious with me for coming here. Well, I'm sick of me for coming here and I'll bet you're a little angry at yourself for last night. We make a pretty cold quartet, you and I." She dabbed some of Betty Jane's perfume behind her ears and stood next to Charley. "Like it?"

"Let's go downstairs, shall we?"

"Not yet."

"Why not?"

Jenny gestured toward the bed. "It's sleepytime down south." She lifted the suitcase, set it on a chair. "Who gets to undress who?"

"I'm sorry."

"Meaning?"

"Meaning no."

"I told you, I've got to take in the talent in the room. Betty Jane's welcome to my sofa bed. Anytime."

"And I told you no."

"Why?"

"I don't think either of us would enjoy it."

"Who said anything about enjoying it?" She switched out the light, undressed, walked straight into his arms, slammed her body up against his. He grabbed her, kneaded her body with his great hands. She guided them toward the bed. They tumbled down on top, rolling around, his hands raiding her flesh until she screamed "You're hurting me!"

"Good."

"I could hurt you—bite you—"

"Do it."

"No, you'd like that, because then she'd see—she'd make the choice, not you. I'll never mark you till you're mine. So hurt me now—I don't care—hurt me all you want to."

Charley did as he was told.

At four the next morning he drove her to New Brunswick. She insisted on lying on the floor of the back seat. All the time he drove she giggled. When they reached the outskirts of New Brunswick, he started laughing too. He let her off and waved goodbye and went back home, making excellent time, considering how long he wasted parking by the side of the road when he was weeping too hard to see to drive.

Charley and Rudy Miller walked through the hot ghetto, skirting swirls of Puerto Ricans, eddies of Jews. Down Rivington Street they went, the late-afternoon sun still visible over the old tenements. Close ahead of them lay the babble of Orchard Street. They turned into the sound. "Yes, I'm happy," Charley said. "Believe me, it's the truth. Listen: there's a reason people have affairs. And the reason is because it's not unenjoyable. Jenny's a great girl. She loves me. I'm really happy. I know what I'm doing and I'm fine."

"Bullshit," Rudy said.

Charley made no reply.

"I'm fresh out!"

"Out of what?"

Rudy raised his arms high and wide and shouted "Instant Pity!" into the air. Then he stopped in front of a pickle stand and held up two fingers.

"Have a whole jar," the pickle lady said. "Special today. Forty cents."

"Two pickles and no lip or I take my business to Levy three stands down."

"It's not good for Jews to be tightwads," the pickle lady said. "Gives the religion a bad name."

"Levy wins me," Rudy said, and he waved a brisk goodbye. "Oh, Charles, if I could manufacture enough Instant Pity I could likely save the world, but it's hard to come by and I had this little bit left only, and as I was walking to the subway stop to meet you this ancient, wretched, leprous cripple hobbled up to me and said, 'Help me, help me, my wife has cancer, my daughter leukemia, my son just ran off with a *shiksa*, my mother heard the news and went insane and the shock of that killed my father on the spot and on top of everything else my piles are acting up.' Could there be a sadder story, Charles? I doubt it, but I didn't weep. I just whipped out my last smidgen of Instant Pity and I gave it to him and said, 'Take this, just add air,' and he downed it, and do you know that inside five seconds not only was he chipper but his piles were gone."

Charley smiled. "Remarkable."

"If only I'd known I would have saved it. If I had it to give you, you'd love me. 'That Rudy,' you'd think. 'Such heart. Such infinite understanding.' But alas, I fail you, Charles. You'll have to bleed alone. What are you having an affair for, fool?"

"I love her."

"Of course you do, you have to. But have you told her?"

"No."

"That would mean subsequent action, yes? You love her, you get divorced. So you can't tell her. Oh, Charles, I have had, believe thee me, affairs, and I know. Hello, Levy."

The pickle man nodded.

"This is my friend Charles Fiske, the famous Gentile. He wants a Levy pickle. I have told him that Levy is the king of cucumbers. Don't disappoint him."

"I saw you," Levy said. "Talking with my competition. You held up two fingers."

"Meaning two centuries," Rudy explained. "I told her that's how long it would take her to match your product. Two hundred years to be your equal, so give my friend a garlic pickle, crisp and sharp. And one for me, while you're at it."

Levy ducked his old hands into the nearest barrel.

"Thief!" Rudy cried. "Those are your soft pickles. Your old, soft, wrinkled, inferior—"

Levy sighed and reached into a different barrel.

Rudy took the pickles, paid for them and handed one to Charley. "Bite."

Charley bit. Then he nodded and made a smile.

"Hardly an ecstatic response," Rudy said to Levy. "But what can you expect from a Gentile?" They started walking again, down the loud street. "What we're not supposed to talk about today is what we're feeling; am I correct, Charles?"

"I suppose so."

Rudy nodded. "When you suggested a walk down Orchard Street and then told me of your high jinks—Orchard Street is hardly the place to bare the soul. What do you want from me, Charles?"

"Cover."

"Explain."

"If you hear from Betty Jane, and she happens to ask did you happen to see me at some particular time, if she wonders were we together—"

"The answer is always yes?"

"The answer is always yes."

"I like her. Why should I lie?"

"No reason."

"Do you like her?"

"I've tried not to do much thinking lately."

"Well, when you were thinking, why did you marry her?"

"Why?"

Rudy stopped in front of a clothing cart and fingered a shirt. "Stein," he said.

Stein nodded.

"You have the finest taste on Orchard Street, you know that? Stein, if I had a million in solid gold I would still buy my clothes from you."

"You'd be a fool," Stein said.

"But a fool with impeccable taste," Rudy said, dropping the shirt, walking again.

"There's a look," Charley said. "A look—I don't mean just a face; I mean a whole kind of *look*—if you're who I am—"

"Who you were—"

"Right. Who I was. If you're who I was—what the hell, Betty Jane looked like my wife. When I first saw her, I can still remember sort of nodding, almost in recognition."

"Some Enchanted Evening," Rudy said.

Charley ignored him, hurrying on. "I had just turned down many millions and my prospects weren't all that limitless and I saw this girl . . ."

Charley stopped and stood there, Rudy watching him, as the people crowded by them, bumping them, pushing them together, forcing them apart. "I saw this girl and she smiled at me and I could tell. It was very goddam romantic, if you want to know the truth." He began shaking his head, sharply, and his eyes quicky closed. "Son of a bitch, son of a bitch, I should have known something was wrong even then—I met her in Schrafft's! How can you be romantic in Schrafft's? She was having a sundae with this girlfriend of hers, Penny, and I walked over to them and said something crazy and we were married before the month was out and how the hell was I supposed to know. You meet someone and fall in love and they're not supposed to turn out stupid. Isn't that right?" He stared at Rudy. The crowd milled around them, tiny Puerto Ricans, ancient Jews. "What am I doing, Rudy? The other day I cried. I was driving and the next thing I couldn't see the road. Will you cover for me? Will you lie? What am I doing? Am I crazy? What's the answer?"

Rudy raised his arms again, raised them high, spread them wide. "The answer is always yes," he said.

"Shall we get comfortable?" Jenny asked, nodding toward the sofa bed. Charles stared at the blue walls. "If you'd like."

"If you would."

"Would you?"

"It's up to you."

"No, really."

"Fair is fair. I made the suggestion; you make the decision."

"I hate these goddam blue walls," Charley said.

Jenny said nothing.

Charley made a smile. "I can decide anything except decisions."

"Have you thought about it, speaking of decisions?"

"Thought about what?" he said.

"The name of the game."

"Oh, that. I have."

"And?"

"Life without you would be unbearable," Charley said. "Have I told you lately?"

"Are you being nasty?"

"I don't know. I just hate these blue walls so, it's hard to tell what I'm being."

"Why don't we paint them?"

"Why don't we?"

"If we painted them, they wouldn't be blue anymore."

"Not unless we painted them blue all over again. Let's get the hell out of here."

"Where?"

"Let's walk along the river."

"Sold." She threw on her coat. "Will you be warm enough?"

"Yes, Mother."

"Well, it's *cold* out. It's practically November."

"You're from the north woods; you're supposed to like it cold."

"I left, didn't I?"

"True." He opened the apartment door, held it for her. They hurried out to the sidewalk, then slipped silently across the street and over to Riverside Drive. They entered the park quickly, walking down to the Hudson, slowing when they reached the promenade along the river. "Betty Jane went to see Rudy," Charley said then. "Yesterday."

"And?"

"He lied. She believes him."

"You're sure?"

"When you want to believe, you believe."

"What did she ask him?"

"Nothing specific. Just was I acting funny. Rudy said he thought I was. Work pressures—that sort of thing. Betty Jane agreed with him completely."

"Is that why he came to the office today? To tell you?"

"I guess so. I don't know. Whenever he's up near the office and feels like it, he drops in. Mostly he stays in the ghetto."

"What's with him?"

"God knows. He crazy, if that's what you mean."

"Why did you pick him? To lie for us?"

"Because I knew he would. He does that kind of thing."

"Lies?"

"No. He just happens to be the kind of guy that if you ask him to do something, he does it."

"You like him?"

"We like each other. I think I can say that."

"Why?"

"What are you so full of questions for?"

"I'm thinking of having an affair with him. He's kind of incredible-looking. Is he a good writer?"

"I think so."

"And you've known him how long?"

"What is it with you?"

"I just want to know a little bit about my savior. How do you know you can trust him? You've known him how long?"

"Ever since I went to work for Kingsway. I was on the slop pile. You know, reading all the unsolicited manuscripts. You never accept any of them, but somebody's got to read them, and I was given the job. I was reading ten books a day, sometimes fifteen—"

"A *day*?"

"You just read them until you know for sure they stink. That only takes a few pages usually. I was going crazy doing that. There's a limit to how much of that suff you can read. I had this Maxwell Perkins image of myself. I wanted to discover somebody. Then I came across *The Nose Is for Laughing*. I can still remember how it began. 'First there was the nose. There were other features: eyes, a sweet mouth, elf's ears. But first, before you could consider them, first there was the nose.' It went something like that."

"Whose nose?"

"The narrator's father. It was just a little book, a novella, about this kid and his father and their life in this delicatessen. The father was very old, and his hearing was bad, and one day he got sick and went *deaf*. It ruined him. He thought he was a freak. The kid loved him, but the father wouldn't believe it. He just wouldn't. So finally the kid clapped his hands over his ears until the drums popped. And he was deaf too. And the father saw the kid did love him, and when he found out, he started to cry, and the kid cried too, and that was how the book ended, the two of them hugging each other and crying in the empty store." Charley smiled. "I would have liked that book if I'd just picked it up at the library, but after a million years of fifteen books a day, it had quite an effect on me."

"What did you do?"

"Well, first off, I ran in to see Dave Boardman." Charley leaned against the railing and looked down at the cold river. "I burst in on Boardman and told him I found this beautiful little novel on the slop pile and he picked up his golf ball out of his desk and started whipping it against the wall and called me feebleminded, but I kept after him until he promised to read the book that night. Just because I liked it didn't mean anything; but if he liked it, then the firm would publish it, so he took the book home with him while I tried calling up the author. R. V. Miller and an address—that's all the book had on it—but there wasn't any R. V. Miller in the telephone directory and the address on the book was way down in the ghetto along Orchard Street. I'd never been there before but I went. I asked people and finally I found this crummy building and the landlady said a Miller lived there and I knocked on this door and knocked and knocked but there wasn't any answer. Just for the hell of it I turned the knob and the door opened and there was this kid looking at me. This beautiful kid. And he said 'Yes?' and I said 'Mr. Miller?' and he said 'Yes?' again and I said that I was with the Kingsway people, and for the third time, he said 'Yes?' and I said 'I loved your book, I loved it!' and the next thing I knew we were both laughing and hugging each other in the empty room, just like the ending of the book all over again."

Jenny kissed him.

"Jenny kiss'd me," Charley said. They started to walk. "Then I found out he was deaf. The book was autobiographical. His father was the old man with the big nose. And he made himself deaf, Rudy did, to prove to his father how much he loved him. But I told you already he was crazy."

"Boardman hated the book, I bet. That's why you didn't publish it."

"No. Boardman liked it. You had to like it; it was that good. Boardman thought it might even sell—the characters were Jews and Jews like reading about themselves, Boardman thinks. 'Jews buy books' is the exact quote. He thought it might sell but I *knew* it would, and I knew everything was going to work out great for both Rudy and me, it couldn't miss jumping straight from the slop pile to the best-seller lists. So we published it and you know what? It sold a big fat eleven hundred and six copies. I think I probably bought half of them. And then I found out that Betty Jane bought the other half. It got reviewed four places, little magazines, all favorably. It was just so sad, eleven hundred and six copies. I did O.K. out of it. Boardman liked me. I guess I more or less became his boy. Anyway, it got me off the slop pile and—" Charley whirled on the river— "eleven hundred and six son-of-a-bitching copies! Everything was going to work out so great—goddammit!"

"What's wrong?"

"She shouldn't have bought those copies! She shouldn't have!"

"Charley—"

"She'll never find out! Not about us. What you want to believe you believe!"

XVIII

Well, it was a blow, the rejection of *Autumn Wells*. Aaron didn't bother trying to deny it. The whole thing could hardly have been worse. His pride was battered, his ego bloody, and for a while he had a little difficulty in getting back into the swing of things. But if wounds don't heal, you die, and he had no intention of doing that, so he drifted around the city, letting the healing process take its own sweet time. He went to museums when he felt like it, and he window-shopped when he felt like it, but mostly he went to the movies.

He loved movies, always had. He knew who the stars were and the supporting players and sometimes the bit players and the writers of course, and occasionally he could come up with the cameraman or even the set designer. There were more than a dozen movies on 42nd Street going almost twenty-four hours a day, their programs changing constantly, and for Aaron 42nd Street was very close to heaven. He saw every Bogart revival, especially *Casablanca*. No one was as good as Bogart except Cary Grant, so he caught all of Cary's films too and he saw *It Happened One Night* and Jimmy Cagney strutting through *Yankee Doodle Dandy* and James Mason dying through *Odd Man Out* and Joanie Crawford in *Mildred Pierce*, and *Gaslight* and *Gunga Din* and *Sergeant York* and *Tarzan and the Slave Girl* and *The Snake Pit* and *The Informer* and *San Francisco* and *Pittsburgh* and *Knute Rockne, All American* and *Scudda Hoo, Scudda Hay* and *Letter to Three Wives* and *All about Eve* and *Asphalt Jungle* and maybe a million more and sometimes, if he felt in the mood, he would wait around the theater lobbies for a little companionship and usually it didn't mean too long a wait. He found quick companions from all over: a farmer from Indiana, a sailor from France and others, with varying occupations, from New Jersey and California and Nebraska and Italy and England and Paris, France, and San Juan, Puerto Rico, although that wasn't much to brag about, and Portland, Des Moines, Denver, and then, one hot summer night, he found a big black jazz dancer from Harlem.

The dancer's name was Walker. He was very muscular and wore a tight white tee shirt and tight white pants. And he swished. Every few steps he would accentuate the movement of his white-covered butt, and Aaron would laugh. It wasn't funny, but Aaron laughed anyway, because he knew he was supposed to, because he knew Walker thought it was simply hysterically hilarious, and he couldn't disappoint Walker. They moved through the summer heat, away from the lights of 42nd, moving west toward Walker's car. Walker was telling a story about his mother and her man, and whenever he was his mother he would drop his voice as deep as he could and whenever he was her man he would swish, his white teeth gleaming in appreciation at Aaron's laughter. Aaron hoped his laughing sounded convincing—Walker's smile seemed to indicate that it did—but it was hard work, laughing at what was not remotely funny, smiling when you weren't laughing, pleasing the swish; it was terribly hard work, for he loathed swishes, Aaron did, absolutely loathed them. (Why did he pick them then? What possible reason?) They swung down Eighth Avenue for several blocks, then west, Walker talking faster than before, his exaggerations even more crude. The air was growing increasingly muggy; a bolt of lightning struck down over New Jersey and after a moment they heard the distant sound of summer thunder. They began moving faster as the thunder died, hurrying along the empty street, crossing Ninth Avenue, heading toward Tenth.

It was then that Aaron had his *gestalt*.

He had first encountered that word years before in a psychology text. An experiment was done, involving a monkey, a chair and a banana. The banana was hung from the ceiling of a room, too high for the monkey to jump for. But, if the monkey set the chair under the banana, he could simply mount the chair and pluck the banana down. The monkey, however, not being possessed of much logic, would jump for the banana, and jump and jump, coming close, but never able quite to grab it. Then came the monkey's *gestalt*. It happened invariably when the monkey saw the chair and the banana in a single visual line. Once that happened, the monkey picked up the chair, placed it under the banana, clambered up and devoured his prize. The two things that Aaron saw in a single visual line were not, of course, a chair and a banana; he saw Walker and a small children's playground. The playground, which they were rapidly approaching, was very dark. And Walker—this is what provoked the gasp from Aaron—Walker, for just an instant, was not swishing. And so, Aaron's *gestalt*: My God, my God, he's going to roll me.

"Hey, man, what's with you?"

"Nothing," Aaron answered. He stopped to light a cigarette. "We're not in a race, you know. Nobody says we have to run."

"Gimme a butt."

Aaron held the cigarettes out. His hands were trembling.

"Nervous in the service," Walker said, holding Aaron's hands steady, extracting a cigarette from the pack. "Light." Aaron struck a match. Walker laughed. "Man, you need Miltown. Fast." He lit his cigarette.

Then they started to walk. The playground was perhaps fifty yards away.

"So where was I?"

"Talking about your mother."

"Man, I know that. But in what precise part of the narrative did I leave off?"

"You were at the part where ... where the guy was ... he was ..." Aaron knew. He knew exactly. But he couldn't quite say it. The playground was thirty yards away.

Aaron stopped.

Walker flashed him a smile, threw an arm around his shoulder and nursed him step by step forward. Twenty-five yards. Now fifteen.

Aaron ducked loose. "My raincoat," he said. "I ought to have my raincoat. I think I left it at the movies. No. It's back at my place. It's going to rain."

"O.K., we'll drive up to your place."

"I don't want to put you to all that trouble."

"Sweetie, it's no trouble." And again the black arm wrapped itself around his thin shoulders. Aaron's whole body was trembling by now and Walker felt it, for he flashed the smile again. "Relax now, hear? Walker'll treat you nice and easy."

I'll report you, Aaron thought. Right to the police. If you even try and roll me I'll report you. I'll give them a description and you'll go straight to jail, black boy. Walker Brown, six foot two, two hundred pounds, twenty-five, scar on left hand, scar on left cheek, jazz dancer, long hair, no mustache, black skin. I'll give that to the police—

No.

He could not report it. Not to the police. Never. "What were you doing in that area, Mr. Fire? With a queer, Mr. Fire? You queer too, Mr. Fire? Sodomy's illegal, Mr. Fire. Didn't you know that, Mr. Fire?"

He could not report it. Not to the police. Not to anyone. If it happened, he was helpless. Nowhere to turn.

The playground lay just ahead of them now, narrow, black and deep.

"Nice and easy," Walker soothed.

"Listen to me a second—"

"Nice and easy," Walker said again, his arm tight around Aaron's neck.

"Listen to me—"

"You talk too much."

"Walker—"

"Too damn much." Walker turned his strong body and led Aaron into the playground.

Aaron tried to laugh. "What's this, a short cut?"

Walker said nothing.

"I don't like playgrounds. Cut it out, Walker. Where's your car?"

Aaron struggled now but Walker only led him deeper into the darkness, his big arm taut, the muscles bulging against Aaron's skin.

"Dammit, let go!"

Walker let go.

"I'm telling you, Walker. You hear me? You better not do it."

"Do what?" Walker said, and then he swung.

His hard fist landed high on Aaron's cheek. Aaron could not remember having been hit like that before and he expected to tumble backward, like in the movies, falling over something, gracefully jumping to his feet, ready for battle. Bogart would have reacted that way. But this was different. Aaron didn't tumble, didn't fall. He simply grunted once and stepped backward one step. "Ow," he said. "Ow," and his hands raced to protect his swelling cheek.

Walker swung again, this time to the mouth.

Aaron tasted blood. His lip was gashed and it hurt, it hurt. He should be fighting back, he knew, hitting out with his own fists, but he didn't know how, and his lip hurt as the blood burst loose. "I haven't got any money," Aaron whispered. "Just enough for the movies, that's all." His breath came in gasps and he wasn't sure the words made any sense until he heard Walker whisper "You better," and then another punch landed, doubling his pain.

The black fist collided with Aaron's neck, slamming at the Adam's apple, and Aaron dropped straight down to his knees. He knelt there, helpless, his long arms dangling until Walker hit him again, then again, punch after punch, bending Aaron over backward with their power. At last an elbow crashed against his cheek and Aaron sprawled full length on the hot pavement. He lay still, trying to breathe, trying to crawl, anything to stop the pain.

"Faggot!" Walker said. "Fuckin' faggot!" and he punched down with his fist, hitting the bloody side of Aaron's face, driving it brutally against the pavement.

After that, Aaron didn't feel much.

Oh, he was aware. He was aware of Walker's black hands as they scurried over his body, finding pockets, ripping out their contents; he was aware of Walker's panting, of his whispered curses; he was aware of the final gratuitous kick that was probably aimed for his face but missed, skimming and scraping his ear, making it bleed. But he didn't feel much. He just lay there. He never lost consciousness. There was no point in trying to move—not for a while. He could not command his brain sufficiently to order his limbs into action. Aaron lay stretched, without thought, without movement, lifeless, alive. Some time later he heard a sound that frightened him, an animal sound, a rhythmic gasping and it took him a while but he finally deduced he was hearing himself and that spurred him into action.

He moved his hand.

Not much, not far, simply from the back to the palm, flip-flop. The cost of the movement was enormous—motionless, he had forgotten the pain; now he remembered it—but it made him proud. See? I can move my hand. Flip-flop. Flip-flop. Hey, everybody, looka me. I can move my hand.

The rain, long promised, finally arrived after an endless prelude of thunder. A deadly bolt of lightning lit the night and then the first drops ticked down, gentle and soft—incongruous following such an introduction. The gentle drops stopped. Nothing. Then with a hiss the rain started, sheet after sheet, cold. Aaron licked the wet pavement with his tongue. The rain picked up tempo, drumming. Puddles began to form, filling the irregularities in the pavement. Aaron called for his right arm and after a moment it drew in under his body. He rested, letting the rain beat down. Then his left arm began to move, not stopping until it too was tucked beneath him. He rested. A bolt of lightning followed a clap of thunder and Aaron strained, pushing himself up on his elbows. Puddles were all around him now and as he looked down, another bolt of lightning exploded and for just an instant Aaron saw himself in water. And seeing, gaped in disbelief. You? Here? Like this? On the ground? At night? Crying in the rain?

Crying? Am I crying?

He was. Big boys didn't, they weren't supposed to, but there he was, a big boy crying, for the first time in ever so long, crying, filling the night with regret, and though he tried to stop—Aaron thrashing, thrashing in the rain—he could not, and at last his long body subsided, and he closed his eyes, and he gave himself up to his tears.

In the morning, shortly after dawn, two small boys entered the playground, bouncing a basketball back and forth between them. They were chattering, but when they saw the gaunt object lying stretched and still, they stopped, advancing on it slowly, standing over it, looking from it to each other, back and forth.

"Hey, mistuh," the first boy said.

Aaron gazed at him.

"You O.K., mistuh?" the second boy said.

Aaron transferred his gaze.

"You bettah go home, mistuh," the first boy said.

Aaron went home.

Aaron sat stiffly in the chair. At the desk, the doctor smiled at him—an encouraging smile. Aaron took out a cigarette and put it in the corner of his mouth but he had difficulty lighting it. Three matches were needed. "I'm nervous," Aaron said.

Gunther nodded.

"I've never done anything like this before. I don't know where to begin."

"Well, why don't you begin with what brought you here?"

Aaron nodded, trying to think. "What brought me here?"

"Yes."

"Well, I don't seem to be getting anywhere."

"Some days I feel that way too," the doctor said, smiling again. "Go on."

"Well," Aaron said. "Well," and then nothing. He was terribly nervous and that was the one thing he shouldn't have been. The social worker at the Institute for Free Therapy had told him that when he was sent out for his interview that he should above all not be nervous. "Just talk," she had said. "Relax and talk." And here he was, at the crucial interview, unable to relax, not able to talk. If he was to get accepted at the clinic, he would have to get this Gunther's approval; if Gunther recommended him for free treatment, and the Institute board passed the recommendation, then he could start. If Gunther said no, then nothing. Gunther was looking at him now, waiting, a pipe in his fat hands. Everything about Gunther was fat. At least three hundred pounds, Aaron guessed. Three hundred pounds and not that tall. Gunther lit the pipe. Aaron stared around the room. The walls were lined with books and the windows looked out over Central Park. The inevitable couch stood in one corner. Aaron glanced back at the books. Say something. Something.

"Well, I just don't seem to be getting anywhere, that's all."

"And that's what brought you here?"

Aaron looked out at the September sun. "No, see, I was robbed. A couple of weeks ago. It upset me. I called the clinic the next day. But they couldn't give me an interview till now."

Gunther nodded. "There is nothing in this world so hard to find as an analyst in August." He paused again, waiting.

"It's very hard," Aaron blurted. "Just all of a sudden talking."

"Well, why don't you tell me about yourself? What do you do?"

"I'm a writer."

"A writer? Wonderful. Will you excuse a stupid question, but have you written anything I should have read?"

"No. I only wrote one book. *Autumn Wells*, I called it. It was rejected."

"When was this?"

"Three years ago."

"And everybody rejected it?"

"No. Just this one place. I never sent it out after that."

"Why?"

"I don't know; I meant to. I just never quite got around to doing it."

"And the past three years?"

"I . . ." A shrug. "I . . ." A quick smile. "Nothing. Nothing."

"All right, we can come back to that. Tell me this. Where—"

"I went to the movies! O.K.? For three years. I went to the movies. Every day. Oh, I did other things, but mostly I just went to the movies. That's all. That's all."

"I hope for your sake you like them."

Aaron laughed. "Of course I like them. I'm not that crazy."

"I'll tell you if you're that crazy," Gunther said, and then he laughed, all of him, shaking up and down. "You're embarrassed about it?"

"Wouldn't you be?"

"Why did you go?"

"It passed the time. No, more than that. I don't know. I just went, that's all."

"And how did you afford this cinematic orgy?"

"Odd jobs, this and that."

"How odd is your present job?"

"I drive a taxi. On weekends. I have the last couple of years. It gets me by."

"Did you go to college?"

"Yessir. Princeton."

"Finish?"

"Yessir."

"How were your grades?"

"Good enough."

"Honors?"

"That's right."

"I thought so." Gunther smiled. "Sometimes I'm terribly acute," he said. "Tell me, Mr. Fire, couldn't you have gotten a better job somewhere in this city?"

"I guess so. I tried one or two. I don't take orders very well."

"You were fired?"

"I was fired."

"Did that please you?"

Aaron lit another cigarette. "I don't understand."

"Let it pass. Where do you live now?"

"West Eighty-fourth Street. Between Amsterdam and Columbus."

"Of your own choice?"

"Yessir."

"That's supposed to be the worst street in the city."

"Yessir, you bet it is."

"Is that why you live there?"

"What does that mean?"

"What do you think it means?"

"I live there—" Aaron jammed out his cigarette—"I live there because when I was looking for a place there was a place there I could afford, so I took it, O.K.?"

"O.K."

"I'm sorry."

"For what?"

"I shouldn't have talked to you like that."

"Why shouldn't you?"

Aaron shrugged.

"Because you're afraid I won't like you and if I don't like you I won't recommend you to the clinic, is that it?"

"Yes."

"Mr. Fire, the last person I recommended was a young woman who was practically a carbon copy of my first wife whom I loathed beyond belief. Does that make you feel any better?"

"Yes."

"Swear at me if you want to, Mr. Fire. Do anything you want, except please stop saying 'I don't know' to questions we both know you know the answers to, O.K.?"

"O.K."

"Now, you said you were robbed."

"Yes."

"Who robbed you?"

"Some guy."

"Where did this happen?"

"Over near Ninth Avenue. Between Ninth and Tenth. At night."

"A slum area?"

"Yes."

"You were walking alone through this slum area at night and some guy robbed you?"

"Yes."

"Are you lying?"

"Yes."

Gunther put his pipe down. "Please, Fire—"

"I don't want to talk about the robbery."

"That's a hell of a thing to tell an analyst. 'I don't want to talk about it.'"

"I don't. It's not important."

"You just finished saying it was what brought you here."

"I was probably lying again."

"Do you lie a lot?"

"Yes, yes, all the ti— No, I don't lie. I never lie, except sometimes I do."

"Well, that about covers it," Gunther said. He emptied his pipe in the wastebasket, then filled it again. "Fire, you want to get accepted at the Institute, don't you?"

"Oh yes. I must."

Gunther lit his pipe. "Tell me about your family, Fire."

"My father's dead."

"And your mother?"

"She's all right. My sister too."

"When did your father die?"

"Long time ago."

"Do you remember anything about it?"

"I don't know."

"You don't know?"

"I mean I haven't tried."

"Try."

"How?"

"Just think about it. Close your eyes. Try and remember."

Aaron closed his eyes. Then he opened them. "No," he said. "Nothing."

"Take your time. Humor me; do it again."

Aaron closed his eyes. He sat very stiffly in the chair, his eyes shut tight. Gunther puffed on his pipe. "The grass," Aaron said, and then he shook his head, eyes wide. "That's funny."

"Funny?"

"All of a sudden my throat—I felt like I wanted to cry."

"Try it again. Please."

Aaron leaned back in the chair, his hands over his eyes. "He died on the grass. It was very green. It—no."

"Go on."

"No. I had that feeling again."

"I've seen tears."

"Not mine, you haven't."

"True, Fire, not yours."

"Look, he died on the grass. He fell down on the grass and he died. That's all there is. I don't want to talk about it."

Gunther smiled. "That and the robbery you don't want to talk about."

"Correct."

"Did you report the robbery?"

"Hell no."

"I would have if I'd been robbed. I would have gone to the police. Why didn't you?"

"Are you trying to insinuate something?"

Gunther said nothing.

"Look, I didn't report it because I didn't want to because I didn't have much money on me so what was the point because who wants to get mixed up with the cops when you don't have to anyway?"

Gunther heaved his bulk around in the chair so that he was facing the desk and jotted down something on a piece of paper.

"What are you doing?"

Gunther finished his note.

"What are you writing down there? Is it about me? What are you writing about me?"

"Anyone ever tell you you're suspicious?"

"What did you write down about me?"

"It's a reminder to myself to pick up my wife's clothes at the cleaner's." He held out the paper. "Read for yourself."

Aaron waved his hand. "No. I'm sorry."

"What did you think I was writing?"

"What do you know about me?"

"Just what you've told me. Precious little."

"I thought you were putting something down about me," Aaron

said. "There's this thing about shrinkers. You never know what they're thinking."

"What in the world are you afraid of?"

"I'm not afraid of anything."

Gunther smiled.

"I'm not. Not of anything."

Gunther watched him, the smile lingering.

"You're the suspicious one," Aaron said. "Not me. Can we get a little air in here? That pipe, it's very strong."

"Help yourself." And Gunther indicated the window.

Aaron rose from the chair, hurrying across the room, yanking the window up. "There. That's a lot better." He stared out. "Central Park," he said. "You take the rest of the city, just leave me Central Park."

"How long have you lived here?"

"Three years."

"And you don't like it?"

"I hate it."

"Why don't you leave?"

Aaron just looked at him. "Leave New York?"

"It's been done."

"I couldn't. I just couldn't. You *come* to New York, you don't *leave* it. I mean, nobody's *from* New York. They're all from Kansas City or Pittsburgh or Roanoke, Virginia. But they come here. They don't like it, but they don't leave either. Nobody likes it here. You're not supposed to like it here. But you gotta come anyway. It's the place. New York's the place. But you're not supposed to like it."

"And you came here to be a writer."

"Yes."

"Are you a good writer?"

Aaron said nothing.

"We haven't got much time, Fire. Now come back and sit down and tell me."

Aaron sat down. "I don't know," he said. "I used to think I was. Once, I was positive. Now I don't know anymore."

"These past three years—have you written?"

"It's hard to write here. To concentrate, I mean. There's so much to do."

"What did you do? I know, you went to the movies. Besides that?"

"I wrote a little. Not much. Nothing, really. I don't know. Things. Like that."

"Social life?"

"Oh, sure. I went out with a lot of girls. I did that. I dated plenty."

"Read?"

"Sure. No, not so much. Like I said, it's hard to concentrate, there's so much to do."

"What are you afraid of?"

"Nothing."

"I've had that answer. What are you afraid of?"

"Not you! I'll tell you that. Not you and your stupid questions."

"Then why won't you answer them?"

"I will! Ask me anything! I'll answer it. Go ahead. Ask me anything!"

"Why didn't you report the robbery to the police?"

Aaron had to laugh. He looked across at the fat bland face and he roared. "I know what you're thinking and you're wrong. As a matter of fact, I'm living with this girl right now. A dancer. She's a dancer and as far as sex is concerned she's practically a nymphomaniac and I'm the first guy she's found who can satisfy her. In her whole life, the first guy."

"How long have you been living with her?"

"Eight, nine months; going on a year."

"You plan to marry her?"

"Hell no."

"Why not?"

"She's a spic! Her name's Chita. You just can't go around marrying a girl named Chita. What do you think my mother would do if I brought some girl named Chita home to marry? Chita Lopez. Boy, that'd be funny if I brought old Chita home. Not that there's anything wrong with the way she looks, you understand. She's great-looking. She's got this incredible body, not skinny like most dancers. I mean she's got these great breasts and a real ass on her. But she's lithe like a dancer. The things she can do with that body. You wouldn't believe what she can do. And her face is pretty. Oh, she's dark, sure, but really pretty. Big black eyes and a nasty mouth. And she's smart, too. Not one of those dumb spics. She had two years of college—she majored in English—she reads all the time. That's how we met, because of the reading. See, I carry a book with me in the cab and she got in and she had a book too and she said was I reading that book—it was *Crime and Punishment* by Dostoevski—and I said I was and she said that that was funny because most cab drivers don't read and I pointed at her book and said neither did most Puerto Ricans and we both laughed and after that we got to talking and she gave me her name and when I got off duty I called her and we went for a walk in Central Park, talking about this and that, books mostly, and when we were done walking we went to her place and she said she really liked me but she wasn't sure we ought to shack up on account of her being, like I said, almost a nymphomaniac that nobody could satisfy but I told her I was the boy so we hit the sack and she was a tiger growling and clawing at me but I stayed with her right to the end riding her down and afterwards she kissed me like a little baby and kept saying I was right, I was her boy, over and over, I was her boy, and then she had to go to work at this club and I went along, sitting at the best table by myself even though the place was packed with all these guys, and when Chita came out they went crazy just from watching her, screaming her name and jumping up and waving money, but she just looked at me and that was something, let me tell you, all these guys going crazy, and I sat there smiling because it was me she wanted, not any of the other guys, just me, I was her boy, so we've been together ever since and she loves me something awful, waits on me, does what I tell her, she really loves me and I suppose she wants to marry me and she really is a great thing, smart and gorgeous, but it's strictly a bed relationship, what we have, at least as far as I'm concerned that's all it can ever be, strictly a bed relationship, even though she loves me and brings me presents and is great-looking with two years of college and . . . and . . ." Aaron closed his eyes. "It's not ringing true, is it?"

"I don't know. Is it?"

"No," Aaron said. "No."

Gunther said nothing.

"I'm homosexual," Aaron said, and he opened his eyes. "Why is that?"

Gunther said nothing.

"It's really crazy, me being homosexual, because I hate it. I hate it so much. The whole dirty life. Everything. It's just so degrading. It humiliates you so. I hate the life but I lead it. And that's crazy. And I hate them too. All of them. The gay boys that swish; the gray boys too. That's my word. I made it up. The gray boys, the shadowy ones, the ones you can't tell by looking at. Like me. I'm gray. You couldn't tell about me, could you? From looking. You didn't know."

"No. Why, is it important to you?"

"Yes." Aaron sank back into the chair, his shoulders sagging, his arms hanging down almost to the floor. "Because I hate them." His voice was very soft. "I hate them." Aaron made a smile. "Myself worst of all. I've hated myself for so long now and I'm tired. Tired of hating myself. That's why the clinic, it's so important. I can't seem to get straightened away. I need help—something. I just don't seem to be able to untangle it. I'm just not getting anywhere."

"Your friends, are they homosexual?"

"No."

"None of them?"

"No friends; I've never had any. Not really what you'd call friends. No, that's not true. I had one once. My senior year in college. Hugh was his name. I liked him. We were very close. For a while."

"What happened to the friendship?"

"I killed it."

"Why?"

"It was very hard. For me to kill it. But I did."

"Why?"

"I did not ... trust ... my feelings toward him. You see, he didn't know about me, that I was ... what I was ... I didn't know it then either, but I suspected, and I cared—you see, he liked me, he really liked me— and I cared for him, but I was afraid ... that he might find out about me ... that I might not be able to ... control ... the way I felt and I could not let him find out that I was ... what I was—that would have humiliated me too much. I couldn't have taken that, for him to find out. He would have been so disappointed in me if he'd ever found out and I couldn't have that. So even though it was very ... hard—really it was, so hard—I killed it."

"How did you do that?"

"I have a gift for cruelty. You see, I'm ... I'm not nice. No, I'm not very nice and I hurt him. I knew where he was weak and I hit him there, just as hard as I could. I hurt him and he tried to make me stop, find out why, but I never let him know. I just hurt him and hurt him until it was dead."

"I'm sorry," Gunther said.

"Yes."

"This gift for cruelty, why do you think you have it?"

"What do you want me to say? That I'm afraid if I don't hurt them first they'll hurt me."

"Say what you want. If that's what you want to say, say that."

"I don't know why. But I do it all the time. I'm good at it. In the Army, there was this rich kid, Branch. Well, he was queer and he ran after me. I never run after people—never. They always come after me. I won't run after them because that way, whatever they get from me, I figure it's their fault; they deserve it. This Branch, I humiliated him. I never did the things to anyone I did to him. He liked it, though, but that's his problem, isn't it?" Aaron closed his eyes. "I have never been like that before, never that sadistic. I hate that word. I think that's the ugliest word. But sometimes I think that's what I am. A sadist. That thought, when I have it, it scares me."

"What scared you about the robbery? You said at the start it's what brought you here."

"The kids, maybe."

"Kids?"

"There were two of them. They had a basketball. They stood over me and told me to go home. This was in the morning. I had spent the whole night lying there I didn't know I'd spent the whole night. Oh, I felt the sun, all right, but I didn't realize how much time had gone, how long I'd been just lying there. One minute it was night, the next minute these kids were there. It made me wonder that maybe I was losing contact— something; I don't know."

"While you were lying there, what were you thinking?"

"I don't want to talk about it."

"Is that what really scares you? Is that what scares you most?"

"I don't want to talk about it."

"All right, Mr. Fire, you can go."

Aaron sat up, "Go?"

"That's right."

"You mean just leave? We're done?"

"That's right."

"Why are you doing this?"

"Our time was almost up anyway."

"You mean you're punishing me? Like I was in kindergarten?"

"You should hear from the clinic in about two weeks. One way or the other."

"Look, I didn't think anything. I just lay there. He'd hurt me, Walker'd hurt me and I wasn't sure I could move so I didn't."

"What kind of a name is Walker?"

"I don't know."

"Was he a Negro?"

"Yes."

"Do you always pick Negroes?"

"No. Never."

"But you did this time."

"Yes."

"Why?"

"I don't know."

"Do you like Negroes?"

"I don't know. Not particularly."

"You look down on them?"

"Sometimes."

"This Walker, did you look down on him?"

"Yes. He swished. Yes."

"You picked up an overt Negro homosexual?"

"Yes."

"Would it be fair to say that you were perhaps trying to degrade yourself? Particularly degrade yourself?"

"Maybe."

"Why were you?"

"I don't know."

"Did anything happen that week?"

"No."

"Did anything happen that day?"

"No."

"Think about it."

"Nothing happened. Nothing."

"Don't answer so quickly. Think. That day. Did anything happen?"

Aaron said nothing.

Gunther sucked his pipe.

"Yes."

"What?"

Aaron did his best to smile.

Gunther waited.

"I saw Branch," Aaron said, louder.

"The boy from the Army?"

"Yes."

"That upset you?"

"Yes," louder.

"Why?"

"It just did."

"But why?"

Aaron mumbled something.

"I didn't hear you."

Aaron said it again.

"Please, I can't hear you. You don't want what?"

"I DON'T WANT TO BE A WHORE! I DON'T WANT TO BE A WHORE!" and he was halfway up out of the chair when Gunther said "Aaron" very softly and probably that stopped him, his name, his name coming for the first time from the lips of the fat man with the pipe, for he froze, his body petrified for just a moment, before he slumped back deep into the chair, talking tonelessly. "He didn't say anything, Branch, really—just was I living here and was I living alone and I said yes, I was, yes, I was, both times, and then he said he was coming and would I wait for him until he got there. Would I wait for him. That was all he said. He's rich, don't you see? He's rich. He'll keep me. He'll get a nice apartment somewhere and he'll keep me. I won't have to do anything but be his whore and we'll all live happily ever after."

"If he calls you, say 'no.' "

Aaron moved his head, slowly, from side to side. "I don't think I could do that. I couldn't do that because, see, I'm not—how can I put it?—see, I *like* nice things. If somebody offers me something, it's very hard for me to turn it down. I'm not strong. Oh, I'm strong on some things, but not here. Because I don't feel much. Nothing warm. I feel cold things only. And when someone offers me something, I take it. I let them use me when I'm really using them, because, see, I have the seeds of the whore in me. I've seen whores. They come out of theaters with their . . . their patrons, and if they're young, then it's not so bad, but I've seen them when they weren't so young anymore and then it's painful. And I have the seeds of the whore in me. In the Army once, this guy—his name was Sergeant Terry—and he was ugly like an ape and he . . . he . . . introduced me to this splendid life and then when Branch came with his money I dumped him, Terry, without even thinking I dumped him, even though he cared for me, and I let Branch wine me and then when Branch got shipped someplace there was this Terry, begging for me to come back, and I couldn't much stand the sight of him but I came back to him for a while because it got me out of the Army. Terry, he had a friend, a doctor up at the post hospital, and so in return for the doctor setting up my discharge I let Terry use me for a little and that was a bad thing to do, a whore thing to do, but I didn't care, I mean they're only touching you on the outside, so what's a little touching, what harm does it do? Except . . . except see . . . it does do you harm because it was just another step toward being . . . It's the one thing in the world that scares me the most, being a whore, and I can feel it happening to me. It's why the clinic, I need the clinic, because I'm not strong enough, I don't think, to resist it by myself and . . . I can just feel it happening . . . me becoming what I most don't want to become . . . and that's why, after Walker, he'd rolled me, I cried. I don't cry much, I really don't, almost never, but it started to rain and I was lying there trying to raise up on my elbows and there was this terrible lightning and after a while I got up on my elbows and in the lightning I saw a puddle with my face in it and I thought that at last I had hit the bottom, nowhere to go but up, but then . . . then . . . I started to cry because . . . I remembered that Branch was coming . . . and I was going to end up a whore . . . nowhere to go but down . . . so I cried because . . . these last three years . . . they're going to be the good years compared with what's coming . . . I know that. These are the good years . . . these years now . . ."

"Let's hope not," Gunther said.

"Yes," Aaron said.

"Let's hope not," Gunther said again.

"Is my time up?"

"Five minutes ago."

Aaron nodded. "Thank you," he said and he stood, said "Thank you" again and walked toward the door.

"Fire."

"Yessir?"

"Fire, I am about to pay you the supreme compliment. I almost never do this. If my other patients heard about it, they would either hate you, hate me or switch analysts. But here it is, the supreme compliment: Fire, I shall walk you to the door." Gunther strained his arms against his chair, pushing, and slowly, very slowly, he got to his feet. "I'm never sure I'll make it," he said, and he exhaled deeply. Then, step by heavy step, he approached the door. "May I tell you something, Fire?"

"Yessir."

"I have had husbands who tried to destroy their wives, wives who wanted to kill their husbands, parents who craved the ruination of their children, so let me tell you—although you probably won't want to hear it and, when you do hear it, probably won't believe it—but you're only trying to destroy yourself, Fire, so you see, in the long run, you're not so bad. You're really not, not compared to the masters I've known, not so bad at all."

"Thank you." Aaron opened the door, stepped out, turned. Then he said, "And I don't think you're a bit overweight, either." Gunther laughed. Aaron smiled.

End of session.

•

Aaron lived the next days on the edge of panic. He fidgeted, tried to read, tried to sleep, smoked his throat raw. Outside his second-floor window, Puerto Ricans paraded, clogging the hot sidewalk, overflowing into the street. Stoop-sitters, they appeared to be; stoop-sitters, window-watchers, penny-pitchers, laughers and gossips. That was how they appeared, and on other crosstown streets, that was what they might have been. But not on 84th Street. Not West 84th. Peddlers, they were, peddlers all, hawking dope or their mothers or their sisters or brothers or wives or, if need be, themselves. For a buck. For the Yankee dollar. And day and night, from behind the semi-safety of sooted glass, Aaron eyed the swarthy Lilliputians, wondering why they had come here, what had possessed them to uproot themselves from their golden beaches and light here as dark strangers in a city of eternal cloud. Why here? What was here? Beyond the relief rolls, what? Was there dignity in pushing a cart through the garment district? Was there honor? Was there pride? Yet here they were, a million of them nearly, thin-bodied, red-eyed, their sole accomplishment being that they had at last given the Negro someone to look down on. Here they were, spindly little things, loathed, huddling in their ghettos, dreaming of golden sand (past imperfect) of green money (future improbable). Here they were, strutting on 84th Street, desperate for violence, cocks with no walk. Here they were born, here they died, the journey swift and chill. That was their great unwanted gift: aging. That was what they did best: age. Not the men. The men were born old. But the women: the smooth-skinned women, flashing and sultry, slender and strong—the women *aged*. Budding at twelve, at fourteen in bloom, fading at sixteen and at twenty gone, used, done. Plucked.

From his window, Aaron watched them wither.

There he would sit, elbows on his desk, smoking and watching. For two days and more, whenever it became clear that he could not concentrate to read, he would slip to the window and stare. Sometimes he could almost lose himself in the restlessness outside, the staccato shouts, the punctuating bursts of sad laughter. He came to recognize some of the faces and he would imagine little stories about them. There was one, a scrawny little girl, thick-legged and homely, but Aaron liked her. For she had eyes. Great black eyes, bright and frightened, frightened, he hoped, because inside she had a mind, and she was afraid she would die in this ghetto before anyone found out, before she ever had a chance to use it.

Her Aaron liked, and his little stories were mostly concerned with chance meetings with men who saw inside the flat body, who ripped her clear of the ghetto and set her down in some cloudless place where she could run and think and be. Carmen, he called her in his mind. Carmen Diaz, a pretty name for a girl with eyes, and when she stood on the street, off by herself, Aaron could almost relax, forget. But every so often, too often, his eyes would flick out like the tongue of a snake, flick toward the phone. And then he would remember what he was waiting for.

And then, panic.

The phone. The phone. The black phone. Silent now, but when it rang, whose voice would follow the ringing? Fat Gunther or bald Branch? How could he fear such a harmless thing, lying there on his floor that needed sweeping, next to his bed that needed making? If Gunther called first, then everything was possible; if Branch, nothing was. Gunther had said two weeks, but that might be too late. What if Branch called first? I'm sorry, Branch, I'm busy, Branch, goodbye, Branch. Just like that. Easy. Easy. Sure.

In the heat, Aaron shivered with the cold.

Gunther had to call first. Gunther liked him. Gunther would push it through fast. A little pressure here, a phone call there; Gunther was a good man, a kind man. If anyone could shake up the clinic, Gunther could. The boy needs help. Let's give it to him. That's our job. To give help. To that boy. Help to that boy because if we don't, then . . . then . . . the boy, in my professional opinion as a doctor, the boy, I feel quite sure, will become just like those people out the window, a peddler, peddling his own flesh to those who can afford him, and I feel, since he is doing his best to help Carmen Diaz, that we, dedicated physicians that we are, should do our best to give, to that boy, hellLLLLPPPPPPP!

In the heat, Aaron waited for the phone.

He waited for two days and three nights, or three days and four nights, leaving his room only once, and then just to rush down the stairs through the slave market to the corner for a fresh carton of cigarettes, first carefully taking the phone off the hook so that if Gunther called he would know from the busy signal that he was only out for cigarettes and would be right back. So Aaron waited, and paced and smoked, and then one morning, either the third or the fourth, Aaron got up from his bed, stretched, glanced down at the phone and started to laugh. He laughed for a long time, standing there, and after that he toppled backward onto his bed and laughed some more, because it was so funny, his waiting for the phone to ring, his dying by inches as he waited for the phone, his tying his life to the single expectancy of a single shrill sound. It was hilarious, his waiting like that. It was.

Because his phone never rang.

Oh, it worked; it was connected; he paid his monthly bill. *But it never rang.* Not if you didn't count wrong numbers. In the past year he had received thirteen wrong numbers, the majority of them asking for a French restaurant on Broadway in the 70s. Thirteen wrong numbers; that was all. Not once from Charlotte; not once from his sister; not once from anybody really, except eight people who wondered if the Château de Lille was open on Mondays and five women who were looking for Kermit, Dutch, Beau-Beau, Blanche and Charlene.

Aaron had the damn phone installed only because you couldn't trust *Cue* as to when movies started, and since he hated being late he ordered the phone because that way you could call the theaters direct and find out exactly. That was all he used it for—to call movie theaters and occasionally Time when his watch stopped or Weather because outside his window it always looked like rain. One call a month, that was his average, and here, after less than a week, he was climbing the walls, begging for lung cancer, so what would he be like if Gunther took *more* than two weeks? Ripe for the loony bin, that much was for sure, and Aaron rolled to one side of the bed and, picking up the telephone, threw it against the wall. It fell with a satisfying crash, the receiver buzzing. He grabbed the receiver and slammed it against the wood floor a while before replacing it in its cradle. Then he stood.

"Enough," Aaron said. Enough of waiting, of smoking, of pacing and staring. The whole city was outside his window and he had to do something to celebrate. But what?

His immediate instinct was to go to the movies, because *Casablanca* had been playing all week on 42nd, together with *The African Queen*, a double dose of Bogie—what could be better? And then, after old Humph, maybe he could find a Cary Grant comedy, one of the great ones with Hepburn or Russell or Dunne, and Aaron grabbed his shirt, threw on his pants, slipped into his loafers and was almost to the door when he did a sharp about-face, marching to the opposite wall. When he got there he executed another about-face and returned to the door. Tired of war games, he moved to the window and stared out through the grime. But that depressed him. Everything suddenly depressed him, so the thing to do was hit the flicks except he had been to the flicks, for three years; he had seen *Casablanca* and *The African Queen* and *all* the Cary Grant comedies more than once, so it wasn't that he was being a fair-weather friend, he wasn't saying "Bogie, goodbye," it was just that maybe there was something else he might do, something of more benefit, more stature maybe, something that might make Gunther smile.

What about writing? Aaron thought.

Well, that wasn't a bad idea. It didn't panic him or anything. Probably he would have written something, except he didn't have any paper or pencils or erasers or anything else. Besides, his desk chair wasn't the right height. It was too low and it gave him a stiff neck if he sat in it for too long and what kind of moron went around looking for that kind of trouble? Just to prove that he was telling the truth, Aaron sat down in his desk chair.

Immediately he could feel his neck muscles start to stiffen. Ten seconds and already he was massaging his neck. Hell, he wasn't imagining anything; the desk was just too low. The only reason for imagining something like that was if you needed an excuse for not writing, if you were afraid and, hell, he wasn't afraid, he was more talented than any of them, Wolfe or F. Scott or big Ernie or little Bill. He could write something fantastic if he wanted to. He could write something so brilliant that Graham would turn Greene and O'Hara would turn in his jock and Aaron got up from the crippling chair and lit a cigarette. He smoked it all the way down and lit another, sticking this one in the corner of his mouth while he scrambled around in the mess in one corner of his room, coming up, somewhat to his dismay, with half a dozen art gums and ten Scriptos and a ream of Eaton's Corrasable, two reams of onionskin, a stack of carbons, plus at least a dozen pads of scratch paper, lined, unlined, yellow, white. Aaron went back and lay down on his bed and threw his cigarette onto the floor and lit another.

If my desk chair were the right height I'd dash off something brilliant, Aaron thought, but it just isn't smart risking a stiff neck. I proved it once, I'll prove it again, and he ran at his desk chair and sat down and it wasn't too low and his neck felt fine, everything was fine except that he was terrified. Because he wasn't sure if he could write his own name anymore and it had been three years since he'd even tried. You could lose a lot in three years, pride as well as time, talent as well as pride. But what the hell, he could still dash off something if he wanted to, a novel, a major novel, long and brilliant and cruel, a critical success, a popular blockbuster, a—

"Cut the crap," Aaron said out loud.

Cold, he began to write a little short story.

It took him almost a week to get warm. By then he knew that the story was about a girl, a woman, twenty-five years old, named Teresa, and the story was about her vacation in New York and it was called "Teresa in Magic Town." She was very plain, Teresa, with thick legs, with bright eyes, with long straight hair already gray. Teresa was from Evansville (Aaron had been there once on pass) and she worked at the J. C. Penney store selling lingerie and she lived with her mother, a harpie named Fern who was always attacking Teresa for being an old maid.

Aaron loathed Fern and as the next days passed, as he took page after page of character notes—how the people talked, how they walked, what they wore—he realized he had to be careful not to let Fern take over the story. Because it was a slender story at best, and what there was of it belonged to poor Teresa, who, in desperation to escape her mother's taunts, agrees to come up to New York for two weeks' vacation, supposedly to see the sights but really (secretly, hopefully, dear God) to find a man. Aaron was not remotely sure if she would find one or not, and he spent a great deal of time trying to make up his mind because old maids ended up old maids, but he liked Teresa and he was pondering the problem when the telephone rang, jangling, interrupting his thoughts, and though he tried to concentrate he found he couldn't, so he pushed back from his desk and stooped, grabbing the black receiver, and while he was raising it to his ear he remembered, remembered that in a moment someone was going to identify himself, Gunther or Branch, Branch or Gunther, and in that moment, as he slid weakly onto his bed, one word went through his mind a thousand times: please.

It was Gunther.

"What do you mean, 'Thank God'?" Gunther said.

"Nothing," Aaron said. "It's just . . ." He rolled around on his bed. "Hey, how the hell are you? You lost any weight or anything? Forget that, it's kind of a stupid question and I'm sorry, it just popped out because it's just so damn good to hear your voice. Of course, I'm not hearing much of your voice, not with me doing all the talking like this, so you go ahead and say something, say anything you want, but first guess what I've been doing. Going to the movies, that's what you were about to say, wasn't it, but you're wrong. I haven't been to one movie. I've been writing. I swear I'm not kidding. Every day and that's probably why I'm a little hopped up now—I mean, with all the writing and not talking to anybody, it gets to you after a while, I guess, because I really feel hopped up now, over this writing, this little story. I call it 'Teresa in Magic Town' and it's about this old—no, she's isn't old—anyway this woman comes to New York and that doesn't sound like much when I say it but it's good. I mean, I don't know if it's good but I think it is. I mean I hope it is. Anyway that's what's new with me what's new with you?"

"The clinic rejected your application. You'll get a letter to that effect tomorrow or the next day. I'm calling you now to prepare you and to see what I can do to help. Aaron?"

Aaron lay flat down on the bed and closed his eyes.

"Aaron?"

"Sir?"

"I take it," Gunther said softly, "I take it that you heard me."

"Yessir."

"I'm sorry, Aaron. It's no fun telling you but I thought it would be better than receiving—"

"Gee," Aaron said. "How could I have been so wrong? I thought, after our talk, I thought sure you'd recommend me. I was counting on that."

"I did recommend you."

"What happened, then?"

"Does it matter? Isn't the result sufficient?"

"Gee, I'd really like to know. I mean, I'd sure like to know, Dr. Gunther. I mean, I might even go so far as to say that it's *important* to me that I know, because I mean, it's important, do you understand?"

"Clinics have their goals, Aaron. They can't accept everybody. They have to be selective as to whom they accept. They have their reasons."

"But why didn't they take me?"

"They don't want any homosexuals this year."

"They don't want any homosexuals this year?"

"Yes. You see, last year they took primarily homosexuals. But they feel they have to diversify. So this year they're looking for manic-depressives."

"Manic-depressives?"

"Yes."

"Is that funny, Doctor? I can't tell, but I think it might be." Lying flat, eyes shut tight, Aaron began to laugh.

"There are a number of places in the city where you might apply for treatment. I have a list of them here, which I'll give you, when you write for an interview I'll write them too, recommending—"

"No."

"I promise you they're every bit as good as our clinic and—"

"No, it's not that, don't you see?" Aaron opened his eyes and watched the ceiling. "I don't need it anymore. Didn't you hear what I've been doing? I'm writing again. I'm fine. I had a bad period, sure, but that's done

with. Everybody has these little slumps now and then, but they pass. Mine
did. I'm fine now. I don't need a shrinker. I'm fine. Really fine."

"Whatever you want, Aaron."

"Right. Well, so long, Dr. Gunther. Thanks."

"Aaron?"

"Yes?"

"If you need me, will you call?"

"No."

"I didn't think you would."

"You're a nice fat man, Dr. Gunther, you know that?"

"I know a compliment when I hear one. Goodbye, Aaron."

"Goodbye." Aaron lay on his back until that bored him and then he
flip-flopped to his stomach and when that bored him he crawled off the
bed for his cigarettes, then crawled back and lit one, sticking it in the corner of his mouth, smoking it down to the butt before lighting another.
Then he went to his desk and sat down and picked up "Teresa in Magic
Town." He glanced through it a few minutes before he decided it was shit.
Corny, crappy, treacly, phony, slick, sentimental shit. He started ripping it
up, every note, every line. He began calmly, ripping with exquisite precision, each page perfectly in half, but presently the precision left him and
he simply clawed the paper, tearing it to bits, throwing it all around the
room, and when all the tiny pieces lay around him he dropped panting to
his knees, grabbing at the bits of paper spitting at him, ripping and tearing until there was nothing left to rip, nothing more to tear. Then he
gathered it all together, every piece of what once had been a page, every
shred of what once had been a note, and he dumped it into his wastebasket and coated it with lighter fluid and set it on fire. For a moment it
flamed up beautifully, hot and red, but soon it died. The ashes glowed
and Aaron watched them weaken, turning black, curling, then turning
again, into gray smoke. Aaron moved into the smoke and stood there until the telephone rang and then he approached the sound, reminding
himself that he must congratulate Branch on his fine sense of timing, and
as he lay down on the bed he picked up the receiver and said "Yes?" into it
with a voice that he did not recognize, but he was alone in the smoking
room, so it must have been his.

"Are you open on Monday?"

"What?"

"I want to know if you're open on Monday. Isn't this the Château de
Lille?"

"The Château de Lille," Aaron said, pushing up on one elbow. *"Mais oui."*

"Well, are you open on Monday?"

"But of course," Aaron said. The voice sounded as if it belonged to a college girl, an intellectual, probably—she had that phony twang. Vassar most likely. Or maybe Bryn Mawr.

"Then I'd like to make a reservation," the girl said. "Seven o'clock. For two. The name is Wickersham."

"I'm sorry, Mr. Wickersham, but—"

"Miss Wickersham."

"Excusez-moi, mademoiselle," Aaron said. He reached for a cigarette and lit it. "But your reservation for seven o'clock. I cannot honor it. We are not open at seven o'clock."

"Oh," the girl said. "Well, what time are you open?"

"Just for two hours. From eight until ten."

"Oh," the girl said again.

"In the morning," Aaron said.

"What?"

"Something is wrong, *mademoiselle?*"

"You mean you're only open in the *morning?*"

"That is correct, *mademoiselle.*"

"What kind of French food do you serve?"

"French breakfast food, *mademoiselle.*"

"Oh," she said. "I didn't know. I mean, I thought you were a regular French res— I mean, well, it all sounds just fascinating."

Vassar, Aaron thought. Definitely Vassar. "It is a good deal more than just fascinating, *mademoiselle.* It is what makes us unique. We are the only French restaurant in all of Manhattan that is only open for breakfast. There is a Spanish restaurant in Queens that is only open for breakfast, but we do not consider them competition. Who can eat *paella* in the morning? The very thought is barbaric, don't you agree?"

"Absolutely, I absolutely agree. And what do *you* serve?"

"Just the one dish, *mademoiselle,* the one that made us famous. The *spécialité de la maison.*"

"What is it?"

Aaron closed his eyes and made French sounds. *"Rue de veau de oiseau sans beaudouisleaioux."*

"My French is a little rusty. Could you please trans—"

"Intestine with orange sauce," Aaron said.

"Intestine—?"

"With orange sauce."

"In the morning?"

"You drink orange juice in the morning, don't you?"

"Yes."

"Well, orange juice, orange sauce, it all comes from the orange."

"Of course it does," the girl said. "Now I see."

"Then would eight-fifteen on Monday be suitable? I can give you two nice seats at the counter."

"Well, speaking for myself, *I'd* love to, but my roommate, I don't know if she likes intestine, so—"

"It has an exquisite flavor, *mademoiselle*. Very like truffle hound. Tell her that."

"Yes," the girl said. "I'll tell her. And then I'll call you back."

"Au revoir, mademoiselle." Aaron dropped the phone into its cradle and fell back diagonally across the bed. Then he started to laugh. He had not laughed full out in several days, and he had almost forgotten how good it felt, so he lay for a while on the bed, laughing, he thought, as hard as he could because when the phone rang again it was all he could do just to pick up the receiver and say "Château de Lille," but a moment later, after Branch had hung up with a muttered, "I'm sorry, I must have the wrong number," Aaron really started to howl. He lay shrieking on the bed, his hands slapping the mattress, tears filling his eyes, so when the phone started ringing again he was much too weak to answer it at first, but it kept on ringing, nine times, ten times, eleven and twelve, so finally he was able to pull the receiver to his mouth and say "United States Weather Bureau forecast for New York City and vicinity—"

"Aaron?"

"The ten A.M. temperature is hot as a bitch, the sky is falling, and it is raining cats and dogs." Then he hung up and collapsed again, whooping and holding his sides. When the phone rang again he picked it up and said, "Good morning, this is your long-distance operator."

"Aaron—"

"To whom did you wish to speak?"

"Aaron, what's the matter with you?"

"I'm sorry, but I cannot give out that information," and he hung up, his hand resting on the receiver until the next call. "Good morning," he said then, "this—"

"All right now, Aaron, just quit it and—"

"This is Radio City Music Hall."

"I'm in a phone booth, Aaron, and I'm running out of dimes."

"This week, by popular demand, we are having a Vera Hruba Ralston festival."

"Aaron—don't hang up, Aaron—"

"Thank you for calling, goodbye," and he sat hunched over the silent phone, staring anxiously down at it, a mother with a strange child, and when it rang he picked it up, listening to the frantic voice on the other end, listening with a smile.

"This is my last dime, Aaron, and it's hot in this phone booth, so—"

"I'm sorry," Aaron said. "Don't get upset. I apologize."

"O.K.," Branch said. "Forget it."

"Where are you? What are you doing in a phone booth?"

"I just took an apartment. The phone doesn't get installed till tomorrow. Besides, my mother's still here. She helped me pick the place. She's up there now, unpacking my stuff; she's leaving tomorrow morning and I wondered if you were free tomorrow afternoon, cocktails, maybe. We might have a drink, christen the apartment, that kind of thing."

"You out of change?"

"Yes."

"Then you better let me call you from here before we get cut off. What's your number?"

"It's Endicott 2-7299."

"Endicott 2-7299," Aaron said. "Gotcha. Call you right back." He hung up and stretched out on the bed, closing his eyes, wondering how long it would take Scudder to realize no call was going to come. Quiet, Aaron waited with a smile. As the wait grew, the smile grew, and seven minutes later when the telephone rang Aaron answered it with cheer. "*Hel*-lo."

"You didn't call me back," Branch managed, the hurt in his voice genuine and lingering. "And I only called you this time for one reason. And that's to say goodbye. You went too far, Aaron. I'm not a kid anymore. You can't treat me like that. You didn't call me back. You just let me sit there. Well, this is goodbye."

"Who is this?" Aaron said. "Who am I talking to?"

"It's too late for games, Aaron. You went too far and—"

"I want to know who I'm talking to."

"Dammit, Aaron—"

"*Who is this?*"

"It's Branch and you know it and—"

"Who?"

"*Branch. Branch* Scudder."

"Oh my God," Aaron said. "*Branch* Scudder. Now I understand. I thought I was talking to Branch *Scudder*. Don't you see my mistake? I never much liked Branch *Scudder* and—"

"If you hang up one more time, Aaron—"

"Shut up. You love it."

"I don't! I don't! Not anymore."

"*Branch* Scudder, well, what do you know. And all the time I thought I was talking to Branch *Scudder*. Well, how are you, *Branch* Scudder? I haven't seen you since my Army days."

"I won't call you back again, Aaron. I promise."

"Oh-oh, I just remembered something."

"I mean it. You hang up again and we'll never see each other. Not ever. I swear."

"What I just remembered was I never much liked *Branch* Scudder either."

"*I'll* hang up on you, Aaron. I will. It'll be goodbye. I'll never call you back and you'll never get a chance to hang up on me again and I'm not kidding either so just—"

"Toodle-oo," Aaron said and he hung up. Licking his lips, he sat huddled over the black phone, his knees pressed against his thin chest, his fingers caressing the receiver. Aaron waited. The phone did not ring. Aaron smiled. You'll call, he thought. Fight the good fight, but you'll call. The phone did not ring. Aaron stood up and stretched. Across from him, the wastebasket had stopped smoking, so he approached it, staring down at the black ashes. He prodded the basket with his foot. The ashes stirred, resettled. Call, Aaron thought, and he smiled again, because Scudder was just so feeble. That was the only word for him. Feeble. Aaron stuck a cigarette in a corner of his mouth and began to pace. Call, dammit. I mean it, Scudder. I don't like being kept waiting, so you better call. Nobody keeps me waiting. Nobody keeps . . . Aaron stopped pacing and began to laugh, because for a moment he pictured Scudder in the phone booth, bald and sweating, feebly trying to keep his feeble hands off the phone, and that picture was so ridiculous he just had to laugh. Here he was, he, Aaron Fire, getting a little worked up over something like that. Tsk-tsk, for shame. Aaron stretched lazily and returned to his bed, lying flat, watching the smoke rise. Poor Scudder. Poor feeble Scudder. Every second he could postpone the call was a minor triumph for him, the closest he would ever come to glory. Scudder, I salute you, Aaron thought, and he raised his fingers in the gesture. He tossed the cigarette onto the floor. He felt relaxed, completely relaxed, except for a vague burning deep behind his eyes. The start of a headache maybe. Too much smoking and not enough sleep—that'll do it every time. Aaron rubbed his eyes. He heard the phone, or thought he did, so he rolled up on one elbow, looking at it, waiting for the next ring, but it didn't come, so it must have been his imagination. Aaron lay flat again, rubbing his eyes harder, because they hurt, but the rubbing only made them worse, so he rolled up on one elbow again and glared at the phone. Scudder, I pity you, you have my pity, a drop of my pity, but, goddammit, call! Call! Call! And he was up again, walking again, smoking again, kneading his hands before him as he went. He hated waiting, hated it, and I'm warning you, Scudder, you just better make the damn call if you know what's good for you. Aaron began clapping his hands out of rhythm with his walking: step-clap-step-clap-clap-step-step—what was it Scudder had said? That he had changed, that he wasn't like that any-more? Impossible. Scudders never changed. Scudders were Scudders. If you pinched them they smiled and you could count on that; it was a given, permanent, a rock resisting the sea. *So why didn't he call?* Aaron ran to the wastebasket and reached down, grabbing out a handful of ashes. He would have looked at them longer had there been something to see, but there wasn't, so he began to rub his hands along his thin arms, black-ening his skin. He grabbed another handful of ashes and when his arms were black and his hands were black he set to work on his face, rubbing his tender eyelids much too hard, trying to reach his brain. He didn't want the call, it wasn't that; he just hated being kept waiting. It was the waiting that got to him, the waiting. Aaron dropped to his knees beside the phone, lifted the receiver and started to dial. What was the number Scudder had said? Endicott? Endicott three? No, two. Two and then three. Or was it five? Seven? Aaron held the receiver until he remembered that if Scudder was trying to call, the line would be busy, so he plunged it back into its cradle and waited on his knees. The waiting. The damn waiting. That was what hell was. Waiting. Just waiting. He didn't want the call. He knew what would follow it and he didn't want that. I don't want it, Aaron thought. I honest to God on my sacred word of honor cross my heart and hope to— "*No!*" Aaron cried and he closed his eyes, blind now, blind and kneeling over the phone.

Because he wanted the call.

He wanted the call.

God, are you going to pay. Scudder, I promise you, I swear, Scudder, on my father's grave, Scudder, you are going to feel regret, Scudder, such regret that I cringe for you, Scudder, for you will writhe, Scudder, I promise you that, endless writhing. That I promise you, and more. The telephone rang. Aaron, on his knees, opened his eyes and slowly lifted the receiver.

"I called you back," Branch whispered. "I called you back. I didn't mean to but I did. I tried not to. I couldn't help it. But I called you back. Here I am. Now what do you want from me?"

"Aaron!" Aaron said. "Aaron, it's me Branch. Branch Scudder."

"What do you want from me?"

"Didn't you hear me, Aaron? This is me. Branch. I just got in town and I thought I'd call you."

"Whatever you're doing, Aaron, don't," Branch said.

"Say hello to me, Aaron. Say hello to Branch."

"Don't," Branch said.

"Say hello to me, Aaron."

"Please."

"Aaron, this is Branch. Say hello. *Say hello!*"

"Hello," Branch whispered.

"Not just 'hello,' Aaron. Say 'hello, Branch.' "

"Hello, Branch."

"Hello, Aaron," Aaron said. "How are you? I'm pretty good. I mean I'm still the same little swish I was in the Army, but other than that I'm pretty good."

"What do you want from me?" Branch said.

"I loathe you, Aaron, do you know that?"

"No."

"But you cause me pain and I love pain."

"Not anymore."

"Will you hurt me, Aaron, if I say please? Pretty please. Pretty please with sugar on it if you hurt me."

"Aaron—"

"And you hate me too, don't you, Aaron? Way down deep, you hate me."

"No."

"Yes, you do. Say it. Say you hate me."

"No."

"Say you hate me or I won't let you hurt me anymore. And you know how you love that. Say you hate me."

"I hate you. I hate you."

"We hate each other, don't we, Aaron?"

"Yes."

"Then will you marry me, Aaron? Will you come and live with me and let me keep you like a whore except you'll be my wife?"

"Aaron—"

"Will you marry me, Aaron? Say you'll marry me."

"Please—"

"This is a proposal, Aaron. Will you be my wife? Say it."

"No."

"Say it."

"Aaron, don't, for God's sake, Aaron, please don't make—"

"*Say it!*"

"All right. I'll say it."

"You'll come and be my wife."

"Yes."

"Yes."

"Then repeat after me: for richer or richer."

"Yes."

"In sickness."

"Sickness."

"Forever and ever."

"Forever."

"From now till doomsday."

"Doomsday."

XIX

"Of course he's queer," Tony said. "My God, how can you even argue the point?" She lay on the sofa and slowly raised her legs until they formed a right angle with her body. Then, effortlessly, she lowered her legs to the cushions, paused a moment, then raised them again.

Walt pushed his glasses up snug against the bridge of his nose with his left thumb. It was two o'clock on a muggy October morning and they were sitting in the living room of Tony's apartment in a new red-brick building on East 53rd Street. "I went to college with Branch," Walt said. "He dated girls as much as most people."

"Nevertheless, dear heart, he's queer," Tony said. She was wearing tight black slacks and a light-gray cashmere cardigan buttoned to the throat and she continued, slowly, to raise and lower her legs.

I know why you're doing that, Walt thought. You're doing it because I happened to run into a college acquaintance of mine walking along Third Avenue and he's been in New York a month and in the excitement I forgot to introduce you until he was gone and I told you I was sorry, but apologies are never enough for someone like you. What you want is for me to make a pass at you so you can get your kicks turning me down. Walt looked closely at her as she lay stretched on the couch, moving her legs. Her skin was dark and clear, her hair black, her lips red. I'm on to you, you teasing bitch. Not this time. I'm not gonna make a pass because if I did you would only remind me, again, of your precious virginity.

"Can't we cut the calisthenics?" Walt said.

"You don't find it attractive?"

"No-no, it's too attractive. I'm liable to go berserk just watching you. See, lady athletes are my weakness. I've got pinups all over my room. Russian lady shot-putters. Tamara Press, she's my dream girl. What a body—65-48-72."

Tony continued moving her legs, up and down, up and down. "Knowing you, I believe it," she said. "Getting back to your *friend*—"

"Boy, you make that sound dirty. Now I know you're very knowledgeable about homosexuals, having taken Perversion I at good old Sarah Lawrence."

Tony sat up on the couch. "What's wrong with Sarah Lawrence?"

"Nothing's *wrong* with Sarah Lawrence. It happens to be a marvelous school. Why, it's probably the only college left in the world where you can still major in Phrenology."

"Ohhhh, hims made a jokey."

"Love that baby talk."

"Hers only does it to get hims vexed."

"Well, hims is vexed, so hers can can it."

"You're my cutesy-wootsy," Tony said, and she lay back on the couch. "The reason I know about Branch or whatever his name is is that I happen to be a girl. Girls can tell things about guys like that. A guy like that, he reacts to a girl different from a guy who isn't like that. That's how I know he's a fag."

"Tony, dammit—"

"What are you so defensive about? Did you have the hots for him or something? Is that why you wouldn't introduce me? Afraid I wouldn't measure up to old Baldy?"

Walt said nothing.

Tony looked at him. "Oh-oh," she said. "You're mad at me. I've gone too far. I keep forgetting what a sensitive creature you are."

"Let's just please change the subject. Talk about something else. How about getting me a cup of coffee?"

"Say you forgive me," Tony said, and she jumped up from the couch and ran behind Walt's chair, throwing her arms around his neck. "Please. You've got to." She leaned over his shoulder until her upside-down face was level with his. "If you don't, I'll fog your glasses," and she tightened her hold on his neck, blowing hard on his lenses until they were steamed up. Then she began to giggle.

"It really isn't funny, y'know."

"Oh yes it is too. You should see yourself." She slipped over the arm of the chair and fell into his lap. "Kiss me, my fool," she said.

Walt kissed her.

Tony jumped to her feet.

"Hey," Walt said.

Tony shook her head. "Only one to a customer." She looked at him. "God, you're a sexy wench, Kirkaby, old foggy Kirkaby, old coffee drinker."

"Forget the damn coffee." And he reached out for her, but she skipped clear of his grasp and disappeared into the kitchen. "Nuts," Walt muttered, and he sat in the chair, all hot and bothered, all bothered and hot. She could always do that to him; no matter how casually he determined to play an evening, she could always shatter his characterization, make him commit himself one way or another, thus enabling her to reject him. Walt made a fist and was about to slam it down against the arm of the chair when he realized that if he did, she would hear, and if she heard, she would be able—with her cat's mind—not only to identify the sound but also to know its reason, and once she knew that, then she would make a sound of her own—not quite stifled laughter—and he had heard her make that sound more than too many times. Slowly, with some difficulty, Walt relaxed his hand.

A lightning flash lit the world outside the window. Then the ensuing thunder.

"What was that?" Tony called.

Walt told her what it was.

Tony stuck her head out from the kitchen. "Gonna rain?"

"Not supposed to."

"Good for the farmers," Tony said, and she disappeared again.

"Good for the farmers," Walt muttered and he stood, moving slowly to the window, gazing out. "Nuts," he whispered, and he turned, starting for the kitchen, but halfway there he detoured left, pausing at the door to

Tony's bedroom. The room was dark until another bolt of lightning lit it long enough for him to see the large double bed. Walt stared at it. Even after the room was dark he continued to stare.

Wistfully.

"Almost ready," Tony called.

Walt made his way to the kitchen. "You are a supreme chef," he said.

"I am that." She nodded. "Pavillon is just dying for my instant-coffee recipe but I'm holding out; I don't think the world's ready for it."

"Tony," Walt said, and then he stepped up behind her and clasped his hands around her waist, kissing her neck.

"Quit with the funny stuff, huh?"

Walt released her. "That was supposed to be sexy."

"Kirkaby, old kirk, that's your trouble: when you're sexy, you're funny."

"And when I'm funny?"

"You're not funny."

"God, you're a bitch."

Tony turned on him. "I don't much like that. I genuinely do not."

"Protest too much lately?"

"All right," she said. "All right. Get this now. *I* didn't start this. *You* did. *You* came in here and *you* had to start making remarks about what a lousy cook I am and *I am* a lousy cook but I don't like being reminded particularly and *you know* I don't like being reminded particularly so what do you do, naturally, but lip off, asking for it, so I give it to you, just like you're asking for, but *that doesn't make me a bitch*. If you would just once grasp that when I'm what you think of as bitchy I'm not being bitchy, just defensive—well, try being sweet sometime, I'll be sweet back. I don't start things. Never. Not me. You. Always you. Always."

"You win," Walt said, and he meant to stop there, but then he said, "You shouldn't but you do," and then he said "Dammit" louder than he ever intended, so he grabbed the cup of instant coffee from her hands and turned back into the living room. Moving to the window, he stared sadly out at the rain.

Why sadly? What in the rain made him sad? Something . . . something . . . Then he remembered that it had to do with Blake and their last night together, and as he remembered he heard Tony's voice.

"What?" Tony asked from the couch.

"I'm sorry. I wasn't listening." Walt gripped his cup.

"You just said 'Oh.' Why?"

"Did I? No reason." He took a sip of coffee and continued to stare at the rain. He was aware that Tony was saying something, and probably he should have listened, answered, but probably, again, what she was saying was only his name, "Walt? Walt?" time after time.

Then she was close behind him, her body pressing lightly against his, her hands clasped tight around his waist. We always seem to come up behind each other, Walt thought. I wonder why that is.

And while he was wondering he stepped clear of her embrace, turning to face her. "The coffee," he said. "It might spill." He moved to the chair and sat down.

She moved to the arm of the chair, hesitated, started to sit, straightened, then sat on the couch. "Coffee all right?"

"Fine," Walt said.

"You're a gentleman and a liar."

"No, really," Walt said. "It's fine."

"What are you thinking?" Tony said, and then she clapped her hand to her mouth. "I hate girls who ask that. Absolutely loathe and despise them. Forgive me?"

"Forgiven." Walt stared out the window at the rain.

"*Merci.*"

Walt made a smile.

"What *are* you thinking?" Tony said. Then: "My God, I just did it again."

Walt made another smile, took a long sip of coffee, put the cup down. "It's about that time," he said, and he stood.

"Asking you twice. You must think I'm just awful."

"No." He walked to the front door. "So I'll call you, O.K.?"

"I'm a leper?" Tony said, standing, hurrying to him. "Take off your glasses."

Walt took off his glasses.

After the kiss, he put them back on. "So I'll call you," he said, and he reached for the doorknob.

"Hey!"

"What?"

"Aren't you forgetting your raincoat?"

"It wasn't supposed to rain," Walt said.

"You'll ruin your clothes."

Walt looked down at his tennis shoes, his khaki pants, his blue button-down shirt. "Not bloody likely."

"You'll catch your death."

"Subway's not far."

"The Lex subway is four blocks away and in this weather that's far. How about my raincoat? Take my umbrella."

"Your raincoat's too small and I lose umbrellas."

"Let's not make a thing out of this."

"By all means."

"It seems silly going all the way down to the Village. Why don't you spend the night here?"

"Here?" Walt said.

"You'll fit on the couch."

"No. Really. Thanks, but no."

"I'm not gonna let you go out in that rain. *I'll* sleep on the couch."

"No."

"I've done it before."

"No means no."

Tony ran her tongue over her lips. Then she shrugged. "What the hell," she said. "It's a big bed."

• • •

Walt lay naked under the covers, listening as Tony brushed her teeth. I'm gonna make it, he thought. I don't know how but I'm gonna make it. What did I do? I wish I knew what I'd done. I'd have done it a long time ago. How long had he been dating Tony? Three months? Five? At least five. Not steady, of course, but still, he'd been giving it the old college try for close to half a year, half his New York stay, and the only time he'd ever come within shouting distance was that night she'd experimented around with martinis for the first (and last *and* only) time but she'd got sick before anything really much had got under way. Walt looked at the bathroom door a moment before turning his head toward the blessed rain. "Good for the farmers," he said.

"Hey out there I'm done in here." She opened the bathroom door a crack.

"Proud of you."

"Well . . ."

"Well what?"

"Turn off the light, dopey."

"The switch is clear across the room and I'm naked."

"Put something on."

"No, I don't think I want to do that."

"You don't think *what*? Listen, you can see through what I'm wearing."

"It's very strange, but I'm absolutely unable to move."

"Oh, a wise guy," Tony said. "God save us all." She gave a very loud sigh. "All right; *I'll* turn out the light. But you can't look."

"Do you honestly expect me not to look?"

"If you didn't look, I'd never forgive you," and she threw the bathroom door open, dashing across the floor to the wall switch, and then the room was dark, but not before Walt had seen the outline of her body beneath the white nylon negligee.

There was no sound in the room, nothing but their breathing, and in the darkness Walt had difficulty seeing her until she stood by the far end of the bed, her body outlined again in the faint gray light from the window. She bent down a moment, pulling back the covers.

Omigod, Walt thought. Omigod.

"Of course you've got to promise not to touch me," Tony said.

"What?"

"You've got to promise to be a good boy. Otherwise you can't stay."

"Sure, I promise."

"You really mean that now; no fooling around."

"I promise, I promise."

"All right then," Tony said, and she jumped into bed, lying stretched out, her back to him. "Sheets are cold," she said, and she began wriggling her body around.

I'm dying, Walt thought.

"Don't you just love listening to the rain?"

"Oh, absolutely."

"Let's listen to the rain, Walt. Let's hold our breath and listen to the rain."

They held their breath a while.

"Hey," Walt said finally.

"Shhh. It's just so beautiful, don't spoil it."

"I won't make a sound," Walt said, and he rose up on one elbow and gently blew on her back.

"Ooooooooo," Tony went.

Walt kissed her back.

"Ooooooooo," Tony went again.

Walt kissed her neck.

"Oh, Walt—"

Walt kissed her ear.

"Walt, you promised."

He kissed her eyes.

"You promised to be a good boy!"

"Just a good-night kiss?"

Tony said nothing.

"Just one?"

"All right," she whispered. "One." And her arms went around him and her mouth pressed up against his and he could feel her fingers digging into his back. They rolled across the bed and he grabbed for her breasts, but almost before his hand made contact she was pushing him away. *"What do you think you're doing?"*

"Kissing you good night."

"Oh God," Tony said. "God, God, God."

"What's the matter?"

"I'm just so disappointed."

"Tony . . ."

"Good night, Walt," and she moved to the far side of the bed.

Walt started after her.

"Stop!"

"Tony, I'm dying."

"Good night, Walt."

"But, Tony—"

"I mean it. Good night."

"Will ya just—"

"Good *night*."

"O.K., O.K., g' night." He lay on his side of the bed, reaching for the blanket.

"I don't think I've ever been so disappointed in anybody in all my life," Tony said.

"Tony . . ."

"Don't talk. I'm half asleep already."

"But I'm only—"

"What *is* it?"

"You've got all the blanket, Tony. Couldn't I have some of the blanket?"

"Oh, take it, take it all."

"Take what you want but just be *quiet*."

"I don't need *all* of it."

Walt began to laugh.

Tony looked over at him. "There's nothing funny," she said.

Walt quieted.

"I'm all tense," Tony said and she started to stretch. She stretched her arms and when she stretched her legs her foot lingered for a moment on Walt's leg. "Sorry," she muttered.

Walt began laughing again. "O.K.," he said. "Game's over. Let's kiss and make up."

"I cannot believe I heard you accurately."

Walt reached out for her. "C'mere," he said.

"I'm going to the couch," Tony said. "Don't make me go to the couch."

"Tony, enough is enough. You're not serious."

"I'm not serious? I'm not serious?"

"Omigod," Walt said. "You are." He gave a long whistle. "I'll be a son of a bitch. What's the matter with you?"

"Not very much."

"Oh, come on. I mean, you don't, by any chance, consider this the least little bit castrating, do you?"

"Now you're calling me a castrator?"

"Oh, not necessarily. I mean, let's make it hypothetical. O.K.? There's this girl, see, and she out of the blue invites this guy to share her sack—"

"Out of the blue? It wasn't raining?"

"All right, it was raining—that's not the point. The point is she invites him to split the bed. With me so far? O.K. Now, after a few preliminaries, such as running around in a nightie you can see through, she—"

"I didn't ask you to turn out the light, I suppose."

"Anyway, they get between the sheets and all of a sudden she says, 'No, no, mustn't touch,' and—"

"I said that *before* I ever got in bed."

"Now this hypothetical guy, he gives it the die-for-Rutgers try, and she's moaning so loud you can hear it in the next apartment and—"

"Oh boy," Tony said. "Go on."

"It gets kinda unpleasant here because all of a sudden this hypothetical girl turns into Frieda Frigid and she's muttering 'God, God, God' like it's downtown Hiroshima two seconds after the bomb."

"It just doesn't pay," Tony said, "to try to be nice to people." She shook her head in the darkness. "No. No. If you try to be nice to people, they take advantage of you." She shook her head again. "No. No. It just doesn't pay."

"All of a sudden I'm the villain?"

"I'm so disappointed I want to cry. There was rain and it was nasty and I thought it might be nice—no, I'll tell you the absolute truth. I thought it would be fun. Oh, if you knew the men who have wanted to trap me in bed."

"What's this got to do with anything?"

Tony sighed. "I always thought it would be such fun to have a man spend the night here. Oh, it's sad."

"You're winning again. I don't know how but you're winning."

"Oh, Walt, it's not a contest. We're not opponents. I'm not fighting you."

"Well, then, keep your eye on the referee because somebody's killing me."

"Poor Walt."

"What's that supposed to mean?"

"Poor Walt."

"Dammit—"

"Give me your hand."

"Why?"

"Just give me your hand."

Walt gave her his hand.

Tony held it. "Come here," she said and she put her arm around him, resting his head on her shoulder. "There," she said. "There." Softly, she began stroking his chest. "You know what I think?"

"What do you think?"

"I think you better go." She continued stroking his chest with just the very tips of her fingers.

"Go?"

"Yes. Leave. Now. It's best. This isn't working out. If you stay . . . well, if you stay you'll just get more upset and what's the point in that? Where are your clothes? In the closet? I think you better put them on and go home. Don't you agree? It's best you go."

"Well . . ."

"Please," and she lightly kissed his cheek. "In the morning you'll see I was right. Go now. Please. For me."

Aw, come on, Walt thought. You can do better than this. I mean, isn't this a little obvious? You tell me to go and all the time you're pawing me and what I'm supposed to do is beg you to stay, but I'm on to you. I mean, you can whistle if you think I'm gonna beg. "You're right." He got out of bed and made his way toward the closet.

"You do think so, don't you?" she said from under the covers.

"Oh, absolutely."

"You're not just doing this?"

He switched on the closet light, grabbed his clothes, headed for the bathroom to dress. "Huh?"

"I meant, you do think I'm right."

"Course you're right," Walt said as he dressed. "This whole thing was a mistake. I should have known better."

"It's as much my fault as yours."

"As a matter of fact, I was about to leave on my own when you suggested it." Walt raced into his clothes.

"You were?"

"That's right."

Tony got out of bed. "I'll see you to the door."

"You don't have to. I'm all dressed. I know the way."

"Never," Tony said and she walked toward his voice in the darkness, took his hand. "I was brought up on Emily Post." She led him out of the bedroom. "I'm really sorry things turned out like this."

"We'll forget it."

"Of course we will."

" 'Night," Walt said when they reached the apartment door.

"I just hate sending you out in the rain like this."

"I'll be all right."

"Oh, it could have been so much fun," Tony said and her hands rested on his shoulders a moment, and then she pressed up against him, holding him tight.

Walt tried to kiss her, but her head was averted. But when his hands found her breasts her head turned toward him and he pressed his mouth down on her mouth and when they broke he could hear her breathing and he said, "Let me stay."

"Don't ask me."

"Please."

"Oh, Walt."

"Please. Please."

"I could never trust myself," she whispered, opening the door. "Good night, darling."

All of a sudden Walt found himself standing in the hallway. He watched as she threw him a kiss. Then her fingers were dancing at him. Then the door closed. Walt waited a moment. He stuck his hands in his pockets, shrugged, turned, ambled to the elevators, paused, then butted the "down" button with his head. A few moments later he walked out into the rain.

He worked his way cautiously to Lexington, darting from doorway to doorway, but in spite of his efforts he was drenched by the time he reached the corner. As he turned onto the avenue he assumed the center of the sidewalk, moving slowly, hands in pockets, stopping occasionally to rub his bruised head, trying to ease the pain. For a moment he was tempted to taxi down to his tiny Village apartment. It was expensive, but who was he kidding? He could afford it. Walt glanced around, saw there were no cabs and broke into a wild run. He was terribly winded when he reached the subway station, and his legs felt weak, even though it had been but four blocks and once upon a time he could have run three times that and smiled. He started down the steps, fished a token from his wet pocket, sneezed and passed through the turnstile. The station was vacant and he nodded in thanks, because it was probably close to three in the morning and that was when the nuts came out and they frightened him. They liked him, the nuts did; they seemed always to seek him out. And that frightened him too.

Walt sat huddled on a bench thinking about Tony, who he really didn't like all that much, not when you came right down to it, so why did he let her bug him like that? It would have been so simple just to end it, end it, cut it off.

"Snip," Walt said.

Except that it wasn't. It should have been, so why wasn't it? 'Cause I want to quit a winner, Walt thought. If only once—one time—he could leave her with the taste of victory stinging his tongue, then he could forget the way to her door easy apple pie. But she was clever. God, she was. Clever and sexy—a tough opponent. Walt sighed as the uptown local stopped in front of him. I wished I lived uptown, he thought. Just for tonight. He stood and walked around the bench, his clothes still wet from the October rain. His body felt very cold and he sneezed again as he sat back down on the bench. "Why are you such a fink, Kirkaby?" he mumbled, and then he shut up fast because a crazy man was descending the stairs at the end of the subway platform.

"God bless Clark Gable!" the crazy man shouted.

Walt huddled up on the bench and closed his eyes.

"God bless Ralph Waldo Emerson!"

The voice was nearer and Walt sneaked a look, glancing at the crazy man and the thinnish spinster lady who was hurrying by him as fast as she could, staying as far away from him as possible. Walt closed his eyes again.

A subway train roared into the station and Walt half stood before he realized it was another uptown local. Walt shook his head. Two in a row just wasn't fair. Not when he was soaked to the skin and there was a crazy man stumbling around nearby. "Nuts," Walt said. Two in a row; why did that seem like the story of his life?

"God bless America!" the crazy man shouted.

"Some people," the spinster lady said, and she sat down at the far end of the bench.

Walt nodded.

"Look at him. Just look at him. They ought to do something. They ought to police these places. A body just isn't safe."

Walt nodded again.

"What about this weather?" the lady went on, and she shook her head. "Terrible. Just terrible."

Walt smiled at her and stood up, because another train was roaring into the station, a downtown local.

"God bless Franklin D. Roosevelt Junior," the crazy man shouted.

"Not a minute too soon," the lady said, indicating the train.

"Right you are," Walt agreed.

"I think it's the bomb causes this weather," the lady said. "Have you read about that?"

"No. Sorry."

"Well, some meteorologists think all this bomb exploding by the Russians has affected the weather."

"Could be," Walt said as the subway doors opened.

"God bless Lucas T. Hathaway!"

"I hate those Russians," the lady said. "Have you ever seen rain like this on Christmas Eve before?"

"No," Walt said and they had stepped inside the train before he remembered that the month was October, and then as he started to turn away she grabbed him by the arm and said, "Would you like to kiss me under the mistletoe? I always carry mistletoe," and she held up a piece but Walt jerked loose and dived for the door which had started to close and it caught him for a moment until he could fight it open and then he was running down the platform, up the steps and back into the rain.

It seemed warmer at first, not quite so punishing. He stumbled through it, eyes half closed. Why were the nuts after him? And why had he begged Tony like that? "Please. Please. Let me stay." Damn her. Damn her and damn the nuts too, and especially damn the rain. Why did the nuts always pick on him? From his very first day in the city, when he was walking toward Times Square and the cripple began following him down the street yelling "Too good to talk to me? Too good to talk to me?" until he had to run to get away, but once he was away he doubled back, following the cripple from across the street for almost half an hour and why had he done that? Walt whirled, spotted a taxi and waved. The cab stopped beside him. Walt stood there with his hand on the door. After a moment the driver rolled down his window.

"What is it?" the driver said.

"What do you mean?"

"Well, you flagged me, buddy, come on now. In or out."

Walt just stood there. Then he said, "I'm sorry. I was just—I need some information. Do you know where there's a subway stop around here?"

"Sure. Four blocks up on Lex."

"Oh," Walt said, dropping his hand. "Thanks." He turned, starting to walk toward the subway stop until the taxi turned a corner. Then Walt stopped, shook his head, reversed direction. "Why did you do that?" he muttered. "What's the matter with you?" He shivered. Then he heard a great roll of thunder and he shivered again. He reached into his back pocket and brought out his handkerchief and tried to dry his glasses but the handkerchief was wet too, so he stopped trying. Walt shook his head. The rain was harder now and very cold. He broke into a run, dodging the tacklers, the football tucked tight against him, and two tacklers were coming at him now, so he twisted his small body past one and stiff-armed the other and then he had clear sailing all the way to the goal line.

Winded, Walt slowed. For a moment he was silent. Then he sang:

> *I got guilt*
> *You got guilt*
> *All God's chillun got guilt*
> *When I get to Heaven gonna lose all my guilt I'm gonna*
> *Bleed all over God's Heaven*
> *Heav'm Heav'mmm*
> *Everybody talkin' 'bout Heav'm ain't a goin' there*
> *Heav'm Heav'mmm gonna*
> *BUH-LEED*
> *All over God's Heav'mmmmm.*

He finished the song as the rain increased in tempo, so he ducked under an awning and stared out and started the song again: I got guilt, you got guilt—

"All right!"

Walt turned, saw the doorman, tried to smile.

"Get on with you."

"Sorry," Walt mumbled, and he was about to explain how he was just a little bit punchy from rain walking and that he hadn't meant to wake any of the tenants or anything like that but the doorman shook his head and started back inside.

"Nut," the doorman muttered.

"You listen!" Walt said and he ran at the doorman. "You don't know. You've got it all wrong. It started with the mistletoe. She had this mistletoe and she asked me if I wanted to kiss her—just like that. I didn't know her, of course—never laid eyes on her—and this guy was yelling God bless people—oh, all kinds of people—" and he could have gone on a lot longer except by now he was listening to himself as the doorman retreated, so in spite of the fact that a vicious wind had started Walt gladly dashed back into the rain.

Forget about it, he told himself as he hurried along. It's not important. In the morning you'll see how funny it is and that's all it is, just funny, so *it's very important that you don't think about it* because if you do, you'll start thinking about how you're not a kid anymore and it's raining like hell and you're catching your death in the middle of Lexington Avenue in the middle of New York in the middle of the night with tennis shoes on yet, at your age, and worse than that, nobody cares, and worse than that, the doorman thinks you're a nut, and worse than that, the nuts think you're their prodigal son, and worse than that, maybe they're right, and worse than that, you've never yet called Imogene even though you told yourself fifty times you were going to and is this what you came to New York for, to end up kissing nuts under mistletoe on a subway car in October and what was it P.T. had said, about a fuckup being a fuck-up no matter where, and Walt stopped dead in the rain, looking around and around, thinking, I'm not a fuckup! I'm a winner! I'm a winner!

Then he began to run.

He ran along Lexington Avenue, ran by the doorman who had called him a nut, ran through the rain, then out of it and into the lobby of Tony's building, then up the elevator and down the corridor and then he was pounding on her door, pounding and ringing, and when he heard her frightened voice ask who it was he said, "Me, Tony, Walt," and she repeated his name, adding the question mark "Walt?" and then the lock clicked and the knob began to turn, so he threw his weight against the door and she gave a startled little cry, retreating a few steps while he closed the door again and then they were alone.

"I've got to talk to you," Walt said.

"Where have you been?"

"Out. You've got to listen to me—"

"But you're soaked."

"It's raining—now listen to me. This is very important. I want you to know something: you were right to send me away."

"What?"

"You did the right thing. Before, I didn't think so. I was pretty upset. When I said I thought you were doing the right thing? I didn't mean it then. But I do now."

"I don't understand. What have you been doing?"

"Nothing. Just—nothing."

"You'll catch your death."

"That doesn't matter. You've got to listen."

"Get in the bathroom and take off those clothes. Right now."

"Not until we've talked."

She hurried to the linen closet and grabbed a towel. "Move."

"Tony—"

"My father's a doctor, remember; I'm very up on modern medicine and they've just discovered that standing around in wet clothes is a no-no."

"Dammit—"

"*Not one more word.*" She pointed to the bathroom.

Walt hesitated, sighed, turned. Then he closed the bathroom door behind him and started to undress.

A moment later, Tony knocked once and opened the door a crack. "Here. It's the best I can do."

"What's that?"

"A brand-new pink flannel nightgown."

"*Yours?*"

"Of course it's mine; what's wrong with that? I bought it big. It'll fit you well enough. Take it."

Walt took it.

"Now I'll go heat you up a can of soup," Tony said.

Walt nodded and continued to undress. O.K., he thought, so far so good. You got her interested and you got control but she thinks *she's* got control and that's great. But you've got to play it right. You'll never score with her otherwise. Play it cool. Build the moment. Nice and easy. Niiiiiice and slow.

"Can you heat vichyssoise?" Tony called. "It seems that's all I've got."

"I don't know."

"Isn't that ridiculous? I feel like such a fool. Vichyssoise."

"I don't really need any soup."

"Yes, you do. I tell you what: I'll heat it and if you don't like it we'll just pitch the whole thing."

"Thanks," Walt called, and he had to smile at the vision of Tony standing over the stove in her transparent white negligee heating up a can of cold potato soup. He finished undressing and slipped the pink night-gown on over his head.

"Well, the fat's in the fire," Tony said. "How you coming in there?"

"All done." He opened the door and stepped out.

"Oh, *Walt*," she said, going by him for a towel. "You haven't touched your hair. Stand still now." She moved up beside him and rubbed the towel back and forth, back and forth. "Well, that's some better. Did you dry yourself at all? You're such an idiot sometimes," and she reached beneath his nightgown, running her hands over his skin.

Walt stood there patiently. "O.K.?" he said.

"Let's just hope you don't get pneumonia." She turned and hurried to the kitchen.

Walt followed her, standing in the doorway.

Tony bent over the stove. "None of your tricks now."

Walt opened his hands. "I'm five feet away."

"Oh," and she glanced at him. "Yes." She poured the boiling white mixture into a cup. "Here."

Walt took it, walked to the living room, stared at the rain. "Something happened to me out there," he said.

"What was it?"

"I guess I shouldn't say something happened. There wasn't an incident or anything like that. What I mean is, I *realized* something out there."

"At the risk of double pneumonia."

Walt watched the rain. "That probably seems nutty to you, I know, but I do that. Not walk in the rain; it's just that I had to think and it happened to be raining. I knew something important was happening to me and I had to give it a chance to get out. It was the same before."

"Before?"

Walt timed his turn. "With her."

"Your wife, you mean?"

Walt made a nod.

"I thought you didn't like to talk about it."

"I don't like to talk about it but sometimes you have to do things you don't like to do. See, after what happened, after the ... incident—after she did what she did, I spent a lot of time around the house. Walking from one room to another, watching TV, reading a little, eating when I was hungry, sleeping at crazy hours, whenever I wanted to sleep. Well, that went on for a while. People got a little worried, I guess. Because they thought I was acting funny. But I knew different; something important was happening to me and I had to give it a chance to get out. Finally, one day, or night—I forget which—I realized that I'd blown everything, that I had to change my life, fast, so I changed it, left, came here, just like that. So maybe it was nutty, spending all the time around the house, but I had to do it, just like tonight I had to walk in the rain. See, what Blake did, it was, well, it was kind of unpleasant." Kind of unpleasant? Did you just say that? How could you use those words? How can you play this scene? Hands just so, eyes just so, select the sad but brave face and freeze it on. How can you use what happened just to try to make this girl you don't even really care for? How can you sully your past like this, you polluting son of a bitch? "Jesus!"

"Don't talk about it," Tony said. "It's just going to upset you."

"Yeah-yeah-yeah," Walt muttered. "Maybe I better stop. I'd like to."

"I'm marvelous at changing subjects. Let's talk about the vichyssoise—"

"I'd like to but I can't! Don't you see? I've got to tell you about what I realized out in the rain but if I just tell you, it'll sound crazy; you won't believe it, and you've got to. It'll only make sense if you know about what happened. At the dance. It was a rainy Saturday night and there's always a dance at the country club but we almost didn't go, because of the rain. We sat around discussing it and finally one of us said 'What the hell,' so we quick got dressed and went. It was a typical club dance, just like all the others, nothing special, and we danced for a little and then broke for a drink and while we were standing around we got to talking with this guy. He was an ordinary guy, big, I guess, but not great-looking or anything. Just a guy. He was a guest at the dance. I don't know, I think he'd gone to college with some member and was paying a visit or maybe he was in town on a business trip. Anyway, he was there. And we talked and drank and talked some more and then he asked would I mind and I said I was never too crazy about the rumba anyway, so off they went onto the floor. They danced well together. I remember noticing that right off. They *glided*, you know what I mean? I watched for a while and then I had another drink and made a little chitchat with the people there. It was pretty crowded—they are, usually—and I knew most of the people there. Either I'd grown up with them or they knew my father, so I was having a good enough time for myself. I'm not that sensational a dancer anyway, when you come right down to it. So I circulated, just shooting the breeze, and I wasn't aware of anything until somebody slapped me on the back with a laugh and asked me what was going on. I didn't know what he meant and he didn't specify but then I thought about it and I realized that they'd been dancing a helluva long time, this guy and my wife, so I looked around trying to locate them."

"And they'd gone," Tony said.

"Gone?" Walt shook his head. "They were so visible I wanted to die. Right in the middle of the floor, and he had his arms around her and she had her arms around him and they might just as well have been in bed and I wanted to die. So I quick started toward them and right then I felt it—everyone, everybody in the goddam place looking at me, seeing what I'd do, and you can't go around making scenes, not in public places, I mean, it just isn't done, especially when all that's happened is your wife is dancing with some stranger and you think that maybe the rest is all your imagination. But I couldn't stop either. I had to keep walking, so I did, with this nutty smile on my face, I walked straight across the floor, right by them, and I made this happy little wave as I passed, as if nothing had ever been righter in the history of the world. And I didn't stop walking until I was at this window and I stared out at the rain until I figured everyone wouldn't be looking at me anymore, and then I made my way back, around the edges of the room. Smiling all the time. I mean, I just had to smile. And I was very up, making jokes and doing imitations, everything, standing by the bar. I was *on* that night, I was really funny, and a little crowd gathered around and I went on entertaining, not ever looking at the dance floor. I didn't have to. The people around me, they were doing that, and I could tell from them just what was going on. As long as they kept laughing I knew the status quo was holding, but then, when I made a couple of good jokes and the laugh wasn't loud, I knew there'd been a change and, sure enough, they'd stopped dancing and he was walking off one way and Blake was coming in my direction. I let her come. Everybody was watching her. She really looked great that night, I thought, one of those things, everything was right, the dress, the hair. And she came up and took me by the hand and started leading me onto the floor and I made with the protest, 'I'm in the middle of a story,' faked like she was dragging me against my will and the people laughed the way I wanted them to and then we started dancing. Or at least I think we did."

"What do you mean, 'you think'?"

"I don't know. It's hard to explain. Oh, we danced. But later, after everything had happened, it seemed so crazy that we had done that. Danced. Danced while we were having that talk. Danced and smiled and waved to people we knew and clapped for the band and dipped and turned. That's *inhuman*. You can't really do a thing like that. It's so civilized. You sully everything when you do a thing like that."

"Sully?"

"Did I say that? It's not important, I don't know." Walt tugged at his pink nightgown. "Oh God, Tony, that was such a great thing you did. Tonight. Throwing me out. It's probably one of the most important things that ever happened to me. You'll see why. Where was I?"

"Dancing with your wife."

"Oh, that's right. That's where I was. Yes."

"Well, go on. What happened? What did you talk about?"

Walt laughed. "That was crazy too. We talked about my garters. See, I hate wearing garters, I almost never wear garters, and a lot of the time my socks fall down on account of that and she used to think that looked kind of grubby, so she'd bought me a pair of garters and I'd worn them that night. I didn't want to, but she'd made a point about it and what the hell, I mean, she'd bought the damn things, so I couldn't put up too much of a protest when she insisted I wear them and we talked about how they felt. And I had to admit I didn't really feel them at all and she said how much better my socks looked, not all down around my ankles all the time, and I said I didn't care, I still hated garters. On principle, you know what I mean. Garters, they're like long underwear. There's nothing *wrong* with long underwear, it just depends on how you see yourself. I never liked me in long underwear. The same with garters. I told her that. That I wasn't the garter type and I didn't care how much better my socks looked. It was insane. Here she's practically put out for some guy in front of God and everyone and we're dancing and talking about garters, and then she said 'I'm sorry' and I said 'What are you sorry about?' and she said 'You know what I'm sorry about' and I said, 'No, I don't, tell me,' and she gave this long sigh and looked at me and said 'I'm sorry about what's going to happen,' and I said 'What's going to happen?' and she pulled me very close and she rested her head on my shoulder and she whispered, 'The worst thing you can think of, that's what's going to happen.' So right away I blurted out—I didn't mean to, it just came—I said, 'You mean you're going to sack with that guy?' and she snuggled up against me and said 'That's right.' See, she knew, she understood that if she really wanted to get to me, really wanted to break things with a bang, that would be the thing to do, sleep around. I don't go for that kind of thing. She knew that. See, there's been a lot of that in my family—sleeping around—and it really upsets the hell out of me, more than anything—call me a prude if you want, I can't help it, it just does. So after she said it we just danced a little without talking. Then she was whispering in my ear again. 'Now I know this probably isn't the time to say this because you're probably upset, but I wish you'd try to remember that I said I was sorry.' And then my voice started getting loud. 'Sorry,' I said, *'sorry,'* and I was about to go on but the number ended, so we had to stop and smile and applaud the band and the bandleader bowed and turned to the musicians and they began some goddam waltz or other. We started waltzing, nice and slow, and I said 'I'll stop you,' and she smiled and came up close to me and said 'Oh, I don't see how, unless you want to make a scene, right here, and you're not about to make a scene, are you, not with everybody watching us, and besides, even if you made a scene I'd still do it.' And I looked around and everybody *was* watching us, or at least I thought they were, I don't know. And then I thought about how my father had hit my mother once. Right out in public. By the pool. He hit her and I saw him. I saw. It was, I don't know, kind of an unpleasant thing, I guess; anyway, everybody was watching us dance around the floor and I said 'I'll stop you' again and she only shook her head and said 'Oh, Walt,' and then she asked did I want her to leave in the middle or did I want to wait till the end of the waltz, and then she said that *she* thought it was better that she just leave now and she asked would I dance her over toward the door please, and right then we bumped smack into another couple and we all had to laugh and I had to make some remark about eight left feet and we all laughed again and then we picked up the waltz again, turning and turning, waltzing toward the door, and all I could think of to say was 'Why are you doing this?' and after I'd said it she paused for a while and then she gave me the smile again, a sweet, distant smile, and she said, 'Why? Maybe it's because I want to have something to remember *too.*' But I never touched her! Never! I swear!"

"You never touched who?" Tony said.

"Imogene. She went to Oberlin with us and one night she and I walked home together . . ." Leave that one alone, you son of a bitch. Don't sully that too.

"You walked home together and what?"

"Nothing. Nothing happened. But Blake, she thought—but I never even kissed Imogene. Not once. How could I? Blake and I were engaged. I was committed. That meant something. It meant something. Can you understand that?"

"Yes," Tony said.

"Blake never could. She was all the time throwing it up to me. And after she'd gone, after she'd left the dance, I stood slopping down the liquor at the bar and I thought, it's just so unfair because I never touched her. I was pretty squiffed by then, and I started getting funny again, and the people were back around, listening to me. I just went like sixty, making with the jokes, and everybody was having a gay old time and that was good, because you just can't let on to people about things. I even got up on the bandstand. It was way after midnight and I remember getting up and clowning with the bandleader, doing a few imitations, a little soft-shoe, hamming it up like I was crazy. I couldn't stop. My wife was in the sack somewhere with some guy but I couldn't stop. I mean, if I'd stopped, someone might have thought something and you just can't let that happen. I closed the dance practically. One, two o'clock. Everybody just about had gone, except there I was, screwing around on the bandstand, and I guess I drove home because I remember sitting on the front steps of our house, sitting in the rain waiting for her. For Blake. I sat there I don't know how long and then I realized what a fool I was, sitting in the rain, so I went upstairs and showered and changed into dry clothes and had a drink of brandy and then I did this crazy thing. I went out and sat in the rain again."

"My God, why? Things weren't bad enough?"

"Well, I thought maybe it might cool me down. I was so angry by then and I began getting afraid I might hit her when I saw her and I didn't want to do that. A man can't hit a woman. It's inexcusable, just like what she was doing was inexcusable and if I hit her I'd be as bad as she was; I'd be sullying myself and that's the worst thing in the world. Besides, I just had to make sure I didn't miss her when she came back."

"You couldn't have waited in the living room just as well?"

"Look, that's not the point. I already said it was crazy, didn't I? I don't know exactly why I did it but I did it; that's the point. I spent the whole night sitting outside and then going inside and getting nice and dry and then going outside again. I couldn't stop me from doing what I did any more than I could have stopped her from doing what she did. I tried. I'd say to myself, 'What, are you cracking up, are you crazy?' but that didn't stop me; once people get something in their heads you can't stop them.

That's the truth. And it's easier to think in the rain, for me anyway, and I thought about our marriage and all the little incidents that led up to her taking off from the dance, things I would have seen if I'd been sharper, but I'm not Peter Perceptive and it's easier to ignore things when they happen, unpleasant things. We never had too great of a marriage, not from the very beginning; I guess it stunk, you might say, but that still didn't excuse her telling me about it before she did it. If she'd just gone ahead and sacked with some guy, well, that happens, but *telling me*, I couldn't excuse that, especially when it was unfair on account of I'd never touched Imogene. It was just the most unfair thing . . . and you'd think she would have said something about that when she came back, at least admitted that it was unfair, but she didn't, not a word. I thought sure she would, as soon as I heard the car door close and then footsteps on the walk. I was sitting there on the steps—I don't know what time it was, six, maybe seven; it was dark but not so dark as it had been—but the rain was just as strong as ever, and the footsteps came closer and they stopped and I stood up and there she was, just a few feet away from me, the both of us there in the rain and she looked at me and I waited for her to say something because I sure didn't see how it was my place to say anything but she didn't, she just looked at me in a way that made me start to think that maybe I wasn't there at all, maybe I was safe upstairs in bed, and she kept on looking at me that way and I hit her and she didn't say anything and I hit her again and she stood there in the rain while I hit her and after a while I stopped and she took a few things from inside and left and we got divorced and I spent a lot of time around the house until I packed up and came here and . . ." Walt looked at Tony's body, visible through the white nylon negligee. "And . . . now, when I tell you what I realized tonight out there—" he gestured at the window—"now you'll believe it. It won't sound so crazy when I tell you . . ." It's not worth it, so why don't you stop? You don't have to say any more. There's no law. Quit!

"All right; tell me."

Walt turned toward the rain.

"What did you realize?"

Silence from Walt.

"Tell me."

"I think I love you," Walt whispered.

Silence from Tony.

"I love you."

Silence.

"Doesn't that mean anything to you?"

"Of course it does, my God."

"A boy tells a girl he loves her, she ought to say something. Is it that you don't believe me? I swear it's true. I never lie. You know that."

"Just give me a chance to think."

"About what? I'm not asking if you love me. Right this second I don't even want to know that answer. I love you; that's all that matters now." He sat beside her on the couch and took her in his arms. "Christ, I'm happy," Walt said. Then he kissed her on the mouth.

"Are you? I'm glad." They lay back on the couch.

"I don't think I've ever been this happy before. I want to say the craziest things to you." He kissed her again. Again. "If you hadn't had me leave tonight, this might never have happened. Thank God you did it. Just thank God."

"Say something crazy to me."

"You might laugh and if you did I'd die, but you could care for me couldn't you? I'm not talking about love, understand. But I'm not so awful that you couldn't someday care?"

"I care for you now."

"I'm gonna burst!" Walt cried and he ran his hand over her negligee until it rested on her breast.

"Crazy Kirkaby," Tony whispered.

"You just can't know how I'm feeling right now."

"Tell me. Try."

"All I can tell you is that when I realized it, see, what you did, having me leave, that was so great, so . . . I don't know, just so goddam *decent*. And then I remembered what Blake did that night and I understood all of a sudden that they were completely the opposite. And then I understood that you were completely the opposite from her. I thought she was decent, and that was important to me because I've got this crazy overworked sense of morality and she wasn't but you are and I love you, I love you," and he began lifting her negligee.

"Can I say—"

"No. Hush."

"But it's im—"

"Hush, I said."

"You have got to listen to—"

"God, I love you. Raise your arms."

"Then will you listen to me?"

"Yes."

Tony raised her arms.

"I love you so." He tossed the negligee aside.

"Then—"

Walt kissed her. *"Mon petite Antoinette."*

"This is very important."

He pulled her close. "You're so perfect."

"You're not listening."

"Of course I am. Oh God, I love—where you going?"

"Over to the chair," Tony said, and she did.

Walt followed her. "I love that chair."

"Stay in it, then," Tony said and she moved back to the sofa. "Because there's something you've got to know about me and it's this—stay, sit, that's better—I'm not perfect, Walt. I'm twenty-five years old and I have more than my share of flaws and less than my share of pride but there's something I'm proud of, and I don't care if you laugh, I don't care how Victorian it sounds. You don't lie. Well, I don't lie either, and I'm twenty-five and these days that's pretty close to old-maid country, and I'm a girl with what I hope are healthy passions and God knows you're attractive, and when I get married and I pray at night someone will have me, I won't have much in the way of dowry. But, goddammit, on my wedding night I'm going to look at him with pride and say 'You are the first. The first. I—am—a—virgin!' "

•   •   •

She wasn't, of course.

Nor had she been since her nineteenth summer, her first as a counselor at the girls' camp in Maine, when Clarkey White's brother had paid a visit. Clarkey White was a gawky little twelve-year-old with eyes that had a tendency to cross whenever she got excited and more money than ninety percent of the rest of the camp put together. She also had a brother. And he had visited her the year before, on her birthday. He had stayed for three nights, dated three girls.

None of them ever admitted to being the same again.

So when Clarkey reported, one hot July noon, that her brother was going to pay another birthday visit, this coming weekend, some of the counselors nodded, a few perhaps flushed, but that was all. When the meal was over, however, the camp store sold out of cleansing cream in fifteen minutes, hair curlers in twenty, and by mid-afternoon there was a going black market in mascara.

Tony, herself, remained unconvinced.

She was, to begin with, no kid anymore (so what if he went to Princeton; wasn't she at Sarah Lawrence?). Besides, she knew how girls were naturally addicted to exaggeration. Finally, among all the boys she had dated—bright boys, college boys, pretty boys, nice boys—she had yet to meet one who was her equal.

She did not change her mind until she saw him.

From a distance. His first morning. She dressed carefully for lunch, choosing white walking shorts and a plain white tee shirt, tucked in tight, and halfway through the meal she excused herself from her campers and walked to the table where Clarkey sat with her brother, and she stood very straight, and she smiled and said "Happy birthday, Clarkey," and as she spoke she felt his eyes, so when he approached her after the meal she was not in the least dumfounded.

"I take it you're not busy tonight."

"What makes you say that?"

"Oh, come on."

"Well, you're wrong."

"It's happened before," and he turned away.

"I wonder something."

"What?"

"Would you be so confident if you weren't so rich?"

"No," he muttered. "Of course not."

"That's better," Tony said. "*Now* I'll go out with you."

And she did. It was a perfect Maine night. They talked and had a soda in town and then they walked through the dark woods and before they sat down he spread his jacket for her. She knew he was working up to a pass; she was prepared for that. What she was not prepared for was wanting him. She accepted his kisses, fended off the rest. For a while. But it was such a splendid night and he was such a splendid creature that she finally tired of fending and thought, What the hell. She was nineteen and she'd read her Hemingway: the sooner the earth moved, the better.

It didn't even tremble.

The whole thing was, in fact, so niggling that she didn't feel guilty that she didn't feel guilty. But that night, as she lay in bed, staring out, hands clasped behind her neck, she shook her head and said, "You weren't a good brownie."

Brownies were little elves that helped the shoemaker, who was a nice man, a craftsman too, but his wife was very sick, his children very small, so he had to spend all of his time taking care of his family, cleaning and tidying, and that left little time for shoemaking, and his business got worse and worse until there was almost no money at all. But then the brownies came. Down the chimney and under the door and through the window and they worked all night, doing the cleaning and tidying, and after that was done they began stitching shoes, and so wondrous was their skill that the King heard of the shoemaker and he ordered a pair of shoes and they were so fine that he ordered more shoes, and more, and the little shoemaker became the King's shoemaker and his wife got better and everyone lived happily, of course, ever after, and as soon as her kindergarten teacher finished telling the story Tony knew that that was what she was going to be, and that night, when she told her parents, her mother said only, "I'll believe it when I see it."

But her father smiled.

So she woke at four the next morning and made her bed and dressed herself and dusted her whole room before going downstairs. And even though it didn't need it, she dusted the living room and fluffed the sofa cushions and would have scoured the entire kitchen except that everything had been done the night before. She crept back upstairs, pausing outside her mother's bedroom, but her mother was asleep, and since brownies never woke anyone, there was nothing she could do, so she hurried down the hall to her father's bedroom and peeked inside. He was snoring, but as she sadly trudged back to the stairs, she heard him snort and sputter, and then he was making his way heavily toward the bathroom.

As the bathroom door closed, Tony darted into the bedroom and made his bed. She tucked it in all the way around and then she was about to start dusting but she heard him returning, so she fled into his closet and half closed the door, holding her breath, peeking out.

He walked to his bed and he started to get in. Then he stopped. Then he squinted. He looked away. He looked back. He lifted the spread. He dropped the spread. He scratched his head, he shook his head. And then he was laughing, laughing and running toward the closet, and then he had her in his arms, tight in his arms, saying "That's a good brownie. That's a good brownie," as he whirled her around and around and around.

This happened on Marlborough Street, in Boston, in the old brick house set close by the Common and the Charles. Tony's father, Roger Last, was a doctor, "one of the more successful young pediatricians," or so her mother used to say. He had a baby face, sweet and fat, and although it undoubtedly looked incongruous, perched as it was on his thin body, Tony thought it perfect. She also thought her mother beautiful, perhaps too strong an adjective for dark Diana; "sultry" was probably closer to the truth. In any case, they were a popular couple, always off to concerts or parties or the tryouts of the plays. And they were a happy couple too, arguing infrequently and then only about money, or, rather, Diana's spending of it.

Then came the war.

Roger was called up early. Diana worried about him, but not Tony. Not when he was stationed in Rhode Island or later, when he was sent to Europe or after that, when he was shifted to the Pacific. Tony had faith. She knew he'd come back. And he did.

But it took five years.

And when he reopened his office he found that the babies he had treated were no longer babies, and they had other doctors. In the almost eleven months he kept his practice going, it seemed that everyone in the entire city of Boston had other doctors.

Roger went back in the Navy.

Diana was not particularly pleased with the decision. She wept and threatened and swore and started taking lengthy cocktail hours because, she said, she "had to get in training to be an officer's wife." Roger kept her company during the cocktail time, drink for drink, but for the most part he said nothing.

Tony didn't see why it mattered much, one way or the other, just so he was happy. He was, after all, still a doctor, except that now, when people asked her what her father did, she got to add that he was a lieutenant commander, and they were good words to roll off your tongue, words with a rhythm all their own, "lieutenant commander." And he looked wonderfully smart in his uniform. And being so important, it wasn't hard for him to pull strings and get himself stationed right in Boston, at the Charlestown Navy Yard, so he actually, if anything, got to spend more time around the house. When they moved from their house, Tony was momentarily unhappy, but they moved only a few blocks, up Marlborough Street toward Massachusetts Avenue, so even if the apartment was smallish, the address was still practically the same.

And besides, she was getting ready for high school. Being a success in eighth grade was one thing; high school had her scared. She used to lie awake nights envisioning herself—slip showing, books dropping, boys laughing, teachers scolding—moving from one humiliation to another.

They never materialized. She was a bigger success in high school than she had ever been in eighth grade. She loved the work and her grades and the teachers. She wasn't that pretty but she knew how to dress; she had, she told herself, *flair*, and the boys loved her. Her first weeks in school it was the shy boys she dated, fellow freshmen, mumbling and stoop-shouldered, acne-ridden. But before the initial grading period ended, the shoulders had straightened, the complexions cleared—she was dating juniors, seniors before the first year ended. Sophomore year she continued with seniors until a freshman math major from M.I.T. spotted her at a basketball game. He lasted almost a month before being replaced by a Harvard poet. By the time she graduated she had, according to her diary, gone out with one hundred and seventeen different boys, sixty-four of whom swore they loved her. Of these, eleven had proposed. Of these, she had kissed five, accepted none.

Summers she worked, often at the Navy Yard, once as a counselor in Maine, her best summer, probably, marred only by the fact that she submitted nightly, for three nights, to the Princeton boy. She continued to submit to him for a while; whenever he called her down to New Jersey, she always obeyed. And there were others too, until one night she stopped submitting, for reasons she chose not to think about.

Sarah Lawrence did not begin well. At first, the other girls troubled her. Not because they were so bright; she was more than willing to compete on that score. But there were so many what she called "phony dilettantes." Tony hated the phony dilettantes. They seemed so confident, so everlastingly smug. Eventually, she saw through them, and then they didn't trouble her anymore. She began to enjoy college. For a time she thought of becoming a modern dancer. She was graceful and the movements came naturally to her, but when she saw the limitations inherent in the field she turned to musical composition; she had taken years of piano lessons and could sight-read like a professional. She could paint too and well, but well enough? She wasn't sure. In the end she chose literature. She had a way with words, and besides, she loved to read.

She moved to New York after graduation. Her father would have preferred her settling in Boston, and she might have, except that he and her mother were getting on so much better by that time that there really wasn't any need. She got a tiny apartment in Greenwich Village and a secretarial job with an advertising agency. But the agency, in grateful recognition of her potential and skill, quickly advanced her to the position of assistant copywriter. The week of her promotion she moved into a new apartment in a new red-brick building off Lexington Avenue. It was far too expensive, so she took a roommate. A series of roommates, actually; one after another they got married or moved to San Francisco, but so long as they paid the rent until a replacement could be found, Tony didn't care. Her social life was busy as ever. She went to all the hit plays, some of them twice, and the good foreign movies, and she ate in the best restaurants and bought her clothes from Jax. So everything was going well, everything was going wonderfully, except every so often, just from time to time, she burst into unaccountable tears.

"What are you crying for?" Walt said. "What's the matter?"

Tony bit her lip, tried to stop. Then she shook her head and sobbed.

"Look, I'm happy you're a virgin. I am. There's no reason to cry."

"I'm sorry. I'm sorry."

"Nothing to be sorry about. Just stop."

Tony hid her face behind her hands.

"Want me to get you something? A washrag?"

"I'll be O.K." She took a deep breath. Another. Finally, she dropped her hands. "There. See? Done."

"What happened?"

"I don't know. Nothing. Forget it." She glanced toward the window. "Maybe it was the rain."

Walt watched it come down.

"It won't happen again. I swear. Sometimes it just does and then I get so disappointed in myself. I'm not a baby. Don't ever disappoint me, Walt."

"I won't."

Tony shook her head. "I don't know," she whispered. "Sometimes my life, it's like a Genet play. Here I am, naked and crying, and there you are, in my nightgown. Take it off. Please."

Walt took it off.

"I'm tired, Walt. Are you tired?"

"Dead."

"Let's go to sleep then, huh?"

"Let's."

They walked into the bedroom.

"No promises this time," Tony said. "You don't have to promise a thing. I'm too tired to fight you off. But you said you loved me—"

"Yes."

"Well, if you love me, you won't touch me."

"I love you."

"Then don't disappoint me. I'm yours, Walt, but if you love me you'll leave me alone."

"Ordinarily I'd ravage you, but I'm probably too tired to do a good job."

"Just remember, I didn't make you promise anything. We've passed that stage, you and I."

"Yes."

They got into bed, turned out the light.

"I don't ever think I've been this tired," Tony said.

He kissed her lightly. "Sleep."

"Yes."

" 'Night."

"Walt?"

"What?"

"One thing? You hurt me. Something you said. When you called me a castrator. I'm not. You see that now, don't you?"

"I was mad. Sometimes you say crazy things when you get that way. I'm sorry. I am."

"Walt?" Her voice was very soft.

"What?"

"Can I sleep in your arms?"

He reached out, held her gently, kissed her forehead. In a moment she was asleep, her naked body warm against his. Walt looked at her. Then he smiled and closed his eyes. Soon he was breathing deeply. Hey, he thought just before he slept. Hey, I won. What do you know about that?

XX

"Charley's sleeping with his secretary," Betty Jane said to Penny Whitsell. They were sitting in the bedroom of Penny's apartment in Peter Cooper Village. It was two weeks before Christmas and Betty Jane had been shopping, successfully for her son and husband, not so for her baby daughter, now six months old.

Penny sighed, picking up her tweezers and her magnifying mirror, zeroing in on the bridge of her nose. "Obviously," she said.

Betty Jane looked at her for a long time. Then, very softly she said, "Will you please stop playing with the bridge of your nose and explain?"

"You know very well I am compulsive about the fact that my eyebrows almost meet and Charley has all the symptoms. Remember last winter you were preg and it was snowing and I was out to your place and you three all frolicked in the snow like gazelles? Well, whenever Ferd that bastard cheated on me, the next time we'd sleep together he'd always bite me to prove his passion. I began feeling like a midnight snack. Ferd's biting, Charley's frolicking: same thing. Dammy!" She pulled a hair from the bridge of her nose.

"Penny, Charley's having—"

"Swing. Have one too. Listen, when Ferd first started, I almost fell apart. Then I realized: what's so great about a junior executive at Gimbels? Plenty of fish, right? Well, after that, whenever Ferd screwed around, little Penny went fishing. Smartest thing I ever did. Try it."

"But you got divorced." She could not keep her hands still.

"Yeah, but that was basically because we disliked each other. We were too competitive; promiscuity had nothing to do with it."

"I love Charley."

"Prove it."

"I love him, I love him, please, *please,* I do," and she turned away, starting to rise, starting to cry.

Penny reached out for her. "I'm sorry," she said. "B.J. B.J. I didn't want you to get upset. You know how it upsets me when you get upset and I figured if I played it cool you might too. Sit down, B.J. Please."

Betty Jane sat silently down on the bed.

"Here." Penny held out a handkerchief.

Betty Jane shook her head, stopped crying. "I just don't know," she said then. "I just feel so bad."

"Is she cute?"

"Built is the word, I think."

"How long have you known?"

"Year. More maybe."

Penny whistled.

"I didn't know exactly. I just knew something. He was working late and . . ." She shrugged.

"And what have you done?"

"Nothing."

"Why?"

Betty Jane shrugged again. "What could I do?"

"Kill him, kill her, leave him, threaten to leave him—"

"Oh, I couldn't."

"Why?"

"I'd be afraid to."

"Afraid of what?"

"Charley might let me go. I'm not right for him. I don't really make him happy, you know that."

"Oh, B.J.—"

"I'm too stupid for Charley."

"Oh, crap."

"I am."

Penny lit a cigarette, then put it out. "You're not stupid. That's a *game* you and Charley play. You say you're stupid and he says you're not, but he says it in such a way as to make you think he thinks you are. It's easier to blame it on stupidity than on the truth." Penny smiled. "Oh, baby, you're not stupid. I couldn't love you if you were. Stupid men, yes, but I loathe stupid women. Stupidity, that's just an excuse you two use. Every marriage needs an excuse in case things don't go well. You remember that afternoon in Schrafft's, when we first met Charley?"

"Of course I remember it. What about it?"

"You smiled at him."

"I did not either smile." Betty Jane held the Schrafft's menu in front of her face.

"You did too smile, Betty Jane Bunnel."

"Did not."

"Did too."

"Not."

"Too—look out, look out, *he's coming over.*" Penny brought her own Schrafft's menu up in front of her face. "We're gonna get in trouble and it's all your fault because you smiled at him."

"Hush," Betty Jane whispered. "He's terribly nice-looking."

The terribly nice-looking man stopped in front of their table. "Are you rich?" he said.

Betty Jane stared straight at the menu.

"You smiled at me," the man said.

"You smiled at me first," Betty Jane said.

"In either case," the man said, "are you rich?"

"I'm well off," Betty Jane answered. "My parents are."

"Don't talk to him he might have escaped from someplace," Penny whispered.

"Just so you're not rich. My name is Charley Fiske and I am drunk."

"I'm Betty Jane Bunnel." She put the menu down.

"You *told* him," Penny said.

Betty Jane kicked her.

"You *kicked* me," Penny said.

"I just broke a very expensive vase," Charley said. "I was having brunch on a terrace looking at the East River. There were many drinks. If I were sober, would you see me?"

Betty Jane looked at him. "Yes."

"I think you both just escaped from someplace," Penny said.

"You're very pretty, aren't you?" Charley said.

Betty Jane shrugged. "I guess so. If you say I am."

"I have never seen anyone as pretty as you. Tonight would you see me?"

Betty Jane nodded, looking at him.

"Well, why don't you both hit the sack right here?" Penny said.

"Shut up," Betty Jane said.

Charley smiled. "Six o'clock? You'll be alone?"

"I promise."

"And we'll just walk? I have no money."

"We'll walk."

"I'll meet you here. Don't change your mind."

"Don't even think that. Why are you smiling?"

"Because I met you and I'm happy," Charley said. "And because I don't do things like this."

"Neither do I," Betty Jane said. She watched him walk away. When he was gone she slumped back in her chair and looked at Penny. "That's the most romantic thing. Ever. In all my life. Don't you think?"

"Romantic with a capital R," Penny said, squinting at her magnifying mirror, plucking with her tweezers at the bridge of her nose. "But do you know what I hoped, that night when I left you alone to meet him at a few minutes before six? And a few weeks later, when I watched you all in white walking down the aisle?"

"What did you hope?"

"That you'd neither of you ever have to go to the bathroom," Penny said.

Betty Jane hesitated a moment, the jar of cold cream in her hands. Then she said to Charley, "I was thinking."

Charley looked at her from the bed. "What about?"

"Going to night school. They have these marvelous night-school courses. Do you think I ought to go to night school?"

"I don't know, honey; what for?"

"Oh, no reason. But it isn't expensive or anything. It's not really actually a formal night school I'm talking about. What it is is a bunch of the wives get together and they pay some expert to lecture to them once a week on whatever they want to learn about. You can take a course in art or music or even sculpture, if you want. The teachers are very good so they say. Real experts—graduate students from Princeton, or some of them come all the way from New York. I was thinking I might take a literature. Books and like that. Novels."

"Are you going to put on that cold cream or aren't you?"

"I don't know. I was just trying to make up my mind."

"Well, hurry up and make it; I'm tired."

Betty Jane started putting on her cold cream. "I can take any kind of literature course I want, practically. I think I'd learn a lot. Everybody says about how much you learn."

"Well, if you feel it's important."

"Oh, I don't care really; it's just an idea. I mean, I've never been to night school or anything since junior college."

"Do what you want, honey."

"There's no telling what I might do," Betty Jane said.

Shivering in the January night, Betty Jane sat in her car and watched the other ladies arrive. She had got to the grammar school early, which was silly of her, and so she sat, waiting as the other cars drove into the teachers' parking lot, and the other ladies got out and entered the school. Betty Jane lit a cigarette. She was, she knew, terribly nervous, and she hoped the teacher would let her alone on this, her first night in class, and not ask her anything. She remembered how, when she was a child, she had averted her eyes whenever the teachers asked a question, whether she knew the answer or not. I feel like I'm back in school again, Betty Jane thought, and then she realized how silly she was, because she *was* back in school again, night school now. If I can only do well, she thought. She had always liked books, so there wasn't any reason for her not to do well, and, besides, having Charley to help her was almost like having a teacher in your very own home.

But of course she couldn't ask him to help her. That would be bad. She must do it all herself, master the books, and then Charley would be proud, and if she became a really marvelous reader, maybe she could even help him out sometime when his work load got too heavy. Maybe she might even take a manuscript without his knowing and read it and then tell him what she thought of it and maybe he would agree with her and then afterward, maybe, he might even *give* her one or two manuscripts to read when he felt he needed help.

It was possible. But don't you count on it, she told herself. Don't you go and ruin everything by counting on it. Betty Jane got out of the car, hoping she didn't have a run in her stockings. Runs rattled her; she was never at her best when her stockings ran, so she checked and double checked and they were both just as straight and perfect as you could want, so she nodded and pressed down the eight crevices between her gloved fingers and marched into grammar school. The novel class met in room 121. Betty Jane said it aloud.

"One twenty-one."

Moving in the proper direction, she gave her stockings another check, removed her gloves, stuffed them quickly into her purse, reached the room. Taking off her coat, Betty Jane straightened her skirt and walked in.

Eleven ladies sat in little desks with arm rests. All eleven turned to look at her and she smiled and scurried to the farthest back seat in the corner.

"Move up, please."

Betty Jane looked at the teacher. He was tall and kind of handsome in a youngish sort of way.

"My throat isn't all it might be tonight. Come down front, Miss . . ."

"Fiske, Mrs."

"Sanders, Mr."

Betty Jane heard the class laughing as she moved down to the front of the room, being very careful not to run her stockings.

"That was a laugh at your expense, Mrs. Fiske; I'm sorry."

Mr. Sanders opened a book and leaned against the blackboard. "All right, ladies; now I'm sure we've all read *The Sound and the Fury*."

Oh dear, oh dear, Betty Jane thought; I've always meant to read that book. If only I had. If only I had.

"Why is it called *The Sound and the Fury,* Mrs. Lauderdale?"

"Why is it called *The Sound and the Fury?*" Mrs. Lauderdale said.

"Mrs. Lauderdale, in the future would you please try not to repeat all of my questions back to me?"

"That's a habit of mine," Mrs. Lauderdale explained. "It gives me a little extra time to think."

"That's certainly very canny of you, Mrs. Lauderdale. Well?"

"I don't know why it's called *The Sound and the Fury.*"

"I do," another lady said.

"Wonderful, Mrs. Bond. Why?"

"It's a quotation."

"And the source?"

Mrs. Bond snapped her fingers softly several times. "I knew it a minute ago."

"You tell us, Mrs. Fiske."

"I don't know," Betty Jane said.

"I'll give you a hint. Whenever anyone asks the source of a quotation, answer either Shakespeare or the Bible and you'll do fine."

"The Bible," Betty Jane said.

"Tsk, tsk, Mrs. Fiske," Mr. Sanders said, and the class laughed at the rhyme. "I apologize again."

"That's all right," Betty Jane said, but she could have killed him.

"Note this, ladies: the quote is from *Macbeth*, and the gist of it is that life is a tale told by an idiot, full of sound and fury, signifying nothing."

Oh, I knew that, Betty Jane thought. What's the matter with me?

"What did you think of the book, Mrs. Fiske?"

"I didn't read it."

"Why?"

"This is my first time here."

"All right, Mrs. Oliver. What did you think?"

"It was crazy. I read the start and it was crazy. That Faulkner writes like a moron if you ask me and besides I don't like Southern writers, they're all the time so pessimistic and dirty."

"It *was* written by a moron, Mrs. Oliver, Benjy is a moron. Remember the quote? A tale told by an idiot? Apt?"

"I couldn't say. I didn't read it."

"Who did read it?" Mr. Sanders wondered.

"I meant to," Mrs. Bond said.

"Close only counts in horseshoes, Mrs. Bond. None of you read it, I see. Ladies, I'm miffed. Shame on you all. Mrs. Fiske has an excuse, but the rest of you . . ." He shook his head.

"I want to talk about J. D. Salinger," Mrs. Lauderdale said. "My husband and I had a big fight about J. D. Salinger."

"Your husband said she was pregnant and you said she wasn't," Mr. Sanders said.

Mrs. Lauderdale looked at him. "That's absolutely right."

Mr. Sanders sighed.

"Who's pregnant?" Betty Jane asked.

"*Franny,*" Mr. Sanders said.

Oh, now, I meant to read that too, Betty Jane thought.

"Do you like Salinger, Mrs. Fiske?"

You shouldn't ask me questions, Betty Jane thought. This is my first time and it isn't fair. "I don't know . . . I guess . . . yes—well, not so much. If you ask me everybody sounds the same."

"Many critics feel he writes the best dialogue since Hemingway but you say all his characters sound the same, is that right?"

Betty Jane stared at the desk top where someone had scratched "Peter is a Fink!" and she heard the class laughing at her and she almost said "They all do talk the same my husband says so too and he's smarter than all of you put together." But she didn't.

What was it she had thought a few minutes ago? Something about mastering the class on her own? How silly. She was stupid and that was all there was to it and what was she doing anyway, sitting in a room talking about books? The only apt thing was the school child's desk and she opened her purse, feeling around for her nail file, and when the point of it found her fingertip, quick tears came to her eyes. Or maybe the tears were there already, what did it matter? Sneaking the file out, Betty Jane stared up at the teacher, who was busy now, in animated conversation with the other ladies, talking all about was Franny pregnant. Betty Jane kept her eyes on the teacher, and she began scratching her initials in the desk top.

My God, she thought, I'm defacing school property. She scratched away, finishing the "B," starting on the curve of the "J." I think if Mr. Sanders caught me I would just die, because he'd probably make some smarty remark and all the others would giggle. They really liked him. Betty Jane watched them watching Mr. Sanders. Well, he was young and sarcastic and that was undoubtedly a change from what they were used to. Betty Jane finished the "J" and wondered what else she should scratch in. What was it she used to do in grammar school? She smiled. Grammar school made her do that—smile. Once, in fourth grade, Penny had made a survey and found that eleven out of seventeen boys in class had scratched "BJB" on their desk tops. Betty Jane Bunnel.

Eleven out of seventeen, Betty Jane thought.

I should have listened! All I did was smile at the boys instead of listening to the teacher and if I'd listened I'd be smart now and if I were smart I would have thought of something just terribly clever to say back to Mr. Sanders and put him in his place. No, I wouldn't either, because if I were smart I wouldn't have to bother with putting him in his place because I wouldn't be here now.

Mr. Sanders glanced at her.

Betty Jane quick hid her nail file.

Mr. Sanders glanced at her again.

I wonder what else he does for a living? Betty Jane thought. Then she thought, I wonder why I wonder what else he does for a living? What possible difference does it make to me what Mr. Sanders does? For a moment Betty Jane paid attention. They were still going on about that silly pregnancy and Mrs. Lauderdale was raising her voice and so was Mrs. Bond and you could just see Mrs. Oliver getting angry and Mr. Sanders was standing in front of the room with his arms crossed, smiling. It would probably be rude for me to get up and leave, Betty Jane thought, sneaking out her nail file, scratching at the desk top. I'll just have to stick it out. Maybe I'll get Robby that new pair of shoes tomorrow. Honestly, that boy goes through shoes like Mr. Sanders—

That boy goes through shoes like Mr. Sanders?

What's happening to me? I've got Mr. Sanders on the brain, and if that isn't silly, I don't know what is. Penny would say . . . What did Penny say? Something about going fishing?

Ridiculous! In the first place, he doesn't attract me. Betty Jane looked closely at her teacher. There certainly wasn't much wrong with his face, and his physique was better than— What are you thinking? Stop it. He's much younger than you are. He doesn't look much past twenty-five. Forget it. Even if you were silly enough to contemplate doing such a ridiculous thing, and even if he decided to do it too, where would you find to go except the back seat of the car?

The back seat of the car?

Betty Jane blushed.

I must pay attention to what they're saying, she decided, so she tuned in as Mrs. Lauderdale was saying, "Listen, I've been pregnant and Franny wasn't!"

"Then why did she get into a foetal position?" Mrs. Bond asked. "Salinger says specifically that she gets into a foetal position!"

"Ladies, I appreciate your enthusiasm but . . ."

The back seat of the car was too dangerous, Betty Jane thought. Even if you parked someplace quiet and out of the way, what was to prevent some policeman from driving by and seeing the car and—

You're married, she thought. Not to mention the mother of two.

And besides, how do you know Mr. Sanders can keep his mouth shut?

What if he blabbed? "Hey, fellas, listen, you'll never believe this but the other night this old bag comes to class—well, not exactly an old bag but she's seen better days—and after class I get in the car with her and—"

I must be going mad, Betty Jane thought. She looked down at her completed initial scratching.

"B.J.—Mr. S."

I *am* going mad, Betty Jane thought, and she prayed for class to end.

"Until next week ladies," Mr. Sanders said. Then he said, "Mrs. Fiske?" and he started walking in her direction.

Betty Jane placed her purse directly above the initials.

"Could you wait a few moments, please?" Mr. Sanders said.

I could not. "Certainly."

Betty Jane sat very still while he dispensed with Mrs. Lauderdale and Mrs. Bond and Mrs. Edson, who hadn't spoken a word but who was terribly upset with all the talk of pregnancy. Betty Jane fidgeted, managing finally to get her gloves on.

When they were alone, Mr. Sanders said, "I went too far with you."

Betty Jane pressed at the crevices between her fingers.

"I'm sorry. Sometimes I do that. I think all his characters sound the same too."

"Well, then, you should have said so."

"I should have."

Betty Jane stood. "You were very nice to apologize." He was really terribly tall, when you were right next to him.

"What I really wanted to find out was will you be here next week?"

"Well, I don't think so."

"I was afraid of that. Because of how I acted?"

"Oh, absolutely not, not at all. It's just, well, I won't be here, what's the point. But I think you're a very good teacher, Mr. Sanders. Goodbye."

"Goodbye."

She picked up her purse and coat and started toward the door.

He had his coat on and moved in the same direction.

She smiled at him quickly, then looked away.

"It's so embarrassing isn't it, when this happens?"

"Yes."

"Goodbyes should be final."

"Yes. Goodbye, Mr. Sanders."

"Goodbye, Mrs. Fiske."

They walked through the door and both turned the same way.

"Oh dear," Betty Jane said, and she stopped.

He stopped beside her.

"I'm going to the parking lot."

"I'm heading that way; I'm going to the train station."

They started walking again, together. "New York or Philadelphia?"

"New York. I'm getting my doctorate at Columbia." He opened the door for her and they walked out into the cold.

"Do you have a car?"

"No."

"Oh, that's right. You said you were going to the train station."

"Yes."

It would be just inhuman not to offer, she thought. In this weather. "Could you use a lift?"

"That would be lovely."

They moved through the parking lot. "Here we are," Betty Jane said. He held the car door open for her.

He's really very well-mannered, Betty Jane thought. One thing about well-mannered people: they know how to keep their mouths shut. "Can you keep a secret, Mr. Sanders?" She drove into the street.

"Mark. Try me."

That's sort of nice—Mark Sanders. "Oh no, I didn't have anything in mind but my eldest—" might as well let him know now—"was asking me if I was good at keeping secrets and I said I thought I was and he said, 'How do you know?' That's a pretty good question. How do you know?"

"You just do and that's all there is to it. I can keep a secret, Mrs. Fiske. I'll prove it to you. I teach several of these night classes. Three a week. Have for two years. I've taught in half a dozen different towns. Would you believe it if I told you that over fifteen women in the course of two years have thrown themselves at me?"

"How interesting," Betty Jane managed.

"I have yet to tell anyone their names."

"What do you do when they 'throw themselves at you'?"

"Try to save their pride. As gently as possible."

"That's very good of you."

"No, it isn't. All of them were married, and most of them were old, and some of them were stupid, and none of them was really what I'd call pretty—turn in at the next street, it's dark."

Betty Jane managed to keep control of the car.

"Turn in."

"I can't."

"Of course you can."

"You don't even know my name."

"What's your name?"

"Betty Jane."

"Turn the damn car, Betty Jane."

Betty Jane turned the damn car.

"Now stop. Right here. No one can see."

She made the car stop.

He took her in his arms and kissed her very hard on the mouth.

"I keep thinking I ought to say 'how dare you?' "

"Say it."

"I can't. How did you know I'd let you?"

"You made it pretty obvious."

"Oh, dear; I was trying not to."

He kissed her again.

"Can I ask you something, please?" Betty Jane said.

"At your service, Mrs. Fiske."

"This isn't what you meant before about saving pride as gently as possible?"

"No; you're not old and you're not stupid and you are what I'd call really pretty. You're only married." He opened her coat and placed his hand on her cardigan sweater over her breast.

I wish Penny could see me now, Betty Jane thought.

He kissed her again.

I really ought to mind this more, Betty Jane decided. His tongue was available, so she bit it.

He started unbuttoning her cardigan and reaching inside.

"That's all there is," Betty Jane said.

"You mean stop?"

"I mean, that's all there is. I'm flat-chested. I didn't want it to come as a surprise."

He kissed her tiny breast.

"How old are you?" Betty Jane said. If he's twenty-three I'll die.

"Twenty-seven."

"Thank God."

He laughed. "How old are you?"

"Old enough to know better." Suddenly she began to shake her head.

"What is it?"

"When I said that, about knowing better, I thought I'd stop this right away. I mean, I do know better. But I don't seem to be stopping. Would you kiss me, please? Anywhere you like."

He laughed again. Then he kissed her.

She closed her eyes and held him very close.

"I'm not married," he said.

"I didn't ask if you were."

"You would have. It always follows 'how old are you?' You're looking for an excuse to stop, aren't you?"

"Yes. Please kiss me."

"Do you know how pretty you are?"

"I used to be."

"I hate people who fish for compliments."

"I'm sorry."

"Are you cold?"

"A little. I don't mind."

"Good."

He kissed her again and she thought about Charley, and then after that she thought about Robby and Paula, and then after that she bit his tongue again. She could feel her body relaxing beneath the pressure of his big hands. "My husband has hands like yours."

"Don't tell me I remind you of him."

"He used to be like you."

"I don't care that you're married."

"I'm sure you mean that."

"I do. I don't care. And I'm not mad for older women either; I thought that might put your mind at rest."

"I'll tell you something about me; I make a very good first impression. But I don't last like some people. That's the truth."

"Please shut up."

"I'm telling you, Mark—I don't like that name—I thought I did but I don't anymore."

"I'll change it."

"I'm not smart. And I say stupid things. And I'm dull. I swear to God."

He made an enormous yawn.

Betty Jane laughed and grabbed him.

They started to lie back, but her shoulders hit the steering wheel. He pulled her back upright and kissed her ear. "Whoever invented the steering wheel ought to be pistooned."

"What is that?"

"I just made it up. It feels good to say. Say it."

"Pistooned," Betty Jane said. "Yes, it does."

"You don't happen to have any friends wintering in Bermuda who asked you to look after their geraniums?"

"No."

"I thought not." He bit her ear.

Betty Jane stiffened.

"What's the matter?"

"I'm not enjoying this."

He pulled away. "I'm sorry."

"*I am, though,*" she cried and she reached for him.

"Betty Jane," he said, then he shook his head. "We'll both change our names."

"Yes."

"Why did you say you weren't enjoying this?"

"Because I thought . . . I should stop."

"Do you know what I hate—this is changing the subject."

"What?"

"Big fat flabby floppy breasts." He covered her tiny breasts with his big hands.

Betty Jane listened to herself breathe.

He kissed her. She closed her eyes. When she opened them again she was momentarily blinded by the headlights of a car.

Betty Jane cried out.

The car cruised by.

"That might have been a policeman," she began.

"Princeton cops always drive convertibles?"

"Well, then, it could have been someone who knows my car. Or someone who thought we looked suspicious and went to get a policeman."

"I don't care."

"Jesus God, neither do I," Betty Jane said. "I don't care. I'm not going to stop! I'm not going to stop!"

That stopped her.

"What's wrong?" he said.

She shook her head, straightened her clothes, started the car.

"Listen," he said as the car picked up speed. "I haven't been doing this just for the hell of it."

"Don't you think I know that?"

"Talk to me then."

"What would happen if I really liked you?"

"Find out."

Betty Jane shook her head.

"Why not?"

"There's the train station," Betty Jane said, and she sped up until she was there. She stopped the car, kept the motor running.

He looked at her. "I wish I could think of some great thing to say."

Betty Jane stared out the windshield.

Then she felt the tips of his fingers touch her lips.

"What did you have to be nice for?" she said as he got out of the car. She started to drive. She drove up the street, looking for him in the rear-view mirror. Then she saw him. He had come into the street after her, waving. They both stopped still in the middle of the street. She stared back at him through the darkness. At that moment she could not imagine a lovelier boy.

Well, I am stupid, she thought as she started to drive away. There's no doubt about it now.

Jenny sat slumped in her acting class, trying to pay attention to Mr. Lee. He was a wonderful teacher and she always found him fascinating to listen to, except lately she had trouble concentrating on things. It was the beginning of March and she hadn't felt well for a long time. Tired. Tired. All the time. It wasn't Charley's fault. You couldn't blame Charley. He loved her. She knew that, even though he'd never actually told her in so many words. It didn't bother her that he'd never told her, only sometimes, like now as she sat slumped in her chair in acting class, she thought she wouldn't mind so much if once or twice he might actually go ahead and tell her, in so many words, just for the hell of it.

Up at the front of the class, Mr. Lee said "Skedaddle," and the minute he did, Jenny hurried to her feet and started for the door. But she was too slow; Bernie Randolph was already there, waiting for her. Bernie Randolph was the best actor in the class, or at least the best male actor. He had already appeared in three Broadway shows and everybody knew it was just a matter of time until he made it big. For five weeks running now he had asked Jenny out for coffee after class. She had always managed one excuse or another, except that it bothered her because she wanted to say yes, because his name had not always been Bernie Randolph and he had spent his youth in a concentration camp and Jenny would have loved to have got to know him.

But back among the blue walls, Charley was waiting. This was Thursday, an easy day for him to stay late in the city, and he wanted her to change to another acting class. And she would have, except that Mr. Lee was one of the best teachers in the whole city and this was the only class of his she could make, Thursdays, from five o'clock to seven-thirty.

Bernie Randolph smiled at her.

I just can't lie to you again, Jenny thought, and she turned abruptly, walking up to Mr. Lee. He was surrounded by other students, but that was fine as far as Jenny was concerned. The more the better. Eventually Bernie would have to tire of waiting. Jenny stood beside Eli Lee, trying to come up with some not so silly question; he was a smart man and the thought of him finding her foolish was instantly unendurable. Eli Lee was fifty, had once been a Communist, had turned to teaching when he could no longer act. Now that the pressure was off he was performing again, character parts only; he had a good, rough face that was instantly familiar to viewers of new television and old movies. Connecting the name with the face was, for some reason, all but impossible: audience referred to him as "that guy," and even his own wife called him "Hey, you" from time to time.

"I've been avoiding this," Eli Lee said.

Jenny looked quickly around to see who he was talking to. But, except for an occasional glimpse of Bernie Randolph waiting in the hall outside, the room was empty.

"I made a mistake with you," Eli Lee went on.

"Auh?"

"You're the least experienced person in this class, you know that, don't you? You're also suddenly the lousiest. I never should have taken you in."

I must say something, Jenny thought. Yes; I must do that. She put her hands to her temples and began to rub, around and around.

"When a girl's as bad as you've been for one week, I figure it's that time of the month. For two weeks I figure she figures she's knocked up, but you don't strike me as that type. With you, all I can figure is that I made a mistake."

Jenny nodded.

"You're no straight ingenue, kid. You're a minority group. Nobody's ever gonna hire you for a sweet young thing unless your leading man plays pro basketball. The chances of your ever working would give Nick the Greek insomnia; the only reason I took you in is because I thought that *if if if* there was ever a part you were right for, you'd play the hell out of it. What you have is size and power but they're nothing without discipline. Where's your discipline gone, kid; where's your concentration gone, kid; what in the hell has happened to you?"

Jenny could think of nothing to say.

"That's all."

Jenny managed to locate the door.

She made her way along the corridor and, holding tight to the railing, down the steps to 44th Street. Outside it was dark, warm for March, and she hesitated, wondering whether to put on her coat or not.

"I left as soon as he started," Bernie Randolph said, standing on the sidewalk.

For a moment Jenny couldn't remember who he was.

"I thought you'd rather no one heard. I could tell from his tone he was going to blast you."

"How have I been?"

"I'm no teacher."

"That bad?"

"You've been better. We've all been better. Coffee?" They started to walk.

"I've had things on my mind," Jenny said.

"That happens. Will you have coffee or not?"

"I didn't know I'd been so awful. Eli said he never should have taken me into class."

"You're very talented. He's told you that too."

"Not today. I don't feel very talented. All my life I wanted to be good at something. I can't think of anything better than being good at something. I can't have coffee with you."

"Why not?"

"Well—"

"Don't make up anything. Just tell the truth; you don't want to."

"I do, though."

"Then let's."

"Well, I can't!"

"You have this evil stepfather and he punishes you whenever—"

"I can't because I've got someone waiting for me. There."

"Ten minutes? One cup?"

"No."

"Sounds like a terrific relationship. Rich with understanding; give and take."

"Bernie—"

"I mean, if you hadn't wasted ten minutes trying to dodge me earlier, not only would you be on your way home now, Eli wouldn't have taken your head off."

"I wasn't trying to dodge you."

"You're a lousy liar."

"All right I was, because I knew you'd ask me for coffee and I wanted to go but I couldn't and I didn't want to lie." She stopped walking. "Why can't I have coffee? I mean it? *Why?* Why can't I, I'd like to know? Class might have run late. So why can't I have a cup of coffee if I want to?"

Bernie applauded softly.

"I'll have two cups if I want to," Jenny said. "I do what I please."

"Great."

"Let me make just one little phone call first." She looked around. Up on the corner she saw a sidewalk telephone booth and they hurried to it. Jenny stepped into the booth, closed the door behind her, dialed. Bernie walked around the outside, glancing in occasionally, sometimes breaking into a quick dance, his heels clicking against the sidewalk. "Charley?" Jenny said. "Listen, would you mind if I was just a few minutes late?"

"You already are."

"All right, a few minutes later. Would you mind?"

He said, "Not at all," in a tone that said he minded.

"Just a few minutes? That's all I'll be."

"I said I wouldn't mind."

"You didn't mean it and you know it."

"Stop the mind reading, will you, please?"

"I don't see why I can't have just one quick cup of coffee."

"Have a goddam potful."

"Why are you mad?"

"I'm not."

"I'll be right home."

"Don't you dare."

"What—"

"If you come home you'll do nothing but complain all evening about how I wouldn't let you have one stinking cup of coffee which isn't the truth in the first place."

"*What do you want me to do?*"

"Whatever you want to do. You're a big girl."

"Why do you have to make such a thing out of this?"

"Jenny, if anybody's making a thing out of this—"

"It isn't me, it isn't!"

"Of course not. It's my fault. Here I've had the supreme bliss of sitting surrounded by these lovely blue walls for many, *many* hours, and when I don't froth at the mouth at the chance of extending my solitary confinement, I automatically come out the bad guy."

"You've got no right to talk to me like that. You knew I had class—"

"I'm not waiting any more Thursdays, Jenny; you can quote me on that."

"Charley—"

"I'm going home now; I'll see you tomorrow."

"You better get ready! You better get ready to choose, Charley! I mean it! That's the God's truth and you can quote me on that too!"

"Slow down."

"I don't like the way you're behaving and using me and not making up your mind and you better make it up and I mean what—"

"You're so sweet I'd have to pick you."

"You"—"bastard" she was going to say, you bastard son of a bitch, except she lost control before she could get it out, and was genuinely amazed at how quickly the gawkers came when you did that in public, lost control, because from all over the gawkers appeared, forming a second wall outside the four walls of the telephone booth, watching her as she turned, crying, around and around and around.

"I just feel so silly," Jenny said as Bernie helped her out of the cab in front of her building. "I'm really all right, Bernie."

Bernie guided her toward the front door.

A figure raced down to meet them.

"Charley, hi," Jenny said. "Charley, this is Bernie. He's that wonderful actor I've told you about."

"Thanks," Charley said to Bernie. "I'll take her now."

Bernie nodded.

"It's just the silliest thing," Jenny said as Charley led her in to her apartment. "All of a sudden I was so upset. It's on account of Eli. He bawled me out, Charley. He said I was just such a terrible actress and that really upset me."

The blue walls surrounded them.

"I'm very tired," Jenny went on, her voice dropping now. "I didn't think I was. But boy, am I ever tired. Eli, he shouldn't have talked to me like that. Not when I wasn't ready or anything. He shouldn't have upset me."

Charley knelt, took off her shoes. Then he got her to lie down and, lying beside her, cradled her gently.

"I just feel . . . well, I haven't felt this silly since I don't know when. Oh, am I the tired one. Back home once I made a cake with baking soda instead of baking powder. I felt pretty silly then, I can tell you. The poor cake, it just lay there. Oh, I've really done some silly things in my time. That poor cake." And she talked on, her voice dropping, and when it was less than a whisper she heard Charley saying something, the same thing, over and over, as he rocked her in his great hands. Jenny listened to him repeat it, and when she realized that was telling her he loved her, she managed a smile. "He loves me," she whispered then. "Oh, I knew you would . . . I did . . . I did. Oh, isn't this a red-letter day . . ."

Jenny stood on the second floor of the customs area of Idlewild, looking down at the lines of people below, trying to find Tommy. His plane had arrived fifteen minutes earlier, so he really ought to be here, she told herself. She made a careful check, staring at all the faces down below, and suddenly it struck her that maybe he was there and she just didn't recognize him. Impossible, she decided. Absolutely impossible. She'd known him all her life; she knew him now.

Jenny straightened her skirt and shook her head and continued her search. It was two o'clock of a May afternoon—she had taken the afternoon off for the occasion—and her stomach growled, which always embarrassed her, especially when it used to happen in school and all the boys around her laughed, Tommy leading the laughter, so she turned away from the window and hurried to the cigar store down the way and bought two candy bars. She wolfed the first one, downed the second in a fashion more ladylike, and returned to her position by the window.

Taking out his letter, she checked the information he had given her as to his arrival. Jenny nodded. Somewhere, down there, Tommy was waiting to pass through customs, and if that very rude boy at the rear of the nearest line would only stop waving at her, she might stand a better chance of finding—

Oh dear, Jenny thought, and she waved back at Tommy.

He held up his suitcase and gestured to it, then to the customs man.

She nodded that she understood.

He mouthed that he loved her.

She cupped her hands around her ear and shook her head.

He mouthed it again.

Jenny waved to him, thinking how wonderfully well and handsome he looked, wishing that she felt well herself, or at least better. She was terribly nervous and had been ever since Tommy's letter arrived, and she wished she were calmer and stronger for this, a difficult day.

Tommy put his hands to his heart.

Jenny whirled her index finger around her ear.

They both smiled and waved at each other as the customs line moved slowly forward. I must do this right, Jenny told herself, going over in her mind what she planned to say. Charley was against her saying anything, but Jenny felt she owed it to Tommy to tell. She opened his letter again and reread the beginning:

Moose:
It dawned on me the other day that in all my world travels, I have yet to meet your equal at Indian wrestling, shot-putting, or tossing the caber. This set me to thinking, which is what we Rhodes scholars do best. I think we ought to get married. I mean, enough is enough. What do you think . . . ?

Jenny looked down at the boy in the customs line. The boy looked back at her, pointed to his watch, then shook his fist at the slow customs man. Jenny smiled. The boy pulled out a pistol and fired six shots at the customs man. Jenny began to giggle. The boy produced a gigantic submachine gun and started blasting away at the customs man. Jenny laughed and laughed, then whirled, racing for the nearest phone, dialing Kingsway, asking for Mr. Fiske, saying, "Do you love your secretary?" when he answered.

"I do."

"Say it."

"I love my secretary."

"More."

"I have loved you more these last two months than I have ever loved anybody in all my life. I take it he's arrived."

"Yes."

"But you haven't talked to him yet. Well, you don't *have* to tell him about us. All he asked you was a question: 'will you marry me?' All you owe him is an answer: 'no.' You don't have to explain a damn thing."

"Yes, I do."

"Why?"

"Because it's Tommy."

"Jenny—"

"Nobody understands me like Tommy. I love you so. Goodbye." She hung up and went back to the window. Tommy looked up at her; he was terribly old now, all bent over, and his hands trembled and he had to squint to see.

Jenny laughed out loud. You're crazy, she thought, just like always. The customs man finally beckoned, so Jenny went downstairs, waiting by the exit door for Tommy to finish. When he was through, he shook the custom man's hand firmly, took his suitcase, ran through the exit door, dropped his suitcase and grabbed Jenny around the waist, crying "Look at you, look at you, for crissakes."

"Stop!"

"You're a goddam sophisticate. My God, I leave a—"

"Tommy—"

"Fat clod and come back and she's chic."

"People can *see* us."

"No, they can't—I've clouded their minds so that they cannot—little trick I learned years ago in the Orient. You will never, in your wildest dreams, guess how much I missed you." They started walking for a taxi.

Jenny wished she felt better.

"You're going to turn me down, aren't you?" Tommy said.

"No one understands me like you do."

"May I ask why?"

Jenny told him. Slowly, with great and gentle care.

"You have a crummy apartment," Tommy said when she was done. He glanced around at the walls. "I think they call this color 'loony house blue.'"

"Don't you want to say anything else?"

"I'd just as soon not talk about it."

"But do you understand?"

"Of course I understand."

"And you're not mad."

"I didn't say I wasn't mad. I said I'd just as soon not talk about it. You really care for this Fiske?"

"I love him."

"And he loves you and's gonna marry you."

"Yes."

"I really hate him, I'm that jealous."

"You'd like him."

"Sure," Tommy said, and then he said, "Got it."

"Got what?"

"I was trying to think of what it was I minded about all this. I just figured it out, that's all."

"I had to tell you. I couldn't just say 'no' and not explain."

"I really appreciate that, Jenny. How long have I been crazy about you? Five years? Closer to ten?"

"I'm sorry about that."

"At first I thought it was the seaminess I minded, but then I figured, if you want to drop your pants, drop 'em, it's not much of my business."

"*Don't talk that way,*" Jenny said and she thought, oh dear, oh dear, this is going to be awful.

"I mean, you want to be the town pump, O.K."

"*Tommy!*"

"But that isn't what I mind, the seaminess. My second thought was—"

I wish he'd raise his voice, Jenny thought. It's like a lecture in a schoolroom and I do wish he'd talk a little loud—

"—the triteness. But that isn't it either. After all, every girl who comes to Manhattan has an affair with her boss—it's practically an entrance requirement—and I figured you—well, I hoped you'd pick somebody a little more original to put out for."

Jenny wished a lot of things.

"What I really mind, though, is the *deceit*. All the love shit; all the crap about how Fiske's gonna marry you."

I must not listen, Jenny told herself. I must be very careful or it's going to be like the telephone booth and I don't know if I can take that and—

"He's never gonna marry you! He's got too good a deal going for him the way it is."

"That's not—"

"I envy the guy. Has he had this setup before? I guess he probably wouldn't tell you that, it might upset you. Admit it: he's never gonna marry—"

"He . . . *is*!" somebody said.

"Aw, Jenny, face it, huh? Come on now."

"It's . . . truth . . . !"

"Jenny, you admitted you've been shacked with him for almost two years now and he hasn't made a move yet and he's not going to and you know it and that's why you're not pushing him into a decision because you know which way the decision's going and if you want to know the truth this whole thing is so bloody ludicrous it's very hard not to laugh."

I must get to the bed and lie down, Jenny told herself, starting on the journey.

"The fact is," Tommy said, "that you're nothing but a lousy whore."

Jenny's mouth opened.

"Don't misunderstand me. I didn't mean lousy in the sense of disgusting; I'd never call you disgusting."

Jenny made it to the bed at last, and she sat down, then lay flat, thinking how much he must care for her, poor Tommy, to talk to her this way, except the realization brought with it no relief, and she closed her eyes, wondering which could last longer, his power to talk or hers to listen.

"Lousy in the sense of inept is what I meant, if you can use lousy that way. I mean, look around you; only an inept whore would live in a place like this. Can't he at least help you out a little on the rent, get you a decent place? Hasn't he got any pride? How can he bring his friends to a place like this?"

Jenny could feel herself starting to go.

Tommy began to cry.

Then he left.

Then there was some time.

Then Charley came.

Jenny lay quietly on the bed. She smiled at him.

"I take it it didn't go well."

"Not so very."

"It's over; look on the bright side." He sat down beside her. "I left work early because I had a feeling it might not go well because I had this overwhelming desire to tell you how much I love you. I love you." He shook his head. "Nope. Desire's still there. *I love you!* There. Better."

Jenny reached up, lightly clasped her hands around his neck. "I'm so happy when I'm with you. That's the most marvelous thing."

"According to latest reports, I am much happier with you than you are with me. What'll we do?"

"When?"

"Now. We owe ourselves some kind of celebration, right? Hey—let's rent a car! Drive someplace. Like that? We could take in a movie maybe."

"Sleep with me?"

"Now?"

"Yes."

"Sure you feel up to it?"

"Please."

He kissed her. "Don't you ever dare say please. The pleasure, for God's sake, is mine." He ran his hands along her body. "You are a real piece and that's the truth." He got up and went to the closet and began to undress.

Jenny slipped out of her clothes.

Charley looked at her. "Don't lose any more weight. That's an order."

When they were both naked she went to him. "Miss Devers desires to be carried to bed."

"In a minute." He kissed her for a while, running his fingertips along her skin. "God, you're a hunk, you know that?" and he lifted her, carried her across the room, gently put her stretched out on the bed. He lay down beside her. "Strange, I have the feeling I've been here before."

Jenny smiled. "How may I excite you?"

"Oh, I don't know." He reached for her breasts. "I'll think of something." They locked in an embrace. "God, I love you," Charley said then.

"We're happy together."

"That we are."

"That's the truth, isn't it?"

"Yes."

"We don't lie, do we? Not to each other."

"I can only speak for myself. I don't."

"That's what he objected to—Tommy. 'Deceit,' he called it."

"Can we just not talk about him? What does he know?"

"Just for a little."

"Why?"

"Because I want to." She kissed him.

"All right. Just for a little."

"Touch my breasts."

"Aye, aye, skipper. Can I ask a question?"

"Don't stop. You may."

"What the hell has touching your breasts got to do with Tommy?"

"You enjoy touching me, don't you?"

Charley laughed. "I'd say it's reasonably pleasurable. If you pinned me to the wall."

"Good; that's what I'd always thought, because you see, that's all to my advantage. And so is being here, lying where we're lying."

"Come again?"

"This is it, Charley. Choose."

Charley smiled.

"Tommy—he said I'd never dare ask that. He said we were liars, that you'd never leave her and that I was afraid to ask, but I'm not afraid to ask, I just proved that. So he was wrong. He was wrong about everything, wasn't he? Now I know this isn't easy, but it had to happen sometime, Charley, so this is as good as any. I mean, we couldn't go on like this for-ever—that wouldn't have been fair to anybody—so choose."

Charley opened his mouth to answer.

"There's a couple of things I think I ought to say before you make anything final, so will you listen? Of course you will. I know everybody always says that divorces are terrible on the children and I guess that's the truth but what nobody says is that it's probably worse having them grow up in a house where you're in love with me, so you bear that in mind when you make your decision."

Charley started to speak.

"One more thing: you probably feel sorry for Betty Jane, but you've got to realize that she lived perfectly well before you came along and she's still prettier than almost anybody, so I wouldn't worry about her—I'd worry about me—of course I'm biased." She gave a little laugh. "But I love you and you love me and we're so happy together, we're good for each other, you know that yourself, you say it all the time—you're at your best when you're with me—that's important! We love each other! That's important too. So what you've got to do is make up your mind one way or the other between Betty Jane and me and if I were you I know who I'd pick. Pick."

Charley nodded.

"One final thing and I swear this is the end. If you pick her—I don't mean this to be a threat, it isn't, it's just a fact and I swear I mean it—but if you decide to stay with her, well, I'm leaving. I have to. You understand that. You won't ever see me again. I'll go. I'll head home. You won't ever see me anymore. Or touch me. Touch me, Charley! Now, touch me, go on, you said it was pleasurable, go on!" His hands began to roam. "Go on, oh, I love that, I love you when you touch me, so touch me, touch me and choose, Charley, her or me, yes or no, now or never."

". . . never . . ."

The green canoe seemed to be flying.

Jenny giggled.

She stood on tiptoe, staring down through the woods as the green canoe flew toward her between the trees. Jenny set her suitcase down on edge, then sat on it and waited, giggling some more. It was really so funny. She had not seen him for a long time, her father, and she remembered him as being particularly big and strong and she was afraid that perhaps her memory was a liar. But here he came, carrying the green canoe, swerving up, up from the lake, cutting through the trees. Jenny put her hand to her mouth, because if she laughed too loudly he might hear and would know she had come and spoil her surprise. Breathlessly, she waited. She could hear him now. Coming closer. Then the canoe knifed in toward her, forty feet away. Jenny sat very still. Twenty feet, ten. Jenny waited.

The canoe stopped, tilted to one side. A face appeared beneath it.

"Auh?"

"Auh." Jenny giggled. "I just knew you were going to say that. I would have bet anything."

"Auh."

"I'm home."

Carl nodded.

"Are you glad?"

Carl smiled.

"How do I look?"

"Skinny."

"Other than that?"

"Tired."

"Other than that?"

"Beautiful."

"I've missed you."

"Same."

"I've been so miserable."

"Shows."

"Oh, Daddy, Daddy, Daddy, take me home."

Carl put the canoe down, picked up his daughter. She slumped against his chest. Carl turned his body, protecting her eyes from the slants of the afternoon sun. Her breathing grew deeper. Deeper.

Soon she slept in her father's arms.

• • •

She woke in her own bed and Tommy was standing over her.

"Hi."

"Hi."

"You were right, Tommy. He wouldn't have me."

"Can't we forget about that?"

"Oh, what a wonderful idea," Jenny said.

Then she slept a day.

Tommy paddled toward the center of Cherokee Lake while Jenny lay on the bottom of the canoe, sunning. "So I know what I'm gonna be," Tommy said.

"What?"

"Lawyer."

"You sure got the mouth for it," Jenny said.

Tommy lifted the paddle and dripped water on her stomach. When she had squirmed sufficiently he put the paddle back in the lake. "I sure do like funny women," he said.

Jenny rolled onto her stomach. "Where?"

"I guess Harvard. You're a good color now. You looked like hell when you got back."

"I was under severe strain. I can't remember why."

"Could we talk?" Tommy said.

"Huh?"

"Privately, I mean."

Jenny looked around. "Are you crazy? We're all alone right here."

"I sure do wish I could think of someplace private to talk," Tommy said, and he began rocking the boat.

Jenny sat up. "What *are*—"

"Rocking the boat," Tommy replied, and then he tipped it over.

Jenny dived into the cool water, came up, looked around, saw nothing. She dived down again, surfacing under the canoe.

Tommy was waiting for her. "Glad you could come," he said, his voice echoing softly.

"Boy," Jenny said, "when you say private, you're not kidding."

"I think this is pretty romantic," Tommy said. "Ever since we were kids I've always thought so. And that's fitting. Henceforth, what I am about to say will be referred to as UTC. Under the Canoe, Up the Creek— take your pick."

"Under the Canoe," Jenny said. Her hands rested on a thwart.

Tommy pulled himself up alongside, put his hands next to hers. Their faces were very close. "This is just to find the mood," Tommy said, and he kissed her gently. "O.K. Here's the thing. I don't expect to get married while I'm in law school. That gives you three years to screw up your life. Have all the breakdowns you want, try suicide, shoot the works, go. *But*—notice I underlined that—but *if* at any time, during that three-year period—I won't wait any longer than that—*but if* during that time you happen to decide that you'd like to marry a brilliant, handsome, reasonably rich, all-around great guy who loves you, I know where you can find one."

"Aren't you the nicest boy," Jenny said.

"Close your eyes."

Jenny closed her eyes.

He ducked her.

She came up furious but he was gone, so she moved outside the canoe and he was beaming at her from the other side.

"You're bu-tee-ful in your wrath," Tommy said. "I learned that line from a John Wayne picture."

"You're gonna get it."

"I meant what I said. You know that."

"I'm gonna really give it to you," and she dived under the boat, coming up on the other side to find they had changed positions. "Come back here."

He started swimming away. "Nobody calls me the nicest boy and gets away with it."

She started to follow him.

"I'm a faster swimmer than you are."

"Oh, that's right," Jenny said and she returned to the canoe.

Tommy swam close to her. "Hey—what would you do if he called?"

"Who?"

"Don't give me that. Your fink editor friend."

"He wouldn't."

"What if he did?"

"Wouldn't bother me."

"He called. Earlier."

"Doesn't bother me," Jenny said.

No sooner had her parents left for the lodge, leaving her alone in the house, than there was a knock at the front door. Jenny opened it, found Tommy. "Yes?"

"Hi."

"What is it?"

"I just thought I might want to talk to you," Tommy said.

"I told you; I feel like sewing tonight."

"Crap."

"You watch—"

"You're crazy, Jenny."

"For not wanting to spend the evening with you? Has it ever dawned on you that you might just possibly bore me?"

"You know he's gonna call again and you just wanna be here and take it. Now admit that."

"I'll do no such thing."

"You're gonna get involved again. I'm telling you—"

"You gave me three years! That's what you said. Well, if I wanna get involved again, I will."

"Do you?"

"No."

"Then what do you wanna talk to him for?"

"You wouldn't understand."

"I'm pretty dumb."

"I want to listen to him squirm," Jenny said.

"Why? Why do you care?"

"I don't care."

"Then why bother talking to him?"

"I told you you wouldn't understand."

"Revenge involves desire," Tommy said.

"Hell hath no fury like a woman spurned."

"Scorned."

"Either! Both! Get out."

"Temper!"

"*Smartypants!*"

Tommy smiled.

"Stop that."

"You care for me. You haven't called me that for years."

Jenny went into his arms. "Of course I care. Now please get out."

"She's using her feminine wiles. Look out."

"He hurt me, Tommy. I want to hurt him. What's wrong with that?"

"Nothing. Actually, I think it's kinda noble."

"I know what I'm doing."

"That's what Custer said."

Jenny kissed him. "I hate you."

The telephone rang.

"Lemme stay."

"Get out."

"Moral supp—"

"Get out. Out! Out! Out! I mean it. Go!"

Tommy went.

Jenny smoothed her hair.

The telephone rang for the third time.

"All right now," Jenny said. You do this right and he'll squirm. This is like class. It is an exercise. This is an exercise in craft and that is all, so get it and get it right. She picked up the phone and after the operator's "Go ahead, please" she said "Hello?"

"Jenny—"

"Oh, Charley, Charley, thank God!—"

"I've been going crazy—"

"I've been just praying for you to call—"

"I called once already."

"Nobody told me. Oh God, Charley—"

"I love you."

"And I love you."

"I've been going crazy, Jenny."

"I haven't stopped crying."

"Oh, Jenny—"

"Tell me, tell me—"

"I love you."

"Oh yes."

"I love you, I love you—"

"Charley?"

"Yes?"

"Charley?"

"Yes?"

"Go to hell, Charley."

There was a considerable pause on the other end of the line.

Jenny giggled. "My, that felt good. Ummm-ummm."

"Come back," Charley said.

"Whaat?"

"I said, come back."

"Didn't you hear me?"

"I heard you. Come back."

"To quote Charley Fiske: '. . . never . . .' "

"Don't you understand? Everything's different now. You win."

"What do I win?"

"Me. I'll divorce her."

"So divorce her."

"Will you come back?"

"Of course not."

"Then I won't divorce her."

"Do you love me?"

"Yes. Yes. So much."

"If you love me, how can you stand living with her? If you love me, you'll divorce her anyway."

"You're very young. There's something you don't know yet: anything is better than nothing."

"Sob, sob."

"Jenny, I made a mistake—*don't hang me!* Come back."

"No."

"Come back."

"No!"

"Jenny—"

"Divorce her."

"I won't divorce her until you come back."

"I won't come back until you divorce her."

"*Then you will come back.*"

"*No. No.*"

"I knew you would."

"I won't."

"You want me."

"So what?"

"That makes all the difference."

"I want Cary Grant too. It means nothing."

"We love each other."

"*Loved* each other. Duh-duh."

"Will you take the bus or fly?"

"Canoe."

"Come tonight."

"I can't."

"Tomorrow then."

"No, not tomorrow."

"Get here by Thursday. I'll send her out to Long Island early."

"*No!*"

"You're protesting too much."

"I'll whisper it, then: no. Better?"

"Don't be afraid."

"I'm not."

"Yes, you are."

"That's funny."

"It's true. If you come back I'll get divorced and then you'll have to take me. I'll be free. You don't want that, though. All you want is the lying and the sneaking around—"

"*That's not so!*"

"Isn't it? Isn't it?"

"Please. No."

"Admit it."

"I admit . . . nothing."

"The deceit. You loved it. *It*, not me."

"No; I loved you."

"Then come back."

"How do I know you'll divorce her?"

"You don't. Come back."

"You can't talk me into this."

"Nobody can *talk* anybody into anything. You *want* to come back."

"Charley—"

"Bus or plane?"

"Neither."

"You've made me suffer. You've said your 'go to hell.' That's enough revenge. Come back."

"I don't know."

"My God don't you want to be happy?"

"I don't know, I don't know."

"Bus or plane?"

"I don't know."

"Make up your mind. If you want to be happy, come back. If you love me, come back."

"Do you think we could be happy?"

"How could we miss? Bus or plane?"

"I need time to think."

"We're fresh out of time. Bus or plane?"

"You can't push me into a decision."

"Who's pushing? Bus or plane?"

"Say something else."

"O.K., plane or bus?"

"Bus by Thursday." Jenny hung up. Well, she thought, that's making him squirm all right.

• • •

Jenny slipped out of the house at dawn. She stood very still, listening. When she heard the steady sound she nodded, followed it until she could see him, Carl, chopping down the tree. He held the ax very delicately, and when he swung it was an easy swing, almost slow. But every time he landed, the tree shuddered.

"Take me for a ride?" Jenny said.

"Auh?" He stopped swinging.

"We could go see the Princess. I've got over an hour."

"Princess?"

"Oh, you know, you remember. She lived in the magic lake and she had long, long hair and said you could fish there anytime."

"She went away."

"She did?"

"Urgent business, so she said." He smiled, turned on the tree again.

"You're mad at me, aren't you? For going back?"

"No."

"He's going to get a divorce. We'll come visit after we're married. You'll like him. He's not really so very different from you."

The ax dug sweetly into the "V."

Jenny stared through the trees as the sun rose. "Daddy," she whispered.

"Auh?"

"Please *stop* me."

"Big," Carl said as he looked at his hands.

"Daddy—"

"See? Big." He spread his hands before her eyes.

They blocked out the sun.

"Always been big. I had it figured once—all scientific—that if I flapped them fast enough, and got a good running start someplace high, that maybe I couldn't fly so good but I could sure glide a long ways."

Jenny listened to her father.

"My father—he died before you—he said he had no objection to me flapping, just so I did it on the ground. I told him I needed a high place like the roof of the house. One-story house. Twelve, maybe fifteen feet high." Again the ax enlarged the "V." "Flat roof. Perfect for a takeoff, I told him. He said no. I explained—all scientific—about my big hands and I told him I was going to do it regardless. He said, O.K., do it. I did it. I waited till I had a good strong following wind, then I ran across the rooftop flapping like crazy."

"What happened?"

"I did good at first."

"Then you fell?"

"Broke two arms and a foot."

"He shouldn't have let you do it."

"That's what I thought. Told him, when I came to. I was all trussed up, casts all over. Couldn't move much. When I told him he just looked at me and shook his head and said, 'Well, now we know the most important thing in life.'"

"What's that?"

"'Who the horse's ass is,' my father said."

The first thing Jenny saw when she got off the bus in Manhattan was three fags and a cripple.

I'm sure it's a great place to visit, she thought, but I'd hate to live here.

Charley met her. They taxied to the Plaza Hotel, where Charley had taken a room in Jenny's name. When they pulled down the shades and turned off all the lights, the room was very dark. She was tired from the trip and when he started pulling off her clothes she sort of wished he'd go easy, but when her clothes were gone and his fingers began lighting on her flesh, she became, quite suddenly, equally filled with enthusiasm. Together, they stripped him down. They grappled for a moment in the darkness. Then her arms went around his neck, her legs around his body. They made it to the bed just in time.

Dot. Dot. Dot.

"I'm not really sure about the calf," Charley said. He ran his hand along her leg, pinching her calf experimentally.

Jenny flicked on the bed lamp and looked at him. "What are you talking about?"

Charley closed his eyes and pinched her other calf. "No; I wouldn't be sure. Now, the thigh—" he placed his hand there—"the thigh is something else again."

"What are—"

"The thigh I'd know anywhere. The curve of the hip, too." He moved his hand upward. "There is a particular angle to the curve of your hip that makes it absolutely distinguishable from any other—"

"Idiot," Jenny said. She switched off the lamp.

"The gut's easy too," Charley went on.

"Please. Stomach."

"I'm very happy," Charley said. "Are you aware that there is a difference in the circumference between your left and right breast?"

Jenny laughed. "No."

"At least half an inch. Damn—" he snapped his fingers—I left my caliper at the office. Come to work tomorrow at your own convenience. I should judge the difference is closer to three-quarters—"

"You mean I can have my job back?"

"Apartment too. Now your shoulders are very commonplace. I would have a helluva time telling your shoulders—"

"How'd you manage that?"

"Everybody takes two weeks' vacation in the summer. That's what I told them at the office. Your landlord too. He's a very nice man."

"You knew I'd be back?"

"I suspicioned. So everything's just like it was. Now your neck—"

"Except that it's different."

"Huh? I'm sorry; your neck had my attention."

"Everything's different."

"That's what I said," Charley said.

* * *

The next morning Charley paid the bill in cash and put Jenny in a taxi. He went to the office; she went home. The blue walls greeted her. As she looked at them she felt something but decided not to find out what. She took her time, unpacked, got settled, ironed a white dress, put it on. Then she subwayed down to Kingsway. Everyone was glad to see her—Mr. Boardman, Mr. Fiske, Mr. Wesker, all the other girls. Even Mrs. Fiske sounded pleased to hear her voice when she called in from Long Island that afternoon to speak to her husband. As the afternoon was about to end, Jenny went in to see Mrs. Fiske's husband. He seemed a bit under the weather.

"Do it beautifully," she said.

The train trip out to his mother-in-law's house on Long Island was not much fun for Charley.

He had to tell Betty Jane, she had to be told, and if only he could do it without seeing her face, he would have felt a lot better. Hers was such a pretty face, too pretty really, and it did not suffer anguish at all well. If only she were stronger, Charley thought (for she was weak), stronger and not so pretty. Of course, if she had been, he never would have married her; he knew that much.

Charley sat sweltering in the clutches of the Long Island Railroad and wondered just how to do it, tell her, get it done. Fastest equals best, no question; in and out, tell the truth, not the whole truth (but nothing but), good guys don't lie, never the good guys. I'm a good guy, Charley Fiske is a good guy—

Ask anybody.

The thing that he knew that nobody else did was that, without him Betty Jane was helpless. That was what made telling her so hard. She had based her life on his, and now, with him about to pull out, he knew there was nothing left for her to do but stumble, tumble and fall and that sounded like a law firm: Stumble Tumble & Fall.

Hands in his lap, eyes staring, Charley laughed out loud.

The lady in the adjoining seat immediately edged as far away from him as possible.

She thinks I'm crazy, Charley thought, and that only made him laugh all the louder. When he stopped laughing he went back to Betty Jane— pretty, sweet, helpless, loving and dumb. No, not dumb. Not really. And maybe she's not helpless either. Maybe she's strong enough to come through this fine. With her looks she could remarry anytime she wanted. If I think she's strong enough, Charley thought, I'll just tell her right out.

What if she isn't strong enough? he wondered.

What if I tell her and she splits into little bits and it's all my fault and I'm supposed to be a good guy, goddammit, so bring me a new jigsaw puzzle somebody, my pieces don't fit. Charley closed his eyes, tried getting relaxed, but after a moment he gave up the thought of relaxation. He was just too nervous, too upset.

He was aware, then, of a certain unhappiness, but the full extent of it escaped him until when he was just a few minutes from his stop, he got up and walked to the men's room, found it in use, the door locked, shrugged, started back for his seat and had gone several steps before he realized he had to hurry, so he whirled and plunged headlong into the ladies' room, falling to his knees in front of the toilet, where he vomited and vomited until his throat was raw.

As soon as she heard Jenny's voice that afternoon, Betty Jane started getting ready. Her first reaction was panic. (When Charley mentioned casually, a few weeks before, that Jenny had gone home, Betty Jane joyously assumed she had her husband back.) Now she assumed that Jenny's return must somehow signal a change in the entire operation. Faced with the reality of losing her husband for good and all, Betty Jane killed her panic, paced and smoked and thought, called her friend Penelope several times to discuss what to do, reached certain conclusions, and that evening after dinner, when Charley said "Let's talk," Betty Jane was able to answer, "Good, good, let's" and actually mean it.

"I'll watch the kiddies," Mrs. Bunnel said. Mrs. Bunnel was just like her daughter, only withered.

"Thanks, Mom. C'mon." Betty Jane held out her hand for Charley and they walked together out of the house down to the shore of Great Peconic Bay. It was dark and warm and there was little wind. "Hold me," Betty Jane said, and she fled into his arms.

Charley held her. "What is it?"

"I'm just so upset," Betty Jane whispered.

"Why?"

"I hate myself when I act this way," she said, and she slipped free and took off her sandals, walking into the water.

"What's upset you?"

"Penny."

"Penny?"

Betty Jane nodded. Then she held out her hand. "Take it?" They started walking down the beach, holding hands, Betty Jane in the water, Charley on the beach. "I love her, you know that. How we've always been so close?"

Charley nodded.

"Well, when she gets rattled—when something happens to her, it sort of happens to me too. Oh, Charley, I feel so sorry for her."

"What happened?"

"Oh, nothing. Nothing really. It's just that she's a friend of mine and I can see what's happening to her. There's this buyer in town and she's going off with him for the weekend. That means sleeping with him—everything."

Charley nodded.

"Oh, it's so dirty. Ever since she got divorced from Ferd, it's gotten dirty. Her whole life. She's sleeping around, she says so herself. She's practically a whore, she says. I grew up with her and I can't help her when she needs me. She never should have gotten divorced from Ferd. Do you remember how when we got married she said we didn't even know each other and she and Ferd went out for years before they got married and look—look who's lasted. *Oh! Oh!* It's just like a funeral!"

"What is?"

"The way I feel. You know how at funerals when people get upset they're upset for themselves. That's how I feel now. All I can think is thank God it happened to them and not us. I know what I'd do if it happened to us."

"That's enough," Charley said.

Betty Jane shook her head; her body started to shiver. She locked her arms across her chest and stared up at the dark sky. *"Crack!"* she said.

"No, you wouldn't," Charley said.

"I would and you know it. Wide open." Betty Jane continued to shiver.

"No, you wouldn't."

"That's right; I'd be fine. *Charley*—"

"Take it easy."

"Why do we torture ourselves?"

"I don't know what you're—"

"It's Penny's problem. It's her life she's ruining."

"That's right."

"You can't help your friends; you can only help yourself."

"That's right," Charley repeated, and then he said "Stop!"

Because Betty Jane had started to cry.

"I don't like you to get all upset," Charley said.

"I'm sorry. I'm sorry."

"I don't like it when you cry, Betty Jane."

She shut her eyes and bit down hard on her lower lip and groped for him.

She was like a little blind bird. He sheltered her in his arms.

"Thank God one of us is strong," Betty Jane said.

"Jesus!" Jenny exploded.

"Take it easy," Charley told her.

"I will like hell take it easy."

"All right. Scream."

Jenny screamed at the blue walls.

Charley put his hands over his ears.

"You had the whole weekend."

"Don't you think I know that?"

"Why didn't you tell her?"

"I didn't, that's all."

"Why?"

"The time wasn't ripe."

"Tell her."

"I will."

"Tell her!"

"When the time is ripe."

"*Tell her!*"

Charley reached out for her body.

She slapped his wrist. "Fat chance," she said.

"What do you think about Robby?" Betty Jane asked her husband.

"What do you mean, what do I think about Robby?"

"He's been acting funny."

"He's fine."

"He doesn't eat, he's nervous, he cries for no good rea—"

"He's fine!"

"Whatever you say, Charley."

"I'm going to lose my temper, Charley." Jenny put down her dictation book.

"Keep your voice—"

"I don't care if half of Kingsway hears. I'm getting angry."

"How do you think you've been acting?"

"That was nothing," Jenny said.

"Ouch," Betty Jane said.

Charley walked into the kitchen. "What's wrong?"

"It's this darn can opener." She held up a bleeding finger. "I just can't make it do anything but cut me."

"Here." Charley took it, opened the can, handed it back.

She kissed him quickly, saying, "Husbands. No home should be without one."

Charley walked in to work and looked at his secretary. Then he shook his head.

His secretary made a sad smile.

He walked into his office and sat behind his desk. She came in a moment later and closed the door. "What's today's reason?" she said.

"No reason."

"But you just didn't tell her."

"I didn't tell her."

Jenny sighed and sat wearily down in a chair. "Oh, Charley."

"I keep thinking she hasn't done anything wrong."

"Meaning I have?"

"Meaning *I* have."

"Charley, you told me on the phone in Wisconsin you'd get a divorce. You promised me."

"I know what I said."

"I'm not a bitch. I don't much like acting like one."

"I know that too."

"Then please tell her."

"I will, I will."

"How do I know you mean it?"

"I always mean it."

"How do I know you'll do it?"

"There's no way."

"Please, Charley."

"I said I would."

"Don't make me act like a bitch."

"What are you getting at?"

"Don't make *me* be the one to tell her."

"Wow," Charley said.

"Don't make me do it."

"Would you?"

"If pressed."

"And I'm pressing you?"

"You are."

"I don't think anybody would be very pleased if you did that."

"I'm so tired, Charley, I don't care anymore who wins, just so everybody loses."

"I don't think you'd tell her."

"Bet me."

"I love you so much. Don't let me ever think why."

He entered his house angry, slammed the door, listened for a feminine voice, heard it in the kitchen. Starting there, he determined to tell Robby to leave and then just let Betty Jane have it quickly and efficiently, because in the long run that was the kindest way. He walked into the kitchen, started to speak, stopped.

"Hello, Mr. Fiske," Mrs. Catton said, sipping tea.

"Where's Betty Jane?" Charley asked the sitter.

"She'll call at seven," Mrs. Catton replied. "Any minute now."

"She's not here?"

Mrs. Catton nodded and continued sipping.

At seven, Betty Jane called.

"I'm with Penny," Betty Jane explained. "You remember that talk we had the other night? Well, she's in sort of a bad way and wondered if I could keep her company. Wasn't I lucky Mrs. Catton was available?"

"Then you won't be home tonight?"

"That's right. I told Mrs. Catton to make you a steak. There's one in the icebox. Are the kids asleep? They should be. Mrs. Catton can sleep in with Paula."

"You're not coming home at all?"

"Tomorrow sometime. You tell Mrs. Catton—what's the joke?"

Charley just couldn't stop laughing. "It's this terrific mood I'm in."

"Oh," Betty Jane said. "Just my luck to miss it. Gotta go, g'bye."

Charley put the phone down and went out to the porch. He sat, staring alternately at Carnegie Lake and his hands, his thumbs in particular, the nails in his thumbs, the edge of the tip of the nail. At some time or other he said, "No, I'm really not hungry, thank you," to Mrs. Catton, and a while after that, "Good night, yes, I'm fine." It was dark on the porch. Charley got a book and, bringing it very close to his eyes, began to read:

So he was to be deaf. A cripple. Stunned, the old man sat alone in the dark delicatessen, surrounded by tinned fish and memory, his great nose motionless, ignoring the aromatic overtures from the friendly pickle barrel. So he was to be a cripple! What he feared most was to be. For he had failed, failed a private image of himself, and though the failing was neither his fault nor of his choosing, it was still his. How could you do this to me? he said, speaking to himself. All this time I thought I knew you; I thought we were friends . . .
Charley put the book down and rubbed his eyes. It was a hot June night and his eyes hurt. He got up and found his flashlight and went outside, feeling under the porch where the lumber was stacked. Selecting three fine logs, he carried them into the living room and set them in the fireplace. He took the morning paper and folded it and wedged it around the three logs. Then he lit a match and had a fire. It crackled quite properly, was properly red, and he watched it until the logs were spent. Then he went upstairs and shook his son. "What shall we play?" Charley said.

Robby rubbed his eyes. "Wuzzatime?"

"Recess."

Robby picked up his clock with the luminous dial. He looked at it, then at his father. Then he put the clock back and lay down again. " 'Night."

"You just name the game," Charley said, "and we'll play it."

Robby shook his head.

"Why don't you eat more? You're too thin."

"Is everything all right?" Mrs. Catton said from the doorway. "I heard voices."

"I was just telling him to eat more," Charley said, and he brushed by her and headed downstairs, picking up a deck chair from the porch, taking it outside. He sat down in the middle of the lawn and waited without sleep for the sun to rise. When it did, he got up and stretched and went inside, shaving, cleaning up, downing an entire pot of coffee. Just before he left for the train Robby came up to him and said, "Sorry."

"What about?" Charley said.

"Last night. I shoulda come down with you. Or talked to you more. But you came in so suddenlike it scared me."

When the boy was gone, Charley swelled his chest. Better and better, he thought; it's not every father who scares his son.

"Gooooooood morning, Miss Devers," he said later that morning.

"You're very chipper today, Mr. Fiske." She shut the office door and leaned against it.

"I've got this funny joke to tell you is why. I didn't tell my wife about divorcing her last night because—and get this now—because she was *sitting up with a sick friend*." Charley laughed and laughed.

Jenny watched him.

"You're not laughing. Where's your sense of humor gone to?"

Jenny shrugged.

"Wait till you tell me a joke; see if I laugh."

"Fine."

"You can't be mad *at me* because my wife takes it into her head not to come home. Fair is fair."

"That's right." Jenny nodded. "What did you do?"

"When?"

"When you found out she wasn't coming home."

"Had the sitter cook me a steak and then went to sleep."

"I couldn't sleep. The last time I looked at the clock it was after three."

"You gotta stay loose, kid. Listen to old Charley, he knows. I tell you, there's a plot on to keep me from telling."

"If you don't tell her tonight, I'll tell her tomorrow."

"Set it to music and we'll dance to it."

"If only I were kidding," Jenny said.

Charley flapped his arms. "Loose as a goose."

When he got home that night Charley found his wife in bed sick.

"What's the matter?" he asked, sitting down beside her.

"Nothing. I'll be up in a sec."

"Like hell you will. Robby said you were sick. What is it?"

"I know better, I do, but I skipped lunch because I was making this little nightie for Paula and then, well, it was hot this afternoon, and I shouldn't have tried painting the porch steps. I just got tired."

"Are you trying to hurt yourself?"

"I said I knew better."

"You work too hard."

"My home and my family; what else have I got?"

"What else has any of us?" Charley wanted to know.

The next morning Jenny said, "Well?"

"Close the door," Charley told her. "I wanna talk."

"Did you tell her?"

"Close the door and *sit down*."

"Did you tell—"

"I said *sit*!"

Jenny sat. "Answer my question."

"All in due time."

"Did you tell her or not?"

"I'm a little sick of the way you've been acting," Charley said.

"*You're* sick of the way *I've*—funny, funny."

"That's your last bitch remark of the morning."

"Charley—"

"My instructions to you are: shut the hell up."

"Are you all right?"

"I am fine."

"Sleep?"

"Sleep is an overrated commodity. I slept wonderfully. I have been, for the last days, sleeping wonderfully. I want to talk about shirts."

"Shirts?"

"Look." Charley took off his cord topcoat. "See this?" He fingered his shirt. "It is a white Oxford-cloth, button-down shirt and it comes from the Brothers Brooks. Eye it. Tell me what you see."

"It's a shirt."

"Pay attention. It is not a shirt; it is a very particular shirt and what is particular about it is that Mr. Myles has done his job to perfection. If you were to look inside this collar you would see a message imprinted: 'No starch.' When I first moved to Princeton—that is years ago now—I found that what laundrymen delighted most of all in doing was ignoring messages on shirt collars. My shirts came back starched, and I would explain that to the laundryman—I'm very particular about my shirts—and he would say that it wouldn't happen again and then a week later back they'd come, starched as hell. This went on and on and then finally, one day, I went to Mr. Myles' laundry and the next week, when I picked them up, there was no starch whatsoever in the shirts!"

"Did you tell her?" Jenny said. "That's all I want to know."

"For a moment, as I fingered the soft collar, I felt absolutely triumphant. I had found my laundryman! The quest was over. But then—then—" Charley shook his head sadly—"I realized my job was not nearly over. The ironing was atrocious. So I set to work. Every Saturday morning, when I went uptown to get my shirts, I would have a little chat with Mr. Myles. One week we would talk about the sleeve board, another the steam iron. We talked and talked and he was a willing man. But it still took months. Then, one Saturday in November—beautiful day, perfect; there was a game in Palmer Stadium, I remember, I heard the cheers—I went in to pick up my shirts and Mr. Myles handed them to me and they were on a hanger, Jenny, and the sleeves had been ironed with a sleeve board and they hung so clean and straight you almost had to *weep*. And Mr. Myles handed them to me and they were on a hanger, Jenny, and on the way back I heard the cheers again—"

"*Did you tell her?*"

"And I started cheering too: Rah, rah, rah-rah-rah—"

"Don't shout, for God's—"

"Rah, rah, rah-rah-rah, rah-rah-rah-rah-ray, *Myles*. And from that day to this, as the storytellers say, I have gone in every Saturday and I pick up my shirts and he hands them to me, hanging straight and clean on hangers, and he says, 'Well, Mr. Fiske?' and I say 'Perfect, Mr. Myles'; and it's not so easy as you think, getting a divorce, because it's not hurting your kids or the gossip or the alimony or moving in town to some crummy apartment or the lawyer's bills or anything else. It's leaving my laundry-man that's going to break my heart."

Jenny picked up the phone and said, "Princeton, New Jersey, please."

"Don't do it," Charley said.

"The number is Walnut 4-3878."

"I'm telling you. Just don't. Hang up the goddam—"

"Yes, it's a business call.

"Jenny—"

"It's too late."

"You won't do it. You're bluff—"

"Don't you know me at all?"

"Give me the damn phone." He reached out for it.

She grabbed it with both hands. "Hello, Mrs. Fiske? This is Jenny at the office."

"Give me the goddam—"

"There something I have to tell you about Charley."

Charley wrenched the phone away. "I'll tell her!"

"He'll tell you!" Jenny shouted.

"It's nothing, honey—just that I feel a little rocky—"

"He'll be right home," Jenny shouted. "To tell you!"

"Jenny's such a worrier. I'll be right home. Yes. Goodbye, honey."

Jenny started him toward the door. "Love, here is your hat," she said.

· · ·

At half past three the call came. Jenny picked up her phone and said "Yes?"

"The bloody deed is done."

"How did it go?"

"Hideously."

"Charley?" Jenny said.

But he was gone.

She sat at her desk for a long time before getting up and clutching her purse and hurrying to the elevators. She went down to the lobby and got a lot of change and went into a telephone booth. Then she called him back. He did not sound pleased to hear her. "How could you have called?"

"I had to talk to you," Jenny said.

"There's no limit to what you *have* to do, is there? Isn't it enough she knows? What if she'd answered the phone? Did you have to gloat that much?"

"*Charley*—"

"I don't want to talk to you."

"I'm sorry about this."

"Like hell you're sorry! You're so glad you had to call to gloat—"

"I'm not, I'm not. Please—"

"I told you I wanted to wait till the time was ripe. But no. No, sir. Old Jenny, she wants blood—"

"Charley, please listen. It had to happen sometime, remember that. No matter when you'd told her it would have been hard for her, but I love you, I do, please, I love you so much, I'll make you happy, don't take this tone with me, please don't talk to me this—"

"You're a great actress, you know that?"

"All I want is for you to love me."

"What you want is for everybody to lose. You got what you want now. Goodbye, Jenny."

"Charley?" Jenny said.

But he was gone again.

The next morning Archie Wesker said, "Hey, lemme see, lemme see."

Jenny flushed.

Archie took her hand, led her to her feet. "Turn around. Turn around. That's got to be a new dress."

Jenny nodded.

"What the occasion?"

"I just felt like it."

"Wait'll Charley sees you. I wish you were my secretary."

Jenny sat back down.

"Just wait till old Charley catches a glimpse."

"Stop saying that."

"Sure thing, baby," Archie said. And then he smiled at her.

"I've got a lot to do, Archie."

"Sure, baby." Archie kept on smiling.

"I mean it, Archie."

"Busy little bee," Archie said. Then he turned and walked away.

When Charley phoned in she said, "Guess what," the finish of which would have been "I'm wearing," because it was a new dress, as Archie had surmised, a very expensive new dress, pale-blue silk, bought the previous afternoon from Lord & Taylor for much too much money.

But Charley wouldn't let her end it. "I won't be in today."

"Why not?"

"Think why not. I can't leave her today, not in her condition, that's why not, goodbye, why not."

Jenny put her head in her hands. "Hotcha," she said.

Charley paced around the blue walls. "What she wants is time."

"Time?" Jenny watched him move.

Charley nodded.

"I'm not sure I understand."

"She loves me. More than I cared to think. And at first, when I told her, all she did was shake her head. Then she started making sounds." He slammed a fist into a palm. "I don't have to explain all the details, do I?"

"No. No."

"Anyway, she didn't think she could make it. She thought she'd crack."

"She'll be fine."

"I told her that. It was a helluva job, convincing her, but I think I've got her set along those lines now. She's just afraid she'll come apart. I don't blame her. She just wants some time before anything definite is done."

"She'll give you the divorce, though."

"She'll give me anything I want. She loves me. She just wants to cut things gradually. She doesn't want anything to change for a while."

"Meaning you'll live together still?"

"We'll share the same house, yes. She thought she might start spending more time out with her mother. Gradually, you understand. She thinks things will work out better. But you're the one that's pushing this. If you want a split now, say so. If she cracks—God, you should have heard the way she said that word—'Crack! Crack!'"

"What did she say about me?"

"About you?" Charley paced a little more. "Nothing much."

"Tell me."

"It wasn't nasty."

"What did she say?"

"I told her I was in love with somebody else. She said 'Jenny?' Right off. Just like that."

"She knew?"

Charley shook his head. "Maybe subconsciously. Then after she said your name she said, 'I can't even hate her.' She admires you, it turns out."

"I've only met her a couple of times."

"I can't help that."

"What about the children?"

"She'll be fair as long as I am."

"Meaning don't push her?"

"I guess so. Do you blame her?"

"No," Jenny said. She gave Charley a kiss. "How can I blame someone for loving you?"

"I'm a real catch," Charley said.

Jenny smiled.

"Anyway, I told her."

"That's the important thing. She can have her time. I don't care, not anymore. I can wait a little now."

That was on the thirtieth of June.

On the eleventh of July, Jenny said, "How long is a little?"

Charley, not listening, said "Huh?"

Jenny decided not to repeat her question.

On the twentieth of July she changed her mind. "How long is a little?"

"I wish I knew," Charley answered.

Then one or the other of them changed the subject.

"Are you sure you trust her?" Jenny asked on the twenty-seventh of July.

"Betty Jane? Why?"

"Well, how do we know she's not trying to win you back or something?"

"She's doing a lousy job if she is."

"Are you sure, though?"

"Last night she said she wasn't sure she loved me anymore."

Jenny nodded. "But are you sure you trust her? was the question."

"Charley?" Jenny began on the first of August.

"She's much better," Charley replied. "We talked about it without emotion. She's thinking of the future. I tell you, I couldn't be more pleased. She may take the family back to Long Island to live. Great for the kids out there. Not that close to town, either. She wouldn't be calling in every other day. I tell you, it's only a matter of time."

"That's all it's ever been," Jenny said.

On the eighteenth of August Jenny said, "I hate to bring up an unpleasant sub—"

"*You think I'm enjoying myself?* Do ya? You think it's funny walking around that house with a woman that's your wife but isn't anymore? You think it's fun looking at the kids and thinking what they don't know? You think I enjoy all the lousy sneaking around we have to do? Goddammit—"

"I'm sorry."

"All right. Forget it."

"It can't be this hard for everybody to get married," Jenny said.

On the twenty-second of August Jenny looked across the room to Charley, who was sitting on her bed beside the blue walls.

Before her mouth was open he cried, *"Quit nagging!"*

"I didn't say anything."

"You had that look—you were going to."

Quick tears came to Jenny's eyes. "Yes," she whispered. "I was." She ran across to him and gave him her body.

He was altogether merciless in his acceptance.

On the fifth of September Jenny said, "I just don't know."

"Know what?"

"How much endurance remains."

"It's so close now," Charley said.

"Are you sure?"

"Didn't I just say so?"

"Don't you just say a lot of things?"

"Why do you want to fight?"

"I don't want to fight."

"Then why are we fighting?"

"Maybe it's because we're good at it," Jenny said.

On the tenth of September Charley said, "I think she's going to threaten me with the children."

"*What?*"

"This morning she said, 'After we're divorced, I think it might be best if you stayed away from the children.' "

"Do you think she means it?"

"I don't know her all that well anymore."

"I told you months ago not to trust her."

Charley nodded.

"She's desperate. When you're desperate you'll do anything."

"Tell me something I don't know," Charley said.

"She wants to go to a *psychiatrist?*" Jenny said on the twenty-fifth of September. "Oh, come on." She kicked at the blue walls.

"That's what she says. She's already made an appointment."

"I thought she was getting so strong and everything."

"So did I. Now she says she wants help."

"That takes *years.*"

"I'm well aware—"

"I cannot stand this another goddam minute!"

"You're shouting."

"Don't say one word to me, buster. I was on to her from the word go. I had her number, yes, I did, you bet I did, but you said, 'Oh, no, she's coming along fine, just fine'; and now—"

"I was wrong. I admit it."

"A fat goddam lot of good that does."

"I love it when you swear."

"Charley, we've got to *do* something."

"I'm going to."

"What?"

"I'll go to see her psychiatrist and find out."

"Find out what?"

"If she's lying or not. He'll tell me that much, when I explain the situation to him. If he thinks she's genuinely unstable, that's one thing, but if he thinks she might be faking or be strong enough to take it, I'll move out the next day."

"I know she's faking and so do you."

"And so will the psychiatrist."

"Then why not move out now?"

"You know she makes me feel guilty—she's good at that. Well, what if that one chance in a thousand were true? What if she really would crack? You'd be racked about it and so would I. Actually it's a break, her making an appointment to see a psychiatrist. At least now we'll *know*."

"That bitch—she's liable to turn out crazy just for spite."

"Don't even think that," Charley said.

At lunch hour, on the twenty-seventh of September, as she was hurrying to have lifts put on her heels, it crossed Jenny's mind that Charley was nothing but a liar, that he had never mentioned to his wife the subject of divorce, that the entire psychiatrist business was simply the latest shovelful in a great pile of bilge, and that she, Jenny, was not one of History's brighter creatures.

Her reactions were both many and varied.

"You saw the psychiatrist?" Jenny said on the fourth of October as Charley entered her apartment.

Charley nodded.

"What did he say?"

Charley slammed a fist against a blue wall.

"Oh, baby, don't," Jenny said, and she hurried to him, kissed the reddened knuckles.

"God," Charley said.

"From the beginning, tell me. Was he nice? What was his name? Everything."

"Adler."

"Was he Viennese, do you know? Did he have an accent or anything?"

"I guess a little one. He spoke English very well."

"I hope he's Viennese. They're supposed to be the best. Go on."

"I don't remember all the terms he used."

"That's all right; just translate."

"She's sick."

"How sick?"

"Very, I take it."

"Go on."

"He's only seen her a couple of times, and besides, he said, she was the patient, not me, so there was a limited amount he could tell."

"But he did say she was sick."

"Psychotic."

"I just knew it—I had a feeling, Charley. She's been acting crazy ever since you told her about us. Go on."

"Betty Jane's very romantic. If I leave her, it may crack what she considers reality."

"He said that, this Adler?"

"More or less."

"Then you can never leave her?"

"Oh no—God no. He's very hopeful, he says. Her problems—they're the kind that respond well to treatment. She's not crazy or anything. It's just that she would crack if I left her. She needs to come to grips with reality more. Her troubles aren't really unusual, he said. They respond to treatment. All it takes is time."

"Thank God for that."

"We'll have to have patience."

"Do you know what love is? Love is supplying what's needed. Right now I've got all the patience in the world."

On the tenth of October Charley managed to say, "You are?"

Jenny made a nod.

"You're sure?"

Another nod.

"Have you taken tests and everything?"

"Rabbit and frog. They both say so."

"Can't fight that," Charley said.

"I've tried not to tell you; it's such a rotten time. That's why I held off until I was sure. That's why we've been fighting, I think; I've been so scared. But I'm gonna start showing pretty soon and, well, it's up to you now, Charley."

Charley smiled. "Something's gotta give," he said.

That weekend was warm, so Charley suggested they all go out and visit Mrs. Bunnel on Long Island. Mrs. Bunnel couldn't have been more pleased when they called with the suggestion, so Saturday morning they got in the car, Charley and Robby and Paula and Betty Jane, and drove out. They played on the beach the entire afternoon, and for supper they had fried chicken and mashed potatoes and a fresh green salad. Charley ate a great deal of food and called attention to the fact, and Betty Jane commented that it was wonderful seeing him so chipper and he agreed, saying several times that he was chipperer than he had been in years, and he even made a joke out of stumbling over "chipperer" in case anyone might possibly forget his splendid spirits. They went to bed not long after dinner, the old and the young first, Charley and Betty Jane a little bit later. Their second-floor bedroom overlooked the bay and the waves' beat lulled her immediately into sound sleep. The magic of the rhythm escaped Charley, and after counting Betty Jane's breaths up to five hundred he found himself bored. Then he remembered the flashlight Mrs. Bunnel always kept in the cabinet by the front door, so he tiptoed down and got it and then scampered back to bed and flashed the light up across the ceiling. It was full of cracks, and they had fabulously wonderful shapes. In the first hour he found seventeen totally different and distinct animals. After that he decided to concentrate on elephants, because he thought he saw a herd lurking in the far corner, so he lay on his back and waved the light and counted and pretty soon he was thinking of *Elephant Boy* and tiny Sabu and then Shirley Temple and the Jackies, Cooper and Coogan, and Coogan led to *City Lights* and the great clown smiling at the end, which was probably the saddest of all endings, and then for a little Charley thought about smiles and decided they were all sad, maybe sadder than anything. Flashlights were sad and elephants were sad and Shirley Temple was sad, but not as sad as a smile, and dawn was sad, and when it came Charley got out of bed quietly and put on his bathing suit and kissed Betty Jane and took a towel and crept out to the water. He walked in up to his chest. It was warm, really surprisingly warm considering the month was October, and that was sad too, warm water in October, sad, and he was about to push off when he remembered that he hadn't left any note.

Should he leave one?

Charley glanced along the completely deserted beach and tried to figure it out. In a minute he shook his head, because why had he bothered stumbling over "chipperer" if he was going to reverse himself and spoil everything and leave a note? No note. The answer was no and that was what had stopped him pushing off before and now nothing was, so he pushed off and began to swim. He was a good swimmer and he was a strong man, so he knew he would have to beat himself down at first, so he plunged his head into the water and began a brutal Australian crawl, his arms cracking into the water, his legs kicking straight and frantically as his big body cut through the bay away from shore. He swam and he swam and as he felt his breath getting harder to catch he stepped up his pace, flailing at the bay with all his considerable might until he could not swim anymore. Then he rolled over onto his back and smiled at the sun, gasping, waiting for his second wind. He had to kill that and completely before he had a chance of going through with anything, and already he could feel his breath coming easier. When he had his second wind he flipped off into the crawl again, and the water was cooler here, and that revived him somewhat more, and he was surprised at what a strong swimmer he was. On he swam, stroking with more speed than he could manage, kicking his powerful legs much too fast, and when his second wind started to go he smiled again and rolled over for a final look at the sun. His throat was on fire, worse than when he had vomited violently that day on the train, and then he thought of the various women in his life and that drove him back into motion again, so he rolled forward, forcing his arms to churn, ordering his legs to kick, and then he began to cramp. His left calf was gone and Charley screamed at the unexpected pain, and he pounded at the calf with what remained of his strength, and he greeted the fact that there was little left with mixed emotions. The cramp eased and he swam again, slower now, slower, then slowly, and then he could barely move his arms and his legs trailed like dead snakes in the water. He slapped feebly with his arms, slapped again, but there was little splash, and he tried for air but he opened his mouth under the water and that surprised him, and with what power remained he clawed his way forward and up, and then he was in the air and gasping and that gave him a final burst of strength and he slapped at the water and kicked at the water and all of a sudden there was nothing left, not a thing, it was over, he was done. He began to sink. He could not stop. He was sinking. One foot. There was nothing he could do. Two feet. He could not stop. Three feet now and Charley felt nothing, nothing at all. He wondered whether he had the strength to open his eyes and see the blue water as he descended and he did, finally, open his eyes, and the water was gold, like the sun, and Charley blinked and blinked, staring dully at the sun, and then he felt he was not sinking anymore and he looked around.

He was on a sandbar.

For a moment he could do nothing. Then he realized how funny it all was, how paralyzingly funny, so he started to laugh, kneeling there in the nice cool water beneath the blinding rise of the sun. He laughed and laughed because it was all so funny, not sad, nothing was sad anymore, least of all him, because he was indestructible now, nothing could touch him, and he laughed and slipped off the bar and started stroking his way back to shore. The water was wonderfully refreshing, and even though there was a steady ache behind his eyes he felt really marvelous and the cramps didn't start actually to worry him until he was almost halfway back. Then at once both of his calves knotted and his stomach grabbed and Charley screamed out loud, sinking down below the surface, balling his hands, hitting at his calves, and they felt just the slightest bit better but his stomach was dragging him down. Charley fought for one sweet breath, got it, sank again, and when the first thought of death as an actuality crossed his mind he was able barely to realize that it would be funny too, if he died now on his way back, just as the sandbar had been funny a little while ago. The next time he made it to the surface he vomited, so the air was of little use, but the time after that was better and his calves were fine now, or almost fine, and if only his stomach would stop he felt he had an excellent chance of floating in to shore. But his stomach would not stop, and he doubled up in agony, vomiting again and again, and he realized what he had to do was straighten, but it hurt more than anything he had ever known and he doubted that he had the strength, but he tried, tried to straighten, and his stomach tightened, fighting him, and he made it to the surface one more time and filled his lungs with air and then, like some great fish, he broke water, jerking back with his head, kicking out with his feet, and his stomach fought him, tried to clench, but he was too much for it, and in a moment it began subsiding. Charley lay stretched straight out in the water facedown. His calves started knotting again but he ignored them easily.

Then he made a suede jacket in his mind and it floated him to shore.

Awakened by a kiss, Betty Jane watched her husband's swim from their second-floor bedroom. At first she thought it was merely odd to swim so far, at dawn, in October. It was only when she found herself glancing around the room for some kind of note that she allowed herself to realize the other ramifications of his jaunt, and by that time he was floating safely, if weakly, in toward shore. He lay spent on the beach, half in, half out of the water, the larger waves covering him briefly with foam. She stared at him for the longest time. Then, when he tried getting to his feet, she hurried to him. He explained that he had gone out too far.

She called him a silly and helped him up to bed.

Cowards die many times before their deaths. "Hi, Jenny."

"Hello, Mrs. Fiske." Jesus—

"Busy, I see." You are through with my husband. I am here to tell you that.

"Oh, not so very." What the hell is she doing here?

Say it. Tell her. Stay away from him. "Good. It never pays to work too hard, I always say."

"Not at these prices." How much do you know?

"You're looking well, Jenny." When you age—when that day comes—when you age and your body sags, the sound you hear will be my laughter.

"So are you." God damn it. "Where's the boss?" Bitch.

"He won't be in today." Slut.

Why? "Oh?"

"Yes; he swam a bit too much over the weekend. He's still exhausted." *You are killing him.*

"Well, we're none of us as young as we used to be." You bitch, you stupid bitch, say something!

"I was just in the area, so I thought I'd drop in; I do that sometimes." You will stay away from my husband. You will keep your sweating whore hands away from Charley.

"Yes." You stupid insipid—

Tell her. *Tell her!* "You really are looking well."

"You'll make me blush." Say what's on your mind. Compose yourself, you clinging bitch, and say something. "Coffee?"

Thank God. "If it's not too much trouble."

"Cart was just here. How do you take it?" He loves me, bitch. The thought of him touching you . . .

"Black." Look at her, slut with a whore's face, and how can he touch a thing like you?

"Be right back." She's here to beg for him. Well beg, bitch. Screw up your courage and beg!

She is killing my husband and destroying me and there is no excuse for her existence in my life. She must be told and told firmly! That he is mine! That she is not wanted! That her services are no longer needed! That she is loathed! That she must leave! Leave! Him! *Take your whore's body and go!*

"Black it is." All right, say it. Say it!

"Jenny—" Tell the whore!

"What?" *Say it.*

"There's something—" THE WHORE MUST BE TOLD!

"What?" SAY IT! SAY IT!

"My heavens, look at the time." Of course, eventually she's got to bore him to distraction. You sleep with a whore but you live with a wife. Nothing to be gained by telling. Not really.

"Can't you stay?" How can he stand it with you? Well, he won't much longer.

"I've really got to dash." I'll never leave him.

"Well, if you have to, you have to." I'll never let him go.

"Take care now, Jenny." God, how I pity you.

"You too." Poor thing.

Both: "Biiiiiiieeeee."

Two days later, when he came to work, Charley stopped by Jenny's desk to report that his wife had left him that morning.

She followed him into his office and requested details.

He demurred, saying there were none, that she simply had packed up the children and gone, asking would he please not follow.

Jenny asked if he was happy.

He said he was.

She wondered why he didn't look it.

He explained it was because of the suddenness of her departure.

She went into his arms and asked did he really think it was over.

He said he really thought it was.

She said she almost felt let down since it ended so quietly.

He agreed, saying a good screaming match might have provided catharsis.

Then she told him her news, how she wasn't pregnant after all.

He mused at the oddity of both the tests being mistaken.

She hastened to inform him of her miscarriage over the weekend.

He nodded.

She explained that she deemed it unwise to contact him over the weekend, and, besides, she wanted him to be there when she told.

He asked after her present health.

She said she was fine.

He said she certainly looked it.

She said how she loved him.

He said how it was his lucky day.

Betty Jane stared at the bay, then jerked around, grabbed for the phone. She told the long-distance operator that she wanted to place a call to a Mr. Mark Sanders in Manhattan. The operator, for some reason, thanked her. Betty Jane gripped the phone, listening to the clatter coming from the kitchen, where her mother was trying to quiet her son from urging her daughter into making an even greater racket with a frying pan.

Paula loved banging frying pans around more than almost anything. Betty Jane took a deep breath and when a man answered she said "Mark?"

"Mark's not here."

"Betty Jane Bunnel—no, Fiske—tell him Mrs. Fiske called and he knew me from school last winter—Princeton, tell him—and would you tell him too to call me? Collect. Please."

"I meant not here, Mrs. Fiske. Mark's in Ann Arbor."

"That's in Michigan," Betty Jane said, though she couldn't for the life of her think why.

"Yes."

"Well, will he be back soon?"

"I don't think so. He was offered a teaching fellowship. I'm a friend of Mark's—I've got his apartment now. Can I help you?"

"No."

"Then it's not important?"

"I didn't say that." She hung up.

"Who was that?" her mother asked.

Betty Jane shook her head.

"Was it Charley?"

"No, it wasn't Charley."

"Well, maybe he'll call soon."

"I told him *not* to, Mother."

"Well, don't bite my head off."

"I'm sorry."

"Thank God Penny's coming."

"What are you talking about?"

Mrs. Fiske glanced at the grandfather's clock in the corner. "She'll be here any minute."

"Oh, for God's sake, Mother. Penny's *my* friend. If *I'd* wanted her here *I'd've* told her to come."

"Mother knows best."

"Never use that phrase to me again!"

"Have you taken your temperature?"

Betty Jane lifted her hands in surrender.

"I don't understand you young people," Mrs. Bunnel said, and when there was a thud followed by a grunt from the kitchen she left to investigate.

Penny arrived shortly after. She poured herself a half glass of Scotch, sat down across from Betty Jane and said, "Are you out of your trick head?"

Betty Jane smiled.

Penny swallowed half her Scotch. "Why the hell didn't you tell me you were out here?"

"Because I didn't and don't want to see or talk to you."

"A friend is someone you can tell to go to hell and they'll understand. I read that some place. Wha hoppen?"

"We're *finito*."

"Why?"

"I don't want to go into it."

"Who cares what you want?"

"Oh, Penny, I went to see that lousy whore secretary and I was all ready to have it out."

"Except you didn't."

"Except I didn't."

"You said nothing whatsoever."

Betty Jane nodded. "I had to leave him. For everybody's health. I got so fed up with myself after I left her without speaking I just all of a sudden later got this urge to pack and run."

"What's health got to do with it?"

"Charley tried suicide. Out there." She pointed toward the bay. "The sandbar saved him."

Penny finished her Scotch. "Where were you when they passed out brains?"

"Meaning?"

"Nobody *tries* suicide."

"What are you talking about?"

"Listen, dumbo, if you really wanna knock yourself off, it's easy. Take any elevator ten floors up, find the nearest window and move out smartly."

"I don't understand you."

"Charley wasn't trying suicide, I'll bet anything. He just wanted you to think he was."

"That's not true."

"When was this?"

"Last weekend. Dawn."

"You're a heavy sleeper. What the hell were you doing up? What woke you?"

Betty Jane looked blank.

"You don't remember?"

"No."

"Well, think about it. How long has Charley been coming here?"

"What's that got to do with anything?"

"Just that everybody knows about the sandbar and where it is. I've been out there and so have you and *so has Charley.*"

"He's not that kind. He wouldn't do a thing like that and you know it."

"Not consciously, maybe. But I'll bet when you remember it'll turn out to be Charley woke you up. And after you remember, just forget about it and get the hell back to him as fast as you can."

"You talked differently a year ago."

"I was younger and thought I had a shot at marrying this buyer from Hudson's in Detroit and I'd spent one year less on the open market. And I haven't even got kids. You got two—count 'em, two—and how the hell can you be sure your looks are gonna last? People age under strain, B.J., even you. He'll get bored with this broad someday. You better be there when he does. I'm telling you, you're crazy to pitch it."

"Charley kissed me!"

"Huh?"

Betty Jane stood and walked to the window, staring out at the bay. "That morning. That's what woke me. Charley kissed me. I remember it so plain." She turned to Penny. "But why would he want me to see?"

Penny shrugged. "I don't know. Maybe so *you'd* get upset and *do* something. I rest my case. Now go make up."

"Not while he has that whore. If I go back now, I hope I die."

"Don't say that. Ever."

"I say what I feel," Betty Jane said.

Jenny tugged at her skirt with one hand and combed her hair with the other. When the doorbell rang she gave up the tugging and concentrated her entire effort on trying to "do something" with her hair. When the doorbell rang a second time she dropped the comb, ran her tongue across her lips and opened the apartment door. Jenny said "How do you do" very politely and gave a little curtsy.

"Miss Devers, I believe," Charley said.

"May I take your coat?"

"Thank you." He gave it to her. She took it and hung it carefully in her closet. "All dolled up," Charley said, and he went to her and began to touch.

"Now you must wait," Jenny said, pressing his hands together. "This is our first date and you must show respect."

"May I molest you later?"

"If you show respect you may do whatever you want to later, but this is our first real human-type date and we must treat it accordingly. May I tell you something? I can almost never remember being so excited. Do you realize we are going to walk out that door *into the open air together*?"

"As they say, 'at last.' "

"At last," Jenny repeated. "Now I have a duty. What was it?" She pressed one hand against her forehead, then giggled. "Oh yes—I'm the hostess. Would you care for anything? A drink?"

"No, thanks."

"Would you like to wash your hands?"

Charley broke out laughing.

"I boned up for tonight," Jenny said. "Don't you dare laugh. It's proper for the hostess to ask if you want to wash your hands or anything."

"My hands are spotless, like my soul." He looked around. "I don't even mind these goddam blue walls tonight so much. And that is remarkable."

"I'm not trying to be a nag, but considering the occasion and all, could you please remember the respect due me and watch your language?"

Charley bowed. "Gosh darn blue walls," he said.

"I love you," Jenny said.

"I love you," Charley said.

Jenny turned to the full-length mirror. "Should I wear a hat, do you think?"

"Hat?"

"Yes. I've got a nice one. An occasion-type hat."

"No."

"I like a man who makes decisions."

"I hate hats on girls. When you're forty, you can wear a hat. What do you want to do first?"

Jenny smiled. "Walk!"

"Where?"

"Where there are people. Where people can see us and say, 'My, what an obviously blissfully fantastically happy couple.' "

"Do you think they'll say that?"

"If they have an ounce of perception."

"An ounce of perception is worth a pound of cure," Charley said. "Those just pop out sometimes. Forgive me."

Jenny forgave him.

"Are we ready?"

"We are. Get our coats?"

Charley went to the closet, got the coats. "Fifth Avenue? Lots of people on Fifth Avenue."

Jenny slipped into her coat. "Fine." They turned out the lights, opened the door. "Hold me," Jenny said then. "Respectfully."

Charley buried his face in her neck.

"Let's go face the world," Jenny said then. "I'm ready now." They walked out of the building to the sidewalk. Jenny stopped. "There's something I must do," she said.

"Do it."

"*Hello, World, we're here!*" Jenny shouted, her hands cupped around her mouth. Across the street some people looked at her. She curtsied toward them. "They think I'm a nut," she whispered to Charley.

"They're right."

"I forgive you only because of your spotless soul. I didn't embarrass you?"

"God no." He hailed a cab. They got in and started toward Fifth Avenue. "I've some news about Betty Jane," Charley said.

"Auh?"

"Yes. It seems her mother invited her best friend out last night to try and talk some sense. She called me today, Penelope did."

"And?"

"Betty Jane has apparently been chipperer. That's to be expected, I guess, but I just hope she isn't going to be venomous when it comes to the settlement terms. Courts generally side with the woman, you know."

Jenny nodded.

"We'll find out soon enough. She sees a lawyer Friday."

"Driver?" Jenny said then.

"Yes, ma'am?" the driver said. He was very old, with hands like a baby's.

"Can you take a look at us? What would you say? Wouldn't you say that we were just the most fantastically blissful couple? Be honest now."

"Yes, ma'am."

"See?" Jenny whispered to Charley. "Would you believe it, Driver, but this is our first real date? We've known each other for years but we've never really been out together before."

"You certainly look like a very nice couple," the driver said.

"Tip him liberally," Jenny whispered. When they got to Fifth Avenue in the fifties Charley told the driver to stop. They got out of the car and began walking. "Hold my hand," Jenny said.

They stopped for a moment by the F.A.O. Schwarz window.

"I feel just like that," Jenny whispered. "A kid. All my life I wanted this one special toy and now I've got it. Are you happy?"

"You know I am."

"Not unless you say so. Don't ever let go of my hand. Promise that."

"I do."

"Oh, Charley, God, we made it. We made it."

"Yes."

"After all these years, we did it. We deserve to be happy. We waited and we deserve it. Hello," she said to a couple walking by.

The couple smiled at them.

"They're talking about us now, Charley. They're saying, 'What a nice thing to say hello to a complete stranger like that. They must be very much in love.' That's what they're saying, Charley. How do you do," she said to an old lady on the corner.

"Lovely night," the old lady said.

They waited on the corner for the light to change. There was no wind and the bright October night was full of stars. "It's not the night," Jenny whispered to Charley. "It's us."

They crossed slowly, holding hands, stopping when they came to the Bergdorf windows. A very tall woman was staring through the glass at a dark-blue dress. "It would be perfect for you," Jenny said.

The woman looked at her.

"I mean it," Jenny went on. "It's made for you. I'm Mrs. Fiske. This is my husband—Charles. Say hello, Charles."

"Hello," Charley said.

"I'm awfully tall," the woman said.

"Admit you're tall," Jenny told her. "I'm tall too but I always wear high heels." They started walking away. "I tell you, you'll regret it if you don't buy that dress *tomorrow*." When no one could hear her, she said, "You didn't mind that I called you 'Mr. Fiske'?" She started to giggle. "Why should you mind, you are Mr. Fiske. What I meant was—" But the giggles had her, so she stopped. When she was able to talk she said, "Are you happy? I'm happy, are you?"

"Yes, I'm happy; no, I didn't mind."

"Let's go see the skating rink. We're going to be married, after all, so I wasn't lying, just jumping the gun, I love you."

"Officer, I swear I didn't know she was on dope."

"You're right," Jenny said. "I am acting all hopped up. I can be lady-like. I can be anything you want, Charley Fiske, so there. Hold my hand."

He held her hand and they started walking down to the skating rink.

"We're out of jail," Jenny said.

Charley nodded.

"Are you happy?"

"Yes."

"Then *say* you are."

"How often?"

"Every so."

"Will do."

"And be careful not to step on any cracks. I've waited so long for this and if you step on a crack, the boogeyman will come and carry you off to sea. That's what stepping on a crack means where I come from."

"I love you," Charley said. "Are you hungry?"

"I will be."

"Let's eat at the Plaza when you are. The Edwardian Room."

Jenny nodded.

Then they walked down to the skating rink. It was crowded but they managed to find a spot near one corner. They wedged their way in and put their elbows on the railing and their chins in their hands and stood quietly watching the skaters.

"Will you please have the decency to stop," Jenny said a few minutes later.

"Huh?"

Jenny pointed down to a woman dressed in red who was jumping and turning and skating around. "At least don't make it so obvious."

"What are you talking about?"

"Stop watching her."

"She's the best skater down there."

"That's not why you're watching her and you know it."

"Jenny—"

"She looks like Betty Jane."

"Are you crazy?"

"She looks exactly like Betty Jane and let's both admit it."

"She doesn't look remotely—"

"I just don't understand," Jenny said.

"She looks about as much like Betty Jane—"

Jenny shook her head. "You've tried to ruin this evening from the very beginning and I just do not understand."

"What?"

"I took it as long as I could, Charley, but when you said let's go eat at the Plaza—"

"*What's wrong with the Plaza?*"

"People . . . are . . . staring."

"What do you want to fight for?"

"I don't want to fight, Charley. You're the one who wants to fight. Why are you trying to ruin tonight?"

"I'm not—"

"I said *people . . . are . . .*"

"You're gaslighting me, for chrissakes."

Jenny broke away from the crowd.

Charley caught her. "Now, dammit—"

"Let's go, they're watching."

"Let them watch."

"Why did you try to ruin tonight?"

"I didn't, I didn't, are you crazy?"

"You knew I wasn't dressed up enough for the Plaza. You wouldn't let me wear a hat. You had to remind me how we sneak around. The last time we were there we snuck upstairs and you paid cash for the room and you had to go back there to humiliate me and I want to know why."

"You shut up! Just shut up and listen! I said let's go to the Plaza because the last time we were there we *did* sneak around and tonight I said let's go to the Edwardian Room because I thought it would be an honest to Christ symbol of the fact that we were free. Now stop this and behave!"

Jenny said nothing.

"Now do you want to eat or watch the skaters or what?"

"I'm not hungry."

He took her arm and they went back to their old position by the railing.

"Don't ask me to apologize," Jenny said.

"I didn't, did I?"

"Well, just see you don't."

"Let's forget it."

"You weren't excited about tonight at all."

"I was too."

"You didn't show it."

"I'm not an actor, for God's sake. I don't show things that way."

"When you came to my apartment you barely even smiled."

"I was thinking about what Penny'd said. I'm sorry."

"Nothing awful will happen," Jenny said. She took his hand. "You should at least have said about how nice I looked."

"I did."

"No, you didn't."

"Jenny, I distinctly remember—"

"What you said, to be specific, because *I happen* to remember, was 'All dolled up.' And that is *all* you said and what have you got to say to that, Charley?"

Charley said nothing.

"Charley?" She nudged him.

"Oh, I'm sorry. I was thinking about—"

"You were not, you were not thinking, *you were watching that girl skating.*"

"No."

"Yes."

"Well, she was doing a spin. It was very difficult and—"

"Watch her till you're dead for all I care!" Jenny bolted to the corner and held her hand up for a cab.

Charley grabbed her. "I'm sorry."

"You wanted to ruin it, you ruined it."

"Jenny, I'm sorry."

"Cab!"

"Jenny—"

"You wanted a cab, lady," a taxi driver said.

"Yes!" Jenny got in and slammed the door and they pulled away.

Charley hurried to Fifth Avenue, waited until he saw another cab, got into it and took it uptown. He got out in front of Jenny's building, paid the driver and wondered whether or not to use his key. He pushed the buzzer, waited for the answering buzz. He went to her door, knocked, and said, " 'Tis I."

"It's open."

Charley walked in. Jenny was wearing slacks and a sweater, and her dress was visible on the floor in the corner. "I was in the area . . ." Charley said.

Jenny went to the kitchen and poured herself a drink.

"Oh, come on; this is silly."

"I know it is. It's just that you really hurt my feelings."

"I'm sorry. That's the God's truth. And I wasn't trying to embarrass you by taking you someplace swanky and I'm sorry if I didn't tell you how pretty you looked because you sure as hell did, and do now, but I stand on my statement about the hat. There. Forgiven?"

Jenny sipped her drink. "I wanted tonight to be—"

"It still can. I'll molest you as never before." He ran his hands across her black sweater. "I totally approve of cashmere."

"You really hurt me," Jenny said.

"I thought I apologized."

"She did look like Betty Jane, didn't she, that skater girl? Admit it."

"If you'll forget about this."

"Tell me."

"There was a certain resemblance, yes. At least from a distance."

"I was right, wasn't I?"

Charley undid the top button of her sweater and kissed her throat. "The customer is always right."

"Why did you say that?" Jenny said.

"Say what?"

"You called me a customer."

"Jenny, cut it out."

"I really wanted tonight to be special," Jenny said. "Whores call people customers."

"She's always been a trifle paranoid, Doctor, but it was only lately I noticed she'd gone completely 'round the bend."

"*It's not funny, Charley.*"

"I love you, shut up."

"If you love me, why did you try to ruin everything tonight?"

"What do you want to fight for?"

"I don't wanna fight, I don't wanna fight, you're the one that wants a fight. Why did you try and ruin tonight? Tell me."

"Oh, for Christ's sake!"

"*Tell me!*"

"You have yelled at me for the last time, lady fair. I mean that."

"You came right in tonight looking to ruin things. You didn't hardly talk—"

"It was kind of tough to get a word in."

"You mean I talked too much."

"If the shoe fits—"

"I wanted tonight to be special and you wanted to ruin it and *I demand to know why.*"

"And I want to know why in the good sweet name of Jesus you want to fight."

"*I don't!*"

"For the first time I'm free, you can have me and you blow the evening with your goddam stupid lunatic ravings."

"Get out!"

"Like hell. That's why, isn't it? Isn't it? Because I'm *free* and you can *have me* and it's just like I told you on the phone—you don't want me, all you want is the lying and the whoring and the sneaking around—"

"*Shut up!*"

"The lying and the whoring appeals to you, but when it comes—"

"*Don't call me a whore.*"

"Don't try and sneak out of it either, goddam it." He grabbed her and started to shake her.

"Let go!"

"Admit it. You want to fight because I'm free, because you can have me and you're afraid. *Admit it.*"

"I said let—"

"I get rid of my wife and all of a sudden you don't want to play."

"Liar. Lying bastard."

"Whore!"

"You never told her about us. You never told her. Liar! Liar!"

"You weren't pregnant!"

"I was."

"Now who's the liar?"

"I had to do something!"

"Liar!"

"Get out! you make me sick! I hate bastard little-boy liar weaklings and you can get out!"

"Try . . . and . . . stop . . . me!"

Charley slammed his way out to the street. "Bitch," he said aloud. "Oh, you lying bitch." He shoved his hands into his pockets and started walking east. The first bar he came to he went in and had a shot of Scotch, then another. After the third shot he paid and walked outside and continued east until he saw another bar. He hesitated outside this one, but it seemed very nice, much nicer than the other, so he paid his respects for a double shot and then took up his journey again. When he got to Central Park he realized that he had got where he had intended to get, but now he had forgotten why. He looked at his watch, calculating whether he could make the next Princeton train, and the thought of Princeton brought Betty Jane to mind, Betty Jane conjured Jenny, and Charley sat down hard.

They were both gone.

For a moment it was hard for him to catch his breath. Both. Gone. After over two years. Charley sagged back against the bench. Two years and all for nothing. Two years and two women and the total was nil. He pictured Betty Jane's face, Jenny's body. Charley put his head in his hands. For a moment he felt overpoweringly lonely. Not that he expected pity; not that he'd earned it; still, he felt lonely. "I have blown it," Charley muttered to the bench. "I have blown it all." Once upon a time he had had a wife with a princess' face. Once upon a time he had had a mistress with melon breasts and sweet thighs. And their love, he had that too. All their love. Now he had nothing. Now they were gone. Both gone. After two long years, both of them gone.

So why am I smiling? Charley wondered.

Am I smiling? He put the tips of his fingers to the edges of his mouth. I am. *I am definitely smiling.* Charley stood. His feet began to move, carrying him deeper and deeper into the park. His feet were dancing. Charley looked down at them. They shuffled along through the park, and every so often a heel kicked up, and a hansom cab went by and Charley cried "Happy New Year" and then his fingers began snapping in time with the rhythm of his feet, and his body began to sway, and he spun through the moonlight, a blissful smile on his face, no weight whatsoever on his good free shoulders, and he laughed and laughed and made a microphone with his left hand and brought it to his lips and said, "Calling all cars! Calling all cars! There's this dancing nut in Central Park!" Charley shrieked with joy.

"And it's me!"

XXI

"Fool!" Aaron said. "You've burned the toast again."

"I'm sorry," Branch muttered.

"I didn't think you were glad about it, Scudder. Burning the toast on purpose—my God, only a Hitler could do a thing like that." He reached across the dining-room table for his pack of cigarettes. "Now here's the point, the important thing, the *thinga importanta,* as we Kurdish scholars say—dammit, the pack's empty."

"Well, don't look at me. It's not my fault you're out of cigarettes."

"Everything's your fault, Scudder," Aaron told him. "Don't you know that yet?" Pushing back from the table, he stood and hurried out of the room, turning left down the corridor to the master bedroom. The bed was unmade, but otherwise the room was neat enough. Aaron stared out the window at the Hudson River, half covered with January ice. Then he turned and started to search. "Where's my cigarette carton?" he called.

"I think it's in there someplace," Branch called back.

"Thanks," Aaron muttered. For a moment he contented himself with opening and closing dresser drawers, but then, quite to his surprise, he found he was angry. He tried to master the anger but he was no match for it, and soon his hands were ripping the sheets and blankets from the mattress and the fat pillows were flying across the room and he had the bed half up on end when Branch shouted at him from the doorway.

"Aaron. Aaron!"

Aaron blinked, then slowly lowered the bed back to the floor. "Trying to find my cigarettes," he managed.

Branch was watching him. "Maybe they're in your study," and he pointed toward the rear bedroom. "You smoke a lot when you write."

Aaron shook his head.

"Are you all right?"

"I'm supreme."

"Come on, then. It's Sunday; let's go finish brunch. You shouldn't smoke when you eat anyway." They walked back to the dining room and Branch sat down and picked up his coffee cup and started to fill it.

"My God," Aaron said. "What's that you're pouring from the coffeepot?"

"Coffee."

"Then why isn't it brown?"

"Oh come on, it's brown."

"Sort of a wan brown, maybe." Aaron cleared his throat. "All right, everybody, it's time for a little community sing. Here we go. 'Wan Brown's body lies a-moldering in the grave. . . .'" He looked at Branch. "Laugh."

"That was very clever, Aaron. Really very—"

"Laugh."

"I don't feel like it. I'm sorry."

"That's the truth, Scudder. You're the sorriest vista on my horizon, I'll tell you that." Aaron poured himself some coffee. "Why didn't you laugh? What's the matter?"

"Nothing."

"Don't be like that. Tell Uncle Aaron. Smile, Branchy-poo. What have you got to be unhappy about except that you're a faggot with halitosis?"

"Do you have to be so unpleasant?"

"That's my job, isn't it? I'm the sadist in this relationship."

"Sometimes you're not so funny, Aaron."

"Watch it there, Scudder, or I'll start being nice to you."

"Dry up."

"That's it!" Aaron cried. "*That's it!* Pencil, pencil," and he got up again, going into the living room, returning a moment later with a pad and pen. "It's poetry. Genius. 'Dry up.' What an image! I'm weak. 'Dry up.' Branch, it's *Shakespearean*! God, you're clever. I hate you for it. I'm supposed to be the writer, but you—*you*—have the talent. Oh, why can't I think of things like that? Why? Why?"

"O.K.," Branch said. "You've embarrassed me. Are you happy?"

Aaron smiled. "Every little bit helps."

"What's with you today?"

"I might ask the same of you. As a matter of fact, I think I did. Something is the matter, isn't it? With both of us. Have you any ideas? Of course you don't. Mongoloids rarely get ideas, and—"

"How about changing the subject?"

"Wonderful. Let's talk about your Oedipus complex."

Branch said nothing.

"Aw, now don't be embarrassed about it, sweetums. Here; let me ask you a few intimate questions."

"I do not have an Oedipus complex."

"Scudder, you are so sick—I mean, what goes on between you and your mumsy—"

"That's enough, Aaron!"

"Ah, but you're a fiery wench, Scudder, you know that?"

"What's the matter with you?"

"*I'm out of cigarettes!* That's symbol as well as fact, so obviously you won't understand, you're so tied up with your own petty problems. All you're worried about is that your mother is pressuring you to get the hell back to Ohio. Well, so what if you go back to Ohio? So what if you live a life of anguish and misery? What does that matter when compared with the fact that I'm out of cigarettes? Your existence was at best meaningless, you measly little fink, but when a man of my stature is out of cigarettes— that's tragedy, Scudder. Cry."

"Aaron—"

"Cry!"

"Shut up!"

"On one condition."

Branch looked at him a moment. "What's the condition?"

"That you admit you have an Oedipus complex."

"Oh, please."

"Admit that your relationship with your mother is so sick that *Freud would have paid you* twenty-five an hour."

"My relationship—I'm really angry, Aaron—my mother and I! Oh, you wouldn't understand. You just wouldn't understand, that's all. What's the point? All you understand is cruelty. You don't know what love is. I happen to have a good warm honest loving relationship with my mother and that's all there is to it."

"Secretly," Aaron whispered. "Secretly—"

"Just don't say any more."

"I'm going to make you admit it, Scudder. I'm going to make you face up to the fact that that 'good, warm, honest, loving relationship' isn't good, honest, warm or even a relationship. But loving? I'm going to make you admit it, Scudder. Watch. I'm gonna trap you, Scudder. Watch. I'm going to make you admit it with your own fat lips."

"Aaron, be nice!"

"I'm—I'm—" Aaron covered his eyes with his hands. "I'm sorry," he whispered then. "Please. I'm sorry."

Branch reached across the table. "Forgiven."

"I don't know what's happening to me," Aaron whispered.

"Look at me."

Aaron shook his head, his hands still over his eyes.

"Aaron, it's all right. I'm not mad anymore."

"It's not all right. I don't know what's happening to me. Sometimes—" He pushed out of the chair and moved to the window. "Branch?"

"What?"

"There's something you've got to do for me. We've been living together almost six months now and I've never asked anything like it before. I won't be bad to you anymore. I swear. I'll change. But you've got to help me, Branch. You've got to do this thing."

"What?"

"Go to the drugstore and get me some cigarettes."

"Huh?"

"Right now. It's got to be right now. I'll be your slave if you go now." Aaron turned. "Well?"

"You son of a bitch," Branch said.

"I don't get it," Aaron said. "Here I promise to be your slave if you'll just go get me a pack of cigarettes and you swear at me."

Branch said nothing.

"I'm so confused," Aaron went on. "Here it is five minutes before twelve and I offer you myself as a slave for a ten-minute jaunt and you say no. I just—" Aaron snapped his fingers. "No, wait, it's Sunday. And who calls on Sunday? On the dot at twelve every goddam Sunday! *Mumsy.* So if you went out for cigarettes, you'd miss her call. Is that why you won't go? Am I getting warm?"

Branch said nothing.

"But wait. I tell you what. You go get the cigarettes and when she calls I'll just tell the operator that you'll be back in a couple of minutes. And if she calls station to station I'll chat with her just until you get back. O.K.? Now will you go?"

"Do you get pleasure out of this?"

"Bet I do, psycho. I'm getting to the juicy part now. I'm getting to the meat, if you know what I mean. Here's the crux coming up. You see, here's this guy who says he's got this great relationship with his mother. And this guy, he's got a roommate, see. And they've lived together almost six months, see. *And the mother thinks he lives alone.* That's why, when she calls at twelve noon Sundays, the roommate can't answer the phone. Raise too many questions. And that's why when this hag comes visiting her little precious, the roommate has to pack up all his worldly goods and sneak off someplace till Lady Macbeth has gone away. *The guy's afraid to tell his mother. He's afraid she'll be jealous.* He's afraid—"

"That's not why! It's not—"

"What is, then?"

"I could tell her. She'd understand. It's just that the subject's never come up. I mean, there's a proper time to tell a thing like that to your mother, that you've got a roommate, and the proper time, it just hasn't—I mean, I could tell her. I could. That's the truth. It is, *damn you!* Why do you attack me like this now? Why do you do this just before she calls me? Don't you understand she's trying to get me to come home? I want to be a producer more than anything else in the world. I want my name to mean something. I want my name to be connected with things that mean something but I'm nobody and Tennessee Williams isn't about to trust me to produce his next play. I've got to find talent and it takes time and I work every day at it and you know it but she doesn't. She's trying to make me come home, so I'm out of cigarettes too, Aaron, so leave me the hell alone."

"You know the sickest thing of all, Scudder?"

"What?"

"We're both enjoying this."

Branch looked at him. "Are we?"

The telephone rang.

"Give her my love," Aaron said.

Branch went into the living room and picked up the phone. "Hello?"

"Hi, hon."

"Howdy, howdy."

"How're ya?"

"Fine. You?"

"How'd everything go this week? Work hard?"

"I tried to."

"Tell me what you've done."

"Well, I read half a dozen scripts. And I had lunch three days with agents. And I spent one whole afternoon, practically, talking with some people down at the Theater Guild. And I went to a couple of off-Broadway plays, just to see if the writers were any good. And I read two novels to see if there might be a play in them. And later today I'm going to a party some other producer's giving and I've got an idea he wants to talk about something. And—"

"In other words," Rose cut in, "nothing—that's what you've done."

"Now, Rosie—"

"Having lunch with people, going to parties—you call that work?"

"Well, as a matter of fact there is something very hot on the fire. But I can't talk about it yet."

"Is this very hot thing the same as what was on the fire last week and the weeks before that too?"

"Finding plays you want to produce—it isn't easy, Rosie."

"I understand that. I also understand your father and I built up this real-estate business with nothing but you in mind. Our gift to you. Along with our love. And you can't run a real-estate business in Ohio from New York City! You want to produce plays—fine. Produce plays. But you've been there a long time. *Long.* And what have you produced?"

"But this thing that's on the fire—"

"I tell you what I think, hon. I think *you* might think about maybe coming home. It's been a reasonable length of time, baby. And there's no sense in wasting your life. Not when there's so much for you back here. You want to come back here, don't you? You like it? With me."

"You know I do."

"We understand each other, baby. We always have."

"Always."

"Gramma misses you. She wishes you were home."

"Give her my love."

"I will. Darling?"

"Yes?"

"Everything's clear?"

"Yes. If this thing that's on the fire doesn't work out, you think I ought to come home."

"That's sort of it."

"I thought it was."

"Bye-bye, baby."

Slowly, Branch hung up.

"That's telling her," Aaron called from the dining room.

Branch stood. Slowly.

Aaron burst into song: "M is for the million things you gave me. O is for—"

"I tried living back home." Branch sat down at the dining-room table. "I did try . . . but I couldn't . . . function. I don't think I can go back there. I just . . ." He shook his head.

"So don't go."

"You don't understand. If I don't find something to produce . . . if I could just find something—"

"Word reaches me there's something terrific on the fire."

"Don't laugh at me. Please."

"What's the big deal? She wants you to come home, tell her no."

"I'm not sure I can do that."

"So what if she stops giving you a little money?"

"It's not that. My God, money's got nothing to do with it. I can always work. It's the other things."

"What other things?"

"I don't know."

"Well, think about it."

"I don't want to."

"If you thought about it, you might find out what you're afraid of."

"That's what I'm afraid of."

"Oh."

"I've got to find a play, Aaron. I can't go home. But I don't know if I can buck her. She's so strong. Stronger than I am, but I can't go home. What should I do?"

"Punt," Aaron advised.

At 5:25 that afternoon, Aaron hurried along East 47th Street with Branch at his heels. "I didn't want to go to this stupid party, Scudder; remember that. I wanted to go see the Humphrey Bogart. You're getting your way. So shut up."

"But we're too *early*."

"Nonsense. The invitation said five-thirty. We'll arrive at five-thirty."

"But you can't go to a cocktail party at the time you're invited. It isn't done."

"Hurry," Aaron said. "I don't want to miss a single second."

"This is important to me, Aaron. Mort Blandings has a play I hear maybe is pretty good. And he might need a co-producer."

"Well, why don't you call him up on the phone and and ask him? That way we can go to the Humphrey Bogart."

"Because calling him up and asking is the best way I know of not getting the deal."

"Here's the address," Aaron said. "And very spiffy too." He walked up the steps of the brownstone and rang a buzzer. After a moment there was an answering buzz, so Aaron pushed the front door open.

"Who is it?" somebody called from the floor above.

"Mort, it's me, Branch Scudder, hi." He walked up to the next landing. Mort Blandings stood in the doorway to his apartment, his necktie in his hand. "Are we early?"

"No-no." Mort Blandings made a smile. "Come on in." He was a big man with a kind face, a kind smile. "How do you do," he said to Aaron.

"Mort, for crissakes, how the hell are ya?" Aaron replied.

"Pardon?" Mort said.

"Mort, this is a friend of mine. Aaron Fire, meet Mort Blandings."

"I understand you and Branch are going to co-produce some play," Aaron said.

"Pardon?" Mort said.

"*Aaron*," Branch said. "Aaron's a novelist, Mort. You know how novelists are."

"We're pretty novel," Aaron said.

Branch looked around. "What a terrific apartment you've got."

"Thanks," Mort said.

"It's incredible what you can do with a cold-water flat," Aaron said.

Mort laughed, but not really. "Would you like a drink?" he said, guiding them over to a table set up as a bar.

"What are you pushing?" Branch wanted to know.

"Very spicy vodka fruit punch," Mort said. "Specialty of the house."

"Branch, are you lucky," Aaron said. "That's his favorite thing in all the world, Mort. Very spicy vodka fruit punch."

"Are you putting me on?" Mort wanted to know.

"I crave it, I crave it!" Branch burst out. "I honestly do."

"What else have you got?" Aaron asked as Mort filled a cup with pale reddish liquid.

"There'll be some hors d'oeuvres in a while."

"You mean if you don't like very spicy vodka fruit punch you're sort of out in the cold, is that it?"

"That's it," Mort nodded.

"I'll wait a while," Aaron said. He started backing away. "You two must have a lot to talk about." Turning, he found his way to the kitchen, where an elderly Negro in a butler's coat was making hors d'oeuvres. "Mr. Blandings needs some more vodka to spice up the spicy fruit punch. He sent me for a bottle."

"In the liquor cabinet," the butler said, gesturing.

Aaron followed the gesture, found the liquor. Skipping past the vodka and several bottles of bourbon, he reached into the farthest corner of the cabinet and brought out a bottle. It was twelve-year-old Ambassador Scotch. "Thanks," Aaron said.

"Welcome."

Branch and Blandings were talking in a corner of the living room when Aaron returned and set the Scotch bottle down on the bar next to the spicy punch. Downstairs, someone pushed the buzzer. Blandings started for the door. "Mind if I help myself to the Scotch?" Aaron called.

"Go right—*Scotch?*"

"Ambassador." Aaron nodded, pouring himself a drink.

Mort Blandings started toward Aaron, but then the buzzer sounded again, so he stopped, turning toward the sound. He looked back and forth, back and forth. Then he said, "Branch, let them in," and hurried to the bar, grabbing the Ambassador bottle.

"It was right next to the punch bowl," Aaron said. "We must have overlooked it."

"Sure we did," Mort Blandings said.

"Let me make you a proposition," Aaron said. Branch opened the apartment door. Voices on the stairs. "If *you* hide that bottle, I'll tell everybody what I'm drinking. If *I* hide it, the word is mum."

"Mort," several people called from the doorway.

"Oh boy," Mort Blandings said. Then: "Hide it, quick, hide it," and he shoved the bottle into Aaron's hand.

With a courtly bow, Aaron turned and headed for the bedroom. Settling himself in a comfortable chair, he tucked the bottle under his coat and began to drink. Branch came in a few minutes later and they talked a while and the number of buzzes grew and Aaron could hear the babble from the next room. By 6:15 he guessed that probably fifty people were congregated in the next room and by half past a dozen or more had spilled into the bedroom, where he sat happily, drinking the twelve-year-old Scotch, smiling at all the people. Branch came and went. Aaron sat still. He got involved in a few conversations, but not for long. The smoke in the bedroom grew thick, and by now he guessed that at least a hundred people were clogging the apartment and several were sitting on the arms of his chair, making it very hard for him to drink, let alone pour. At a quarter of seven Aaron decided that enough was enough, so he got up from his chair and began searching for the bathroom, his plan being to lock the door and get in the tub and drink in privacy. He left the bedroom and pushed his way into the living room, looking through the smoke for Branch because it was important Branch know he would be in the bathtub in case Branch ever decided to leave. The room was wildly stuffed with people and from somewhere there was the sound of recorded music and a few couples were trying to dance and Aaron was having a terrible time finding Branch but he kept on looking around and around and the next thing he knew the bottle of Scotch had crashed to the floor and the next thing he knew after that was that two people were pointing at him and laughing, saying, "Get him. September Morn," and Aaron recognized the validity of their joke, because he was standing like that, but he couldn't help it and even though the joke was funny he couldn't laugh either, because what had happened to him was that he had realized that there were only men at the party, and it was very hard for him to feel merry after that, so he stood there, just stood there, trying to duck his face whenever anyone pushed him or shoved him and it was only when Branch wandered by that Aaron moved.

"What is it?" Branch said. "You're hurting, Aaron, let go, what is it?"

Aaron whispered, "There are no women at this party."

"So?"

"You don't understand. There aren't any women here."

"What kind of a game are you playing now?"

"Branch—"

"I'm really a little tired of this, Aaron, you and your games. Acting the way you did when we came in. Stealing the Scotch."

"There aren't any women here, Branch. It's a fairy party. He invited you to a fairy party. How could he humiliate you like that? I'll kill him. I'll kill that son of a bitch."

"*Behave.*"

"I'm just trying—Branch? Branch?"

"Let go!"

"You didn't know . . . it was going to be like this . . . tell me you didn't."

"Of course I knew, now—"

"*How could you do this to me?*"

"You're drunk."

"How could you do this to me?"

"Lower your voice."

"Humiliate me. Humiliate me. Let all these—these *creatures* know, let these *things* know . . . what . . . I am . . . what I am is my business. My secret."

Branch dropped his voice. "Doesn't it bother you at all that everybody's looking at you?"

"Bother me? Bother me? *It kills me!*" And he pushed away from Branch, turning blindly toward the door, shoving, fighting his way through the crowd of male bodies. Or at least he began that way, but by the time he had crossed to the middle of the room the male bodies were aware, and they fell back, away from his flailing arms, so Aaron moved faster, half running, runing down the sudden aisle, running to the door, to the stairs, to the street, to the night.

His legs hurt. High up, in the hip area, they ached, forcing him to slow down. Aaron shook his head. He walked along 47th Street shaking his head over and over and over. At the corner he screamed, "I'm better than that!" while he waited for the light to change.

After that, he began to nod.

When he entered the hotel lobby he was a bit surprised, but when he saw it was the Biltmore everything seemed to make a kind of sense, or, as he hurried toward the clock, at least he hoped it did. The inevitable girl was sitting and waiting and Aaron saluted her. "Inevitable girl, good evening."

She glanced at him from the bench.

"This is not," Aaron went on, "a pickup."

She looked him up and down. "I'll say it isn't."

"My name is Aaron."

"Change it."

Aaron sat down beside her. "Do you mind if I sit down beside you?"

She didn't answer. But she didn't move away.

"You're really kinda brave, aren't you?" Aaron said.

"Brave? Are you kidding? What're ya gonna do, attack me under the *clock* at the *Biltmore*? C'monnnnn."

"City College?" Aaron asked.

She shook her head. "I'm an unconventional Barnard girl."

"This is your lucky day, unconventional Barnard girl; did you know that?"

"No. How drunk are you?"

"Oh, I'm quite drunk. Do you know why this is your lucky day?"

"I feel it only fair to tell you that my boyfriend is fantastically jealous. Of course, he's sort of small, but capable of frenzies, nonetheless. Why is it my lucky day?"

"Because—what's your name?"

"Judy—but I'm not at all like that."

"I can tell, because—how jealous would he be if I bought you a drink?"

"He's a Marvin and you know how jealous they can get."

"A Marvin," Aaron said. Then: "What the hell—I'll risk it."

"You're sure this isn't a pickup?"

They moved under the clock toward the tables and sat down. As the waiter approached, Aaron turned to the girl and said, "I know all about you—you're nineteen and you're beyond bourbon and ginger ale but not up to Scotch and soda. You're at the whisky-sour stage."

"I'm not nineteen till next month. Otherwise you're impeccable."

"Scotch on the rocks, please, and a whisky sour." The waiter nodded and went away. "Because for the first and perhaps last time in your little life, Judy-who-isn't-at-all-like-that, you have a chance to help someone."

"You just lost me."

"Your lucky day. That's why."

"Aw, I thought meeting you was what made it lucky, Spoiler."

"Look at me and tell me what you see."

"Well . . ." She squinted at him a moment. "It's this way, Aaron: you're too old for a boyfriend and too young for a father figure."

"No! Tall, right? And thin. Emaciated, almost. But *human*. Not odd—nothing bizarre or grotesque—a human."

"What happened? Did you just break up with your girl, is that it?"

"I belong—Aaron belongs—to the race—"

"Y'know, I'm getting just a little bit afraid—"

"Someone has got to say that Aaron belongs—an unbiased being. Do you know the word *freak*? Do you know what *freak* means? A *freak* is an abnormal person, plant or thing and—"

"Judging from the weight of the evidence thus far presented it is the opinion of this tribunal that Aaron is not an abnormal person, plant or thing. There. Dismissed. Are you always like this? I like you, why is that? Do you like me? My father thinks I'm beautiful."

"Your father is a man of taste."

"Except I'm not beautiful. Bad nose. Little squinty eyes. I hope Marvin gets lost on the subway."

"I hope Marvin has an endless happy life on the subway," Aaron said, and when the waiter came, they drank to it: "To Marvin's eternal underground bliss," Aaron toasted and Judy touched his glass with hers, and for just a moment he was tempted to take her hand.

"Live," Judy said.

Aaron took her hand.

"Are you embarrassed now? You look embarrassed now."

"No," Aaron said. "Yes," Aaron said. "I don't know," Aaron said. "But I'm sure as hell cheerful."

"I have that effect on people. Tell me more."

"If I had the money I'd hire you. Keep you around. For the freak days. You could banish them, you know that? Make them fly. You could—" Aaron held his breath.

"What's the matter?"

"Nothing."

"Then why did you stop?"

"No reason." But there was, because over in the far corner a man was sitting, a lone man, and for just a moment he looked at Aaron, and Aaron saw the look and he saw what it meant. The man in the corner knew; you could fool all of the people some of the time and some of the people all of the time, but you couldn't fool the man in the corner. So Aaron said it again, just before he paid for the drinks, just before he kissed the girl on the cheek, just before he fled back into the obliterating night:

"No reason."

•   •   •

Branch stayed at the party until it was over. Then he and Mort Blandings and two others went out for Chinese food. Branch had eaten Chinese food the night before and he certainly did not want it again. But he also didn't want to be alone. And he was afraid to return to his apartment. Afraid what Aaron might say.

Or do.

So he dawdled over dinner, and when it was finally done he convinced the others that a drink was in order, on him, of course, and when they agreed he led them to a lively Third Avenue bar where they all had a terrible time till after midnight. Then everybody went home.

When Branch reached the front door of his apartment he paused. Slowly he reached into a pocket for the key, took it out, aimed it toward the lock. He experienced a bit of difficulty inserting it, because his hand was trembling, and that made him angry. "Nobody pushes me around," Branch muttered, and he threw the door open and slammed it behind him.

Aaron was sitting in the living room. Quiet. Smiling.

"I hope you know you made a spectacle of yourself," Branch began.

Aaron sat quietly. Smiling.

"Ass would be a better word. You made an ass of yourself. I mean it. You know why I'm so late? Because I had to apologize to half the civilized world about you and the assy way you behaved. I've never seen anything like it. When you left it was like some leper. You should have seen the way everyone was looking at you. And if you think it was fun for me to explain that *I* was the one who brought you, well, you're crazy. I'd like an apology, Aaron." Branch waited.

Quietly, Aaron smiled.

"I want an apology. Right now. Say something."

"Nineteen," Aaron said.

"Oh my, get him." Branch began to pace. "Off on one of his silly damn games. Well, I'm on to you, Aaron. I'm supposed to ask what nineteen means and then you'll tell me and it'll turn out that it's some way of insulting me, right? Well, tough. I don't care what nineteen means, so you can say nineteen all you please, it doesn't bother me."

"Twenty," Aaron said.

"I want an apology! I'm ashamed of you. You're just not adult enough to go into civilized society. Everything's such a game with you. You're one of the biggest babies. Stealing the Scotch like that. You're just not old enough to play with the big boys."

"Twenty-one," Aaron said.

"I can see there's just no point in trying to deal with you rationally. Good night, Aaron."

"Twenty-two," Aaron said.

Branch turned and went to the bedroom. He took off his jacket and hung it carefully in the closet. Then he took off his tie. He slipped off his trousers, unbuttoned his shirt. Then he crept to the doorway and held his breath. The apartment was completely quiet. No sound.

"Twenty-four."

Branch whirled and hurried to the bathroom. He washed his face and brushed his teeth and put on his pajamas. After that he left the bathroom and turned out the light in the bedroom and slipped under the covers.

"Twenty-eight."

Branch pulled the blankets over his head and closed his eyes, but after a moment he realized it was just too stuffy under there, so he threw the blankets back and carefully fluffed his pillow and then sank his head into it so that his ears were covered. He stared at the ceiling. Then he thought he heard footsteps, so he lifted his head from the pillow.

"Thirty."

"*What are those numbers?*" Branch jumped from the bed and tore down the corridor into the living room, grabbing Aaron's shoulders, shaking them, shaking them hard.

"Synonyms for stupid."

"Well, stop it."

"Bonehead. That makes thirty-one."

"Stop."

"Eventually. Clod. Thirty-two."

"I'm not a clod. Why am I a clod?"

"Thirty-three."

"What word did you just think of?"

"Beetlebrain. How long have we lived together?"

"Six months maybe. Why?"

"And what have you been looking for all that time? Thirty-four and five."

"What do you mean, what have I been looking for? A play?"

"Thirty-four and five, by the way, were boob and booby. That's right, a play. And what do I do?"

"Drive a cab?"

"What else?"

"Write?"

"Not 'Write' question mark. 'Write' exclamation point. Write! And *that* is why you are stupid. Because only a genuine cretin could live with a writer and look for a play and never put two and two together."

"You're a novelist. You don't write plays."

"Have you asked?"

"No, but—"

"Ask."

"All right; have you got a play?"

"I might have."

"But you don't."

"I didn't say that."

Branch turned. "I'm going to sleep. Good night."

"Thirty-six, thirty-seven, thirty-eight."

"Where's it take place, this play of yours?" Branch's voice was very loud.

"A college town!" Aaron shouted back. "Here. Manhattan. Yes. Up near Columbia. One of those big old buildings near the Columbia campus."

"Make up your mind, Aaron. Manhattan isn't everyone's idea of a college town."

"Up near Columbia," Aaron said again. "That's the set. The living room of a big run-down apartment between Broadway and West End."

"And what's it about?"

"What's it about?"

"That's right."

"Well, that's a little difficult to put into words, so—"

"You're making this up as you go along. Admit it."

"Love!" Aaron cried. "Love!"

"Boy, that's an original theme," Branch said. "That's what I call breaking new ground."

"Five characters, one set. Five people. Two men, three women. The men don't count for much. One of them's a make-out man, the other's kind of a backward rich kid. The women have the big parts. Two of them anyway. The two young ones."

"I'm already confused."

"Well, shut up and maybe you won't be. The three women live in this apartment, O.K.? A mother, her daughter and a boarder. The daughter's name is Loretta—her mother named her after Loretta Young. Her mother had great plans for her, O.K.? But the daughter didn't turn out quite pretty enough. Oh, she's attractive, Loretta is, but not the knockout her mother needed. See the mother, she lives all the time in the sweet by and by, when she was belle of the ball, before she got married and her looks started going and her hair turned gray—"

"Dreamy mother with big plans for her daughter. Aaron, come on, it's *The Glass Menagerie.*"

"Like hell it is. Listen. The daughter's one main character: lonely Loretta. *Can't stand being alone.* And the boarder's the other main character. Lemme tell you about her. Name's Claire. A young old maid, but great: bright and funny and smart and not really ugly except she's a cripple. Clubfoot. Clubfoot Claire. She and Loretta, they're like good sisters: close.

And they all work around the Columbia campus. Claire, she works in a bookshop. And Loretta, she waits table in a little restaurant. The mother— she's got no name, just the mother—she works in a dress shop—women's clothing. So there's the people, Scudder—five of 'em. The animal make-out man, the rich-kid grad student, the mother and lonely Loretta—and Clubfoot Claire."

"I can hardly keep my eyes open," Branch said.

"You're gonna pay for your lip, Scudder—" Aaron sat limp in the chair, arms dangling, eyes closed—"but right now it's Act One and we meet the girls! Dinner's over, Loretta's getting ready for a date, Claire's teasing her, and the mother's blabbing on about when she was a girl. And here we get the mother's big word: *eligible.* I told you how she had big plans for Loretta? Well, her plans are marriage and marriage with an *eligible* man. For *eligible* read loaded. And in comes the animal. He's a grease-ball and no genius, but handsome, and it's obvious Loretta's got the hots for him, and the mother, she almost tosses her cookies after they're gone. He's a poor Dago Catholic, three strikes is *out.* And she goes into this big spiel to Claire about *eligibility.* And suddenly we realize that she may be an old bag, the mother, but on this subject, at least, there's passion left. Her daughter *will marry an eligible man*—she *means* it. That night, when the animal brings Loretta home, they neck a little—a dash of sex for the butter-and-egg man, Scudder—and the animal paws her and every time he touches her body she *writhes.* She's like a bitch in heat when he fingers her flesh, and when he takes off, Loretta goes and gets Claire out of bed and they chitchat about how crazy Loretta is for the animal and how the old lady is agin it, but mostly what you get here is how close the girls are—they *read each other*, they *care.* Kind of a sweet scene. And then, late afternoon a couple of weeks later, in comes the mother like gangbusters because it has happened! He has come! The eligible man has appeared! This rich-kid grad student, he walked into the shop to buy his mother a birthday present and they started to talking and he's very shy but nice-looking and loaded and—surprise—she's invited him to dinner. That night! Well, there's surprise, all right, and irritation, but the mother rides roughshod through it all and then the doorbell rings and in comes this richie—Frank Fink in the flesh. Shy and not very handsome and what they have is cocktails without liquor. It's a really funny scene except it's all sort of horrible to Loretta, who's acting kind of out of it, and then, as the mother continues pumping the rich kid about his background and ex-plaining what a *fabulous catch* any daughter of hers would be, Loretta comes down to the very front of the stage with Claire and the lights start to fade and in the background the mother is going at it hot and heavy and maybe some sweet wistful music starts to play and Claire says, 'You don't have to tell me, I know,' and Loretta starts maybe a little to weep and Claire says, 'How far gone are you?' and Loretta says 'A month' and then the mother and the richie come swooping down on them, laughing and happy and noisemaking like crazy and we have an intermission."

"That's a good curtain," Branch said. "But there better not be—"

"Good *curtain*! You ass, the whole thing's marvelous."

"*There better not be* a big abortion scene—I'm bored with them already."

"Yours is a common mind, Scudder. Get me a drink."

"Get it yourself."

Aaron threw back his head and howled. "Such pain he's going to suffer; my heart bleeds." Then he got up and made himself a drink. "So we come up on Loretta and the animal." Aaron gestured with his glass, pacing around, glancing out the window at the black Hudson. "Loretta tells him how she really cares for him but that means nothing, he's used to adoration, and then she tells him again how she's swelling with his carelessness, and he says tough. He's been through this kind of thing before and he's cool as hell. *They don't even talk about abortion, Scudder*—he never even goes so far as to make an offer—and Loretta's terribly shook by all this and she says how he's got to marry her and he says how he's on to whores like her and then he says there's probably twenty guys at least who might be the little old papa and she's sorta hysterical by now and swears he's the first, which is corny but true, and he only laughs and then he *really* pours on the venom and reduces her to rubble and then Claire and the old lady come in from the flicks and the old lady doesn't know why they're fighting but she jumps right in and chews the animal up and down and tells him never to come back and this strikes him as being the funniest joke of all time and he gives his love to everybody and takes off. And the mother says thank God he's gone because things have been going really well between Loretta and the richie—he's taken her out a couple of times the past week—and the mother just knows that everything is gonna work out great and Loretta says she's pregnant and without a word the mother whips a hand across her daughter's face. Loretta just sits there like a lump, she's that far gone. Whip! The mother creams her again, harder. Whip! Whip! Whip! She slaps on and on and probably she would've killed her kid if Claire hadn't pulled her off. Then there follows this looonnnnnnng pause, and then the mother says that she is just stunned and furious that the rich kid would knock up her daughter. Loretta tells her it wasn't the rich kid but the animal and the mother says no, it was the richie, and Loretta says it wasn't the richie and the mother says how can you be sure and Loretta says on account of he's never touched me and then the mother says, *'That can be remedied!'*—and whammo, we're off into this fantastic scene where the mother says screw with the richie and Loretta says no, no, no, and she's really hysterical when in from left field dashes Claire—*and on the mother's side*—and that's the clincher. Claire convinces Loretta to do it and finally Loretta just nods and nods and the mother is smiling and saying over and over and over, 'Love will find a way. Love will find a way.' "

"What a wild idea," Branch said. "Where do you get ideas like that?"

"I'm a writer, Scudder. I got imagination. Catch this next scene: the seduction. Loretta alone in the house. Nervous and scared. In comes the richie. They talk. The talk gets personal. Loretta says that she thinks that maybe they oughta break up and he says why and she explains that she thinks he's attractive but obviously he doesn't find her that way and that that's no basis for a relationship so maybe they ought to just stop seeing each other now before she gets hurt. And he says, no-no, he finds her fantastically attractive but he was afraid she'd rebuff him and *that's* why he hasn't made a pass. And she says then that maybe they shouldn't break up after all and that's great with him and they talk a little and she says that she's found out something: her mother keeps a bottle. Really? he says. They quick go get it and have a few *schlugs* and he asks a few what he thinks are clever questions trying to find out where the others are. When he learns they're alone, he grabs her and kisses her and she like melts in his arms and he kisses her again and again and then he tears around, dousing the lights until there's just one left on, and then he comes back and kisses her some more. Then very slow and nervous, they start to undress. Loretta's upset as hell and the richie's scared to death and nobody sees Claire as she steps out of the shadows. Nobody knows she's there. She watches as they kiss and touch and undress. Loretta's standing by the couch with not very much on and the richie comes up and they sink slowly down but just before he grabs her Claire—back in the darkness— she holds out her empty arms to Loretta and like a ball bat you know she loves her, Claire loves Loretta, really loves her, and when I say love, Scudder, I mean love, curtain."

"Lesbians," Branch said. "Jesus."

"Sensational?"

"Go on."

"Now he wants me to go on. Before he was all lip, but now he's interested. Maybe I don't feel like going on, Scudder. Get me a drink."

Branch hurried up and got Aaron a drink.

Aaron took it and laughed.

"Shut up. Go on, go on."

"*Curtain up on the three ladies sitting!* It's weeks later. Doorbell rings. In comes the richie. Claire and the old lady leave Loretta alone with him. She tells him. She's pregnant and he better do something and at first he's stunned, then he starts to argue that not enough time has gone by and, besides that, is she sure she's pregnant and is she sure it's him because he's a very careful fella and Loretta isn't doing any too great when *in comes the cavalry,* Claire and the old lady, both spitting fire, and they roll over the richie like an avalanche and just before the blackout he mumbles that he'll marry her. Lights up and they're hot to trot to city hall. Loretta's ready and so's the old lady and the richie's at his place getting ready too and Claire gets on stage alone and she picks up the phone and dials and then she says, in a crazy, strange voice, 'She lies. She lies. It isn't your baby. *It isn't your baby!*'"

"God," Branch said. "What a thing to do. Where'd you ever get—"

"I told you, I'm a writer, shut up. Because what happens now is the other two come in and sit down and wait. And wait. And the lights dim and then come up bright and then dim and time is passing, time is passing, and the richie hasn't come and the mother keeps trying to joke it off but terrible things are beginning to show on her face and the lights keep dimming and getting bright and then finally a telegram comes from the richie and Loretta reads it out loud and it says that he's never coming because it isn't his baby and Loretta puts the wire down and says 'I'm almost glad' and the mother snaps, 'Glad! Glad! You goddam whorechild!' and she takes off in a frenzy, control gone, and Loretta just sits there and takes it because she's too tired to move and the vituperation builds and builds and the mother goes out screaming that if Loretta's there when she comes back she'll kill her dead and invite the flies in for a feast and we black out for a second, but then we're bright again and Loretta has a suitcase in her hand and is looking around like a little lost sheep when in comes old Clubfoot Claire, all packed too, and Loretta says 'Where are you going?' and Claire says 'With you' and Loretta says 'Why?' and Claire says 'Because the child will need a father, love,' and Loretta just gapes and Claire says 'Come to me, love,' and Loretta bolts for the door and her hand's on the knob when Claire cries '*You'll die out there alone!*' Loretta freezes and

Claire starts to talk in this crazy whisper about loneliness and how some people die of it and how Loretta's one of those people, and it's true, and Loretta just stands there while Claire goes on about being alone and pregnant in the city and slowly dying and then she talks about how strong her love is, and how long it's lasted already and how it would always last, always, always, and finally she comes to a stop and just says one more word: 'Well?' Loretta stands there. She looks at Claire. She shakes her head. Then, almost as if she can't control it, her hand goes out. She looks at the hand almost in disbelief. Claire reaches for that hand. Claire takes it. They turn toward each other, hands touching. They almost smile. They walk together out the door. Curtain." Aaron emptied his glass. "Well?"

For a long time Branch was silent. Then he turned and walked away.

"Where you going?" Aaron said.

"To get someone off my back," Branch said, picking up the phone, calling Ohio. "Rosie?" he said when she came on the line. "Rosie, it's happened!"

"Branch?"

"That thing I told you that was on the fire? That terrific thing? Did I wake you? I had to—you had to know. It's happened, Rosie. I've got a play. I've just read it and it's absolutely fantastic."

"You got a play?"

"Aren't you excited?"

"Yes, yes, you know I am, you woke me is the thing. Who wrote it?"

"This young writer, Aaron Fire."

"*Brilliant* young writer," Aaron whispered.

"He's brilliant," Branch said.

"What's it called?"

"It's called . . ." He put his hand over the receiver and whispered, "What's the title?"

"Beats the shit out of me." Aaron said.

"It's more or less untitled at present," Branch said to his mother.

"*Madonna with Child*," Aaron said then.

"*Madonna with Child*," Branch repeated.

"Sounds religious," Rose said. "What's it about?"

"The playwright says it's about love, Mother."

"What else?" Rosie said.

"What else?" Branch looked at Aaron.

"What else is there?" Aaron answered.

Part V

XXII

Aaron was up.

In the first place, it was a good party. He stood still in the center of the enormous living room and let the people swirl around him. The living room was in the Dakota, at 72nd and Central Park West. Aaron glanced out at the park and smiled. I am going to live in the Dakota, he decided. When I have sufficient *argent*, home will be here. He was reminded of the fiddler who only played one note on one string and, when asked why, replied, "Everybody else is looking for the right place; I've found it." So the setting was perfect, the April night at least as fine, the women and the whisky beyond reproach, the women being bundled in either Bonwit's, Bergdorf's or Bendel's, the whisky being Chivas Regal, Wild Turkey, Coates Plymouth Gin, plus some authentic imported Polish vodka if you felt the need for being "in."

The girl he had been talking to said something, and Aaron, not listening, nodded and smiled. She was a religion major from Southern Methodist University and totally pretty, if you could stand the Dallas accent. Her escort was somewhere across the room and that was fine with Aaron because he liked the way people looked at them, first at her, then at him, then at her again, then a farewell glance at him, usually accompanied by a shrug and a shake of the head.

I deserve her, you bastards, I'm pretty tonight too. "Do you find me ravishing?" he said to the girl.

"Pardon?" the girl said in three syllables.

"Just say yes."

"Yes," she said in two.

"How flawless your taste," he told her. Of course, as he glanced around, he realized again that he was the only man at the party not in a suit, but that only reminded him of Princeton and his yellow corduroy. His trousers were pressed reasonably well and his shoes were shined (Branch had shined them) and his dark brown jacket was of the finest tweed. The jacket thrilled him. It was his first Brooks Brothers item. Branch had got it for him. As a surprise gift. For finishing the play.

And that, of course, was the real reason for his mood. The play. Talking it aloud to Branch, winging it—that had been one thing. Writing it was a horse of a different et cetera, and now that it was done, now that his labors were completed, he could only smile. He had swept the stables clean, and brilliantly. The play, the first thing he had written in years, was the best thing he had written, ever.

Aaron was up.

"Are you an actor or a writer or what?" the girl asked him. "Everybody here seems to be one or the other."

"Neither," Aaron told her. Then he began to laugh.

"What is it?"

"Nothing," Aaron said. "I was just thinking of this funny thing that happened to me back in rabbinical school."

"You're a *rabbi*?"

Aaron stuck a cigarette in the far corner of his mouth. "Reform," he said.

"Good for you," the girl said.

"I try not to think of it as being noble. A job is a job. May I get you a drink?"

She held up her glass. "It's just ginger ale. I'm a Baptist."

"Good for you," Aaron said. "Excuse me." He started for the bar. The room was crowded and he made his way slowly, pausing for a moment by the piano. The piano player, handsome but turning to flesh, was singing what must have been an original composition:

> *"Your touch*
> *Is just too much*
> *For such as I . . ."*

"This party is a drag," the girl sitting by the piano player said. She pointed to a fat balding figure lurking behind the curve of the piano. "That's my boyfriend. He's afraid to come out. He's a worse drag than this party is." The piano player nodded and went on singing:

> *"Your touch*
> *In our small hutch*
> *Would make me cry:*
> *Heaven."*

"That doesn't make any sense," a girl sportswriter wandering by said.

"The hell it doesn't," the piano player told her.

"A 'hutch' is a box or coop for confining a small animal. Why are you putting your sweetheart in a coop? It just doesn't make any sense. That's a lousy song."

"You know what you can do, dontcha?" the piano player said.

"Sticks and stones," the girl sportswriter told him, walking away.

Aaron continued on to the bar. He held up his glass, said "Scotch" to the bartender, then waited, looking around. There must have been several hundred people in the various rooms, many of them with famous faces. Across from the bar half a dozen uniformed domestics were busily setting up a buffet of turkey and great slabs of roast beef and glazed ham and salvers of relishes and salads and bowls of fruit and melon balls and thick wedges of imported cheese. "My thanks," Aaron said to the bartender, taking his filled glass.

"Don't look now but I'm back," the religion major said to him. She gestured to a corner. "That's my escort. He's talking about the Chicago Bears. Whenever he finds anybody who'll talk about the Chicago Bears he completely ignores me."

Aaron followed her gesture. "He's got yellow teeth and he doesn't look at who he's talking to."

The religion major nodded. "Sometimes I spend an entire evening just staring at the whites of his eyes. Otherwise, he's very nice." She glanced at the buffet. "My, my, will you look at that food."

"Who's giving this party?"

"Oh, somebody. My escort told me but I forget."

"Lee Strasberg!" an aficionado of the Actors' Studio was saying to the girl who had been sitting by the piano player. "Lee Strasberg is the most important single force in the American theater today."

"What about Gadge?" the girl said.

"Gadge," the aficionado said. "Gadge. Jesus, you might just as well say Josh, for crissakes."

"Josh! Josh! Josh!" the girl said. "You're a worse drag than my boyfriend." She went back to the piano.

> *"Your touch*
> *Makes me clutch*
> *My heart . . .*
> *If you leave*

> *I'll be in dutch*
> *With my heart . . ."*

"Now you *know* what *happens* when you *drink martinis*," the wife of a saxophone player said to her husband, smiling while she said it. "And *that's* your *fourth.*"

"But it's free booze," the saxophone player said.

"All right," his wife said. "All right. But let's just not try for any sympathy in the morning. We've been warned, after all, so let's just not beg for any back rubs or temple massages or along those lines."

The saxophone player sighed. "Girls never understand about free booze," he said.

> *"I'll need no crutch*
> *For your touch*
> *Makes me strong . . ."*

"You must get invited to a lot of parties, being a rabbi," the religion major said.

Aaron smiled. "Hundreds."

"You must like them, then."

"I'm a very jovial rabbi," he admitted. "I was voted that. Back at school. Most jovial. I was the gay blade of Hebrew Union College."

"Oh, oh, oh," the girl whispered, "will you just look."

Aaron turned. A famous fifty-year-old action-movie star had just entered the room, a dazzling young girl on his arm.

"He's handsomer even than in the movies, don't you think? My mother's crazy for him too. Oh, isn't he virile-looking, though."

Aaron smiled. "He's a fag."

"He is?"

"He is."

"But he's married."

"Of course he's married. It's just a smoke screen. That only proves it."

"It does?"

"It does."

"But he's been married three times."

"That just shows how desperate he is."

"But he's all the time having affairs with beautiful young starlets."

"Some men will go to any lengths to keep a secret."

"They will?"

"They will."

"But he loves big-game hunting."

"Obviously."

"You mean that proves it too?"

"Don't you know about big-game hunters?"

"He used to play professional football, though."

"Oh, you are young," Aaron said.

"But he's got *seven children.*"

Aaron smiled. "It's such an obvious case of protesting too much. Who else but a fag would have seven children?"

The girl looked at him.

Aaron laughed, put his arm around her. "We have just sung our national anthem," he said.

Branch walked by on his way to the bar. "Having any fun?"

"Getting any lovin'?" Aaron answered.

Branch laughed. "What a pretty jacket," he said.

"A gift from an admirer."

Branch nodded, smiled, continued on toward the bar.

For a moment Aaron watched him. They had not fought or even argued in weeks, since he'd finished the play. At first Scudder's good humor was a little tough to take, but now he had come almost to enjoy it. Aaron fingered the soft tweed.

"It is a lovely jacket," the girl said.

"My wife gave it to me," Aaron explained.

"Oh, you're—"

"Before she died," Aaron said softly.

"I'm sorry," she said.

"Yes, she died last week," Aaron went on. "Horribly and—"

"*Last week?*"

"You're wondering how I can be out like this tonight, aren't you, laughing and drinking and smiling at the world? You're wondering what possible reason I can have for gadding about with my wife barely chill in the ground."

"Well, if you must know, yes."

Aaron was about to tell her when Branch screamed.

Branch had screamed once already that day.

Late afternoon, and he had been alone in the apartment. Aaron was off at some movie revival and along about half past five Branch had felt drowsy. He had taken off his shoes and sprawled across the bed and, in a moment, he was dreaming.

The dream he had had before.

All his life, it seemed.

He was a prisoner, standing helpless, great snakes knotted tight around his hands and feet. In front of him was his captor, a bloodless white maggot, bigger than the sun. The maggot was capable of unbelievable cruelties and there was, in all the universe, only one thing it feared.

The beautiful black prince.

Branch's black prince. The beautiful black prince with the silver sword that could cut any body, any thing. And now, from halfway across the world, the black prince was coming. And the white maggot knew it and it knew that if it was ever going to have its victim it would have to move, fast, else the black prince would come with his silver sword.

The maggot began to move.

Branch struggled, but the snakes tightened their knots, tightened them until his hands and feet were blue and dying and nothing could loosen them except the silver sword and the maggot picked up speed, coming closer and closer, and its mouth seemed full of claws and the snakes cut into Branch's skin and from halfway around the world the black prince was coming, the beautiful black prince was coming, but so was the white maggot, like the wind, and the maggot had never been this close before, and where was the black prince? The maggot was so close now than Branch could see it had a breast, two breasts, great hanging things, and its claw mouth opened and started coming down, covering his face, and then there was a *crack!* as the jaws snapped shut and his head was gone and Branch rose up from the bed, wet, wide-eyed and screaming. For a moment he stood trembling in the middle of his bedroom. Then he fell back on the bed, not daring to close his eyes.

The black prince had left him. The black prince was gone.

Branch was down.

> *"Your touch*
> *In our small hutch*
> *Would make me cry:*
> *Heaven."*

Branch sipped his Polish vodka and looked at all the people. How pretty some of them were. Across the room Aaron had a lovely brunette in conversation, and although usually he, Branch, would have found tonight his element, now it was all he could do to smile whenever he thought Aaron might possibly be looking at him. He had to keep his feelings from Aaron. His true feelings.

Branch was down.

After twenty years his black prince was leaving him alone at the mercy of the white maggot. And Rose was scandalized by *Madonna with Child.* It was a mistake, sending her a copy, he knew it at the time, but she had to read it. If she was going to back it, the least he could do was let her read what she was backing. Of course, he had no intention of making her put up the money. He would certainly try to raise it elsewhere first. But lacking success, Rose would have to angel. And loathing the play the way she did . . . Naturally he had argued with her, had told her what a lovely thing it was, Aaron's *Madonna.*

Had, in other words, lied.

The play was wretched.

The January night that Aaron had outlined it, it seemed potentially fine. But on paper, on paper . . .

> *"Your touch*
> *Makes me clutch*
> *My heart . . ."*

Aaron was so proud of it too. That was one of the difficult things: Aaron actually thought it was *good.* Branch shook his head. Sooner or later he was going to have to send the play out, let people read it, try and get some money somehow. But so far Rose was the only one to have read it and Branch intended keeping things that way, for just as long as he could. He was not looking forward to any literary criticism, not about *Madonna with Child.* Of course, he knew he could always change his mind and pitch the project. Except if he did, Rose would drag him home forever. She would take two stubby fingers and pinch his ears and drag him across Pennsylvania to Ohio and—Branch suddenly wondered if Aaron might be looking at him.

Taking no chances, he smiled.

He grinned from ear to ear, cursing his cowardice. I loathe the public me, Branch thought. The private me, he's not so bad; he's sweet and gentle and I try to make him kind. He's really all right. Not perfect, but decent enough. The public me, though, fawns and cringes and sometimes he stutters and I find him despicable. Letting the smile die, he quickly downed his Polish vodka.

"I'll need no crutch
For your touch
Makes me strong . . ."

Branch moved to the window and stared unblinking out at Central Park.

"Archie, hi."

"Hello there, Betty Jane Fiske."

Branch glanced at the man talking with the exceptionally pretty woman.

"Just get here?" the man said.

"Just."

"Charley?"

"Hanging up coats."

"Lemme getcha a drink." They moved off.

I could just tell him right now, Branch thought. I could just say, "Aaron, it stinks" and then I could go call Rose and tell her the same thing and that I wasn't coming home. I could do that. I could free myself. There would be no more snakes knotting at my wrists. I could be free of any and all maggots with great swaying breasts and jaws that go click! and I wouldn't suffer so at the hands of that cruel skeleton. I could kill the public me! I could kill! I have that power! I have—

"Oh dear," Branch said out loud.

His eyes were wet. With tears of despair.

It was sad but it was true, so it was funny. Here he thought grand murderous thoughts and all the while his eyes were filling with tiny tears and if Aaron saw them he would be altogether merciless. Branch got out his handkerchief and made a show of wiping his forehead. Then he turned, spotted Aaron, turned away and quickly dried his eyes. Then he wiped his forehead again, said, "It's really hot in here," out loud, and headed for the bar.

Aaron was muttering something about a national anthem, his arm around some girl's shoulder.

"Having any fun?"

"Getting any lovin'?"

"What a pretty jacket," and the words "A gift from an admirer" trailed after him as he continued on to the bar. Branch tried very hard not to think about the jacket. It had cost twice too much and he had bought it in desperation after he had finished reading *Madonna with Child.* He had bundled Aaron up and they had zoomed down in a taxi to Brooks and they had got the jacket and Aaron had worn it with such obvious pride that, as he paid for it, Branch almost managed to convince himself that buying it had been a good idea.

Why did you buy it, fool?

I was afraid. I was afraid.

Of what?

Of . . .

Of what?

"Vodka, please," Branch said. The bartender filled his glass. Branch leaned down on his elbows and cupped his glass between his hands. Then he closed his eyes.

"Charley . . ." It was the voice of the exceptionally pretty woman.

Branch opened his eyes.

"Charley, Rudy—over here."

Branch glanced toward the two men. The one called Charley he ignored. The one called Rudy made him weak.

Branch screamed.

His black prince stood in the doorway.

Branch had the sense to drop his glass. It shattered. Then Aaron was beside him. "What happened?"

"Nothing."

"You screamed. Why?"

"No reason."

A crowd was growing around them. Aaron supported Branch as best he could but neither was Branch light nor Aaron strong. "Are you all right?"

"Lie . . . down."

"Help me, then." Aaron draped Branch's arm around his shoulder and started to move. The crowd was bigger now, everyone was watching, so Aaron said, "A little too much too fast, O.K.? Clear the way, huh? That's right. Thank you," and they moved from the bar down a wide hall into a bedroom filled with rented coat racks. Aaron shoved the racks aside and lowered Branch gently to the bed.

"Thank you," Branch whispered.

"You going to be all right?"

"Fine."

"Haven't you any idea what happened?"

"Just . . . got dizzy."

"Well, Jesus, Scudder, you're my producer; you can't go folding up on me."

Branch smiled, closed his eyes.

"Want me to stay with you?"

"No . . . I'll join you in a little . . . don't let me spoil the party . . . just close the door . . . and thank you, Aaron."

"Take it easy," Aaron said, closing the door behind him.

Alone, Branch waited a moment. Then he whirled off the bed, eyes bright, arms out, turning, turning, circling the room, dancing a wild dance. "Any way I can get it," he replied.

Half hidden by a doorway, Branch held his breath and stared at the three people surrounding the boy with the hearing aid—an exceptionally pretty woman, a large handsome man, another man who looked a lot like Robert Mitchum. They were talking, the quartet, and Branch was very careful to look at only the other three. Then the black prince glanced away. Branch stared at him. The black prince glanced back. Branch looked away.

"You're sure you're all right?" Aaron said, coming up from behind.

"Yes."

"You look flushed."

Branch held up his glass. "Just water now. Too much drinking. I'm fine."

Aaron nodded and started away, saying, "I think I'll go bait the piano player."

Branch resumed his vigil. The party was getting louder now as more and more people entered the enormous apartment. Still hidden, Branch stared as the deaf boy looked away, looked away as the deaf boy glanced in his direction. Then the exceptionally pretty woman smiled and excused herself and crossed out of sight. Branch followed her, watched as she entered the powder room, waited a few moments until she came out, fresh lipstick on her perfect mouth. "There you are," Branch said then. "I've been wanting to apologize to you. I'm Branch Scudder."

She looked at him.

Branch laughed. "I'm the one who practically fell apart on top of you back there by the bar. Too much drinking." He held up his glass. "Just water now. Feel a lot better. I really owe you an apology, Mrs. . . ."

"Betty Jane Fiske. I didn't place you at first."

"Mrs. Betty Jane Fiske. Isn't this a marvelous apartment? I love the Dakota. You must let me show you the view." He escorted her to a window. "I really do apologize, Mrs. Fiske."

Betty Jane laughed. "You do it very nicely."

"Thank you. Your husband, is he an actor? He looks perhaps like he might be one."

Betty Jane laughed again. "No, he's an editor. At Kingsway Publishers."

"That's wonderful. I do admire people ignoring their handicaps, if you'll pardon my saying that."

"I don't understand."

"The last thing that happened before my scandalous exhibition of a little bit ago was you calling to those two men and I just *assumed*—he is deaf, your husband?"

"No; that's Rudy Miller. He's a writer friend of Charley's."

Branch smiled. "How silly of me. Well, then, how wonderful of Mr. Miller, ignoring *his* handicap, writing all those mysteries the way he does."

"Rudy doesn't write mysteries," Betty Jane said. "He's just written one book—"

"I'm just getting everything wrong tonight. I would have sworn— well, perhaps it's because it's such a common name, Miller."

"Rudy's R. V. Miller. V for Valentino. It's really very easy to remember."

"I'm just horrible with names," Branch told her. "Would you believe me? I've forgotten it already."

". . . still, it must be fascinating, working with writers the way you do, Mr. Wesker. Would you like a slice of ham?"

"Call me Archie. Yeah, I'd like a hunk, thanks." They moved slowly through the buffet line. "You're Branch, right?"

"Right."

"Well, I'll tell you about writers, Branch. Basically—should I shovel you some turkey?"

"Please."

"Basically, writers are the most ungrateful sons of bitches on the face of the earth. It's the editor that makes the book, and you'd think just *once* a goddam writer would have the decency to admit it. Will you look at that roast beef? I'll bust."

"I think I'll have some too." Branch forked a slab of rare beef onto his plate, then one onto Archie's. "I suppose once they make all that money and move into those big country houses—"

"They don't all live like that, lemme tell you."

"Where do they live, I wonder?"

"Depends. All over."

"I think I'll have to pass up the lobster. For example, are there any writers here? Where do they live? If you'll take my ham, I can have some crabmeat."

"Done. Sam Dunnaway lives at Eightieth and West End, Rudy Miller at Orchard off Rivington, Ed—hey, you're spilling—"

"Sometimes I'm clumsy," Branch told him.

". . . basically, it has to do with sacrifices for your art," Branch said as Charley gave his glass to the bartender. "And when I happened to be talking to your lovely wife earlier, and she happened to mention that you were an editor, well, I just had to talk to you."

"My pleasure," Charley said.

"Well, now, I'm a producer, and that's sort of in the arts, and certainly your writers are artists, and you see, I think it's best—until one is established—not to get married and have a family. It applies too many pressures. What do you think?"

"Don't you think it depends on the individual?" Charley said.

"Well, for example, if a man is a writer, and he only has himself to support, he can write whatever he wants. If he has a wife and family, then there's pressure. Terrible pressure. Are most of your writers married?"

"That's kind of impossible to answer."

"Then let's take a specific. Your lovely wife mentioned that the deaf boy was a writer."

"Rudy's single," Charley said.

"Is he engaged?" Branch said, too quickly.

Charley looked at him.

Branch laughed. "I mean, is he, for example—well, you see, to support my thesis—well, if someone were living with a young lady, that would be the same as . . . being married; it would apply pressure and—"

Charley took his drink from the bartender. "I've left my wife stranded," he said. "You'll have to excuse me."

"Of course. A pleasure."

"Yes." Charley crossed away from the bar. Betty Jane was talking with Archie. Rudy stood beside them. "You have an admirer," Charley said. "Or something."

Rudy said nothing.

Charley glanced back at Branch, turned to Rudy. "I'll describe him, then you can look. But don't look now; he's watching you."

"I always know who's watching me," Rudy said.

That night, when Aaron was almost asleep, Branch said, "We've got to talk."

Aaron muttered something about the morning.

"Now."

Aaron muttered something about going to hell.

Branch turned on his reading lamp. "I mean it, Aaron."

Aaron whirled over. "Turn that—"

"It's about the play. About *Madonna with Child*."

"What about it?"

"You've got to change it."

"Change it?"

"That's right."

"Why?"

"Because it needs changing."

"I thought you said you loved it."

"I do love it. It's brilliant. But it's got to be changed."

"Blow it out."

"You mean you won't change it?"

"I won't change it."

"Then I won't produce it." Branch turned off his reading lamp. "Good night, Aaron."

Aaron lay very still. Then he turned on his reading lamp. "What the hell do you mean, you won't produce it?"

"Just what I said."

"Scudder—"

"I'm not kidding, Aaron."

"The play's perfect the way it is."

"Then you won't have any trouble getting another producer, will you?"

"Goddam right I won't."

"How wonderful it must be to have such confidence. Sleep tight, Aaron."

"I will, don't worry." He switched off his bed lamp.

"You know what I think, Aaron?" Branch said then.

"It's after four, let's knock it off."

"I think you're taking a terrible chance." He switched on his bed lamp. "I love your play. I think it's brilliant and needs just a few minor little teeny changes. You think it's perfect. What if we're both wrong? What if nobody else will touch it?" He switched off his bed lamp. "I sure hope you're right."

Aaron made a snore.

"You know what else I think? I think for the first time since we met I've got something you want."

"What have you got besides dandruff?"

"The endurance to suffer your insults. But that's minor. The theater's a funny place. What's important, what's *crucial*, is getting done. Being seen. Being heard. It doesn't matter if the play's another *Hamlet* or the actor Kean. What matters is if your talent shows. And if it does, then sometimes other things come. But if you're never seen or heard, then nothing. And what I've got that you want, Aaron, is the desire to do your play. And if I do it, even if it stinks, somebody might think you had some talent. Other things might come. But if I don't, and if nobody else does either, then nothing. But of course, like you said, the play is perfect, so I'll shut up. Good night, Aaron."

Aaron turned on his bed lamp. "All right, smart ass, what changes?"

"There are just two."

"What are they? Get going."

Branch turned on his bed lamp and arranged his pillows beneath his back. "The first one involves Clubfoot Claire, the boarder in love with Loretta."

"Don't summarize my own play, Scudder. What about her?"

"She's the best character in the play. Potentially."

"*But?*"

"These changes are very small, Aaron. They require next to no rewriting."

"*Tell me, goddammit.*"

"Well, Claire has this lesbianic love for Loretta, right?"

"Right."

"The lesbian stuff has got to go," Branch said.

Aaron grabbed for a cigarette. "You're out of your trick head, Scudder."

"There is no audience for a lesbian play. It's too sick. Nobody wants to see one and I don't want to produce one."

"There's no play if she's not a dike. You can't justify her calling up the rich kid and telling the truth. Love's the only reason."

"I couldn't agree more," Branch said.

"When girls love each other they're lesbians, Scudder."

"Who says Claire had to be a girl?"

"What are you talking about?"

"Make her a boy. It's so easy, Aaron, don't you see? Make her a boy and you don't even have to change her name—Clare can be a man's name too. It's perfect. The lesbianism goes—just like that—and you've got to admit a boy *could* make that call."

Aaron had to smile.

"Well?"

"It's crazy, Scudder. What the hell's a guy doing living in close quarters like that with a mother and daughter? It's a little rigged, if you ask me."

"Not if he's her brother," Branch said.

Aaron broke out laughing.

"It's not funny, Aaron."

"I'm laughing at something else."

"Well, stop."

In time, Aaron did.

"What do you think if Clare's her brother?" Branch said then.

"Scudder, that's incest."

"So?"

"Lesbianism's sick but incest is ginger peachy?"

"There's all the difference in the world. Lesbianism is cheap, sensational. Incest—Ford did it three hundred years ago—*'Tis Pity She's a Whore*. You'd just be giving new life to an old myth, Aaron. There's nothing cheap about that."

"I hope your boots are waterproof," Aaron said, " 'cause it's getting kinda deep in here." He began laughing again.

"Aaron, I'm not kidding!"

Aaron stopped. Quickly this time. "All right; what's the other change?"

"You'll do the first one, then?"

"I didn't say that. I just asked about the other."

"It's about Clare too. Aaron, I just don't think an audience—this is from a producer's point of view, remember—people have got to pay money to see this play, and I just don't think an audience is going to enjoy looking at a character club-footing his way around all evening long. It's painful to see, Aaron. And besides, that's not what the play's about. Clare doesn't have to have a clubfoot."

"There's got to be some kind of infirmity!"

"I couldn't agree more," Branch said. "What if he were deaf?"

"Deaf?"

"I think that's a perfect solution. From both of our points of view. There's nothing wrong with looking at a person who's deaf—you can barely see a hearing aid nowadays—and you've got to admit it's certainly an infirmity."

Aaron nodded. He put out one cigarette, lit another. "Why are we having this talk now?"

"Because we didn't have it a week ago."

"Meaning?"

"There's something you don't know, Aaron. You think my mother's the only one who's read the play. She loved it, and you think she's all, but she isn't. I gave it to some people two weeks ago. Very bright people. Rich and bright."

"And?"

"Well, they had some interesting comments."

"They hated it, didn't they?"

"Now, Aaron—"

"Goddammit, admit it—they hated it!"

"I'm not going to say anything as long as you insist on shouting."

Aaron lit a cigarette.

"That makes two," Branch said.

"I'll light fifty if I want," Aaron said. He flicked both burning cigarettes across the room.

"You're just crazy sometimes," Branch said. He got out of bed and retrieved the cigarettes.

Aaron had another lit and in his mouth.

Branch went to the bathroom, dropped the cigarettes down the toilet, flushed it. When he came back he said, "That was to give you time to calm down."

"It's a good play," Aaron said, his lips barely moving. Then: "Isn't it?"

"Of course it is."

"I had a bad experience once," Aaron went on softly. "With the novel I wrote. I don't think I could stand it if something like that happened again. I tried on this play, Branch. I really tried. Just as hard as I could."

"Aaron, it's a wonderful piece of work and it's going to be even better."

"But they did hate it?"

"Hate's a very strong word."

"I really tried on this play, Branch. Did you tell them that?"

"They all had lovely things to say about your talent, Aaron. Believe me."

"But they hated the lesbian part?"

"All of them. Yes."

"How many people did you give it to?"

"Five, six. It doesn't matter. Nobody liked the lesbian thing and nobody liked the idea of spending all night with a cripple. One of them suggested the deafness."

"They didn't want to invest any money?"

"Aaron, the money's my responsibility, so forget it." He lay back down in bed and turned off his bed lamp.

Aaron grabbed him. *"Now you tell me what they said!"*

"They said I was crazy to produce it. There. Now you know."

Aaron turned off his bed lamp. His cigarette glowed in the darkness.

"I'm sorry I had to tell you that, Aaron."

Aaron's cigarette glowed brighter.

"I want you to know if you try and take it to other producers, I won't hold a grudge."

"Will you produce it?"

"Will you change it?"

"I'll change it."

"I'll produce it."

"You know what, Scudder?"

"What?"

"You beat me."

"I guess I did."

"For the very first time."

"Probably won't happen again."

"I'm not so sure."

"Time will tell."

"Doesn't it always?"

• • •

The day Aaron started rewriting, Branch took the subway down to Orchard Street. He wandered around until, after about an hour, he saw what he was looking for. Up ahead of him, the other boy cut through the crowd and Branch followed, careful not to be seen. When the other boy entered an old building, Branch hurried across the street, hoping to find the floor, and a moment later the dark face appeared momentarily in a second-floor window. Then the face withdrew, down came the shade. Branch stood on the opposite sidewalk, his hands behind his back, staring. A little later he bought himself a paper and read it, staring up, every few lines, at the shade on the second-floor window. That was what he saw that day, and in the days ensuing: the shade. What he did not see was the dark figure on the roof behind him who crept onto the top of the fire escape—graceful, quiet, sad, still: watching.

The room was very small. There was a chair and a desk and a sink. The room was warm. Outside, there was no wind on Orchard Street. The boy lay on the bed, his head hurting. He wore white pants and a tee shirt and was barefoot. He got up and crossed the room, spinning the "cold" spigot on the sink, but the coolness could not seep behind his eyes. He spun the spigot the other way, turning it as far off as it got. The dripping was audible to him only when he stood nearby. He crossed back to his bed, lay down, closed his eyes. The knock came then.

"Mr. Miller?"

"The door is open."

"My card."

He half sat, taking the card from the balding man who smiled at him, dressed impeccably in gray suit and blue shirt and striped red tie and shined cordovans. "Yes, Mr. Scudder?"

"This is really the most incredible coincidence. I mean that. Coincidence of the very purest kind. You were outside a bit earlier this morning, yes?"

"Yes."

"Well—can you hear me? Am I speaking loudly enough?"

"Yes."

"The reason I ask is—that's where the coincidence part comes in—you see, I'm a producer—theatrical producer for now—and I've got this play I'm doing—brilliant thing, *Madonna with Child*—and the main part, you see, it calls for a young man about your age and looks and—here's the incredible part now—the script calls for him to be deaf, hard of hearing, whatever, you understand? And the second I saw you something just clicked and I thought, 'There's your actor, Branch'—you may call me Branch—it's really quite warm in here, isn't it? May I open the window?"

"It is open."

"Of course, of course, with the shade down I couldn't tell. Well, to go on, it would make the most marvelous publicity story—you understand, producer just wandering along, sees—well, you must read the play for yourself. I probably sound like an absolute lunatic going on this way, but you see I've *read* the play and I can just tell from talking to you now how perfect you are—it's one of those crazy wonderful coincidences that just happens sometimes, you understand—it's a superb part, best in the play—it will *make* whoever plays it—but why am I rambling on when you can see for yourself. Here—" and he handed over a typed manuscript— "see for yourself, read it. It's hot off the presses, as they say—this is the only true copy—I haven't even had time to have it mimeographed yet, the rewrites were just finished late last night and aren't I the lucky one, casting the crucial part just like that—go on, take it, take it, take it."

"Thank you very much, Mr. Scudder, but—"

"No buts now, no buts, no-no, you just do as I say, take it and—"

"I'd really rather not, thank—"

"Listen, I promise you I'm not as crazy as I may sound to you right now. I *know a certain amount* about the theater—I've wanted all my life to produce plays—and *I know whereof I speak*. Now, I understand your reticence and all that—I mean, if I came bursting in on me like this, I'd be reticent too—but you must have confidence in my judgment—can't you stop the sink from dripping? Really, it's maddening." He glared at the sink. "Forget it, it's not important. What is important is that you have faith in me and in my judgment and in this absolutely phenomenal coincidence that has brought us both together—and don't you worry if you're not experienced—ninety percent of the stars of this world can't act, but they have something else—they have what you have—I could tell it as soon as I saw you and now that I've talked to you I know it, I swear to Jesus God I'm telling the truth—*you can't take your eyes off them*—you watch them—that's what makes them special—not experience—no— *they dominate*—wherever they are, the circle forms around them—that is their essence, and it is yours—"

"Go away."

"If I were that easy to get rid of I wouldn't be much of a producer, would I now, Rudy? You don't mind my calling you that? You call me Branch and—"

"Go . . . *away*."

"I didn't expect this to be simple—"

"*Leave! Me! Alone!*"

"All right, you don't have to shout. After all, if that's the way you're going to feel I certainly don't want to bring the walls down around our heads now, do I? Perhaps we'll talk again, Rudy and—*wait! Wait just one second!* Didn't I see you once before? Weren't you at a party at the Dakota? Isn't that funny? It's the name—I heard somebody call the name

'Rudy' and when I just said it, well, something clicked. Why, we've probably got lots of friends in common." Branch smiled. "New York's nothing but a small town and that's the truth."

No reply.

"You believe me, don't you?"

No reply.

"Do you feel all right? You look tired. Are you tired? I've picked the wrong time, haven't I? I'll tell you what. Nap. Nap and I'll wait around and then we'll discuss all the people we probably know in common and I'll convince you that reading this script and playing the part is the most important single thing you've ever done in your entire—that damn sink, it's enough to drive you crazy." He pulled at his necktie, yanked it down. "Listen: you've got to do this." Branch grabbed for his handkerchief, wiped his neck. "I get a terrible shaving rash on my neck if—you'd think I wouldn't have much of a shaving problem." He touched the top of his head. "After all, I don't have much of a combing problem." He smiled, walked to the window, lifted the shade. "The truth is," he whispered suddenly, "that I saw you at the party and checked up on you because you're perfect for my play and I would have approached you then and there except we were in the midst of final rewrites and I couldn't." He turned to face the room. "There. Now you know." He wiped his neck again. "Is it getting red?" He gestured to his neck. "In the heat this shaving rash comes out and it kills me. I'm sorry I lied to you before—all that coincidence business—but I didn't want you to think that—well, the trouble with the truth sometimes is that it sounds so damn *premeditated.*" Perspiration poured down his forehead and he blinked and wiped his eyes and smiled. "I'm glad it's out in the open. I don't like lying—do you mind if I try fixing that damn sink?" He ran to it, twisted with both hands. The dripping continued. "I could deaden the sound with my handkerchief, but what would I wipe my neck with? I'm really caught, aren't I? If I used the handkerchief—I'll admit I wanted to get to know you too. Sometimes you just see people and you think they'd be interesting to know. The author of this play of mine, we met in the Army and got to know each other really only because I thought he was the kind of person that would be interesting to know. It happens." Branch laughed. "It shouldn't be this hot this time of year, you know that? Congress should enact some kind of— my neck is so sore already I can feel it burning." He pulled his necktie all the way off and stuck it in his coat pocket. "The truth is . . . the truth is . . . the truth is that . . . Isn't that crazy? I can't seem to say anything." He slumped into the chair and dropped the manuscript to the floor. "I tell you with this rash and that dripping sink and the way the heat digs at you . . ." He pushed to his feet and grabbed at the shade, pulling it back down. "Do you want it up? I shouldn't have just pulled it down without asking. Of course, it was down to begin with, so maybe you do—my neck is just on fire." He put his hands over his ears. "It must be a blessing, not having to listen to that sound all the time, that dripping, it's all I can hear and that's the truth . . . the truth . . . is too frightening . . . too . . . frightening . . . yes . . . and that's the first true thing I've said." He fell into the chair again, eyes closed, head down. "No . . . that about my neck . . . that was true . . . the heat . . . the rash . . . since I was ten . . . nine . . . eight . . . all my life I have dreamed of a black prince . . . and now you have come." Branch opened his eyes and stared at Rudy.

Rudy closed his eyes. "But I'm not like you."

"I would never come near you . . . never . . . you're my black prince . . . I would never touch you . . . you're not like the others . . . I've waited all my life for you . . . and now you've come . . . do you know what that means?"

Rudy turned his face to the wall.

"Help me . . . I've waited . . . help me . . . so long . . . you must . . . you can't refuse . . ."

"How did you know that?" Rudy said.

•   •   •

It was late afternoon and Aaron sauntered along 72nd Street, his Brooks Brothers tweed jacket tossed over his shoulder. It was really too warm to carry the tweed, but the idea of putting it away till autumn somehow saddened him, so he took it with him wherever he went, tossing it across his arm or over his shoulder, touching it every few minutes with his fingertips, the rough texture a never-failing balm. Aaron stuck a cigarette in the far corner of his mouth and lit it. Then he said, "Play it, Sam," because he had just seen *Casablanca* for the eleventh time and was—the usual effect from that picture—in a state of euphoria. Aaron entered his and Branch's building and pushed for the automatic elevator. It was on the eighth floor and it refused to budge. Aaron glared at the lighted "8" and inhaled. He and the elevator were at war and it was maddening. He pushed the button again, started to anger, stopped, said, "Not today." Shaking his finger at the machine, he smiled, turned, started walking up the six flights to their apartment. "You must remember this," Aaron said, "a kiss is still a kiss, a siiiigh is still a siiiigh. The fundamental things apply, as time goes by." He paused on the third-floor landing and lit another cigarette. He tossed the tweed jacket over his left arm and continued the rest of the way in silence. When he reached their apartment he unlocked the door and walked into the living room.

"Hi," Branch said.

"*Ingrid, it's you!*"

"Listen—"

"Why did you come to Casablanca? Out of all the bars in the world—"

"I took the script off to the mimeographers."

"Play it, Sam."

"*Aaron, I've got news!*"

"You're gonna take a bath? Not a second too soon, Scudder."

"I've got our Clare."

"Hmm?"

"I've found him, Aaron. He's going to be brilliant."

"You got an actor for the play?"

"If you'd shut up and listen—"

"Who-who-who?"

"Rudy Miller."

"Never heard of him."

"You will. Believe me, everybody will. He's a trifle inexperienced, but, oh, Aaron, God, the talent."

"You work fast, Scudder, I'll say that. Where'd you find him?"

"Just a silly bunch of coincidences. The point is, we've got him; he's ours."

"What's he done? Have I ever seen him?"

"Like I said, he's a trifle inexperienced, but we can compensate for that. As a matter of fact, I think the best thing would be to have him move in here. Right into the thick of things, so to speak."

Aaron looked out the window at Riverside Park. "Jesus, Branch, isn't that liable to make things just a little crowded?"

Branch sat down on the couch at the opposite end of the room. "That's a good point, Aaron." He wiped his neck with his handkerchief. "You're absolutely right. And I thought that maybe you wouldn't mind moving someplace for a little. It's all for the good of the play."

Aaron nodded. "If it's all for the good of the play, how could I mind? It won't be for long, though, will it?"

"Of course not."

"I tell you, Scudder, this guy better really be fantastic, evicting me like this."

"Take my word."

"Hell, I do. There's just one thing I'd like to know, though."

"Ask me?"

"What the fuck's going on?"

"Now, Aaron—"

"Who is he?"

"I told you—Rudy—"

"*Who is he?*"

"This fantastic find—"

"Where'd he come from?"

"His home, you mean?"

"You know goddam well what I mean." He crossed the room, grabbed Branch.

"Let go."

"Where?"

"I met him at a party."

"What party?"

"I forget."

"What par—"

"At the Dakota."

"Who was he?"

"I don't think you met him."

"What does he look like?"

"Just like our Clare, Aaron, now let me—"

"Describe him!"

"He's dark. And quite handsome, I think you'd have to say. And—let go of me, Aaron; I just don't understand you sometimes—he's perfect for us. Aaron, he's even deaf."

Aaron dragged Branch to his feet.

"Let go!"

"Yes, yes, I remember him—yes, he's quite handsome, you moldy lying bastard, and you think you're going to can me and bring him in, well, Scudder, tough, Scudder, you're not throwing Aaron out in the hot, not for him or any other black beauty you think you can get your hands on because I like it here, it's nice here, and if you want it less crowded *you* move out. I'm staying!"

"I've got you a room at the Y," Branch said.

Aaron broke out laughing.

"I'm not kidding, Aaron."

"Listen—*I* do not get thrown out by people like *you*! It does not happen that way. Not in this world."

"Aaron, I'm sorry about this."

"*There is nothing to be sorry about. Nothing is going to happen. There are to be no changes.*"

"Like I said, I got you a room at the Y. Take it or leave it."

"Consider it left."

"Aaron, this is *my* apartment, *I* pay the bills, I have the right—"

"You have *no* rights."

"Get out."

Aaron sat down in a chair. "Bring me a drink, Scudder. Scotch. Just a dash of soda."

"Get out!"

"And some Ritz crackers if we have any."

"I'll call the police. They'll come—"

Aaron started laughing again. "Insist on faggot coppers; they're apt to be a bit more understanding."

"Aaron, get out of my house now!"

"You made me a whore. You can't unmake me. I'm here."

Branch turned and hurried from the room.

"Where you going?"

Branch made no reply. In a moment he reappeared, carrying two suitcases. "I think I packed all your stuff," he said. "If I missed anything, well, you can pick it up later." He put the suitcases down in the living-room doorway. "Come along now, Aaron."

Aaron lit a cigarette. "I am going to punish you severely, Scudder. You had the audacity to touch my belongings. Here's how I'm going to punish you. Listen carefully. You put each item back, exactly where it was, and if you get it all perfect, I will suspend sentence. *But,* for each necktie out of place, each rumpled hankie, *you will pay and pay—*"

"Don't make me do something drastic," Branch said.

Aaron inhaled.

Branch crossed to him. "This is your last chance, Aaron. Or I'll throw you out. Yes, I will. I'll do that."

Aaron held up his cigarette. "If you reach for me, Scudder, I'll burn you."

Branch reached.

Aaron burned him. He brought the cigarette down onto the back of Branch's hand.

Branch yelled. "Aaron!"

"I warned you, Scudder."

"*And . . . I . . . warned . . . you!*" Branch fell on him, knocking the cigarette away, and they wrestled, struggling in the chair until it tipped over backward, dumping them onto the floor. They were neither of them fighters, and when Branch regained his feet first he didn't know what to do, so he waited, circling until Aaron was up, and then Branch charged and Aaron managed to sidestep and Branch careened into the sofa. Aaron fell on him there, striking down with rabbit punches at the back of Branch's neck, but most of them hit his head and Aaron cried out loud with the pain. Branch pushed him off and they circled again and then he charged, and this time Aaron got only half out of the way and they both fell down, tripping over the coffee table in front of the sofa, and Branch yelled "Dammit!" when his head hit the floor. Aaron crawled on him and started slapping. He slapped all over Branch's face and there was blood streaming from Branch's nose and Aaron kept slapping and slapping until his arms were tired. Then he lunged at Branch and they rolled kicking and screaming over the floor and Branch was slapping now and pulling Aaron's hair and shaking him, and when they were on their feet Aaron staggered back until the wall could hold him up and he gasped as Branch came at him, slapping at his face. Aaron fell, more from fatigue than the slapping, and Branch dropped on top of him and slapped him some more, but then his arms got tired and he lay on top of Aaron until Aaron managed to get loose. They both got slowly to their feet, panting, and Aaron was trying to curse but his wind was gone and Branch blinked one eye because the blood blinded him and Aaron stood still and then Branch closed his other eye and charged, catching Aaron in the stomach, carrying him along until they both collided with the wall and Aaron grunted and Branch shrieked and then everybody fell down.

Branch moved.

Aaron lay still.

Branch got to his knees, fell back, pushed up again, made it to his feet. He found the wall and followed it, out of the living room and down the hall and into the bedroom and out of that and then at last to the bathroom, where he dropped to his knees by the shower bath and leaned over the edge of the tub and turned the shower spigot on cold and after a moment he used the spigot as a brace and pushed himself up to his feet under the cold water. The blood washed from his eyes. He blinked. He stuck his face up close to the shower head and when he found that uncomfortable he fell to his knees and lay down in the tub, letting the water spray him as a little strength returned. Then he muttered "Aaron" and took a towel, wet it and made his way back to the living room.

Aaron was moaning. Branch lay the cool towel across Aaron's bloody face, wiping it clean. Aaron whispered, "Thank you."

Branch helped him to the sofa. Then he sat down beside him and they both stayed like that, very still, listening to their panting subside. When he could move, Aaron got to his feet. He was still unsteady.

"Take your time," Branch said.

"No. I better go," Aaron answered. "Do you think I ought to change shirts?"

Branch studied him. "Yes. The blood."

Aaron nodded.

"Let me help you," Branch said. He unbuttoned Aaron's shirt and slipped it off Aaron's bony shoulders. Aaron got another shirt from one of the suitcases. Branch held it up for Aaron to slip into. Aaron buttoned the shirt and tucked it inside his trousers "That's a hundred percent better," Branch said.

Aaron looked slowly around the apartment. "This is all sort of sad, you know?"

"I know."

"How long have we been together, off and on?"

"Long time," Branch said.

Aaron shook his head. "They don't have divorce laws for people like us. That would make everything easier somehow; I could worry about paying the legal bills and alimony and things like that. Take my mind off the central condition. The Y on Sixty-third?"

"Yes."

"What about the play?" Aaron said.

"The play is more important than ever now."

Aaron nodded, picked up his two suitcases. "I feel like Willy Loman," he muttered. "Can I call you tomorrow?"

"Please. You can meet Rudy then and everything. He's going to be brilliant, Aaron."

"I'm sorry about burning you. And the fighting. I just went sort of crazy. Nobody likes getting jilted, I guess." He walked slowly to the front door, then stopped. "One thing: people like us—everybody thinks we're flighty. I'm not and don't you be either. I haven't got many friends, Branch. I don't want to lose you. Promise me we'll stay that way."

"I promise," Branch said. "I swear."

Aaron took a last look around. "I've liked it here. It's been a home to me." Then he shrugged and smiled. "So I'll just have to find another, right?"

"Right."

"Thank God I can lose," Aaron said, opening the door. "You know, for a minute there I almost got sentimental. Me." He pushed for the automatic elevator. "I'm a lousy winner, I admit that, but when I lose, goddammit, I lose beautifully."

Dear Mrs. Scudder:
I hope you remember me. My name is Annie Withers and I went to Oberlin and did that dancing and stuff in that musical comedy tent, do you remember? I hope so. Anyway, pardon me for interrupting your busy life like this, but I just had to drop you a line and this is it. I am married now and living very happily with my husband who is a dear sweet boy and studying to be an electrical engineer (did I spell that wrong? isn't it terrible, not being able to spell your husband's occupation, but I've had trouble with that word ever since I was a child in grammar school).

Aaron lit a cigarette and tried to remember if there was anything else that Branch had ever mentioned about Annie Withers. Placing the cigarette in the far corner of his mouth, he closed one eye and continued typing.

Anyway, Mrs. Scudder, the thing is, I was just visiting in New York City the other day and who should I run into and spend a little time with but your son Branch. We talked and laughed about how we used to date and all the fun we had and—and—Mrs. Scudder I'm beating around the bush and here's why—

I'M WORRIED ABOUT BRANCH.

Oh, his health is fine and he's still the same handsome wonderful son you've always known and loved and who I was so crazy about but something's happened to him—

HE'S GOT A ROOMMATE.

"Careful," Aaron said out loud. He inhaled five or six quick times until the heat from the cigarette began hitting his lip. Then he lifted a glass ashtray and flicked his tongue, knocking the butt into the center of the glass. Aaron smiled at his trick, lit another cigarette, stuck it in the corner of his mouth, shut one eye and reached for his thesaurus. Opening it to the entry on "Sex," he began jotting down possible euphemisms. "You must remember this," he sang softly, "a kiss is still a kiss, a siiiigh, is still a siiiigh . . ." He looked at the letter again. "Be brilliant," he commanded, and began to type.

> *Mrs. Scudder, I have always been the kind of person who hated gossipy things, and I swear to you that I am not the kind of person who tells tales out of school, especially when I don't know exactly all the details of the tale I'm telling, and so what I will do is stick to the facts (like they're always saying on television) and let the chips fall where they may—This roommate's name is Rudy Miller and I don't quite know how to describe him to you. He's a strikingly handsome person and he is supposed to be an actor, except he's never I don't think acted in anything so how he got the lead in that brilliant play (so I hear) your son is producing, I'll never know.*

"And when two lovers woo, they still say I love you . . ." I wonder if the old bag's an anti-Semite?

> *Now I certainly think it is commendable of Branch, taking in an untrained Jewish actor and making him the star of his play, but I don't see why Branch has to support him at the same time, do you?*

"She'll pop her cork," Aaron said, starting to laugh. "Moonlight and love songs, never out of date; hearts full of passion, jealousy and hate . . ."

> *MRS. SCUDDER THAT BOY HAS SOME UNNATURAL HOLD ON BRANCH, I'M JUST ABSOLUTELY CONVINCED OF IT.*

> *Now I don't know what it is, and I'm the first to admit that this is none of my business, but I know how you love Branch and . . . well . . . to tell you the truth I guess I loved him too once and I hate to see this happening to him, whatever it is. But that Miller boy has something unnatural about him. He orders Branch around like Branch was his slave practically, and all the time Branch is paying for the food he puts in his mouth. It's unnatural.*

If I can just figure out how to use the word "unnatural" enough times, perhaps I can bring on menopause. Or, considering old Rose, bring it back. "It's still the same old story, a fight for love and glory . . ."

Well, Mrs. Scudder, I guess that's all I have to say. Please don't tell anybody about this and please don't above all do anything on just my saying that Branch is supporting this Jewish actor who's got some unnatural hold on him. I wish I had a prettier story to tell, Mrs. Scudder, but I know everything will work out just fine for all concerned. Branch is such a sweetheart as we both know and the unnatural people of this world, they sometimes try to take advantage of the sweethearts, but God looks after us all, Mrs. Scudder, and Thank God for that . . .

ANNIE

Rose read the letter in her living room. Or started it. Because, when she was halfway through, she jerked her head back and forth, put stubby fingers to paper and began to tear. She tore the letter into strips, the strips into shreds and then, with one wild gesture, scattered it across the floor. Rose stared at the mess, scowling. Then she gave a cry.

A moment later she was on her knees.

She crawled around the rug, gathering the bits, and when she had them all she smoothed them as best she could and began to order them back the way they were. It was laborious work, and her knees began to feel the strain, but she kept on, having trouble only with the word "unnatural," which seemed to appear a million times, and it was difficult to puzzle which one went where. By the time she realized the word meant the same in any sentence, the letter was back in some kind of legible form. Rose read it.

Over and over.

Mother Scudder came in in her wheelchair. She looked at her daughter-in-law. "Can I play?" Mother Scudder said.

"Play?"

Mother Scudder wheeled close. "The game," she said excitedly. "The game. With the puzzle pieces."

"It's a letter," Rose said.

"We could put it on the card table and play. I bet I beat you, Rose."

"It isn't a game, Mother."

Mother Scudder wheeled closer and squinted down. "Well, it certainly looks like a game. What is it?"

"A letter."

"Why didn't you say so in the first place?"

Rose stared at the pieces of paper.

"Who's it from? Good news or bad? What, what, what?"

Rose looked up. "Branch is coming home," she said.

Rose was the first one off the plane at Idlewild. She had no luggage, so she was almost to the taxi area before she remembered the way she must look. Doubling back, she entered the ladies' lounge and looked at herself in the mirror.

She had never been a beauty, but she looked as well now as she ever had in her life. She had kept her figure, and that hadn't been easy, because she was big-boned and tended naturally to gain, but she hated fat people—fat people looked old—so no matter the strain from her almost continual dieting, the knowledge that her waist was the same twenty-five and a half it had been on her wedding day provided an almost continual reward. Her legs—her best feature—were still as slender and shapely as any girl's, and her breasts, never large, were still firm. Rose unbuttoned the jacket of her raw-silk suit. It was dark green, and the china-silk print blouse beneath picked up the color. Rose took off the jacket, tucked in the blouse. Then she smoothed the blouse, running her stubby hand down from the swell of her breasts to the flat of her stomach. She put her hands on her hips and inhaled. She stood five-four and had yet to weigh a hundred and thirty pounds, and she nodded to her image as she took a comb and began fluffing her brown hair into place. She found her lipstick, dabbed just a trace of it onto her thin lips, ran her tongue across her lips until they glistened. Then she put her jacket back on, hurried out into the May afternoon, and took a taxi to 72nd Street.

Branch was surprised to see her. "Rosie!" he said.

"Hi, hon."

"*Rosie!*" Branch said again.

"Aren't you gonna invite me in?"

Branch bowed. "Come in, come in."

Rose moved through the foyer into the living room. Then she held out her arms. "Aren't you gonna give me a kiss?"

Branch went to her, kissed her cheek, hugged her. "You look *fantastic.*"

Rose smiled.

"Twenty years old at the outside."

"You've got your father's charm." She sat down on the sofa, tapped the empty cushion beside her.

Branch sat down beside her. "I'm giving you three to tell me."

"Tell you what, hon?"

"Will you get her?" Branch said. "Appears from the blue without a word of warning and then says, 'Tell you what, hon?' " Branch took her hand and examined the palm. "Can't read a thing," he said. "I give. Why're you here?"

"You're glad, aren'tcha?"

Branch smiled. "Horrified."

Rose dropped her voice and looked around. "Are we alone?"

"Course we're alone. My God, who do you think should be here?"

Rose shrugged. "I just wondered."

Branch got out a handerkerchief and snapped it at her playfully. "You still haven't told me." He began drying his neck.

"I won a contest," Rose said, and she stood up and stretched and started walking around the room.

"You won a what?"

" 'Scuse me a sec," Rose said, and she left the room, walking down the corridor to the bedroom.

Branch followed her. "What can I do for you?"

"Just want to freshen up," Rose answered, and she moved into the bathroom and closed the door.

"Lemme get you a fresh towel," Branch called through the door.

"I'm fine," Rose said. "How are your teeth?"

"My teeth?"

"One toothbrush is all I ever needed."

"Oh," Branch said. "That. Well, I've been having a little gum trouble."

"You never told me. We talked every Sunday and you never once mentioned it. I thought we didn't keep secrets."

"I didn't want to worry you," Branch called. He hurried into his bedroom and got out another handkerchief from his top right-hand bureau drawer.

"It's that serious?" Rose said.

"No-no—the whole point is it *isn't* serious. I didn't want to upset you over a trifle. My gums have been bleeding and I got a different toothbrush, a softer bristle, you see, so that my gums wouldn't bleed so much. The dentist I go to suggested it. It helps a lot."

"That's good," Rose said. She opened the bathroom door. "I feel ever so much better now."

"Now what about this contest?" Branch said.

Rose took his arm and held it against her as they strolled back through the bedroom into the living room. "Oh. Well, they had this contest in West Ridge. To see who wanted the most to come visit New York

City. The Best Reason Contest, it was called. And I won. I had the best reason for coming to New York. Guess what it was?"

They sat back down on the sofa. "I give up," Branch said.

"To see you, silly; that was all I put down and I won the contest."

"I don't understand."

"Well, pay *attention*, Branch. There was this contest in West Ridge to see who had the best reason—"

"You're fooling around with me."

"You mean lying to you, don't you?"

"Mother—"

"You don't believe about the contest. Well, you're right, except you say I'm fooling around and I call it lying. I'm lying to you. Do you ever lie to me?"

"Of course not."

"I know, Branch. Let me ask it again: do you ever lie to me?"

"*We never lie to each other and you know it.*" He got up and walked to the window.

"Don't get so excited, hon."

Branch mopped his neck. "I just don't like the whole tenor of things. You come in here surprising me—which isn't like you—and then you all but practically *accuse* me of lying—and that isn't like either of us, and—"

"Honey . . . honey . . . didn't you hear me? I said 'I know.' "

"Know what, for God's sake?"

"About the Jew."

Branch stared out at the Hudson. "I know I'll wake up any minute. My own mother, the world's most levelheaded lady, comes in from nowhere and starts talking some gibberish about some nonexistent Jewish—"

"Miller; isn't that the name? Rudy Miller? Something like that."

"I can just feel myself waking up any minute now."

"*Branch!*"

"My neck is just absolutely giving me fits."

"*Turn around. Branch. Now. Look at me.*"

Branch turned. "Yes, Mother?"

"Don't make me get upset. Please."

"All right, Mother."

"Where is he?"

"Out."

"Good."

"He should be back in a while."

"That doesn't matter."

Branch looked at her.

"We'll be long gone," Rose said.

Branch leaned against the window.

"Get in there and pack," Rose said, and she gestured with her thumb toward the bedroom.

"How did you find out?"

"Never mind. Get in there and pack."

Branch ran to her. "Now you listen, Rosie—"

"Branch—"

"Rosie, you've got to listen!"

"All right, hon; go ahead. Rosie's all ears."

"I didn't think there was any reason to tell you. He's just been here a little, that's all. He's going to be in my play."

"I know, hon. Go on."

"How did you know?"

"Go on, hon. You've got your mother's attention; take it while you got it."

"He's very inexperienced. Brilliant, but everyone thought it would be a good idea if he were here for a little where I could help whenever he needed—"

"I knew it was a mistake letting you come here in the first place. Sometimes I think I should just have my head examined for—"

"There's nothing wrong with taking in a roommate, Rosie."

"That's right, hon. Let's go pack." She stood up.

Branch stood beside her. "You don't mean go home, do you? You can't mean leave town. Not now!"

"Just take enough to scrimp by on. I'll take care of the rest later." She started in toward the bedroom.

Branch followed her. "This thing is all out of proportion in your mind, Rosie. My God—"

Rose opened the first closet she came to. "Good," she said, and she picked out a canvas suitcase. "This'll be fine."

"Rosie, you're acting silly—"

"Look!" Rose whirled. "Ya see? Ya see my hands?" She dropped the suitcase, held her stubby fingers before her child's eyes. "Tell me what they're doing."

"Shaking."

"That's right. They are shaking! And I am trying to keep them under control! I am trying to keep them still but I can't. I can't control my hands! Now I'm asking you, Branch, as a favor—don't make me get upset. *Please!*" She grabbed the suitcase, hurled it onto the bed.

Branch stayed in the doorway, staring at it.

"Honey," Rose whispered. "Please do as I say."

Branch moved to the bed.

"Mother knows best," Rose said.

Branch opened the suitcase, spread it flat. Then he said, "I'm not a kid anymore, Rosie. You can't just order me around any way you like."

"You're only wrong for one reason," Rose said.

Branch waited.

"Money," Rose said.

Branch said nothing.

"As long as Rosie pays the bills, Rosie gives the orders."

"I'll pay you back every penny."

"No need, hon. I do with my money what I want. I don't put my son in debt. I just look out for his well-being, that's all."

"My God, Mother, eighty trillion guys in Manhattan have roommates. It's no sin."

"Pretty view," Rose said, staring out the window at the Hudson. "I'll watch it while you pack."

"I've got some little stocks. I'll sell them."

"Sure you have. Sure you will."

"I don't need your money, Mother."

"We're having kind of a cool May," Rose said. "Pack accordingly."

"Mother, you can't make me go home just because I've got a roommate for probably a few days at the outside. You just can't."

"Branch, please pay attention—I don't like losing my temper. It frightens me when I do. I mean that and you know I do. I hate it. I hate it. Please. For me, Branch, look at my hands—see?" The hands were trembling worse now, and Rose's face was starting to drain of color. "It's not on account of roommates—" she started moving in on him—"and you know it and I know it and there are some things you just don't say and they will not be said now." She was almost on top of him, circling around the bed, advancing while he backed away. "And I like being a woman and when I lose my temper I feel almost like a man and I hate that, *so do as I say, Branch, or dare the consequences!*"

"All right," Branch whispered. "All right."

Rose smiled.

Branch closed his eyes. "I never could fight you."

Rose gave him a quick hug. "That's because when we argue—not fight, baby—we don't fight, we just argue sometimes—but when we do, Rosie's right and you know it and that's why you give in to Rosie, 'cause she's right, baby."

Branch nodded and started opening his bureau drawers.

"I'll fill you in on gossip from home," Rose said, crossing the room, returning to the window.

Branch took socks and underwear and folded them into the blue canvas case.

"Mother's taking to her chair just like a duck to water. Wait till you see her scoot around corners and things. I tell her I'm going to enter her at Indianapolis for that speedway and she just laughs and laughs."

Branch got some handkerchiefs and neckties and pressed them down on top of the underwear.

"And business. Well, West Ridge, you'd think it was Valhalla or they'd just discovered oil. People are moving in from all over. There's that new factory out at the edge of town—isn't that silly, I forget what it makes, but they're responsible for some of the growth."

Branch was perspiring from the effort and his shirt was soaked in the middle of his back and under his arms, so he ripped it off and got a towel, drying his skin before going back and packing some more.

"Then, of course, there's the developers," Rose said.

Branch was having difficulty breathing.

Rose noticed it. "What's the matter?"

Branch shook his head.

"Tell me."

"No."

"Tell me."

"I just did," Branch gasped. "No." He sat down hard on the bed.

Rose went to him and put her hand to his forehead. "You feel hot."

"I'm not going with you, Rosie."

"You shouldn't sit around half naked like that. You're just asking to catch something."

"I'm not going with you, Rosie."

"You just rest. I'll help you pack," Rose said. She unbuttoned her green silk jacket.

"Hear me!"

"Now, you've got socks and ties and hankies. Shirts. Shirts you need. Which drawer do you keep—"

Branch put his head in his hands. "I'm not going," he whispered.

"That's right, hon; you just rest." She got some shirts, started to fold them into the case, paused, took off her jacket, tucked in her blouse.

Branch stood up. "I'm not leaving."

"That makes kind of a stalemate, hon. 'Cause I'm not leaving you here."

"I've got enough money for a while. I'll be fine."

Rose smoothed her blouse, running her hands over the curve of her breasts to her flat hard stomach. "I'm not leaving you here," she said.

"Goodbye, Rosie."

"Not with him," Rose said.

"*Goodbye,* Rosie."

"Not with the likes of him. Your father and I didn't work all our lives so our money could be spent on people like him."

"You don't even know him."

"I know enough."

"What do you know?"

"Let's not go into it, Branch."

"*What do you know?*"

"You're supporting a pervert," Rose said, "and I'm not leaving you here."

"You're funnier than Jackie Gleason, you know that, Rose?" He started to laugh.

"Shut up."

"What kind of a pervert is he, Rose?"

"I said shut up!"

"Is he a peeping Tom, a *voyeur*? Is he—"

"Branch, stop!" Rose cried. "Now." She ran at him, her stubby hands searching for his mouth.

Branch fought her off. "He's a fag, that's what you mean."

"I don't know that word—"

"Ho-mo-sex—"

"*Some things are not said!*"

"*He's* not—*he's* not. *I* am!"

"Never!"

"Always—" Branch said.

"The girls are crazy for you—"

"Never—"

"Always—" Rose said.

"Watch me walk, Mother—watch me swish—I can swish if I want

to—I'm good at it—" he dropped his wrist, shot a hip out, started to walk—"See?"

"Stop." Rose closed her eyes.

"Watch!"

Rose's eyes opened.

Branch paraded for his mother.

"I'll kill him," Rose whispered.

"You will?"

"I'll kill him with my hands."

"Why?"

"He did this to you. I'll kill him."

"Now, Rosie," Branch said, "we all know who did what to who, don't we?" He started toward her.

"Branch—"

"Remember when you put me in your clothes? Fun? I'll tell you something—"

"I brought you up to be a man. Like your father. That's all I ever did, I swear to God."

"The last guy I *kept*—"

"Big and strong," Rose mumbled. "I swear."

"Aaron—anyway, old Aaron, he kept trying to make me admit that I had an Oedipus complex—you understand, don't you?—that I wanted my mother. Well, I used to deny it because frankly, Rose, you fill me with the shudders—every time you've touched me, every time you've ever pinched me or patted me or run your stubby hands across your goddam breasts it has filled me with such revulsion—"

"Some things . . . are . . . not spoken aloud . . ."

Branch grabbed her. "Let's face the music and dance," he said, and with that he began to spin with her, out of the bedroom and down the corridor, around and around and around.

Rose began to cry.

"*Put your arms around me, honey, hold me tight.*" Branch bawled the words out. "Sing, Rosie. We're together at last, Rosie. You've got a real shape, you know that, Mother? It's too bad I'm queer, Mother, or I could go for a mother like you, Mother," and he whirled her into the living room. "Do you know how I have felt year after year cowering in front of you, Rosie?"

Rose slipped to her knees.

Branch dropped beside her. "I don't think the orchestra's quite finished, Mother, sweet Mother, come home to me now, Mother, sweet Rosie o'mine, stop crying, stop crying, listen, you should be happy I'm queer, I mean never any daughter-in-law problems, look on the bright side." He shook her with his hands. "Touch me, go on, don't you want to sure you do all these years admit it go on I'm here no one can see go on touch me touch me—"

"*Jesus!*" Rose screamed and she shoved at him, pushing him back and down, and she tried scrambling to her feet, but he recovered and pulled at her, pulled her down, his hands grabbed and she struggled but he was strong, too strong, and for a long moment their mouths were very close—

Branch gagged.

Rose ran screaming.

Branch doubled up on the living-room floor, his hands around his knees.

XXIII

Walt lay in his bed, trying not to sneeze, but as the urge grew he sat up and began grunting, "Huh-huh-huh—"

"Quick put your finger under your nose!" Tony said.

Walt quick put his finger under his nose, held it there until he sneezed. "You're what they call a help," he muttered then. "*Merci.*" He was wearing red-striped pajamas and he lay down flat again, listening to Tony doing things in the kitchen. His Greenwich Village apartment consisted of a living room–bedroom, a kitchen and a bath. The bathroom was small, but it was bigger than the kitchen, and the two of them together were almost equal in square footage to the living room–bedroom. His lease described the place as a 3½, and Walt wondered for a long time what that could possibly mean, before he finally decided it referred to the distance in feet from the floor to the ceiling.

Tony shrugged. "Sometimes it works."

Walt pulled the quilt up to his neck. "Who gets colds in the middle of May? Ridiculous."

"Fools and Kirkabys," Tony told him, and she hurried to the bed, holding a large steaming glass. "Drink this."

Walt took it, looked at it dubiously. "What's in it?"

"Tea and honey and sugar and brandy and lemon."

"No saltpeter?"

"You poor feeble creature, your body supplies enough of that naturally."

Walt slapped the empty side of the bed. "Put your money where your mouth is."

Tony sat down in the one overstuffed chair. "Drink the drink."

Walt slapped the bed again. "I dare you."

"Oh God," Tony said. "Ever since I was *fool* enough last fall to let you spend the night you haven't given me a moment's peace."

Again Walt slapped the bed. "A moment's piece—that's what I'm talking about."

Tony got up from the chair. She wore a white blouse and tight black slacks and sandals. "If you're not going to drink that, I'll take it back to the—you should pardon the expression—kitchen."

As she reached the bed, Walt grabbed for her.

"Now, dammit! You get me to come down here tonight because you're so sick. All right, I came. That's my part of the bargain. Now you act sick, phony."

"I *am* sick," Walt said. He coughed for her. "Hear that?" He took a sip of the drink. "Yum."

Tony went back and sat down. "Your apartment depresses me."

Walt glared at her. "It so happens I'm not a big-deal copywriter jingle girl."

"I don't mind that it's small. I don't even mind the corny way you've got it decorated." She gestured to the Lautrec prints and the bullfight posters. "I simply object to the dirt, Walt. Is that so terrible?" She shook her head. "I mean, I passed my Village phase. Why can't you?"

"You're no Jane Russell," Walt said.

"What?"

Walt sighed. "Nossir, you haven't got half the compassion Jane Russell had."

"What are you talking about? I said that you should grow up and get out of Greenwich Village and live someplace *clean* and—"

"Jane Russell had heart."

"Will you shut up about Jane Russell?"

Walt locked his lips and threw the key away.

"Explain first."

Walt gestured to his closed lips and shook his head.

"You know it drives me *right* up the walls when you do this."

Walt nodded vigorously.

"All right, if I get you the key, will you talk?"

Walt continued to nod.

Tony got up, mimed finding a key on the floor, handed it to Walt.

Walt reached for a pad and paper and wrote, "That's the wrong key" and handed it to Tony.

"The horrible thing is you really think you're funny." She got another key and handed it over.

"When-Billy-the-Kid-got-sick-in-*The-Outlaw*-Jane-Russell-got-in-bed-with-him-so-he'd-feel-better-faster-because-she-had-heart-and-compassion-not-like-some-people-I-might-mention!"

"*I don't want to get in bed with you!*" She began to pace around the room.

"I'm very sick," Walt said. "I'm not responsible for my actions."

Tony sank into the chair and stared at the cracked ceiling.

"Now don't say, 'Maybe we're seeing too much of each other, Walt.' "

"You have an amazing gift for anticipating me, you know that?"

"Just 'cause we're fighting a little doesn't mean anything. Lots of people fight a little." He pushed his glasses up snug against the bridge of his nose with his left thumb. "I'm only kidding about the sack. I'm glad you're a virgin; you know that."

Tony shook her head. "You're trying to make me ashamed of what I am and I don't like it all that much."

"The only thing I don't like about your being a virgin is the word 'virgin.' It's got to be one of the ten worst words in the language, along with 'crotch' and 'pimple' and 'bowels.' Please say you believe me."

Tony nodded. "I do. And 'belly.' "

"And 'urine specimen,' " Walt said.

"And 'fungus.' "

And the phone rang. "Yeah," Walt said. "Yeah. Hi . . . Yeah, yeah, yeah. Sure. Great. . . . All the way west on Eleventh. When you hit the Hudson, swim back half a block and you're here. S'long." He hung up. "Branch Scudder," he said. "What do you know?"

"Who he?"

"You know; that guy I didn't introduce you to that night, remember? The one I put the show on with back at Oberlin. To this day, so I'm told, we are fondly remembered."

"What did he want?"

Walt shrugged. "Beats me. Branch claims to be like an off-Broadway producer, except what that is is probably wish fulfillment." He looked at Tony. "Don't say it."

"Don't say what?"

"That I claim to be a director but that's wish fulfillment too."

"I wasn't going to say a thing like that. I would never—"

"Oh, come on, admit it; it was on the tip of your tongue. I don't blame you. I say I'm in the theater but who'm I kidding? Every time I think of that show we did and how easy it was and how well it went and I think about now and the way things are going—" He pounded one fist suddenly into the other. "Goddam but I was a stupid bastard in those days. It's so humiliating. It just is."

"You are really paranoid if you think I would have said a thing like you said I was about to say."

"Yeah-yeah-yeah, maybe I am," Walt said, getting out of bed. He went to the bathroom and turned on the hot water and took off his pajama top.

"What are you shaving for? You hot for this guy or something? You don't shave for me."

Walt splashed some water on his face. "Maybe it's business."

Tony folded her arms. "I'm insulted."

"Well, don't be. Branch and me, we've got what you call a 'New York Relationship.' We never see each other, and when we do, what we talk about is how we never see each other, and then we never see each other again for a while." He spread lather on his face and started shaving.

Tony stood up and stretched. "I shall disappear discreetly into the night."

"Hang around."

"You said it might be business."

"Just don't listen. If we handle it right, maybe he'll taxi you back up-town."

Tony sat back down. "Sold," she said.

"I wonder what he wants," Walt said. "It's after nine o'clock. You'd think it could've waited till morning. Maybe it's important, what do you think?" He continued to shave.

Tony watched him. "What a build," she said.

Walt made a muscle, did a double-take, then started looking around for it. "I could've sworn it was here this morning."

Tony smiled. "Boys like talking about girls' bodies all the time, don't they?"

"Some do. Frankly, I have never stooped to anything so common." He finished shaving, splashed on some cold water, then some aftershave. "What the hell could old Jiggles want?" he muttered as he put on his pajama top and walked past Tony, back to the bed.

"That does it," Tony said.

"Huh?"

"For the first time all night you look like a human being and you walk right by me without even—"

"Baby," Walt said, and he grabbed for her, brought her into his arms, tried to kiss her.

"Don't," Tony said. "I can't afford to catch your cold."

Walt held her tight with one hand, tried unbuttoning her blouse with the other.

"Not that either," Tony whispered. "Your friend's coming, remember?"

Walt let her go. "What can I do?"

"You can't kiss me on the mouth and you can't take my clothes off." She held out her arms to him. "Anything else is fine," she whispered.

"I don't know what's left but it's a deal," Walt said, and he buried his head in her neck, then blew in her ear.

"You must shave more often," Tony said. "You're practically irresistible."

"Damn that 'practically,'" Walt said. His hands moved across her white blouse until they reached her breasts.

"Oh, Walt, God," Tony whispered.

"Stay after he's gone," Walt said. Gently, he squeezed her breasts, started backing her toward the bed. "I'll get rid of him fast." Again he blew in her ear.

"What *is* that aftershave?"

"Aphrodisiac Number Six," Walt whispered. "I love you."

"Why do you only say that when we're having physical contact?"

"Only a Sarah Lawrence girl could ask a question like that at a time like this." He held her very tight, pressed her close.

"Answer me."

"Lemme kiss you."

"No; you're sick."

"I'm dying this way." He lowered her to the bed, followed her down.

"You think I'm not?"

"Stay when he's gone? Promise? I'll have him out of here so fast—"

"No, business is business; it's liable to be important. You said so."

"You're all that's important, dammit, so please—"

"Don't ask me—"

"I've gotta kiss you. I can't just touch you and not kiss you—I can't and survive," and he reached for her face.

"No." Tony sat up and took a deep breath. She ran her hands through her hair. "What must I look like? Oh God, why is he coming?" She hurried to the bathroom and shut the door.

Walt lay in bed, eyes closed, and mouthed the word "bitch" over and over.

When the buzzer sounded a few minutes later, Tony was sitting prettily in the overstuffed chair. Walt went to the door, opened it, buzzed back. "Jiggles," he said then, stepping into the hallway.

"Egbert," Branch said.

"*Egbert?*" from inside the room.

"Me and my big mouth," Walt said, following Branch into the apartment. "Tony Last, this is Branch Scudder. Branch—Tony."

Tony glanced at the top of his head. "Hi," she said.

"How do you do," Branch said, smiling.

Tony got up and walked over to the Lautrec poster. "I won't hear a word," she promised.

Branch smiled again, rubbed his bald head, turned to Walt. "Good to see you. We never see each other."

"We never do." Walt nodded. "We've gotta start." He lay down in bed.

"Yes," Branch agreed. "Are you sick?"

Walt shook his head. "Just one of these damn spring colds. What's up?"

Branch handed him a mimeographed manuscript. "Read this, would you please?"

Walt glanced at the title. "*Madonna with Child.*"

"Will you read it?"

"Course I will, if you ask me to."

Branch sat down on the bed. "Here are the facts," he said, his voice very low. "The script is brilliant. The money is *all raised.* I need a director. If you like it, if you're *genuinely enthusiastic,* we'll go right into production off-Broadway."

"Into production?"

Branch nodded.

"You mean, if I like it, I can *do* it? The money's all raised and everything's set and like that?"

"If you're *genuinely enthusiastic,* it's yours."

Walt lay back and closed his eyes. "You really think I'm the one to direct this? You think I can do it right and everything?"

"We were successful once; I don't see any reason why we shouldn't be again." He stood. "It's going to *make* the off-Broadway season, Walt, I just know it. Take your time, read it, think about it, then call me."

Walt nodded, started to get up.

"No-no, stay in bed. I'll let myself out." Branch turned toward the door.

"Walt tells me you're from Oberlin too," Tony said.

Branch looked at her and nodded.

"Are you another Greenwich Villager?"

"Oh no; I live up on West Seventy-second Street," Branch said.

"I lived in the Village once but I passed that phase; I keep wishing Walt would reach it. You couldn't drag me back here."

"Where do you live now?" Branch asked.

"Sort of just across the park from you."

Walt lay very still, watching them, but mostly her.

"Could I give you a lift or anything?" Branch asked.

"Gee, wouldn't that be nice," Tony said. "You're sure it's not inconvenient?"

"Fine," Branch said.

"Well, I was going to leave anyway . . ." She turned to Walt. "You sure you're gonna be all right? I mean you won't need me for anything more?" She looked back at Branch. "I'm sort of nursemaid for the night."

Branch smiled at her.

So did Walt.

"I'll stay if you like, Walt; if you need me, just say the word."

"I'll survive," Walt told her. "Thanks, Branch."

"My pleasure."

Tony kissed Walt on the cheek. "Love me," she whispered. Then she waved and skipped on out the door. "This is really awfully nice of you," she said to Branch as they started outside.

Branch smiled at her.

"You're looking at me a lot," Tony said. "May I ask why?"

Branch flushed. "No reason. Because you're pretty. I'm sorry."

Tony laughed. "Listen; did I say I didn't like it?"

Branch smiled at her. They walked on outside into the May night. Branch stopped and looked back at Walt's building. Then he shook his head. "I don't understand," he said.

"What don't you?"

"Oh, Walt's living that way."

"I don't like it either. He's promised me that as soon as he hits with something, he'll move."

"I don't know," Branch said. "Everybody's got his own problems, but I'll tell you, if my father owned the Kirkaby stores, I wouldn't wait."

"Now I don't understand."

"The stores. The discount houses."

"Oh," Tony said. "Those. Well . . ." And she shrugged.

"I suppose I've never really understood Walt, though. Back in college, when we were doing that show . . ." And he went on talking.

Tony found it very hard to pay attention.

When their taxi reached her building, she thanked Branch and hurried inside, waiting impatiently for the elevator, jabbing her thumb at the call button again and again. She rode up to her apartment in silence, unlocked the door, went to the bedroom, fell on the bed. She undressed lying flat, kicking her clothes to all sides. Then she went into the bathroom, turned on the tub, poured in a double portion of bubble bath. She went to the kitchen, poured a double portion of Grand Marnier, went back to the bathroom, got in the tub. "Damn," she said, scrambling out, running wet and naked to the magazine rack in the living room, grabbing *The Reporter*, putting it back, taking *Vogue* instead, dashing back into the tub, lying down, saying "Ahhhhh" half a dozen times unconvincingly. She snapped her fingers then, said "Ronnie Lewin" and dashed out of the tub again, clutching a towel around her, running to her bed phone, picking up the address book. "Lewin, Lewin, Lewin," she said, turning pages. "Yes," she said, spreading the book before her, starting to dial. "No!" she said when the number began to ring. She slammed the phone down. *"It doesn't matter!"* Her voice was very loud in the quiet apartment. She looked down at the puddle on the floor, dropped the towel, dried the puddle by moving the towel with her feet, then picked it up between her toes, grabbed it, and carried it back into the bathroom. She sat down in the tub for the third time, opened *Vogue*, stared at a few of the models. "You're not fooling me—you're all boys in drag," Tony said, and she pitched the magazine onto the floor.

Humming, she bathed and shaved her legs and played catch with the handfuls of bubbles, and then she undid the stopper with her toes and stood up, looked around and said "Moron," because she had used the only towel to dry the puddle and that meant she had to run out naked again, this time to the linen closet, grabbing a fresh towel, commencing to rub her body. When she was dry, she walked to the telephone again, picked it up, checked Ronnie Lewin's number just to make sure she had it right, said it out loud, "Yukon 8-5737" and hung up the phone. Tony trekked back to the bathroom singing, "Here she is, Miss America, here she is, your ideal . . ." She put on a perfumed body lotion, covered it with talcum. Then she spread cleansing cream all over her face, took it off with a tissue, put on an astringent with a cotton ball, covered that with a night cream because her skin was getting dry, and set to work on her hair. She fumbled with curler after curler, finally getting them as right as she ever would, grabbed her fluffy blue night cap, spread it over the works and flicked out the bathroom light. She dialed for the correct time, got it, moved her alarm clock ahead two minutes, set the alarm for half past seven so she could reset it again for eight when half past seven came, pulled off her bedspread, folded it neatly, dropped it on the floor and fell into bed. She fluffed the pillow, put the cooler side up, lay gently down into it, adjusted the sheet over her and closed her eyes. She yawned and stretched and yawned again. Then she said "Who are you kidding?" and called Ronnie Lewin on the phone. "Ronnie . . . ? Hi, it's me. . . . Me, silly—Tony Last. Hi. Here's the thing, Ron. . . . No, I couldn't wait until tomorrow at the office, and I'll tell you why if you just h-u-s-h—because I'm in an absolute *frenzy of rage.* . . . You're from St. Louis, aren't you? . . . I sort of remembered that. . . . So *listen,* Ron . . . Ron, you may *not* have my body—*lisssss*-on. I was out with some old bag couple from St. Louis tonight. . . . Their names don't really matter, Ron. . . . Herman or Franklin something—I can't remember hers at all—but what they did was what every hick from out of town does, they *knock* New York. . . . Ron, if I could remember their names I wouldn't tell you—what if you knew them or something, huh? . . . So anyway, I got in this argument with this old-bag lady, who said everything about New York was stinko. . . . I don't know why I did it, Ron, I just did it, and she started with the stores—you know, I mean, New York's *world famous* for its stores—and this fink lady from St. Louis kept saying Bergdorf's stunk and . . . of course *I* hate Macy's, Ron—how everyone who's ever shopped at Macy's hates it—the point is I couldn't back down and let this harpie think she was right. . . . Ron, their names are of *absolutely no importance* will you just listen I *told* you I was in a *frenzy.* . . . You needn't apologize, Ron, just *fermez* the old *bouche* and we'll get along fine. . . . The reason I'm pausing is because I'm embarrassed, Ron, because we finally got into an argument, this harridan and yours truly, a real screamer, and I'm embarrassed to tell you what we argued about. Ready? Don't laugh now. *Discount houses.* . . . I mean it, we argued about discount houses—*me* defending Korvette's, can you picture it? . . . But she really got to me, gassing on about some store in St. Louis, Kirkahead's, and . . . What, Ron? . . . Kirkaby's? Well, same difference, who cares, the point is, she *swore* it was not only better than Korvette's, but bigger too, and I said she was out of her trick head and I thought you being from St. Louis . . . I mean, I just had to be proved right or I knew I'd never sleep tonight. . . . It is a big chain? . . . Really big, Ron? Well, what do you know; not as big as Korvette's, though, right? In other words, Ron, what you're saying is that there is a big chain of stores in St. Louis named Kirkaby's but that it doesn't compare in size to Korvette's, so that in actuality this woman was full of it just like I thought. . . . Thanks, Ron, it's always nice to be proved right. . . . I tell you, I feel like a real nut, calling you this way. . . . You're a good brownie, Ron, night-night."

Tony went into the bathroom for her Grand Marnier glass, emptied it, went to the kitchen and filled it again. She carried it to bed and sipped it, staring at the darkness. In time, the glass was empty. Tony felt languid. She set the glass down and fluffed her pillow. She lay very still. With what energy remained to her she said, *"It means nothing!"* again, louder than before.

That night she dreamt of diamonds.

Walt neither dreamt nor slept.

By one in the morning he had the play read and, stopping only to heat a cup of consommé, he started all over again, Act One, Scene One, taking notes this time, jotting down things in the margin. This was a slower reading, and it was almost five o'clock before he finally put the manuscript down. He turned off the lights and lay quiet for a moment before switching the lights back on. Sleep was out of the question, because maybe it wasn't a brilliant play; maybe it wasn't even good.

But, goddammit, I can make it work!

I can, I think. I think I can I think Ican IthinkIcan IthinkIcanI thinkIcan.

"I got a play!" Walt shouted.

Madonna with Child, directed by Walt Kirkaby. Directed by E. Walters Kirkaby. Directed by Egbert Walters Kirkaby. Directed by Egbert Goddam Walters Kirkaby. Directed by *Me*.

"Me-me-me-me-me," Walt sang. "Do-re-me-fah-*me-me-me-me-me-me!*" He looked at his watch. Five-ten. What were the odds on old Branchereeno being up at ten past five? About the same as *anybody* being up at ten past five. Crummy. Walt pushed his glasses up snug against the bridge of his nose with his left thumb. Then he whirled from bed, threw on some clothes and took off out the door. He had gone half a block before he began to sneeze, and that made him remember his cold, so he dashed back to his apartment and grabbed a scarf and tied it around his neck. Then he took off for outside again, sneezing as soon as he hit the street, but now his conscience was clear.

Hands in pockets, Walt skipped his way through Greenwich Village.

Good morning, all you failures and faggots and fugitives from Bennington and Haverford and Swarthmore and Smith and Harvard and for crissakes Rutgers, this is Kirkaby giving you the word. And the word for today is goodbye. I'm leaving, I'm paying my dues, I'm kissing you one and all a big fat so long, because *I got a play*. I ain't like you no more. I ain't gonna sit around and piss and moan, not no more, on account of I'm going to work. *I got a play*. I am joining the ranks of the ex-unemployed. I am about to earn the right to fail. Or succeed. Or any little old spot along the way.

"I got a play!" Walt shouted.

He began to shiver. It was really stupid, coming out in the practically freezing dawn when you're already dying with a common cold, but it wasn't every day somebody trusted you. Took a chance that maybe, just possibly, don't quote me, boys, but it is within the realm of possibility that you might have: t?-a?-l?-e?-n?-t? Wouldn't that be wonderful? Walt thought. After all these years of crapping around wouldn't it be just the most fantastic thing?

"Goodbye," he said then, waving at the Village buildings. "I can't visit witcha no longer." Because that was what you did to the Village: you visited it, for the sole and only purpose of staying like a youngster. One year of kindergarten not enough for ya? Dissatisfied with eight years of grammar school and four years of high school and four years of college? Tell ya what I'm gonna do. I'll let you live in Greenwich town, and if you're lucky you can stay a student seventy, maybe eighty years. Never grow up, never age, just stay as sweet as you are, sucking from the book of life.

"How's that for an image, ya bastards?" Walt shouted down the street. Then he looked at his watch, saw it was almost six and cut left at the next corner, heading for Angie's. Angie ran the stationery store nearest Walt's apartment. He was a fat Italian, probably old and he made the best egg creams, if he liked you, south of 23rd Street. Walt picked up a *News* and a *Times* and walked inside the store, fishing in his pocket for change. "Morning, Ange," Walt said.

Angie was looking at a girlie magazine. He held up a large picture for Walt to see. "Willya looka them boobs?" Angie said.

"Jesus, Ange, how can you look at boobs at this hour of the morning?"

Angie appeared genuinely puzzled. "Whatsa time gotta do with look-inat boobs?"

"*Times* and *News*," Walt said.

Angie went back to the magazine. "Putter onna counter."

Walt nodded, put his change down. "So it looks like I'm gonna direct a play," he said.

Angie glanced up. "Yeah?"

Walt shrugged.

"Goodfuckin'luck, buddy," Angie said.

"Thanks, Ange," Walt said, and he tucked the *Times* under his arm and opened the *News*. Some people could read the *Times* on their feet, but he had never been able to master the art. "I only read the *Times* while sedentary," says E. Walters Kirkaby, famed director.

Walt started sneezing again, so he broke into a run back down the block to his place, and when he got there he took two aspirins and set a pan of water to boiling on the stove. Then he lay down in bed, turned quick to the *Times* theater section, read it and flipped to James Reston. By the time he was finished, not only was he infinitely wiser but the water was boiling, so he poured it into a cup, heaped in too much instant, blew on it as he took it back to bed with him. He read the entire entertainment section, skimmed the sports, dented as much of the front page as he could, interspersing it all with trips to the kitchen for more of what-ever you called what he was drinking. After his fourth cup he looked at his watch. Eight minutes of seven. For a moment he hesitated. His father had always been an early riser, but just to be on the safe side, wait till seven on the nose. Walt reopened the *Times*, closed it and went to the kitchen and turned on some more water, came back, glanced through the *News*, went back to the kitchen because he just couldn't stomach any more of that stuff he was drinking, wondered what was on the television, decided nothing probably any good, lay down, stretched out, relaxed, whistled a little, tossed his pillow to the ceiling and at 6:56 put in a call to St. Louis.

"Hey, Dad," he said when he heard P.T.'s voice.

"Arnold?"

"It's me, Dad. Walt."

"*Walt?*"

"I got good news, Dad. I've got this play."

"That you, Walt?"

"Dad, didja hear?"

"You're in New York, right?"

"That's right. Dad—"

"Walt, it's five-fifty-nine here. What the hell's going on?"

"Nuts," Walt said. "I woke you, huh?"

"Just gimme a sec."

"Dad, I forgot about the lousy time change. I'm sorry."

"I'm gonna go put some cold water on my face, O.K.?"

"O.K., Dad." He tucked the phone under his chin. " 'I only forget the time change while sedentary,' says E. Walters Kirkaby, internationally renowned—"

"What is it, kid?"

"I got a play, Dad. To direct. How about that?"

"A real play?"

"A real play."

"Well, God damn," P.T. said. "Wouldn't your mother be proud."

"I bet you never thought I'd get one, didja? I don't blame you, I guess. I bet you thought I was just wasting all my time here, huh?"

"I'm really glad, Walt."

"Just thought I'd let you know."

"Don't run off."

"I got a lot to do," Walt said.

"Course you do. Walt?"

"Huh?"

"Call me sometime?"

"Sure."

"Call me?"

Walt blinked.

"A real play," P.T. said. "How about that?"

After they'd hung up, Walt began to shiver from the cold, so he slipped under his quilt and stared at his bullfight poster. He began to sneeze again, and when the seizure was over he ran to the kitchen and took two more aspirins. Then he hopped back into bed and dialed Branch. "Jiggles?"

"Walt?"

"I am genuinely enthusiastic. Now go back to sleep." He hung up.

A moment later the phone rang. "That *was you*?" Branch said.

" 'T was."

"And you're—"

"I am."

"Lovely," Branch said. "Let's both go back to sleep."

Walt hung up, shook his head, dialed. "Hey, I'm sorry to bother you and this is my last phone call, but let's get together sometime like soon."

"This afternoon?"

"I'll be here sneezing." Walt hung up, dialed again. "Branch?" he said.

"Yes, Walt."

"This is really the last time, but I thought you might set up a meeting between me and the author in the not so distant future."

"It will be done."

"Good. S'long." Walt hung up and pulled the quilt under his chin. He was shivering again and he touched the back of his hand to his forehead, but he had never been able to tell his temperature that way, so he picked up the phone and dialed Branch again. "Whenever I'm really excited I act like a horse's ass," he said.

"Yes, Walt."

"I just wanted to tell you that I understand this play. I mean that. I can make it work. I just know I can."

"I just know it too."

"S'long, Branch."

"Bye, Walt."

"Isn't this just something," Walt said, and he hung up. His head was aching now, and he decided to take his temperature, but then he remembered that he didn't have a thermometer because before it didn't matter if he was sick or not but now it did, now it mattered like hell, so he threw on some clothes again and ran outside and around the corner but it was not quite seven-thirty and the drugstore didn't open till eight and he was disgusted with himself until he remembered that Tony always set her alarm for seven-thirty and that if he ran like crazy he could call her before she was back asleep.

Walt ran like crazy.

When he heard Tony's voice on the other end of the phone he said, "I'm waking up everybody this morning, so you're nothing special to me."

"You didn't wake me. I was dreaming and then the alarm went off. I was just resetting it when you called. I miss you."

"I gotta catch your act in the morning more often," Walt said. "Tell me that again."

"I miss you," Tony said. "I thought about you all last night, lying there sniffling."

Walt sneezed.

"Did you sleep well?" Tony said.

"Not a wink," Walt whispered. "Tony, Tony, it's happened."

"What?"

"It's happened, it's happened, I'm gonna direct a play." He waited. "Well?"

"Just getting a cigarette, dopey."

"I read it, and then I read it again, and I've talked with Branch, and the thing is *I've got a play*, Tony, isn't that—you're not interrupting me."

"Why should I do that?"

"No reason—just that you usually interrupt me a lot. Not criticizing, you understand—I mean, I interrupt you too a lot—say something."

"Don't get excited."

"I am excited. Don't tell me not to get excited, just say something—"

"I did, honey. 'Don't get excited.' That was a specific statement, not a general overall comment."

"I don't get you," Walt said.

"All I mean, Walt, is that if you don't get so excited now, you may not be so disappointed later."

"Later? Later? Why would I be disappointed? I'm not saying it's *Salesman* or *Streetcar*. All I'm saying is that if we cast it halfway decent and if I'm worth a damn, we might just have something."

"What about money?"

"*The money's all raised,* don't you understand? This is a cinch thing. It's going to happen."

"I just don't want you to be disappointed in case—"

"Goddammit, there's nothing that can disappoint me."

"Walt, I'm sorry, it's just too fishy. I mean, why would this package just drop *boom* in your lap? There are other directors and it just doesn't sound right and I don't want you getting disappointed—"

"I know there are other directors—don't you think I'm aware of— what the hell's the matter with you anyway?"

"Nothing's the matter with me."

"Why are you all the time so damn destructive?"

"I just don't want you getting hurt, that's all."

"I was so excited when I called you and—"

"Calm down."

"Every time I ever get excited about anything you have to come along and knock the props out—"

"I said calm down."

"*You always do this.*"

"You're getting incoherent."

"You just go to hell, huh?"

"This conversation was just terminated," Tony said.

"You're too late," Walt told her, "I'm hanging up on you."

"You hang up on me and you're going to be very sorry—"

"So long, kiddo."

"I mean it, Walt. I can be very stubborn. I'll never call you again—"

"I'm gonna hang up now."

"You'll come crawling back inside five minutes," Tony said. "You always do."

Walt slammed the phone down on her laughter.

His throat felt dry and he really wished he knew exactly what you were looking for when you put the back of your hand to your forehead, because if he got sick now, well, he just wouldn't and that was all there was—*damn her!* He should have known she'd put him down before he ever called her. He understood Tony. Every time they were together and he got excited over a movie or a painting or a great-looking mother walking with a baby—every time anything like that happened she'd put him down. Cut at him, draw blood some way, any way. She had to. Walt understood Tony. *She* had to be what caused excitement, whether by use of her body or her mind, and the minute anything else crept in, she had to kill it. Like last night, when he'd wondered why Branch was coming down and had started getting excited, she'd made herself almost available to him, got him hot and bothered, the juices flowing like crazy, until he'd begged her to stay, until she was back in stage center again. Hell, he understood her all right.

He just couldn't do anything about it.

Walt sighed, listening to the echoes of Tony saying, "You'll come crawling like you always do." Walt nodded. "Like always," he said. He knew she'd never call him, not ever again, or make any kind of appearance until he called; she was that stubborn. God, she could get to him. Walt ran his hand over his eyes. He felt really rotten and he would have loved not to call her, loved to finesse crawling just once, but what had to be done had to be done, so he reached for the phone and was halfway through dialing before he wondered if maybe the last scene of the play, the one where the brother Clare goes off with the pregnant sister, Loretta, oughtn't be longer, a fuller scene. Walt scrambled out of bed for a yellow pad and pencil and made five column headings at the top of a blank page, one for each of the five characters in the play. Then he wrote, "Who wants what and why?" and began noting down answers for the five people until his eyes really hurt and he put his pencil down and in a second he was asleep.

He woke at half past two, rubbed his eyes, thought immediately, "Hey,

I never called Tony, how about that" and immediately after that he got back to work on his note-taking, filling page after page. He stopped and made himself a sardine sandwich and took four aspirins just to be on the safe side and wrote down more notes until close to five when Branch buzzed.

Walt let him in and put his finger to his lips. "I gotta tell you something," he said. "Before we say a word." He got back in bed and pulled the quilt up. "I'm a little fuzzy, so don't hold this against me, but I gotta explain why I was a horse's ass on the phone this morning."

"But you don't—"

"Please," Walt said, almost whispering. "This'll just take a sec. See, I came here like everybody, running away—it doesn't matter from what— and I said I was a director and then I sat on my ass a few years. Because I didn't know if I was a director or not, and if I just sat quietly long enough, I figured, I'd never have to prove it. One way or the other. Now this—" he touched the manuscript—"this scared me, Branch, because all of a sudden the possibility of failure was there. Well O.K. it's there, I accept it, I'll take the chance and gladly. This is going to sound very corny, Branch, but I *belong* in the theater now, and God knows what that's worth, but thank you."

Branch nodded.

"O.K., let's get to work."

"First there's something," Branch said. "A little trouble."

"What kind?"

"Money," Branch said. "My backers are gone."

Walt said nothing. Then he said, "Wait'll Tony hears, won't she smile?"

"I'm sorry," Branch said.

"When did this happen?"

"Just this afternoon. I got several totally unexpected phone calls and . . ." He shrugged. "Gone. All my contacts. Gone."

Walt pulled the quilt up around his neck. "Nuts," he said.

Branch sat down in the overstuffed chair and rubbed his neck with his handkerchief.

"I feel like such a fool," Walt whispered. "How my little speech must have embarrassed you. I had no right to do that, Branch. I'm sorry."

Branch continued to mop his neck.

"Hey, I tell you what. Let's go to the drugstore and get me a thermometer." He started to get out of bed. "I just regret being an ass, that's all!"

"I never had the money," Branch said then. "It was never raised. I lied."

Walt lay back down.

"I don't like lying. I'm not that good at it. I didn't mean to upset you like this, Walt. I'm the one that's sorry."

"Tell me."

Branch jammed his handkerchief into his pocket. "I thought, whenever I needed the money, that my mother would, well, assist me, but . . . we aren't on the best of terms just now. I tried getting the money other places . . . but all my contacts failed me. No one saw enough in the play. They turned me down, but I did try."

"So you came to me because you knew I had loot."

"No. I came to you because I *wanted* you to direct the play. And because I knew you had loot."

Walt nodded.

"There's something else you ought to know. The part of the deaf boy. Clare. It's already cast."

"Why tell me?"

Branch sat forward. "This play is . . . highly important to me . . . I cannot stress that enough . . . I have . . . of my own money . . . six thousand dollars . . . I'll keep one to live on . . . leaving five . . . the play will cost approximately ten . . ."

"And I'm supposed to put up the other five?"

Branch nodded. "If you believe in the play . . . No one would ever know, I promise you. You put up five and all the money will be raised."

"Why do you think I live this way, Branch?"

"I don't know."

"I live this way because I swore I would never get anywhere in this world because I bought my way in."

"This . . . kind of thing happens . . . frequently."

"I called my father!" Walt said. "What the hell kind of fool would do a thing like that?" He began rolling back and forth across the bed.

"I have only . . . that money I spoke of . . . You have so much more . . . If I'm willing to risk . . . everything . . . I should think you might do the same with . . . a fraction."

"You came to me because I had money and that's the only reason!"

"No! I want you to do this play. If you were . . . just rich, I would never . . . are you all right?"

"I feel kinda funny, that's all." He tried sitting up, made it.

Branch crossed to him. "What can I do?"

Walt shook his head. "Nothing. Too many sardines maybe. What the hell do I need a thermometer for?"

"Say 'the money's all raised,' Walt. No one will know ... ever ... please ..."

"I took some notes. They're here someplace and you're welcome—*who?*" he shouted as there was a knock on the door.

"Western Union with a singing telegram."

"Nuts," Walt said.

Branch let Tony in. "Hmmmmm," she sang, getting the pitch. Then: "To the tune of 'Happy Birthday': We apologize to you, we apologize to you, we apologize, Egbert Kirkaby, we apologize to you." She smiled quickly at Walt. "Somehow I thought that might draw applause."

"There's been a little trouble with the play," Branch explained.

"Walt, I'm sorry," Tony said, and she ran to him.

He looked at her.

"I am, I am. I really am. I'm not going to say I told you so. I'm just so sorry, Walt, I swear to God."

"It's just that Branch and I don't quite see how to cast the girl," Walt said, still looking dead at her. "Hell, it's not important, not really, not when you consider that the money's all raised."

"Well, what ... did you think?" Branch asked as soon as the three men were alone. Walt pushed his glasses up snug against the bridge of his nose with his left thumb. Aaron stared at the wall.

"Obviously she's a helluva good actress," Walt said.

Branch mopped his neck with his handkerchief. "I liked her," he said. They were sitting in the rear of a rehearsal hall in midtown. It was almost three o'clock and they had been holding auditions since a little after nine. "Her quality, I mean."

Walt nodded.

Branch continued mopping his neck. "What was her name again?"

Walt consulted a three-by-five card. "Devers. Jenny."

"Shall we sign her?" Branch said. He gestured up to the front of the room where the actors had auditioned. "She certainly works well with Rudy, don't you think?"

"I'm not worried about Rudy," Walt said. "Rudy's gonna be fine no matter who he plays against. In this part he's a natural."

"Of course," Branch said. "He's been wonderful auditioning with all the Lorettas we've looked at. I just thought . . . up there . . . something happened between those two."

"Balls," Aaron said.

Walt looked at him. "That's your considered opinion?"

"Nothing *happened* up there," Aaron said. "That's a lot of crap— 'something happened.' " He lit a cigarette and stuck it in the far corner of his mouth. "Some broad comes in and reads a few lines and all of a sudden Branch has gotta make it a mystical experience."

"You didn't like her, then," Walt said to Aaron.

"I liked her," Branch said. "I liked her quality."

"Her quality reminded me of European toilet tissue," Aaron said.

"We must put that line in the play," Branch said.

"You're such an ass," Aaron said.

"And you're a phony," Branch said. "You've never even been to Europe, so—"

"What is it with you two?" Walt wanted to know. "Let's stick to business. What about this Devers girl?"

"I'm satisfied with her," Branch said.

"No, *nein*, negative, never." Aaron inhaled deeply, then coughed.

Branch mopped his neck with his handkerchief. "You're so obvious, Aaron, really you are."

"Why is he obvious?" Walt said.

"Oh, because if I'd said I didn't like her, then he would have fallen down and *died* unless we hired her on the spot."

"Try me," Aaron said.

"What *is* it with you two?" Walt wanted to know. "Come on now. Let's act professional just for five minutes." He got up and began to pace.

"We've only got five minutes," Branch said. "She was the last audition today, and if we wait much longer we'll have to pay for the room another hour."

"O.K.," Walt said. "I'm not sure about her. She's a good actress." He ran over and got the three-by-five card. "She studies with Eli Lee and he's tops. Experience? She understudied in *The Left Hand Knows*, the Stagpole thing."

"That was years ago," Aaron said.

"Right." Walt nodded. "The point is, somebody else at some time or other must have thought she had talent. She does. She's good. Whether she's good for us or not, I'm not sure."

"I liked—" Branch began.

"If you say you liked her quality one more time," Aaron cut in, "I'm gonna bust you one."

Branch mopped his neck. "I was *going to say* I liked the way she worked with Rudy."

"I told you," Walt said. "Don't worry about him. He's a natural; he's like the part was written for him."

"I'm dying of the heat," Aaron said, starting to pace. "Let's get the hell out of here."

"We've still got almost four minutes," Branch said. "Let's be thrifty and finish our discussion here."

"*There is nothing to discuss.* I will not have that girl in my play!"

"Why?" Walt asked.

Branch got up and started to pace.

"Because *I said so*," Aaron answered. "I'm the playwright. I'm allowed unlimited preemptive refusals."

"Will you listen to that?" Branch said. "Will you all just please listen to that?"

"Why?" Walt repeated.

"I don't have to answer you," Aaron said. "I don't have to do anything but give my opinion. You've got my opinion, so let's get the hell out of here."

"What have you got against her?" Walt asked.

"Aside from the fact that I liked her quality," Branch said.

Aaron lit another cigarette, jammed it between his lips. "Goddammit, I just don't like her, that's all. She's too big, for crissakes. How's that?"

"Go on," Walt said. "What else?"

Aaron turned on him. "What? Now you're on Branch's side all of a sudden?"

"I'm not on anybody's side! We're all on the same side, Aaron! *What is it with you two?* Whatever it is, please stop it. We-are-all-on-the-same-side-Aaron-goddammit!"

"I'm sorry," Aaron said. "It's a hot day. She's just too big, Walt. She's nine feet tall with boobs out to here. That's not Loretta."

"I agree with the descriptive passages," Walt said. "I'm not quite so sure about the conclusion." He started walking quickly in a circle. "What else?"

Aaron started his own circle on the far side of the room. "She's clumsy."

"I don't think so," Walt said. "What else?"

"She's not pretty enough," Aaron said. "Loretta's supposed to be pretty."

"Correction," Walt said. "Loretta's supposed to be *attractive*. This girl's attractive. In our society, anybody with boobs out to here—"

"What are you getting at?" Branch said, choosing a straight line between the circles, tracing it back and forth across the room, mopping his neck with a fresh handkerchief now.

"I don't know," Walt said. "I don't know. I just want to hear Aaron."

"She's not what I picture, that's all," Aaron said. "I don't see her in the part."

"I think she'd be wonderful," Branch said.

"Nobody cares what you think," Aaron said.

"Aaron's spoken," Branch said. "I must face east a while."

"Goddammit, you two—"

"He gets to me sometimes," Aaron said, circling around and around.

Walt followed his own perimeter. "Did you think she was sad, Aaron? Think a minute. Did you find her at all poignant? Or lost? Anything like that?"

Before Aaron could answer, Branch said, "Not so much."

Aaron glared at him. "Yes. I did."

"We've really got to decide soon," Branch said. "They're liable to throw us right out on our canny-can-cans."

Walt waved him quiet. "I'll tell you what I think," he said. "Aaron, you listen, all right?"

"All right."

"All right!" Walt stopped circling. "Now Loretta is a girl who gets pregnant, solid? And she can't make the man she wants, the man who did it, marry her. Not only that, she gets bulldozed into trying to slip it to this innocent rich guy, solid? O.K., now what can we say about a girl like that? What conclusions can we draw? I really think I'm onta something." He began circling again, around Aaron now, who turned as Walt walked, the two of them turning, keeping face to face. "She is *weak*! Right!"

"Right," Aaron said.

"O.K., now get this: Ordinarily you want to cast a weak girl—you get some goddam skinny ingenue and have her flutter around the stage and the audiences says, 'I get it, I've seen her before, she's weak.' So what I say, Aaron old buddy, is that we cast this Amazon. Yeah. Remember *Of Mice and Men*? Lenny? He broke your heart because he was so goddam big and strong. Who'd have given a crap if he'd been little? I mean it. It's great casting. Great big weak girl—that's fresh. Little teeny weak girl—I've been there before. What do you think, huh, Aaron, huh?"

Aaron said nothing.

"I think you're really off the track there, Walt," Branch said.

"Let's hire her," Aaron said.

"Just in time," Branch said, skipping out of the room and down the stairs, trying not to laugh too loud. Rudy was waiting on the sidewalk. "I got her the part," Branch said.

Rudy nodded. "Thank you."

Early that evening there was a knock on the door of the apartment on Seventy-second Street. Then the doorbell rang. Then the knock again, louder this time. Branch answered. "Yes?"

"Rudy Miller."

"You're the editor," Branch said. "Fiske."

"That's right. And I want to talk to Rudy."

"He's not feeling all that well," Branch said. "I'll see if he'll see you." He turned and walked down the corridor while Charley moved into the living room and looked out the window at the Hudson. Then Branch came back. "This way, please."

Charley followed him down the corridor. The first room on the right was the kitchen. Then, on the left, a large bedroom, also facing the Hudson. Then, past that on the right, a small, dark study. Branch gestured toward the study. Charley entered it and looked around. "Rudy?" he said.

"I was expecting you."

Charley went to the window. "Jenny quit this afternoon."

Rudy sat on a step of the fire escape, staring out, his legs tucked up tight, his chin on his knees. He said, "I know."

"You got her a job in this play, that right?"

"She would have gotten it anyway." He turned his head slowly, looked at Charley.

"What the hell business was it of yours?"

"None."

"You had to butt in?"

"Yes."

"You had no business! People should be left the hell alone. Since when are you Jesus?"

Rudy said nothing.

"I want to know why you did it! You shouldn't have, you shouldn't have; you've bitched it all up now!"

Rudy stared out. "That doesn't surprise me. I don't think I've ever in my whole life done anything right. I mean that factually, Charles. I think it's true. Come out? We'll talk. It's good to see you."

Charley grabbed him through the window. "I came here to hurt you."

"And you are."

"We were happy."

"I know that, Charles. That's why she took the part to get away."

Charley dropped his arms.

"It's really very cool out here," Rudy said.

Charley shook his head. "It was silly to come. I ought to catch a train."

"Goodbye, then."

"It's just we've been together for so long, Jenny and me. And today I got the feeling, for the first time I got it, that we were done."

"Would that be so terrible?"

Charley gestured to the fire escape. "I'd get my suit dirty."

"Yes."

"No, of course not. We should have stopped it years ago. We just somehow never got around to it."

"That happens, Charles."

"Can you see the sunset?"

"It's over."

"But if it wasn't, could you see it?"

"No."

"I'll bet maybe you could if you tried," Charley said. He pushed his big frame through the window and stood on the fire escape, looking around. "I'm really upset, Rudy. I don't know what to do." He sat down on the step below Rudy. Their heads were level.

"I'm sorry, Charles."

"Look at this suit," Charley said, fingering the khaki material. "Filthy already." He shook his head.

"It seems to me I've spent most of my life on one fire escape or another. I can't remember any of them being clean."

"It's probably for the best," Charley muttered. "I never would have married her. Maybe I would, I don't know."

"They're very cool, though, aren't they?"

"Very," Charley said. "What are we doing, any of us?"

Rudy closed his eyes. "I'm an actor; you're ending an affair."

"You're a writer."

"No. I wrote a book; that doesn't make me a writer. I loved my grandfather; I put it down; that's all."

"Father, he was."

Rudy smiled. "My father's back in Chicago someplace, my mother too; I haven't seen them in what must be ten years, so here we are,

Charles—dear friends—and we know nothing. I cannot remember ever having been this tired." He closed his eyes.

Branch knocked on the window. "Are you all right?"

"Yes."

"You're sure?"

"Yes."

"Can I do anything for you?"

"No."

"You're sure?"

"I'm talking to an old friend. Everything is fine. Thank you."

Branch looked at Charley. Then he went away.

"What's with him?" Charley asked.

"He loves me. It's very sad. And hates you, most likely, for being out here with me."

"What are you mixed up in?"

"Nothing I can handle."

"Get out of it, then."

"*I am afraid to go to sleep!*" He reached out and grabbed the rusted rails and clung to them with both hands. "*I am afraid!*"

"What is it?"

"Not in my dreams. I can ignore them. And my thoughts I can control. It's in between. That waiting period when the mind starts to go. You are lulled and warm and walking along some path and suddenly, Charles, *things* speak to me. Stones, waves, blades of grass. And they all say the same words. '*Have you had enough? Are you ready now?*' Things. And when they speak I wake and I pace and think and wait until I can drop like a rock through that in-between place. And then too soon it's morning. '*Have you had enough? Are you ready now? Have you had enough? Are you ready now?*' I used to answer *No!* so loudly. Now the reply is rather on the quiet side."

"You're talking about dying, aren't you?"

"Yes."

"What do you want to die for?"

"I don't want to, Charles. It's just that I've lost some of my enthusiasm for the alternative."

A sudden thrust of air enveloped them. Rudy turned his face to the wind. Charley watched him. "Do you know what's going to happen?"

Rudy shook his head. "My guess: catastrophe."

"Get out of it. Before it gets awful, get out."

"Did you with Jenny?"

"That's different."

"No. Oh, you're more stable than I, Charles, but otherwise it's all the same. I am afflicted, Charles. I have the great disease. I'm a damaged man."

"You mean deaf?" Charley said.

"I mean damaged. Like you. Like me. Like our director, a lovely boy, divorced painfully, but with a new love now, a new love just like the old, so Branch informs me. Or look at Branch. Or Aaron, who you don't know. Or poor sweet Betty Jane, who let you lie to her all these years without ever letting on she knew you lied. What makes us different is the knowledge of our damages. We're like little children suffering our first wounds. Before that cut we never thought ourselves capable of bleeding. Afterwards, we'll accept it as a fact. But you and I, Charles—all of us—we are living at the instant of incision—to us the world seems to be nothing but blood—so we wallow. . . ."

FROM the New York *Times*, JUNE 30, PAGE 23

INITIAL VENTURE

A new play goes into rehearsal today at the Greenwich Street Theatre. It is "Madonna With Child," by Aaron Fire. Sponsor Branch Scudder describes the drama as "a different kind of play about family life." E. Walters Kirkaby will direct and the featured roles of a brother and sister will be played by Rudy Miller and Jenny Devers. "Madonna With Child" is a maiden effort for all concerned. Previews will begin the first of August, with the formal opening set for the twelfth.

XXIV

"Jenny Devers," Jenny said, lying flat in bed, reading from the New York *Times*. It was morning of the first day of rehearsal. "The part of the sister will be played by Jenny Devers. The crucial and terribly difficult part of the sister will be played by that brilliant new star of stage, screen and radio, Jenny—"

The telephone rang.

Jenny jumped.

She had been expecting the call, was indeed braced for it, still, when it rang, she jumped and gasped, reacting in general like a dumb heroine in a silent film. Jenny gazed at the blue walls and quickly closed her eyes. Charley had promised not to call her, never to call her; she had made him swear it but even as he swore she doubted his strength. Now, as the phone rang again and again, his weakness was proven and Jenny sighed because it was all so cheap and false. He was better than this and so was she; they were both of them better than this and, aware of her own weakness, she got out of bed and wearily answered the phone, saying "What do you want?" in a voice that was not warm.

"It's only me, Moose."

"Oh God, Tommy—"

"Continuing their lifelong talent for just missing each other, Miss Devers and Mr. Alden spoke briefly on the phone. 'What do you want?' she said, thinking him to be not who he was but someone else entirely."

"Are you in town?"

"I'm in Boston, oaf—I'm being funny on my own money and you don't even smile. You're not smiling, I can tell."

"How are you?"

"You're a fantastic conversationalist, y'know that?"

Jenny smiled.

Tommy said, "I just called to say that I seen ya name inna papuhs and I think it's terrif."

"Thank you," Jenny said.

"Aren't you over that guy yet? Jesus, Jenny—"

"We're getting there. That's a promise."

"You know what I wish?"

"What do you wish?"

"You remember back home when we were kids and I tried raping you?"

"I really miss you, Tommy."

"Shut up. What I wish is that you hadn't been stronger than me. What I wish is that I'd raped you and gotten you pregnant and we'd had to get married. I think in the long run we both would have been one helluva lot happier. Goddammit!"

"What's the matter, Tommy?"

"Nothing, nothing."

"Yes, there is. I know you, now—"

"Nothing."

"Tommy—"

"Nothing is the matter. I just called to say congratulations and wish you luck and all the rest of the crap."

"Thank you, Tommy."

"Big old moose, anyway." He hung up.

Jenny held the phone for a moment, then quietly thrust it back into its cradle because if Charley called it wouldn't do for the line to be busy. She took a step away, whirled back and grabbed the receiver then, dropping it to the floor, because if Charley called the line would have to be busy because if it wasn't they would start up again, and where would that get them? Jenny undressed and sat on the edge of the sofa bed, looking at her name. She heard a sound, a steady irritating sound, and in a moment realized it was the telephone demanding to be put back. Jenny hesitated only a moment. Then she got up and put it back. Because it didn't matter if he called. Because there was no strength left, not for Charley. She was tired, too tired for any more of that.

She felt, suddenly, old.

Silly, she told herself, you're not. But on the way to the shower she stopped and looked at her face in the mirror. That is not an old face, she decided. But neither was it young. And suddenly she thought of the face that had listened so carefully to the old lady on the bus. Luke, Paul, Matthew, Luke, Paul, Matthew—Jenny retreated and stared at her body. If anything, it was better now than then. The legs were just as long and hard, the shoulders as broad, the breasts as large and firm. The waist, astonishingly small then, was even smaller now, baby fat gone, and the hips were as full, as rounded as before.

It was a remarkable body.

Jenny hated it, of course, now more than ever. But still, it was a remarkable body . . .

Aaron raced Mrs. Santiago for first use of the communal bathroom on their floor of their tenement on West 84th Street. My God, Aaron thought. At least three hundred pounds and she's carrying her baby and she's beating me.

The lavatory door slammed in his face.

Aaron pounded on it. From inside, Mrs. Santiago's baby giggled. Aaron groaned. He stood there, a towel over his thin shoulders, razor and instant-lather can in his hands, and he shouted, "Mrs. Santiago, you've got to let me in."

"*Quien es?*" Mrs. Santiago asked.

"You know damn well who it is, Mrs. Santiago. You just raced me for the bathroom—it's me."

"*Quien es?*" Mrs. Santiago said again.

"*El Americano,* for crissakes," Aaron shouted. "I've got my first re-hearsal today and I'm late, Mrs. Santiago. You've got to let me shave."

"*Momentito,*" Mrs. Santiago sang over the splash of running water.

"I've got to shave, Mrs. Santiago, so easy on el hot water!"

"*Momentito.*"

"I swear I'll be out in two minutes, Mrs. Santiago. One minute. Please," Aaron said, though it was fruitless and he knew it because she spoke no English. He had long since left the Y, moving back to West 84th Street (and hello to you, Dr. Gunther) into a building in which no one spoke more than a few words of the language—they were all Puerto Rican—and though being the sole Caucasian in the dump was not his vision of Heaven, it had certain advantages which he happily used in moments of particular wrath. "You're a lousy slut, Mrs. Santiago," Aaron said, sweetly singsong.

"*Momentito.*"

"Your husband is deceiving you, Mrs. Santiago, did you know that? He spends afternoons with Mrs. Rodriguez." It was true; Aaron could hear them rolling on the bed in the room above his, chattering passion.

"*Momentito.*"

Aaron scowled and kicked the door, then turned, stalking back to his room. "Puerto Rico is not free," he muttered, kicking the door shut behind him. He fell on his filthy bed and glared at the filthy rotting ceiling and then at his watch and he was late. There was just no time, so, taking a deep breath, he squirted some instant lather onto his fingertips and spread it across his skin. Then he took his razor, moved to his tiny mirror and brought the razor to his face. "Ouch," Aaron said as the razor scraped down. "Ow. Ow. Ooooooo. Ow. Ow . . ."

Tony lodged the phone against her neck.

"What's wrong?" she heard Walt say.

"Just trying to light this dopey cigarette," she replied. Striking another match, she got the cigarette lit and inhaled, coughing as the smoke hit her throat.

"Sounds good," Walt said. "So listen, tonight being special—I mean, I don't go into rehearsal every day—what I figured was if you'd wait for me at your place I would go on record as promising to pick you up and take you someplace so jazzy you can't stand it."

"Walt . . ." Tony said, waiting for him to interrupt her.

"What's wrong? What's wrong? You've got that tone—"

"Well . . ." she said, using the tone again.

"Dammit, Tony, say it."

"Would you be terribly upset if—"

"If what? If what? You're killing me."

"If I brought someone along tonight?"

"Tonight? A man? You're kidding."

"Yes, a man; no, I'm not kidding."

"*Who?*"

"Oh . . ." She sipped some instant coffee, noting that directly to the right of the announcement about the play was an advertisement that the Thalia Theater was having a Vittorio De Sica double bill, *The Bicycle Thief* and *Miracle in Milan*. "Nobody special," Tony concluded.

"Tony, ever since I got involved with this play your life has been bugged with guys, all of them 'nobody special,' and I wish they'd leave you the hell alone. Now who's this one, I demand to know?"

"Oh, this Italian I met at the agency. He's just in town for a little and—"

"Tony, *you knew* today was the first day I've ever had a play in rehearsal in the city of New York. Did it never cross your small square mind that I might possibly wish to celebrate said event? Now use your head. Would I be upset? Think."

"You're right, dopey. I'm sorry. I'll call him back and break it. I'm such a cretin sometimes. Forgive me, Egbert?"

"What is with you—asking would I be a trifle miffed if you brought along some lousy greaseball—"

"*Vittorio* is *not* a greaseball! Actually, he's almost blond."

"Oh, those albino Italians," Walt said. "Ask him if he's got a sister and we'll double."

"He hasn't got a sister. He's an only child, terribly handsome and the heir to a considerable fortune."

"*Will you quit talking about him please before I come up there and throttle you?* See you tonight?"

"He forgives me," Tony said. She made the sound of a kiss. "I'll be waiting Vittorioless." She kissed him again.

"Go to hell," Walt mumbled.

Tony hung up, smiling. Then she laughed. Vittorio. Vittorio! Such a funny name . . .

"Misquoted," Branch said, pointing to the article in the paper. "And by the New York *Times*. I never said anything like that."

Rudy stared out at the Hudson.

Branch came up behind him. "Should I do something? Do you think it matters?"

"No. Nothing matters."

Branch turned him around. "You mean everything matters."

"Yes," Rudy nodded. "That too."

"Well, here we are," Walt said.

He stood on the bare stage of the Greenwich Street Theatre and looked out at the people, at Branch standing in the rear, a smile frozen on; at Aaron, already pacing, a cigarette jammed in the far corner of his mouth; at Jenny and Rudy, sitting together off to one side; at Jim Masters, who played the animal and insisted on combing his hair like Marlon Brando; at Ed Ritchie, who played the timid wealthy student and was to become known, inevitably, as Ritchie the richie; at Carmella Spain, who played the mother and almost drank too much and who, once, many painful years before, had been Walter Huston's leading lady in a short-lived play uptown.

"You're probably wondering why I've gathered you together," Walt said, pausing for the laugh. "What we're gonna do," he went on when it had ended, "is read the play and then break for lunch and then come back and block as much of the first act as we have time for." He wiped his forehead. "It's gonna stay hot like this, so get used to it, relax, and while you're doing that I thought I might gas a little about what the play's about. Now, our producer—" he pointed back to Branch—"or I should say 'sponsor,' although he claims he was misquoted, says it's 'a different kind of play about family life.' I don't think it is and I don't think it's a play about incest either." Walt grabbed a chair and sat down. "Consider," he said. "There's this girl, Loretta, and she gets with child, and the guy who did it says 'tough,' and she tries to rope this other guy into playing papa, and it almost works. Almost. But then her brother does this *incredible* thing. He louses up the works, tells the richie it's not his baby, and then, when the mother pitches the daughter out into the cold, the brother goes along, 'cause he loves her. And then *she* does this incredible thing: she lets him. She knows he loves her and she knows he's her brother and *she still lets him.* Two people, two incredible things. Too much? I don't think so. Not one bit.

"We all do incredible things." Walt paused.

"The reason for that pause," he said when he went on, "is because I think that's important. We all do incredible things. Now, the word 'incredible'; here's what I say it means: beyond belief. Not 'unbelievable.' 'Unbelievable' means *'that which I do not believe.'* 'Incredible' means *'that which I did not know I believed.'* A girl comes to town and she thinks, I may not be much but I'm pure, and pretty soon she's having an affair with a married man. Happens all the time, solid? Incredible? A guy comes from a good decent family, he comes to town and in two shakes of a dead lamb's tail, he's shacked up with some other guy, who's probably also from a good decent family. Happens all the time, solid? Incredible?

"This is a play about what people will do when they have to. Here we do it for love; sometimes we do it for money, sometimes for revenge, which I guess is love bass-ackwards. Anyway, we all do things we don't do; when we have to, we can do incredible things."

Carmella Spain had fallen asleep.

Walt smiled and shook her gently.

Then they began.

They read the play out loud and broke for lunch, and coming back, Ed Ritchie said "What do you think?" to Carmella Spain and Carmella told him, "Sonny, you can't do nothing without the people," and that afternoon Walt started to block. He worked quickly, telling the actors what he wanted, listening when they questioned, then answering, moving on, and by the end of the day most of the first act was blocked, and after he dismissed the actors he conferred with Aaron and they decided that even though it was much too early to tell anything they both thanked God the first day was over and then Branch came up with news of a lunatic idea sprung on him that day by Katz, the costume designer, and Walt, also saying so long to Aaron, decided, with Branch, that Katz had to go and, that done, he dashed into a taxi up to Tony's and he took her, without a word, down to the waiting cab and from there they went to a *nouveau riche* building on East End Avenue and took the elevator to the twelfth floor, unlocked the door to the E apartment: living room, bedroom, kitchen, terrace, the latter with an almost unobstructed view of the East River.

"I sublet it for the summer, furnished," Walt said. "I mean why not, what the hell?"

"Why not what the hell indeed?" Tony said.

"You're probably wondering—" Walt began.

"Discount houses, schmiscount houses," Tony said. "I've known all along and frankly, the way you've acted today—deal mysterious—I liked you better poor." She turned quickly for the terrace. Walt followed her.

"Doesn't matter to me that you're loaded," she said, hands on the railing. "As a matter of fact—" she turned; Walt came toward her—"if you're a nice boy I'll try not to hold it against you," and with that she was in his arms.

Walt finished blocking the first act the second day, the second act the third, and the morning of the fifth day the entire play was blocked when they broke for lunch. "What do you think?" Branch asked him as they went out for a sandwich and Walt said, "Can't tell, can't tell," and after lunch he told the actors they had three more days to get the books out of their hands and have their parts memorized, which frightened Carmella Spain, because she didn't remember things as well as she used to. She complained about the heat and how it gave her a headache and how she was a human being, and how she wasn't going to work until the management made things cool enough, and Walt took her aside and said that he agreed with her completely but that he wished she wouldn't quite give vent like that, because he was worried about the other actors being able to get the books out of their hands in time, all of them being so inexperienced, and he put his arm around her shoulder and whispered that it was up to them, Walt and Carmella, to lead the strays and he asked would she please be the last to take the book out of her hand so as not to embarrass those with less experience, and Carmella whispered that she would do her best to shape up the kids and Walt said he knew she would, that's why he asked her, and after that the day went as smoothly as days can go when you're in rehearsal and nobody knows if anything's any good or not. Two days later the five performers had all put down their scripts, and although nobody still knew if the play was any good or not, they all were more than aware of something else:

Jenny was sensational.

"And you didn't want her, for crissakes!" Walt whispered, pounding Aaron on the arm. They stood in the back of the theatre, watching the second scene of the first act, where Loretta comes home and talks to Clare after her date with the animal.

"I was wrong, don't remind me, shut up," Aaron said.

"You're a stupid bastard," Walt said.

"I'm a stupid bastard," Aaron agreed.

Midway through the second week Rudy started getting good. Walt, who had previously been praising him, took note of the change and started shaking his head after Rudy's scenes. "Can't you do better than that?" Walt asked. "Can't you?"

Rudy said nothing, only nodding, doing better.

"Aren't you being a little hard on Rudy?" Branch asked.

"Shut up and produce," Walt told him.

Branch produced. At any particular time on any particular day he was liable to be talking, arguing or screaming at or with the scene designer; the costume designer, Katz, who, horrified at being fired, successfully begged forgiveness; the lighting and sound man, a bearded wonder who lacked only the brains to be a genius; the business manager, who loathed the press agent; the press agent, who was nothing if not verbal concerning his highly negative feelings about the business manager; several representatives of several unions; a Japanese carpenter who claimed to be able to produce any prop at less than no cost at all. Along with these came Mrs. Toledo, who owned the building that housed the theater and whose name was not really Toledo, but then, neither had it been the name of Mr. Toledo, the Italian numbers runner with whom she had lived for several years before his somewhat unusual demise and whose greatest fear was that some thoughtless member of the cast should set her building on fire, so she was either calling Branch constantly, ordering him to check on the obedience to all "No Smoking" signs, or dropping in constantly, pointing a slender finger at whoever was breaking the law, always Aaron, who always paced around the rear of the seats, a cigarette always between his lips, except when Mrs. Toledo's sudden "Ah-*hahs*" made him douse the butt until after she had triumphantly exited, leaving him free to light up again. And Branch also had to deal with Mrs. Plotkin, who claimed she could print his tickets for so little money that if the show was a hit she would starve; and also Branch saw and spent too much time with Jay Roget, who claimed to be distantly related to the thesaurus man and was a rummy painter, but talented, and who was designing the poster for the show for no dough, just booze, which wasn't as good a deal as Branch thought when he made it. And he also had to see and soothe the box-office man (whose name Branch could never remember), who was constantly getting his feelings hurt by Aaron, and through the box-office man Branch met Trixie, a remarkably disturbed thirteen-year-old girl who was the best in the entire Village at the art of Poster Placement, claiming no less than two hundred shop windows as practically her very own, with more to come if the money was right. So Branch produced, running here, there, slapping his bald head when the set designer realized he'd made the set too big, slapping both his cheeks when the stage manager got hepatitis and had to be replaced. Branch got up early, worked late, running, always running, with barely a moment in which to sit and rest.

But when they came, those moments, he sat and rested in the dark theater. And he stared up onto the stage. At Rudy. And sometimes he stared at the other people. As they stared at Rudy.

And then everything seemed worthwhile.

"I don't think Rudy should have an understudy," Branch whispered to Walt one evening as they were about to stop.

Walt pushed his glasses up snug over the bridge of his nose with his left thumb. "You don't hire understudies for a production like this till after you open, so what are you talking about?"

"Well, I just don't think Rudy should have an understudy, that's all."

"If you want my opinion, I wouldn't much care to see this play without Jenny in it."

"Wonderful," Branch said. "Then we won't get one for her either."

"We won't get them for anybody, Branch; how's that?"

"Always glad to get things settled," Branch said.

"What did we settle?" Walt said. Then they all quit for the day.

"Hi," Aaron said one morning during break.

Jenny sipped her coffee and nodded.

Aaron sat down beside her.

"All right, all right, two minutes," Walt bawled.

"I just want you to know it's a pleasure," Aaron said softly.

"What is?"

"Watching you."

"A pleasure?" Jenny said. "Well, fancy that."

Aaron got up and started away.

"Aaron," Jenny whispered.

He dropped his head down to hers. "What?"

"Aren't you sweet."

"No. But aren't you pretty to think so."

Toward the end of the second week, Walt lost his temper for the first time. "Goddammit no!" he said and glared at Branch.

"But why not?" Branch asked. It was lunch break and they were alone in the theater.

"Because," Walt shouted, tromping across the stage, "because when I direct there will be nobody watching. And that means nobody."

"But we don't know what we've got. A few people here to watch a run-through—that's not much to ask."

"Nobody sees this show till I say it's ready to be seen or I quit," Walt said.

"You can't quit, you're the backer," Branch whispered.

"You bet I am," Walt said.

Branch sighed.

"The first of August," Walt said. "That first preview. Then we'll know."

"The first of August," Branch agreed. He looked at his watch. "Two weeks away. Walt? Why am I looking at my watch for the date?"

" 'Cause you're a producer. They do that kind of thing."

"Walt? What if it stinks?"

"What if it doesn't?" Walt said . . .

That afternoon, for the first time, Rudy and Jenny changed parts. Walt gave them scripts and they read each other's roles, and after they did it Jim Masters, the animal, changed parts with Ritchie the richie, and Carmella, protesting all the while, finally tried it, changing roles with Rudy, playing the son to his mother. At the first break, Carmella came up to Walt and put her arm around him and said very softly that *she* understood exactly just what the hell he was doing but that some of the youngsters were a little confused and she thought he might tell *them* just exactly what the hell he was doing and clear it up for *them* and would he mind if she listened just for the hell of it, so before they started back to work Walt told them all that since they knew the words it was time to try to find the meaning, and that was all the switching was, just a little game to try and help.

"Obviously," Carmella said.

That night Branch asked, "What's the matter with you?"

Rudy rubbed his eyes. "I'm not doing well? I'm sorry."

"No-no-no; you're wonderful. Even Walt says so. But you look so tired."

"I don't know why that should be," Rudy said.

Aaron and Jenny walked slowly through Riverside Park. "So what happened after you broke up?" Aaron asked.

Jenny squinted at the moon. "Oh, we made up the next day. It was all very funny. His wife made up with him that same day too."

"If I'd been Fiske, I'd have married you," Aaron said. "I think."

Jenny laughed. "That's the way his mind worked too. 'Yes, I'll do it, maybe.' "

"Go on," Aaron said.

"No. It only got uglier and uglier. Just before I got this part, the week before, Charley and I got invited out as a couple. This other editor, Archie, he had a place and so, I guess out of desperation, Charley asked could he use it and Archie was delighted. We'd fooled him for so long, he just loved it that we were sneaking around. He thought it was funny, us sneaking around and all the time pretending to be so moral and upright. He used to ride me about it in the office. Leave little notes for me, things like that. Then, the week before I got this part, Archie invited Charley and me out as a couple. As soon as I heard the invitation, I broke out crying. Isn't that terrible?"

Aaron said nothing.

"I just couldn't help it, though. All I saw for myself was this lifetime of sneaking around, forever, and I bawled like a baby."

"Poor Jenny," Aaron said.

"Someone else said that to me once: 'Poor Jenny.' " She shrugged.

"It's got to be good," Aaron said.

"We'll know in ten days," Jenny told him.

"I'll know who to blame if it isn't."

"Oh, Aaron."

"I hate him."

"Why? He's good in the play and you know it."

"When I was a kid," Aaron said, "my mother used to let me pick one food each year I didn't have to eat. Squash, turnips, spinach, goddam brussels sprouts. Every year I got to hate any one food I wanted to and whenever it was served I didn't have to eat it. My hate food, we called it. Well, I'm that way with people too. Every year I get to hate one person free. I don't have to give out any reason. All I have to do is hate, O.K.? Well, Rudy—this year, he's *mine*."

"Poor Aaron," Jenny said.

"I'll tell you something: if this play bombs . . ." He took Jenny's hand. "What do you know about me?"

"What do you mean?"

"Oh dammit, Jenny, answer my question."

"You mean with girls? Yes."

"Well, I must tell you something. I like you. You don't know how funny that is, coming from me, but just take my word. You see, my *condition*, it does not of necessity fill me with joy."

"I really don't want to hear this."

"Shut up. It's not what you think—I'm not going to tell you about some priest seducing me in the sacristy, for crissakes." He tightened his hold on her hand and they stopped, close in the darkness. "But from when I was young I made an *assumption* about myself. I *assumed* I was gifted, one of the chosen, a *spécialité de la maison*. There is already some indication that I may have erred in my assumption. This play, if it is bad, would make it more than an indication. I would more or less have to take it as proof of my mistake. And if I were mistaken, if it turns out after all that I am nothing but a common garden-variety faggot—"

"Aaron—"

"Shut up, I said. I like you. *Listen to me.* Well, if that is the case, I don't think I can face it, at least not alone, so therefore I would have to do my best to initiate general suffering, you understand? This is an apology, Jenny. In advance. I will not enjoy hurting you. Because you're very honest and I care. I almost wish I were straight or you weren't—" He made a smile. "Smile at me," he said.

Jenny looked at him instead. "You would hurt me? Even though you care?"

"Alas."

Two nights later Tony appeared down at the theater, arriving just exactly when Walt had told her to, and Walt, on seeing her, stretched and said "Take off, everybody," and he couldn't help smiling when he said it, because it was nice to think things revolve around your whims, even though it was time to quit anyway. Being the boss didn't knock him out all that much, except sometimes it was nice to remind yourself just who was who. He took Tony by the hand and introduced her around.

Aaron took one good, long, close look at her.

Then he beamed. . . .

The next day Walt took Aaron and Jenny and Rudy aside, and he told them that they had better get ready to *work*, really *work* now, because there wasn't much time left, and the scene they were going to work on more than any other was the long last scene, the scene where Loretta is about to go off by herself when her brother tells her how he feels and they talk and finally, at the end, they touch hands and go on out the door together, and Walt explained that the crucial thing wasn't that they were brother and sister, what really mattered was that by the time the play was over they would both have done incredible things, the boy and the girl, for love, and people do incredible things, and if the audience didn't come to understand and feel that, then the whole play had been for nothing, and Rudy and Jenny nodded and Aaron jammed a fresh cigarette into the corner of his mouth and the meeting broke up and then they *worked*. Everybody. They ran the play once a day all the way through without stopping and then Walt worked on the individual scenes, but mostly on that long last one with Jenny and Rudy, and he had them change roles and he had them sing the scene as if it was an opera and not a play, and then he had them do the scene in gibberish, and when they did that their bodies began moving differently because the words weren't there, and he had them race the scene, saying the words justasfastastheycould, and then he had them mime the scene, and then he had them speak again, but as slowly as they could without going cra zy, and then he had them play it as if it were all the funniest scene in the world and Rudy was looking terribly tired now but he was playing, Walt thought, remarkably well and Jenny was so fine he sometimes could only watch her work and nod and when there were six days to go he took her aside and told her to get everybody she ever knew down to see her and fast and she said yes she would do that, thank you, and then the sets came and everybody got nervous and then the costumes and everybody got more nervous and when there were three days left Walt announced that there would be a complete run-through at noon on the day of the first preview and then Branch announced that there would be a little party for the cast from four to seven the day of the first preview, at his apartment on Seventy-second Street, and bring your friends, just so they buy tickets for later, and then they had to start work all over again, with the sets and costumes making everything different and strange and one blurred morning Jenny remembered that it had been Stagpole who had said "Poor Jenny" and then she wondered if he might come down and see her and then she wondered, if he would, would he come to the party beforehand, so she asked Branch if it would be all right to ask and he said "My God, certainly," so she called a secretary at Kingsway and found who Stagpole's agent was and then she called the agent and left the complete message, both invitations, to the play and the party beforehand, but as she gave the message to the agent's secretary she felt sort of like a fool, and she told the secretary to sign the message "Jenny Devers, the Algonquin, friend of Mr. Alden," and that made her feel like such a fool she almost yelled "Forget the whole thing," except she didn't, and later at the theater, she and Rudy worked again, so hard, with Walt driving them, and Rudy was quiet now, never talking, and then all of a terrible sudden it was the first of August, August the first, preview day.

And a scorcher.

Branch woke early, walked into the living room, found Rudy there, staring. "Come down to the theater with me? Of course you will."

Rudy made no motion.

"Sleep well?"

Rudy nodded. Yes.

"Nervous?"

Rudy shook his head. No.

"Don't be." Branch came toward him. "This is our day. Your day and mine and nothing can go wrong."

They taxied to the theater, arriving before ten, and Branch got busy on the phone. Rudy sat alone in a corner of the theater, his eyes closed, staying like that until the box-office man appeared, calling his name, and then Rudy followed the box-office man out of the theater into the lobby where someone was waiting. Rudy saw who, stopped, leaned against the wall and the wall whispered, *"Have you had enough? Are you ready now?"*

"Son," Sid said.

The day was to his father's advantage.

In the sweltering lobby Rudy stared at his father, who, natty in a blue suit, dapper in a straw hat, innocent blue eyes brighter than stars, smiled through the heat.

"Son," Sid said again, his voice lower, dropping still more into a whisper. "Rudy, my Rudy, my only son."

Rudy stood still, his arms down.

Sid embraced him. "After all these years. The prodigal father. The beautiful son. Someone should paint a picture. Yes . . . yes . . ."

Rudy began to cry.

Branch walked in.

Sid held out a hand. "Sid Miller. Father of the star." He smiled.

Branch muttered his name, stared at Rudy.

"He's fine," Sid said. "Overcome with emotion. We haven't seen each other. I came a thousand miles for this, would you believe it, Mr. Scudder?"

Branch reached for Rudy. "He shouldn't get upset. Not today."

Sid held tight to his son. "I tell you he's fine. It's just the surprise. Can I talk to my son alone, Mr. Scudder? It's been years and—"

Branch looked at his watch. "There's a run-through at noon."

"It's not ten yet," Sid said. "I'll have him back, I swear."

"Rudy," Branch said. "Do you want to go?"

"I've come *a thousand miles.* Can you refuse your father when he's come a thousand miles?"

Rudy wiped his eyes, shook his head.

"Come," Sid said, and he led him out of the lobby into the sun. "Hot," Sid said. "The heat is no place for a father and son." They walked up Greenwich to Seventh and Sid hailed a cab, said "Sherry-Netherland" to the driver. "You know what, Rudy? I got a suite in that hotel. Me—a suite in the Sherry-Netherland, pretty snazzy? What do you think of your old man, kid? I got a view of Central Park would knock your eyes out." He put his arm around his son. "Rudy, Rudy," Sid crooned. "We're back together, thank God, thank God, you and me."

Rudy closed his eyes, his head on his father's shoulder. "I'm very tired," he whispered.

Sid stroked him. "That's all right, it's all right, you're safe now."

"So tired. So . . . don't please . . . don't ask . . . not for anything."

"All I want is to be with my son," Sid said. He began to croon again, "Safe and sound . . . safe and sound . . . my little deaf baby's all safe and sound . . ."

When Rudy opened his eyes again, they were at the Sherry-Netherland.

Sid paid the driver and they stood a moment on the sidewalk. "You know what I would enjoy to do?" Sid said. "More than anything else in the world right now?"

Rudy shook his head.

"Walk in the park with my son. Would you do that, Rudy? Would you walk in the park with your father?"

The boy nodded.

"Good. Goddam hotel room, the air-conditioning's enough to freeze you. Look." He gestured across the street to Central Park. "Doesn't that look cool, Rudy? Shadows and trees and nice sweet wind. Come." They crossed the street into the park. "This is for us, Rudy; this is for my son and me. Yes?"

They started to walk.

"How you been?" Sid said.

"Fine," Rudy said. "How is mother?"

Sid shrugged. "Esther we can talk about later. Now is our time. How you been? You look so tired, Rudy." Sid stopped. "Aw, isn't that pretty?" He pointed down toward the lagoon. "Is that a swan, do you think? Look at it glide, Rudy. Aw, isn't that something to see?"

"How did you find me?" Rudy said.

"A father plays golf, a golfing partner reads papers from New York. There's a certain similarity in names. The father is interested. He makes inquiries. The play is about a deaf boy. A father can put together two and two. Smile for me, Rudy. Don't make me feel a bad father. I've changed, Rudy. I'm a different man. See me as I am now and smile."

"And you came all this way . . . ?"

"To see my son. To walk in the park. To watch you smile." They turned slowly away from the lagoon, started walking again, uptown. "Why did you leave?"

"It seemed best."

"That was all a mistake, Rudy. That terrible Lou Marks—forgive me for speaking ill of the dead, but it's true—he lied. He admitted it. The whole thing. He forced his wife into going along. They had a terrible marriage, Rudy. You were the one who suffered for it."

"It seemed best," Rudy said again. He wiped his forehead clear of perspiration, but before his hand had dropped, his brow was wet again.

"Omigod look, Rudy—" Sid pointed—"a pony ride. A pony ride. Isn't that a wonderful thing? Do you want a pony ride? I'll buy you one. I'll buy you a thousand pony rides. You—" Sid called to the attendant— "how much for a thousand pony rides?"

Rudy smiled.

"See my Rudy smile?" Sid said. "Oh yes. Oh yes."

They continued to walk, slowly, slowly through the heat.

"The zoo!" Sid cried. "What a wonderful city to have a zoo in its middle. This I have heard of, Rudy—the zoo and the carousel—those I must see." They stopped by the first cage. "Hello, Yak," Sid said. He looked at his watch. "You must not be late getting back," he explained. "I promised. Such an ugly animal. How is your play?"

"We'll know tonight."

"And you? I wanted you to be an actor once. But for me, you chose not to perform. Well, life goes on, we change. Tell me about these years, Rudy. What have you done?"

Rudy shrugged. "You?"

"I have made money," Sid said. They moved down a couple of cages. "A camel in the park," Sid said. "How amazing." Then he smiled. "Though why a camel in the park is more amazing than a yak in the park I can't imagine. Sometimes I'm such a fool. I play golf, now. Bad. I'm on the board at Greentree. Big deal. Ten, fifteen years ago I would have sold my soul. This fall I'm going to ask them to replace me. Dull. Bores me. I'm worth a lot of money, Rudy, would you believe it? It's all for you when I die. This suit cost two hundred. A summer suit! What do you think of that?"

"Wonderful, Father."

Sid pointed. "Are those porpoises?"

"Seals, maybe."

Sid hurried to the sea-lion pool. "Aren't they the cutest things?" He gripped the railing. "You don't think it's wonderful?"

"If it pleases you, then it is, Father. I mean that."

Sid lowered his body down, resting his chin on the railing. Like a small boy he watched the sea lions play. "I'll tell ya," he whispered.

Rudy crouched beside him.

"I'll never see fifty again. Not fifty-five either.

"I've done a lot of terrible things in my life. I'm trying to set my house in order, Rudy. You remember Solomon's?"

"Solomon's?"

Sid closed his eyes. "The corned-beef place. I bought you corned beef once when you were little. We stuffed you, Esther and I. We made you eat yourself sick, you remember that?" He reached out for his son. "I have suffered for that lately, believe me, I have suffered what I call torture for some of the things I done." He turned abruptly, straightened, started to walk again, stopping in front of the lions. "Big goddam cats," Sid muttered. "Look." He pointed to the signs about the animals' names. "*Felis Leo, Felis Tigris,* lion and tiger. Same family, I bet, but a different cage. That's like us, Rudy. Same family but we lived in different cages too long. Would you come home? After this thing? Yes?"

"No, Father."

"Why? You don't love me?"

"I do."

"Then why?"

"It's easier for me to love you if I don't have to see you every day."

Sid laughed, flung an arm around his son. "I'll buy that," he said, and he glanced at his watch. "Tell me you're glad I came. Tell me it was worth the thousand miles."

Rudy smiled.

"I'm tired of the zoo. Let's get out of the zoo." They walked up the steps, past the brown and black and polar bears, and Sid said, "There's a sign says we're headed for the carousel. Friedsam Memorial Carousel. That must make them very happy, the Friedsam people, knowing they gave a thing like that away. All these years, tell me what you done."

"Hid, Father."

Sid looked at him. "Where?"

"All over. First I went back to the deli, but it wasn't there anymore. I stayed around, though. For a while. I don't mind ghettos. Not really. I went west a while. I came east. I even wrote a book once, did you know?"

Sid shook his head. "What about?"

"Grandfather."

"Turk?"

The boy nodded.

"What the hell kind of a book can you write about a man with a big nose? You make any money out of it?"

"Not so much."

"I read *Exodus.* You read *Exodus*? Terrific. How do you make a living?"

"I don't need much. Odd jobs. What do you want from me, Father?"

Sid pointed. "What is that?"

Rudy stared up at the circular enclosure on the top of a hill. "That's where old people go. They play chess there."

Sid glanced at his watch. "I'd love to see that. We got time." He started up the steps.

"What do you want from me?"

"*What makes you think I want something, goddammit?* What makes you think I just didn't come a thousand miles because I'm old and I want my son to say I love you? Why does everybody always have to want something from you?"

"*I don't know! I don't know!*"

"*Maybe I don't!*"

"*But you do!* It's happened before. Over and over and I know the signs. I feel things. I know. So tell me, it doesn't matter, because I'm just too tired, I can't do anything for anybody anymore."

Sid hurried to the top of the stairs, found a bench, sat. Rudy slumped beside him. All around them, old men looked up from their chess games. "Ya got to," Sid whispered.

"No, Father."

"It'll be the one best thing you ever did."

"No, Father."

"You won't fail me."

"No, Father."

"Don't say that till you know what it is."

"No, Father."

"*Don't say that till you know what it is.*"

"What is it, then? Tell me."

"Esther—she's crazy, kid. I want you to commit your mother."

The old men were watching them, wet eyes staring.

"It's not what you think," Sid said.

Rudy tried to stand.

Sid held him. "It's not what you think," and twenty feet away a black knight moved across a chessboard, whispering, *"Have you had enough? Are you ready now?"* and Sid said, "I don't mean to any dump. I mean to the most expensive places in the country. I checked around already. Twenty thousand a year it would cost me, maybe more, but worth every penny. It's best. It's best."

"*Why?*" The old men were nodding now, watching them and nodding, their tired heads moving like chickens after grain.

"Because she's crazy and she needs peace and if she gets put away she'll have it."

"Put her away, then."

"I need *you*—"

"No, you don't. You don't . . . make them stop looking at us."

"Forget them. Listen." He grabbed his son. "Listen, Rudy, you know how it is with Esther and me—how it's always been. I say 'sit,' she's gotta stand—you know that's true. *You're* the only one. If *you* told her it would bring her peace to go, she would go. *You* she would believe. Me, never. She thinks I got other reasons. She's gotta be put away. She's gotta have peace, kid, and—"

"What are they, your other reasons?"

"*Go back to your games!*" Sid cried, and immediately the old heads turned away. "Old cockers. They should play their silly games and leave us—"

"I know you, Father. So tell me. The reasons. The reasons."

"Sid Miller don't lie! Not no more. Sure, I got reasons. The best reasons. The best in the whole world—you think I would come all this way to ask a favor *if it didn't matter?* My God, *this is the most important thing in my whole life*—yes."

"Leave me alone . . . Father, please, Father . . ."

"You got to do this."

"Can't you understand? *I'm tired.*"

"This you can do—"

"I'm really . . . very tired, Father."

"*This you can do!* This—*you old cockers!* Play your games! Leave my son and me alone!"

The old heads turned away.

"This you got to do," Sid said. "Listen—when I was a youngster, pushing cutlery and like that door to door, shop to shop, I screwed all the broads—the broads, they fell ker-plunk for little Sidney, but not Esther, so whatever the reasons it was a mistake but we married—"

"Please . . ."

"We married and we fought, and her health went and I clawed for every penny and by Christ I got pennies now, and I got a place on the board of Greentree Country Club, and servants I got, and a house in the country and land I got, but I also got a crazy wife, and then, Rudy—are you getting this?—now—listen—the most wonderful thing at last has happened to me—at last the only thing I never had I got—*I'm in love, Rudy*—me—Sid—in love—and she loves me—the widow Marks loves me—'Sid and Dolly and everything's jolly'—ya see?—ya see?—little poems I make up—her too—we're *that* happy—at last I got someone who loves me—I never had that—neither did she ever have what we got now—*we love each other*—"

The old faces were watching again. Rudy closed his eyes.

Sid began to whisper. "But Esther ruins it . . . *she follows us.* Always. Always. Wherever we try and go—*Esther's there*—whenever we try and meet—*Esther's there*—so don't you see what it would mean, Rudy—it would mean love for me and peace for Esther and everybody could live happily ever after—don't deprive me of my happiness, Rudy—don't deprive your mother of peace—we've suffered—we have—release us, Rudy—from our suffering—let us go—"

"I could never," Rudy whispered.

"Why?"

Rudy shook his head. "Never."

"But *why?*"

"She's not crazy."

"You haven't seen her in ten years. How do you know?"

"She has headaches. That doesn't make her crazy."

"But if she was, you would help me to put her away. You would tell her 'go.' "

"If she was, you wouldn't need me. You could get doctors. They would do it."

"All that matters, Rudy, is what is *best* for her."

"Yes."

Sid grabbed him. "You agree, then. If she is crazy, then it would be *best* to put her away."

"No, no, you should never put anyone—"

"These are fine places of which I'm speaking. Hot-and-cold-running doctors. She would be happy. You'll help me. If you think she's crazy."

"No."

"You mean yes."

"Leave me alone, Father."

"Rudy—"

"*I mean it!*"

"*Stare if you want to, old fools!*" Sid shouted at the chess men. "You're tired," he said, patting his son. "We'll talk more about this later."

"No."

"You can't disappoint me. I know my son."

"I've got to get back," Rudy said. "You can go back too."

"You mean leave? Before this is settled?"

"This is settled. The answer is forever no." He started to walk.

Sid caught up, put an arm around his shoulder. "I've tired you. I'm a fool. Forgive me." Sid pointed to a sign. "The Friedsam Memorial Carousel. What a poetic name almost." They walked away from the old men and down across a road and in the distance they saw the carousel. "Can you hear?" Sid said.

Rudy shook his head.

"Such beautiful music," Sid said. "Sets your feet right to tapping."

"I can't hear."

"Rudy—"

"You came a thousand miles for nothing. Don't ask me anymore. It's over. You want to put her away, do it, do it, but not with me. Never mention it again to me."

"I'm in love, Rudy. And Esther needs peace. The world's too much for her now. It beats her all the time. It hurts her, Rudy. She's suffered. God knows we both have. Please—"

"I say never mention it and you go right on. Why must you do that?"

"Because I am in love! Because I am desperate. Look at the carousel, Rudy. Isn't it a wonderful thing?" They moved up close to it and the sound of children joined the music. Sid looked at his watch. "Eleven almost on the button," he said, then he waved.

Esther waved back.

"Surprise," Sid said.

"She's *here*?"

Esther started toward them.

Rudy turned.

Sid grabbed him. "Talk to her. Talk to her. You'll see how crazy. How she needs peace. You'll see."

"Rudy . . ." Esther called. "Rudy . . ." closer.

"Talk to her. You'll see."

"Rudy . . ." Esther said. She stopped in front of him.

Rudy just stood there.

Esther wept.

"Eleven o'clock it is, Tootsie," Sid said. "Did I lie?"

Esther clutched her son. "I must stop crying," she said. "I will ruin my makeup. Everything runs when you cry."

"Talk to her, Rudy," Sid said.

She looked as young and pretty as he could ever remember. He told her so.

"You two talk," Sid said, smiling, waving as he backed off. "Look—" and he pointed— "there's horseshoe players. I'll go watch the horseshoe players. You two just talk as much as you want to."

Esther watched him go. "What did he want from you?"

". . . nothing . . ."

"Watch out. He has some scheme in mind. I know him. Oh . . ." She looked down at the sidewalk where her purse had fallen. "I do that. I drop things."

Rudy picked up her purse. "You really look wonderful, Mother."

"I have no more headaches."

"Oh, what a blessing, what a blessing."

"I have no more headaches. No more. I drop things. I just somehow forget I have things in my hands and they open and something drops. Are you hot? I'm hot. I love you, Rudy." She moved to a bench by the carousel and sat down. "I love the carousel, don't you?" There were two little blond children at the far end of the bench. "Hello," Esther said. "What are your names?"

They said nothing.

"This is my son," Esther went on. "Rudy, say hello to the young ladies."

"Hello." Rudy smiled.

"I have no more headaches, isn't that a blessing?" Esther put the tips of her fingers to her eyes. "We said that. Yes. I drop things and I can't remember much unless it was a long time ago, isn't that funny?"

Rudy smiled. "It's so hot today. That's probably why."

The carousel stopped. Children streamed off, others waited to get on. The noise was high and very loud. "Do you remember Eli Shapiro? Of course you don't, why should you? He was the undertaker—he buried your grandfather—oh . . ." She looked down at the sidewalk.

Rudy picked up her purse and gave it back to her and smiled.

"He was the last man to take me on a carousel. Eli Shapiro, I loved him so much, Rudy, why did he leave me?"

Rudy made another smile.

"I wonder what Sid wants from you? Where is Sid? Probably off with that Dolly. Did you hear? Everybody talks about it—the spectacle they're making of themselves—terrible." She shook her head. "I do my best to save them from criticism: The wife of Eli Shapiro can do no less than to try and save her friends from criticism." The little blond girls hurried away. Esther stared after them. "Rudy? Why didn't they tell me their names?"

"They were just nervous."

"No. I did something, I could tell. You can tell when people like you. They didn't like me. Oh . . ."

Rudy picked up her purse.

"It's so hot here in Chicago." Esther laughed. "Do you remember how it was over the deli? We sweltered so, remember? Our whole house is air-conditioned now, Rudy. Every nook. We don't use it, though. Only maybe twice a year. That's all it ever gets so hot you need to turn it on. And sometimes when I have a bad headache, we use it then too."

"Good," Rudy said.

Esther shook her head. "That's three," she said. "Three mistakes I've made. Now wait—what tune is that from the carousel? 'Put On Your Old Gray Bonnet'?"

"I can't tell. Perhaps."

Esther closed her eyes and mouthed "One, two, three." She opened her eyes. "Three mistakes is correct. I said I was the wife of Eli Shapiro. I said this was Chicago. I switched about the headaches. Three."

"I didn't notice," Rudy said.

"The doctor says I must try to catch them. He doesn't mind if I say them, but I must catch them and think about why I made them. Now Eli, he I daydream about, and Chicago I said because . . . because the heat reminded me and I switched about the headaches because . . ." She paused. "Why did I make that one? Why did I make that one?" She clapped her hands. "Yes, I said it because I don't want the headaches. There. A memory, a daydream and a wish." She smiled. "I got them all."

"Yes," Rudy said.

"Oh . . ."

Rudy picked up her purse.

"I really do look well, don't I? Tell me the truth."

"I have. Yes."

Esther nodded. "I can tell. My mirror tells me so. I'm just so placid in the face. If only my hands weren't so forgetful. If only you could kiss them and make them well. Didn't I do that to you all the time? When you were little?"

Rudy kissed her hands. "There. All well."

"I always *meant* to do it, Rudy. I never did though, did I?"

"It doesn't matter."

"We must ride the carousel. Then later I can say, 'Remember when we rode the carousel?' and I won't have to think I never did but only meant to. Oh . . ."

Rudy picked up her purse and took her arm, guiding her to the ticket window. He signaled for two, paid, and they got in line with the children. When the time came, he led her in, helping her onto a white horse, mounting the neighboring black himself. Everyone waited for the music.

All around them were the children.

The carousel at last began to turn.

"They should have told me their names," Esther said, and she tried not to, but in a moment she was weeping.

"It's all right," Rudy shouted over the music. "They *did* tell. You just didn't hear. Their names were Janie and Jeannie and they liked you very much. They liked you. They told me so."

Esther could not stop crying.

Sid appeared outside, watching them, mouthing the word "See? See?" to Rudy and Esther cried and Sid might just as well have shouted "SEE? SEE? SEE?" and the children shrieked with laughter and the music grew louder and the carousel turned faster and the noise hurt Rudy's ears; his mother's tears, his father's shouts, the shrieking and the music that wasn't "Put On Your Old Gray Bonnet" and he clung to the great black horse but it bucked and threw him to the ground, thundering "HAVE YOU HAD ENOUGH? ARE YOU READY NOW?" and then it tried to crush him with the weight of its mighty hoofs, but he was fast, too fast, and he squirmed out from under and off the machine and over the railing and then he was free, Rudy Miller in the park, sprinting through the heat, running like crazy.

XXV

Walt stood sweating in front of the theater, and when Rudy appeared at the end of the block, turning the corner, running toward him, Walt shouted, "Let's go, let's go, it's after twelve, you're late," and Rudy, when he reached him, stopped and muttered that he was sorry. Walt shepherded him into the lobby and through it to the rear of the theater. He pushed his glasses up snug against the bridge of his nose with his left thumb and looked at Rudy. "You O.K. and everything?"

"Fine. Yes."

"Good; go get ready."

Rudy dashed toward the dressing rooms.

Walt started in the direction of the stage where Katz, the costume designer, was having words with the light man, but before he was halfway there he turned abruptly and slipped out the side exit of the theater. "Rudy's here," he said to Tony. "Can't be long now."

Tony nodded, continuing to smoke.

"I haven't mentioned you to Branch yet, but I will. I just couldn't wait till tonight. Once the lights are out, I'll sneak you in."

Tony stepped on her cigarette, lit another. "Pack two for the day," she said. "When I called in sick this morning I gave as my malady smoker's hack."

Walt wiped his forehead. "So you be honest, huh? Tell me what you think no matter what?"

Tony raised her right hand.

"S'long." He started back inside.

"Boy, are some people in big trouble."

Walt stopped. "Huh?"

"Here I am, wearing a *brand-new titillatingly filmy watermelon-colored cotton chiffon shirt-waist creation* bought at the cost of *an arm and a leg* from Jax spatzel for the occasion, and *you say not one word.*"

"You look good," Walt said.

Tony laughed and hugged him, kissed his cheek. "I promised to be biased in your favor," she whispered. "I love the play already."

"May I?" Walt said, looking around, his hands moving up from her waist.

Tony looked around too, whispered "You may."

Walt touched her breasts. "Very titillatingly filmy," he allowed. "You've spurred me on to victory." He turned and walked into the door. "Nuts," he said.

Tony could not stop laughing.

Walt made it through the door the second time, pausing to admire the chaos. Jenny was trying to study her script, but Katz insisted on readjusting the length of her skirt and now the stage manager was yelling at the light man and Aaron was pacing around with the inevitable cigarette jammed in the corner of his mouth and Carmella was dogging him, telling him (again) about what a prince Walter Huston was and Branch was talking with some old fat bag who needed a better girdle and then Katz was crying out that he would not allow his name to appear on the program if people were going to tamper with his creations and the light man was yelling back at the stage manager and Walt started toward Branch, who left the old lady and they met halfway up an aisle and before Branch could talk Walt whispered, "I got Tony stashed outside. I'm gonna sneak her in this aft—I'll tell you after what she says. O.K.?"

"I think . . . I'll uh . . . go on up to . . . uh Seventy-second now," Branch said.

"You mean after the rehearsal, dontcha?"

"No; the party's got to be set . . . up and everything."

"You're not gonna watch your own dress rehearsal?" Walt said.

"Someone has . . . got to take care . . . of getting the party set . . . up, you know."

"Branch, it's just—I mean, it's not a formal gathering. We can set it all up when we get there after rehearsal. Don't work so hard."

"I'm not."

"But—"

"Mother will help me," Branch managed, gesturing toward the fat old lady in green. He hurried back to her. Then they hurried away.

Walt stared after Mrs. Scudder. Her cheeks were fat and her eyes puffy and her stomach bulged and the seams of the green dress strained to contain her and the still slender legs supporting all that flesh were ludicrous, painful to look upon. They belonged to a young girl, those legs; they had no business being beneath a wrinkled body.

"What's with Scudder?" Aaron asked Walt, coming up behind.

"I don't know. He and his mother are gonna set the party up, I guess. Beats the hell outta me."

"That was Scudder's *mother*?"

Walt nodded.

Aaron sat down. He jammed a cigarette into a corner of his mouth and looked around. "Where's Rudy?"

"Getting ready."

"Ought to be a fun party," Aaron said.

Walt shrugged, moved up onstage, settled the argument with Katz, settled the argument with the light man, walked over and whispered into Jenny's ear that he loved her madly and she smiled and went on studying her script, and when Rudy came onstage Walt asked would everyone please shut up, because he had a few words to say. "I am not a believer in last-minute pep talks," he said. "If the work has been done decently, it'll show; if not, not. What is it, Rudy?"

"I . . . want to say something."

"Go."

"I want to say—"

"Louder," Carmella shouted.

"I'm . . . sorry," Rudy said.

"What's the matter?" Jenny said, going to him.

"Nothing. Please." Rudy closed his eyes. "Earlier, I did some running. I'm fine. What I want to say is . . . there is a man—he was let in here earlier—this man—" His fingers flew to his earpiece. "He is . . . my father and we do not get on as well as we might and . . . if he returns—and he will—please, I don't want to see him—don't let him in, please—and if he asks where I am, please say you know nothing—I must not see him and he is very . . . persuasive and . . . if this were not important to me . . . I would not embarrass you like this by speaking out in such a manner. I'm sorry."

Walt waited. When it was clear that Rudy was finished, he said, "Everybody got that? O.K. Now just one word about the party. As you know, you're all invited, and it's for after this rehearsal, at Branch's place on Seventy-second Street. Six A is the apartment number and there's booze and if I choose to get bombed, that's O.K., but none of the performers, solid?" He began to pace "The party's Branch's notion. It worked once in college and everybody got relaxed and performed well and we could do with some of that too, relaxed performances, and I think we're gonna get 'em. We've had a lot of fun working on this play and tonight some lousy people are going to come and spoil all that fun. Just because they pay *money* they have the gall to expect to be *entertained*. Shall we entertain them? I say yes." He hurried off the stage into the auditorium. "Hit it!"

The minute the lights went out, Walt went to the side exit and cracked the door for Tony, who slipped in and sat in the farthest back corner. Walt moved down closer and sat, watching as he had watched so many times, taking notes, shaking his head when a line was fluffed, laughing when he thought something was funny. From the start it was clear that Rudy was off, but Jenny was very solid, and before the first act ended Rudy was good again, and Carmella was playing well, and the other two boys too, and Walt sat there, mouthing the words now along with the actors, trying to remember what he thought of Tony's taste, because if she liked it, fine, but if she didn't, what then, but in the second act Jenny was so good he began to relax, because you couldn't do much else but like it, and then he remembered that Tony's taste was excellent, not necessarily commercial, but critically it was sound (God bless all Sarah Lawrence girls) and then at the start of the third act Rudy was nervous again, and Walt gnawed at his fingernails, because if Rudy blew the last scene, the big scene, the whole thing was out the window and he stopped taking notes, stopped mouthing, just watching now as the big scene began, Jenny appearing in the doorway, lonely lost Loretta, a suitcase clutched in her hands, and then here came deaf Clare and they began talking and Walt thought halfway through my God I'm a helluva director and three-quarters of the way he started to smile, because Rudy was as good as he'd ever been and Jenny was as good as she always was and they touched hands and went on out the door together and as he turned to look at Tony, Walt wasn't sure but what he didn't catch a tear in her eye. He bounded up on-stage, told the actors they were fine and to get ready for the party and that he wouldn't bother giving notes just then and with that he raced on back to Tony, who sat alone in the rear of the darkened theater, smoking. "Well?" Walt said. He sat down beside her.

Tony said " 'Well?' 'Well?' You just can't say 'well?' and expect me to talk, not coherently anyway." Visibly excited, she ground out her cigarette with her shoe, immediately lit another, inhaled, exhaled, inhaled again. "Maybe you better ask me questions or along those lines, what do you think?"

"Just tell me," Walt said smiling. "Just talk."

"You bastard, you've got talent."

"Why does that make me a bastard?"

"I don't know, it just does. I'm competitive and I don't like for my boyfriends to be talented. I like for my boyfriends to be goons. I don't want this cigarette." She dropped it, ground it out. "I don't want this ciga-rette either," she said, lighting another.

"Go on. Start with the little things. Rudy was nervous at the start, but that's all I'm gonna tell you."

"I don't know much about sets or costumes, Walt. I liked them, but I don't know beans; it doesn't mean anything."

"Go on."

"Well, the acting . . . the two boys with the little parts, they're really O.K., I thought."

"So do I. Go on."

"It's very hard just trying to be coherent like this when you're all in-volved and everything."

"You're doing great. Go on."

"The old lady's—well, basically I hate that kind of person—in real life, I mean—but I thought she was good. Very solid."

"I'm with you."

"And Rudy—well . . ."

"Now remember he was nervous at the start. He can do that a lot better than today," Walt said.

"In the first place, he's so goddam fantastic-looking and he's natural and he's deaf and so's the part and that helps—he's *really* very good, Walt. I mean, he's marvelous and if it weren't for Jenny he'd steal the play easy."

"Isn't she something?"

"I would love to be her agent," Tony said. She finished the cigarette, coughed, started to light another.

"Why not smoke?" Walt said.

"Terrific idea," Tony said, smiling at him, finishing lighting the cigarette, inhaling deeply, coughing again. "They are so marvelous together, the two of them. I don't know what other parts she's right for on account of her size, but, Walt, she's really something. I mean, he's good, but she's—"

"I tell you," Walt said, "It's a pleasure watching her. Sometimes—"

"You're really talented," Tony cut in. "I'm really mad at you, you bastard, I could almost hate you, it's just one helluva good production."

"You don't know—"

"Everything that could be done's been done."

"Just hearing you say—what do you mean?"

"What do you think I'm so upset for? All this effort and love spent on this play. You wash garbage, it's still garbage." All of a sudden there were tears in her eyes. "What do you think's so upsetting? No one's going to know you can do anything at all. They're just going to kill you, Walt. They're going to take this thing apart and tromp all over it." She threw up her hands. "What can I tell you? It's a shitty play."

I didn't hear that, Aaron thought, behind them in the darkness, lurking.

The doorbell rang.

"Honey, honey, *please*," Rose said. "Someone's here. Answer the door."

Branch lay still in the dark study, his arms across his eyes. "Get it, will you, Mom?"

"Branch, the party's started. Please. Get *up*."

"Get it, will you, Mom?"

"But what'll I say?"

"I don't care, Mom."

The doorbell rang again.

"I had to come, honey. I *had* to see you. And you would've said 'no' if I'd called and asked. Wouldn't you?"

"Answer the door, Mom. Before they go 'way."

"You're all I got, Branch." Rose gave her head a quick shake, shut her puffy eyes. "I mean all I had. An' I just couldn't stand . . . not hearing from you *at all* an'—"

"*Mom*—"

"Awright, awright, I'll go." She touched her skirt. "Tell me I look O.K."

"Never better, Mom," Branch said, and as she closed the door he lay still a moment in the darkness. Then, with a strength that took him completely by surprise, he arched his body up, arched it so that he rested on his heels and the base of his neck. He stayed like that until it began to hurt, and when that happened he fell back to the bed and just thought, Never better. Jesus.

God, Rose thought, standing one last moment before the foyer mirror. "Coming," she called, trying to pull her dress down and suck in her stomach and it all began that day after she got home from New York the last time. The day after her return and she saw that fudge in Custer's Bakery and why had she been such a fool as to buy it? Once you started Custer's fudge, you just couldn't stop when you wanted to. Not if you had a real sweet tooth. I'll just have to go on one of those crash diets, Rose decided. Just as soon as I get home, that's what I'll do. Meanwhile, she pulled in her stomach, or tried to, and got her dress to look right, or tried to, and made her hair lie flat, or tried to, and thought, God.

Tony thought: Fool. She stood outside the door of apartment 6A and she cursed herself for her honesty. I never should have told him. Never. Fool to speak truth. Lies he wanted and you gave him the truth, Tony baby, both goddam barrels, and you better watch it now because he's angry, old Kirkaby is, and at you. Not for any good reason; just because you spoke the stupid truth, so you watch it, kiddo, or you'll blow it all, sweetheart, and you don't want that to happen, do you, dumpling? She took Walt's hand and looked at him and smiled.

Walt returned it warmly, the word "bitch" very prominent in his mind.

"Coming" from inside.

Walt held on to Tony's hand even though it was too hot to hold on to anything, and he tried to think about how much he hoped Branch's apartment would be air-conditioned, but he was only partially successful, and the taxi ride up from the theater kept steaming through his mind, one dollar and sixty cents' worth of solid criticism from Tony. She had opened her mouth with the drop of the meter and not closed it till the checker cruised to a halt before the building. *How* could you have done a play like this? *Where's your taste?* How did they raise *the money?* Walt raised Tony's hand to his lips.

"You devil," Tony said.

The word "bitch" kept coming back. He dropped her hand, wiped his wet forehead. What he objected to, when you came right down to it, wasn't the criticism. It really wasn't. He didn't mind her knocking him. What bothered him a great deal more than the words was the fact that while she spoke he could never, at no time since he'd known her, ever remember her having seemed quite so goddam blissfully happy.

"Hi, I'm Rose."

"Hello, Mrs. Scudder. You remember me? I'm Walt Kirkaby. And this is Tony Last."

"Come *in.*"

"Thank you," Tony said. "What a lovely apartment."

"I'll show you around if you like," Rose said. "Except we can't go in the study now. Branch is terribly busy in there. Last-minute things, you understand." They stopped in the living room. "This is the living room," Rose said. "Isn't that some view?" They all moved to the windows and stared out at Riverside Park and the Hudson.

"Beautiful," Tony said. She looked at Walt. "It really is."

"Do you think that looks all right?" Rose said, gesturing to two card tables, one of which held liquor and ice, the other cold cuts and rye bread and a large blue container of Morton's salt. "I couldn't find the salt shakers," Rose said, "and Branch was so busy with last-minute things, I didn't want to bother him. Do you think it looks all right or not? Branch is usually the decorator in the family."

"Lovely," Tony said.

"I just had to do everything, Branch being so busy. Back in college, he did a show. Oh, it was terribly successful, and he had a party before the first performance and he swore then and there he'd always do that, but of course doing it in New York is a lot different from doing it in Ohio."

Walt nodded.

Rose took Tony's hand. "Like a tour? This is the living room, and the foyer you've seen already." They walked back into it, turned left and moved down the hall. "Then here's the bedroom," Rose said. "It's got the same view as the other." She gestured to the river. "And then behind it— that's the study where we can't go 'cause Branch is so busy, and this—in between the bedroom and the study is the bathroom. Do you want to see the bathroom? Why bother, it's a bathroom, and now back we go." They re-entered the hall. "And here's the kitchen. It's just the four rooms—living, bed, kitchen, study."

"But they're all a lovely size," Tony said.

Rose lowered her voice. "Branch wouldn't live in a place unless it was the very best. That's what he's used to and that's what he gets."

The doorbell rang.

Rose called "Coming."

Tony walked back into the living room. Walt stood alone, staring out the window. Tony stopped and pointed, whispering, "By George, he's even handsomer in person than on the silver screen." Then as he turned and smiled, she walked toward him.

Walt watched her, deciding, as she approached, that in her watermelon-colored whatever it was she looked better than he had ever seen her. A sexy bitch, no denying, and as she smiled at him he wondered if he was going to have to marry her, which would serve him right, because he was such a goddam fool, picking virginity as an admirable virtue, in this, the twentieth century.

Jenny wondered if she should ring again. "What do you think?" she asked Rudy.

Rudy said he didn't know.

Jenny raised her hand toward the buzzer, then dropped it. "Don't you live here?" she asked.

Rudy remembered that he did.

"Then don't you have a key?"

Rudy produced it as Rose opened the door.

They looked at each other.

"Hi, I'm Rose," Rose said.

Rudy wished someone had told him.

"Jenny Devers. And this is Rudy Miller."

"Hi," Rose said, and she reached out a stubby hand, and Rudy was about to take it when a silver ring on her finger asked *Have you had enough? Are you ready now?* which startled him so that her stubby hand hung in midair, untouched, and then, embarrassed, she withdrew it, but he grabbed it, grabbed it hard with both of his, and said, "I'm sorry, I'm sorry," and then Jenny's voice was saying "He's very tired," and Rose's: "Of course, my, yes, why shouldn't he be?" and then Jenny was saying "Can I do anything" and Rose told her "I think everybody's in the living room," and Rudy watched her go and then Rose was whispering, "You've got to help me. Got to."

Rudy kept an eye on her silver ring.

Rose led him down the corridor, whispering, "I had to come. You understand that. Make him not be mad at me. Make him understand. You can do that. I know you can do that. You're the only one who can do that." They stopped by the study door. "Tell him that I love him. I can't take the way he looks at me. You tell him that I love him. You tell him. You make him believe."

The study door opened and they walked into the darkness.

"Hon, it's Rudy. I brought him to you."

Branch said nothing.

"You tell him," Rose whispered, and then she was gone.

"Did you see her?" Branch said then. *"Did you see her? I did that."* He lay on the bed, breathing quietly.

Rudy stood in the center of the darkness.

"I almost got sick when I saw her. She walked in down there and . . . and . . . *why didn't her legs get fat too?"*

"I'm sorry," Rudy said, and then he said "Don't cry," because Branch was, and then he said "Stop," because Branch couldn't, and then he said "Stay," because Branch was crawling toward him, and then, just before Branch touched him, he said "Please," and when the darkness rumbled *"Have you had enough? Are you ready now?"* he was not in the least bit surprised.

"Coming," Rose called as the doorbell rang.

Tony left Walt and went over to the food table and said "I thought you were so wonderful" to Jenny.

Jenny smiled. "You saw the play, then? How is it?"

"Bits and pieces," Tony said quickly. "Not enough to tell. What I saw was just excellent."

That bad, Jenny thought.

"I really loved you, though."

Jenny looked at the dark girl, neat and cool in her watermelon-colored dress, and she felt, as she stood there, hot and messy, and, clutching the makings of a bologna sandwich in her big hands, she felt—now cut it out, Jenny told herself—you're too big to be a waif! Just say thank you and finish making your sandwich. "Thank you," Jenny said, and she turned quickly back to the table.

Tony went back to Walt, who, drenched, was still staring out the window. "Hey," she whispered. "I could be wrong. Smile."

Walt shook his head. "You're not wrong. If you were wrong," he whispered, "then why did I tell—" and he nodded to Jenny—"to get people down to see her as soon as possible? Nope; you're right and I knew it."

"You can still smile," Tony said.

"You smile," Walt told her. "You do it so nicely. Smile like you smiled in the cab coming up. I loved that smile."

Aaron appeared in the living-room doorway, sweating and happy. "I'm looking for the seventh layer," he said, mopping his forehead.

What I must do, Jenny thought, piling pickle relish on top of her lettuce, which was on top of her tomato, which was on top of her bologna, is just pray we run long enough so I don't go back to Charley. No. What I must do is just pray that someone comes and sees me and likes me and says come act for me someplace far away from Charley. She nodded, wondering what the odds on that were.

Aaron made himself a drink and walked over to Walt and Tony. "How'd you like it?" he said.

"She loved it," Walt said quickly.

Aaron smiled. "Thank God."

Tony nodded. "Yes."

Aaron said, "Tell me."

"I'm no critic," Tony replied. "I just know what I like." She laughed.

"And you really loved it?"

"She did, she did," Walt said.

Aaron could not stop smiling.

Walt wiped his face.

Rose came over. "How's everybody doing?"

"Where's Branch?" Aaron asked.

"In the study, beavering away," Rose said. She pulled at her green dress, straightened her hair.

Aaron looked at Jenny. "I could have sworn I saw Rudy leave with her."

"Oh, Rudy's in helping Branch right now," Rose said.

"Wouldn't you just know it," Aaron said. "I tel! you, friendship is such a wonderful thing, don't you agree, Mrs. Scudder?"

"Yes. Yes."

"I tell you, Branch and Rudy—well, it's just amazing when two guys can get to be such friends in such a short time." He smiled.

Rose tried to.

"These days where you find Rudy, you're a cinch to find Branch, and where you find Branch—well, guess where Rudy is?" He started to laugh. "Right, Walt?"

"Huh?" Walt said. "I wasn't listening."

"They're so close sometimes when I'm just sitting around bulling with them—well, Mrs. Scudder, they can almost guess each other's thoughts. I tell you, it's *unnatural*."

Rose looked at him. "You mean uncanny."

"Of course," Aaron said. "What did I say? *Unnatural?*" He laughed again. "Silly of me."

"Coming," Rose called as the doorbell rang, almost running across the room.

"You look marvelous," Aaron said to Tony. "Of course, that just might be because you loved my play. 'Scuse," and he went back to the bar. When he got there, he looked at Walt and then at Tony and then he laughed. He made himself a Scotch and water, looked back at them again, laughed louder.

Walt walked over. "What's so funny?"

"Tell you sometime," Aaron answered, and then he shouted "Carmella!" as the rest of the cast and crew streamed into the room. "Lemme bartend," Aaron said, and he set to making drinks for everybody, taking time out, every so often, to gaze at Walt and Tony and shake his head, or laugh, or smile. Sweat poured down his thin face, but he ignored it, or licked out with the tip of his tongue, or took his damp kerchief and wiped his eyes. "I can get bombed!" Aaron roared. "I'm the writer." He looked at Walt and broke out laughing.

Walt walked over again. "Dammit, Aaron, what is it?"

"Nothing, nothing," Aaron muttered, and then he looked around, finding Rose, hurrying toward her. "We were having that lovely talk about friendship," Aaron began.

"The kitchen," Rose said. "Some things," and she left him.

Branch appeared.

Aaron engulfed him. "I was just having this lovely conversation with your mother about friendship," he began.

Branch didn't seem to hear. "Where's Mother, do you know?"

"I believe the kitchen."

Branch turned and went away.

The doorbell rang.

Rudy stood quietly in a corner of the living room.

"Coming," Rose called, and she ran and opened the door. "Hello, I'm Rose."

"Sid and Esther Miller, parents of the star."

"How do you do," Esther said.

"Rudy . . ." Sid cried. "Rudy . . ." He charged toward his son.

"How the hell did they get here?" Walt said to Tony.

Across the room, Aaron smiled.

Sid clasped an arm around his son's shoulder. "So are you nervous?" he said aloud, dropping his voice, whispering, "Coward, coward to run like that, coward."

"Please," Rudy said.

"Will you do it? Yes? What I want? Yes?"

"Please."

"Rudy . . ." Esther said.

"Talk to your mother, Rudy."

"Why did you run, Rudy?"

"Excuse—" the boy began, starting to turn, but Sid anticipated, and when the boy made the turn there was Sid's face, and there were Sid's lips whispering "She's crazy, you saw that, commit her, help me," and Rudy closed his eyes, brushing by, and then he was safe in the corridor, heading toward the quiet of the bedroom, but when he got there he heard Esther's voice, and he smiled at his mother and said "I don't know" when she said, "What does he want from you?"

"What could it be?" Esther went on. "It must be something. Why did you run?"

"I shouldn't have. I'm sorry."

"Sid says I made you run. Did I?"

"No."

"Why did you run, then?"

"No reason. Mother—" he took her hands—"please, you are not as weak as you seem. I know, I know, you must be strong—"

"Yes," Esther said. "I must be strong." Then: "How do I do that? Why did you run from me?"

"You two talking?" Sid said from the bedroom door. "Tell her, Rudy."

"Tell me what?"

"Nothing."

"Tell her what you told me, Rudy. Remember—"

"I said nothing—nothing."

"Tell me what?"

"Excuse me," Rudy said, and he dashed by Sid, back into the living room and the heat and the noise.

Branch grabbed him.

Rudy broke free.

Sid came after him. *"Obey me. Tell her. Obey me for once in your life!"*

"Rudy . . ." Esther called.

"I mean it, Aaron," Walt said. "I'm getting sick and tired of the way you're looking at Tony and me."

"Sorry," Aaron said, smiling, walking away.

Tony stopped Aaron. "Do you know me?"

"Of course I do. You're Walt's girlfriend."

"Rudy—" Branch said.

"Rudy!" Sid said.

Esther called, "Rudy . . . Rudy . . ."

"I mean," Tony said, "do I look familiar?"

Aaron said, "I don't know, do you?"

Tony said, "That's not an answer."

"That's right," Aaron replied.

Rose called, "Can I get anybody anything?"

"Tell her," Sid whispered. "Rudy, if you love me, if you love her, tell her—it would bring her such peace. You know she's crazy—you knew it when you ran—so tell her, tell her—"

"Oh . . ." Esther said, and she looked down for her purse.

Rudy scrambled after it.

"Thank you," Esther said. She put her fingertips to her temples. "Thank you."

"Tell her," Sid whispered. "For the love of God—"

"Oh . . ." Esther said, looking down.

Rudy stood very still.

Then the whole room turned and stared at him. All the things turned, the walls turned and the glasses and the rings on stubby fingers, and the floor buckled, staring up at him, and the windows turned and the furniture shifted so as to see him better, and then there was a deadly pause, and after it came the voices, the infinite whispering voices, all at once wondering if, by any chance, he might have had enough; did he think, just possibly, he might be ready now?

Rudy ran.

Sid started after him, Branch too, and for a moment they blocked each other, and Esther also went after him, first scooping up her purse, then trying to run, and Sid said "Have you seen Rudy?" to Rose and Rose said "Yes, I think he's in the living room" and Sid said "Maybe" but ran on to the bedroom where Jenny said when asked, "No, he hasn't been in here" and Esther looked all over the study and Branch scoured the kitchen but he wasn't there either and then Rose said, "We're out of soda, perhaps he went for that," and Sid was hot from the chase and Branch was perspiring terribly and Esther feebly fanned herself, and Branch, after staring for a moment at his mother's slender legs, turned violently away and Esther said "Oh . . ." and Sid got her purse and smiled, saying, "We'll find him, Tootsie, don't cave in now," and Esther answered, "No, I must be strong."

Branch, completing his violent turn, aimed for the bedroom, where Jenny sat alone, smiling, because she had just realized that what she was was the biggest fool in all the world, because if the play failed and nobody came to see her she would just go off and marry Tommy Alden, which was what she should have done in the first place, years ago, because he loved her, and then she thought that even if the play was a hit and *every-body* came to see her, she would *still* marry Tommy, and *then* she thought, *well,* if the play was a hit and *everybody* came to see her and offered her some *just fabulous part,* what she would do would be to act in it for *just a little* bit and *then* marry Tommy.

"Have you seen Rudy?" Branch asked again.

Jenny just smiled in the terrible heat, because no matter what happened now, she had nothing to lose anymore.

Above her, on the fire escape, Rudy soared. He dashed up past the tenth floor, the eleventh, the twelfth, past the fourteenth, all the way to the top of the building, and then he sat and stared down, but only for a moment, because his feet were alive, his feet needed movement, so he was off again, flying again, down the rusted steps, jumping six at a time, eight, sometimes ten, landing catlike in the heat, whirling around a corner, darting down another and another floor. When he reached the sixth, he rested above the window, out of sight. Across from him was the dark side of another building; below him, a darker alleyway, with one or two cars parked, single file. But the cars, like the windows across, were empty. No one could see him, so no one could catch him. Of course, even if someone did see, he would still be uncatchable. No one could ever catch him, not on a fire escape, not as long as he stayed just right where he was, winded and warm, rust-surrounded, safe.

Aaron poured himself another shot of Scotch and threw his arm around Walt's shoulder. He gestured toward Tony, who was talking to a sweating Sid. "What color's that dress?" Aaron wondered.

"Watermelon, word reaches me."

"Whatever it is, she sure looks cool."

Walt nodded.

"She's sure something," Aaron went on. He slapped Walt on the back. "Boy, you must be tired."

"We're all tired, Aaron. You too, I bet."

Aaron smiled. "You must just be beat down to the ground."

"Well, like I said—"

"What I'm trying to say," Aaron went on, "is that your little ole ass has just got to be dragging." He grinned in Tony's direction.

"I don't get you," Walt said.

"Is she still such a fabulous fuck?" Aaron wanted to know.

Walt shook his head. "*What'd* you say?"

"My buddy Hugh White used to fuck her and he said—"

"*Aaron*—"

"—she was the finest fuck in Sarah Lawrence hist—"

Walt grabbed Aaron.

"And Hugh—well, Hugh, believe me, was a connoisseur."

Walt shoved Aaron against the wall.

"You don't believe me?"

"Shut your goddam mouth!"

"Ask her."

"I said—"

"Afraid?"

"Aaron, I'll kill you, so help—"

"Ask her if she fucked for Hugh White or not. Go on. Back at Princeton—"

"God damn you, *shut up!*"

"I'll ask her, then. Hey, Tony. Tony—"

Tony hurried over. "What is it?"

"Nothing," Walt told her. "Nothing."

"Walt wants to know—" Aaron began.

"Aaron, I'm warning you, God damn you, shut your—"

"*What is it?*" Tony said.

"Walt wonders if you remember Hugh White," Aaron said.

Tony stopped dead.

Walt let go of Aaron, dropped his hands.

"Oh my God," Tony said, and she stared at Aaron. "You were somebody's blind date."

Aaron laughed. "See, Walt? Am I a liar?"

Walt said nothing.

Tony looked at him. "What did he tell you?"

"I was very complimentary," Aaron assured her.

"*What did you say?*"

"I mentioned certain intimacies is all," Aaron answered.

"You son of a bitch!" Tony said.

"I'll allow that," Aaron said. "But I'm not a liar. Am I? Am I?"

Tony said nothing.

Walt excused himself.

Aaron smiled.

"Can I get anybody anything?" Rose called. "Except soda." She hurried into the foyer after her son. "Branch?"

Branch walked away.

"Branch, what's the matter with you?"

"Nothing. I'm looking for somebody."

"Well, please don't run away whenever I come near."

"*I'm just looking for somebody, Mother.*"

Rose, in the foyer, whispered, "Please."

Walt, at the bar, filled a glass with ice cubes, then with gin. The heat was unbearable now, and the cigarette smoke stung his eyes, and after the first large swallow of gin he came close to gagging. He remembered that he had not eaten much that day, so he slapped some bologna on a piece of rye and wolfed it down, then gulped the glass of gin.

Aaron watched him, then turned and stared out the window at the Hudson. The view, as always, was lovely, and he wondered how much longer he could take it living among the spics on 84th Street. What I need, he thought, is a fairy godmother, and he smiled at his joke, turning for another drink. Walt was still at the bar, refilling his glass, so Aaron decided to wait a while.

Esther sank down onto the living-room sofa and pinched at the bridge of her nose. "I want my Rudy," she said. "Sid, where is Rudy?"

"Easy, Tootsie," Sid said, giving her a little kiss. "He'll be back."

Rudy sat, his feet dangling in space, and he thought about his grandfather, about that great nose and the pickle barrel and reading tuna-fish labels and playing Seek the Seltzer, and Rudy said, "So, Joel, what now?" because below him was the silent babble of the party, and probably she was crazy, but he knew he could never commit her and he knew also that he was too tired either to deny his father or to run away. "So, Joel, what now?" Rudy said again, and then he closed his eyes because it was very hot and because he was very tired and because once you've seen the earth you've seen it all.

I have tried, dear God, to play this game of yours, but I am no one to carry the flag. I am tired, God, a poor Jew, tired, so let me please lie down. Give me a bed, God, because there is a limit to love and mine has long ago been reached, so just give me a bed to lie alone in. I have failed them, all who ever loved me, and for this last I have clung for dear life to life, but now I find it not so dear. I have had enough. I am ready now.

He vaulted up, balancing on the top of the railing.

Across were the empty windows, below the cars. Alive, he was nothing, a bringer of pain; dead, he was nothing too, but dead she was uncommitted. Sid defied.

Rudy smiled a final smile.

And dead, perhaps, perhaps someday in someone's mind, he might flicker for an instant: a quick sweet memory.

Rudy looked down the six floors. A wink was all it would be, a speedy jaunt, one way, and he suddenly felt at such peace that he had begun his drop through space before it crossed his gentle mind that the shock of his death would likely send his mother mad.

He turned, grabbing for the railing.

Too late, too late.

Wanting to rise, he fell, screaming "No!" every hot inch of the way.

His body caromed off the curving roof of the rear car, spun in the air, dropped. He landed on his face. Blood came quickly, from all over; it seemed not to have a central source. Rudy did not move, and probably would not have had not his pain been sufficient to force a gasp. The gasp made him realize that he was still alive, and that seemed to him such a cruel, such a God-less trick that he began to cry. He wept and tried to rise and, weeping, fell back. Then, through his tears, he saw the bottom of the fire escape and he knew he would always be safe if he was on a fire escape, so he turned his attention to getting there. It took much time and more pain, but he had plenty of that and to spare, and once he had done it, gotten there, once his broken hands had closed around the railings, he set his mind to pushing up that first step and, that conquered, the next. It seemed a foolish voyage he was on, but foolish or not, he was on it, and he only hoped that someday it would end.

Stagpole's appearance at the party came as a complete surprise to Jenny. Not that she had forgotten her invitation; it was the possibility of his acceptance she had dismissed, so when she opened the door to the apartment and saw the red-haired writer she could only say, "My God, you came."

"My God, it isn't air-conditioned," Stagpole said.

"Just fancy that," Jenny said, and she closed the door behind him.

Stagpole lingered in the foyer, dabbing a monogrammed handkerchief at his hairline. "It's a genuine inferno," he said.

"Come into the living room," Jenny said.

Stagpole sighed.

Actually, he loved entering rooms.

His red hair was eye-catching and his face was a famous one and there was always that moment after his entrance when everything froze and he knew that all eyes were on him. That frozen moment he relished because, with quick practiced flicks of his green eyes, he could catch and discard twenty faces in an instant. And sometimes if a proper, an appealing face appeared—well, that was enough to make a day. Originally he was quite catholic about which faces he found proper, but now that he was fifty he insisted that the face be young. And thin; gaunt, if possible.

And, of course, masculine.

Now, as he entered the steaming living room, the frozen moment came. Stagpole's green eyes flicked out like a serpent's tongue and when he saw the gaunt face by the window he smiled because his last lover had certainly been thin but this—*this* was going to be like making love to a cadaver.

Aaron, by the window, spun his face toward the glass, whispering exultantly, "I got him. *I got him!*"

Walt had begun feeling sick to his stomach before Stagpole's appearance, and he was aware, as Jenny led the red-haired man around the room, that what he didn't need was anything more to drink. Still, he stooped over the bar and poured himself another glass of gin, because he hoped it might help him think of something to say when his turn came, because he *was* a fan of Stagpole's, and that always made saying anything difficult. Walt sipped the gin, not looking at Tony, who still stood across the room from him, staring at him, waiting probably for him to run over and drop to his knees and beg forgiveness. The gin tasted funny, and Walt looked at his glass for a moment before he realized that he had poured the gin from a Scotch bottle, which very likely meant it wasn't gin at all, which probably had a good deal to do with why it tasted funny.

Also it was warm.

Warm Scotch, Walt thought, ummmm-boy, and he was reaching for some ice cubes when his stomach took a turn for the worse and Walt hurried out of the room. When he reached the corridor he ran down it, whirling into the bedroom and out of it to the bathroom floor, dropping to his knees, his head over the bowl.

Closing his eyes, Walt waited.

Tony said, "I'm going."

"Go."

"Not until we've talked," Tony said.

"We're talking."

"Not until you've listened, then," she said, and she closed the bathroom door and locked it.

"Tony, I don't feel so goddam well if you don't mind."

"My father's a doctor." She sat on the edge of the tub.

Walt opened his eyes and looked at her. Even now, in the stifling heat of the bathroom, she managed to appear, in her goddam watermelon whatever it was, almost cool. "Would you please let me vomit in peace?" Walt said. And then he said, "Look, you want to drop for some guy, terrific, it's none of my business. Don't bother apologizing, you don't hafta."

"What else do you want to say?"

"I don't want to say anything. I frankly do not care who you put out for. I just wanna upchuck alone, O.K.? Now can I have a little privacy or can't I?"

Tony said nothing.

Walt stuck his finger down his throat.

"I've watched operations, Walt; you're not going to make me sick that easy."

Walt removed his finger but stayed, head down, over the bowl.

"It's that I lied, isn't it?" Tony said.

Walt, eyes closed, nodded. "That's got a little to do with it. I mean, I would rather you hadn't shacked up with half the adult population of New Jersey but it does bug me somewhat—" Walt began to gag.

Tony knelt down beside him.

Walt pushed her away. "Dammit, can't you leave—"

"Why do you think I lied?"

"Because you're a liar. Why else?"

"I did it—"

"Oh boy, I can hardly wait—"

"—because I couldn't get you any other way. Not if I told the truth. Because I love you, Walt."

"That'll make me vomit if the Scotch won't."

"*Goddammit, you're gonna believe me!*" She moved up next to him. "That's the only thing I care about left, and you are going to believe me when I leave here and say good goodbye. That I loved you. I love you in spite of the fact that you're funny-looking and not all that sweet and—"

"Tony—" Walt said.

She grabbed his shoulders. "I don't suppose you care that this big thing that's making you fall to pieces happened when I was just a kid and I don't care either because it doesn't matter. What matters is *you* blew it, *you*, buddy, you threw it all away, what we had, *you* pitched it all—" And her voice built in the steaming tiled room and Walt, sick, tried turning toward the toilet, saying, "Look out, huh, look out, look out, *Tony*—"

Then nobody said anything.

"It doesn't matter," Tony whispered finally.

"All over you," Walt said. "All over your dress."

"It doesn't matter," Tony said again.

"You moved right into me," Walt said. "I tried making it to the toilet but you moved right in my way."

Tony shook her head and slowly began to unbutton her dress.

Walt knelt over the bowl and threw up again. "I really feel crummy," he whispered.

Tony took off her dress and looked at herself in the mirror. "Oh dear," she muttered, "you got the slip too." She took it off.

"I'm sorry."

"It's all right."

Walt gripped the sides of the bowl. "I'm sorry, I'm sorry."

"Shhh, baby," Tony told him. "You just take care."

Walt reached out for her. "I'm sorry, I am, but why did you have to lie?"

Tony knelt beside him, took him gently in her arms. "Because I was in love, baby, and people in love do desperate things." She began to rock him.

Walt, eyes closed, lowered his face against her bra. "Do you really, do you?"

"Here," Tony whispered, and she reached behind her back, unhooked her bra, lifted it gently up, giving his mouth a better grip.

Then there were three screams.

The first one when it came, came from Stagpole.

But that was only natural, since he had maneuvered himself into a position with his back to the window and his face, therefore, to the door. Everyone else in the room was grouped around him, facing him, which he rather liked, and he told them stories and they laughed, and if it weren't for the heat he would really have almost enjoyed it, what with the eye play he was managing between himself and the gaunt young man called Fire, but then the thing appeared crawling slowly through the doorway and Stagpole screamed. *"Jesus!"*

Rudy stopped and for a moment, lifted his bloody face, trying to locate something, and then he started to crawl again, saying "Father . . . ? Father . . . ?" as he moved painfully along.

Everybody scattered and Esther clutched her heart but Sid, frozen, retreated toward the window, watching his son crawl toward him.

"Father . . . ? Father . . . ?"

When Rudy was almost on him, Sid supplied the second scream.

"DIE!"

The third scream came immediately after, and it was Branch's, and probably he meant some word but none was distinguishable. He simply ran across the room, and when he was above the quiet form he dropped beside it and gathered it into his arms and began to keen, and when Rose came over and tried to lead him away she discovered Branch would not let go.

In a moment all save five people had moved quietly out of the room, standing like cattle in the hot foyer. Branch, of course, had not moved, continuing to keen, his face now buried in the neck of the dead. And Sid was still standing by the window. Esther, still clutching her heart, stared at her husband, and Rose, panting from her labors, tried dislodging her son.

But Branch just would not let go.

Jenny watched it all from the foyer. Then she whirled, bolting for the bedroom phone, calling Boston. She waited, eyes closed. When she got the law firm where Tommy was working the summer she said, "Mr. Alden, please," and then, when his voice came on the line, she said, "Tommy?"

"Hello, Jenny. How's the play?"

"Well, there's been some . . . a postponement, maybe, and I wondered if you loved me."

"Yes."

"Then marry me."

"I'm married."

"Auh?"

"I didn't know how to tell you, Jenny. I guess I was trying to hint around that day when I called you after your name was in the paper. See, it's all kind of, I don't know, a mess, except she's very nice except it more or less had to happen, the marriage, if you get what I mean, and I haven't told anybody but I'm thinking of going north around Labor Day and surprising people."

"You be happy," Jenny said.

"You too, Moose."

"I am."

"So'm I."

"Good for us," Jenny said, and after she'd hung up she went over to the bed and lay down. She had no idea how long she stayed there, but the next thing she knew a slender Negro was asking her please to come to the living room and, since he was a policeman, she went, and he thanked her, explaining that someone in the neighboring building had seen something on the fire escape and had called the police, and, as she was leaving the room, Tony appeared from the bathroom in what probably was Branch's bathrobe, and Tony asked what was going on, and when Jenny told her Tony went into the bathroom and told Walt, green by now, that Rudy was dead and Branch had likely cracked and there was a Negro cop outside asking questions.

Walt, in pain over the bowl, only wondered what the punch line was.

The questioning took a long time. Nobody knew much of anything, but they had to be asked anyway, and the eventual conclusion was that R. V. Miller had probably slipped from the fire escape where he was wont to linger and was, in any case, dead. Long before the questioning was concluded a doctor was summoned and, after brief consultation with the police and Mrs. Scudder, gave her son a shot, which soon loosened his hold, and he was then carried unconscious to the bedroom and allowed to rest there. Charley Fiske of Kingsway Press arrived shortly before the doctor, having been summoned, he said, by the playwright Aaron Fire, who, as the police were finishing up, gave a moving speech about the future of *Madonna with Child*, that future being, as far as he was concerned, absolutely and totally nil, since the script had been more or less commissioned by Branch Scudder and since Branch, even if he were in condition to continue with the production, would never do so, since he saw only the deceased in one of the two central roles. Consequently, the playwright concluded, out of respect for the dead and the maimed, he was withdrawing the play from presentation, which was his contractual right. The actress in the other central role was more than a little upset by the playwright's moving gesture but was at least partially soothed by the editor of the deceased. The question of body disposal was settled quickly, when Esther Miller said "The boy will be buried beside his grandfather!" with such force that Sidney Miller argued but briefly about interstate costs, and, that over, Campbell's Funeral Church was called and soon came, and Sid urged them on to their greatest effort, and Campbell's, used to parental grief, agreed to do its best.

By the conclusion of all this, the rising of the moon was complete, and as the police released them the people scattered. Walt and Tony were among the first to go and Walt did fine on the elevator trip down, supporting himself, but outside, the first strong breath of night heat made him woozy. He grabbed a building façade for support, stayed there gasping until Tony slipped her arm around his shoulder, shifted the brunt of his weight against her hip. Walt was still reluctant to leave the safety of the building, but at Tony's urging he gathered courage and in a moment, when he felt himself properly propped, he let go and leaned on her completely as they moved along.

"Don't let go," Walt told her.

Tony said "Never."

Jenny left as soon as she heard Charley calling Princeton. She dashed out the door, and when the automatic elevator was slow to obey she ran down the six flights and out into the night. Charley, when he ran down the stairs a few minutes later, found her sitting on the front steps of the building.

"I'm through running," Jenny explained. "I'm through hiding. I can say good night to you like a human being. That's why I stopped."

Charley sat down beside her. "I couldn't agree more" he said. "That was what I was running to tell you."

"We had our chances," Jenny said. "They are gone. I'll never get involved with you. Not again."

"Don't worry; I'm involved with another woman now and thank God this time it's my wife."

"I'll never work for you again either."

"I wouldn't fire my new girl. She's forty-five and homely and we get along just fine. We're staffed completely, except Archie has an opening coming up."

"He does?" She shook her head. "I could never work for Archie Wesker."

Charley stood. "I'm gonna be rude and not even offer to walk you home. And I'm sorry about the play."

Jenny nodded. "I wonder if it was any good," she said. "Only one person ever really saw it. It's kind of silly to take the word of one person." She stood. "Good night, Charley. And I'm glad you're not walking me home." She shook his hand and started across the street into Riverside Park.

"Is that safe at night?" Charley called.

"I hope so," Jenny called back. "I only go through the park for half the way."

"I'll walk you halfway home, then."

Jenny waited for him to cross to her.

They slipped into the shadows.

Sid and Esther were the last to leave. They sat quietly in the living room, talking softly to Rose, or rather Sid talked, Esther remaining silent, coddling her grief in private, Sid assumed. So they talked, scrambling for things in common, all the time staring at that one thing they did share, the spot on the rug where their children had lain. The spot held them, and though once they certainly would have fought over it, or over what it represented, now they just sat, old and tired and staring. But finally, inevitably, Sid said "Well . . ." and Rose answered him in kind, "Well . . ." and though no one made a move, the ending was at hand.

"So if you're ever near Chicago," Sid said, leaving the rest.

"Thank you. Or you Cleveland."

"Who can tell?" Sid muttered.

So did Rose. "Who can tell?"

Then they stood, Sid helping Esther, Rose accompanying them to the door. "I'm sure your son will be fine," Sid said.

Rose nodded. "Oh yes. Once I get him home."

"So will Rudy," Esther said. "Once I get him home."

Sid opened the door. "I meant that about Chicago." He pushed for the automatic elevator.

"If you're ever near Cleveland," Rose said, and she waved and said good night and shut the door. Sighing, she moved toward the bedroom, taking off her green dress as she went. She took off her girdle and heaved another sigh, and then she took a bathrobe from her son's closet. Rose went into the bedroom. The moonlight was very bright and she pulled a chair up close beside the bed and lowered herself into it.

Branch had such a lovely face. Rose smiled, put her hands on her stomach, preparing herself for her nightlong vigil. Softly, in a voice so sweet it surprised her, she began to sing:

> *"Comin' home . . .*
> *Comin' home . . .*
> *Branch is comin' home . . .*
> *Mother's there . . .*
> *Gramma too . . .*
> *All the friends we knew . . ."*

When the automatic elevator finally came, Sid bowed Esther into it, entered himself, pushed the button marked "Main." They rode down in silence, and when they were almost ready to get out Esther said, "Murderer!"

Sid, lost in thought, didn't hear her quite.

"Murderer!"

"What are you talking about, Tootsie?"

"Murderer! *Murderer!*"

"Esther—"

"You killed my son!"

Sid pulled her through the lobby. "Get you to the hotel," he said. "Fast."

On the street, Esther hollered, "Murderer!"

"You don't know what you're saying, shut up—"

"Oh God," Esther said, and she moved in on him. "You killed my Rudy. I know it. I know it. You made him die."

"Esther, for crissake—"

"I have never *dreamed* I could hate you the way I hate you now!"

"We've all had a helluva shock, Es—"

"I love it. I love it. I love it, Murderer!"

Sid started walking away up the street.

"Murderer! Murderer!"

Sid whirled. "You want to get us both arrested?"

"You and your goddam Dolly. You and your goddam girlfriend, you can kiss her goodbye, Sid. I'll never leave you, Sid. Never for an instant. Never. I'll be with you always, Murderer!"

"You're crazy." Starting to panic, Sid backed away.

Esther ran at him, eyes bright. "I'll never leave you. Never leave your side. Oh God, Sid, I'm so happy—" Esther clapped her hands, and for a moment, as she reached out for her husband, she looked almost young. She took his arm, locked it in hers. "Isn't it wonderful?" Esther crowed. "I've got something to live for at last!"

XXVI

I was born for caviar, Aaron decided.

It was the twelfth of August and he stood in a corner of Stagpole's stateroom, piling a cracker indecently high with fresh Beluga caviar. He downed it, quickly filled a slender glass with iced champagne, downed that too. Delicately, Aaron wiped his mouth. Glancing around the room, he counted a grand total of eleven people, ten of them famous. Well, Aaron thought, give me time.

In the center of the room, Stagpole inserted a cigarette into his holder, then looked at Aaron.

Aaron hesitated, trying not to redden. Hurrying forward, he lit Stagpole's cigarette. As he moved he was conscious of all the other men's eyes.

"Thank you, dear boy," Stagpole said, inhaling.

Aaron said nothing, moving quickly back to his place in the corner by the food. Again he was aware that everyone was watching him, probably comparing him with previous "secretaries" of Stagpole's. And, the snotty bastards, they were laughing at him too. Aaron knew that. Every burst of laughter was in one way or another directed at him.

"Dear boy," Stagpole called out, "do you think it might be time for more champagne?"

Aaron flushed deeper, silently cursing himself for reddening. They were all watching him again, so he casually picked up a bottle of champagne and took a very long time to study the label. The words meant nothing to him. I must learn about such things, Aaron decided. I must become *une frigging connoisseur*. Then he toured the room as fast as he could, filling a few glasses before returning to his place in the corner.

"Thank you, dear boy," Stagpole said to him, smiling.

That makes forty-two "dear boys" today so far, Buster, and for every one of them, buddy old pal, you are going to *pay*. He smiled back at Stagpole, wishing that the boat would sail, that everyone would get the hell out and stop smirking at him.

A uniformed flunky appeared in the doorway. "Packages for Mr. Stagpole," he said.

Stagpole interrupted his conversation with a wavy-haired symphony conductor, a bearded choreographer and a dirty-fingernailed young Broadway lyricist long enough to snap his fingers at Aaron.

Eyes down, Aaron hurried to the door, listening as a derisive burst of laughter exploded behind him. Finger snaps count as five "dear boys," Aaron thought, and that makes forty-seven I owe you. "I'm Mr. Stagpole's secretary," he said to the uniformed flunky. Aaron looked at the pile of boxes stacked in the corridor. "All for Mr. Stagpole?"

The flunky nodded.

"Well, bring them in, bring them in," Aaron said, snapping his fingers, pointing toward the corner of the room already containing Stagpole's luggage. When the boxes were neatly piled, Aaron said "You may go" as haughtily as he could, considering everyone was watching him and laughing at him and he was the one man out of eleven who wasn't famous.

The warning whistle blew for the third time and, in a moment, a slow general movement began toward the stateroom door. "Oh, must you?" Stagpole said. He sighed. "I suppose you must. That or come along," and he gave a light laugh, moving to the doorway then, nodding and smiling, gripping each passing hand, giving each a meaningful little squeeze. "Dear heart . . . take care . . . you too . . . goodbye . . . we must . . . by all means . . . you know I will . . . don't you dare . . . so good of you . . ." and the men filing out said "Goodbye" or "Nonsense" or "Till Bimini, then" or "Remember me to Nadia." When they were gone Stagpole closed the door and leaned against it.

Stagpole smiled at Aaron.

Aaron turned his back, piled another cracker high with caviar, took his time about eating it because, in truth, he was a bit flustered since, through his own skillful maneuverings, he had managed never to be alone with Stagpole before.

"The first time we've really been alone," Stagpole said.

Aaron turned. "Is it?"

Stagpole nodded. "I wanted it that way. I wanted our initial venture to take place on water. Don't ask me why."

"Repression is the better part of valor," Aaron said.

Stagpole laughed. "May I use that? Thank you. Why don't you like my friends?"

"Same reason I don't like you: natural good taste."

Stagpole stopped laughing. "Please. Don't be nervous."

"Nervous?" Aaron laughed. "May I use that? Thank you."

Stagpole smiled, went to the windows, drew the curtains. "I feel like I've been standing up for hours," he said, lying on one of the twin beds. "Massage my feet, would you, Aaron?"

"Who was your nigger last year? You can massage your own feet."

"Please?"

"Look," Aaron said, pouring himself another glass of champagne. "You needed a secretary, I know how to type—"

"Massaging my feet is not such an incredible request."

"I signed on as secretary, not a goddam masseur."

"Surely you didn't think answering mail and such would be your only duties?"

"Don't worry, you'll get your jollies every now and again."

Stagpole shook his head. "You're a stern young man," he said. "Very stern." He got up and moved to the corner where the boxes were. "You remember my having your measurements taken?" he said. "Sit down, Aaron. Please."

Aaron sat on the other bed.

Stagpole began opening boxes. He opened them and threw the contents on the bed, starting with silk underwear and cashmere socks, a dozen pairs, and Aaron grabbed them, but then he had to let them go because Stagpole put down a dozen silk shirts and after the shirts came three lizard belts and bench-made shoes and trousers of imported woolens and cashmere jackets, one brown, one white, and Aaron began putting clothes half on, throwing them off, donning something else more splendid, and when Stagpole opened the cashmere overcoat of darkest blue Aaron almost wept as he paraded before the full-length mirror. He ran back and jumped onto the bed and threw the clothes up in the air and when they landed, threw them again and then he returned to the mirror and Stagpole, watching, only smiled.

"Am I not breathtaking?" Aaron yelled. "Am I not divine?" He whirled on Stagpole. "Why? I love it, but why?"

Stagpole lay back down, his hands beneath his fiery hair. "People like us, we have no heirs to leave our money to. We need only satisfy the government; the rest is for our whims. You—" and he pointed at Aaron— "are my very dearest whim."

"I'm gonna enter the goddam Miss America contest," Aaron said. He paraded before the mirror. "Miss America, that's me," and he made smiling faces toward the mirror till Stagpole spoke again.

"Please massage my feet, Aaron."

Aaron took off the cashmere coat, dropped it to the stateroom floor, kicked it in Stagpole's direction. "Kiss my rosy red rectum," he said.

"I'm sorry," Stagpole muttered, and he sighed and picked up the coat and carried it back to Aaron, handing it to him with his left hand, and as Aaron reached out for it Stagpole made his right hand rigid and, swinging suddenly, crashed it against Aaron's throat.

Aaron reeled backward, slammed into the mirror, fell.

Stagpole walked slowly after him, reached down, lifted him gently and, with his left hand this time, dealt another blow to Aaron's throat. Aaron fell full length, gagging, his hands across his Adam's apple. When Stagpole picked him up a third time Aaron whispered, "Don't."

"Ah, but I must," Stagpole said, and then he turned Aaron gently around, brought his knee up fast, slamming it into the small of Aaron's back.

Aaron gave a quiet cry. Then he lay sprawled out, very still.

"Now we'll have a little talk if we may," Stagpole said, moving to the bed, taking off his shoes. He started to massage his feet. "You see, Aaron, you were quite right: I can do it myself." Stagpole smiled. "But of course, the central question here is not one of manipulation but of obedience." Stagpole removed his socks and started rubbing his little pink toes. "Pudgy fingers, pudgy toes," he said, holding up his hands for Aaron to see. "Am I boring you?"

Aaron lay still.

"In a little you'll be fine, don't worry," Stagpole said. "In the meantime, let me point out that you, according to your own biased reports, have written one novel which nobody published and one play which nobody saw. I, on the other hand, have written many novels and many plays; the novels sell, the plays run. I am not bragging, Aaron—"

Aaron made a sound.

Stagpole rubbed his toes harder. "I'm not, really. I'm just trying to indicate something to you: *I am a master,* Aaron. You could not begin to lick the shoes of an apprentice and *I am a master!*"

"Your breath smells," Aaron whispered.

"Wonderful," Stagpole applauded. "Not only stern but spunky." He left the bed and pulled a chair over beside Aaron. Then he sat down, reached out, made a finger stiff and jabbed it at just below Aaron's left ear.

Aaron groaned.

"What is a writer actually," Stagpole asked, "but an exposer of nerves?" He pressed down again, and again Aaron groaned. "There are various places on your body, Aaron, which, when pressed will cause certain rather unpleasant reactions. I am going to press, from time to time, those places. Now hear me: if you suffer silently, I will let up. If you are audible, well, so much the worse for you." He reached down quickly, jammed a knuckle into Aaron's neck.

Aaron yelled.

Stagpole jabbed again, much harder.

Aaron bit his lip.

"Splendid," Stagpole said.

Aaron panted, color draining.

Stagpole sat up and lit a cigarette, inserting it into an elegant holder. "Mustn't have you fainting, Aaron," he said. "Not before the ship has even sailed. I hate rushing things, don't you?"

Aaron managed to lick the perspiration from his lips.

"Now what we have in you, Aaron," Stagpole went on, "what you are is a writer and a sadist and a pervert. Well, small world, so am I. Except that *I am a master of those crafts! I am unexcelled.* And you . . ." Stagpole shook his head. "Well, it's just too bad about you."

"What do you mean?"

"Would you like to know your future? I'll tell you. If you'd like."

Aaron said nothing.

Stagpole bent down, pressed a finger lightly on Aaron's eye. "Say you'd like."

Aaron bit his lip. "Tell me."

"That one is almost too painful, isn't it?" He pressed down again.

Aaron bit his lip while perspiration sprang all across his forehead.

"I must begin with myself, when I was your age, Aaron. I wrote a novel and suddenly I found myself famous. It was a book about people like us, Aaron, and with the money I made I determined to take a trip around the world. You see, what I didn't know then was that people like us, we form a special club. We more or less take care of our own. And when I got to Europe, oh, Aaron, I was feted, believe me. I did such things as only a young man dreams. I met the mighty men of Europe, Aaron; I saw sights, kissed kings—oh God, it was a journey to remember. And the most memorable sight pertains to you."

Aaron lay still, panting.

"I don't remember quite the country. I'm terrible at geography, flunked it in the seventh grade, would you believe it?"

Aaron said nothing.

Stagpole pressed down with a finger. "That was a question, Aaron."

Aaron bit his lip, then muttered that he wouldn't have believed it.

"In the East it was," Stagpole said. "In the East, a village square, at dawn. Dust rising. White buildings all around. People scurrying back and forth across the square. And then, at a signal—are you listening, Aaron?—the children appeared! Ten years old, some of them less, eight or nine, some of them perhaps thirteen. They appeared with their parents, and their parents pushed them into the middle of the village square, with the dust rising and the white buildings all around. The children stood huddled together. Panicked. Not a sound. And then, Aaron, then came the foreign legionnaires. Because that is what I was witnessing—a flesh sale. A flesh sale at dawn, human flesh. The legionnaires walked in among the children, they began to examine them. They checked their teeth and their calf muscles and they tested their arms and they carefully scrutinized their genitals, and all the while, Aaron, there was not a sound. The legion officers, you see, needed houseboys. Boys to cook and clean and dust and, on steamy nights, Aaron, other things. The head officers, they each had a boy all to themselves, while the lower ones had to share. And here before me at dawn, Aaron, the officers of the foreign legion tested these children and made their choices and paid the asking price to the parents and then led their prizes off into the day. That movement brought back the dust. The sun became blinding. Soon the square looked like a village square somewhere in the East. White buildings, dust, hot sun." Stagpole stood.

Aaron struggled to his knees.

"And now, Aaron, we come to the pertinent part, the part that tells your future. Because I'm certain you've noted the parallel, so I assume you're more than a little interested in what happens to the boys."

Aaron licked his lips. "Tell me."

"They disappear! They get *used* and *used* and *used* until they are *all used up*. Then they simply disappear."

"And that's gonna happen to me?"

Stagpole lifted him roughly. "By the time that I am done with you, there will be nothing left. I . . . will . . . use . . . you . . . up, believe me, trust me, trust my skill. *I am a master.* Do you believe that?"

"I . . . I believe . . ."

Stagpole smiled, then, gently, he patted Aaron's face. "Prepare to live in splendor," he said, leading Aaron to the cashmere-covered bed. "For a while. Now go anoint your body. I must make ready."

"What do you mean, 'make ready'?"

Stagpole shrugged. "Nothing, really. You'll get used to it. Costumes, apparatus, various bits of paraphernalia. Here, a final gift for you," and he opened a suitcase, removed a monogrammed silk robe. "Now go. Beautify yourself." He escorted Aaron to the bathroom door. "I'll call you when I'm ready."

As the door closed behind him, Aaron felt a momentary urge to scream for help, so he ran to the tiny porthole, fought it open, peered out. But the robe was purest silk and soft to the touch. Aaron closed the porthole and slowly undressed.

The great ship began to move.

Aaron opened the medicine chest. Stagpole had filled it with oils, and Aaron almost enjoyed bathing as he covered his gaunt body with first one sweet-smelling liquid, then another. He took a long time, but still there was no word from Stagpole, and as he waited Aaron felt the screaming urge again, and he ran back to the tiny porthole, throwing it open, staring out as the borough of Manhattan glided by. A young girl stood staring at the giant buildings as they glistened in the noonday sun.

"You—" Aaron said. "You—listen."

She said, *"Je ne parle pas."*

"Of course you don't," Aaron said, and he thought, son of a bitch, I'm gonna disappear, it's enough to make you believe in God.

The girl pointed to the glistening city. *"Belle, oui?"*

"Oui," Aaron agreed. "And the streets, *les boulevardes*, they are paved with shit."

"Oui?" the girl said.

Aaron nodded. *"Oui."*

The girl smiled and was gone.

"If you ask me you're a lousy place to visit!" Aaron shouted.

"I'm ready, Aaron," Stagpole said from beyond, his voice different and strange.

Aaron closed his eyes.

"Aaron. I'm ready."

Aaron entered into agony.

About the Author

WILLIAM GOLDMAN has been writing books and movies for more than forty years. He has won two Academy Awards (for *Butch Cassidy and the Sundance Kid* and *All the President's Men*), and three Lifetime Achievement awards in screenwriting. His novels include *Marathon Man*, which has made him very famous in dentists' offices around the world, *The Temple of Gold*, and *The Princess Bride*.